Work

Work

Émile Zola

MINT EDITIONS

Work was first published in 1901.

This edition published by Mint Editions 2021.

ISBN 9781513281025 | E-ISBN 9781513286044

Published by Mint Editions®

 MINT
EDITIONS

minteditionbooks.com

Publishing Director: Jennifer Newens
Design & Production: Rachel Lopez Metzger
Project Manager: Micaela Clark
Translated by Ernest Alfred Vizetelly
Typesetting: Westchester Publishing Services

Contents

BOOK I

I

As Luc Froment walked on at random after emerging from Beauclair, he went up the Brias road, following the gorge in which the Mionne torrent flows between the two promontories of the Bleuse Mountains. And when he found himself before the Abyss, as the Qurignon steel-works are called in the region, he perceived two dark and puny creatures shrinking timidly against the parapet at the corner of the wooden bridge. His heart contracted. One was a woman looking very young, poorly clad, her head half hidden by some ragged woollen stuff; and the other, nestling amidst her skirts, was a white-faced child, about six years old, and scarcely clothed at all. Both had their eyes fixed on the door of the works, and were waiting, motionless, with the mournful patience of despairing beings.

Luc paused and also looked. It would soon be six o'clock, and the light of that wretched, muggy, mid-September evening was already waning. It was a Saturday, and since Thursday the rain had scarcely ceased to fall. It was no longer coming down at present, but across the sky an impetuous wind was still driving a number of clouds, sooty ragged clouds, athwart which filtered a dirty, yellowish twilight, full of mortal sadness. Along the road over which stretched lines of rails, and where big paving-stones were disjointed by continuous traffic, there flowed a river of black mud, all the gathered moistened dust of the neighbouring coal-works of Brias, whose tumbrels were for ever going by. And that coal-dust had cast a blackness as of mourning over the entire gorge; it fell in patches over the leprous pile of factory buildings, and seemed even to besmirch those dark clouds which passed on interminably like smoke. An ominous melancholy swept by with the wind; one might have thought that the murky quivering twilight was bringing the end of the world in its train.

Luc had stopped short at a few paces from the young woman and the boy, and he heard the latter saying with a shrewd decisive air, like one who was already a little man: "I say, *ma grande*,[1] would you like me to speak to him? P'r'aps he wouldn't get so angry with me."

---

1. Literally "my big one," *i.e.* "big sister." We have no exact equivalent for this expression as a form of endearment, nor for the ensuing one, *frérot*, little brother.—*Trans.*

But the young woman replied: "No, no, *frérot*, those are not matters for little boys."

Then again they continued waiting in silence, with an air of anxious resignation.

Luc was now looking at the Abyss. From professional curiosity he had visited it when first passing through Beauclair the previous spring. And during the few hours that he had again found himself in the district, suddenly summoned thither by his friend Jordan, he had heard through what a frightful crisis the region had just passed. There had been a terrible strike of two months' duration, and ruin was piled up on either side. The establishment had greatly suffered from the stoppage of work, and the workmen, their rage increased by their powerlessness, had almost starved. It was only two days previously, on the Thursday, that work had been resumed after reciprocal concessions, wrung from either party with the greatest difficulty after the most furious wrangling. And the men had gone back like joyless, vanquished beings enraged by defeat, retaining in their hearts only a recollection of their sufferings and a keen desire for revenge.

Under the wild flight of the mourning clouds the Abyss spread its sombre piles of buildings and sheds. It was like a monster which had sprung up there, extending by degrees the roofs of its little town. One could guess the ages of the various structures by the colour of those roofs which arose and spread out in every direction. The establishment now occupied a surface of many acres and employed a thousand hands. The lofty, bluish, slated roofs of the great halls with coupled windows, overtopped the old blackened tiles of the earlier buildings, which were far more humble. Up above one perceived from the road the gigantic hives of the cementing-furnaces, ranged in a row, as well as the tempering tower, seventy-eight feet high, where big cannon were plunged on end into baths of petroleum. And higher still ascended smoking chimneys, chimneys of all sizes, a very forest, whose sooty breath mingled with the flying soot of the clouds, whilst at regular intervals narrow blast-pipes, with strident respiration, threw out white plumes of steam. All this seemed like the breathing of the monster. The dust, the vapour that it incessantly exhaled, enveloped it as in an everlasting cloud of the perspiration of toil. And there also the beating of its organs, the impact, the noise of its every effort: the vibration of machinery, the clear cadence of helve-hammers, the great rhythmical blows of steam-hammers resounding like huge bells and making the soil shake. And at the edge of the road, in the depths of a little building, where the first Qurignon had first forged iron, one could hear the violent, desperate dance of two tilt-hammers which were beating there like the very pulse of the colossus, every one of whose life-devouring furnaces flamed afresh.

In the ruddy and dismal crepuscular mist which was gradually submerging the Abyss, not a single electric lamp as yet lighted up the yards. Nor was there any light gleaming through the dusty windows. Alone, through the gaping doorway of one of the large halls, there burst a vivid flame which transpierced the gloom with a long jet of light, like that of some fusing star. A master puddler had doubtless opened the door of his furnace. And nothing else, not even a stray spark, proclaimed the presence of the empire of fire, the fire roaring within that darkened city of toil, the internal fire which heated the whole of it, the trained, subjected fire which bent and fashioned iron like soft wax, and which had given man royalty over the earth ever since the first Vulcans had conquered it.

At last the clock in the little belfry surmounting the offices struck six o'clock. And Luc then again heard the poor child saying: "Listen, *ma grande*, they will be coming out now."

"Yes, yes, I know well enough," the young woman answered. "Just you keep quiet."

As she moved forward to restrain the child, her ragged wrapper fell back slightly from before her face, and Luc remarked the delicacy of her features with surprise. She was surely less than twenty. She had fair hair all in disorder, a poor, thin little face which to him seemed ugly, blue eyes blurred by tears, and a pale mouth that twitched bitterly with suffering. And what a light, girlish frame there was within her old threadbare dress! And with what a weak and trembling arm did she press to her skirts the child, her little brother, who was fair like herself and equally ill-combed, but stronger-looking and more resolute! Luc felt his compassion increasing, whilst the two poor creatures on their side grew distrustfully anxious about that gentleman who had stopped so near, and was examining them so persistently. She, in particular, seemed embarrassed by the scrutiny of that young fellow of five-and-twenty, so tall and handsome, with square-set shoulders, broad hands and a face all health and joy, whose firmly-marked features were o'ertopped by a straight and towering brow, the towering brow of the Froment family. She had averted her gaze as it met the young man's brown eyes, which looked her frankly in the face. Then she once more stole a furtive glance, and seeing that he was smiling at her in a kindly way, she drew back a little more, in the disquietude born of her great distress.

The clang of a bell was heard, there was a stir in the Abyss, and then began the departure of the day-shifts which the night-shifts were about to replace; for never is there a pause in the monster's devouring life; it flames and forges both by day and night. Nevertheless there was some delay in the departure of the day-hands. Although work had only been resumed on the Thursday, most of them had applied for an advance, for after that terrible strike of two months' duration great was the hunger in every home. At last they began to appear, coming along one by one or in little parties, all gloomy and in a hurry, with their heads bent whilst in the depths of their pockets they stowed away their few dearly earned silver coins which would procure a little bread for wife and children. And in turn they disappeared along the black highway.

"There he is, *ma grande*," the little boy muttered. "Can't you see him? He's with Bourron."

"Yes, yes; keep quiet."

Two men, two puddlers, had just left the works. The first, who was accompanied by Bourron, had a cloth jacket thrown over his shoulders. He was barely six-and-twenty; his hair and beard were ruddy, and he was rather short, though his muscles were strong. Under a prominent brow he showed a hook nose, massive jaws, and projecting cheek-bones, yet he could laugh in a very agreeable way, which largely accounted for his success with women. Bourron, five years the elder, and closely buttoned in an old jacket of greenish velveteen, was a tall, dry, scraggy fellow, whose equine face, with long cheeks, short chin, and eyes set almost sideways, expressed the quiet nature of a man who takes life easily, and is always under the influence of one or another mate.

Bourron had caught sight of the mournful woman and child standing across the road at the corner of the wooden bridge, and, nudging his companion with his elbow, he exclaimed: "I say, Ragu, Josine and Nanet are yonder. Be careful if you don't want them to pester you."

Ragu ragefully clenched his fists. "The —— girl! I've had enough of her, I've turned her out! Just let her try to come dangling after me again and you'll see!"

He seemed to be slightly intoxicated, as always happened indeed on those days when he exceeded the three quarts of wine which he declared he needed to prevent the heat of the furnace from drying up his skin. And in his semi-intoxication he yielded the more especially to a cruel boastful impulse to show his mate how he treated girls when he no longer cared for them.

"I shall send her packing," said he, "I've had enough of her."

With Nanet still among her skirts Josine was now gently, timidly, stepping forward. But she paused on seeing two other workmen approach Ragu and Bourron. They belonged to a night-shift, and had just arrived from Beauclair. Fauchard, the eldest, a man of thirty, looking quite ten years older, was a drawer, and seemed already "done for" by his terrible work. His face had the appearance of boiled flesh, his eyes were scorched, the whole of his big frame burnt and warped by the ardent glow of the furnaces when he drew out the fusing metal. The other, his brother-in-law Fortuné, was a lad of sixteen, though he would hardly have been thought twelve, so puny was his frame. He had a thin face and discoloured hair, and looked as if he had ceased growing, as if, indeed, he were eaten into by the mechanical toil which he ever performed, perched beside the lever of a helve-hammer amidst all the bewilderment born of blinding steam and deafening noise.

On his arm Fauchard carried an old black osier basket, and he had stopped to ask the others in a husky voice: "Did you go?"

He wished to ascertain if they had gone to the cashier's office and obtained an advance there. And when Ragu, without a word, slapped his pocket in which some five-franc pieces jingled, the other made a despairing gesture and exclaimed: "Thunder! To think that I've got to tighten my belt until to-morrow morning, and that I shall be dying of thirst all night unless my wife by some miracle or other contrives to bring me my ration by-and-by."

His ration was four quarts of wine for each day or night-shift, and he was wont to say that this quantity only just sufficed to moisten his body, to such a degree did the furnaces drain all the blood and water from his flesh. He cast a mournful glance at his basket, in which nothing save a hunk of bread was jolting. The failure to secure his usual four quarts of wine meant the end of everything, black agony amidst overpowering unbearable toil.

"Bah!" said Bourron complacently, "your wife won't leave you in the lurch; she hasn't her equal for getting credit somewhere."

Then, all at once, the four men standing in the sticky mud became silent and touched their caps. Luc had seen a kind of bath-chair approaching, propelled by a servant; and ensconced within it sat an old gentleman with a broad face and regular features around which fell an abundance of long white hair. In this old gentleman the young fellow recognised Jérôme Qurignon, "Monsieur Jérôme" as he was called throughout the region, the son of Blaise Qurignon, the drawer, by whom the Abyss had been founded. Very aged and paralysed, never speaking, Monsieur Jérôme caused himself to be carted about in this fashion, no matter what might be the weather.

That evening, as he passed the works on his way back to his daughter's residence, La Guerdache, a neighbouring estate, he had signed to his servant to go more slowly, and with his still bright, living eyes he had then taken a long look at the ever-busy monster, at the day hands departing homeward, and at the night hands arriving, whilst the vague twilight fell from the livid sky besmirched by rushing clouds. And his glance had afterwards rested on the manager's house, a square building standing in a garden, which his father had erected forty years previously, and where he himself had long reigned like a conquering king, gaining million after million.

"Monsieur Jérôme isn't bothered as to how he will get any wine to-night," resumed Bourron in a sneering whisper.

Ragu shrugged his shoulders: "My great-grandfather and Monsieur Jérôme's father," said he, "were comrades. Yes, they were both workmen and drew iron here together. The fortune might have come to a Ragu just as well as to a Qurignon. It's all luck, you know, when it isn't robbery."

"Be quiet," Bourron muttered, "you'll be getting into trouble."

Ragu's bounce deserted him, and when Monsieur Jérôme, passing the group, looked at the four men with his large, fixed, limpid eyes, he again touched his cap with all the timorous respect of a toiler who is ready enough to cry out against employers behind their backs, but has long years of slavery in his blood and trembles in the presence of the sovereign god from whom he awaits the bread of life. The servant meanwhile slowly pushed the bath-chair onward, and Monsieur Jérôme disappeared at last down the black road descending towards Beauclair.

"Bah!" said Fauchard philosophically by way of conclusion, "he's not so happy after all, in that wheelbarrow of his. And besides, if he can still understand things, that strike can't have been very pleasant to him. We each have our troubles. But thunder! I only hope that Natalie will bring me my wine."

Then he went off into the works, taking with him little Fortuné, who had not spoken a word, and looked as bewildered as ever. Already

ÉMILE ZOLA

feeling weary, they disappeared amidst the increasing darkness which was enveloping the buildings; whilst Ragu and Bourron set out again, the former bent on leading the latter astray, to some tavern in the town. But then, dash it all, a man surely had a right to drink a glass and laugh a bit after undergoing so much misery!

However, Luc, who, from compassionate curiosity had remained leaning against the parapet of the bridge, saw Josine again advance with short unsteady steps to bar the way to Ragu. For a moment she had hoped that he would cross the bridge homeward bound, for that was the direct road to Old Beauclair, a sordid mass of hovels in which most of the workpeople of the Abyss lived. But when she understood that he was going down to the new town, she foresaw what would happen: the money he had obtained would be spent in some wine-shop, and she and her little brother would have to spend another whole evening waiting, dying of starvation, amidst the bitter wind in the streets. And her sufferings and a fit of sudden anger lent her so much courage that, puny and woeful though she was, she went and took her stand before the man.

"Be reasonable, Auguste," said she; "you can't leave me out-of-doors."

He did not answer, but stepped on in order to pass her.

"If you are not going home at once, give me the key, at any rate," she continued. "We've been in the street ever since this morning, without even a morsel of bread to eat."

At this he burst forth: "Just let me be! Haven't you done sticking to me like a leech?"

"Why did you carry off the key this morning?" she answered. "I only ask you to give me the key, you can come in when you like. It is almost night now, and you surely don't want us to sleep on the pavement."

"The key! the key! I haven't got it, and even if I had I wouldn't give it you. Just understand, once for all, that I've had enough of it, that I don't want to have anything more to do with you, that it's quite enough that we starved together for two months, and that now you can go somewhere else, and see if I'm there!"

He shouted those words in her face, violently and savagely; and she, poor little creature, quivered beneath his insults, whilst gently persevering in her efforts with all the woeful desperation of a wretch who feels the very ground giving way beneath her.

"Oh! you are cruel! you are cruel!" she gasped. "We'll have a talk when you come home to-night. I'll go away to-morrow if it's necessary. But to-day, give me the key just for to-day."

Then the man, infuriated, pushed her, thrust her aside with a brutal gesture. "Curse it all!" he cried, "doesn't the road belong to me as much as you? Go and croak wherever you like! I tell you that it's all over." And as little Nanet, seeing his sister sob, stepped forward with his air of decision, his pink face and tangle of fair hair, Ragu added: "What! the brat as well! Am I to have the whole family on my shoulders now? Wait a minute, you young rascal; I'll let you feel my boot somewhere."

Josine quickly drew Nanet towards her. And they both remained there, standing in the black mud, shivering with woe, whilst the two workmen went their way, disappearing amidst the gloom in the direction of Beauclair, whose lights, one by one, were now beginning to shine. Bourron, who at bottom was a good-natured fellow, had made a movement as if to intervene; then, however, in a spirit of imitation, yielding to the influence of his rakish companion, he had let things take their course. And Josine, after momentarily hesitating, asking what use it would be to follow, made up her mind to do so with despairing stubbornness as soon as the others had disappeared. With slow steps she descended the road in their wake, dragging her little brother by the hand, and keeping very close to the walls, taking indeed all sorts of precautions, as if she feared that on seeing her they might beat her to prevent her from dogging their steps.

Luc, in his indignation, had almost rushed on Ragu to administer a correction to him. Ah! the misery of labour!—man turned to a wolf by overpowering and unjust toil, by the difficulty of earning the bread for which hunger so wildly contends! During those two months of the strike, crumbs had been fought for amidst all the voracity and exasperation of daily quarrels. Then, on the very first pay-day, the man rushed to Drink for forgetfulness, leaving his companion of woe, whether she were his wife or a girl he had seduced, in the streets! And Luc remembered the four years which he had lately spent in a faubourg of Paris, in one of those huge, poison-reeking buildings where the misery of the working classes sobs and fights upon every floor! How many tragedies had he not witnessed, how many sorrows had he not attempted to assuage! The frightful problem born of all the shame and torture attending the wage system had often arisen before his mind; he had fully sounded that system's atrocious iniquity, the horrible sore which is eating away present-day society, and he had spent hours of generous enthusiasm in dreaming of a remedy, ever encountering, however, the iron wall of existing reality. And now, on the very evening of his return to Beauclair, he came upon that savage scene, that pale and mournful creature cast starving into the streets through the fault of the all-devouring monster, whose internal fire he could ever hear growling, whilst overhead it escaped in murky smoke rolling away under the tragic sky.

A gust of wind passed, and a few rain-drops flew by in the moaning wind. Luc had remained on the bridge, looking towards Beauclair and trying to take his bearings by the last gleams of light that fell athwart the sooty clouds. On his right was the Abyss, with its buildings bordering the Brias road; beneath him rolled the Mionne, whilst higher up, along an embankment on the left, passed the railway line from Brias to Magnolles. These filled the depths of the gorge, between the last spurs of the Bleuse Mountains, at the spot where they parted to disclose the great plain of La Roumagne. And in a kind of estuary, at the spot where the ravine debouched into the plain, Beauclair reared its houses: a wretched collection of working-class dwellings, prolonged over the flat by a little middle-class town, in which were the sub-prefecture, the town-hall, the law-courts, and the prison, whilst the ancient church, whose walls threatened to fall, stood part in new and part in old Beauclair. This town, the chief one of an arrondissement,[2] numbered barely six thousand souls, five thousand of them being poor humble souls in suffering bodies, warped, ground to death by iniquitous hard toil. And Luc took in everything fully when, above the Abyss, half-way up the promontory of the Bleuse Mountains, he distinguished the dark silhouette of the blast furnace of La Crêcherie. Labour! labour! ah! who would redeem and reorganise it according to the natural law of truth and equity so as to restore to it its position as the most noble, all-regulating, all-powerful force of the world, and so as to ensure a just division of the world's riches, thereby at last bringing the happiness which is rightly due to every man!

Although the rain had again ceased Luc also ended by going down towards Beauclair. Workmen were still leaving the Abyss, and he walked among them as they tramped on, thinking of that rageful resumption of work after all the disasters of the strike. Such infinite sadness born of rebellion and powerlessness pervaded the young man that he would have gone away that evening, indeed that moment, had

---

2. Each French "department" or county is for administrative purposes divided into two, three, or four "arrondissements"; and the arrondissements in their turn are subdivided into "cantons."—*Trans.*

he not feared to inconvenience his friend Jordan. The latter—the master of La Crêcherie—had been placed in a position of great embarrassment by the sudden death of the old engineer who had managed his smeltery, and he had written to Luc, asking him to come, inquire into things, and give him some good advice. Then, the young man, on hastening to Beauclair in an affectionate spirit, had found another letter awaiting him, a letter in which Jordan announced a family catastrophe, the sudden, tragical death of a cousin at Cannes, which obliged him to leave at once and remain absent with his sister for three days. He begged Luc to wait for them until Monday evening, and to instal himself meanwhile in a pavilion which he placed at his disposal, and where he might make himself fully at home. Thus Luc still had another two days to waste, and for lack of other occupation, cast as he was in that little town which he scarcely knew, he had gone that evening for a ramble, telling the servant who waited on him that he should not even return to dinner. Passionately interested as he was in popular manners and customs, fond of observing and learning, he felt that he could get something to eat in any tavern of the town.

New thoughts came upon him, whilst under the wild tempestuous sky he walked on through the black mud amidst the heavy tramping of the harassed, silent workmen. He felt ashamed of his previous sentimental weakness. Why should he go off, when here again he once more found, so poignant and so keen, the problem by which he was ever haunted? He must not flee the fight, he must gather facts together, and, perhaps, amidst the dim confusion in which he was still seeking a solution, he might at last discover the safe, sure path that led to it. A son of Pierre and Marie Froment, he had learnt, like his brothers Mathieu, Marc and Jean, a manual calling apart from the special study which he had made of engineering. He was a stone-cutter, a house-builder, and having a taste for that avocation, fond of working at times in the great Paris building-yards, he was familiar with the tragedies of the present-day labour-world, and dreamt, in a fraternal spirit, of helping on the peaceful triumph of the labour-world of to-morrow. But what could he do, in which direction should he make an effort, by what reform should he begin, how was he to bring forth the solution which he felt to be vaguely palpitating within him? Taller and stronger than his brother Mathieu, with the open face of a man of action, a towering brow, a lofty mind ever in travail, he had hitherto embraced but the void with those big arms of his which were so impatient to create and build. But again a

　　　　　　　　　　　　　　　　　　　ÉMILE ZOLA

sudden gust of wind sped by, a hurricane blast, which made him quiver as with awe. Was it in some Messiah-like capacity that an unknown force had cast him into that woeful region to fulfil the long-dreamt-of mission of deliverance and happiness?

When Luc, raising his head, freed himself of those vague reflections, he perceived that he had come back to Beauclair again. Four large streets, meeting at a central square, the Place de la Mairie, divide the town into four more or less equal portions; and each of these streets bears the name of some neighbouring town towards which it leads. On the north is the Rue de Brias, on the west the Rue de Saint-Cron, on the east the Rue de Magnolles, and on the south the Rue de Formerie. The most popular, the most bustling of all—with its many shops stocked to overflowing— is the Rue de Brias, in which Luc at present found himself. For in that direction lie all the factories, from which a dark stream of toilers pours whenever leaving-off time comes round. Just as Luc arrived, the great door of the Gourier boot-works, belonging to the Mayor of Beauclair, opened, and away rushed its five hundred hands, amongst whom were numbered more than two hundred women and children. Then, in some of the neighbouring streets, were Chodorge's works, where only nails were made; Hausser's works, which turned out more than a hundred thousand scythes and sickles every year, and Mirande's works, which more particularly supplied agricultural machinery.

They had all suffered from the strike at the Abyss, where they supplied themselves with raw material, iron and steel. Distress and hunger had passed over every one of them, the wan, thin workers who poured from them on to the muddy paving-stones had rancour in their eyes and mute revolt upon their lips, although they showed the seeming resignation of a hurrying, tramping flock. Under the few lamps, whose yellow flames flickered in the wind, the street was black with toilers homeward bound. And the block in the circulation was increased by a number of housewives who, having at last secured a few coppers to spend, were hastening to one or another shop to treat themselves to a big loaf or a little meat.

It seemed to Luc as if he were in some town, the siege of which had been raised that very evening. Hither and thither among the crowd walked gendarmes, quite a number of armed men, who kept a close watch on the inhabitants, as if from fear of a resumption of hostilities, some sudden fury arising from galling sufferings, whence might come the sack of the town in a supreme impulse of destructive exasperation.

No doubt the masters, the *bourgeois* authorities, had overcome the wage-earners, but the overpowered slaves still remained so threatening in their passive silence that the atmosphere reeked of bitterness, and one felt a dread of vengeance, of the possibility of some great massacre, sweeping by. A vague growl came from that beaten, powerless flock, filing along the street; and the glitter of a weapon, the silver braid of a uniform shining here and there among the groups, testified to the unacknowledged fear of the employers, who, despite their victory, were bursting into perspiration behind the thick, carefully drawn curtains of their pleasure houses; whilst the black crowd of starveling toilers still and ever went by with lowered heads, hustling one another in silence.

Whilst continuing his ramble Luc mingled with the groups, paused, listened, and studied things. In this wise he halted before a large butcher's shop open on the street, where several gas-jets were flaring amidst ruddy meat. Dacheux, the master butcher, a fat apoplectical man, with big goggle eyes set in a short red face, stood on the threshold keeping watch over his viands, evincing the while much politeness towards the servants of well-to-do customers, and becoming extremely suspicious directly any poor housewife came in. For the last few minutes he had kept his eyes upon a tall slim blonde, pale, sickly, and wretched, whose youthful good looks had already faded, and who, whilst dragging with her a fine child between four and five years old, carried upon one arm a heavy basket, whence protruded the necks of four quart-bottles of wine. In this woman Dacheux had recognised La Fauchard, whose constant appeals for little credits he was tired of discouraging. And as she made up her mind to go in, he all but barred the way.

"What do you want again, you?" he asked.

"Monsieur Dacheux," stammered Natalie, "if you would only be so kind—my husband has gone back to the works you know, and will receive something on account to-morrow. And so Monsieur Caffiaux was good enough to advance me the four quarts I have here, and would you be so kind, Monsieur Dacheux, as to advance me a little meat, just a little bit of meat?"

At this the butcher became furious, his blood rushed to his face, and he bellowed: "No, I've told you no before! That strike of yours nearly ruined me! How can you think me fool enough to be on your side? There will always be enough lazy workmen to prevent honest folk from doing business. When people don't work enough to eat meat, they go without it!"

He busied himself with politics, and like a narrow-minded hot-tempered man, one who was greatly feared, he was on the side of the rich and powerful. On his lips the word "meat" assumed aristocratic importance: meat was sacred, it was a luxury reserved to the happy ones of the earth, when it ought to have belonged to all.

"You owe me four francs from last summer," he resumed; "I have to pay people, I have!"

At this Natalie almost collapsed, then she again strove to touch him, pleading in a low prayerful voice. But an incident which occurred just then completed her discomfiture. Madame Dacheux, an ugly, dark, insignificant-looking little woman, who none the less contrived to make her husband the talk of the town, stepped forward with her little daughter Julienne, a child of four, plump, healthy, fair, and full of gaiety. And the two children having caught sight of one another, little Louis Fauchard, despite all his wretchedness, began to laugh, whilst the buxom Julienne, feeling amused, and doubtless as yet unconscious of social inequalities, drew near and took hold of his hands. In such wise that there was sudden play, fraught with childish delight, as at the prospect of some future reconciliation of the classes.

"The little nuisance!" cried Dacheux, who had quite lost his temper. "She's always getting between my legs. Go and sit down at once!"

Then, turning his wrath upon his wife, he roughly sent her back to the cash desk, saying that the best thing she could do was to keep an eye on the till, so that she might not be robbed again, as she had been robbed only two days previously. And, haunted as he was by that theft, of which he had never ceased to complain with the greatest indignation during the last forty-eight hours, he went on, addressing himself to all the people in the shop: "Yes, indeed, some kind of beggar woman crept in and took five francs out of the till whilst Madame Dacheux was looking to see if the flies laughed. She wasn't able to deny it, she still had the money in her hand. Oh! I had her taken into custody at once. She's at the gaol. It is frightful, frightful; we shall be utterly robbed and plundered soon if we don't keep our eyes open."

Then with suspicious glances he again watched his meat to make sure that no starving wretches, no workwomen out of work, should carry any pieces away from the show outside, even as they might carry away precious gold, divine gold, from the bowls in the windows of the money-changers' shops.

Luc saw La Fauchard grow alarmed and retire; she feared, no doubt, that the butcher might summon a gendarme. For a moment she and her little Louis remained motionless in the middle of the street, amidst all the jostling, their faces turned the while towards a fine baker's shop, decorated with mirrors and gaily lighted up, which faced the butcher's establishment. In one of its windows, which was open, numerous cakes and large loaves with a crust of a golden hue were freely displayed under the noses of the passers-by. Before those loaves and cakes lingered the mother and the child, deep in contemplation. And Luc, forgetting them, became interested in what was taking place inside the shop.

A cart had just stopped at the door, and a peasant had alighted from it with a little boy about eight years old and a girl of six. At the counter stood the baker's wife, the beautiful Madame Mitaine, a strongly-built blonde who at five-and-thirty had remained superb. The whole district had been in love with her, but she had never ceased to be faithful to her husband, a thin, silent, cadaverous-looking man who was seldom seen, for he was almost always busy at his kneading trough or his oven. On the bench near his wife sat their son, Évariste, a lad of ten, who was already tall, fair, too, like his mother, with an amiable face and soft eyes.

"What, is it you, Monsieur Lenfant!" said Madame Mitaine. "How do you do? And there's your Arsène, and your Olympe. I need not ask you if they are in good health."

The peasant was a man in the thirties, with a broad sedate face. He did not hurry, but ended by answering in his thoughtful way, "Yes, yes, their health is good; one doesn't get along so badly at Les Combettes. The soil's the most poorly. I shan't be able to let you have the bran I promised you, Madame Mitaine. It all miscarried. And as I had to come to Beauclair this evening with the cart, I thought I'd let you know."

He went on giving expression to all his rancour against the ungrateful earth, which no longer fed the toiler, nor even paid for sowing and manuring. And the beautiful Madame Mitaine gently nodded her head. It was quite true. One had to work a great deal nowadays to reap but little satisfaction. Few were able to satisfy their hunger. She did not busy herself with politics, but, *mon Dieu*, things were really taking a very bad turn. During that strike, for instance, her heart had almost burst at the thought that a great many poor people went to bed without even a crust to eat when her shop was full of loaves. But trade was trade, was it not? One could not give one's goods away for nothing, particularly as in doing so one might seem to be encouraging rebellion.

ÉMILE ZOLA

And Lenfant approved her. "Yes, yes," said he, "everyone his own. It's only fair that one should get profit from things when one has taken trouble with them. But all the same there are some who want to make too much profit."

Évariste, interested by the sight of Arsène and Olympe, had made up his mind to quit the counter and do them the honours of the shop. And like a big boy of ten he smiled complaisantly at the little girl of six, whose big round head and gay expression probably amused him.

"Give them each a little cake," said beautiful Madame Mitaine, who greatly spoilt her son, and was bringing him up to kindly ways.

And then, as Évariste began by giving a cake to Arsène, she protested jestingly: "But you must be gallant, my dear. One ought to begin with the ladies!"

At this Évariste and Olympe, all confusion, began to laugh, and promptly became friends. Ah! the dear little ones, they constitute the best part of life. If some day they were minded to be wise they would not devour one another as do the folk of to-day. And Lenfant went off, saying that he hoped to be able to bring some bran after all, but, of course, later on.

Madame Mitaine, who had accompanied him to her door, watched him climb into his cart and drive down the Rue de Brias. And at this moment Luc noticed Madame Fauchard dragging her little Louis with her, and suddenly making up her mind to approach the baker's wife. She spoke some words which Luc did not catch, a request no doubt for further credit, for beautiful Madame Mitaine, with a gesture of consent, immediately went into her shop again, and gave her a large loaf, which the poor creature hastened to carry away, close-pressed to her scraggy bosom.

Dacheux, amidst his suspicious exasperation, had watched the scene from the opposite foot pavement. "You'll get yourself robbed!" he cried. "Some boxes of sardines have just been stolen at Caffiaux's. They are stealing everywhere!"

"Bah!" gaily answered Madame Mitaine, who had returned to the threshold of her shop. "They only steal from the rich!"

Luc slowly went down the Rue de Brias amidst the flocklike tramping which ever and ever increased. It now seemed to him as if a Terror were sweeping by, as if some gust of violence were about to transport that gloomy, silent throng. Then, as he reached the Place de la Mairie, he again saw Lenfant's cart, this time standing at the street corner, in front of some large ironmongery stores, kept by the Laboques, husband and wife. The doors of the establishment were wide open, and he heard some violent bartering going on between the peasant and the ironmonger.

"Good heavens! why, you charge as much for your spades as if they were made of gold! Why, for this one you ask two francs more than usual."

"But, Monsieur Lenfant, there has been that cursed strike. It isn't our fault if the factories haven't worked and if everything has gone up in price. I pay more for all metal goods, and, of course, I have to make a profit."

"Make a profit, yes, but not double prices. Ah! you do drive a trade! It will soon be impossible to buy a single tool."

Laboque was a short, thin, wizened man, extremely active, with a ferret's snout and eyes; and he had a wife of his own size, a quick, dusky creature, whose keenness in money-earning was prodigious. They had both begun life at the fairs, dragging with them a hand-cart full of picks, rakes, and saws, which they hawked around. And having opened a little shop at Beauclair ten years back, they had managed to enlarge it each succeeding twelvemonth, and were now at the head of a very important business as middle-men between the factories of the region and the consuming classes. They retailed at great profit the iron of the Abyss, the Chodorges' nails, the Haussers' scythes and sickles, the Mirandes' agricultural appliances. They battened on a waste of wealth and strength with the relative honesty of tradespeople who practised robbery according to established usage, glowing with satisfaction every evening when they emptied their till and counted up the money that they had amassed, levied as tribute on the needs of others. They were like useless cogwheels in that social machine, which was now fast getting out of order; they made it grate, and they consumed much of its remaining energy.

Whilst the peasant and the ironmonger were disputing furiously over a reduction of a franc which the former demanded, Luc again began to examine the children. There were two in the shop—Auguste, a big, thoughtful-looking boy of twelve, who was learning a lesson, and Eulalie, a little girl, who seemed to be scarcely five years old, and who, grave and gentle, sat quietly on a little chair as if judging all the folk who entered. She had shown an interest in Arsène Lenfant from the moment he crossed the threshold. Finding him to her taste, no doubt, she greeted him like the good-hearted little body she was. And the meeting became complete when a woman entered, bringing a fifth child with her. This woman was Babette, the wife of Bourron the puddler, a plump, round, fresh-looking creature, whose gaiety nothing would ever dim, and who held by the hand her daughter Marthe, a little thing but four years old, who seemed as plump and as gay as herself. The child, it should be said, at once quitted her mother and ran to Auguste Laboque, whom she doubtless knew.

Babette meantime promptly put an end to the bartering between the ironmonger and the peasant, who agreed to halve the franc over which they had been disputing. Then the woman, who had brought back a saucepan purchased the previous day, exclaimed: "It leaks, Monsieur Laboque. I noticed it directly I put it on the fire. I can't possibly keep a saucepan that leaks, you know."

Whilst Laboque, fuming, examined the utensil and decided to give another in exchange, Madame Laboque began to speak of her children. They were perfect pests, said she, they never stirred, one from her chair, the other from his books. It was quite necessary to earn money for them, for they were not a bit like their parents, nobody would ever find them up and doing to earn a pile. Meantime Auguste Laboque, listening to nothing, stood smiling at Marthe Bourron, and Eulalie Laboque offered her little hand to Arsène Lenfant, whilst the other Lenfant, Olympe, thoughtfully finished eating the cake which little Mitaine had given her. And it was altogether a very pleasant and moving scene, instinct with good fresh hope for to-morrow amidst the burning atmosphere of battle and hatred which heated the streets.

"If you think one can gain money with such affairs as this, you are mistaken," resumed Laboque, handing another saucepan to Babette. "There are no good workmen left, they all scamp their work nowadays. And what a lot of waste and loss there is in a place like ours! Whoever chooses comes in, and what with having to set some of our goods outside, in the street, it's just like the Fair of Take-what-you-like. We were robbed again this afternoon."

Lenfant, who was slowly paying for his spade, expressed his astonishment at this. "So all those robberies one hears about really take place then?" said he.

"Really take place! Of course they do. It isn't we who rob, it's others who rob us. They remained out on strike for two months, you know, and as they haven't the money to buy anything they steal whatever they can. Only a couple of hours ago some clasp-knives and paring-knives were stolen out of that case yonder. It isn't tranquillising by any means."

And he made a gesture of sudden disquietude, turning pale and quivering as he pointed to the threatening street, crowded with the gloomy throng, as if he feared some hasty onrush, some invasion which might sweep him, the owner and tradesman, away and despoil him of everything.

"Clasp-knives and paring-knives!" repeated Babette with her sempiternal laugh. "They're not good to eat. What could people do with them? It's just like Caffiaux over the way—he complains that a box of sardines has been stolen from him. Some urchin just wanted to taste them, no doubt."

She was ever content, ever convinced that things would turn out well. As for that Caffiaux, he was surely a man whom all the housewives ought to have cursed. She had just seen her man Bourron go into his place with Ragu, and Bourron would certainly break up a five-franc piece there. But when all was said it was only natural that a man should amuse himself a bit after toiling so hard. And having given expression to this philosophical view she took her little girl Marthe by the hand again and went off, well pleased with her beautiful new saucepan.

"We ought to have some troops here, you know," resumed Laboque, explaining his views to the peasant. "I'm in favour of giving a good lesson to all those revolutionaries. We need a strong government with a heavy fist to ensure respect for respectable things."

Lenfant jogged his head. With his distrustful common sense he hesitated to express his opinions. At last he too went off, leading Arsène and Olympe away and saying: "Well, I hope that all these affairs between the *bourgeois* and the workmen won't end badly!"

For the last minute or two Luc had been examining Caffiaux's establishment over the road, at the other corner of the Rue de Brias and the Place de la Mairie. At first the Caffiaux, man and wife, had simply kept a grocery, which now had a very flourishing appearance with its display of open sacks, its piles of tinned provisions and all sorts of comestible goods protected by netting from the nimble fingers of marauders. Then the idea had come to them of going into the wine business, and they had rented an adjoining shop and had fitted it up as a wine-shop and eating-house, where nowadays they literally coined gold. The hands employed at all the neighbouring works, notably the Abyss, consumed a terrible amount of alcohol. There was an endless procession of them going in and coming out of Caffiaux's establishment, particularly on the Saturdays when they were paid. Many lingered and ate there, and many came away dead drunk. The place was a den of poison, where the strongest lost the use of both their heads and their arms. Thus the idea at once occurred to Luc to enter it to see what might be going on inside. It was a very simple matter; as he was to dine out, he might as well dine there. How many times in Paris had not his passion to learn everything about the "people," to dive to the depths of their misery and suffering, impelled him to enter the very worst dens and spend hours in them?

He quietly installed himself at one of the little tables near the huge zinc bar. The room was large, a dozen workmen stood up drinking, whilst others, seated at table, drank, shouted, and played cards, amidst the thick smoke from their pipes, a smoke in which the gas-jets merely looked like red spots. And at the very first glance around him Luc recognised Ragu and Bourron seated face to face at a neighbouring table, and shouting violently at one another. They had doubtless begun by drinking a quart of wine, then they had ordered an omelet, some sausages and some cheese; and the quart bottles having followed one after another, they were now very drunk. What particularly interested Luc, however, was the presence of Caffiaux, who stood near their table talking. For his part the young man had ordered a slice of roast beef, and whilst eating it he listened.

Caffiaux was a fat, podgy, smiling man with a paternal face. "But I tell you," said he, "that if you had held out only three days longer you would have had the masters bound hand and foot at your mercy! Curse it all! you're surely not unaware that I'm on the side of you fellows! Yes, indeed, you won't upset all those blackguardly exploiters a bit too soon."

Ragu and Bourron, who were both greatly excited, clapped him on the arm. Yes, yes, they knew him, they were well aware that he was a good, a true friend. But all the same a strike was too hard to bear, and it always had to come somehow to an end.

"The masters will always be the masters," stammered Ragu. "So you see we have got to put up with them, whilst giving them the least we can for their money. Another quart, Caffiaux—you'll help us to drink it, eh?"

Caffiaux did not decline. He sat down. He favoured violent views because he had noticed that his establishment expanded after each successive strike. Nothing made one so thirsty as quarrelling, the worker who was exasperated rushed upon Drink, rageful idleness accustomed toilers to tavern life. Besides, in times of crisis, he, Caffiaux, knew how to be amiable. Feeling certain that he would be repaid, he opened little credit accounts for needy housewives, and did not refuse the men a glass of wine on "tick," thus winning the reputation of being good-hearted, and at the same time helping on the consumption of all the poison he retailed. Some folks said, however, that this Caffiaux, with his jesuitical ways, was a traitor, a spy of the masters of the Abyss, who had helped him financially to set up in business, in order that he might make the men chatter whilst he was poisoning them. And it all meant fatal perdition; the wretched, pleasureless, joyless, wage-earning life necessitated the existence of taverns, and taverns finished by rotting the wage-earning class. Briefly, here was a bad man and a bad place, a misery-breeding shop which ought to have been razed to the ground and swept clear away.

Luc's attention was for a moment drawn from the conversation near him by the opening of an inner door communicating with the grocery shop, and the appearance on the threshold of a pretty girl about fifteen years of age. This was Honorine, the Caffiaux's daughter, a short, slim brunette, with fine black eyes. She never stayed any time in the tavern, but confined herself to serving grocery. And on now entering she merely called her mother, a stout, smiling woman, as unctuous as her husband, who stood behind the large zinc bar. All those tradesfolk, so eager for gain, all those hard egotistical shopkeepers seemed to have very fine children, thought Luc. And would those children for ever and ever remain as grasping, as hard, and as egotistical as their forerunners?

But all at once a charming and mournful vision appeared before the young man. Amidst the pestilential odours, the thickening tobacco-smoke, the noise of a scuffle which had just broken out before the bar, he saw Josine standing, so vague and blurred, however, that at the first moment he did not recognise her. She must have slipped in furtively, leaving Nanet at the door. Trembling, and still hesitating, she stood behind Ragu, who did not see her; and for a moment Luc was able to scrutinise her, so slim in her wretched gown, and with so gentle and shadowy a face under her ragged *fichu*. But he was struck by something which he had not observed over yonder near the Abyss: her right hand was no longer pressed against her skirt, and he could see that it was strongly bandaged, wrapped round to the wrist with linen, doubtless a bandage for some injury which she had received.

ÉMILE ZOLA

At last Josine mustered up all her courage. She must have followed as far as Caffiaux's shop, have glanced through the windows and have seen Ragu at table. She drew near with her little, faltering step, and laid her girlish hand upon his shoulder. But he, in the glow of his intoxication, did not even feel her touch, and she ended by shaking him until he at last turned round.

"Thunder!" he cried. "What! is it you again? What to the—do you want here?"

As he spoke he dealt the table such a thump with his fist that the glasses and the quart-bottles fairly danced.

"I have to come, since you don't come home," she answered, looking very pale and half closing her large frightened eyes in anticipation of some act of brutality.

But Ragu was not listening to her, he was working himself into a frantic passion, shouting by way of showing off before all the mates who were present.

"I do what I choose!" he cried, "and I won't have a woman spying on me! I'm my own master, do you hear? And I shall stop here as long as I please!"

"Then give me the key," she said despairingly, "so that at any rate I may not have to spend the night in the street."

"The key! the key!" shrieked the man, "you ask me for the key!" And with furious savagery he rose up, caught hold of her by her injured hand and dragged her down the room to throw her into the street.

"Haven't I told you that it's all over, that I don't mean to have anything more to do with you?" he shouted. "The key, indeed! just go and see if it isn't in the street!"

Josine, bewildered and stumbling, raised a piercing cry of pain. "Oh! you have hurt me!"

Ragu's violence had torn the bandage from her right hand, and the linen was at once reddened by a large bloodstain. But none the less the man, blinded, maddened by drink, threw the door wide open and pushed the woman into the street. Then returning and falling heavily upon his chair before his glass, he stammered with a husky laugh: "A fine time of it we should have, and no mistake, if we listened to them!"

Beside himself this time, quite enraged, Luc clenched his fists with the intention of falling upon Ragu. But he foresaw an affray, a useless battle with all those brutes. And feeling suffocated in that vile den he hastened to pay his score, whilst Caffiaux, who had taken his wife's place at the bar, tried to arrange matters by saying in his paternal way that some women were very clumsy. How could one hope to get anything out of a man who had been tippling? Luc, however, without answering, hurried out and inhaled with relief the fresh air of the street, whilst searching among the crowd on all sides, for in leaving the tavern so hastily his one idea had been to rejoin Josine and offer her some help, so that she might not remain perishing of hunger, breadless and homeless, on that black and stormy night. But in vain did he run up the Rue de Brias, return to the Place de la Mairie, dart hither and thither among the groups: Josine and Nanet had disappeared. Terrified perchance by the thought of some pursuit, they had gone to earth somewhere; and the rainy, windy darkness wrapped them round once more.

How frightful was the misery, how hateful were the sufferings to be found in spoilt, corrupted labour, which had become the vile ferment whence every degradation sprang! With his heart bleeding, his mind clouded by the blackest apprehensions, Luc again wandered through the threatening crowd whose numbers still increased in the Rue de Brias. He once more found there that vague atmosphere of terror which had come from the recent struggle between the classes, a struggle which never finished, whose near return one could scent in the very air. That resumption of work was but a deceptive peace, there was low growling amidst all the resignation of the toilers, a silent craving for revenge; their eyes still retained a gleam of ferocity, and were ready to flash once more. On both sides of the way were taverns full of men; drink was consuming their pay, poisonous exhalations were pouring into the very street, whilst the shops never emptied, but still and ever levied on the meagre resources of the housewives that iniquitous and monstrous tribute called "commercial gain." Everywhere, upon every side the toilers, the starvelings, were exploited, preyed upon, caught and crushed in the works of the ever-grating social machine, whose teeth proved all the harder now that it was falling to pieces. And in the mud, under the wildly flickering gaslights, as on the eve of some great catastrophe, all Beauclair came and went, tramping about like a lost flock, going blindly towards the pit of destruction.

Among the crowd Luc recognised several persons whom he had seen on the occasion of his first visit to Beauclair during the previous spring. The authorities were there, for fear no doubt of something being amiss. He saw Mayor Gourier and Sub-Prefect Châtelard pass on together. The first, a nervous man of large property, would have liked to have troops in the town; but the second, an amiable waif of Parisian life whose intellect was sharper, had wisely contented himself with the services of the gendarmes. Gaume, the presiding judge of the local court, also went by, accompanied by Captain Jollivet, an officer on the retired list, who was about to marry his daughter. And as they passed Laboque's shop they paused to exchange greetings with the Mazelles, some former tradespeople who, thanks to a rapidly acquired income, had finally been received into the high society of the town. All these folks spoke in low voices, with scarcely confident expressions on their faces, as they glanced sideways at the heavily tramping toilers who were still keeping up Saturday evening. As Luc passed near the Mazelles he heard them also speaking of the robberies, as if questioning the Judge and the Captain on the subject. Tittle-tattle was indeed flying from mouth to mouth. A five-franc piece had been taken from Dacheux's till; a box of sardines had been abstracted from Caffiaux's shop; but the gravest commentaries were those to which the theft of Laboque's paring-knives gave rise. The terror which was in the air gained upon sensible people. Was it true then that the revolutionaries were arming themselves, and purposed carrying out some massacre that very night, that stormy night which hung so heavily over Beauclair? That disastrous strike had put everything out of gear, hunger was impelling wretches hither and thither, the poisonous alcohol of the taverns was breeding destructive and murderous madness. Truly enough, right along the filthy, muddy roadway, along the sticky foot-pavements one found all the poisononsness and degradation that come from iniquitous toil, the toil of the greater number for the enjoyment of the few—labour, dishonoured, hated, and cursed, the frightful misery that results therefrom, together with theft and prostitution which are its monstrous parasitic growths. Pale girls passed by, factory girls whom some unprincipled men had led astray and who had afterwards sunk to the gutter; and drunken men went off with them through all the puddles and the darkness.

Increasing compassion, rebellion compounded of grief and anger, took possession of Luc. Where could Josine be? In what horrid dark nook had she sought refuge with little Nanet? But all at once a clamour arose, a hurricane seemed to sweep over the crowd first, making it whirl and then carrying it away. One might have thought that an attack was being made upon the shops, that the provisions exposed for sale on either side of the street were being pillaged.

Gendarmes rushed forward, there was scampering hither and thither, a loud clatter of boots and of sabres. What was the matter? What was the matter? Questions pressed one upon the other, flew about in stammering accents amidst the growing terror, whilst answers came back wildly from every side.

At last Luc heard the Mazelles saying, as they retraced their steps, "It's a child who has stolen a loaf of bread."

The snarling, excited crowd was now rushing up the street. The affair must have taken place at Mitaine's shop. Women shrieked, an old man fell down and had to be picked up. One fat gendarme ran so impetuously through the groups that he upset two persons.

Luc himself began to run, carried away by the general panic. And as he passed near Judge Gaume he heard him saying slowly to Captain Jollivet: "It's a child who has stolen a loaf of bread."

That answer came back again, punctuated as it were by the rush of the crowd. But there was a great deal of scrambling and nothing could yet be seen. The tradespeople standing on the thresholds of their shops turned pale, and thought of putting up their shutters. A jeweller was already removing the watches from his window. Meantime, a general eddying took place around the fat gendarme, who was busy exerting his elbows.

Then Luc, beside whom Mayor Gourier and Sub-Prefect Châtelard were also running, again detected the words, the pitiful murmur rising amidst a little shudder: "It's a child who has stolen a loaf of bread."

At last, as the young man was just reaching Mitaine's shop in the wake of the fat gendarme, he saw him rush forward to assist a comrade, a long, lanky gendarme, who was roughly holding a boy, between five and six years old, by the wrist. And in this boy Luc at once recognised Nanet, with his fair tumbled head, which he still carried erect with the resolute air of a little man. He had just stolen a loaf of bread from beautiful Madame Mitaine's open window. The theft could not be denied, for the lad was still holding the big loaf, which was nearly as tall as himself. And so it was really this childish act of larceny which had upset and excited the whole Rue de Brias. Some passers-by having noticed it had denounced it to the gendarme, who had set off at a run. But the lad on his side had slipped away very fast, disappearing among the groups, and the gendarme, raising a perfect hullabaloo in his desperation, had nearly turned all Beauclair topsy-turvy. He was triumphant now, for he had captured the culprit, and had brought him back to the scene of the theft to confound him.

"It's a child who has stolen a loaf of bread," the people repeated.

Madame Mitaine, astonished at such an uproar, had come once more to the door of her shop. And she was quite thunder-struck when the gendarme, addressing her, exclaimed: "This is the young vagabond who just stole a loaf of yours, madame."

Then he gave Nanet a shake in order to frighten him. "You'll go to gaol, you know," he said. "Why did you steal that loaf, eh?"

But the little fellow was not put out. He answered clearly, in his flute-like voice: "I've had nothing to eat since yesterday, nor my sister either."

Meantime Madame Mitaine had recovered her self-possession. She was looking at the little lad with her beautiful eyes so full of indulgent kindness. Poor little devil! And his sister, where had he left her? For a moment the baker's wife hesitated, whilst a slight flush rose to her cheeks. Then, with the amiable laugh of a handsome woman accustomed to be courted by all her customers, she said in her gay quiet way: "You are mistaken, gendarme—that child didn't steal the loaf, I gave it him."

Without relaxing his hold on Nanet, the gendarme stood before her, gaping. Ten people had seen the boy take the loaf and run off with it. And all at once butcher Dacheux, who had crossed the street, intervened, in a furious passion. "But I saw him myself. I was looking this way at the very moment. He threw himself on the biggest of the loaves, and then took to his heels. That's how it happened. As true as I was robbed of five francs the day before yesterday, as true as Laboque and Caffiaux have been robbed to-day, that little vermin has just robbed you, Madame Mitaine, and you can't deny it."

Quite pink from having told a fib, the baker's wife none the less repeated gently: "You are mistaken, neighbour, it was I who gave the child that loaf. He did not steal it."

Then, as Dacheux flew into a temper with her, predicting that by her foolish indulgence she would end by having them all pillaged and massacred, Sub-Prefect Châtelard, who had judged the scene at a glance like a shrewd man, approached the gendarme and made him release Nanet, to whom, in a loud, ogre-like whisper, he said: "Off with you quick, youngster."

The crowd was already growling. Why, the baker's wife herself declared that she had given the boy the loaf! A poor little beggar, no higher than a jack-boot, who had been fasting since the previous day! Exclamations and hisses arose, and suddenly a thunderous voice made itself heard above every other.

"Ah! curse it! so little urchins six years old have to set us the example now? The child did right. When one's hungry one may take whatever one wants! Yes, everything in the shops is ours, and if you are all starving it's simply because you are cowards!"

The throng swayed about and eddied back, as when a paving-stone is flung into a pond. "Who is it?" people asked. And at once came back replies, "It's Lange, the potter." Amidst the groups which drew aside, Luc then saw the man who had spoken, a short, thick-set man, barely five-and-twenty, with a square-shaped head, bushy with black hair and beard. Of a rustic appearance but with a glow of intelligence in his eyes, he went on speaking, proclaiming the dream of his life aloud, in soaring but unpolished language, like a poet yet in the rough. And he made no gestures, but quietly kept his hands in his pockets.

"Provisions and money and houses and clothes," said he; "they have all been stolen from us, and we have a right to take them all back! And not to-morrow, but this very evening, if we were men, we ought to resume possession of the soil, the mines, the factories, all Beauclair indeed! There are no two ways of doing it, there is only one—to throw the whole edifice on the ground at one blow, to poleaxe and destroy authority everywhere, so that the people, to whom everything belongs, may at last build up the world anew!"

Women took fright on hearing this. Even the men, in presence of the aggressive vehemence of Lange's words, became silent and retreated, anxious as to the consequences. Few of them really understood, the greater number, beneath the century-old grinding bondage of the wage-earning system, had not as yet reached such a degree of embittered rebellion. What was the good of it? They would none the less die of starvation and go to prison, they thought.

"Oh! you don't dare, I know it!" continued Lange, with terrible sarcasm. "But there are others who will dare some day. Your Beauclair will be blown up unless it falls to pieces from sheer rottenness. Your noses can't be worth much if you are unable to smell this evening that everything's rotten, and stinks of putrefaction! There is only so much dung left; and one doesn't need to be a great prophet to predict that the wind which blows will some day sweep away the town and all the thieves and all the murderers, our masters! Ah! may everything tumble down and break to pieces! To death, to death with all of it!"

The scandal was becoming so great that Sub-Prefect Châtelard, though he would have preferred to treat the matter with indifference, found himself obliged to exercise his authority. Somebody had to be arrested, so three gendarmes sprang upon Lange, and led him off down a gloomy, deserted side street, where their heavy footfalls died away. The crowd itself had shown but vague, contradictory impulses, which were promptly quieted. And the gathering was broken up and the tramping began afresh, slow and silent through the black mud from one to the other end of the street.

But Luc had shuddered. That prophetic threat had burst forth like the frightful fated outcome of all that he had seen, all that he had heard, since the fall of daylight. Such an abundance of iniquity and wretchedness called for a final catastrophe, which he himself felt approaching from the depths beyond the horizon, in the form perchance of some avenging cloud of fire which would consume and raze Beauclair to the ground. And with his horror of all violence Luc suffered at the thought of it. What! could the potter be right? Would force, would theft and murder, be necessary for mankind to find itself once more within the pale of justice? In his distracted state it had seemed to Luc that, amidst all the harsh, sombre faces of the toilers, he had seen the pale countenances of Mayor Gourier, Judge Gaume, and Captain Jollivet flit past him. Then, too, the faces of the Mazelles, perspiring with terror, darted by in the flickering light of a gas-lamp. The street horrified him, and only one compassionate consolatory thought remained, that of overtaking Nanet, following him, and ascertaining into what dark nook the unhappy Josine had fallen.

The lad was walking on and on with all the courage of his little legs. Luc, who had seen him go off up the Rue de Brias in the direction of the Abyss, overtook him fairly rapidly, for the dear little fellow had great difficulty in carrying his big loaf. He pressed it to his chest with both his hands, from fear of dropping it, and from fear too lest some evil-hearted man or some big dog might tear it from him. On hearing Luc's hasty footsteps in the rear, he no doubt felt extremely frightened, for he attempted to run. But on glancing round he recognised by the light of one of the last gas-lamps the gentleman who had smiled at him and his big sister, and thereupon he felt reassured, and allowed himself to be overtaken.

"Shall I carry your loaf for you?" the young man asked.

"Oh, no! I want to keep it. It pleases me," said the boy.

They were now on the high road beyond Beauclair, in the darkness falling from the low and stormy sky. The lights of the Abyss alone gleamed forth some distance off. And one could hear the child splashing through the mud, whilst he raised his loaf as high as possible, so that it might not get dirty.

"You know where you are going?" asked Luc.

"Of course."

"Is it very far?"

"No—it's somewhere."

A vague fear must have been stealing over Nanet again, for his steps slackened. Why did the gentleman want to know? Feeling that he was his big sister's only protector, the little man sought to devise some ruse. But Luc, who guessed his feelings, and wished to show him that he was a friend, began to play with him, catching him in his arms at the moment when he narrowly missed stumbling in a puddle.

"Look out, my boy! You mustn't get any mud-jam on your bread."

Conquered, having felt the affectionate warmth of those big brotherly arms, Nanet burst into the careless laugh of childhood and said to his new friend: "Oh! you are strong and kind, you are!"

Then he went trotting on, without showing further disquietude. But where could Josine have hidden herself? The road stretched out, and in the motionless shadow of each successive tree Luc fancied he could see her waiting. He was drawing near the Abyss, the ground already shook with the heavy blows of the steam-hammer, whilst the surroundings were illumined by a fiery cloud of vapour traversed by the broad rays of the electric lights. Nanet, without going past the Abyss, turned towards the bridge and crossed the Mionne. Thus Luc found himself brought back to the very spot where he had first met the boy and his sister earlier in the evening. But all at once the lad rushed off, and the young man lost sight of him and heard him call, whilst once more laughing playfully:

"Here, big sister, here big sister! look at this, see how fine it is."

Beyond the bridge the river bank became lower, and a bench stood there in the shadow cast by some palings facing the Abyss, which smoked and panted on the other side of the water. Luc had just knocked against the palings when he heard the urchin's laughter turn into cries and tears. He took his bearings, and understood everything when he perceived Josine lying exhausted, in a swoon, upon the bench. She had fallen there overcome by hunger and suffering, letting her little brother go off, and scarcely understanding what he, with the boldness of a lad of the streets, had intended to do. And now the child, finding her cold, as if lifeless, sobbed loudly and despairingly.

ÉMILE ZOLA

"Oh! big sister, wake up, wake up! You must eat, do eat, there's bread now."

Tears had come to Luc's eyes also. To think that so much misery, such a frightful destiny of privation and suffering, should fall upon such weak yet courageous creatures! He quickly descended to the Mionne, dipped his handkerchief in the water, and came back and applied it to Josine's temples. Fortunately that tragic night was not a very cold one. At last he took hold of the young woman's hands, rubbed them, and warmed them with his own; and finally she sighed and seemed to awaken from some black dream. But in her prostrate condition, due to lack of food, nothing astonished her; it appeared to her quite natural that her brother should be there with that loaf, accompanied too by that tall and handsome gentleman, whom she recognised. Perhaps she imagined that it was the gentleman who had brought the bread. Her poor weak fingers could not break the crust. He had to help her break the bread into little pieces, which he passed her slowly, one by one, so that she might not choke herself in her haste to quiet the atrocious hunger which griped her. And then the whole of her poor, thin, spare figure began to tremble, and she wept, wept on unceasingly whilst still eating, thus moistening each mouthful with her tears ere she devoured it voraciously, evincing the while the shivering clumsiness of some eager beaten animal which no longer knows how to swallow. Luc, distracted, with a pang at his heart, gently restrained her hands whilst still giving her the little pieces which he broke off the loaf. Never could he afterwards forget that communion of suffering and kindliness, that bread of life thus given to the most woeful and sweetest of human creatures.

Nanet, meantime, broke off his own share, and ate like a little glutton, proud of his exploit. His sister's tears astonished him—why did she still weep when they were feasting? Then, having finished, quite oppressed by his ravenous feast, he nestled close beside her and was overpowered by sudden somnolence, the happy sleep of childhood, which beholds the angels in its dreams. And Josine pressed him to her with her right arm, leaning back against the bench and feeling a trifle stronger, whilst Luc remained seated by her side, unable to leave her like that alone in the night with that sleeping child. He had understood at last that some of the clumsiness that she had shown in eating had been due to her injured hand, around which, as well as she could manage, she had again wound her bloodstained bandage.

"You have injured yourself?" he said.

"Yes, monsieur, a boot-stitching machine broke one of my fingers and I had to have it cut off. But it was my fault, so the foreman said, though Monsieur Gourier gave me fifty francs."

She spoke in a somewhat low and very gentle voice, which trembled at moments as with a kind of shame.

"So you worked at the boot-factory belonging to Monsieur Gourier, the Mayor?"

"Yes, monsieur, I first went there when I was fifteen—I'm eighteen now. My mother worked there more than twenty years, but she is dead. I'm all alone, I've only my little brother, Nanet, who is just six. My name's Josine."

And she went on telling her story, in such wise that Luc only had to ask a few more questions to learn everything. It was the commonplace, distressful story of so many poor girls; a father who goes off with another woman, a mother who remains stranded with four children, for whom she is unable to earn sufficient food. Although she luckily loses two of them, she dies at last from the effect of over-work, and then the daughter, just sixteen years of age, has to become a mother to her little brother, in her turn killing herself with hard work, though at times she is unable to earn bread enough for herself and the boy. Then comes the inevitable tragedy which dogs the footsteps of a good-looking workgirl—a seducer passes, the rakish Ragu, on whose arm she imprudently strolls each Sunday after the dance. He makes her such fine promises, she already pictures herself married, with a pretty home, in which she brings up her brother together with the children that may come to her. Her only fault is that one evening in springtime she stumbles; how it was she hardly remembers. And six months later she is guilty of a second fault, that of going to live with Ragu, who speaks no more to her of marriage. Then her accident befalls her at the boot-works, and she finds herself unable to continue working at the very moment when the strike has rendered Ragu so rageful and spiteful that he has begun to beat her, accusing her of being the cause of his own misery. And from that moment things go from bad to worse, and now he has turned her into the street, and will not even give her the key so that she may go home to bed with Nanet.

Whilst the girl went on talking it seemed to Luc that if she should have a child by Ragu he might become attached to her and make up his mind to marry her. However, when the young man hinted this to Josine she speedily undeceived him. No, nothing of that was at all likely. Then silence fell, they no longer spoke. The certainty that Josine was not a mother, that she would never bear children to that man Ragu, brought Luc, amidst his dolorous compassion, a singular feeling of relief, for which he was unable to account. Vague ideas arose in his mind, whilst his eyes wandered far away over the dim scene before him, and he again discerned that gorge of Brias which he had viewed in the twilight before it was steeped in shadows. On either side where the Bleuse Mountains reared their flights of rocks the darkness became more dense. Midway up the height behind him the young man now and again heard the passing rumble of a train which whistled and slowed down as it approached the station. At his feet he distinguished the glaucous Mionne, rippling against the stockade whose beams upheld the bridge. And then, on his left, came the sudden widening of the gorge, the two promontories of the Bleuse Mountains drawing aside on the verge of the vast Roumagne plain, where the tempestuous night rolled on like a black and endless sea beyond the vague eyot of Beauclair, where constellated hundreds of little lights, suggesting sparks.

But Luc's eyes ever came back to the Abyss in front of him. It showed forth like some weird apparition under clouds of white smoke, fired, so it seemed, by the electric lamps in the yards. Through open doorways and other apertures one at times perceived the blazing mouths of the furnaces, with now a blinding flow of fusing metal, now a huge ruddy glare; all the internal, hellish flames indeed of the monster's devouring, tumultuous work. The ground quaked all around, whilst the ringing dance of the tilt-hammers never ceased to sound above the dull rumbling of the machinery, and the deep blows of the great steam-hammers, which suggested a far-away cannonade.

And Luc, with his eyes full of that vision, his heart lacerated by the thought of the fate that had befallen that hapless Josine, now reclining in utter abandonment and wretchedness on that bench beside him, said to himself that in this poor creature resounded the whole collapse of labour, evilly organised, dishonoured, and accursed. In that supreme suffering, in that human sacrifice ended all his experiences of the evening, the disasters of the strike, the hatred poisoning men's hearts and minds, the egotistical harshness of trade, the triumph of drink which had become necessary to stimulate forgetfulness, the legitimation of theft by hunger, the cracking and rending of old-time society beneath the very weight of its own iniquities. And he fancied that he could again hear Lange predicting the final catastrophe which would sweep away that Beauclair, which was rotten itself and which rotted everything that came in contact with it. And he saw once more also the pale girls wandering over the pavement, those sorry offspring of manufacturing towns, where the vile wage-system invariably brings about the ruin of the better-looking factory hands. Was it not to a similar fate that Josine herself was drifting? He could divine that she was a submissive, a loving creature, one of those tender natures that give courage to the strong and prove their reward. And the thought of abandoning her on that bench, of doing nothing to save her from accursed fate, filled him with such revolt, that he would have for ever reproached himself had he not offered her a helping and a brotherly hand.

"Come, you cannot sleep here with that child," he said. "That man must take you back. For the rest we'll see afterwards. Where do you live?"

"Near by, in the Rue des Trois Lunes, in Old Beauclair," she replied.

Then she explained things to him. Ragu occupied a little lodging of three rooms in the same house as one of his sisters, Adèle, nicknamed La Toupe. And she suspected that if Ragu really had not got the key with him, he must have handed it to La Toupe, who was a terrible creature. When the young man spoke of quietly going to her and asking her for the key, Josine shuddered.

"Oh, no! you must not ask her. She hates me. If one could only come upon her husband, who's a good-natured man, but I know that he works at the Abyss to-night. He's a master puddler, named Bonnaire."

"Bonnaire!" Luc repeated, a recollection awakening within him; "why I saw him when I visited the Abyss last spring. I even had a long talk with him—he explained the work to me. He's an intelligent fellow, and, as you say, he seemed to me to be good-natured. Well, it's quite simple, I will go and speak to him about you."

Josine raised a cry of heartfelt gratitude; she was trembling from head to foot, and she clasped her hands as her whole being went out towards the young man. "Oh! monsieur, how good you are!—how can I ever thank you!"

A sombre glow was now rising from the Abyss, and Luc, as he glanced at her, saw her, this time bare-headed, for her ragged wrapper had fallen over her shoulders. She was no longer weeping, her blue eyes gleamed with tenderness, and her little mouth had found once more its youthful smile. With her supple graceful slimness she had retained quite a childish air, she looked like one who was still playful, simple, and gay. Her long fair hair, of the hue of ripe oats, had fallen, half unbound, over the nape of her neck, and lent her quite a girlish and candid appearance in her abandonment. He, infinitely charmed, by degrees quite captivated, felt moved and astonished at the sight of the winning creature that seemed to emerge from the poor beggarly being whom he had met badly clad, frightened, and weeping. And, besides, she looked at him with so much adoration, she surrendered to him so candidly her soul, like one who at last felt herself succoured and loved. Handsome and kind as he was, he seemed to her a very god after all the brutality of Ragu. She would have kissed his very footprints; and she stood before him with her hands still clasped, the left pressing the right, the mutilated hand round which was wrapped the bloodstained bandage. And something very sweet and very strong seemed to bind her and him together, a link of infinite tenderness, infinite affection.

"Nanet will take you to the works, monsieur," she said; "he knows every corner of them."

"No, no, I know my way. Don't awake him, he will keep you warm. Wait here for me quietly, both of you."

He left her on the bench, in the black night, with the sleeping child. And as he stepped away a great glow illumined the promontory of the Bleuse Mountains on the right above the park of La Crêcherie, where stood Jordan's house. The sombre silhouette of the blast furnace could be seen on the mountain side. A "run" of metal flowed forth, and all the neighbouring rocks, even all the roofs of Beauclair, were illumined by it as by some bright red dawn.

II

Bonnaire, the master puddler, one of the best hands of the works, had played an important part in the recent strike. A man of just mind, indignant with the iniquity of the wage-earning system, he read the Paris newspapers and derived from them a revolutionary education in which there were many gaps, but which had made him a fairly frank partisan of Collectivist doctrines. As he himself, with the fine equilibrium of a hard-working healthy man, very reasonably said, Collectivism was the dream whose realisation they would some day seek; and meantime it was necessary to secure as much justice as might be immediately obtained in order to reduce the sufferings of the workers to a minimum.

The strike had been for some time inevitable. Three years previously, the Abyss having nearly come to grief in the hands of Monsieur Jérôme's son, Michel Qurignon, the latter's son-in-law, Boisgelin, an idler, a fine Paris gentleman, had purchased the works, investing in them all that remained of his jeopardised fortune on the advice of a poor cousin, a certain Delaveau, who had positively undertaken to make the capital invested yield a profit of thirty per cent, per annum. And for three years Delaveau, a skilful engineer and a determined hard worker, had kept his promise, thanks to energetic management and organisation, strict attention to the minutest details, and absolute discipline on all sides. Michel Qurignon's ill success in business had been partly due to the difficulties which had beset the metal market of the region ever since the manufacture of iron rails and girders had there ceased to be remunerative, owing to the discovery of certain chemical processes which in Northern and Eastern France had enabled ironmasters to make use very cheaply of large quantities of ore which previously had been regarded as too defective. The Beauclair works could not possibly turn out the same class of goods so cheaply as their competitors; ruin therefore seemed inevitable, and Delaveau's stroke of talent consisted in changing the character of the output, in giving up the manufacture of rails and girders which Northern and Eastern France could supply at twenty centimes the kilogramme,[1] and confining himself to the manufacture of high-class things, such indeed as projectiles and

---

1. That is about 1*d*. per pound.

ÉMILE ZOLA

ordnance, shells and cannon, which brought in from two to three francs per kilogramme. Prosperity had then returned, and Boisgelin's investment brought him in a considerable income. Only it had been necessary to obtain a quantity of new plant, and to secure the services of more careful and attentive workmen, who necessarily required to be better paid than others.

In principle the strike had been brought about by that very question of better pay. The men were paid by the hundred kilogrammes,[2] and Delaveau himself admitted the necessity of a new wage tariff. But he wished to remain absolute master of the situation, desiring above all things to avoid anything which might seem like surrender on his part to the pressure of his workpeople. With a specialist mind, very authoritative in disposition, and stubborn with respect to his rights, whilst striving to be just and loyal, he regarded Collectivism as a destructive dream, and declared that any such utopian doctrine would lead one direct to the most awful catastrophes. The quarrel on this point between him and the little world of workers over whom he reigned became a fierce one directly Bonnaire succeeded in setting a defensive syndicate on foot. For if Delaveau admitted the desirability of relief and pension funds, and even of co-operative societies supplying cheap provisions and other necessaries, thus recognising that the workman was not forbidden to improve his position, he at the same time violently condemned all syndicates and class grouping designed for collective action.

From that moment then the struggle began; Delaveau showed great unwillingness to complete the revision of the tariffs, and thought it necessary in his turn to arm himself, in some measure, decreeing a "state of siege" at the Abyss. Soon after he had begun to act thus rigorously the men complained that no individual liberty was left to them. A close watch was kept on them, on their thoughts and opinions as well as on their actions, even outside the works. Those who put on a humble flattering manner and perchance became spies, gained the management's good graces, whilst the proud and independent were treated as dangerous men. And as the manager was by instinct a staunch conservative, a defender of the existing order of things, and openly evinced the resolve to have none but men of his own views in the place, all the underlings, the engineers, foremen, and inspectors

---

2. 220 ½ lbs.

strove to surpass one another in energy, displaying implacable severity with regard to obedience, and what they chose to call "a proper spirit."

Bonnaire, hurt in his opinions, his craving for liberty and justice, naturally found himself at the head of the malcontents. It was he who with a few mates waited on Delaveau to acquaint him with their complaints. He spoke out very plainly, and, indeed, exasperated the manager without obtaining the rise in wages that he asked for. Delaveau did not believe in the possibility of a general strike among his hands, for the metal workers do not readily lose their tempers, and for many years there had been no strike at all at the Abyss, whereas among the pitmen of the coal mines of Brias strikes broke out continually. When, therefore, contrary to Delaveau's anticipations, a general strike did occur among his own men, when one morning only two hundred out of a thousand presented themselves at the works, which he had to close, his resentment was so great that he stubbornly held to the course he had chosen and refused to make the slightest concession. When Bonnaire and a deputation of the syndicate ventured to go to him he began by turning them out of doors. He was the master, the quarrel was between his workmen and himself, and he intended to settle it with his workmen and with nobody else. Bonnaire therefore returned to see him accompanied only by three mates. But all that they could obtain from him were arguments and calculations, tending to show that the prosperity of the Abyss would be compromised if he should increase the men's wages. Funds had been confided to him, a factory had been given him to manage, and it was his duty to see that the factory paid its way and that the funds yielded the promised rate of interest. He was certainly disposed to be humane, but he considered that it was the duty of an honest man to keep his engagements, and extract from the enterprise he directed the largest amount of gain possible. All the rest, in his opinion, was visionary, wild hope, dangerous utopia. And thus, each side becoming more and more stubborn after several similar interviews, the strike lasted for two long months, full of disasters for the wage-earners as well as for the owner, increasing as it did the misery of the men whilst the plant was damaged by neglect and idleness. At last the contending parties consented to make certain mutual concessions, and came to an agreement respecting a new tariff. But throughout another week Delaveau refused to take back certain workmen, whom he called the "leaders," and among whom, of course, was Bonnaire. The manager harboured very rancorous feelings towards the latter, although

ÉMILE ZOLA

he recognised that he was one of the most skilful and most sober of his hands. When he ultimately gave way, and took Bonnaire back with the others, he declared that he was being compelled to act in this manner against his inclinations, solely from a desire to restore peace.

From that moment Bonnaire felt that he was condemned. Under such circumstances he was at first absolutely unwilling to go back to the works at all. But he was a great favourite with his mates, and when they declared that they would not return unless he resumed work at the same time as themselves, he appeared to resign himself to their wishes, in order that he might not prove the cause of some fresh rupture. In his estimation, however, his mates had suffered quite enough; he had fully made up his mind and intended to sacrifice himself in order that none other might have to pay the penalty of the semi-victory which had been gained. And thus, although he had ended by returning to work on the Thursday, it had been with the intention of taking himself off on the ensuing Sunday, for he was convinced that his presence at the Abyss was no longer possible. He took none of his friends into his confidence, but simply warned the management on Saturday morning of his intention to leave. If he were still working at the Abyss that night it was solely because he wished to finish a job which he had begun. He desired to disappear in a quiet, honest way.

Luc having given his name to the door porter, inquired if he could speak to master-puddler Bonnaire; and the porter in reply contented himself with pointing out the hall where the puddling-furnaces and rolling-machines were installed at the further end of the second yard on the left. The yards, soaked by the recent rain, formed a perfect cloaca, what with their uneven paving-stones and their tangle of rails, amongst which passed a branch line connecting the works with Beauclair railway station. Under the lunar-like brightness of a few electric lamps, amongst the shadows cast by the sheds and the plunging tower, and the vaguely outlined cementing furnaces, which suggested the conical temples of some barbarous religion, a little engine was slowly moving about and sending forth shrill whistles of warning in order that nobody might be run over. But what more particularly deafened the visitor from the moment he crossed the threshold was the beating of a couple of tilt-hammers installed in a kind of cellar. Their big heads—the heads, it seemed, of voracious beasts—could be seen striking the iron with a furious rhythm; they bit it, as it were, and stretched it into bars with all the force of their desperate metal teeth. The workmen beside them led calm and silent lives, communicating with one another by gestures only amidst the everlasting uproar and trepidation. Luc, after skirting a low building where some other tilt-hammers were also working ragefully, turned to the left and crossed the second yard whose ravaged soil was littered with pieces of scrap metal, slumbering in the mud until collected for re-casting. A railway truck was being laden with a large piece of wrought work, a shaft for a torpedo boat, which had been finished that very day, and which the little engine was about to remove. As this engine came up whistling, Luc, in order to avoid it, took a pathway between some symmetrically disposed piles of pig-iron, and in this wise reached the hall of the puddling-furnaces and the rolling-machines.

This hall or gallery, one of the largest of the works, resounded in the daytime with the terrible rumbling of the rollers. But the latter were now at rest, and more than half of the huge place was steeped in darkness. Of the ten puddling-furnaces only four were at work, served by two forge-hammers. Here and there a meagre gas-light flickered in the draught; huge shadows filled the place; one could scarcely distinguish the great smoked beams upholding the roof above. A sound of dripping water emerged from the darkness; the beaten ground which served as a flooring—all bumps and hollows—was in one part so much fœtid mud, in another so much coal-dust, in another, again, a mass of waste stuff. On every side one noticed the filth of joyless labour, a labour hated and accursed, performed in a black, ruinous, ignoble den, pestilential with smoke and grimy with the dirt of every kind that flew through the air. From the nails driven into some little huts of rough boards hung the workmen's town-clothes, mixed with linen vests and leather aprons. And all that dense misery was only brightened when some master puddler happened to open the door of his furnace, whence emerged a blinding flow of light which, like the beaming of some planet, transpierced the darkness of the entire gallery.

When Luc presented himself Bonnaire was for the last time stirring some fusing metal—some four hundred and forty pounds' weight of cast iron, which the furnace and human labour between them were to turn into steel. The whole operation of steel puddling required four hours, and this stirring at the expiration of the first hours of waiting was the hardest part of the work. Grasping an iron rod of fifty pounds' weight and standing in the broiling glare, the master puddler stirred the incandescent metal on the sole of the furnace. With the help of the hook at the end of his bar he raked the depths and kneaded the huge sun-like ball or "bloom," at which he alone was able to gaze, with his eyes hardened to the intense glow. And he had to gaze at it, since it was by its colour that he ascertained what stage the work had reached. When he withdrew his bar the latter was a bright red, and threw out sparks on all sides.

With a motion of his hand Bonnaire now signed to his stoker to quicken the fire, whilst another workman, the companion puddler, took up a bar in order to do a stir in his turn.

"You are Monsieur Bonnaire, are you not?" asked Luc, drawing near.

The master puddler seemed surprised at being thus accosted, but nodded affirmatively. He looked superb with his white neck and pink face full of victorious strength amidst the glare of his work.

Scarcely five-and-thirty years of age, he was a giant of fair complexion, with close-cropped hair and a broad, massive, placid face. His large firm mouth and big peaceful eyes expressed great rectitude and kindliness.

"I don't know if you recognise me," Luc continued, "but I saw you here last summer and had a talk with you."

"Quite so," the master puddler at last replied; "you are a friend of Monsieur Jordan."

When, however, the young man with some embarrassment explained the motive of his visit, how he had seen the unhappy Josine cast into the street, and how it seemed that he, Bonnaire, could alone do something for her, the workman relapsed into silence, looking embarrassed on his side also. Neither spoke for a time; there came an interval of waiting, prolonged by the noise of the forge-hammer near them. And when the master puddler was at last able to make himself heard he simply said: "All right, I'll do what I can—I'll go with you as soon as I've finished, in about three-quarters of an hour."

Although it was nearly eleven o'clock already, Luc resolved to wait; and at first he began to take some interest in a cutting-machine, which in a dark corner near at hand was cutting bar-steel with as much quiet ease as if steel were butter. At each motion of the machine's jaws, a little piece of metal fell, and a heap was soon formed, ready to be carried in a barrow into the charging-chamber, where each charge of sixty-six pounds' weight was made up in order to be removed to the adjacent hall, where the crucible furnaces were installed. And with the view of occupying his time, attracted as he was by the great pink glow which filled that hall, Luc entered it.

It was a very large and lofty place, as badly kept, as grimy and as much out of repair as the other. And on a level with the bossy ground, littered with scrap, were the openings of six batteries of furnaces, each divided into three compartments. Those narrow, long, glaring pits whose brick walls occupied the whole basement, were heated by a mixture of air and flaming gas, which the head caster himself regulated by means of a mechanical fan. Thus, streaking the beaten ground of the shadowy hall, there appeared six slits, open above the internal hell, the ever-active volcano, whose subterranean brazier could be heard rumbling loudly. Covers, shaped like long slabs, bricks bound together by an iron armature, were laid across the furnaces. But these covers did not join, and from each intervening space sprang an intense pinkish light, so many sunrises as it were, broad rays starting from the soil and darting in a sheaf to the dusty glass of the roofing. And whenever a man, according to the requirements of the work, removed one or another of the covers, one might have thought that some planet was emerging from all obstacles, for the hall was then irradiated by a brightness like that of aurora.

It so happened that Luc was able to see the operations. Some workmen were loading a furnace, and he saw them lower the crucibles of refractory clay, which had previously been heated till they were red, and then by means of a funnel, pour in the charges, sixty-six pounds of metal for each crucible. For some three or four hours fusion would be in progress, and then the crucibles would have to be removed and emptied, which was the terrible part of the work. As Luc drew near to another furnace, where some men provided with long bars had just assured themselves that the fusion was perfect, he recognised Fauchard in the drawer whose duty it was to remove the crucibles. Livid and withered, with a bony, scorched face, Fauchard had none the less retained strong herculean arms and legs. Physically deformed by the terrible labour— ever the same—which he had been performing for fourteen years already, he had suffered yet more considerably in his intelligence from the machine-like life to which he had been condemned: perpetually repeating the same movements, without need of thought or individuality of action, becoming as it were merely an element of the struggle with fire. His physical defects, the rise of his shoulders, the hypertrophy of his limbs, the scorching of his eyes, which had paled from constant exposure to flaming light, were not his only blemishes—he was also conscious of intellectual downfall; for caught in the monster's grasp at sixteen years of age, after a rudimentary education suddenly cut short, he remembered that he had once possessed intelligence, an intelligence which was now flickering and departing under the relentless burden of a labour which he performed like some blinded beast crushed down by destructive baleful toil. And he now had but one sole craving, one sole delight, which was to drink—to drink his four quarts of wine at each shift, to drink so that the furnace might not burn up his baked skin like so much old rind, to drink so that he might escape crumbling into ashes, so that he might enjoy some last felicity by finishing his life in the happy stupor of perpetual intoxication.

That night Fauchard had greatly feared that the fire would boil some more of his blood. But, already at eight o'clock he was agreeably surprised to see Natalie, his wife, arrive with the four quarts of wine which she had obtained on credit from Caffiaux, and which he had no longer expected. She expressed regret that she had not a little meat to give him also, but Dacheux, she said, had shown himself pitiless. Ever in low spirits, and greatly given to complaining, she expressed her anxiety as to how they would manage to get anything to eat on the morrow. But her husband, who was well pleased at having secured his wine, dismissed her saying that he should apply to the manager for an advance as his mates had done. A crust of bread sufficed him as food, he drank, and at once found himself full of confidence. When the time to remove the crucibles arrived he tossed off another half-quart at a gulp, and went to the water cistern to soak the large linen apron that enveloped him. Then, with big wooden shoes on his feet and wet gloves on his hands, armed too with long iron pincers, he stood astride the furnace, resting his right foot on the cover, which had just been pushed aside, his chest and stomach being exposed the while to the frightful heat which arose from the open volcano. For a moment he appeared quite red, blazing like a torch in the midst of a brazier. His wooden shoes steamed, his apron and his gloves steamed, the whole of his flesh seemed to melt away. But without evincing any haste, he looked below him. His eyes, accustomed to the brightest glare, sought the crucible in the depths of the burning pit. Then he stooped slightly in order to seize it with his long pincers, and with a sudden straightening of the loins, with three supple rhythmical movements—one of his hands opening and gliding along the rod until the other joined it—he drew up the crucible, raising easily, at arm's length, that weight of one hundred and ten pounds—pincers and crucible combined—and deposited it on the ground, where it looked like some piece of the sun, at first of dazzling whiteness, which speedily changed to pink. Then he began the operation afresh, drawing the crucibles forth one by one amidst the increasing glow, with more skill even than strength, coming and going amidst that incandescent matter without ever burning himself, without seeming even to feel the intolerable heat.

They were going to cast some little shells, of one hundred and thirty-two pounds. The bottle-shaped moulds were ranged in two rows. And when the assistants had skimmed the slag off the crucibles with the aid of iron rods, which came away smoking and dropping purple slaver, the head caster quickly seized the crucibles with his large, round-jawed pincers, and emptied two into each mould. And the metal flowed like white lava, with just a faint pinkish tinge here and there amidst a shooting of fine blue sparks as delicate as flowers. It might have been thought that the man was decanting some bright, gold-spangled liqueur; all was done noiselessly, with precise and nimble movements, amidst a blaze and a heat that changed the whole place into a devouring brazier.

Luc, who was unaccustomed to it all, felt stifling, unable to remain there any longer. At a distance of twelve and even fifteen feet from the furnaces his face was scorched, and a burning perspiration streamed from him. The shells had interested him, and he watched them cooling, asking himself what men they would some day kill. And going on into the next hall, he there found himself among the steam hammers and the forging-press. This hall was now asleep, with all its monstrous appliances. Its press of a force of two thousand tons and its hammers of lesser power spread out, showing in the depths of the gloom their black squat silhouettes, which suggested those of barbarian gods. And here Luc found more projectiles, shells which that very day had been forged under the smallest steam-hammer, on leaving the moulds after annealing. Then he became interested in the tube of a large naval gun, more than nineteen feet long, which was still warm from having passed under the press. Billets totalling two thousand two hundred pounds of steel had spread out and adapted themselves like rolls of paste to form that tube, which was waiting chained, ready to be lifted by powerful cranes and carried to the turning-lathes, which were farther off, beyond the hall where the Martin furnace and some of the steel-casting plant were installed.

Luc went on to the end, across that hall also, the most spacious of them all, for there the largest pieces were cast. The Martin furnace enabled one to pour large quantities of steel in a state of fusion into the cast-iron moulds, whilst eight feet overhead two rolling bridges worked by electricity gently and easily moved huge pieces weighing many tons to every requisite point. Then Luc entered the lathe workshop, a huge closed shed which was rather better kept than the others, and where on either hand he found a series of admirable appliances in which incomparable delicacy and power were blended. There were planes for naval armour-plates which finished off metal-work even as a carpenter's plane gives a finish to wood. And there were the lathes of precise if intricate mechanism, as pretty as jewels, and as amusing as toys. Only some of them worked at night-time, each lighted by a single electric lamp, and giving forth but a faint sound in the deep silence. Again did Luc come upon projectiles. There was one shell which had been fixed to a lathe, to be calibrated externally. It turned round and round with a prodigious speed, and steel shavings which suggested silver curls flew away from under the narrow motionless blade. Afterwards it would only have to be hollowed internally, tempered, and finished. But where were the men that would be killed by it, after it had been charged? As the outcome of all that heroic human labour, the subjugation of iron bringing royalty to man and victory over the forces of nature, Luc beheld a vision of massacre, all the bloodthirsty madness of a battle-field! He walked on, and at a little distance came upon a large lathe, where a cannon similar to the one whose forged tube he had just seen was revolving. This one, however, was already calibrated externally, and shone like new money. Under the supervision of a youth who leant forward, attentively watching the mechanism, like a clock-maker that of a watch, it turned and turned interminably with a gentle humming, whilst the blade inside drilled it with marvellous precision. And when that gun also should have been tempered, cast from the summit of the tower into a bath of petroleum oil, to what battle-field would it journey to kill men—how many lives would it mow down, that gun made of steel which men in a spirit of brotherliness should have fashioned only into rails and ploughshares!

Luc pushed a door open, and made his escape into the open air. The night was damply warm, and he drew a long breath, feeling refreshed by the wind which was blowing. When he raised his eyes he was unable to distinguish a single star beyond the wild rush of the clouds. But the lamp globes shining here and there in the yard replaced the hidden moon, and again he saw the chimneys rising amidst lurid smoke, and a coal-smirched sky, across which upon every side, forming as it were some gigantic cobweb, flew all the wires which transmitted electric power. The machines which produced it, two machines of great beauty, were working close by in some new buildings. There were also some works for making bricks and crucibles of refractory clay; there was a carpenter's shop for model-making and packing, and numerous warehouses for commercial steel and iron. And Luc, after losing himself for a time in that little town, well pleased when he came upon deserted stretches, black peaceful nooks where he seemed to revive to life, suddenly found himself once more inside the inferno. On looking around him he perceived that he was again in the gallery containing the furnaces for the crucibles.

Another operation was now being executed there. Seventy crucibles were being removed at the same moment for some big piece of casting which was to weigh over three thousand nine hundred pounds. The mould with its funnel was waiting in readiness in the pit, in the neighbouring hall. And the procession was swiftly organised, all the helpers of the various squads took part in it, two men for each crucible, which they raised with pincers and carried off with long and easy strides. Another, then another, then another, the whole seventy crucibles passed along in a dazzling procession. One might have thought it some ballet scene, in which vague dancers with light and shadowy feet passed two-by-two carrying huge Venetian lanterns, orange-red in hue. And the marvellous part of it all was the extraordinary rapidity, the perfect assurance of the well-regulated movements in which the bearers were seen gambolling, as it were, in the midst of fire, hastening up, elbowing one another, marching off and coming back, juggling all the while with fusing stars. In less than three minutes the seventy crucibles were emptied into the mould, whence arose a sheaf of gold, a great spreading bouquet of sparks.

When Luc at last returned to the hall containing the puddling furnaces and the rollers, after a good half-hour's promenade, he found Bonnaire finishing his work.

"I will be with you in a moment, monsieur," said the puddler.

On the glaring sole of the furnace, whose open door was blazing, he had already on three occasions isolated one quarter of the incandescent metal, that is a hundredweight of it, which he had rolled and fashioned into a kind of ball with the aid of his bar; and those three quarters had gone one after the other to the hammer. He was now dealing with the fourth and last portion. For twenty minutes he had been standing before that voracious maw, his chest almost crackling from the heat of the furnace, his hands manipulating his heavy hooked bar, and his eyes clearly seeing how to do the work aright in spite of all the dazzling flames. He gazed fixedly at the fiery ball of steel which he rolled over and over continuously in the centre of the brazier; and in the fierce reverberation which gilded his tall pinkish form against the black background of darkness, he looked like some maker of planets, busily creating new worlds. But at last he finished, withdrew his flaming bar, and handed over to his mate the last hundredweight of the charge.

The stoker was in readiness with a little iron chariot. Armed with his pincers the assistant puddler seized hold of the ball, which suggested some huge fiery sponge that had sprouted on the side of a volcanic cavern, and with an effort he brought it out and threw it into the chariot, which the stoker quickly wheeled to the hammer. A smith at once caught it with his own pincers and placed and turned it over under the hammer, which all at once began working. Then came a deafening noise and a perfect dazzlement. The ground quaked, a pealing of bells seemed to ring out, whilst the smith, gloved and bound round with leather, disappeared amidst a perfect tornado of sparks. At some moments the expectorations were so large that they burst, here and there, like canister shot. Impassive amidst that fusillade, the smith turned the sponge over and over in order that it might be struck on every side and converted into a "lump," a loaf of steel, ready for the rollers. And the hammer obeyed him, struck here, struck there, slackening or hastening its blows without a word even coming from his lips, without anyone even detecting the signs which he made to the hammer-lad who sat aloft in his little box with his hand on the starting-lever.

Luc, who had drawn near whilst Bonnaire was changing his clothes, recognised little Fortuné, Fauchard's brother-in-law, in the hammer-lad thus perched on high, motionless for hours together, giving no other sign of life than a little mechanical gesture of the hand amidst the deafening uproar which he raised. A touch on the right-hand lever so that the hammer might fall, a touch on the left-hand lever so that it might rise, that was all; the little lad's mind was confined to that narrow space. By the bright gleams of the sparks one could for a moment perceive him, slim and frail, with an ashen face, discoloured hair, and the blurred eyes of a poor little being whose growth, both physically and mentally, had been arrested by brutish work, in which there was nothing to attract one, in which there was never a chance of any initiative.

"If monsieur's willing, I'm ready now," said Bonnaire, just as the hammer at last became silent.

Luc quickly turned round, and found the master puddler before him, wearing a jersey and a coarse woollen jacket, whilst under one of his arms was a bundle made up of his working-clothes and certain small articles belonging to him—all his baggage in fact, since he was leaving the works to return to them no more.

"Quite so—let us be off," said Luc.

But Bonnaire paused for another moment. As if he fancied that he might have forgotten something he gave a last glance inside the plank hut which served as a cloakroom. Then he looked at his furnace, the furnace which he had made his own by more than ten years of hard toil, turning out there thousands of pounds of steel fit for the rollers. He was leaving the establishment of his own free will, in the idea that such was his duty towards both his mates and himself, but for that very reason the severance was the more heroic. However, he forced back the emotion which was clutching him at the throat, and passed out the first in advance of Luc.

"Take care, monsieur," he said; "that piece is still warm—it would burn your boot."

Neither spoke any further. They crossed the two dim yards under the lunar lights, and passed before the low building where the tilt-hammers were beating ragefully. And as soon as they were outside the Abyss the black night seized hold of them again, and the glow and growl of the monster died away behind them. The wind was still blowing, a wind carrying the ragged flight of clouds skyward; and across the bridge the bank of the Mionne was deserted, not a soul was visible.

When Luc had found Josine reclining on the bench where he had left her, motionless and staring into the darkness, with Nanet asleep and pressing his head against her, he wished to withdraw, for he considered his mission ended, since Bonnaire would now find the poor creature some place of shelter. But the puddler suddenly became embarrassed and anxious at the idea of the scene which would follow his homecoming when his wife, that terrible Toupe, should see him accompanying that hussy. The scene was bound to be the more frightful since he had not told his wife of his intention to quit the works. He foresaw, indeed, that a tremendous quarrel would break out when she learnt that he was without work, through throwing himself voluntarily out of employment.

"Shall I accompany you?" Luc suggested; "I might be able to explain things."

"Upon my word, monsieur," replied the other, feeling relieved, "it would perhaps be the better if you did."

No words passed between Bonnaire and Josine. She seemed ashamed in presence of the master puddler, and if he, with his good nature, knowing too all that she suffered with Ragu, evinced a kind of fatherly pity towards her, he none the less blamed her for having yielded to that bad fellow. Josine had awakened Nanet on seeing the two men arrive, and after an encouraging sign from Luc, she and the boy followed them in silence. All four turned to the right, skirting the railway embankment, and thus entering Old Beauclair, whose hovels spread like some horrid stagnant pool over the flat ground just at the opening of the gorge. There was an intricate maze of narrow streets and lanes lacking both air and light, and infected by filthy gutters which the more torrential rains alone cleansed. The overcrowding of the wretched populace in so small a space was hard to understand, when in front of it one perceived La Roumagne spreading its immense plain where the breath of heaven blew freely as over the sea. The bitter keenness of the battle for money and property alone accounted for the niggardly fashion in which the right of the inhabitants to some little portion of the soil, the few yards requisite for everyday life, had been granted. Speculators had taken a hand in it all, and one or two centuries of wretchedness had culminated in a cloaca of cheap lodgings, whence people were frequently expelled by their landlords, low as might be the rents demanded for certain of those dens, where well-to-do people would not have allowed even their dogs to sleep. Chance-wise over the ground had risen those little dark houses, those damp shanties of plaster-work, those vermin and fever-breeding nests; and mournful indeed at that night hour, under the lugubrious sky, appeared that accursed city of labour, so dim, so closely-pent, filthy too, like some horrid vegetation of social injustice.

Bonnaire, walking ahead, followed a lane, then turned into another, and at last reached the Rue des Trois Lunes, one of the narrowest of the so-called streets. It had no footways, and was paved with pointed pebbles picked from the bed of the Mionne. The black and creviced house of which he occupied the first floor had one day suddenly "settled," lurching in such wise that it had been necessary to shore up the frontage with four great beams; and Ragu, as it happened, occupied the two rooms of the second story, whose sloping floor those beams supported. Down below, there was no hall; the precipitous ladder-like stairs started from the very threshold.

"And so, monsieur," Bonnaire at last said to Luc, "you will be kind enough to come up with me."

He had once more become embarrassed. Josine understood that he did not dare take her to his rooms for fear of some affront, though he suffered at having to leave her still in the street with the child. In her gentle resigned way she therefore arranged matters. "We need not go in," she said; "we'll wait on the stairs up above."

Bonnaire immediately fell in with the suggestion. "That's best," said he. "Have a little patience, sit down a moment, and if the key's in my place, I'll bring it to you, and then you can go to bed."

Josine and Nanet had already disappeared into the dense darkness enveloping the stairs. One could no longer even hear them breathing, they had ensconced themselves in some nook overhead. And Bonnaire in his turn then went up, guiding Luc, warning him respecting the height of the steps, and telling him to keep hold of the greasy rope which served in lieu of a hand-rail.

"There, monsieur, that's it. Don't move," he said at last. "Ah! the landings aren't large, and one would turn a fine somersault if one were to fall."

He opened a door and politely made Luc pass before him into a fairly spacious room, where a little petroleum lamp shed a yellowish light. In spite of the lateness of the hour La Toupe was still mending some house linen beside this lamp; whilst her father, Daddy Lunot, as he was called, had fallen asleep in a shadowy nook, with his pipe, which had gone out, between his gums. In a bed, standing in one corner, slept the two children, Lucien and Antoinette, one six, the other four years old, and both of them fine, big children for their respective ages. Apart from this common room, where the family cooked and ate their meals, the lodging only comprised two others, the bed-room of the husband and wife, and that of Daddy Lunot.

La Toupe, stupefied at seeing her husband return at that hour, for she had been warned of nothing, raised her head, exclaiming: "What, is it you?"

He did not wish to start the great quarrel by immediately telling her

ÉMILE ZOLA

that he had left the Abyss. He preferred to settle the matter of Josine and Nanet first of all. So he replied evasively: "Yes, I've finished, so I've come back." Then, without leaving his wife time to ask any more questions, he introduced Luc, saying: "Here, this gentleman, who is a friend of Monsieur Jordan's, came to ask me something—he'll explain it to you."

Her surprise and suspicion increasing, La Toupe turned towards the young man, who thereby perceived her great likeness to her brother Ragu. Short and choleric, she had his strongly marked face, with thick ruddy hair, a low forehead, thin nose and massive jaws. Her bright complexion, the freshness of which still rendered her attractive and young-looking at eight-and-twenty years of age, alone explained the reason which had induced Bonnaire to marry her, though he had been well acquainted with her abominable temper. That which everybody had then foreseen had come to pass. La Toupe made the home wretched by her everlasting fits of anger. In order to secure some peace her husband had to bow to her will in every little matter of their daily life. Very coquettish, consumed by the ambition to be well-dressed and possess jewellery, she only evinced a little gentleness when she was able to deck herself in a new gown.

Luc, being thus called upon to speak, felt the necessity of gaining her good will by a compliment. From the moment of crossing the threshold, however bare might be the scanty furniture, he had remarked that the room seemed very clean, thanks undoubtedly to the housewife's carefulness. And drawing near to the bed he exclaimed: "Ah! what fine children, they are sleeping like little angels."

La Toupe smiled, but looked at him fixedly and waited, feeling thoroughly convinced that this gentleman would not have put himself out to call there if he had not had something of importance to obtain from her. And when he found himself obliged to come to the point, when he related how he had found Josine starving on a bench, abandoned there in the night, she made a passionate gesture, and her jaws tightened. Without even answering the gentleman, she turned toward her husband in a fury: "What! What's this again? Is it any concern of mine?"

Bonnaire, thus compelled to intervene, strove to pacify her in his kindly, conciliatory way.

"All the same," said he, "if Ragu left the key with you, one ought to give it to the poor creature, because he's over yonder at Caffiaux's place, and may well pass the night there. One can't leave a woman and a child to sleep out of doors."

At this La Toupe exploded: "Yes, I've got the key!" said she. "Yes, Ragu gave it to me, and precisely because he wanted to prevent that hussy from installing herself any more in his rooms, with her little scamp of a brother! But I don't want to know anything about those horrors! I only know one thing, it was Ragu who confided the key to me, and it's to Ragu that I shall return it."

Then, as her husband again attempted to move her to pity, she violently silenced him. "Do you want to make me take up with my brother's fancies then?" she cried. "Just let the girl go and kick the bucket elsewhere, since she chose to listen to him. A nice state of things it's been, and no mistake! No, no, each for himself or herself; and as for her, let her remain in the gutter; a little sooner, a little later, it all amounts to the same thing!"

Luc listened, feeling hurt and indignant. In her he found all the harshness of the virtuous women of her class, who show themselves pitiless towards the girls that stumble amidst their trying struggle for life. And in La Toupe's case, ever since the day when she had learnt that her brother had bought Josine a little silver ring, there had been covert jealousy and hatred of that pretty girl whom she pictured fascinating men and wheedling gold chains and silk gowns out of them.

"One ought to be kind-hearted, madame," was all that Luc could say, in a voice that quivered with compassion.

But La Toupe did not have time to answer, for all at once an uproar of heavy stumbling footsteps resounded on the stairs, and hands fumbled at the knob of the door, which opened. It was Ragu with Bourron, one following the other like a pair of good-humoured drunkards who, having wetted their whistles in company, could no longer separate. Nevertheless Ragu, who had some sense left him, had torn himself away from Caffiaux's wine-shop, saying that, however pleasant it might be there, he none the less had to go back to work on the morrow. And thus he had looked in at his sister's with his mate, in order to get his key.

"Your key!" cried La Toupe sharply, "there it is! And I won't keep it again, mind. I've just had a lot of foolish things said to me in order to make me give it to that gadabout. Another time when you want to turn somebody out of the house just do it yourself."

Ragu, whose heart had doubtless been softened by liquor, began to laugh: "She's so stupid, is Josine," he said. "If she had wanted to be

ÉMILE ZOLA

pleasant she would have drunk a glass with us instead of snivelling. But women never know how to tackle men."

He was unable to express himself more fully, for just then Bourron, who had fallen on a chair, laughing at nothing with his everlasting good humour, inquired of Bonnaire: "I say, is it true then that you're leaving the works?"

La Toupe turned round, starting as if a pistol had been fired off behind her. "What! He's leaving the works!" she cried.

Silence fell. Then Bonnaire courageously came to a decision. "Yes, I'm leaving the works; I can't do otherwise."

"You're leaving the works! you're leaving the works!" bawled his wife, quite furious and distracted as she took her stand before him. "So that two months' strike, which made us spend all our savings, wasn't enough, eh? It's for you to pay the piper now, eh? So we shall die of starvation, and I shall have to go about naked!"

He did not lose his temper, but gently answered: "It's quite possible that you won't have a new gown for New Year's Day, and perhaps too we shall have to go on short commons. But I repeat to you that I'm doing what I ought to do!"

She did not give up the battle as yet, but drew still nearer, shouting in his face: "Oh, bunkum! you needn't imagine that folks will be grateful to you! Your mates don't scruple to say that if it hadn't been for that strike of yours they'd never have starved during those two months. Do you know what they'll say when they hear that you've left the works? They'll say that it serves you right, and that you're only an idiot! I'll never allow you to do such a foolish thing! You hear, you'll go back to-morrow!"

Bonnaire looked at her fixedly with his bright and steady eyes. If as a rule he gave way on points of domestic policy, if he allowed her to reign despotically in ordinary household matters, he became like iron whenever any case of conscience arose. And so, without raising his voice, in a firm tone which she well knew, he answered: "You will please keep quiet. Those are matters for us men; women like you don't understand anything about them, and so it's better that they shouldn't meddle with them. You're very nice, but the best thing you can do is to go on mending your linen again if you don't want a quarrel."

He thereupon pushed her towards the chair near the lamp, and forced her to sit down again. Conquered, trembling with wrath which she knew would henceforth be futile, she took up her needle, and made a pretence of feeling no further interest in the questions from which she had been so decisively thrust aside. Awakened by the noise of voices, Daddy Lunot her father, without evincing any astonishment at the sight of so many people, lighted his pipe once more and listened to the talk with the air of an old philosopher who had lost every illusion; whilst in their little bed the children Lucien and Antoinette, likewise roused from their slumber, opened their eyes widely, and seemed to be striving to understand the serious things which the big folk were saying.

Bonnaire was now addressing himself to Luc, as if to invoke his testimony.

"Each has his honour, is that not so, monsieur? The strike was inevitable, and if it had to be begun over again, I should begin it over again—that is, I should employ my influence in urging my mates to try to secure justice. One can't let oneself be devoured—work ought to be paid at its proper price, unless men are willing to become mere slaves. And we were so much in the right that Monsieur Delaveau had to give way on every point by accepting our new wage tariff. But I can now see that he is furious, and that somebody, as my wife puts it, has got to pay for the damage. If I were not to go off willingly to-day, he'd find a pretext for turning me out to-morrow. So what? Am I to hang on obstinately and become a pretext for everlasting disputes? No, no! It would all fall on my mates, it would bring them all sorts of worries, and it would be very wrong of me. I pretended to go back, because my mates talked of continuing the strike if I didn't. But now that they are all back at work and quite quiet I prefer to take myself off. That will settle everything; none of them will stir, and I shall have done what I ought to do. That's my view of honour, monsieur—each has his own."

He said all this with simple grandeur, with so easy and courageous an air that Luc felt deeply touched. From that man whom he had seen black and taciturn, toiling so painfully before his furnace, from that man whom he had seen gentle and kindly, tolerant and conciliatory in household matters, there now arose one of the heroes of labour, one of those obscure strugglers who have given their whole being to the cause of justice, and who carry their brotherliness to the point of immolating themselves in silence for the sake of others.

Without ceasing to draw her needle La Toupe meanwhile repeated violently: "And we shall starve."

"And we shall starve, it's quite possible," said Bonnaire, "but I shall be able to sleep in peace."

ÉMILE ZOLA

Ragu began to sneer. "Oh! starve, that's useless, that's never done any good. Not that I defend the masters—a pretty gang they are, all of them! Only as we need them we always have come to an understanding with them, and do pretty well as they want."

He rattled on, jesting, and revealing his true nature. He was the average workman, neither good nor bad, the spoilt product of the present-day wage system. He cried out at times against capitalist rule, he was enraged by the strain of the labour imposed on him, and was even capable of a short rebellion. But prolonged atavism had bent him; he really had the soul of a slave, respecting established traditions and envying the employer—that sovereign master who possessed and enjoyed everything; and the only covert ambition that he nourished was that of taking the employer's place some fine morning in order to possess and enjoy life in his turn. Briefly his ideal was to do nothing, to be the master so that he might have nothing to do.

"Ah! that pig Delaveau!" he said, "I should like to be just a week in his skin and to see him in mine. It would amuse me to see him smoking one of those big cigars of his while making a ball. But everything happens, you know, and we may all become masters in the next shake-up!"

This idea amused Bourron vastly; he gaped with admiration before Ragu whenever they had drunk together. "That's true, ah! dash it, what a spree it will be when we become the masters!"

But Bonnaire shrugged his shoulders, full of contempt for that base conception of the future victory of the toilers over their exploiters. He had read, reflected, and he thought he knew. Excited by all that had just been said, wishing to show that he was right, he again spoke. In his words Luc recognised the Collectivist idea such as it is formulated by the irreconcilable ones of the party. First of all the nation had to resume possession of the soil and all instruments of labour in order to socialise and restore them to one and all. Then labour would be reorganised, rendered general and compulsory, in such wise that remuneration would be proportionate to the hours of toil which each man supplied. The matter on which Bonnaire grew muddled was the practical method to employ in order to establish this socialisation, and particularly the working of it when it should be put into practice; for such intricate machinery would need direction and control, a harsh and vexatory State police system. And when Luc, who did not yet go so far as Bonnaire did in his humanitarian cravings, offered some objections, the other replied with the quiet faith of a believer: "Everything belongs to us; we shall take everything back, so that each may have his just share of work and rest, trouble and joy. There is no other reasonable solution, the injustice and the sufferings of the world have become too great."

Even Ragu and Bourron agreed with this. Had not the wage-system corrupted and poisoned everything! It was that which disseminated anger and hatred, gave rise to class warfare, the long war of extermination which capital and labour were waging. It was by the wage-system that man had become wolfish towards man amidst the conflict of egotism, the monstrous tyranny of a social system based on iniquity. Misery had no other cause. The wage-system was the evil ferment which engendered hunger with all its disastrous consequences, theft, murder, prostitution, the downfall and rebellion of men and women cast beyond the pale of love, thrown like perverse, destructive forces athwart society. And there was only one remedy, the abolition of the wage-system, which must be replaced by the other, the new, dreamt-of system, whose secret to-morrow would disclose. From that point began the battle of the systems, each man thinking that in his own system rested the happiness of the coming centuries; and a bitter political *mêlée* resulted from the clashing of the Socialist parties, each of which sought to impose on the others its own plans for the reorganisation of labour and the equitable distribution of wealth. But none the less the wage-system in its present form was condemned by one and all, and nothing could save it; it had served its time, and it would disappear even as slavery, once so universal, had disappeared when one of the periods of mankind's history had ended by reason of the ever-constant onward march. That wage-system even now was but a dead organ which threatened to poison the whole body, and which the life of nations must necessarily eliminate under penalty of coming to a tragic end.

"For instance," Bonnaire continued, "those Quirignons who founded the Abyss were not bad-hearted people. The last one, Michel, who came to so sad an end, tried to ameliorate the workman's lot. It is to him one owes the creation of a pension fund, for which he gave the first hundred thousand francs, engaging also to double every year such sums as were paid in by the subscribers. He also established a free library, a reading-room, a dispensary where one can see the doctor gratis twice a week, a workshop, too, and a school for the children. And though Monsieur Delaveau isn't at all so well disposed towards the men, he has naturally been obliged to respect all that. It has been working for years now, but when all is said it's of no good at all. It's mere charity; it isn't justice! It may go on working for years and years without starvation and misery being any the less. No, no, the people who talk of 'relieving' distress are simply good-natured fools; there's no relief possible, the evil has to be cut off at the root."

At this moment old Lunot, whom the others thought asleep again, spoke from out of the shadows: "I knew the Qurignons," said he.

Luc turned and perceived him on his chair, vainly pulling at his extinguished pipe. He was fifty years old, and had remained nearly thirty years a drawer at the Abyss. Short and stout as he was, with a pale, puffy face, one might have thought that the furnaces had swollen instead of withering him. Perhaps it was the water with which he had been obliged to drench himself in the performance of his work that had first given him the rheumatics. At all events he had been attacked in the legs at an early age, and now he could only walk with great difficulty. And as he had not fulfilled the necessary conditions to obtain even the ridiculous pension of three hundred francs a year[3] to which the new workmen would be entitled later on, he would have perished of starvation in the streets, like some old stricken beast of burden, if his daughter, La Toupe, on the advice of Bonnaire, had not taken him in, making him pay for her generosity in this respect by subjecting him to continual reproaches and all sorts of privations.

"Ah, yes," he slowly repeated, "I knew the Qurignons. There was Monsieur Michel, who's now dead and who was five years older than me. And there's still Monsieur Jérôme, under whom I first went to the works when I was eighteen years old. He was already forty-five at that time, but that doesn't prevent him from still being alive. But before Monsieur Jérôme, there was Monsieur Blaise, the founder, who first installed himself at the Abyss with his tilt-hammers nigh on eighty years ago. I didn't know him myself. But my father Jean Ragu, and my grandfather, Pierre Ragu, worked with him; and one may even say that Pierre Ragu was his mate, since they were both mere workmen with hardly a copper in their pockets when they started on the job together, in the gorge of the Bleuse Mountains, then deserted, near the bank of the Mionne, where there was a waterfall. The Qurignons made a big fortune, whereas here am I, Jacques Ragu, with my bad legs and never a copper, and here's my son, Auguste, who'll never be any richer than I am after thirty years' hard work, to say nothing of my daughter and her

---

3. 12*l.*

children, who are all threatened with starvation, just as the Ragus have always been for a hundred years or more."

It was not angrily that he said these things, but rather with the resignation of an old stricken animal. For a moment he looked at his pipe, surprised at seeing no smoke ascend from it. Then, remarking that Luc was listening to him with compassionate interest, he concluded with a slight shrug of the shoulders: "Bah! monsieur, that's the fate of all of us poor devils! There will always be masters and workmen. My grandfather and father were just as I am, and my son will be the same too. What's the use of rebelling? Each of us draws his lot when he's born. All the same, one thing that's desirable when a man gets old is that he should at least have the means to buy himself sufficient tobacco."

"Tobacco!" cried La Toupe, "why you've smoked two sous' worth to-day! Do you imagine that I'm going to keep you in tobacco, now that we sha'n't even be able to buy bread?"

To her father's great despair she rationed him with respect to tobacco. It was in vain that he tried to get his pipe alight again; decidedly only ashes were left in it. And Luc, with increasing compassion in his heart, continued looking at him as he sat there, huddled up on his chair. The wage-system ended in that lamentable wreck of a man, the worker done for at fifty years of age, the drawer condemned to be always a drawer, deformed, hebetated, reduced to imbecility and paralysis by his mechanical toil. In that poor being there survived nothing save the fatalist sentiment of slavery.

But Bonnaire protested superbly: "No, no! It won't always be like that, there won't always be masters and toilers; the day will come when one and all will be free and joyful men! Our sons will perhaps see that day, and it is really worth while that we the fathers should suffer a little more if thereby we are to procure happiness for them to-morrow."

"Dash it!" exclaimed Ragu, in a merry way. "Hurry up, I should like to see that. It would just suit me to have nothing more to do, and to eat chicken at every meal!"

"And me too, and me too!" seconded Bourron in ecstasy. "Keep me a place!"

With a gesture expressive of utter disillusion, old Lunot silenced them in order to resume: "Let all that be, those are the things one hopes for when one's young! A man's head is full of folly then, and he imagines that he's going to change the world. But then the world goes on, and he's swept away with the others. I bear no grudge against anybody, I don't.

ÉMILE ZOLA

At times, when I can drag myself about a bit, I meet Monsieur Jérôme in his little conveyance, which a servant pushes along. And I take off my cap to him, because it's only fit that one should do so to a man who gave one work to do, and who's so rich. I fancy, though, that he doesn't know me, for he contents himself with looking at me with those eyes of his, which seem to be full of clear water. But when all's said the Qurignons drew the big prize, so they are entitled to be respected."

Ragu thereupon related that Bourron and he, on leaving the works that very evening, had seen Monsieur Jérôme pass in his little conveyance. They had taken off their caps to him, and that was only natural. How could they do otherwise without being impolite? All the same, that a Ragu should be on foot in the mud, with his stomach empty, bowing to a well-dressed Qurignon with a rug over him and a servant wheeling him about like a baby who'd grown too fat, why that was enough to put one in a rage. In fact it gave one the idea of throwing one's tools into the water and compelling the rich to shell out, in order that one might take one's turn in doing nothing.

"Doing nothing, no, no! That would be death," resumed Bonnaire. "Everybody ought to work, in that way happiness would be won, and unjust misery would at last be vanquished. One must not envy those Qurignons. When they are quoted as examples, when people say to us: 'You see very well that with intelligence, toil, and economy, a workman may acquire a large fortune,' I feel a little irritated, because I understand very well that all that money can only have been gained by exploiting our mates, by docking their food and their liberty; and a horrid thing like that is always paid for some day! The excessive prosperity of any one individual will never be in keeping with general happiness. No doubt we have to wait if we want to know what the future has in reserve for each of us. But I've told you what my idea is—that those youngsters of mine in the bed yonder, who are listening to us, may some day be happier than I shall ever be, and that later on their children may in turn be happier than they. To bring that about we only have to resolve on justice, to come to an understanding like brothers, and secure it, even at the price of a good deal more wretchedness."

As Bonnaire said, Lucien and Antoinette had not gone to sleep again. Interested apparently by all those people who were talking so late, they lay, plump and rosy, with their heads motionless on the bolster, a thoughtful expression appearing in their large eyes, as if indeed they could understand the conversation.

"Some day happier than us!" said La Toupe viciously. "Yes, of course, that is if they don't perish of want to-morrow, since you'll have no more bread to give them."

Those words fell on Bonnaire like a hatchet-stroke. He staggered, quailing amidst his dream beneath the sudden icy chill of the misery which he seemed to have sought by quitting the works. And Luc felt the quiver of that misery pass through that large bare room where the little petroleum lamp was smoking dismally. Was not the struggle an impossible one? Would they not all—grandfather, father, mother, and children—be condemned to an early death if the wage-earner should persist in his impotent protest against capital? Heavy silence came, a big black shadow seemed to fall chilling the room, and for a moment darkening every face.

But a knock was heard, followed by laughter, and in came Babette, Bourron's wife, with her dollish face which ever wore a merry look. Plump and fresh, with a white skin and heavy tresses of a wheaten hue, she seemed like eternal spring. Failing to find her husband at Caffiaux's wine-shop, she had come to seek him at Bonnaire's, well knowing that he had some trouble in getting home when she did not lead him thither herself. Moreover, she showed no desire to scold; on the contrary she seemed amused, as if she thought it only right that her husband should have taken a little enjoyment.

"Ah! here you are, father Joy!" she gaily cried when she perceived him. "I suspected that you were still with Ragu, and that I should find you here. It's late, you know, old man. I've put Marthe and Sébastien to bed, and now I've got to put you to bed too!"

Even as she never got angry with him, so Bourron never got angry with her, for she showed so much good grace in carrying him off from his mates.

"Ah! that's a good 'un!" he cried. "Did you hear it? My wife puts me to bed! Well, well, I'm agreeable since it always has to end like that!"

He rose, and Babette, realising by the gloominess of everybody's face, that she had stumbled upon some serious worry, perhaps even a quarrel, endeavoured to arrange matters. She, in her own household, sang from morning till night, showing much affection for her husband, consoling him and telling him triumphant stories of future prosperity whenever he felt discouraged. The hateful want in which she had been living ever since childhood had made no impression upon her good

ÉMILE ZOLA

spirits. She was quite convinced that things would turn out all right, and for ever seemed to be on the road to Paradise.

"What is the matter with you all?" she asked. "Are the children ill?"

Then, as La Toupe once more exploded, relating that Bonnaire was leaving the works, that they would all be dead of starvation before a week was over, and that all Beauclair, indeed, would follow suit, for people were far too wretched and it was no longer possible to live, Babette burst forth into protests, predicting no end of prosperous days of sunshine, in her gay and confident manner.

"No, no, indeed!" she cried. "Don't upset yourself like that, my dear. Everything will settle down, you'll see. Everybody will work and everybody will be happy."

Then she led her husband away, diverting him as she did so, saying such comical and affectionate things that he, likewise jesting, followed her with docility, his inebriety being subjugated and rendered inoffensive.

Luc was making up his mind to follow them when La Toupe, in putting her work together on the table, there perceived the key which she had thrown down for her brother to pick up.

"Well, are you going to take it?" she exclaimed. "Are you going to bed or not? You've been told that your hussy's waiting for you somewhere. Oh! you're free to take her back again if you choose, you know!"

For a moment Ragu, in a sneering way, let the key swing from one of his thumbs. Throughout the evening he had been shouting in Bourron's face that he did not mean to feed a lazybones who had stupidly lost a finger in a boot-stitching machine, and had not known how to get sufficient compensation for it. Since his return, however, he had become more sober, and no longer felt so maliciously obstinate. Besides, his sister exasperated him with her perpetual attempts to dictate a proper line of conduct to him.

"Of course I can take her back if I choose," he said. "After all she's as good as many another. One might kill her and she wouldn't say a bad word to one." Then turning to Bonnaire, who had remained silent: "She's stupid, is Josine," he said, "to be always getting frightened like that. Where has she got to now?"

"She's waiting on the stairs with Nanet," said the master puddler.

Ragu thereupon threw the door wide open to shout: "Josine! Josine!"

Nobody replied, however, not the faintest sound came from the dense darkness enveloping the stairs. In the faint gleam of light which the lamp cast in the direction of the landing one could see merely Nanet, who stood there, seemingly watching and waiting.

"Ah! there you are, you little rascal!" cried Ragu. "What on earth are you doing there?"

The child was in no wise disconcerted, he did not so much as flinch. Drawing up his little figure, no taller than a jackboot, he bravely answered: "I was listening so as to know."

"And your sister, where's she? Why doesn't she answer when she's called?"

"*Ma grande*? She was upstairs with me, sitting on the stairs. But when she heard you come in here, she was afraid that you might go up to beat her. So she thought it best to go down again, so that she could run away if you were bad-tempered."

This made Ragu laugh. Besides the lad's pluck amused him. "And you, aren't you frightened?" he asked.

"I? If you touch me, I'll shriek so loud that my sister will be warned and able to run away."

Quite softened, the man went to lean over the stairs, and call again: "Josine! Josine! Here, come up, don't be stupid. You know very well that I sha'n't kill you."

But the same death-like silence continued, nothing stirred, nothing ascended from the darkness. And Luc, whose presence was no longer requisite, took leave, bowing to La Toupe, who with her lips compressed stiffly bent her head. The children had gone off to sleep again. Old Lunot, still with his extinguished pipe in his mouth, had managed to reach the little chamber where he slept, hugging the walls on his way. And Bonnaire, who in his turn had sunk upon a chair, silent amidst his cheerless surroundings, his eyes gazing far away into the threatening future, was waiting for an opportunity to follow his terrible wife to bed.

"Keep up your courage, *au revoir*," said Luc to him, whilst vigorously shaking his hand.

On the landing Ragu was still calling, in tones which now became entreating: "Josine! come, Josine! I tell you that I'm no longer angry."

And as no sign of life came from the darkness he turned towards Nanet, who meddled with nothing, preferring that his sister should act as she pleased: "Perhaps she's run off," said the man.

"Oh! no, where would you have her go? She must have sat down on the stairs again."

Luc was now descending, clinging the while to the greasy rope and feeling the high and precipitous stairs with his feet for fear lest he should fall, so dense was the darkness. It seemed to him as if he were descending into a black abyss by means of a fragile ladder placed between two damp walls. And as he went lower and lower he fancied that he could hear some stifled sobs rising from the dolorous depths of the gloom.

Overhead Ragu resumed resolutely: "Josine! Josine! Why don't you come—do you want me to go and fetch you?"

Then Luc paused, for he detected a faint breath approaching, something warm and gentle, a light, living quiver, scarcely perceptible, which became more and more tremulous as it drew nearer. And he stepped back close to the wall, for he well understood that a human creature was about to pass him, invisibly, recognisable only by the discreet touch of her figure, as she went upward.

"It is I, Josine," he whispered, in order that she might not be frightened.

The little breath was still ascending, and no reply came. But that creature, all distress and misery, passed, brushing lightly, almost imperceptibly against him. And a feverish little hand caught hold of his own, a burning mouth was pressed to that hand of his, and kissed it ardently, in an impulse of infinite gratitude instinct with the gift of a soul. She thanked him, she gave herself, like one unknown, veiled from sight, full of the sweetest girlishness. Not a word was exchanged; there was only that silent kiss, moistened by warm tears, in the dense gloom.

The little breath had already passed, the light form was still ascending. And Luc remained overcome, affected to the depths of his being by that faint touch. The kiss of those invisible lips had gone to his heart. A sweet and powerful charm had flowed into his veins. He tried to think that he simply felt well pleased at having at last helped Josine to secure a resting-place that night. But why had she been weeping, seated on the step of the stairs on the very threshold of the house? And why had she so long delayed returning an answer to the man overhead, who offered her a lodging once more? Was it that she had experienced mortal grief and regret, that she had sobbed at the thought of some unrealisable dream, and that in going up at last she had simply yielded to the necessity of resuming the life which fate condemned her to lead?

For the last time Ragu's voice was heard up above. "Ah! there you are—it's none too soon. Come, you big stupid, let's go up. We sha'n't kill one another to-night, at any rate."

Then Luc fled, feeling such despair that he instinctively sought the why and wherefore of that frightful bitterness. Whilst he found his way with difficulty through the dim maze of the filthy lanes of Old Beauclair he pondered over things and gave rein to his compassion. Poor girl! She was the victim of her surroundings, never would she have led such a life had it not been for the crushing weight and perverting influence of misery and want. And, picturing mankind as plough land, Luc thought how thoroughly it would have to be turned over in order that work might become honour and delight, in order that strong and healthy love might sprout and flower amidst a great harvest of truth and justice! Meantime, it was evidently best that the poor girl should remain with that man Ragu, provided that he did not ill-treat her too much. Then Luc glanced upward at the sky. The tempest blast had ceased blowing, and stars were appearing between the heavy and motionless clouds. But how dark was the night, how great the melancholy in which his heart was steeped!

All at once he came out on the bank of the Mionne near the wooden bridge. In front of him was the Abyss ever at work, sending forth a dull rumble amidst the clear dancing notes of its tilt-hammers which the deeper thuds of the helve-hammers punctuated. Now and again a fiery glow transpierced the gloom, and huge livid clouds of smoke passing athwart the rays of the electric lamps showed like a stormy horizon about the works. And the nocturnal life of that monster whose furnaces were never extinguished brought back to Luc a vision of murderous labour, imposed on men as in a convict prison, and remunerated, for the most part, with mistrust and contempt. Then Bonnaire's handsome face passed before the young fellow's eyes; he perceived him as he had left him, in the dim room yonder, overcome like a vanquished man in presence of the uncertain future. And without transition there came another memory of his evening, the vague profile of Lange the potter, pouring forth his curse with all the vehemence of a prophet, predicting the destruction of Beauclair beneath the sum of its crimes. But at that hour the terrorised town had fallen asleep, and all one could see of it on the fringe of the plain was a confused dense mass where not a light gleamed. Nothing indeed seemed to exist save the Abyss, whose hellish life knew no respite; there a noise as of thunder continually rolled by, and flames incessantly devoured the lives of men.

Suddenly a clock struck midnight in the distance. And Luc then crossed the bridge and again went down the Brias road on his way back to La Crêcherie, where his bed awaited him. As he was reaching it a mighty glow suddenly illumined the whole district, the two promontories of the Bleuse Mountains, the slumbering roofs of the town, and even the far-away fields of La Roumagne. That glow came from the blast furnace whose black silhouette appeared half way up the height as in the midst of a conflagration. And as Luc raised his eyes it once more seemed to him as if he beheld some red dawn, the sunrise promised to his dream of the renovation of humanity.

III

On the morrow, Sunday, just as Luc had risen, he received a friendly note from Madame Boisgelin, inviting him to lunch at La Guerdache. Having learnt that he was at Beauclair, and that the Jordans would only return home on the Monday, she told him how happy she would be to see him again, in order that they might chat together about their old friendship in Paris, where they had secretly conducted some big charitable enterprises together in the needy district of the Faubourg St. Antoine. And Luc, who regarded Madame Boisgelin with a kind of affectionate reverence, at once accepted her invitation, writing word that he would be at La Guerdache by eleven o'clock.

Superb weather had suddenly followed the week of heavy rain by which Beauclair had almost been submerged. The sun had risen radiantly in the sky, which was now of a pure blue, as if it had been cleansed by all the showers. And the bright sun of September still diffused so much warmth that the roads were already dry. Luc was, therefore, well pleased to walk the couple of thousand yards which separated La Guerdache from the town. When, about a quarter past ten, he passed through the latter—that is, the new town, which stretched from the Place de la Mairie to the fields fringing La Roumagne—he was surprised by its brightness, cheerfulness, and trimness, and sorrowfully recalled the dismal aspect of the poverty-stricken quarter which he had seen the previous night. In the new town were assembled the sub-prefecture, the law court, and the prison, the last being a handsome new building, whose plaster-work was scarcely dry. As for the church of St. Vincent, an elegant sixteenth-century church astride the old and the now towns, it had lately been repaired, for its steeple had shown an inclination to topple down upon the faithful. And as Luc went on he noticed that the sunlight gilded the smart houses of the *bourgeois*, and brightened even the Place de la Mairie, which spread out beyond the populous Rue de Brias, displaying a huge and ancient building which served as both a town hall and a school.

Luc, however, speedily reached the fields by way of the Rue de Formerie, which stretched straight away beyond the square like a continuation of the Rue de Brias. La Guerdache was on the Formerie road, just outside Beauclair. Thus Luc had no occasion to hurry; and indeed he strolled along like one in a dreamy mood. At times he even turned round, and then, northward, beyond the town, whose houses descended a slight slope, he perceived the huge bar of the Bleuse Mountains parted by the precipitously enclosed gorge through which the Mionne torrent flowed. In that kind of estuary opening into the plain one could distinctly perceive the close-set buildings and lofty chimneys of the Abyss as well as the blast-furnace of La Crêcherie—in fact, quite an industrial city, which was visible from every side of La Roumagne, leagues and leagues away. Luc remained gazing at the scene for some little time, and when he slowly resumed his walk towards La Guerdache, which he could already discern beyond some clusters of magnificent trees, he recalled the typical history of the Quirignons, which his friend Jordan had once told him.

It was in 1823 that Blaise Quirignon, the workman by whom the Abyss had been founded, had installed himself there, on the bank of the torrent, with his two tilt-hammers. He had never employed more than a score of hands, and making but a small fortune, had contented himself with building near the works a little brick pavilion in which Delaveau, the present manager, now resided. It was Jérôme Quirignon, the second of the line, born in the year when his father founded the Abyss, who became a real king of industry. In him met all the creative power derived from a long ancestry of workmen, all the incipient efforts, the century-old growth and rise of "the people." Hundreds of years of latent energy, a long line of ancestors obstinately seeking happiness, wrathfully battling in the gloom, working themselves at times to death, now at last yielded fruit, culminated in the advent of this victor who could toil eighteen hours a day, and whose intelligence, good sense, and will swept all obstacles aside. In less than twenty years he caused a town to spring from the ground, gave employment to twelve hundred workpeople, and gained millions of francs. And at last, stifling in the humble little house erected by his father, he expended eight hundred thousand francs[1] on the purchase of La Guerdache, a large and sumptuous residence in which ten families might have found accommodation, whilst around it stretched a park and a farm, the whole forming in fact a large estate. Jérôme was convinced that La Guerdache would become as it were the patriarchal home of his descendants, all the bright and loving couples who would assuredly spring from his wealth as from some blessed soil.

---

1. £32,000.

For them he prepared a future of domination based on his dream of subjugating labour and utilising it for the enjoyment of an *élite*; for was not all the power that he felt within him definitive and infinite, and would it not even increase among his children, free from all danger of diminution and exhaustion during long, long years? But all at once a first misfortune fell upon this man, who seemed to be as vigorous as an oak-tree. Whilst he was still young—in his very prime, indeed, only two and fifty years of age—paralysis deprived him of the use of both his legs, and he had to surrender the management of the Abyss to Michel, his eldest son.

Michel Qurignon, the third of the line, was then just thirty. He had a younger brother, Philippe, who, much against his father's wishes, had married in Paris a wonderfully beautiful but very flighty woman. And between the two boys there was a girl, Laure, already five-and-twenty years old, who greatly distressed her parents by the extreme religiosity into which she had fallen.

Michel for his part had, when very young, married an extremely gentle, loving, but delicate woman, by whom he had two children, Gustave and Suzanne, the former being five and the latter three years old when their father was suddenly obliged to assume the management of the Abyss. It was understood that he should do so in the name and for the benefit of the whole family, each member of which was to draw a share of the profits, according to an agreement which had been arrived at. Although Michel did not in the same high degree possess his father's admirable qualities, his power of work, his quick intelligence, and his methodical habits, he none the less at first proved an excellent manager, and for ten years succeeded in preventing any decline in the business, which, indeed, he at one moment increased by replacing the old plant by new appliances. But sorrows and family losses fell upon him like premonitory signs of a coming disaster. His mother died, his father was not only paralysed and wheeled about by a servant, but sank into absolute dumbness after experiencing a difficulty in uttering certain words. Then Michel's sister, Laure, her brain quite turned by mystical notions, took the veil, in spite of all the efforts made to detain her at La Guerdache amidst the joys of the world. And from Paris, too, Michel received deplorable tidings of the affairs of his brother Philippe, whose wife was taking to scandalous adventures, dragging him, moreover, into a wild life of gambling, extravagance, and folly. Finally Michel lost his own delicate and gentle wife, which proved, indeed, his supreme loss, for it threw him off his balance and cast him into a life of disorder. He had already yielded to his passions, but in a discreet way, for fear of saddening his wife, who was always ill. But when death had carried her away, nothing was left to restrain him, and he took freely to a life of pleasure, which consumed the best part of his time and his energies.

Then came another period of ten years during which the Abyss declined, since it was no longer directed by the victorious chief of the days of conquest, but by a tired and satiated master who squandered all the booty it yielded. A feverish passion for luxury now possessed Michel, his existence became all festivity and pleasure, the spending of money for the merely material joys of life. And the worst was that in addition to this cause of ruin, in addition, moreover to bad management and ever-increasing loss of energy, there came a commercial crisis, in which the whole metallurgie industry of the region nearly perished. It became impossible to manufacture steel rails and girders cheaply enough in face of the victorious competition of the works of Northern and Eastern France, which, thanks to a newly discovered chemical process, were now able to employ defective ore which formerly it had been impossible to utilise. Thus, after a struggle of two years' duration, Michel felt the Abyss crumbling to pieces beneath him, and one day, when he was already unhinged by having to borrow three hundred thousand francs to meet some heavy bills then reaching maturity, a horrible drama drove him to desperation.

He was then nearly fifty-four years old, and was madly in love with a pretty girl whom he had brought from Paris and concealed in Beauclair. At times he indulged in the wild dream of fleeing with her to some land of the sun, far away from all financial worries. His son Gustave, who after failing in his studies led an idle life at seven-and-twenty years of age, resided with him on a footing of friendly equality, well acquainted with the intrigue, about which indeed he often jested. He made fun also of the Abyss, refusing to set foot amongst all that grimy, evil-smelling old iron, for he greatly preferred to ride, hunt, and shoot, and generally lead the empty life of an amiable *fin-de-race* young man, as if he could count several centuries of illustrious ancestry. And thus it happened that one fine evening, after "lifting" out of a *secrétaire* the single hundred thousand francs which his father had as yet managed to get together for his payments, Master Gustave carried off the pretty girl, who had flung her arms around his neck at the sight of so much money. And on the morrow Michel, struck both in heart and brain by this collapse of his passion and his fortune, yielded to the vertigo of horror and shot himself dead with a revolver.

Three years had already elapsed since that suicide. And the speedy downfall of one Qurignon had been followed by that of another and another, as if by way of example to show how great might prove the severity of destiny. Shortly after Gustave's departure it was learnt that he had been killed in a carriage accident at Nice, a pair of runaway horses having carried him over a precipice. Then Michel's younger brother Philippe likewise disappeared from the scene, being killed in a duel, the outcome of a dirty affair into which he had been drawn by his terrible wife, who was said to be now in Russia with a tenor, whilst the only child born to them, André Qurignon, the last of the line, had been sent perforce to a private asylum, since he suffered from an affection of the spine complicated by mental disorder. Apart from that sufferer and Laure, who still led a cloistral life, so that she also seemed to be dead, there remained of all the Qurignons only old Jérôme and Michel's daughter, Suzanne.

She, when twenty years of age—that is, five years before her father's death—had married Boisgelin, who had met her whilst visiting at a country house. Although the Abyss was then already in peril, Michel in his ostentatious way had made arrangements which enabled him to give his daughter a dowry of a million francs. Boisgelin on his side was very wealthy, having inherited from his grandfather and father a fortune of more than six millions, amassed in all sorts of suspicious affairs, redolent of usury and theft—by which he, however, was not personally besmirched, since he had lived in perfect idleness ever since his entry into the world. He was held in great esteem and envy, and people were always eager to bow to him, for he resided in a superb mansion near the Parc Monceau in Paris, and led a life of wild display and extravagance. After seeking distinction by remaining invariably the last of his class at the Lycée Condorcet,[2] which he had astonished by his elegance, he had never done anything, but imagined himself to be a modern-style aristocrat, one who established his claim to nobility

---

2. The Lycée Condorcet (formerly Bonaparte) has always been both the most elegant and the most literary of all the Paris State colleges. Th. de Banville, Dumas fils, the brothers de Goncourt, the younger Guizots, Eugène Sue, Taine, Alphonse Karr, Prévost-Paradol, &c., were educated there; and among those who sat on the forms in my time there—during the Second Empire—were many who have since become distinguished French journalists, authors, and statesmen.—*Trans.*

ÉMILE ZOLA

by the magnificence he showed in spending the fortune acquired by his forerunners without even lowering himself to earn a copper. The misfortune was that Boisgelin's six millions no longer sufficed at last to keep his establishment on the high footing which it had reached, and that he allowed himself to be drawn into financial speculations of which he understood nothing. The Bourse was just then going mad over some new gold mines, and he was told that by venturing his fortune he might treble it in two years' time. All at once, however, came disaster and downfall, and for a moment he almost thought that he was absolutely ruined, to such a point indeed as to retain not even a crust of bread for the morrow. He wept like a child at the thought, and looked at his hands, which had ever idled, wondering what he would now be able to do, since he knew not how to work with them. It was then that Suzanne his wife evinced admirable affection, good sense, and courage, in such wise as to set him on his feet again. She reminded him that her own million, her dowry, was intact. And she insisted on having the situation retrieved by selling the Parc-Monceau mansion, which they would now be unable to keep up. Another million was found in that way. But how were they to live, particularly in Paris, on the proceeds of two millions of francs, when six had not sufficed, for temptation would assuredly come again at the sight of all the luxury consuming the great city? A chance encounter at last decided the future.

Boisgelin had a poor cousin, a certain Delaveau, the son of one of his father's sisters, whose husband, an unlucky inventor, had left her miserably poor. Delaveau, a petty engineer, occupied a modest post at a Brias coal-pit at the time when Michel Qurignon committed suicide. Devoured by a craving to succeed, urged on too by his wife, and very well acquainted with the situation of the Abyss, which he felt certain he could restore to prosperity by a new system of organisation, he went to Paris in search of capitalists, and there, one evening in the street, he suddenly found himself face to face with his cousin Boisgelin. Inspiration at once came to him. How was it that he had not previously thought of that wealthy relative who, as it happened, had married a Qurignon? On learning what was the present position of the Boisgelins, now reduced to a couple of millions which they wished to invest as advantageously as possible, Delaveau extended his plans, and at several interviews which he had with his cousin displayed so much assurance, intelligence, and energy, that he ended by convincing him of success. There was really genius in the plan he had devised. The Boisgelins must profit by the catastrophe which had fallen on Michel Qurignon, buy the works for a million francs when they were worth two millions, and start making steel of superior quality which would rapidly bring in large profits. Moreover, why should not the Boisgelins also buy La Guerdache? In the forced liquidation of the Qurignon fortune they would easily secure it for five hundred thousand francs, although it had cost eight hundred thousand; and Boisgelin out of his two millions would then still have half a million left to serve as working capital for the Abyss. He, Delaveau, absolutely contracted to increase that capital tenfold and supply the Boisgelins with a princely income. They would simply have to leave Paris, and live happily and comfortably at La Guerdache, pending the accumulation of the large fortune which they would assuredly possess some day, when they might once more return to Parisian life to enjoy it amidst all the magnificence they could dream of.

It was Suzanne who at last secured the compliance of her husband, who felt anxious at the idea of leading a provincial life in which he would probably be bored to death. She herself was delighted to return to La Guerdache, where she had spent her childhood and youth. Thus matters were settled as Delaveau had foreseen. The liquidation of the Qurignon estate took place; and the fifteen hundred thousand francs which the Boisgelins paid for the Abyss and La Guerdache proved barely sufficient to meet the liabilities, in such wise that Suzanne and her husband became absolute masters of everything, having no further accounts to render to the other surviving heirs—that is, Aunt Laure the nun, and André, the infirm and mentally afflicted young fellow who had been sent to a private asylum. On the other hand Delaveau carried out all his engagements, reorganised the works, renewed the plant, and proved so successful in his management that at the end of the first twelve months the profits were already superb. In three years the Abyss recovered its position as one of the most prosperous steel works of the region; and the money earned for Boisgelin by its twelve hundred workpeople enabled him to instal himself at La Guerdache on a footing of great luxury: he had six horses in his stables, five carriages in his coach-house, and organised shooting-parties, dinner-parties, and all sorts of festivities, to which the local authorities eagerly sought invitations. Thus he who during the earlier months had gone about idle and dreary, quite Paris-sick, now seemed to have accustomed himself to provincial life, having discovered as it were a little empire, where his vanity found every satisfaction. Moreover there was a secret cause behind all other things, an element of victorious conceit in the quietly condescending manner in which he reigned over Beauclair.

Delaveau had installed himself at the Abyss, where he occupied Blaise Qurignon's former house with his wife Fernande and their little girl Nise, who at that time was only a few months old. He had then completed his thirty-seventh year, and his wife was ten years younger. Her mother, a music teacher, had formerly resided on the same floor as himself in a dark house of the Rue Saint-Jacques in Paris. Fernande was of such dazzling, sovereign beauty that for more than a twelvemonth, whenever Delaveau met her on the stairs, he drew back trembling against the wall like one who felt ashamed of his ugliness and his poverty. At last, however, salutes were exchanged, and an acquaintance having sprung up, the girl's mother confided to him that she had lived for twelve years in Russia as a governess, and that Fernande was her daughter by a Russian prince by whom she had been deceived. This prince, who was extremely attached to her, would certainly have dowered her with a fortune, but one evening at the close of a day's hunt he was accidentally shot dead, and she then had to return penniless to Paris with her little girl, and once more give lessons there. Only by the most desperate hard work did she manage to bring up the child, for whom, in spite of everything, she dreamt of some prodigious destiny.

Fernande, reared amidst adulation from her cradle, convinced that her beauty destined her for a throne, encountered in lieu thereof the blackest wretchedness, unable to throw her worn-out boots aside since she knew not how to replace them, and being for ever obliged to repair and refurbish her old gowns and hats. Anger and such a craving for victory soon took possession of her, that from her tenth year onward she did not live a day without learning more and more hatred, envy, and cruelty, in this wise amassing extraordinary force of perversity and destructiveness. The climax came when, imagining that her beauty was bound to conquer by virtue of its all-mightiness, she yielded to a man of wealth and power who, on the morrow, refused to have anything more to do with her. This adventure, which she sought to bury in the bitterest depths of her being, taught her the arts of falsehood, hypocrisy, and craftiness, which she had not previously mastered. She vowed that she would not stumble in that way again, for she was far too ambitious to lead a life of open shame. She realised that it was not sufficient for a woman to be beautiful; that she must find the proper opportunity to display her beauty, and must meet a man such as she could bewitch and turn into her obedient slave. And her mother having died after trudging for a quarter of a century through the mud of Paris to give lessons which barely yielded enough money to buy bread, she, Fernande, felt a first opportunity arise on finding herself in presence of Delaveau, who, whilst neither handsome nor rich, offered to marry her. She did not care a pin for him, but she perceived that he was very much in love with her, and she decided to avail herself of his arm to enter the world of respectable women in which he would prove a support and a means towards the end that she had in view. He had to buy her a trousseau, taking her just as he found her, with all the faith of a devotee for whom she was a goddess. And from that time forward destiny followed its course even as she, Fernande, had desired. Within two months of being introduced at La Guerdache by her husband, she designedly entered upon an intrigue with Boisgelin, who had become passionately enamoured of her. In that handsome clubman and horseman she found the ideal lover for whom she had sought, the lover all vanity, folly and liberality, who was capable of the worst things in order to retain his beautiful mistress beside him. And it so happened, moreover, that she thus satisfied all sorts of spite and rancour, the covert hatred which she bore her husband, whose toilsome life and quiet blindness humiliated her, and the growing jealousy which she felt towards the quiet Suzanne, whom she had detested from the very first day; this, indeed, being one of the reasons why she had listened to Boisgelin, for she hoped thereby to make Suzanne suffer. And now all was festivity at La Guerdache: Fernande reigned there like a beautiful guest, realising her dream of a life of display, in which she helped Boisgelin to squander the money which Delaveau wrung in perspiration from the twelve hundred toilers of the Abyss. And, indeed, she even hoped that she would some fine day be able to return to Paris and triumph there with all the promised millions.

Such were the stories which occupied Luc's thoughts as, sauntering along, he repaired to La Guerdache in accordance with Suzanne's invitation. If he did not know everything as yet, he at least already suspected certain matters, which the near future was to enable him to fathom completely. At last, as he raised his head, he perceived that he was only a hundred yards or so from the fine park whose great trees spread their greenery over a large expanse. Then he paused, whilst before his mind's eye there arose above all other figures that of Monsieur Jérôme, the second Quirignon, the founder of the family fortune, the infirm paralysed man whom only the day before he had met in his bath-chair, pushed along by a servant near the very entrance of the Abyss. He pictured him with his lifeless, stricken legs, his silent lips, and his clear eyes which for a quarter of a century had been gazing at the disasters that overwhelmed his race. There was his son Michel, hungering for pleasure and luxury, imperilling the works, and killing himself as the result of a frightful family drama. There was his grandson Gustave, carrying off his father's mistress and dashing his brains out in the depths of a precipice, as beneath the vengeful pursuit of the Furies. There was his daughter Laure, in a convent, cut off from the world; and there was his younger son Philippe, marrying an unworthy woman, gliding with her into the mire, and losing his life in a duel after the most disgraceful adventures; and there was his other grandson André, the last of the name, a cripple, shut up amongst the insane. And yet even now the disaster was continuing; the annihilation of the family was being completed by an evil ferment, that Fernande who had appeared among them as if to consummate their ruin with those terrible, sharp, white teeth of hers. Amidst his long silence Jérôme had witnessed and was witnessing all those things. But did he remark them, did he judge them? It was said that his mind had become weak, and yet how deep and limpid were his eyes! And if he could think, what thoughts were those that filled his long hours of immobility? All his hopes had crumbled; the victorious strength amassed through a long ancestry of toilers, the energy which he thought he was bound to bequeath to a long line of descendants whose fortune would ever and ever increase, had now blazed away like a heap of straw in the fire of worldly enjoyment! In three generations the reserve of creative power which had required so many centuries of wretchedness and effort to accumulate had been gluttonously consumed. Amidst the eager satisfaction of material cravings, the nerves of the race had become unstrung, refinement had led to destructive degeneracy. Gorged too quickly, unhinged by possession, the race had collapsed amidst all the folly born of wealth. And that royal domain La Guerdache, which he Jérôme had purchased, dreaming of some day peopling it with numerous descendants, happy couples who would diffuse the blessed glory of his name, how sad he must feel at seeing half its rooms empty, what anger he must experience at seeing it virtually handed over to that strange woman, who brought the final poisonous ferment in the folds of her skirts! He himself lived there in solitude, keeping up an affectionate intercourse solely with his granddaughter Suzanne, who was the only person still admitted to the large room which he occupied on the ground floor. She, when only ten years old, had already helped to nurse him there, like a loving little girl touched by her poor grandpapa's misfortune. And when she had returned to the spot, a married woman, after the purchase of the family property, she had insisted on her grandfather remaining there, although nothing belonged to him, for he had divided his whole property among his children at the time when paralysis had fallen on him like a thunderbolt.

Suzanne was not without scruples in this matter. It seemed to her that in following Delaveau's advice she and her husband had despoiled the two remaining members of the family, Aunt Laure and André, the cripple. As a matter of fact they were provided for; and thus it was on grandfather Jérôme that she lavished her affection, watching over him like a good angel. But although a smile would appear in the depths of his clear eyes when he fixed them upon her, there remained as it were but two cavities seemingly full of spring water in his frigid, deeply marked countenance, directly the wild life of La Guerdache flitted past him. Was he conscious of it, and did he think about it, and if so were not his thoughts compounded of despair?

Luc found himself at last before the monumental iron gate opening into the Formerie highway at a point whence started a road leading to the neighbouring village of Les Combettes, and he simply had to push a little side gate open in order to reach the royal avenue of elm-trees. Beyond them one saw the château, a huge seventeenth-century pile, quite imposing in its simplicity, with its two upper stories each showing a line of twelve windows, and its raised ground floor, which was reached by a double flight of steps, decorated with some handsome vases. The park, which was of great extent, all copses and lawns, was traversed by the Mionne, which fed a large piece of ornamental water where swans swam to and fro.

Luc was already going towards the steps when a light welcoming laugh made him turn his head. Under an oak-tree, near a stone table surrounded by some rustic chairs, he then perceived Suzanne, who sat there with her son Paul playing near her.

"Why, yes, my friend!" said she, "I have come down to await my guests, like a countrywoman who is not afraid of the open air. How kind of you to accept my abrupt invitation!"

She smiled at him while offering her hand. She was not pretty, but she was charming, very fair and small, with a delicate round head, curly hair, and eyes of a soft blue. Her husband had always considered her to be somewhat insignificant, never suspecting, it seemed, all the delightful kindness of heart and sterling good sense which lurked beneath her great simplicity.

Luc had taken her hand, and retained it for a moment between both his own.

"It was you who were kind to think of me! I am very, very pleased to meet you again," he said.

She was three years his elder, and had first met him in a wretched house in the Rue de Bercy, where he had resided when beginning life as an assistant engineer at some adjacent works. Very discreet, and practising charity in person and by stealth, she had been in the habit of calling at this house to see a mason who had been left a widower with six children, two of them little girls. And the young man being in the garret, with these little girls on his knees, one evening when she had brought some food and linen, they had become acquainted. Luc had afterwards had occasion to visit her at the mansion near the Parc Monceau in connection with other charitable undertakings in which they were both interested. A feeling of great sympathy had then gradually drawn them together, and he had become her assistant and messenger in matters known to them alone. Thus he had ended by visiting the mansion regularly, being invited to most of the entertainments there during two successive winters. And it was there too that he had first met the Jordans.

"If you only knew how people regret you, how your departure was lamented!" he added by way of allusion to their former benevolent alliance.

Suzanne made a little gesture of emotion, and replied in a low, voice: "Whenever I think of you, I am distressed that you are not here, for there is so much to be done."

Luc, however, had just noticed Paul, who ran up with some wild flowers in his hand; and the young man burst into exclamations at seeing how much the boy had grown. Very fair and slim, he had a gentle, smiling face, and greatly resembled his mother.

"Well," said the latter gaily, "he will now soon be seven years old. He is already a little man."

Seated and talking together like brother and sister in the warm radiance of that September day, Luc and Suzanne became so absorbed in their happy recollections that they did not even perceive Boisgelin descend the steps and advance towards them. Smart of mien, wearing a well-cut country jacket, and a single eye-glass, the master of La Guerdache was a brawny coxcomb with grey eyes, a large nose, and waxed moustaches. He brought his dark brown hair in curls over his narrow brow, which was already being denuded by baldness.

"Good day, my dear Froment," he exclaimed, with a lisp which he exaggerated so as to be the more in the fashion. "A thousand thanks for consenting to make one of us."

Then, without more ado, after a vigorous hand-shake *à l'Anglaise*, he turned to his wife: "I say, my dear, I hope orders were given to send the victoria to Delaveau's."

There was no occasion for Suzanne to reply, for just then the victoria came up the avenue of elms, and the Delaveaus alighted before the stone table. Delaveau was a short, broad-shouldered man, possessing a bull-dog's head, massive, low, and with projecting jaw-bones. With his snub nose, big goggle eyes, and fresh-coloured cheeks half hidden by a thick black beard, he carried himself in a military, authoritative manner. A delightful contrast was presented by his wife Fernande, a tall and supple brunette with blue eyes and superb shoulders. Never had more sumptuous or blacker hair crowned a more pure or whiter countenance, with large azure eyes of glowing tenderness, and a small fresh mouth whose little teeth seemed to be of unchangeable brilliancy, and strong enough to break pebbles. She herself, however, was proudest of her delicately shaped feet, in which she found an incontestable proof of her princely origin.

She immediately apologised to Suzanne, whilst making a maid alight with her daughter Nise, who was now three years of age and as fair as her mother was dark, having a curly tumbled head, eyes blue like the sky, and a pink mouth which was ever laughing, dimpling the while both her cheeks and her chin.

"You must excuse me, my dear," said Fernande, "but I profited by your authorisation to bring Nise."

"Oh, you have done quite right," Suzanne responded; "I told you there would be a little table."

The two women appeared to be on friendly terms. One could scarcely detect a slight fluttering of Suzanne's eyelids when she saw Boisgelin hasten to Fernande, who, however, must have been sulking with him, for she received him in the icy manner which she was wont to assume whenever he tried to escape one of her caprices. Looking somewhat anxious, he came back to Luc and Delaveau, who had made one another's acquaintance during the previous spring, and were now shaking hands together. Nevertheless, the young man's presence at Beauclair seemed somewhat to upset the manager of the Abyss.

"What! you arrived here yesterday? Of course then you did not find Jordan at home, since he was so suddenly called to Cannes. Yes, yes, I was aware of that, but I did not know that he had sent for you. He has some trouble in hand with respect to his blast-furnace."

Luc was surprised at the other's keen emotion, and divined that he was about to ask him why Jordan had summoned him to La Crêcherie. He did not understand the reason of such sudden disquietude, and so he answered chancewise: "Trouble, do you think so? Everything seems to be going on all right."

However, Delaveau prudently changed the subject, and gave Boisgelin some good news. China, said he, had just purchased a stock of defective shells which he had intended to recast. And a diversion came when Luc, who was extremely fond of children, made merry on seeing Paul give his flowers to Nise, who was his very particular friend. "What a pretty little girl!" exclaimed the young man, "she is so golden that she looks like a little sun. How is it possible when her papa and mamma are so dark?"

Fernande, who had bowed to Luc, while giving him a keen glance to ascertain if he were likely to prove a friend or an enemy, was fond of having such questions put to her; for, putting on a glorious air, she invariably replied by some allusions to the child's grandfather, the famous Russian prince.

"Oh! a superbly built man, very fair and fresh-coloured. I am sure that Nise will be the very image of him."

By this time Boisgelin had apparently come to the conclusion that it was not the correct thing to await one's guests under an oak tree—only commonplace *bourgeois* after retiring from business into the country could venture to do so—and accordingly he led the whole party towards the drawing-room. At that moment Monsieur Jérôme made his appearance, in his little conveyance propelled by a servant. The old man had insisted on living quite apart from the other inmates of La Guerdache; he had his own hours for rising, going to bed, and going out; and he invariably took his meals by himself. He would not let the others occupy themselves with him, and indeed it was an established rule in the house that he should not even be spoken to. Thus, when he suddenly appeared before them they contented themselves with bowing in silence, Suzanne alone smiling and giving him a long and affectionate glance. On his side Monsieur Jérôme, who was starting on one of those long promenades which at times kept him out of doors the whole afternoon, gazed at the others fixedly like some forgotten onlooker who has ceased to belong to the world and no longer responds to salutations. And beneath the cold keenness of the old man's stare Luc felt his uneasiness, his torturing doubts return.

The drawing-room was a rich and extremely large apartment, hung with red brocatelle and furnished sumptuously in the Louis-Quatorze style. The party had scarcely entered it when some other guests arrived, Sub-Prefect Châtelard, followed by Mayor Gourier, the latter's wife Léonore, and their son Achille. Châtelard, who at forty could still claim to be a good-looking man, was bald, with an aquiline nose, a discreet mouth, and large eyes which shone keenly behind the glasses he wore. He was a piece of Parisian wreckage, who, after losing his hair and his digestion in the capital, had secured the sub-prefecture of Beauclair as an asylum, thanks to an intimate friend who had been pitchforked into office as a minister of state. Deficient in ambition, suffering from a liver complaint, and realising the necessity of rest, he had fallen upon pleasant lines there through making the acquaintance of the beautiful Madame Gourier, with whom he carried on an unclouded *liaison*, which was favourably viewed by those he governed, and even accepted, it was said, by the lady's husband, the latter's thoughts being given elsewhere. Léonore was still a fine-looking woman at eight-and-thirty, fair, with large regular features, and she outwardly displayed extreme piety, prudishness, and coldness; though according to some accounts an everlasting brazier of passions blazed within her. Gourier, a fat, common-looking man, ruddy, with a swollen neck and a moon-like face, spoke of his wife with an indulgent smile. He paid far more attention to the girls of his boot factory, which he had inherited from his father, and in which he had personally made a fortune. The only remaining tie between his wife and himself was their son Achille, a youth of eighteen, who, although he was very dark, had his mother's regular features and fine eyes, and evinced an amount of intelligence and independence which confounded and annoyed both his parents. On whatever terms they themselves lived together, they at all events showed perfect agreement in the presence of strangers; and, indeed, since Châtelard had made their acquaintance the happiness of their household was cited as an example. Moreover, the administration of the town was greatly facilitated by the close intercourse that prevailed between the sub-prefect and the mayor.

But other guests were now arriving; for instance, Judge Gaume, accompanied by his daughter Lucile, and followed by the latter's betrothed, Jollivet, a captain on the retired list. Gaume, a man with a long head, a lofty brow, and a fleshy chin, was barely five-and-forty, but seemed desirous of remaining forgotten in that out-of-the-way nook Beauclair on account of the terrible tragedy which had wrecked his life. His wife, forsaken by a lover, had one evening killed herself before him, after confessing her fault. And however frigid and severe the judge might seem to be, he had really remained inconsolable, tortured by that terrible catastrophe, and at the present time full of fears for the future of his daughter, to whom he was extremely attached, and who, as she grew up, had become more and more like her mother. Short, and slight, and refined, and of an amorous disposition, with melting eyes set in a bright face crowned with hair of a golden-chestnut hue, Lucile ever reminded her father of her mother's transgression, and for fear lest something similar should happen to her, he had betrothed her as soon as she was twenty to Captain Jollivet, though he realised in doing so that it would be painful for him to part with her and that he would afterwards sink into bitter solitude.

Captain Jollivet, though he looked rather worn for a man only five-and-thirty years old, was none the less a handsome fellow with a stubborn brow and victorious moustaches. Fever contracted in Madagascar had compelled him to send in his papers; and having just then inherited an income of twelve thousand francs a year, he had decided to establish himself at Beauclair, his native place, and marry Lucile, whose cooing turtle-dove ways had quite upset him. Gaume, who had no fortune of his own, and lived poorly on his pay as a presiding judge, could not decline the proposals of such a suitor. Yet his secret despair seemed to increase, for never had he evinced more severity in applying the law, rigorously following the strict, stern wording of the Code. People said, however, that implacable as he might seem to be, he was really a disheartened man, a disconsolate pessimist who doubted everything, and particularly human justice. If that were true, what must have been his sufferings, the sufferings of a judge who, while asking himself if he has any right to do so, passes sentences on unhappy wretches who are really the victims of everybody's crime?

Soon after the Gaumes came the Mazelles with their daughter Louise, a child three years of age, another guest for the little table. These Mazelles were a perfectly happy couple, two stout folks of the same age—that is, little more than forty—and they had grown so much alike in course of time that each now had the same rosy smiling face, the same gentle parental way as the other. They had spent a hundred thousand francs to install themselves in true *bourgeois* fashion in a fine substantial house surrounded by a fairly large garden near the sub-prefecture; and they lived therein on an income of some fifteen thousand francs a year derived from investments in Rentes, which to their fancy alone seemed safe. Their happiness, the beatitude of their life, which was now spent in doing nothing, had become proverbial. Often were people heard to say: "Ah! if one could only be like Monsieur Mazelle who does nothing! He's lucky and no mistake!"

To this he answered that he had worked hard during ten years, and was fully entitled to his fortune. The fact was that, after beginning life as a petty commission agent in the coal trade, he had found a bride with a dowry of fifty thousand francs, and had been skilful or perhaps simply lucky enough to foresee the strikes, whose frequent recurrence over a period of nearly ten years were destined to bring about a considerable rise in the prices of French coal. His great stroke had consisted in making sure at the lowest possible prices of some very large stocks of coal abroad and in re-selling them at a huge profit to French manufacturers when a sudden failure in their own supplies was forcing them to close their works. At the same time Mazelle had shown himself a perfect sage, retiring from business when he was nearly forty—that is, as soon as he found himself in possession of the six hundred thousand francs which, according to his calculation, would ensure his wife and himself a life of perfect felicity. He had not even yielded to the temptation of trying to make a million, for he was far too much afraid that fortune might play him false. And never had egotism triumphed more serenely, never had optimism a greater right to say that everything was for the best in the best of worlds, than in the case of these perfectly worthy people, who were very fond of one another and of that tardy arrival, their little girl. Fully satisfied, free from all feverishness, having no further ambition to satisfy, they presented a perfect picture of happiness—the happiness which shuts itself up and does not even glance at the unhappiness of others. The only little flaw in this happiness lay in the circumstance that Madame Mazelle, a very plump and blooming dame, imagined that she was afflicted with some serious, nameless, undefinable complaint, on which account she was all the more coddled by her ever-smiling husband, who spoke with a kind of tender vanity about "my wife's illness" in the same way as he might have spoken of "my wife's wonderful golden hair." Withal, this supposed illness gave rise to no sadness or fear. And it was simply with astonishment that the worthy couple contemplated their little girl, Louise, who was growing up so unlike either of them—that is, dark, thin, and quick, with an amusing little head, which, with its obliquely set eyes and slender nose, suggested that of a young goat. This astonishment of theirs was rapturous, as if the child had fallen from heaven as a present, to bring a little life into their sunshiny house, which fell asleep so easily during their long hours of placid digestion. Beauclair society willingly made fun of the Mazelles, comparing them to pullets in a fattening pen, but it none the less respected them, bowed to them, and invited them to its entertainments; for with their fortune, which was so safe and substantial, they reigned over the workers, the poorly, paid officials, and even the millionaire capitalists, since the latter were always liable to some catastrophe.

At last the only other guest expected at La Guerdache that day, Abbé Marle, the rector of St. Vincent, the rich parish of Beauclair, arrived, none too soon, however, for the others were about to enter the dining-room. He apologised for being late, saying that his duties had detained him. He was a tall, strong man, with a square-shaped face, a beak-like nose, and a large firm mouth. Still young, only six-and-thirty, he would willingly have battled for the Faith had it not been for a slight impediment of speech which rendered preaching difficult. This explained why he was resigned to burying himself alive at Beauclair. The expression of his dark stubborn eyes alone testified to his past dream of a militant career. He was not without intelligence, he perfectly understood the crisis through which Catholicism was passing, and whilst preserving silence with respect to the fears which he sometimes experienced when he saw his church deserted by the masses, he clung strictly to the letter of the Church's dogmas, feeling certain that the whole of the ancient edifice would be swept away should science and the spirit of free examination ever effect a breach in it. Moreover, he accepted the invitations to La Guerdache without any illusions concerning the virtues of the *bourgeoisie*. Indeed, he lunched and dined there in some measure from a spirit of duty, in order to hide the sores whose existence he divined there under the cloak of religion.

Luc was delighted with the gay brightness and pleasant luxuriousness of the spacious dining-room which occupied one end of the ground floor, and had a number of large windows overlooking the lawns and trees of the park. All that verdure seemed to belong to the room, which, with its pearl-grey woodwork and hangings of a soft sea-green, became like the banqueting-hall of some idyllic *féerie champêtre*. And the richness of the table, the whiteness of the napery, the blaze of the silver and crystal, the flowers, too, spread over the board, were a festival for the eyes amidst a wondrous setting of light and perfume. So keenly was Luc impressed by it all, that his experiences on the previous evening suddenly arose before his mind's eyes, and he pictured the black and hungry toilers tramping through the mud of the Rue de Brias, the puddlers and drawers roasting themselves before the hellish flames of the furnaces, and particularly Bonnaire in his wretched home, and the woeful Josine seated on the stairs, saved from starving that night, thanks to the loaf which her little brother had stolen. How much unjust misery there was! And on what accursed toil, what hateful suffering was based the luxury of the idle and the happy!

At table, where covers were laid for fifteen, Luc found himself placed between Fernande and Delaveau. Contrary to proper usage, Boisgelin, who had Madame Mazelle on his right, had placed Fernande on his left. He ought to have assigned that seat to Madame Gourier, but in friendly houses it was understood that Léonore ought always to be placed near her friend Sub-Prefect Châtelard. The latter naturally occupied the place of honour on Suzanne's right hand, Judge Gaume being on her left. As for Abbé Marle, he had been placed next to Léonore, his most assiduous and preferred penitent. Then the betrothed couple, Captain Jollivet and Lucile, sat at one end of the table facing young Achille Gourier, who, at the other end, remained silent between Delaveau and the abbé. And Suzanne, full of foresight, had given orders for the little table to be set behind her, so that she might be near to watch it. Seven-year-old Paul presided over it between three-year-old Nise and three-year-old Louise, who both behaved in a somewhat disquieting fashion, for their little paws were continually straying over the plates and into the glasses. Luckily a maid remained beside them, while at the larger table the waiting was done by the two valets, whom the coachman assisted.

As soon as the scrambled eggs, accompanied by sauterne, had been served, a general conversation was started. Reference was made to the bread supplied by the Beauclair bakers.

"It was impossible for me to get used to it," said Boisgelin. "Their fancy bread is uneatable, so I get mine from Paris."

He said this in the simplest manner possible, but they all glanced with vague respect at their rolls. However, the unpleasant occurrences of the previous evening still haunted every mind, and Fernande exclaimed: "By the way, do you know that they pillaged a baker's shop in the Rue de Brias last night?"

Luc could not help laughing. "Oh, madame, pillaged!" said he, "I was there. It was simply a wretched child who stole a loaf."

"We were there too," declared Captain Jollivet, ruffled by the compassionate, excusing tone of the young man's voice. "It is much to be regretted that the child was not arrested, at least for example's sake."

"No doubt, no doubt," Boisgelin resumed. "It seems that there has been a lot of thievery since that wretched strike. I have been told of a woman who broke open a butcher's till. All the tradespeople complain that prowlers fill their pockets with things set out for sale. . . And so our beautiful new prison is now receiving tenants—is that not so, Monsieur le Président?"

Gaume was about to answer when the Captain violently resumed: "Yes, theft unpunished begets pillage and murder. The spirit predominating among the working-class population is becoming something frightful. Some of you were out in the town yesterday evening like I was. Didn't you notice that spirit of revolt, of passing menace—a kind of terror that made the town tremble? Besides, that Anarchist, Lange, did not hesitate to tell you what he intended doing. He shouted that he would blow up Beauclair and sweep away the ruins. As he, at any rate, is under lock and key, I hope that he will be sharply looked after."

Jollivet's outspokenness astonished everybody. What was the use of recalling that gust of terror of which he spoke, and which the others like himself had felt passing—why revive it, as it were, at that pleasant table laden with such nice and beautiful things? A chill spread round; the threat of what the morrow might bring forth resounded in the ears of all those nervous *bourgeois* amidst the deep silence, whilst the valets came and went, offering trout.

Realising that the silence was embarrassing everybody, Delaveau at last exclaimed: "Lange shows a detestable spirit. The Captain's right; as the rascal is under lock and key he should be kept there."

But Judge Gaume was wagging his head. At last, in his severe way, his countenance quite rigid, in such wise that one could not tell what might lurk behind his professional stiffness, he retorted, "I must inform you that this morning the investigating magistrate, acting on my advice, after subjecting the man to a simple interrogatory, made up his mind to release him."

Protests arose, concealing real fear beneath humorous exaggeration: "Oh, do you want us all to be murdered then, Monsieur le Président?"

Gaume replied by slowly waving his hand, a gesture which might mean many things. After all, the wise course was certainly to refrain from imparting, by some uproarious trial at law, any excessive importance to the words which Lange had cast to the winds, for the more those words were spread, the more would they bear fruit.

Jollivet, who had calmed down, sat gnawing his moustaches, for he did not wish to contradict his future father-in-law openly. But Sub-Prefect Châtelard, who had hitherto contented himself with smiling, in the affable way of a man who puts faith in nothing, exclaimed: "Ah! I quite understand your views, Monsieur le Président. What you have done is, in my opinion, excellent policy. The spirit of the masses is not worse at Beauclair than it is elsewhere. That spirit is everywhere the same; one must strive to accustom oneself to it; and the proper course is to prolong the present state of things as much as possible, for it seems certain that when a change comes it will be for the worse."

Luc fancied that he could detect some jeering irony in the words and manner of that ex-reveller of Paris, who was doubtless amused by the covert terror of the provincial *bourgeois* around him. Moreover, Châtelard's practical policy was summed up entirely in what he had said; apart from that he evinced superb indifference, no matter what minister might be in office. The old Government machine continued working from force of acquired motion; there was grating and there were jolts, and things would fall to pieces and crumble into dust as soon as the new social system might appear. There would be a nasty tumble at the end of the journey, as Châtelard, laughing, was wont to say among his intimates. The machine rolled on because it was wound up, but at the first really serious jolt it would go to the deuce. Even the vain efforts that were attempted to strengthen the crazy old coach, the timid reforms which were essayed, the useless new laws which men voted without even daring to put the old ones into force, the furious surging of ambitions and personalities, the wild, rageful battling of parties, were only calculated to aggravate and hasten the supreme agony. Such a *régime* must feel astonished every morning at finding itself still erect, and must say to itself that the downfall would surely occur on the morrow. He, Châtelard, being in no wise a fool, arranged matters so as to last as long as the *régime* did. A prudent Republican, as it was needful to be, he represented the Government just sufficiently to retain his post, doing only what was necessary, and desiring above all things to live in peace with those under his jurisdiction. And if everything should topple over, he at all events would try not to be under the ruins!

"You see very well," he concluded, "that the unfortunate strike which rendered us all so anxious has ended in the best manner possible."

Mayor Gourier was not endowed with the sub-prefect's caustic philosophy, although as a rule they agreed together in such wise as to facilitate the administration of the town. He now protested: "Allow me, allow me, my dear friend, too many concessions might carry us a long way. I know the working classes, I am fond of them, I am an old Republican, a democrat of the early days. But if I grant the workers the right to improve their lot, I will never accept the subversive theories, those ideas of the Collectivists, which would bring all civilised society to an end."

In his loud but trembling voice rang out the fears which he had lately experienced, the ferocity of a threatened *bourgeois*, the innate desire for repression which had at one moment displayed itself in a desire to summon the military, in order that the strikers might be forced to resume work under the penalty of being shot.

"Well, for my part, I've done everything for the workpeople at my factory," he continued; "they've got relief funds, pension funds, cheap dwellings, every advantage imaginable. So what more can they want? It seems as if the world were coming to an end—is that not so, Monsieur Delaveau?"

The manager of the Abyss had so far continued eating ravenously, and listening, scarcely taking part in the conversation.

"Oh, coming to an end," said he, in his quiet energetic manner; "I certainly hope that we sha'n't allow the world to end without fighting a little to make it last. I am of the same opinion as Monsieur le Sous-Préfet, the strike has ended very well. And I have even had some good news. Bonnaire, the Collectivist, the leader whom I was compelled to take back, has done justice to himself—he quitted the works last night. He is an excellent workman, no doubt; but he's wrong-headed—a dangerous dreamer. And it is dreaming that leads one to precipices."

He went on talking, striving to appear very loyal and just. Each had a right to defend his own interests. By going out on strike the workmen fancied that they were serving their interests. He, as manager of the works, defended the capital, the plant, the property entrusted to him. And he was willing to show some indulgence, since he felt himself to be the stronger. His one duty was simply to maintain what existed, the working of the wage-system such as it had been organised by the wisdom born of experience. All practical truth centred in that; apart from it there were but criminal dreams, such as that Collectivism, the enforcement of which would have brought about the most frightful catastrophes. He also spoke of workmen's unions and syndicates, which he resisted energetically, for he divined that they might prove a powerful engine of war. At the same time he triumphed like an active hard-working manager, who was well pleased that the strike had not caused greater ravages or become a positive disaster, in such wise as to prevent him from carrying out his engagements with his cousin that year.

Just then the two valets were handing round some roast partridges, whilst the coachman, acting as butler, offered some St. Émilion.

"And so," said Boisgelin, in a bantering way, "you promise me that we sha'n't be reduced to potatoes, and that we may eat those partridges without any twinges of remorse?"

A loud burst of laughter greeted this jest, which was deemed extremely witty.

"I promise it," gaily said Delaveau, who laughed like the others. "You may eat and sleep in peace—the revolution which is to carry away your income won't take place to-morrow."

Luc, who remained silent, could feel his heart beating. That was indeed the position, the wage system, the capitalist exploiting the labour of the others. He advanced five francs, made them produce seven francs, by making the workmen toil, and spent the two francs profit. At least, however, that man Delaveau worked, exerted his brain and his muscles; but by what right did Boisgelin, who had never done anything, live and eat in such luxury? Luc was struck, too, by the demeanour of Fernande, who sat beside him. She appeared to be greatly interested in that conversation, though it seemed little suited to women. She grew both excited and delighted over the defeat of the toilers and the victory of that wealth which she devoured like the young wolf she was. Her red lips curved over, displaying her sharp teeth while she laughed the laugh of cruelty, as if indeed she were at last satisfying her rancour and her cravings, in front of the gentle woman whom she was deceiving, between her foppish lover, whom she dominated, and her blind husband, who was gaining future millions for her. She seemed to be already intoxicated by the flowers, the wines, and the viands, intoxicated especially by perverse delight at employing her radiant beauty to bring disorder and destruction into that home.

"Isn't there some question of a charity bazaar at the sub-prefecture?" asked Suzanne of Châtelard in a soft voice. "Suppose we talk of something else besides politics?"

The gallant sub-prefect immediately adhered to her views: "Yes, certainly, it is unpardonable on our part. I will give every *fête* you may desire, dear madame."

From that moment the general conversation ceased; each reverted to his or her favourite subject. Abbé Marle had contented himself with nodding approvingly in response to certain declarations made by Delaveau. The priest behaved with great prudence in that circle, for he was distressed by the misconduct of Boisgelin, the scepticism of the sub-prefect, and the open hostility of the mayor, who made a parade of anti-clerical ideas. Ah! how the abbé's gorge rose at the thought of that social system which he was called upon to support, and which ended in such a *débâcle*! His only consolation was the devout sympathy of Léonore, who sat beside him, muttering pretty phrases whilst the others argued. She likewise transgressed, but at least she confessed her faults, and he could already picture her at the tribunal of penitence, accusing herself of having derived too much pleasure at that lunch from the attentions of Sub-Prefect Châtelard, who sat on her other hand.

Like the priest, worthy Monsieur Mazelle, who remained almost forgotten between Judge Gaume and Captain Jollivet, had only opened his mouth to take in quantities of food, which he chewed very slowly, owing to his fears of indigestion. Political matters no longer interested him, since, thanks to his income, he had placed himself beyond the reach of storms. Nevertheless he was compelled to lend ear to the theories of the captain, who was eager to pour forth his feelings on such a quiet listener. The army, so the captain said, was the school of the country. France, in accordance with her immutable traditions, could only be a warlike nation, and would only recover equilibrium when she reconquered Europe and reigned by force of arms. It was stupid of people to accuse military service of disorganising labour. What labour, whose labour, indeed? Did anything of that exist? Socialism! why it was a stupendous farce! There would always be soldiers, and down below there must be people to do the fatigue duties. A sabre could at any rate be seen, but who had ever seen the Idea, that famous Idea, the pretended Queen of the Earth. The captain laughed at his own wit; and worthy Mazelle, who felt profound respect for the army, complacently laughed with him; whilst Lucile, his betrothed, examined him in silence with the side-long glances of an enigmatical *amorosa*, smiling faintly and strangely the while, as if amused to think what a husband he would make. Meantime, at the other end of the table, young Achille Gourier immured himself in the silence of a witness and a judge, his eyes gleaming with all the contempt which he felt for his parents and the friends with whom they compelled him to take lunch.

However, at the moment when a *pâté* of ducks' liver, a perfect marvel, was being served, another voice arose, and was heard by everybody—it was that of Madame Mazelle, hitherto silent, busy with her plate and her mysterious complaint which required ample nourishment. Finding herself neglected by Boisgelin, whose attention was given entirely to Fernande, she had ultimately fallen on Gourier, to whom she gave particulars about her home, her perfect agreement with her husband, and her ideas of the manner in which she meant to have her daughter Louise educated.

"I won't let them worry her brain, ah! no, indeed! why should she worry? She's an only child, she will inherit all our Rentes."

All at once, without reflecting, Luc yielded to his desire to protest: "But don't you know, madame," said he, "that they are going to suppress the right of inheritance? Oh yes, very soon, directly the new social system is organised."

All round the table it was thought that he was jesting, and Madame Mazelle's stupefaction was so comical to behold that everybody helped on the joke. The right of inheritance suppressed! How infamous! What! the money earned by the father would be taken from the children, and they in their turn would have to earn their own bread? Why, yes, of course, that was the logical outcome of Collectivism. Mazelle, quite scared by it all, came to his wife's help, saying that he did not feel anxious, for his whole fortune was invested in State Rentes, and nobody would ever dare to touch the national ledgers.

"That's just where you make a mistake, monsieur," Luc quietly resumed; "the national ledgers will be burnt and Rentes will be abolished. It is already resolved upon."

ÉMILE ZOLA

At this the Mazelles nearly suffocated. Rentes abolished! It seemed to them that this was as impossible as the fall of the sky upon their heads. And they were so distracted, so terrified by the threat of such an inversion of the laws of nature that Châtelard good-naturedly decided to reassure them. Turning slightly towards the little table, where, in spite of Paul's fine example, the little girls Nise and Louise had not behaved particularly well, he said in a bantering fashion: "No, no, all that won't happen to-morrow; your little girl will have time to grow up and have children of her own—only it will be as well to clean her, for I fancy that she has been dipping her face in the whipped cream."

They went on jesting and laughing. Yet one and all had felt the great breath of To-morrow passing, the breeze of the Future blowing across the table, whence it swept away iniquitous luxury and poisonous enjoyment. And they all rushed to the help of Rentes and capital, the *bourgeois* and capitalist society based upon the wage system.

"The Republic will kill itself on the day it touches property," said Mayor Gourier.

"There are laws, and everything would crumble to pieces on the day they might cease to be enforced," said Judge Gaume.

"Dash it! the army's there at all events, and the army won't allow the rogues to triumph," said Captain Jollivet.

"Let God act, He is all kindness and justice," said Abbé Marle.

Boisgelin and Delaveau contented themselves with approving, for it was to their help that all the social forces hastened. And Luc understood the position clearly: it was the Government, the administration, the magistracy, the army, the clergy which sustained the decaying social system, the monstrous structure of iniquity in which the murderous toil of the greater number fed the corrupting sloth of the few. This was another phase of the terrible vision which he had beheld the previous day. After gazing upon the rear he now saw the front of that rotting social edifice which was collapsing upon every side. And even here, amidst all that luxury and those triumphal surroundings, he had again heard it cracking. He could detect that those people were all anxious but strove to forget and to divert their minds whilst rushing on towards the precipice.

The dessert was now being served, and the table was covered with pastry and magnificent fruit. The better to bring back the good spirits of the Mazelles, the others, as soon as the champagne was poured out, began to sing the praises of idleness, divine idleness, which belongs not to this world. And then Luc, as he continued reflecting, suddenly understood what it was that weighed upon his mind: it was the problem of how the future might be freed, in presence of those folks who represented the unjust and tyrannical authority of the past.

After coffee, which was served in the drawing-room, Boisgelin suggested a stroll through the park as far as the farm. Throughout the repast he had been prodigal in his attentions to Fernande, but she still gave him the cold shoulder, refraining even from answering him, and reserving her bright smiles for the sub-prefect seated in front of her. Matters had been like this for a week past, and were always so when he did not immediately satisfy one of her caprices. The real cause of their present quarrel was that she had insisted on his giving a stag-hunt for the sole delight of showing herself at it in a new and appropriate costume. He had taken the liberty to refuse, as the expenses would be very great; and, moreover, Suzanne, having been warned of the matter, had begged him to be a little reasonable. Thus a struggle had ended by breaking out between the two women, and it was a question which of them would win the victory, the wife or the other.

During lunch Suzanne's sad and gentle eyes had missed nothing of Fernande's affected coldness and her husband's anxious attentions. And so when the latter proposed a stroll she understood that he was simply seeking an opportunity to be alone with her sulky rival, in order to defend himself and win her back. Greatly hurt by this, but incapable of battling, Suzanne sought refuge in her suffering dignity, saying that she should remain indoors in order to keep the Mazelles company. For they, from considerations of health, never bestirred themselves on leaving table. Judge Gaume, his daughter Lucile, and Captain Jollivet also declared that they should not go out; and this led to Abbé Marle proposing to play the judge a game of chess. Young Achille Gourier had already taken leave, under pretext that he was preparing for an examination, but in reality to indulge freely in his favourite reveries as he strolled about the country. And so only Boisgelin, the sub-prefect, the Delaveaus, the Gouriers, and Luc repaired to the farm, walking slowly towards it under the lofty trees.

On the way thither things passed off very correctly; the five men walked on together, whilst Fernande and Léonore brought up the rear, deep apparently in some confidential chat. Among the men Boisgelin had now begun to bewail the misfortunes of agriculture: the soil was becoming bankrupt, said he, and all who tilled it were hastening to ruin.

Châtelard and Gourier agreed that the terrible problem for which no solution had hitherto been found lay in the direction of agriculture: for in order that the industrial workman might produce, it was necessary that bread should be cheap, and if corn fetched only a low price, the peasant, reduced to beggary, could no longer purchase the products of industry. Delaveau, for his part, believed that a solution might be found in an intelligent system of protection. As for Luc, who took a passionate interest in the matter, he did his utmost to make the others talk, and Boisgelin ended by confessing that his own despair came largely from the continual difficulties that he had with his farmer Feuillat, whose demands increased year by year. He would doubtless have to part with the man when the renewal of the lease was discussed, for the farmer had asked for a reduction of terms amounting to no less than ten per cent. The worst was that, fearing his lease might not be renewed, he had ceased to take proper care of the land, which he no longer manured, since it was not for him, he said, to work for his successor's benefit. This, of course, meant the sterilisation of the property, whose value would thus be annihilated.

"And it's everywhere the same," continued Boisgelin; "people don't agree; the workers want to take the places of the owners, and agriculture suffers from the quarrel. At Les Combettes now, that village yonder, whose land is only separated from mine by the Formerie road, you can't imagine what little agreement there is among the peasants, what efforts each of them makes to harm his neighbour, paralysing himself the while! Ah, there was something good in feudality after all! Those fine fellows would walk straight enough if they had nothing of their own, and were convinced that they would never have anything!"

This abrupt conclusion made Luc smile. Nevertheless, he was struck by the unconscious confession that the pretended bankruptcy of the soil came from a lack of agreement among those who tilled it. The party was now quitting the park, and the young man's glance ranged over the great plain of La Roumagne, formerly so famous for its fruitfulness, but now accused of growing cold and sterile, and of no longer yielding sustenance for its inhabitants. On the left spread the extensive lands of Boisgelin's farm, whilst on the right Luc perceived the humble roofs of Les Combettes, around which were grouped many small fields, cut up into little morsels by repeated partition amongst numerous heirs, in such wise that the whole resembled a stretch of patchwork. And Luc asked himself what could possibly be done in order that cordial agreement might return, in order that from so many contradictory and barren efforts a great impulse of solidarity might spring, with universal happiness for its object.

It so happened that as the promenaders were approaching the farmhouse, a large and fairly well-kept building, they heard some loud swearing and thumping of fists upon a table—in fact, all the uproar of a violent quarrel. Then they saw two peasants, one stout and heavy, and the other thin and nervous, come out of the house, and after threatening one another for a last time, go off, each by a different path, through the fields towards Les Combettes.

"What's the matter, Feuillat?" Boisgelin inquired of the farmer who had come to his threshold.

"Oh! it's nothing, monsieur; only two more fellows of Les Combettes who had a dispute about a boundary, and wanted me to umpire between them. The Lenfants and the Yvonnots have been disputing together from father to son for years and years past, and it maddens them nowadays merely to catch sight of one another. It's of no use my talking reason to them. You heard them just now! They'd like to devour one another. And, *mon Dieu*, what fools they are! they'd be so happy and well off if they would only reflect and agree together a little bit."

Then, sorry, perhaps, that he had allowed this remark to escape him, for it was not one which the master should have heard, Feuillat let his eyelids fall, and with an expressionless, impenetrable face, resumed in a husky voice: "Would the ladies and gentlemen like to come in and rest a moment?"

Luc, however, had previously seen the man's eyes glittering. He was surprised to find him so wan and dry, as if his tall slim figure were already grilled by the sunlight, although he was but forty years of age. At the same time Feuillat was possessed of quick intelligence, as the young man soon discovered on listening to his conversation with Boisgelin. When the latter, in a laughing way, inquired if he had thought over the matter of the lease, the farmer wagged his head and answered briefly, like a careful diplomatist desirous of gaining his point. He evidently kept back his real thoughts—the thought that the land ought to belong to those who tilled it, to one and all of them, in order that they might once more love and fertilise it. "Love the soil!" said he, with a shrug of the shoulders. His father and his grandfather had loved it passionately, but what good had that done to them? For his part, his love could wait until he was able to fertilise the soil for himself and his kindred, and not for a landlord, whose one thought would be to raise the rent as soon as the crops should increase. And there was something else beneath the man's reticence, something that he pictured whenever he tried to peer into the future: a reasonable agreement among the peasantry, the reunion of all the subdivided fields so that they might be worked in common, so that tillage might be carried on upon a vast scale with the help of machinery. Such, indeed, were the few ideas which had gradually come to his mind, ideas which were best kept from the *bourgeoisie*, but which, all the same, occasionally escaped him.

The promenaders had ended by entering the farmhouse to sit down there and rest a moment; and Luc there again found the coldness and bareness, the odour of toil and poverty with which he had been struck so much on the previous evening at Bonnaire's home in the Rue des Trois Lunes. Dry and ashen, like her man, La Feuillat stood there in an attitude of silent resignation beside her one child, Léon, a big boy of twelve, who already helped his father in the fields. And it was evident to Luc that on all sides, among the peasants as among the industrial workmen, one found labour accursed, dishonoured, regarded as a stain, a disgrace, since it did not even provide food for the slave, who was riveted to his toil as to a chain. In the neighbouring village of Les Combettes the sufferings were certainly greater than at that farm; the dwellings there were sordid dens, the life was that of domestic animals fed upon sops; the Lenfants, with their son Arsène and their daughter Olympe, the Yvonnots, who also had two children, Eugénie and Nicolas, all found themselves in filthy abject wretchedness, and added to their woes by their rageful passion to prey on one another. Luc, listening and glancing around him, pictured all the horrors of that social hell, telling himself the while, however, that the solution of the problem lay in that direction, for as soon as a new social system should be perfected one would necessarily have to come back to the earth, the eternal nurse, the common mother who alone could provide men with daily bread.

At last, on leaving the farm, Boisgelin said to Feuillat: "Well you must think it over, my good fellow. The land has gained in value, and it's only just that I should profit by it."

"Oh! it's all thought over now, monsieur," the farmer answered. "It will suit me just as well to starve on the road as in your farm." That was his last word.

On the way back to La Guerdache, by another more solitary and shady road of the park, the party of ladies and gentlemen broke up. The sub-prefect and Léonore lingered in the rear, and soon found themselves far behind the others, whilst Boisgelin and Fernande gradually drew upon one side, and disappeared as if mistaking their way, straying into lonely paths amidst their animated conversation. Meantime the two husbands, Gourier and Delaveau, placidly continued following the avenue, talking as they went about an article on the end of the strike that had appeared in the "Journal de Beauclair," a little print with a circulation of five hundred copies which was published by a certain Lebleu, a petty clerical-minded bookseller, and which counted among its contributors both Abbé Marle and Captain Jollivet. The mayor deplored that the Deity should have been introduced into the affair, though, like the manager of the Abyss, he approved of the general tone of the article, which was a perfect chant of triumph celebrating the victory of capital over the wage-earners in the most lyric style. Luc, walking near the others, grew weary of hearing their comments on this article; and at last, after manœuvring so as to let them distance him, he plunged among the trees, confident that he would find La Guerdache again as soon as was necessary.

How charming was the solitude amidst those dense thickets through which the warm September sun sent a rain of golden sparks! For a time the young man wandered at random, well pleased at finding himself alone, at being able to breathe freely in the midst of nature, relieved of the load that had oppressed him in the presence of all those folks who weighed upon his mind and heart. Yet he was thinking of joining them once more, when all at once near the Formerie road he came out into some extensive meadows through which a little branch of the Mionne coursed, feeding a large pond. And the scene which he there encountered greatly amused him, fraught as it was with charm and hope.

Paul Boisgelin had obtained permission to take his two little guests, Nise Delaveau and Louise Mazelle, to this spot. The maids in charge of them were lying down under a willow and gossiping, paying no further attention to the children. But the great feature of the adventure was that the heir of La Guerdache and the young ladies in bibs had found the pond in the possession of some working-class invaders, three youngsters who had either climbed a wall or slipped through a hedge. To his surprise Luc found that the leader and soul of the trespassing expedition was Nanet, behind whom were Lucien and Antoinette Bonnaire. Evidently enough it was Nanet who, profiting by the freedom of Sunday, had led the others astray far from the Rue des Trois Lunes.

ÉMILE ZOLA

And the explanation of it all was simple enough. Lucien had fitted a little boat with a mechanism that carried it over the water; and Nanet having offered to take him to a fine pond he knew, one where nobody was ever met, the little boat was now sailing unaided over the clear unrippled pool. To the children it seemed quite a prodigy.

Lucien's stroke of genius had simply consisted in adapting the wheels and clockwork springs of a little toy cart to a boat which he had fashioned out of a piece of deal. This boat travelled quite thirty feet through the water without the spring requiring to be wound afresh; but unfortunately, in order to bring the boat back again it was necessary to use a long pole, which on each occasion almost made the little vessel sink.

Speechless with admiration, Paul and his young lady friends stood on the bank of the pond, watching the wonderful boat. But Louise, with her eyes glittering in her slender face, which suggested that of a playful little goat, was soon carried away by a boundless desire to possess the toy, and thrusting out her little fists she cried repeatedly: "Want it! Want it!"

Then, as Lucien, with the aid of his pole, brought the boat back to shore, in order to wind up the spring afresh, she eagerly ran towards him. Good nature and the pleasure of play brought them together.

"I made it, you know," said the lad.

"Oh! let me see! give it me!" replied the damsel.

But that was asking him too much, and he energetically defended the boat from the approach of her pillaging hands.

"No, no," said he, "it gave me too much trouble. Leave go or you'll break it."

However, finding her very pretty and gay, he became more cordial, and said to her: "I'll make you another one if you like."

Then he put the boat in the water again, and the wheels once more began to revolve, whilst Louise accepted his offer, clapping her hands and sitting down on the grass by his side, in her turn won over, and treating him as if he were an habitual playfellow.

Meantime it vaguely occurred to Paul, who was the oldest of the whole party, quite a little man of seven, that he ought to find out who the others were. Noticing Antoinette, he felt emboldened by her amiable demeanour, her healthy, pretty face, so he inquired: "How old are you?"

"I'm four years old, but papa says I look as if I was six."

"Who's your papa?"

"Who is papa? why, papa, of course, silly!"

The little minx laughed in such a pretty way that Paul regarded her answer as decisive, and questioned her no further, but sat down by her side, in such wise that they at once became the best friends in the world. She looked so pleasant with her good health and pert expression that he doubtless failed to notice that she wore a very simple woollen frock devoid of all pretensions to elegance.

"And your papa," said she. "Do all these trees belong to him? What a lot of room you have to play in! We got in through the hole in the hedge over there, you know."

"It isn't allowed," said Paul. "And I'm not often allowed to come here, since I might fall into the water. But it's so amusing! You mustn't say anything, because we should get punished if you did."

But all at once a dramatic incident occurred. Master Nanet, who was so fair and wavy-haired, had been standing in admiration before Nise, who was yet fairer and more wavy-haired than himself. They looked like two toys, and they speedily ran towards one another, as if indeed it were needful that they should pair off, and had been awaiting that meeting. Catching hold of each other's hands they laughed face to face, and played at pushing. Then Nanet, in a spirit of bravado, exclaimed: "There's no need of a pole to get his boat. I'd go and fetch it in the water, I would!"

Stirred to enthusiasm, Nise, who likewise favoured extraordinary diversions, seconded the proposal: "Yes, yes, we all ought to get into the water! Let's all take our shoes off!"

Then, however, as she leant over the pond she almost fell into it. At this, all her girlish boastfulness abandoned her, and she raised a piercing shriek when she saw the water wetting her boots. But the lad bravely rushed forward, caught hold of her with his little arms, which were already strong, and carried her like a trophy to the grass, where she again began to laugh and play with him, the pair of them rolling about like a couple of romping kids. Unfortunately the shrill cry which Nise had raised in her fright had roused the maids from their forgetful gossiping under the willow. They rose, and were stupefied at the sight of the invaders, those youngsters who had sprung they knew not whence, and who had the impudence to romp with the children of well-to-do *bourgeois*. The servants hurried up with such angry mien that Lucien hastened to take possession of his boat, for fear lest it should be confiscated, and ran off as fast as his little legs would carry him, followed by Antoinette and even Nanet, who was likewise panic-stricken. They rushed to the hedge, fell flat upon their stomachs, slipped out and disappeared, whilst the servants returned to La Guerdache with their three charges, agreeing between themselves that they would say nothing of what had occurred, in order that nobody might be scolded.

Luc remained alone, laughing, amused by the scene that he had thus come upon, under the paternal sun, in the midst of friendly nature. Ah! the dear little ones, how soon they agreed together, how easily they overcame all difficulties, ignorant as they were of all fratricidal struggles; and what hope of a triumphant future they brought with them!

In five minutes the young man reached La Guerdache again, and there he once more fell into the horrible present, reeking of egotism, the hateful battle-field un which all evil passions contended. It was now four o'clock, and the Boisgelins' guests were taking leave.

Luc was most struck, however, on perceiving Monsieur Jérôme reclining in his bath-chair on the left of the flight of steps. The old gentleman had just returned from his long promenade, and had signed to his servant to leave him there a little while in the warmth of the sun, as if indeed he desired to witness the departure of the guests invited to the house that day. On the steps, amongst the ladies and gentlemen all ready to depart, stood Suzanne, waiting for her husband, who had lingered in the park with Fernande. Some minutes had elapsed after the return of the others when she at last saw Boisgelin appear with the young woman. They were walking quietly side by side, and chatting together as if their long stroll were the most natural thing in the world. Suzanne asked no explanations, but Luc plainly saw that her hands trembled, and that an expression of dolorous bitterness passed over her face between her smiles, for she had to play the part of a good hostess and affect amiability. And she felt keenly wounded, and could not help starting when Boisgelin, addressing Captain Jollivet, declared that he should soon go to see him, in order that they might consult together and organise that stag-hunt which hitherto he had but vaguely thought of. Thus the die was cast, the wife was defeated, the other had won the day, had imposed her foolish and wasteful whim upon her lover during that long stroll which for impudence was tantamount to a publicly given assignation. Suzanne's heart rose rebelliously at the thought of it all. Why should she not take her son and go away with him? Then by a visible effort she calmed herself, becoming very dignified and lofty, bent on shielding the honour of her name and her house with all the abnegation of a virtuous woman, relapsing into the silence of heroic affection, that silence in which she had resolved to live, since it would protect her from all the mire around her. Luc, who could divine everything, now only detected her torment in the quiver of her feverish hand when he pressed it on bidding her good-bye.

Monsieur Jérôme, meanwhile, had watched the scene with those eyes of his, clear like spring water, in which one wondered whether there yet lingered intelligence to understand and judge things. And he afterwards witnessed the departure of the guests—that departure which suggested a *défilé* of all the elements of human power, all the social authorities, the masters who served as examples to the masses. Châtelard went off in his carriage with Gourier and Léonore, the latter of whom offered a seat to Abbé Marle, in such wise that she and the priest sat face to face with the sub-prefect and the mayor. Then Captain Jollivet, who drove a hired tilbury, carried off Judge Gaume and his betrothed Lucile, the former anxiously watching his daughter's languishing turtle-dove airs. Next the Mazelles, who had arrived in a huge landau, climbed into it again as into a soft bed, where they lay back, completing their digestion. And Monsieur Jérôme, to whom they all bowed in silence, according to the custom of the house, watched them all go, like a child may watch passing shadows, without the faintest expression of any feeling appearing on his cold face.

Only the Delaveaus remained, and the manager of the Abyss insisted on giving Luc a lift in Boisgelin's victoria, in order to spare him the necessity of walking. It would be easy enough to set the young man down at his door, since they would pass La Crêcherie on their way. As there was only a folding bracket seat Fernande would take Nise on her lap, and the maid would sit beside the coachman.

"Come, Monsieur Froment, it will be a real pleasure for me to drive you home," Delaveau insisted in his most obliging way.

Luc ended by accepting the offer. Then Boisgelin clumsily referred to the hunt again, inquiring if the young man would still be at Beauclair in order to attend it. Luc answered that he could not tell how long he might be in the district, but at all events they must not rely on him. Suzanne listened with a smile. Then, her eyes moistening at the thought of his brotherly sympathy, she again pressed his hand, saying: "*Au revoir, my friend.*"

ÉMILE ZOLA

When the victoria eventually started, Luc's eyes for the last time met those of Monsieur Jérôme, which, it seemed to him, were travelling from Fernande to Suzanne, slowly taking note of the supreme destruction with which his race was threatened. But was not that an illusion on Luc's part, was there not in the depths of those eyes merely the emotion, the vague smile which always gleamed therein whenever the old man looked at his dear granddaughter, the only one whom he still loved, and whom he was still willing to recognise?

Whilst the victoria was rolling towards Beauclair Luc promptly learnt why Delaveau had been so anxious to drive him home, for the manager again began to question him about his sudden journey—what its purpose might be, and what Jordan would do with reference to the management of his blast-furnace now that the old engineer Laroche was dead. One of Delaveau's secret projects had been to buy the blast-furnace as well as the extensive tract of land which separated it from the steel-works, in such wise as to double the value of the Abyss. But the whole constituted a big mouthful, and as he did not expect to have the necessary money for such a purchase for a long time to come, he had only thought of slow, progressive extension. On the other hand, the sudden death of Laroche had now quickened his desires, and he had fancied that he might perhaps be able to come to arrangements with Jordan, whom he knew to be immersed in his favourite scientific studies, and desirous of ridding himself of a business which brought him a deal of worry. This was why the sudden arrival of Luc in response to a summons from Jordan had greatly disturbed Delaveau, who feared that the young man might upset the plans of which he had hitherto only spoken indirectly. At the first questions which the manager put to him in a good-natured way, Luc, although unable to understand everything, became suspicious, and he therefore replied evasively:

"I know nothing, I have not seen Jordan for more than six months," said he. "As for his blast-furnace, why, I suppose that he will simply confide the management to some clever young engineer."

Whilst he spoke, he noticed that Fernande's eyes never left him. Nise had fallen asleep on the young woman's lap, and she kept silence, seemingly greatly interested in the conversation of the others, as if she could divine that her future was at stake, for she had already detected that this young man was an enemy. Had he not sided with Suzanne in the matter of the hunt; had not she, Fernande, seen them in cordial agreement, with their hands clasped like brother and sister? Then, feeling that war was virtually declared between them, she smiled a keen, cruel smile, like one determined on victory.

"Oh! I merely mention the matter," repeated Delaveau, beating a retreat, "because I was told that Jordan thought of confining himself to his studies and discoveries. Some of the latter are admirable!"

"Yes, admirable!" repeated Luc, with the conviction of an enthusiast.

At last the carriage stopped before La Crêcherie, and the young man alighted, thanked Delaveau, and found himself alone. He again felt the great quiver that had come upon him during those two days which beneficent destiny had granted him since his arrival at Beauclair. He had there seen both sides of the hateful world whose framework was falling to pieces from sheer rottenness: the iniquitous misery of some, the pestilential wealth of others. Work, badly remunerated, held in contempt, unjustly apportioned, had become mere torture and shame when it should have been the very nobility, health, and happiness of mankind. Luc's heart was bursting at the thought of it all, and his brain seemed to open as if to give birth to the ideas which he had felt within him for months past. And a cry for justice sprang from his whole being. Ay, there was no other possible mission nowadays than that of hastening to the succour of the wretched, and setting a little justice once more upon the earth.

IV

The Jordans were to return to Beauclair on the Monday by a train arriving in the evening. And Luc spent the morning of that day in strolling through the park of La Crêcherie, which was not more than fifty acres in extent, though its exceptional situation, its watercourses and superb greenery, made it quite a paradise, famous throughout the whole region.

The house, a by no means large building of brick, of no particular style, had been erected by Jordan's grandfather in the time of Louis XVIII on the site of an old château destroyed during the Revolution. Close behind it rose the range of the Bleuse Mountains, that steep gigantic wall which jutted out like a promontory at the point where the Brias gorge opened into the great plain of La Roumagne. Protected in this wise from the north winds, and looking towards the south, the park was like a natural hot-house where eternal springtide reigned.

Thanks to a number of springs gushing forth in crystalline cascades the rocky wall was covered with vigorous vegetation, and goat-paths, flights of steps cut in the stone, ascended to the summit amidst climbing plants and evergreen shrubs. Down below, the springs united, and flowing on in a slow river, watered the whole park, the great lawns, and the clumps of lofty trees, which were of the finest and most vigorous kinds. Jordan had virtually left that luxuriant corner of nature to look after itself, for he only employed one gardener and two lads, who, apart from attending to the kitchen garden and a few flower-beds below the house-terrace, simply had to keep things somewhat tidy.

Jordan's grandfather, Aurélien Jordan de Beauvisage, was born in 1790 on the eve of the Reign of Terror. The Beauvisages, one of the most ancient and illustrious families of the district, had then already fallen from their high estate, and of their formerly vast territorial possessions they only retained two farms—now annexed to Les Combettes—and between two and three thousand acres of bare rock and barren moor, a broad strip indeed of the lofty plateau of the Bleuse Mountains. Aurélien was less than three years old when his parents were compelled to emigrate, abandoning their flaming château one terrible winter's night. And until 1816 Aurélien had his home in Austria, where his mother and then his father died in swift succession, leaving him in a fearful state of penury, reared in the hard school of manual toil, with no other bread to eat than that which he earned as a worker in an iron mine. He had just completed his twenty-sixth year when, under Louis XVIII, he returned to Beauclair and found the ancestral property still further diminished, for the two farms were lost, and there now only remained the little park and the two or three thousand acres of stones which nobody cared for. Misfortune had democratised Aurélien, who felt that he could no longer be a Beauvisage. Henceforth then he simply signed himself Jordan, and he married the daughter of a very rich farmer of Saint-Cron, his wife's dowry enabling him to build on the site of the old château the *bourgeoise* brick residence in which his grandson now dwelt. But he had become a worker, his hands were still grimy, and he remembered the iron mine and blast-furnace where he had toiled in Austria. Already in 1818 he began to look around him, and, at last, among the desolate rocks of his domain, he discovered a similar mine, the existence of which he had been led to suspect by certain old stories told him by his parents. And then, half-way up the ridge on a kind of natural landing or platform, above La Crêcherie, he installed his own blast-furnace, the first established in the region. From that moment he became absorbed in industrial toil, though without ever realising any very large profits, for he lacked capital, and his life proved one continual battle from that cause. His only title to the gratitude of the district was that by the presence of his blast-furnace he brought thither the iron-workers who had created all the great establishments of the present time, among others being Blaise Qurignon, the drawer by whom the Abyss had been founded in 1823.

Aurélien Jordan had but one son, Séverin, born to him when he was more than five-and-thirty, and it was only when this son replaced him after his death in 1852 that the blast-furnace of La Crêcherie became really important. Séverin had married a Demoiselle Françoise Michon, daughter of a doctor of Magnolles, and his wife proved a woman of exquisite kindliness and very superior intelligence. In her were personified the activity, wisdom, and wealth of the household. Guided, loved, and sustained by her, her husband excavated fresh galleries in his mine, increased the output of ore tenfold, and almost rebuilt the furnace in order to endow it with the most perfect plant then known. And thus, amidst the great fortune which they acquired, the only grief of the Jordans was to remain for many years childless. They had been married ten years, and Séverin was already forty, when a son, Martial, was at last born to them; and ten years later they finally had a daughter,

Sœurette. This belated fruitfulness crowned their lives; Françoise, who had been so good a wife, proved also a most admirable mother, one who battled victoriously against death on behalf of her son, a weakling, and endowed him with her own intelligence and kindliness. Doctor Michon, her father, a humanitarian dreamer, full of divine charitableness, a Fourierist and Saint-Simonian of the first days, withdrew in his old age to La Crêcherie, where his daughter built him a pavilion, the one indeed which Luc had lately occupied. There it was that the doctor died among his books, amidst all the gaiety of sunshine and flowers. And until the death of Françoise, the fondly loved mother, which occurred five years after that of the grandfather and father, La Crêcherie lived on amidst all the joy of never-failing prosperity and felicity.

Martial Jordan was thirty years of age, and Sœurette was twenty, when they first found themselves alone; and five years had now elapsed since that time. He, in spite of his indifferent health, the frequent illnesses of which his mother had cured him by force of love, had passed through the Polytechnic School. But on his return to La Crêcherie, finding himself master of his destiny, thanks to the large fortune he inherited, he had relinquished all thoughts of official appointments, and had taken passionately to the investigations which the application of electricity offered to studious scientists. On one side of the house he built a very spacious laboratory, installed the necessary machinery for powerful motive force in an adjacent shed, and then gradually took to special studies, surrendering himself almost completely to the dream of smelting ore in electrical furnaces in a practical way adapted to the requirements of industry. And from that time he virtually cloistered himself, lived like a monk, absorbed in his experiments, his great work, which became as it were his very life. Beside him, his sister had now taken his dead mother's place; and indeed, before long Sœurette was like his faithful guardian, his good angel, one who took every care of him, and set round him all the warm affection that he needed. Moreover she managed the household, spared him many material worries, served him as a secretary and assistant-preparator, rendered all sorts of help ever gently and quietly with a placid smile upon her face. The blast-furnace luckily gave no trouble, for the old engineer Laroche, a bequest of Aurélien Jordan, the founder, had been there more than thirty years, in such wise that the present owner, deeply immersed in his studies and experiments, was able to detach himself entirely from business matters. He left the worthy Laroche free to manage the blast-furnace in accordance with the routine of years; for he himself had ceased to bother about possible ameliorations, since he cared nothing for mere relative, transitory improvements now that he had begun to seek the radical change, the art of smelting by electrical means, which would revolutionise the whole world of metallurgical industry. Indeed, it was often Sœurette who had to intervene and come to a decision on certain matters with Laroche, particularly when she knew that her brother's mind was busy with some important investigation, and she did not wish him to be disturbed by any outside matters. Now, however, Laroche's sudden death had so thoroughly upset the usual well-regulated order of things, that Jordan, who deemed himself sufficiently rich, and had no ambition apart from his studies, would willingly have rid himself of the blast-furnace by at once opening negotiations with Delaveau, whose desires were known to him, had not Sœurette more prudently obtained from him a promise that he would in the first place consult Luc, in whom she placed great confidence. Thence had come the pressing call addressed to the young man which had brought him so suddenly to Beauclair.

Luc had first met the Jordans, brother and sister, at the Boisgelins' residence in Paris, in which city they had established themselves one winter in order to prosecute certain studies successfully. Great sympathy had arisen between them, based, on Luc's side, upon his great admiration for the brother, whose scientific talent transported him, and upon deep affection mingled with respect for the sister, who seemed to him like some divine personification of goodness. He himself was then working with the celebrated chemist Bourdin, studying some iron ores overcharged with sulphur and phosphates which it was desired to turn to commercial use. And Sœurette recalled certain particulars that he had given her brother on this subject one evening which she well remembered. Now, for more than ten years the mine discovered by Aurélien Jordan on the plateau of the Bleuse Mountains had been abandoned, as in the veins reached by the workers sulphur and phosphorus prevailed to such a point that the ore no longer yielded enough metal to pay the cost of extraction. Thus the working of the galleries had ceased, and the smeltery of La Crêcherie was now fed by the Granval mines near Brias; a little railway line bringing the ore, which was of fairly good quality, as well as the coal of the neighbouring pits, to the charging platform of the furnace. But all this was very costly, and Sœurette often thought of those chemical methods, the employment of which, according to what Luc had said, might perhaps enable them to work their own mine afresh. And in her desire to consult the young man before her brother came to a positive decision, she felt too that she ought to know the real value of what would be ceded to Delaveau should a deed of sale indeed be arranged between La Crêcherie and the Abyss.

The Jordans were to arrive at six o'clock, after twelve hours' travelling, and Luc went to wait for them at the railway station, driving thither in the carriage which was to bring them home. Jordan, short and puny, had a somewhat vague, long, and gentle face, with hair and beard of a faded brown. He alighted from the train wrapped in a long fur overcoat, although that fine September day was a warm one. With his keen, penetrating black eyes, in which all his vitality seemed to have taken refuge, he was the first to perceive his friend Luc.

"Ah, my dear fellow!" said he, "how kind of you to have waited for us! You can't have an idea of the catastrophe that took us away, that poor cousin of ours, dying like that, all alone, yonder, and we having to go and bury him, when there's nothing we hate so much as travelling. . . Well, it's all over now, and here we are."

"And the health's good and you are not over-tired?" asked Luc.

"No, not too much. I was fortunately able to sleep."

But Sœurette was in her turn coming up, after making sure that none of the travelling-rugs had been left inside the carriage. She was not pretty: like her brother she had a very slight figure, and was pale, complexionless, indeed insignificant after the fashion of a woman who is resigned to being a good housewife and nurse. And yet her tender smiles lent infinite charm to her face, whose only beauty dwelt in its passionate eyes, in the depths of which glowed all the craving for love which lurked within her, but of which she herself was as yet ignorant. Hitherto she had loved none excepting her brother, and him she loved after the fashion of some cloistered maid, who for the sake of her Deity renounces the whole world. Before even speaking to Luc she called: "Be careful, Martial—you ought to put on your scarf."

Then, turning towards the young man, she showed herself charming, at once giving proof of the keen sympathy she felt for him: "How many apologies we owe you, Monsieur Froment! What can you have thought of us when you found us gone on your arrival! Have you been comfortable at all events, have you been properly cared for?"

"Admirably—I've lived like a prince."

"Oh! you are jesting. Before I started I took good care to give all necessary orders so that you might lack nothing. But all the same I was absent and unable to watch; and you cannot imagine how vexed I felt at the idea of abandoning you like that in our poor empty house."

They had got into the carriage, and the conversation continued as they drove away. Luc fully reassured them at last by telling them that he had spent two very interesting days, of which he would give them full particulars later on. When they reached La Crêcherie, although the night was falling, Jordan looked eagerly around him, so delighted at returning to his wonted life that he gave vent to cries of joy. It seemed to him as if he were coming back after an absence of several weeks. How could one find any pleasure in roaming, said he, when all human happiness lay in the little nook where one thought, where one worked, freed by habit of the cares of life? Whilst waiting for Sœurette to have the dinner served, Jordan washed himself in some warm water, and then insisted on taking Luc into his laboratory, for he himself was eager to return thither, saying with a light laugh that he should have no appetite for dinner if he did not first of all breathe the air of the room in which his life was spent.

The laboratory was a very large and lofty place, built of brick and iron, with broad bay-windows facing the greenery of the park. An immense table laden with apparatus was set in the centre, and all round the walls were appliances, machine tools, with models, rough drafts of plans, and electrical furnaces on a reduced scale in the corners. A system of cables and wires hanging overhead from end to end of the room brought the electrical motive force from the neighbouring shed and distributed it among the appliances, tools, and furnaces, in order that the necessary experiments might be made. And beside all this scientific severity was a warm and cosy retreat in front of one of the windows, a retreat with low bookcases and deep armchairs, the couch on which the brother dozed at appointed hours, and the little table at which the sister sat while watching over him or assisting him like a faithful secretary.

Jordan touched a switch, and the whole room became radiant with a rush of electric light.

"So here I am!" said he. "Really now, I only feel all right when I'm at home. By the way, that misfortune which compelled me to absent myself happened just as I was becoming passionately interested in a new experiment—I shall have to begin it again. But, *mon Dieu!* how well I feel!"

He continued laughing; colour had come to his cheeks, and he showed far more animation than usual. Leaning back on the couch in

ÉMILE ZOLA

the attitude he usually assumed when yielding to thought, he compelled Luc also to sit down.

"I say, my good friend," he continued, "we have plenty of time—have we not?—to talk of the matters which made me so desirous to see you that I ventured to summon you here. Besides, it is necessary that Sœurette should be present, for she is an excellent counsellor. So if you are agreeable we will wait till after dinner, we will have our chat at dessert. And meantime, how happy I feel at having you there in front of me to tell you how I am getting on with my studies! They don't progress very fast, but I work at them, and that's the great thing, you know. It's enough if one works two hours a day."

Then, this usually taciturn man went on chatting, recounting his experiments, which as a rule he confided to nobody, excepting the trees of his park, as he sometimes jestingly exclaimed. An electrical furnace being already devised, he had at first simply sought how it might be practically employed for the smelting of iron ore. In Switzerland, where the motive power derived from the torrents enabled one to perform certain work inexpensively, he had inspected furnaces which melted aluminium under excellent conditions. Why should it not be possible to treat iron in the same way? To solve the problem it was only necessary to apply the same principles to a given case. The blast-furnaces in use gave scarcely more than 1,600 degrees of heat,[1] whereas 2,000 were obtained with the electrical furnaces, a temperature which would produce immediate fusion of perfect regularity. And Jordan had without any difficulty planned such a furnace as he thought advisable, a simple cube of brickwork, some six feet long on each side, the bottom and crucible being of magnesia, the most refractory substance known. He had also calculated and determined the volume of the electrodes, two large cylinders of carbon, and his first real find consisted in discovering that he might borrow from them the carbon necessary to disoxygenate the ore, in such wise that the operation of smelting would be greatly simplified, for there would be but little slag. If the furnace were built, however, or at least roughed out, how was one to set it working and keep it working in a practical, constant manner, in accordance with industrial requirements?

"There!" said he, pointing to a model in a corner of the laboratory. "There is my electrical furnace. Doubtless it needs to be perfected; it is

---

1. It may be presumed that M. Zola means centigrade degrees.—*Trans.*

defective in various respects, there are little difficulties which are not yet solved. Nevertheless, such as it is, it has given me some pigs of excellent cast iron, and I estimate that a battery of ten similar furnaces working for ten hours would do the work of three establishments like mine kept alight both by day and night. And what easy work it would be, without any cause for anxiety, work which children might direct by simply turning on switches. But I must confess that my pigs cost me as much money as if they were silver ingots. And so the problem is plain enough: my furnace, so far, is only a laboratory toy, and will only exist with respect to industrial enterprise when I am able to feed it with an abundance of electricity at a sufficiently low cost to render the smelting of iron ore remunerative."

Then he explained that for the last six months he had left his furnace on one side to devote himself entirely to studying the transport of electrical force. Might not economy already be realised by burning coal at the mouth of the pit it came from, and by transmitting electrical force by cables to the distant factories requiring it? That again was a problem which many scientists had been endeavouring to solve for several years, and unfortunately they all found themselves confronted by a considerable loss of force during transit.

"Some more experiments have just been made," said Luc with an incredulous air. "I really think that there is no means of preventing loss."

Jordan smiled with that gentle obstinacy, that invincible faith which he brought into his investigations during the months and months which he at times expended over them before arriving at the slightest grain of truth.

"One must think nothing before one is quite certain," said he. "I have already secured some good results; and some day electrical force will be stored up, canalised, and directed hither and thither without any loss at all. If twenty years' searching is necessary, well I'll give twenty years. It's all very simple: one sets to work anew every morning, one begins afresh until one finds—whatever should I myself do if I did not begin again and again?"

He said this with such naïve grandeur that Luc felt moved as by a deed of heroism. And he looked at Jordan, so slight, so puny of build, ever in poor health, coughing, pain-racked under his scarves and shawls, in that vast laboratory littered with gigantic appliances, traversed by wires charged with lightning, and filled more and more each day by colossal labour—the labour of a little insignificant being who went to and fro, striving, battling to desperation, like an insect lost amidst the dust of the ground. Where was it that he found not only intellectual energy but also sufficient physical vigour to undertake and carry through so many mighty tasks, for the accomplishment of which the lives of several strong, healthy men seemed to be necessary? He could hardly trot about, he could scarcely breathe, and yet he raised a very world with his little hands, weak though they were, like those of a sickly child.

However, Sœurette now made her appearance, and gaily exclaimed: "What! aren't you coming to dinner? I shall lock up the laboratory, my dear Martial, if you won't be reasonable."

The dining-room, like the *salon*—two rather small apartments as warm and as cosy as nests, in which one detected the watchful care of a woman's heart—overlooked a vast stretch of greenery, a panorama of meadows and ploughed fields spreading to the dim distant horizon of La Roumagne. But at that hour of night, although the weather was so mild, the curtains were drawn. Luc now again noticed what minute attentions the sister lavished on the brother. He, Martial, followed quite an intricate regimen, having his special dishes, his special bread, and even his special water, which was slightly warmed in order to "take the chill off it." He ate like a bird, rose and went to bed early, like the chickens, who are sensible creatures; then during the day came short walks and rests between the hours that he gave to work. To those who expressed astonishment at the prodigious amount of work that he accomplished, and who thought him a terrible labourer, toiling from morning till night and showing himself no mercy, he replied that he worked scarcely three hours a day, two in the morning and one in the afternoon. And even in the morning a spell of recreation came between the two hours that he gave to work; for he could not fix his attention upon a subject for more than one hour at a stretch without experiencing vertigo, without feeling as if his brain were emptying. Never had he been able to toil for a longer time, and his value rested solely in his will-power, his tenacity, the passion that he imported into the work which he undertook, and with which he persevered, on and on, in all intellectual bravery, even if years went by before he brought it to a head.

Luc now at last discovered an answer to that question which he had so often asked himself; wherever did Jordan, who was so slight and weak, find the strength requisite for his mighty tasks? He found it solely in method, in the careful, well-reasoned employment of all his means, however slight they might be. He even made use of his weakness, using it as a weapon which prevented him from being disturbed by outsiders. But above all else, he was ever intent on one and the same thing, the work he had in hand. To that work he gave every minute at his disposal, without ever yielding to discouragement or lassitude, but sustained by the unfailing desperate faith which raises mountains. Is it known what a mass of work one may pile up when one works only two hours a day on some useful and decisive task, which is never interrupted by idleness or fancy? Such work is like the grain of wheat which, accumulating, fills the sack, or like the ever-falling drop of water which causes the river to overflow. Stone by stone, the edifice rises, the monument grows, until it o'ertops the mountains. And it was thus, by a prodigy of method and personal adaptation, that this sickly little man, wrapped in rugs and drinking his water warm for fear lest he should catch cold, accomplished work of the mightiest kind, and this although he gave to it only the few hours of intellectual health that he succeeded in wresting from his physical weakness.

The dinner proved a very friendly and cheerful repast. The household service was entirely in the hands of women, for Sœurette found men too noisy and rough for her brother. The coachman and groom simply procured assistants on certain occasions when some very heavy work had to be done. And the servant-girls, all carefully selected, pleasant-looking, gentle and skilful, contributed to the happy quiescence of that cosy dwelling, where only a few intimates were received. That evening, for the return of the master and mistress, the dinner consisted of some clear soup, a barbel from the Mionne with melted butter, a roast fowl and some salad—all very simple dishes.

"So you have really not felt over-bored since Saturday?" Sœurette inquired of Luc when they were all three seated at the table.

"No, I assure you," the young man answered, "And besides, you have no notion how fully my time has been occupied."

Then he first of all recounted his Saturday evening, the covert state of rebellion in which he had found Beauclair, the theft of a loaf by Nanet, the arrest of Lange, and his visit to Bonnaire, the victim of the strike. But by a strange scruple, at which he afterwards felt astonished, he virtually skipped his meeting with Josine, and did not mention her by name.

"Poor folks!" exclaimed Sœurette compassionately. "That frightful strike reduced them to bread and water, and even those who had bread were lucky. What can one do? How can one help them? Alms give

ÉMILE ZOLA

but the slightest relief, and you don't know how distressed I have been during the last two months, at feeling that we, the rich and happy, are so utterly powerless."

She was a humanitarian, a pupil of her grandfather Dr. Michon, the old Fourierist and Saint-Simonian, who when she was quite little had taken her on his knees to tell her some fine stories of his own invention, stories of phalansteries established on blissful islands, of cities where men had found the fulfilment of all their dreams of happiness amidst eternal springtide.

"What can be done? What can be done?" she repeated dolorously, with her beautiful, soft, compassionate eyes fixed upon Luc. "Something ought to be done, surely."

Then Luc, emotion gaining on him, raised a heartfelt cry. "Ah! yes, it's high time, one must act."

But Jordan wagged his head; he, immersed in the cloistered life of a scientist, never occupied himself with politics. He held them in contempt, and unjustly—for after all it is necessary that men should watch over the manner in which they are governed. He, however, living amidst the absolute, regarded passing events, the accidents of the day, as mere jolts on the road, and consequently of no account. According to him it was science alone which led mankind to truth, justice, and final happiness, that perfect city of the future towards which the nations plod on so slowly, and with so much anguish. Of what use, therefore, was it to worry about all the rest? Was it not sufficient that science should advance? For it advanced in spite of everything—each of its conquests was definitive. And whatever might be the catastrophes of the journey, at the end there rose the victory of life, the accomplishment of the destiny of mankind. Thus, though he was very gentle and tender-hearted like his sister, he closed his ears to the contemporary battle, and shut himself up in his laboratory, where, as he expressed it, he manufactured happiness for to-morrow.

"Act?" he declared in his turn. "Thought is an act, and the most fruitful of all acts in influence upon the world. Do we even know what seeds are germinating now? The sufferings of all those poor wretches are very distressing, but I do not allow myself to be disturbed by them, for the harvest will come in its due season."

Luc, feverish and disturbed as he himself felt, did not insist on the point, but went on to relate how he had spent his Sunday, his invitation to La Guerdache, the lunch there, the people he had met at table, and what had been done and what had been said. But whilst he spoke he could see that the brother and sister were becoming cold, as if they took no interest in all those folks.

"We seldom see the Boisgelins now that they are living at Beauclair," Jordan exclaimed, with his quiet frankness. "They showed themselves very amiable in Paris, but here we lead such a retired life that all intercourse has gradually ceased. Besides, it must be acknowledged that our ideas and our habits are very different from theirs. As for Delaveau, he is an intelligent and active fellow, absorbed in his business as I am in mine. And I must add that the fine society of Beauclair terrifies me to such a point that I keep my door closed to it, delighted at its indignation and at remaining alone like some dangerous madman."

Sœurette began to laugh. "Martial exaggerates a little," said she. "I receive Abbé Marle, who is a worthy man, as well as Doctor Novarre and Hermeline the schoolmaster, whose conversation interests me. And if it is true that we remain simply on a footing of courtesy with La Guerdache, I none the less retain sincere friendship for Madame Boisgelin, who is so good, so charming."

Jordan, who liked to tease his sister at times, thereupon exclaimed: "Why don't you say at once that it is I who compel you to flee the world, and that if I were not here you would throw the doors wide open!"

"Why, of course!" she answered gaily, "the house is such as you desire it to be. But if you wish it I am quite willing to give a great ball, and invite Sub-Prefect Châtelard, Mayor Gourier, Judge Gaume, Captain Jollivet, and the Mazelles and the Boisgelins and the Delaveaus. You shall open the ball with Madame Mazelle!"

They went on jesting, for they felt very happy that evening, both on account of their return to their nest and of Luc's presence beside them. At last, when the dessert was served, they proceeded to deal with the great question. The two silent servant-girls had gone off in their light felt slippers, which rendered their footsteps inaudible; and the quiet dining-room seemed full of the charm of affectionate intimacy, when hearts and minds can be opened in all freedom.

"So this, my friend," said Jordan, "is what I ask of your friendship. I wish you to study the question, and tell me what you yourself would do if you were in my place."

He recapitulated the whole business, and explained how he himself regarded it. He would long since have rid himself of the blast-furnace if it had not, so to say, continued working of its own accord in the jog-trot manner regulated by routine. The profits remained sufficient, but holding himself to be rich enough he did not take them into account. And on the other hand, had he been minded to increase them, double or treble them as ambition might dictate, it would have been necessary to renew a part of the plant, improve the systems employed, and in a word devote oneself to them entirely. That was a thing which he could not and would not do, the more particularly as those ancient blast-furnaces, whose methods to him seemed so childish and barbarous, possessed no interest for him, and could be of no help in the experiments of electrical smelting in which he was now passionately absorbed. So he let the furnace go, occupied himself with it as little as possible, whilst awaiting an opportunity to get rid of it altogether.

"You understand, my friend, don't you?" he said to Luc. "And now, you see, all at once old Laroche dies, and the whole management and all its worries fall on my shoulders again. You can't imagine what a lot of things ought to be done—a man's lifetime would scarcely suffice if one wished to deal with the matter seriously. For my part nothing in the world would induce me to relinquish my studies, my investigations. The best course, therefore, is to sell, and I am virtually ready to do so; still, first of all, I should much like to have your opinion."

Luc understood Jordan's views, and thought them reasonable.

"No doubt," he answered, "you cannot change your work and habits, your whole life. You yourself and the world would both lose too much by it. But at the same time I think you might give the matter a little more thought, for perhaps there are other solutions possible. Besides, in order to sell you must find a purchaser."

"Oh! I have a purchaser," Jordan resumed. "Delaveau has long desired to annex the blast-furnace of La Crêcherie to the steel-works of the Abyss. He has sounded me already, and I have only to make a sign."

Luc had started on hearing Delaveau's name, for he now at last understood why the latter had shown himself so anxious and so pressing in his inquiries. And as his host, who had noticed his gesture, inquired if he had anything to say against the manager of the Abyss, he responded, "No, no, I think as you yourself do, that he is an active and intelligent man."

"That is the very point," continued Jordan; "the business would be in the hands of an expert. It would be necessary, I think, to come to certain arrangements, such as agreeing to payments at long intervals, for Boisgelin has no capital at liberty. But that doesn't matter. I can wait, a guarantee on the Abyss would suffice me." Then looking Luc full in the face, he concluded: "Come, do you advise me to finish with the matter, and treat with Delaveau?"

The young man did not immediately reply. A feeling of uneasiness and repugnance was rising within him. What could it be? Why should he experience such indignation, such anger with himself, as if, by advising his friend to hand the blast-furnace over to that man Delaveau, he would be committing some bad action which would for ever leave him full of remorse? He could find no good reason for advising any other course. Thus he at last replied: "All that you have said to me is certainly very reasonable, and I cannot do otherwise than approve of your views. And yet you might do well in giving the matter a little more thought."

Sœurette had hitherto listened very attentively, without intervening. She seemed to share Luc's covert uneasiness, and now and again glanced at him anxiously, whilst waiting for his decision.

"The smeltery is not alone in question," she at last exclaimed; "there is also the mine, all that rocky land which cannot be separated from the furnace, so it seems to me."

But her brother, eager to get rid of the whole affair, made an impatient gesture, saying: "Delaveau shall take the land as well, if he desires it. What can we do with it? A mass of peeling calcined rock, amongst which the very nettles refuse to grow! It has no value whatever nowadays, since the mine can no longer be worked."

"Is it quite certain that it can no longer be worked?" insisted Sœurette. "I remember, Monsieur Froment, that you told us one evening in Paris that the ironmasters in Eastern France had managed to make use of most defective ore by subjecting it to some chemical treatment. Why has that process never been tried here?"

Jordan raised his arms towards the ceiling in a fit of despair. "Why? why, my dear?" he cried. "Because Laroche was deficient in all initiative; because I myself have never had time to attend to the matter; because things worked in a certain way and could not be got to work otherwise. If I'm selling the property it's precisely because I don't want to hear it mentioned again, for it is radically impossible for me to direct the business, and the mere thought of it makes me ill."

He had risen, and his sister seeing him so agitated, remained silent for fear lest in provoking a dispute she might throw him into a fever.

"There are moments," he continued, "when I think of sending for

Delaveau so that he may take everything whether he pays or not. I am not hard up for money. It's like those electrical furnaces which so greatly impassion me; I have never once thought of employing them myself and of coining money with them, for as soon as I solve all the difficulties in my way, I shall give my invention to everybody, so as to help on universal prosperity and happiness... Well then, it is understood. As our friend considers my plan to be a reasonable one, we will study the conditions of sale together to-morrow, and then I'll finish everything."

Luc made no response; a feeling of repugnance still possessed him, and he did not wish to pledge himself too far. But Jordan became yet more excited, and ended by suggesting that they should go up to see the furnace, the more especially as he wished to ascertain how things had gone there during his three days' absence.

"I am not without anxiety," said he. "Although Laroche has been dead a week I have not replaced him—I have let my master-smelter, Morfain, direct the work. He is a capital fellow! He was born up yonder, and grew up amidst the fires! Nevertheless the responsibility is heavy for a mere workman such as he is."

Sœurette, alarmed by her brother's suggestion, intervened entreatingly. "Oh, Martial!" she cried, "you have only just come back from a long journey, and yet, tired as you must be, you want to go out again at ten o'clock at night."

Jordan thereupon became very gentle again, and kissed her. "Don't worry, little one," said he; "you know that I never attempt more than I feel I can do. I assure you that I shall sleep the better after making certain that things are all right. It is not a cold night, and, besides, I will put on my fur coat."

Sœurette herself fastened a thick scarf about his neck, and accompanied him and Luc down the steps in order to make sure that the night was really mild. It was indeed a delightful one, the trees, the rivulets, and the fields all slumbered beneath the heavens, which spread out like a canopy of dark velvet spangled with stars.

"I am confiding him to your care, Monsieur Froment," said Sœurette, referring to her brother. "Do not let him remain out late."

The two men at once began to climb a narrow stairway which was cut out in the rocks behind the house, and ascended to the stony landing whereon the furnace stood, half-way up the huge ridge of the Bleuse Mountains. It was a labyrinthine stairway of infinite charm, winding between pines and climbing plants. At each bend, on raising one's head, one perceived the black pile of the smeltery standing forth more and more plainly against the blue night-sky, the strange silhouettes of various mechanical adjuncts showing forth fantastically around the central pile.

Jordan went up the first with light short steps, and as he was at last reaching the landing he paused before a pile of rocks among which a little light gleamed like a star.

"Wait a minute," he said, "I want to make sure whether Morfain is at home or not."

"Where, at home?" asked Luc in astonishment.

"Why here, in these old grottoes, which he has turned into a kind of dwelling-place, to which he clings most obstinately with his son and daughter, in spite of all the offers that I have made of providing him with a little house."

All along the gorge of Brias quite a number of poor people dwelt in similar cavities. Morfain for his part remained there from taste, for there forty years previously he had first seen the light; and, moreover, he was thus close beside his work, that furnace which was at once his life, his prison, and his empire. Moreover, if he had chosen a prehistoric dwelling, he had behaved like a civilised man of the caves, closing both sides of his grotto with a substantial wall and providing a stout door and some windows fitted with little panes of glass. Inside, there were three rooms, the bedroom shared by the father and the son, the daughter's bedroom, and the common room, which served at once as kitchen, dining-room, and workshop. And all three chambers were very clean, with their walls and their vaulted roof of stone, and their substantial, if roughly hewn, furniture.

As Jordan had said, the Morfains from father to son had been master-smelters at La Crêcherie. The grandfather had helped to found the establishment, and after an uninterrupted family reign of more than eighty years the grandson now kept watch over the tappings. Like some indisputable title of nobility the hereditary character of his calling filled Morfain with pride. His wife had now been dead four years, leaving him a son then sixteen, and a daughter then fourteen years of age. The lad had immediately begun to work at the furnace, and the girl had taken care of the two men, cooking their meals, sweeping and cleaning the dwelling-place like a good housewife. In this wise had the days gone by; the girl was now eighteen and the lad twenty, and the father quietly watched his race continuing pending the time when he might hand over the furnace to his son, even as his father had transmitted it to him.

"Ah! so you are here, Morfain," said Jordan, when he had pushed open the door, which was merely closed by a latch. "I have just returned home, and I wanted to know how things were getting on."

Within the rocky cavity, lighted by a small and smoky lamp, the father and son sat at table eating some soup—a mess of broth and vegetables—before starting on their night's work, whilst the daughter stood in the rear, serving them. And their huge shadows seemed to fill the place, which was very solemn and silent. At last in a gruff voice Morfain slowly answered, "We've had a bad business, Monsieur Jordan, but I hope that things will be quiet now."

He rose to his feet, as did his son, and stood there between the lad and the girl, all three of them strongly built and of such lofty stature that their heads almost touched the rough smoky stone vault, which served as a ceiling to the room. One might have taken them for three apparitions of the vanished ages, some family of mighty toilers whose long efforts throughout the centuries had subjugated nature.

Luc gazed with amazement at Morfain, a veritable colossus, one of the Vulcans of old by whom fire was first conquered. He had an enormous head, with a broad face, ravined and scorched by the flames. His brow was a bossy one, his eyes glowed like live coals, his nose showed like an eagle's beak between his cheeks, which looked as if they had been ravaged by some flow of lava. And his swollen, twisted mouth was of a tawny redness like that of a burn; while his hands had the colour and the strength of pincers of old steel.

Then Luc glanced at the son, Petit-Da,[2] as he was called, this nickname having been given him because in childhood he had been accustomed to pronounce certain words badly, and, further, had one day narrowly missed losing his little fingers in some "pig" which was scarcely cold. He again was a colossus, almost as huge as his father, whose square face, imperious nose, and flaming eyes he had inherited. But he had been less hardened, less marked by fire; and, besides, he could read, and his features were softened and brightened by dawning powers of thought.

Finally Luc gazed at the daughter, Ma-Bleue, as her father had ever lovingly called her, so blue indeed were her great eyes, the eyes

---

2. The meaning is "Little Dolt," "Da" being a contraction of "Dadais."—*Trans.*

of a fair-haired goddess, lightly and infinitely blue, and so large that in all her face one was conscious of nothing else save that celestial blueness. She was a goddess of lofty stature, of simple yet magnificent comeliness, the most beautiful, the most taciturn, the wildest creature of the region, yet one who in her wildness dreamt, read books, and saw from afar off the approach of things that her father had never seen, and the unconfessed expectation of which made her quiver. Luc marvelled at the sight of those three creatures of heroic build, that family in which he detected all the long overpowering labour of mankind on its onward march, all the pride begotten of painful effort incessantly renewed, all the ancient nobility that springs from deadly toil.

But Jordan had become anxious. "A bad business, Morfain!" said he, "how was that?"

"Yes, Monsieur Jordan, one of the twyers got stopped up. For two days I fancied that we were going to have a misfortune, and I didn't sleep for thought of it. It grieved me so much that a thing like that should happen to me just when you were away. It's best to go and see if you've the time. We shall be 'running' by-and-by."

The two men finished their soup standing, hastily swallowing large spoonfuls of it whilst the girl already began to wipe the table. They rarely spoke together, a gesture or a glance sufficed for them to understand each other. Nevertheless the father, affectionately softening his gruff voice, said to Ma-Bleue: "You can put out the light, you need not wait for us, we shall have a rest up above."

Then whilst Morfain and Petit-Da went off in front, accompanying Jordan, Luc, who was in the rear, glanced round, and on the threshold of that barbarian home he perceived Ma-Bleue, standing erect, tall and superb, like some *amorosa* of the ancient days, whilst her large azure eyes wandered dreamily far away into the clear night.

The black pile of the furnace soon arose before the young man's view. It was of a very ancient pattern, heavy and squat, not more than fifty feet in height. But by degrees various improvements had been added, new organs, as it were, which had ended by forming a little village around it. The running hall, floored with fine sand, looked light and elegant with its iron framework roofed with tiles. Then on the left, inside a large glazed shed, was the blast apparatus with its steam engine; whilst on the right rose the two groups of lofty cylinders, those in which the combustible gases became purified, and those in which they served to warm the blast from the engine, in order that it might reach the furnace burning hot, and in this wise hasten combustion. And there were also a number of water-tanks and a whole system of piping, which kept moisture ever trickling down the sides of the brick walls in order to cool them and diminish the wear and tear of the awful fire raging within. Thus the monster virtually disappeared beneath the intricate medley of its adjuncts, a conglomeration of buildings, a bristling of iron tanks, an entanglement of big metal pipes, the whole forming an extraordinary jumble which, at night-time especially, displayed the most barbarous, fantastic silhouettes. Above, beside the rock one perceived the bridge which brought the trucks laden with ore and fuel to the level of the mouth of the furnace. Below, the kieve reared its black cone, and then from the belly downward a powerful metal armature sustained the brickwork which supported the water conduits and the four twyers. Finally, at the bottom there was but the crucible, with its taphole closed with a bung of refractory clay. But what a gigantic beast the whole made, a beast of disquieting, bewildering shape, which devoured stones and gave out metal in fusion.

Moreover, was there scarcely a sound, scarcely a light. That mighty digestion apparently preferred silence and gloom. One could only hear the faint trickling of the water running down the sides of the bricks, and the ceaseless distant rumbling of the blast apparatus in the engine-shed. And the only lights were those of three or four lanterns gleaming amidst the darkness, which the shadows of the huge buildings rendered the more dense. Moreover, only a few pale figures were seen flitting about, the eight smelters of the night-shift, who wandered hither and thither whilst waiting for the next "run." On the platform of the mouth of the furnace up above one could not even discern the men who, silently obeying the signals sent them from below, poured into the furnace the requisite charges of ore and fuel. And there was not a cry, not a flash of light; it was all dim, mute labour, something mighty and savage accomplished in the gloom.

Jordan, however, moved by the bad news given him, had reverted to his dream; and pointing to the pile of buildings, he said to Luc, who had now joined him: "You see it, my friend; now am I not right in wishing to do away with all that, in wishing to replace such a cumbersome monster, which entails such painful toil, by my battery of electrical furnaces, which would be so clean, so simple, so easily managed? Since the day when the first men dug a hole in the ground to melt ore by mingling it with branches which they set alight, there has really been little change in the methods employed. They are still childish and primitive. Our blast-furnaces are mere adaptations of the prehistoric pits, changed into hollow columns and enlarged according to requirements. And one continues throwing in the ore and the combustible pell mell, and burning them together. One might take such a furnace to be some infernal animal, down whose throat one is for ever pouring food compounded of coal and oxide of iron, which the beast digests amidst a hurricane of fire, and which it gives out down below in the form of fused metal, whilst the gases, the dust, the slag of every kind goes off elsewhere. And observe that the whole operation rests in the slow descent of the digested substances, in total absolute digestion, for the object of all the improvements hitherto effected has been to facilitate it. Formerly there was no blast, no blowing apparatus, and fusion was therefore slower and more defective. Then cold air was employed, and next it was perceived that a better result was obtained by heating the air. At last came the idea of heating that air by borrowing from the furnace itself the gases which had formerly burnt at its mouth in a plume of flames. And in this wise many external organs have been added to our blast-furnaces, but in spite of every improvement, in spite of their huge proportions, they have remained childish, and have even grown more and more delicate, liable to frequent accidents. Ah! you can't imagine the illnesses which fall upon such a monster. There is no puny, sickly little child in the whole world whose daily digestion gives as much anxiety to his parents as a monster like this gives to those in charge of it. Day and night incessantly two shifts, each of six loaders up above and eight smelters down below, with foremen, an engineer, and so forth, are on the spot, busy with the food supplied to the beast, and the output it yields; and at the slightest disturbance, if the metal run out should not be satisfactory, everybody is in a state of alarm. For five years now this furnace has been alight; never for a single minute has the internal fire ceased to perform its work; and it may burn another five years in the same way before it is extinguished to allow of repairs being made. And if those in charge tremble and watch so carefully over the work, it is because there is the everlasting possibility that the fire may go out of itself, through some accident of unforeseen gravity in the monster's bowels. And to go out, to become extinguished, means death. Ah! those little electrical furnaces of mine, which lads might work, they won't disturb anybody's rest at nights, and they will be so healthy, and so active and so docile!"

Luc could not help laughing, amused by the loving passion which entered into Jordan's scientific researches. However, they had now been joined by Morfain and Petit-Da, and the former, under the pale gleam of a lantern, pointed to one of the four pipes which, at a height of nine or ten feet, penetrated the monster's flanks.

"There! it was that twyer which got stopped up, Monsieur Jordan," he said, "and unfortunately I had gone home to bed, so that I only noticed what was the matter the next day. As the blast did not penetrate a chill occurred, and a quantity of matter got together and hardened. Nothing more went down, but I only became aware of the trouble at the moment of tapping, on seeing the slag come out in a thick pulp which was already black. And you can understand my fright; for I remembered our misfortune ten years ago, when one had to demolish a part of the furnace after a similar occurrence."

Never before had Morfain spoken so many words at a stretch. His voice trembled as he recalled the former accident, for no more terrible illness can fall on the monster than one of those chills which solidify the ore and convert it into so much rock. The result is deadly when one is unable to relight the brasier. By degrees the whole mass becomes chilled and adheres to the furnace; and then there is nothing else to be done but to demolish the pile, raze it to the ground, like some old tower chokeful of stones.

"And what did you do?" Jordan inquired.

Morfain did not immediately answer. He had ended by loving that monster whose flow of glowing lava had scorched his face for more than thirty years. It was like a giant, a master, a god of fire which he adored, bending beneath the rude tyranny of the worship that had been forced upon him the moment he reached man's estate as his sole means of procuring daily bread. He scarcely knew how to read, he had not been touched by the new spirit which was abroad, he experienced no feelings of rebellion, but cheerfully accepted his life of hard servitude, vain of his strong arms, his hourly battles with the flames, his fidelity to that crouching colossus over whose digestion he watched without ever a thought of going out on strike. And his barbarous and terrible god had become his passion; his faith in that divinity was instinct with secret tenderness, and he still quivered with anxiety at the thought of the dangerous attack from which he had saved his idol, thanks to extraordinary efforts of devotion.

"What I did!" he at last responded. "Well, I began by trebling the charges of coal, and then I tried to clear the twyer by working the blast apparatus as I had sometimes seen Monsieur Laroche do. But the attack was already too serious, and we had to disjoint the twyer and attack the stoppage with bars. Ah! it wasn't an easy job, and we lost some of our strength in doing it. All the same, we at last got the air to pass, and I was better pleased when, among the slag this morning, I found some remnants of ore, for I realised that the matter which had set had got broken up again and carried away. Everything is once more well alight now, and we shall be doing good work again. Besides it will soon be easy to see how things are; the next run will tell us."

Although he was well-nigh exhausted by such a long discourse, he added in a lower voice: "I really believe, Monsieur Jordan, that I should have gone up above and flung myself into the mouth if I had not had better news to give you this evening. I'm only a workman, a smelter, in whom you've had confidence, giving me a gentleman's post, an engineer's post. And just fancy me letting the furnace go out and telling you on your return home that it was dead! Ah! no, indeed, I'd have died too! I haven't been to bed for two nights now; I've kept watch here, like I did beside my poor wife when I lost her. And at present, I may admit it, the soup which you found me eating was the first food I had tasted for forty-eight hours, for I couldn't eat before, my own stomach seemed to be stopped up like the furnace's. I don't want to apologise, but simply to let you know how happy I feel at not having failed in the confidence you put in me."

That big fellow, hardened by perpetual fire, whose limbs were like steel, almost wept as he spoke those words, and Jordan pressed his hands affectionately, saying: "I know how valiant you are, my good Morfain; I know that if a disaster had happened you would have fought on to the very end."

Meantime Petit-Da had stood listening in the gloom, intervening neither by word nor gesture. He only moved when his father gave him an order respecting the tapping. Every four-and-twenty hours the metal was run out five times, at intervals of nearly five hours. The charge, which might be eighty tons a day, was at that moment reduced to about fifty, which would give runs of ten tons each. By the faint light of the lanterns the needful arrangements were made in silence; channels and panels for casting were prepared in the fine sand of the large hall; and then before running out the metal the only thing remaining to be done was to get rid of the slag. Thus the shadowy forms of workmen were seen passing slowly, busily engaged in operations which could be only dimly distinguished, whilst amidst the heavy silence which prevailed within the squatting idol, one still heard nothing save the trickling of the drops of water which were coursing down its sides.

"Monsieur Jordan," Morfain inquired, "would you like to see the slag run out?"

Jordan and Luc followed him, and a few steps brought them to a hillock formed of an accumulation of waste. The aperture was on the right-hand side of the furnace, and the slag was already pouring out in a flood of sparkling dross, as if the cauldron of fusing metal were being skimmed. The matter was like thick pulp, sun-hued lava, flowing slowly along and falling into waggonets of sheet iron, where it at once became dim.

"The colour's good, you see, Monsieur Jordan," resumed Morfain gaily. "Oh! we are out of trouble, that's sure. You'll see, you'll see."

Then he brought them back to the running-hall in front of the furnace, whose vague dimness was so faintly illumined by the lanterns. Petit-Da, with one lunge of his strong young arms, had just thrust a bar into the bung of refractory clay which closed the tap-hole, and now the eight men of the night shift wore rhythmically ramming the bar in further. Their black figures could scarcely be discerned, and one only heard the dull blows of the rammer. Then, all at once, a dazzling star, as it were, appeared, a small peep-hole through which showed the inner fire. But as yet there was only a faint trickling of the liquid metal, and Petit-Da had to take another bar, thrust it in, and turn it round and round with herculean efforts in order to enlarge the aperture. Then came the *débâcle*, the flood rushed out tumultuously, a river of fusing metal rolled along the channel in the sand, and then spread out, filling the moulds, and forming blazing pools, whose glow and heat quite scorched the eyes of the beholders. And from that channel and those sheets of fire rose a crop of sparks, blue sparks, of delicate ethereality, and fusees of gold, delightfully refined, a florescence of cornflowers, as it were, amidst a growth of wheat-ears. Whenever any obstacle of damp sand was encountered both the sparks and the fusees increased in number, and rose to a great height in a bouquet of splendour. And all at once, as if some miraculous sun had risen, an intense dawn burst over everything, casting a great glare upon the furnace, and throwing a glow as of sunshine upward to the roof of the hall, whose every girder and joist showed forth distinctly. The neighbouring buildings, the monster's various organs, sprang out of the darkness, together with the men of the night-shift, hitherto so phantom-like and now so real, outlined with an energy and splendour never to be forgotten, as if, obscure heroes of toil that they were, they suddenly found themselves enveloped by a nimbus of glory. And the great glow spread to all the surroundings, conjured the huge ridge of the Bleuse Mountains out of the darkness, threw reflections even upon the sleeping roofs of Beauclair, and died away at last in the distance far over the great plain of La Roumagne.

"It is superb," said Jordan, studying the quality of the metal by the colour and limpidity of the flow.

Morfain took his triumph modestly. "Yes, yes, Monsieur Jordan," said he, "it's good work, such as we ought to turn out. All the same, I'm glad you came to have a look. You won't feel anxious now."

Luc also was taking an interest in the proceedings. So great was the heat that he felt his skin tingling through his clothes. Little by little all the moulds had been filled, and the sandy hall was now changed into an incandescent sea. And when the ten tons of liquid metal had all poured forth, a final tempest, a huge rush of flames and sparks, came from the cavity. The blowing-apparatus was emptying the crucible, the blast sweeping through it in all freedom like some hurricane of hell. But the pigs were now growing cold, their blinding white light became pink, next red, and then brown. The sparks, too, ceased to rise, the field of azure cornflowers and golden wheat-ears was reaped. Then gloom swiftly fell once more, blotting out the hall and the furnace and all the adjoining buildings, whilst it seemed as if the lanterns had been lighted up afresh. And of the workmen one could again only distinguish some vague figures actively bestirring themselves—they were those of Petit-Da and two of his mates, who were again plugging the tap-hole with refractory clay, amidst the silence which was now deeper than ever, for the blast machinery had been stopped to permit of this work being performed.

"I say, Morfain, my good fellow," Jordan suddenly resumed, "you will go home to bed, won't you?"

"Oh! no, I must spend the night here," the man answered.

"What! you mean to stay, and pass a third sleepless night here?"

"Oh! there's a camp bedstead in the watch-house, Monsieur Jordan, and one sleeps very well on it. We'll relieve each other, my son and I; we'll each do two hours' sentry duty in turn."

"But that's useless, since things are now all right again," Jordan retorted. "Come, be reasonable, Morfain, and go and sleep at home."

"No, no, Monsieur Jordan, let me do as I wish. There's no more danger, but I want to make sure how things go until to-morrow. It will please me to do so."

Thus Jordan and Luc, after shaking hands with him, had to leave him there. And Luc felt extremely moved, for Morfain had left on him an impression of great loftiness in which met long years of painful and docile labour, all the nobility of the crushing toil which mankind had undertaken in the hope of attaining to rest and happiness. It had all begun with the ancient Vulcans, who had subjugated fire in those heroic times which Jordan had recalled, when the first smelters had reduced their ore in a pit dug in the earth, in which they lighted wood. It was on that day, the day when man first conquered iron and fashioned it, that he became the master of the world, and that the era of civilisation first began. Morfain, dwelling in his rocky cave, and for whom nothing existed apart from the difficulties and the glory of his calling, seemed to Luc like some direct descendant of those primitive toilers, whose far-off characteristics still lived by force of heredity in him, silent and resigned as he was, giving all the strength of his muscles without ever a murmur, even as his predecessors had done at the dawn of human society. Ah! how much perspiration had streamed forth and how many arms had toiled to the point of exhaustion during thousands and thousands of years! And yet nothing changed—fire, if conquered, still made its victims, still had its slaves, those who fed it, those who scorched their blood in subjugating it, whilst the privileged ones of the earth lived in idleness, in homes which were fresh and cool! Morfain, like some legendary hero, did not seem even to suspect the existence of all the monstrous iniquity around him; he was ignorant of rebellion, of the storm growling afar; he remained quite impassive at his deadly post, there where his sires had died and where he himself would die. And Luc also conjured up another figure, that of Bonnaire, another hero of labour, one who struggled against the oppressors, the exploiters, in order that justice might at last reign; and who devoted himself to his comrades' cause even to the point of giving up his daily bread. Had not all those suffering men groaned long enough beneath their burdens, and, however admirable might be their toil, had not the hour struck for the deliverance of the slaves in order that they might at last become free citizens in a fraternal community, amidst which peace would spring from a just apportionment of labour and wealth?

However, as Jordan, whilst descending the steps cut in the rock, stopped before a night-watchman's hut to give an order, an unexpected sight met Luc's eyes and brought his emotion to a climax. Behind some bushes, amidst some scattered rocks, he distinctly saw two shadowy forms passing. Their arms encircled each other's waist and their lips were meeting in a kiss. Luc readily recognised the girl, so tall she was, so fair and so superb. She was none other than Ma-Bleue, the maid whose great blue eyes seemed to fill her face. And the lad must assuredly be Achille Gourier, the mayor's son, that proud and handsome youth whose demeanour he, Luc, had noticed at La Guerdache—that demeanour so expressive of contempt for the rotting *bourgeoisie* of which he was one of the revolting sons. Ever shooting, fishing, and roaming, he spent his holidays among the steep paths of the Bleuse Mountains, beside the torrents or deep in the pine woods. And doubtless he had fallen in love with that beautiful, shy, wild girl, around whom so many admirers prowled in vain. She, on her side, must have been conquered by the advent of that Prince Charming, who brought her something that was beyond her sphere, who set all the delightful dreams of to-morrow amidst the sternness of that desert. To-morrow! to-morrow! Was it not that which dawned in Ma-Bleue's blue eyes, when, with her gaze wandering far away, she stood so thoughtful on the threshold of her mountain cave? Her father and her brother were watching over their work up yonder, and she had escaped down the precipitous paths. And for her to-morrow meant that tall, loving lad, that *bourgeois* stripling, who spoke to her so prettily as if she had been a lady, and vowed that he would love her for ever.

At first, amidst his amazement, Luc felt a heart-pang at the thought of how grieved the father would be should he hear of that sweethearting. Then a tender feeling took possession of the young man's heart, a caressing breath of hope came to him at the sight of that free and gentle love. Were not those children, who belonged to such different classes, preparing amidst their play, their kisses, the advent of the happier morrow, the great reconciliation which would at last lead to the reign of justice?

Down below, when Luc and Jordan reached the park, they exchanged a few more words.

"You haven't caught cold, I hope?" said the young man to his friend. "Your sister would never forgive me, you know."

"No, no, I feel quite well. And I am going to bed in the best of spirits, for I've quite made up my mind. I intend to rid myself of that

ÉMILE ZOLA

enterprise, since it does not interest me, and proves such a constant source of worry."

For a moment Luc remained silent, for uneasiness had returned to him, as if, indeed, he were frightened by Jordan's decision. However, as he left his friend he said, shaking his hand for the last time, "No, wait, give me to-morrow to think the matter over. We will have another talk in the evening, and afterwards you shall come to a decision."

Then they parted for the night. Luc did not go to bed immediately. He occupied—in the pavilion formerly erected for Dr. Michon, Jordan's maternal grandfather—the spacious room where the doctor had spent his last years among his books; and during the three days that he had occupied this chamber the young man had grown fond of the pleasantness, peacefulness, and odour of work that filled it. That evening, however, the fever of doubt, by which he was possessed, oppressed him, and throwing one of the windows wide open he leant out, hoping in this wise to calm himself a little before he went to bed. The window overlooked the road leading from La Crêcherie to Beauclair. In front spread some uncultivated fields strewn with rocks, and beyond them one could distinguish the jumbled roofs of the sleeping town.

For a few minutes Luc remained inhaling the gusts of air which arose from the great plain of La Roumagne. The night was warm and moist, and athwart a slight haze a bluish light descended from the starry sky. Luc listened to the distant sounds with which the night quivered; and before long he recognised the dull, rhythmical blows of the hammers of the Abyss, that Cyclopean forge whence day and night alike there came a clang of steel. Then he raised his eyes and sought the black, silent smeltery of La Crêcherie, but it was now mingled with the inky bar which the promontory of the Bleuse Mountains set against the sky. Lowering his eyes he at last directed them upon the close-set roofs of the town, whose heavy slumber seemed to be cradled by the rhythmic blows of the hammers—those blows which suggested the quick and difficult breathing of some giant worker, some pain-racked Prometheus, chained to eternal toil. And Luc's feeling of uneasiness was increased by it all; he could not quiet his fever; the people and the things that he had beheld during those last three days crowded upon his mind, passed before him in a tragic scramble, the sense of which he strove to divine. And the problem which possessed his spirit now tortured him more than ever. Assuredly he would be unable to sleep until he found a means of solving it.

But down below his window, across the road, amongst the bushes and the rocks, he suddenly heard a fresh sound, something so light, so faint, that he could not tell what it might be. Was it the beating of a bird's wings, the rustle of an insect among some leaves? Luc gazed down, and could see nothing save the swelling darkness that spread far, far away. No doubt he had been mistaken. But the sounds reached his ears again, and even seemed to come nearer. Interested by them, seized with a strange emotion which astonished him, he again strove to penetrate the darkness, and at last he distinguished a vague, light, delicate form which seemed to float over the grass. And still he was unable to tell what that form might be, and was willing to believe himself the victim of some delusion, when, with a nimble spring like that of some wild goat, a woman crossed the road and lightly threw him a little nosegay, which brushed against his face like a caress. It was a little bunch of mountain pansies, just gathered among the rocks, and of such powerful aroma, that he was quite perfumed by it.

Josine!—he divined that it was she, he recognised her by that fresh sign of her heart's thankfulness, by that adorable gesture of infinite gratitude! And it all seemed to him exquisite in that dimness, at that late hour, though he could not tell how she had happened to be there, whether she had been watching for his return, and how she could have contrived to come, unless indeed Ragu were working at a night-shift. Without a word, having had no other desire than that of expressing her feelings by the gift of those flowers, which she had so lightly thrown him, she was already fleeing, disappearing into the darkness spread over the uncultivated moor; and only then did Luc distinguish another and a smaller form, that assuredly of Nanet, bounding along near her. They both vanished, and then he again heard nought save the hammers of the Abyss, ever rhythmically beating in the distance. His torment was not passed, but his heart had been warmed by a glow which seemed to bring him invincible strength. It was with rapture that he inhaled the little nosegay. Ah! the power of kindness, which is the bond of brotherhood, the power of tenderness, by which alone happiness is created, the power of love, which will save and make the world anew!

V

Luc went to bed and put out the light, hoping that his weariness of mind and body would bring him sound and refreshing sleep, in which his fever would at last be dispelled. But when the large room sank into silence and obscurity around him he found himself quite unable to close his eyes—they stared into the darkness, and terrible insomnia kept him burning hot, still a prey to his one obstinate, all-consuming idea.

Josine was ever rising before him, coming back again and again with her childish face and doleful charm. He once more saw her in tears, standing, full of terror, as she waited near the gate of the Abyss; he again saw her standing in the wine-shop, then thrown into the street by Ragu in so brutal a fashion that blood gushed from her maimed hand; and he saw her too on the bench near the Mionne, forsaken amidst the tragic night, satisfying her hunger like some poor wandering animal, and having no prospect before her save a final tumble into the gutter. And now, after those three days of unexpected, almost unconscious inquiry, to which destiny had led him, all that he, Luc, had beheld of unjustly apportioned toil—toil derided as if it were shame, toil conducting to the most atrocious misery for the vast majority of mankind, became in his eyes synthetised in the distressing case of that sorry girl whose misfortunes wrung his heart.

Visions arose, thronging around him, pressing forward, haunting him to the point of torture. He beheld terror careering through the black streets of Beauclair, along which tramped all the disinherited wretches, secretly dreaming of vengeance. He saw reasoned, organised, and fatal revolution dawning in such homes as the Bonnaires' cold, bare, sorry rooms, where even the mere necessaries of life were wanting, where lack of work compelled the toiler to tighten his waistband, and left the family starving. And, on the other hand, he beheld at La Guerdache all the insolence of corrupting luxury, all the poisonous enjoyment which was finishing off the privileged plutocrats, that handful of *bourgeois* satiated with idleness, gorged to stifling point with all the iniquitous wealth which they stole from the labour and the tears of the immense majority of the workers. And even at La Crêcherie, that wildly lofty blast-furnace, where not one worker complained, the long efforts of mankind were stricken, so to say, by a curse, immobilised in eternal dolour, without hope of any complete freeing of the race, of its final deliverance from slavery, and the entry of one and all into the city of justice and peace. And Luc had seen and heard Beauclair cracking upon all sides, for the fratricidal warfare was not waged only between classes, its destructive ferment was perverting families, a blast of folly and hatred was sweeping by, filling every heart with bitterness. Monstrous dramas soiled homes that should have been cleanly, fathers, mothers, and children alike rolled into the sewers. Folk lied unceasingly, they stole, they killed. And at the end of wretchedness and hunger came crime perforce: woman selling herself, man sinking to drink, all human kind becoming a rageful beast that rushed along intent solely upon satisfying its vices. Many were the frightful signs that announced the inevitable catastrophe; the old social framework was about to topple down amidst blood and mire.

Horror-stricken by those visions of shame and chastisement, weeping with all the human tenderness within him, Luc then again saw the pale phantom of Josine returning from the depths of the darkness and stretching out arms of entreaty. And then, in his fancy, none but her remained; it was upon her that the worm-eaten, leprous edifice would fall. She became, as it were, the one victim, she, the puny little workgirl with the maimed hand, who was starving and who would roll into the gutter, a pitiable yet charming creature, in whom seemed to be embodied all the misery that arose from the accursed wage-system. He now suffered as she must suffer, and, above all else, in his wild dream of saving Beauclair there was a craving to save her. If some superhuman power had made him almighty he would have transformed that town, now rotted by egotism, into a happy abode of solidarity, in order that she might be happy. He realised at present that this dream of his was an old one, that it had always possessed him since the days when he had lived in one of the poor quarters of Paris, among the obscure heroes and the dolorous victims of labour. It was a dream into which entered secret disquietude respecting the future, that future which he dared not predict, and an idea that some mysterious mission had been confided to him. And all at once, amidst the confusion in which he still struggled, it seemed to him that the decisive hour had come. Josine was starving, Josine was sobbing, and that could be allowed no longer. He must act, he must at once relieve all the misery and all the suffering, in order that things so iniquitous might cease.

Weary as he was, however, he at last fell into a doze, in the midst of which it seemed as if voices were calling him. Thus before long he awoke with a start, and then the voices seemed to gather strength, as if wildly summoning him to that urgent work for which the hour had struck, and the imperious need of which he fully recognised, though how to accomplish it he could not tell. And above all other appeals, he finally heard the call of a very gentle voice, which he recognised— the voice of Josine, lamenting and entreating. From that moment again she alone seemed to be present, he could feel the warm caress of the kiss which she had set upon his hand, and could smell the little bunch of pansies which she had thrown him as he stood at the window. Indeed, the wild fragrance of the flowers now seemed to fill the whole room. Then he struggled no longer. He lighted his candle, rose, and for a few minutes walked about the room. In order to rid his brain of the fixed idea which oppressed it he strove to think of nothing. He looked at the few old engravings hanging from the walls, he looked at the old-fashioned articles of furniture which spoke of Doctor Michon's simple and studious habits, he gazed around the whole room, in which a deal of kindliness, good sense, and wisdom seemed to have lingered. At last his attention became riveted on the bookcase. It was a rather large one, with glass doors, and therein the former Saint-Simonian and Fourierist had gathered together the humanitarian writings which had fired his mind in youth. All the social philosophers, all the precursors, all the apostles of the new Gospel figured there: Saint-Simon, Fourier, Auguste Comte, Proudhon, Cabet, Pierre Leroux, with others and others—indeed, a complete collection, down to the most obscure disciples. And Luc, candle in hand, read the names and titles on the backs of the volumes, counted them, and grew astonished at their number, at the fact that so much good seed should have been cast to the winds, that so many good words should be slumbering there, waiting for the harvest.

He himself had read widely, he was well acquainted with the chief passages of most of those books. The philosophical, economical, and social systems of their authors were familiar to him. But never as now, on finding these authors all united there in a serried phalanx, had he been so clearly conscious of their force, their value, the human evolution which they typified. They formed, so to say, the advance guard of the future century, an advance guard soon to be followed by the huge army of the nations. And on seeing them thus, side by side, peaceably mingling together, endowed by union with sovereign strength, Luc was particularly struck by their intense brotherliness. He was not ignorant of the contradictory views which had formerly parted them, of the desperate battles even which they had waged together, but they now seemed to have become all brothers, reconciled in a common Gospel, in the unique and final truths which all of them had brought. And that which arose from their words like a dawning promise was that religion of humanity in which they had all believed, their love for the disinherited ones of the world, their hatred of all social injustice, their faith in Work as the true saviour of mankind.

Opening the bookcase, Luc wished to select one of the volumes. Since he was unable to sleep, he would read a few pages, and thus take patience until slumber should come to him. He hesitated for a moment, and at last selected a very little volume, in which one of Fourier's disciples had summed up the whole of his master's work. The title "Solidarité" had moved the young man. Would he not find in that book a few pages brimful of strength and hope such as he needed? Thus, he slipped into bed again, and began to read. And soon he became as passionately interested in his reading as if he had before him some poignant drama in which the fate of the whole human race was decided. The author's doctrines thus condensed, reduced to the very essence of the truths they contained, acquired extraordinary power. Fourier's genius had in the first place asserted itself in turning the passions of man into the very forces of life. The long and disastrous error of Catholicism had lain in ever seeking to muzzle the passions, in striving to kill the man within man, to fling him like a slave at the foot of a deity of tyranny and nothingness. In the free future society conceived by Fourier the passions were to produce as much good as they had produced evil in the chained and terrorised society of the dead centuries. They constituted immortal desire, the energy which raises worlds, the internal furnace of will and strength which imparts to each being the power to act. Man deprived of a single passion would be mutilated, as if he were deprived of one of his senses. Instincts, hitherto thrust back and crushed, as if they were evil beasts, would when once they were freed become only the various needs of universal attraction, all tending towards unity, striving amidst obstacles to meet and mingle in final harmony, that ultimate expression of universal happiness. And there were really no egotists, no idlers; there were only men hungering for unity and harmony, who would march on in all brotherliness as soon as they should see that the road was wide enough for all to pass along it at ease and happily. As for the victims of the heavy servitude that oppressed the manual toilers who were angered by unjust, excessive, and often inappropriate tasks, they would all be ready to work right joyfully as soon as simply their logical chosen share of the great common labour should be allotted to them.

Then another stroke of genius on Fourier's part was the restoration of work to a position of honour, by making it the public function, the pride, health, gaiety, and very law of life. It would suffice to reorganise work in order to reorganise the whole of society, of which work would be the one civic obligation, the vital rule. There would be no further question of brutally imposing work on vanquished men, mercenaries crushed down and treated like famished beasts of burden; on the contrary, work would be freely accepted by all, allotted according to tastes and natures, performed during the few hours that might be indispensable, and constantly varied according to the choice of the voluntary toilers. A town would become an immense hive in which there would not be one idler, and in which each citizen would contribute his share towards the general sum of labour which might be necessary for the town to live. The tendency towards unity and final harmony would draw the inhabitants together and compel them to group themselves among the various series of workers. And the whole mechanism would rest in that: the workman choosing the task which he could perform most joyously, not riveted for ever to one and the same calling, but passing from one form of work to another. Moreover, the world would not be revolutionised all of a sudden, the beginnings would be small, the system being tried first of all in some township of a few thousand souls. The dream would then approach fulfilment, the phalange, the unit at the base of the great human army would be created; the phalanstery, the common house, would be built. At first, too, one would simply appeal to willing men, and link them together in such wise as to form an association of capital, work, and talent. Those who now possessed money, those whose arms were strong, and those who had brains would be asked to come to an understanding and combine, putting their various means together. They would produce with an energy and an abundance far greater than now, and they would divide the profits they reaped as equitably as possible, until the day came when capital, work, and talent might be blended together and form the common patrimony of a free brotherhood, in which everything would belong to everybody amidst general harmony.

At each page of the little book which Luc was reading the loving splendour of its title "Solidarité" became more and more apparent.

Certain phrases shone forth like beacon-fires. Man's reason was infallible; truth was absolute; a truth demonstrated by science became irrevocable, eternal. Work was to be a festival. Each man's happiness would some day rest in the happiness of others. Neither envy nor hatred would be left when room was at last found in the world for the happiness of one and all. In the social machine, all intermediaries that were useless and led to a waste of strength would be suppressed; thus commerce, as it is now understood, would be condemned, and the consumer would deal with the producer. All parasitic growths, the innumerable vegetations living upon social corruption, upon the permanent state of war in which men now languish, would be mown down. There would be no more armies, no more courts of law, no more prisons! And, above all, amidst the great Dawn which would thus have risen, there would appear Justice flaming like the sun, driving away misery, giving to each being that was born the right to live and partake of daily bread, and allotting to one and all his or her due share of happiness.

Luc had ceased reading: he was reflecting now. The whole great, heroic Nineteenth Century spread out before his mind's eye, with its continuous battling, its dolorous, valiant efforts to attain to truth and justice. The irresistible democratic advance, the rise of the masses filled that century from end to end. The Revolution at the end of the previous one had brought only the middle classes to power; another century was needed for the evolution to become complete, for the people to obtain its share of influence. Seeds germinated, however, in the old and often ploughed monarchical soil; and already during the days of '48 the question of the wage-system was plainly brought forward, the claims of the workers becoming more and more precise, and shaking the new *régime* of the *bourgeois*, whom egotistical and tyrannical possession was in their turn rotting. And now, on the threshold of the new century, as soon as the spreading onrush of the masses should have carried the old social framework away, the reoganisation of labour would prove the very foundation-stone of future society, which would only be able to exist by a just apportionment of wealth. The violent crisis which had overthrown empires when the old world passed from servitude to the wage-system was as nothing compared with the terrible crisis which for the last hundred years had shaken and ravaged nations, that crisis of the wage-system passing through successive evolutions and transformations, and tending to become something else. And from that something else would be born the happy and brotherly social system of to-morrow.

Luc gently put down the little book and blew out his light. He had grown calmer now, and could feel that peaceful, restoring sleep was approaching. True, no precise answers had come to the urgent appeals which had previously upset him; but he heard those appeals no more. It was as if the disinherited beings who had raised them were now conscious that they had been heard, and were taking patience. Seed was sown and the harvest would rise. Luc himself was troubled with no more feverishness, he felt that his mind was pregnant with ideas, to which indeed it might give birth on the very morrow if his night's slumber should be good. And he ended by yielding to his great need of repose, and fell with delight into a deep sleep, visited by genius, faith, and will.

When he awoke at seven o'clock on the following morning his first thought on seeing the sun rise in the broad clear sky was to go out without warning the Jordans and climb the rocky stairway leading to the smeltery. He wished to see Morfain again, and obtain certain information from him. In this respect he was yielding to a sudden inspiration. With reference to the advice which Jordan had asked of him, he desired above all to arrive at some precise opinion respecting the old abandoned mine. The master-smelter, a son of the mountains, must know, he thought, every stone of it. And indeed Morfain, whom he found up and about, after his night spent beside the furnace, which decidedly had now recovered from its ailment, became quite impassioned directly the mine was mentioned to him. He had always had an idea of his own, which nobody would heed, although he had often given expression to it. To his thinking, old Laroche, the engineer, had done wrong in despairing and forsaking the mine directly the working of it had failed to prove remunerative. The vein which had been followed had certainly become an abominable one, charged with sulphur and phosphates to such a degree that nothing good came out in the smelting. But Morfain was convinced that they were simply crossing a bad vein, and that it would be sufficient to carry the galleries further, or to open fresh ones at a point of the gorge which he designated, in order to find once more the same excellent ore as formerly. And he based his opinion upon observation, upon knowledge of all the rocks of the region, which he had scaled and explored for forty years. As he put it, he was not a man of science, he was only a poor toiler, and did not presume to compete with those gentlemen the engineers. Nevertheless he was astonished that no confidence was shown in his keen scent, and that his superiors should have simply shrugged their shoulders without consenting to test his predictions by a few borings.

The man's quiet confidence impressed Luc the more especially since he was inclined to pass a severe judgment on the inertia of old Laroche, who had left the mine in an abandoned state even after the discovery of the chemical process which would have allowed the defective ore to be profitably utilised. That alone showed into what slumberous routine the working of the furnace had fallen. The mine ought to be worked again immediately, even if they had to rest content with treating the ore chemically. But what would it be if Morfain's convictions should be realised, and they should again come upon rich and pure lodes! Thus Luc immediately accepted the master-smelter's proposal to take a stroll in the direction of the abandoned galleries, in order that the other might explain his ideas on the spot. That clear and fresh September morning, the walk among the rocks, through the lonely wilds fragrant with lavender, was delightful. During three hours the two men climbed up and down the sides of the gorges, visiting the grottoes, following the pine-covered ridges where the rocks jutted up through the soil like portions of the skeleton of some huge buried monster. And by degrees Morfain's conviction gained upon Luc, bringing him at least a hope that there in that spot lay a treasure which man in his sloth had passed by, and which earth, the inexhaustible mother, was prepared to yield to those who might seek it.

As it was more than noon when the explorations terminated Luc accepted a proposal to lunch off eggs and milk up in the Bleuse Mountains. When about two o'clock he came down again, delighted, his lungs inflated by the free mountain air, the Jordans received him with exclamations, for not knowing what had become of him they had begun to grow anxious. He apologised for not having warned them, and related that he had lost his way among the tablelands, and had lunched with some peasants there. He ventured to tell this fib because the Jordans, whom he found still at table, were not alone. As was their custom every second Tuesday of the month, they had with them three guests, Abbé Marle, Doctor Novarre, and Hermeline, the schoolmaster, whom Sœurette delighted to gather together, laughingly calling them her privy councillors, because they all three helped her in her charitable works. The doors of La Crêcherie which were usually kept closed, Jordan living there in solitude like some cloistered scientist, were thrown open for those three visitors, who were treated as intimates. It could not be said, however, that they owed this favour to their cordial agreement, for they were perpetually disputing together. But, on the other hand, their discussions amused Sœurette, and indeed rendered her yet more partial to them, since they proved a distraction for Jordan, who listened to them smiling.

"So you have lunched?" said Sœurette, addressing Luc. "Still, that won't prevent you from taking a cup of coffee with us, will it?"

"Oh! I'll accept the cup of coffee," he answered gaily. "You are too amiable—I deserve the bitterest reproaches."

They then passed into the drawing-room. Its windows were open, the lawns of the park spread out, and all the exquisite aroma of the great trees came into the house. In a horn-shaped porcelain vase bloomed a splendid bouquet of roses—roses which Doctor Novarre lovingly cultivated, and a bunch of which he brought for Sœurette each time that he lunched at La Crêcherie.

Whilst the coffee was being served a discussion on educational matters began afresh between the priest and the schoolmaster, who had not ceased battling on this subject since the beginning of the lunch.

"If you can do nothing with your pupils," declared Abbé Marle, "it is because you have driven religion out of your schools. God is the master of human intelligence; one knows nothing excepting through Him."

Tall and sturdy, with his eagle beak set in a broad, full, regular face, the priest spoke with all the authoritative stubbornness born of his narrow doctrines, placing the only chance of the world's salvation in Catholicism, and the rigid observance of its dogmas. And, in front of him, Hermeline, the schoolmaster, slim of build and angular of face, with a bony forehead and pointed chin, evinced similar stubbornness, being quite as formalist and authoritative as the other in the practice of his own mechanical religion of progress, which last was to be arrived at by dint of laws and military discipline.

"Don't bother me," said he, "with your religion, which has never led men to aught but error and ruin. If I get nothing out of my pupils it is because, in the first place, they are taken from me too early, to be placed in the factories. And secondly, and more particularly, it is because there is less and less discipline, because the master is left without any authority. If a child is whipped nowadays the parents shriek like a pack of fools. But if I were only allowed to give those youngsters a few good canings I think I should open their minds a little."

Then, as Sœurette, quite affected by this theory, began to protest, he explained his views. For him, given the general corruption, there was only one means of saving society, which was to subject the children to the discipline of liberty, insert belief in republican principles in them by force, if necessary, and in such a manner that they should never lose it. His dream was to make each pupil a servant of the State, a slave of the State, one who sacrificed to the State his entire personality. And he could picture nothing beyond one and the same lesson, learnt by all in one and the same manner, with the one object of serving the community. Such was his harsh and doleful religion, a religion in which the democracy was delivered from the past by dint of punishments, and then again condemned to forced labour, happiness being decreed under penalty of being caned.

But Abbé Marle obstinately repeated: "Outside the pale of Catholicism there is only darkness."

"Why, Catholicism is toppling over!" exclaimed Hermeline. "It's for that very reason that we have to raise another social framework."

The priest, no doubt, was conscious of the supreme battle which Catholicism was waging against the spirit of science, whose victory spread day by day. But he would not acknowledge it; he did not even admit that his church was gradually emptying. "Catholicism!" he resumed, "its framework is still so solid, so eternal, so divine, that you copy it when you talk of raising I know not what atheistical State in which you would replace the Deity by some mechanical contrivance appointed to instruct and govern men!"

"Some mechanical contrivance, why not!" retorted Hermeline, exasperated by the touch of truth contained in the priest's attack. "Rome has never been aught but a wine-press, pressing out the blood of the world!"

When their discussions reached this violent stage Doctor Novarre usually intervened in his smiling and conciliatory way. "Come, come, don't get heated!" said he. "You are on the point of agreeing, since you have got so far as to accuse one another of copying your religions one from the other."

Short and spare, with a slender nose and keen eyes, the doctor was a man of a tolerant, gentle, but slightly sarcastic turn of mind, one who, having given himself to science, refused to let himself be excited by political and social questions. Like Jordan, whose great friend he was, he often said that he only adopted truths when they had been scientifically demonstrated. Modest, timid, too, as he was, without any ambition, he contented himself with healing his patients to the best of his ability, and his only passion was for the rosebushes which he cultivated between the four walls of the garden of the little dwelling where he lived in happy peacefulness.

Luc had hitherto contented himself with listening. But at last he recalled what he had read the previous night, and he then spoke out: "The terrible part of it," said he, "is that in our schools the starting-point is invariably the idea that man is an evil being, who brings into the world with him a spirit of rebellion and sloth, and that a perfect system of punishments and rewards is necessary if one is to get anything out of him. Thus education has been turned into torture, and study has become as repulsive to our brains as manual labour is to our limbs. Our professors have been turned into so many gaolers ruling a scholastic penitentiary, and the mission given to them is that of kneading the minds of children in accordance with certain fixed programmes, and running them all through one and the same mould, without taking any account of varying individualities. Thus the masters are no longer aught but the slayers of initiative; they crush all critical spirit, all free examination, all personal awakening of talent beneath a pile of ready-made ideas and official-truths, and the worst is that the characters of the children are affected quite as badly as their minds, and that the system of teaching employed produces in the long run little else but dolts and hypocrites."

Hermeline must have fancied that he was being personally attacked, for he now broke in rather sharply: "But how would you have one proceed then, monsieur? Come and take my place, and you will soon see how little you will get out of the pupils if you don't subject them one and all to the same discipline, like a master who for them is the embodiment of authority."

"The master," continued Luc with his dreamy air, "should have no other duty than that of awakening energy and encouraging the child's aptitude in one or another respect by provoking questions from him and enabling him to develop his personality. Deep in the human race there is an immense insatiable craving to learn and know, and this should be the one incentive to study without need of any rewards or punishments. It would evidently be sufficient if one contented oneself with giving each pupil facilities for prosecuting the particular studies that pleased him, and with rendering those studies attractive to him, allowing him to engage in them by himself, then progress in them by the force of his own understanding, with the continually recurring delight of making fresh discoveries. For men to make their offspring men by treating them as such, is not that the whole educational problem which has to be solved?"

Abbé Marle, who was finishing his coffee, shrugged his broad shoulders; and, like a priest whom dogma endowed with infallibility, he remarked: "Sin is in man, and he can only be saved by penitence. Idleness, which is one of the capital sins, can only be redeemed by labour, the punishment which God imposed on the first man after the fall."

"But that's an error, Abbé," quietly said Doctor Novarre. "Idleness is simply a malady when it really exists, that is, when the body refuses to work, shrinks from all fatigue. You may be certain then that this invincible languor is a sign of grave internal disorder. And apart from that, where have you ever seen idle people? Take those who are so-called idle people by race, habit, and taste. Does not a society lady, who dances all night at a ball, do greater harm to her eyesight and expend far more muscular energy than a workwoman who sits at her little table embroidering till daylight? Do not the men of pleasure, who are for ever figuring in public, taking part in exhausting festivities, work in their own way quite as hard as the men who toil at their benches and anvils? And remember how lightly and joyfully, on emerging from some repulsive task, we all rush into some violent amusement or exercise which tires out our limbs. The meaning of it all is that work is only oppressive when it does not please us. And if one could succeed in imposing on people only such work as would be agreeable to them, as they might freely choose, there would certainly be no idlers left."

But Hermeline in his turn shrugged his shoulders, saying: "Ask a child which he prefers, his grammar or his arithmetic. He will tell you that he prefers neither. The whole question has been threshed out; a child is a sapling which needs to be trained straight and corrected."

"And one can only correct," said the priest, this time in full agreement with the schoolmaster, "by crushing everything in any way shameful or diabolic that original sin has left in man."

Silence fell. Sœurette had been listening intently, whilst Jordan, looking out through one of the windows, let his glance stray thoughtfully under the big trees. In the words of the priest and the schoolmaster Luc recognised the pessimist conceptions of Catholicism adopted by the sectarian followers of progress, which the State was to decree by exercise of authority. Man was regarded as a child ever in fault. His passions were hunted down: for centuries efforts had been made to crush them, to kill the man which was within man. And then again, Luc recalled Fourier, who had preached quite another doctrine: the passions, utilised and ennobled, becoming necessary creative energies, whilst man was at last delivered from the deadly weight of the religions of nothingness, which are merely so many hateful social police systems devised to maintain the usurpation of the powerful and the rich.

And Luc, as though reflecting aloud, thereupon resumed, "It would be sufficient to convince people of this truth, that the greater the happiness realised for all, the greater will be the happiness of the individual."

But Hermeline and Abbé Marle began to laugh.

"That's no use!" said the schoolmaster. "To awaken energy, you begin by destroying personal interest. Pray explain to me what motive will prompt man to action when he no longer works for himself? Personal interest is like the fire under the boiler, it will be found at the outset of all work. But you would crush it, and although you desire man to retain all his instincts you begin by depriving him of his egotism. Perhaps you rely on conscience, on the idea of honour and duty?"

"I don't need to rely on that," Luc answered in the same quiet way. "Truth to tell, egotism, such as we have hitherto understood it, has given us such a frightful social system, instinct with so much hatred and suffering, that it would really be allowable to try some other factor. But I repeat that I accept egotism if by such you mean the very legitimate desire, the invincible craving, which each man has for happiness. Far from destroying personal interest, I would strengthen it by making it what it ought to be in order to bring about the happy community in which the happiness of each will be the outcome of the happiness of all. Besides, it is sufficient that we should be convinced that in working for others we are working for ourselves. Social injustice sows eternal hatred, and universal suffering is the crop. For those reasons an agreement must be arrived at for the reorganisation of work based upon the certainty that our own highest felicity will some day be the result of felicity in the homes of our neighbours."

Hermeline sneered, and Abbé Marle again broke in: "'Love one another,' that is the teaching of our Divine Master. Only He also said that happiness was not of this world, and it is assuredly guilty madness to attempt to set the Kingdom of God upon this earth when it is in heaven."

"Yet that will some day be done," Luc retorted. "The whole effort of mankind upon its march, all progress and all science, tend to that future city of happiness."

But the schoolmaster, who was no longer listening, eagerly assailed the priest: "Ah! no, Abbé, don't begin again with your promises of a celestial paradise; they are only fit to dupe the poor. And besides, Jesus of Nazareth really belongs to us; you stole Him from us, and arranged His sayings and everything else in order to suit the purposes of your domination. As a matter of fact, He was simply a revolutionary and a free-thinker!"

Thus the battle began anew, and Doctor Novarre had to calm them once more by showing that one was right in certain respects and the other in others. As usual, however, the various questions which had been debated remained in suspense, for no final solution was ever arrived at. The coffee had been drunk long since, and it was Jordan who, in his thoughtful manner, put in the last word.

"The one sole truth," said he, "lies in Work; the world will some day become such as Work will make it."

Then Sœurette, who, without intervening, had listened to Luc with passionate interest, spoke of a refuge which she thought of establishing for the infant children of factory women. From that moment the doctor, schoolmaster, and priest engaged in quiet and friendly conversation as to how this asylum might best be organised, and the abuses of similar establishments avoided. And, meantime, the shadows of the great trees lengthened over the lawns of the park, and the wood-pigeons flew down to the grass in the golden September sunshine.

It was already four o'clock when the three guests quitted La Crêcherie. Jordan and Luc, for the sake of a little exercise, accompanied them as far as the first houses of the town. Then, on their way back across some stony fields which Jordan left uncultivated, the latter suggested that they should extend their stroll a little in order to call upon Lange the potter. Jordan had allowed him to instal himself in a wild nook of his estate below the smeltery, asking no rent or other payment from him. And Lange, like Morfain, had made himself a dwelling in a rocky cavity which some of the old torrents rushing past the lower part of the Bleuse Mountains had excavated in the gigantic wall formed by the promontory. Moreover, he had ended by constructing three kilns near the slope whence he took his clay; and he lived there without God or master amidst all the free independence of his work.

"No doubt he's a man of extreme views," added Jordan, in answer to a question from Luc, who felt greatly interested in Lange. "What you told me about his violent outburst in the Rue de Brias the other evening did not surprise me. He was lucky in getting released, for the affair might have turned out very badly for him. But you have no notion how intelligent he is, and what art he puts into his simple earthen pots, although he has virtually had no education. He was born hereabouts, and his parents were poor workpeople. Left an orphan at ten years of age, he worked as a mason's help, then as an apprentice potter, and now, since I've allowed him to settle on my land, he is his own employer, as he laughingly puts it. . . I am the more particularly interested in some attempts he is making with refractory clay, for, as you know, I want to find the clay best suited to resist the terrible temperature of my electrical furnaces."

At last, on looking up, Luc perceived Lange's dwelling-place among the bushes. Faced by a little parapet of dry stones, it suggested a barbarian camp. And as the young man saw a tall, shapely, dark-oomplexioned girl erect upon the threshold he inquired: "Is Lange married, then?"

"No," replied Jordan, "but he lives with that girl, who is both his slave and his wife. It is quite a romance. Five years ago, when she was barely fifteen, he found her lying in a ditch, very ill, half dead in fact, abandoned there by some band of gypsies. Nobody has ever known exactly where she came from; she herself won't answer when she's questioned. Well, Lange carried her home upon his shoulders, nursed her and cured her, and you can't imagine the ardent gratitude that she has always shown him since. She lacked even shoes for her feet when he found her. Even to-day she seldom puts any on, unless indeed she is going down into the town; in such wise that the whole district and even Lange himself call her "Barefeet." She is the only person that he employs, she helps him with his work and even in dragging his barrow when he goes about the fairs to sell his pottery, for that is his way of disposing of his goods, which are well known throughout the region."

Erect on the threshold of the little enclosure, which had a gate of open fencing, Barefeet watched the gentlemen approach, and thus Luc on his side was well able to examine her with her dark regular-featured face, her hair black as ink, and her large wild eyes, which became full of ineffable tenderness whenever they turned upon Lange. The young man also remarked her bare feet, childish feet, of a light bronze hue, resting in the clayey soil, which was always damp. And she stood there in working costume, that is, barely clad in garments of grey linen, and showing her shapely legs and muscular arms. When she had come to the conclusion that the gentleman accompanying the owner of the estate was a friend, she quitted her post of observation, and, after warning Lange, returned to the kiln which she had previously been watching.

"Ah! it's you, Monsieur Jordan," exclaimed Lange, in his turn presenting himself. "Do you know that since that affair the other evening Barefeet is for ever imagining that people are coming to arrest me. I fancy that if any policeman should present himself here he would not escape whole from her clutches. . . You have come to see my last refractory bricks, eh? Well, here they are—I'll tell you the composition."

Luc readily recognised the knotty little man, of whom he had caught a glimpse amidst the gloom of the Rue de Brias whilst he was announcing the inevitable catastrophe, and cursing that corrupt town of Beauclair, whose crimes had condemned it. Only, as he now scrutinised him in detail, he was surprised by the loftiness of his brow, over which fell a dark tangle of hair, and the keenness of his eyes, which glittered with intelligence, and at times flared up with anger. Most of all, however, the young fellow was surprised at divining beneath a rugged exterior and apparent violence a man of contemplative nature, a gentle dreamer, a simple rustic poet, who, urged on by his absolute ideas of justice, had finally come to the point of desiring to annihilate the old and guilty world.

After introducing Luc as an engineer, a friend of his, Jordan asked Lange with a laugh to show the young man what he called his museum.

"Oh! if it can interest the gentleman, willingly," said Lange; "they are merely things which I fire for amusement's sake—there, all that pottery under the shed. You may give it all a glance, monsieur, while I explain my bricks to Monsieur Jordan."

Luc's astonishment increased. Under the shed he found a number of faïence figures, vases, pots, and dishes of the strangest shapes and colours, which, whilst denoting great ignorance on the maker's part, were yet delightful in their original *naïveté*. The firings had at times yielded some superb results; much of the enamel displayed a wondrous richness of tone. But what particularly struck the young man among the current pottery which Lange prepared for his usual customers at the markets and fairs, the crockery, the stock-pots, the pitchers and basins, was the elegance of shape and charm of colour which showed forth like some florescence of the popular genius. It seemed indeed as if the potter had derived his talent from his race, that those creations of his, instinct with the soul of the masses, sprang naturally from his big fingers, as though in fact he had intuitively rediscovered the primitive models, so full of practical beauty.

When Lange came back with Jordan, who had ordered of him a few hundred bricks with which it was intended to try a new electrical furnace, he received with a smile the congratulations tendered him by Luc, who marvelled at the gaiety of the faïences, which looked so bright, so flowery with purple and azure, in the broad sunlight.

"Yes, yes," said the potter, "they set a few poppies and cornflowers, as it were, in people's houses. I've always thought that roofs and house-fronts ought to be decorated in that style. It would not cost very much, if the tradesmen would only leave off thieving; and you'd see, too, how pleasant a town would look—quite like a nosegay set in greenery. But there's nothing to be done with the dirty *bourgeois* of nowadays!"

Then he at once lapsed into his sectarian passion, plunged into the ideas of Anarchy which he had derived from a few pamphlets that by some chance had fallen into his hands. First of all one had to destroy everything, seize everything in revolutionary style. Salvation would only be obtained by the annihilation of all authority, for if any, even the most insignificant, remained standing, it would suffice for the reconstruction of the whole edifice of iniquity and tyranny. Next the free commune, without any government whatever, might be established by means of agreement between different groups, which would incessantly be varied and modified, according to the desires and needs of each. Luc was struck at finding in this theory much that had been devised by Fourier, and indeed the ultimate dream was the same, even if the roads to be followed were different. Thus the Anarchist was but a Fourierist, a disabused and exasperated Collectivist, who no longer believed in political means, but was resolved to use force and extermination as his instrument to reach social happiness, since centuries of slow evolution seemed unlikely to achieve it. And thus, when Luc mentioned Bonnaire, Lange became quite ferocious in his irony, showing more bitter disdain for the master-puddler than he would have shown for a *bourgeois*. Ah, yes, indeed! Bonnaire's barracks, that famous Collectivism in which one would be numbered, disciplined, imprisoned as in a penitentiary! And stretching out his fist towards Beauclair, whose roofs he overlooked, the potter once more poured his lamentation, his prophetic curse, upon that corrupt town which fire would destroy, and which would be razed to the very ground in order that the city of truth and justice might at last rise from its ashes.

Astonished by this violence, Jordan looked at him curiously, saying: "But, Lange, my good fellow, you are not so badly off."

"I, Monsieur Jordan, I'm very happy, as happy as one can be. I live in freedom here, and it's almost the realisation of anarchy. You have let me take this little bit of earth, the earth which belongs to us all, and I'm my own master; I pay rent to nobody. Then, too, I work as I fancy; I've no employer to crush me, and no workman for me to crush; I myself sell my pots and pitchers to good folk who need them, without being robbed by tradesmen or allowing them to rob customers. And when I'm so inclined I've still time to amuse myself by firing those faïence figures and ornamental pots and plates, whose bright colours please my eyes. Ah! no, indeed, we don't complain, we feel happy in living when the sun comes to cheer us. Isn't that so, Barefeet?"

The girl had drawn near, with her hands quite pink from removing a pot from the wheel. And she smiled divinely as she looked at the man, the god whose servant she had made herself, and to whom she wholly belonged.

"But all the same," resumed Lange, "there are too many poor devils suffering, and so we shall have to blow up Beauclair one of these fine mornings in order that it may be built again properly. Propaganda by deeds is the only thing that is of any good; only bombs can rouse the people. And do you know that I've everything here that's necessary to prepare two or three dozen bombs which would prove wonderfully powerful. Some fine day, perhaps, I shall start off with the barrow, which I pull in front, you know, while Barefeet pushes it behind. It's fairly heavy when it is laden with pottery, and one has to drag it along the bad village roads from market to market. So we take a rest now and again under the trees, at spots where there are springs handy. Only, that day, we sha'n't quit Beauclair, we shall go along all the streets, and there'll be a bomb hidden in each stock-pot. We shall deposit one at the sub-prefecture, another at the town-hall, another at the law courts, then another at the church, at all the places in fact where there's anything in the shape of authority to be destroyed. The matches will burn, each will last the necessary time. Then all at once Beauclair will go up! A frightful eruption will burn it and carry it away. Eh? What do you think of that, of my little promenade, with my barrow, and my little distribution of the stock-pots I'm making to bring about the happiness of mankind?"

He laughed a laugh of ecstasy, his face all aglow with excitement, and as the beautiful dark girl began to laugh with him he turned and said to her: "Isn't that so, Barefeet? I'll pull and you shall push, and it will be even a finer walk than the one we take under the willows alongside the Mionne when we go to the fair at Magnolles!"

Jordan did not argue the point, but made a gesture as much as to say that he, as a scientist, regarded such a conception as imbecility. But when they had taken leave and were returning to La Crêcherie Luc quivered at the thought of that black poem, that dream of ensuring happiness by destruction, which thus haunted the minds of a few primitive poets among the disinherited classes. And thus, each deep in his own meditations, the two men went homeward in silence.

On repairing direct to the laboratory they there found Sœurette quietly seated at a little table, where she was making a clean copy of one of her brother's manuscripts. She just raised her head and smiled at him and his companion, then turned to her task once more.

"Ah!" said Jordan, throwing himself back in an arm-chair, "it is quite certain that my only good time is that which I spend here among my appliances and papers. As soon as I come back to this laboratory, hope and peace seem to rise to my heart once more."

He glanced affectionately around the spacious room, whose large windows were open, the glow of the setting sun entering warmly and caressingly, whilst between the trees one saw the roofs and casements of Beauclair shining in the distance.

"How wretched and futile all those disputes are!" Jordan resumed, whilst Luc softly paced up and down. "As I listened to the priest and the schoolmaster after lunch I felt astonished that people could lose their time in striving to convince one another when they viewed questions from opposite standpoints, and could not even speak the same language. Please observe, that they never come here without beginning precisely the same discussions afresh, and reaching absolutely the same point as on the previous occasion. And besides, how silly it is to confine oneself to the absolute, to take no account of experience, and to fight on simply with contradictory arguments! I am entirely of the opinion of the doctor, who amuses himself with annihilating both priest and schoolmaster by merely opposing one to the other! And then, as regards that fellow Lange, can one imagine a man dreaming of more ridiculous things—losing himself in more manifest, dangerous errors, all through bestirring himself chancewise, and disdaining certainties? No, decidedly, political passions do not suit me; the things which those people say to one another seem to me devoid of sense, and the biggest questions which they broach are in my eyes mere pastimes for amusement on the road. I cannot understand why such vain battles should be fought over petty incidents, when the discovery of the smallest scientific truth does more for progress than fifty years of social struggling!"

Luc began to laugh. "You are falling into the absolute yourself," said he. "Man ought to struggle, politics simply represent the necessity in which he finds himself to defend his needs and ensure himself the greatest sum of happiness possible."

"You are right," acknowledged Jordan, with his simple good faith. "Perhaps my disdain for politics merely comes from some covert remorse, some desire to live in ignorance of the country's political affairs in order to avoid being disturbed by them. But, sincerely now, I think that I am still a good citizen in shutting myself up in my laboratory, for each serves the nation according to his lights. And assuredly the real revolutionaries, the real men of action, those who do the most to ensure the advent of truth and justice in the future, are the scientists. A government passes and falls; a people grows, triumphs, and then declines; but the truths of science are transmitted from generation to generation, ever spreading, ever giving increase of light and certainty. A pause of a century does not count, the forward march is always resumed at last, and in spite of every obstacle mankind goes on towards knowledge. The objection that one will never know everything is ridiculous; the question is to learn as much as we can in order that we may attain to the greatest happiness possible. And so, I repeat it, how unimportant are those political jolts on the road in which nations take such passionate interest. Whilst people set the salvation of progress in the maintenance or fall of a ministry, it is really the scientist who determines what the morrow shall be by illumining the darkness of the multitude with a fresh spark of truth. All injustice will cease when all truth has been acquired."

Silence fell. Sœurette, who had put down her pen, was now listening. After pondering for a few moments, Jordan, without transition, resumed: "Work, ah! work, I owe my life to it. You see what a poor, puny little being I am. I remember that my mother used to wrap me in thick rugs whenever the wind was at all violent; yet it was she who set me to work, as to a *régime*, which was certain to bring good health. She did

ÉMILE ZOLA

not condemn me to crushing studies, forms of punishment with which growing minds are so often tortured. But she instilled into me a habit of regular, varied, and attractive work. And it was thus that I learnt to work as one learns to breathe and to walk. Work has become like the function of my being, the necessary natural play of my limbs and organs, the object of my life, and the very means that enables me to live. I have lived because I have worked; some sort of equilibrium has been arrived at between the world and me; I have given it back in work what it has brought me in the form of sensations, and I believe that all health lies therein, that is in well-regulated exchanges, a perfect adaptation of the organism to its surroundings. And, however slight of build I may be, I shall live to a good old age, that's certain, since like a little machine I have been carefully put together and wound up, and work logically."

Luc had paused in his slow perambulation. Like Sœurette he was now listening with passionate interest.

"But that is only a question of the life of beings, of the necessity of good hygiene, if one is to have good life," continued Jordan. "Work is life itself; life is the continual work of chemical and mechanical forces. Since the first atom stirred to join the atoms near it, the great creative work has never ceased; and this creative work, which continues and will always continue, is like the very task of eternity, the universal task to which we all contribute our store. Is not the universe an immense workshop, where there is never an 'off day,' where matter from the simplest ferments to the most perfect creatures acts, makes, brings forth unceasingly. The fields which become covered with crops work; the slowly growing forests work; the rivers streaming through the valleys work; the seas rolling their waves from one to another continent work; the worlds, carried by the rhythm of gravitation through the infinite, work. There is not a being, not a thing that can remain still, in idleness; all find themselves carried along, set to work, forced to contribute to the common task. Who or whatever does not work, disappears from that very cause, is thrust aside as something useless and cumbersome, and has to yield place to the necessary, indispensable worker. Such is the one law of life, which, upon the whole, is simply matter working, a force in perpetual activity tending towards that final work of happiness, an imperious craving for which we all have within us."

For another moment Jordan reflected, his eyes wandering far away. Then he resumed: "And what an admirable regulator is work, what orderliness it brings with it whomever it reigns! It is peace, it is joy, even as it is health. I am confounded when I see it disdained, vilified, regarded as chastisement and shame. Whilst saving me from certain death, it also gave me all that is good in me. And what an admirable organiser it is, how well it regulates the faculties of the mind, the play of the muscles, the rôle of each group in a collectivity of workers. It would of itself suffice as a political constitution, a human police, a social *raison d'être*. We are born solely for the sake of the hive: we none of us bring into the world more than our individual, momentary effort. All other explanations would be vain and false. Our individual lives appear to be sacrificed to the universal life of future worlds. No happiness is possible unless we set it in the solidary happiness of eternal and general toil. And this is why I should like to see the foundation of the Religion of Work—a hosannah to work which saves, work in which is to be found the one truth, and sovereign health, joy, and peace!"

He ceased speaking and Sœurette raised a cry of loving enthusiasm: "How right you are, brother, and how true! how beautiful it is!"

But Luc seemed more moved even than she. He had remained standing there, motionless, his eyes gradually filling with light, as if he were some apostle illumined by a suddenly descending ray. And all at once he spoke: "Listen, Jordan, you must not sell your property to Delaveau, you must keep everything, both the blast-furnace and the mine. That's my answer, I give it you now because I have quite made up my mind upon the subject."

Surprised by those words, the connection of which with what he had just said escaped him, the master of La Crêcherie started slightly and blinked. "Why so, my dear Luc?" he asked. "Why do you say that? Explain yourself."

The young man, however, remained silent for a moment, overcome as he was by emotion. That hymn, that glorification of pacifying and reorganising work had suddenly raised him, carried him away in spirit, at last showing him the great horizon, which hitherto had been clouded in mist. To his eyes everything now acquired precision, grew animated, assumed absolute certainty. Faith also glowed within him, and his words came from his lips with extraordinary power of persuasion.

"You must not sell the property to Delaveau," he repeated. "I visited the abandoned mine to-day. Such as the ore is in the present veins, one can still derive good profit from it by subjecting it to the new chemical processes. And Morfain has convinced me that one will find excellent lodes on the other side of the gorge. There is incalculable wealth there.

ÉMILE ZOLA

The blast-furnace will yield cast iron cheaply, and if it be completed by a forge, some puddling furnaces, rolling mills, steam hammers and so forth, one may again begin making rails and girders in such a way as to compete victoriously with the most prosperous steel-works of the north and the east."

Jordan's surprise was increasing, becoming sheer consternation. "But I don't want to get any richer," he protested; "I've too much money already; and if I desire to sell the place it is precisely in order to escape from all the cares of gain."

With a fine, passionate gesture Luc broke in: "Let me finish, my friend. It isn't you that I desire to enrich, it is the disinherited ones, the workers whom we were speaking of just now, the victims of iniquitous and vilified labour! As you have said, work ought of itself alone to be a social *raison d'être*. At the moment I heard you, the path to salvation became manifest to me. The happy community of to-morrow can only be brought about by such a reorganisation of work as will lead to an equitable apportionment of wealth, the only solution by which our misery and sufferings may be dispelled lies in that. If the old social fabric, now cracking and rotting, is to be replaced by another it must be upon the basis of work, shared by all and benefiting all, accepted, indeed, as the universal law. Well, that is what I should like to attempt here, a reorganisation of work on a small scale, a brotherly enterprise, a rough draft, as it were, of the social system of to-morrow, which I should contrast with the other enterprises, those based upon the wage system, the ancient prisons where workmen are regarded as slaves and tortured and dishonoured."

He went on speaking in quivering accents, outlining his dream, all that had germinated in his mind since his recent perusal of Fourier's theories. There ought to be an association between capital, work, and talent. Jordan would provide the money required, Bonnaire and his mates would give their arms, and his, Luc's, would be the brain that plans and directs. Whilst speaking, the young man again began to walk up and down, pointing vehemently the while towards the neighbouring roofs of Beauclair. It was Beauclair that he would save, extricate from the shame and crime in which he had seen it sinking for three days past. As he gradually unfolded his plan of action he marvelled at himself, for he had not thought that he had all this in him. But he at last saw things clearly, he had found his road. And he now replied to all the distressing questions which he had put to himself during his insomnia without then finding any answer to them. In particular he now responded to those appeals from the wretched which had come to him from out of the darkness. At present he distinctly heard those cries, and he went forward to succour the poor beings who raised them; he would save them by regenerated work, by work which would no longer divide men into inimical, all-devouring castes, but would Unite them in one sole brotherly family, wherein the efforts of each would be directed to obtaining the happiness of all.

"But the application of Fourier's formula," said Jordan, "does not destroy the wage-system. Even among the Collectivists little of that system is changed excepting the name. To annihilate it, one would have to go as far as anarchy."

Luc was obliged to admit the truth of this objection; and in doing so he passed his feelings and opinions in review. The theories of Bonnaire, the Collectivist, and the dreams of Lange, the Anarchist, still lingered in his ears. The discussions between Abbé Marle, schoolmaster Hermeline, and Doctor Novarre, also seemed to begin afresh and continue endlessly. The whole made up a chaos of contrary opinions, particularly as Luc likewise recalled the objections exchanged by the precursors of Socialism, Saint-Simon, Auguste Comte, and Proudhon. Why was it then that amongst so many formulas he himself should choose those of Fourier? No doubt he was acquainted with a few fortunate applications of them, but he also knew how slowly attempts progressed, and what difficulties stood in the way of any decisive result. Perhaps his choice was due to the fact that revolutionary violence was quite repugnant to him personally, since he had set his scientific faith in ceaseless evolution, which has all eternity before it to achieve its ends. Moreover, a complete and sudden expropriation of present-day possessors could not be effected without terrible catastrophes which would increase the present sum of misery and sorrow. Would it not be best therefore to profit by the opportunity of such a practical experiment as lay before him, an attempt in which he would find contentment for his whole being: his own native goodness of heart and his faith in man's goodness also? He was upbuoyed by some exalted heroic feeling, a faith, a kind of prescience, which seemed to make success a certainty. And, besides, even if the application of Fourier's formulas should not bring about the immediate end of the wage-system, it would at least be a forward step, it would tend towards the final victory, the destruction of capital, the disappearance of mere traders, commercial middle-men, and the annihilation of the power of money, that source of all evils whose uselessness would be proved. The great quarrel of the socialist schools is one as to the means which should be employed. The schools are all agreed as to the object in view, and they will all be reconciled when some day the happy community is at last established. It was the first foundations of that community which Luc desired to lay, by collecting scattered forces, associating men of good will together, and he was convinced that, given the frightful massacre now going on, there could be no better point of departure.

Jordan remained sceptical, however. "Fourier had flashes of genius," said he, "that is certain. Only he has now been dead more than sixty years, and if he still retains a few stubborn disciples I see no sign of his religion conquering the world."

"Catholicism took four centuries to conquer a small part of it," Luc quickly retorted. "Besides, I don't adopt the whole of Fourier's views; I regard him simply as a wise man, to whom one day a vision of the truth appeared. Moreover, he is not the only one; others helped to prepare the formula and others will perfect it. One thing which you cannot deny is that the evolution now proceeding so rapidly dates from far back. The whole of our century has been given to the laborious engendering of the new social system which will arise to-morrow. Each day for a hundred years past the workers have been born a little more to social life, and to-morrow they will be masters of their destinies by virtue of that scientific law which ensures life to the strongest, healthiest, and worthiest. It is all that which we nowadays behold, the final struggle between the privileged few by whom wealth has been stolen, and the great toiling masses who wish to recover the possession of wealth of which they have been despoiled for long centuries. History teaches us how a few seized on the greatest happiness possible—to the detriment of all the others; and how since then all the wretched despoiled ones have never ceased to struggle furiously, eager to reconquer as much happiness as they could. For the last fifty years the contest has become merciless, and one now sees the privileged folk seized with fear, and slowly relinquishing of their own accord certain of their privileges. The times are approaching, one can feel it by all the concessions which the holders of land and wealth make to the people. In the political sphere much has been given it already, and it will also be necessary to give it much in the economic sphere. One sees nothing but new laws favouring the workers, humanitarian measures of all kinds, the triumphs too of associations and unions, and all announce the coming era. The battle between labour and capital has reached such an acute crisis that one can already predict the defeat of the latter. In time, the disappearance of the wage-system is certain. And this is why I feel convinced that I shall conquer by helping on the advent of that something else which will replace the wage-system, that reorganisation of work, which will give us more justice and a loftier civilisation."

He was radiant with benevolence, faith, and hope. And continuing he went back to history, to the robberies perpetrated by the stronger in the earliest days of the world, the wretched multitude being reduced to slavery and the possessors piling crime upon crime in order that they might not be obliged to restore anything to those who were despoiled, and who perished by starvation or violence. And he showed the accumulation of wealth increased by time, and still now in the hands of a few, who held the country estates, the houses in the towns, the factories of the industrial centres, the mines where coal and metal slumber, the means of transport by road, canal, and rail, and then the Rentes, the gold and the silver, the millions which circulate through the banks, briefly the whole wealth of earth, all that constitutes the incalculable fortune of mankind. And was it not abominable that so much wealth should only lead to the frightful indigence of the greater number? Did not such a state of things demand justice? Could one not see the inevitable necessity of proceeding to a fresh apportionment of wealth? Such iniquity, in which on the one hand one beheld idleness gorged with possession, and on the other pain-racked labour, agonising in misery, had made man wolfish towards man.

Instead of uniting to conquer and domesticate the forces of nature, men wolfishly devoured one another. Their barbarous social system cast them to hatred and error and madness; infants and aged beings were abandoned, and woman was crushed down, to become a beast of burden for some, and a mere instrument of pleasure for others. The workers themselves, corrupted by example, accepted their servitude, bending their heads amidst the universal cowardice. And how frightful, too, was the waste of human fortune, the colossal sums spent on warfare, and all the money given to useless functionaries, to judges and to gendarmes! And then there was all the money winch without necessity remained in the hands of the traders, those parasite intermediaries, whose gains were levied on the consumers! But, after all, this was only the daily loss of an illogical, badly constructed social system. Apart from it there was downright crime, famine deliberately organised by those who detained the instruments of labour, in order to protect their profits. They reduced the output of a factory, they imposed off-days upon miners, they created misery for purposes of economic warfare, in order to keep up high prices. And yet people were astonished that the machine should be cracking and collapsing beneath such a pile of suffering, injustice, and shame!

"No, no!" cried Luc, "that cannot last, unless mankind is to disappear in a final attack of madness. The social compact must be changed, each man that is born has a right to life, and the earth is the common fortune of us all. The instruments of work must be restored to all, each must do his own share of the general labour. If history, with its hatreds, its wars, its crimes, has hitherto been nothing but the abominable outcome of original theft, of the tyranny of a few thieves who had to urge men on to murder one another, and institute law courts and prisons to defend their deeds of rapine, it is time to begin history afresh, and to set, at the dawn of the new era, a great act of equity, the restoration of the wealth of the earth to all men, work once again becoming the universal law of human society, even as it is that of the universe, in order that peace may be made among us and happy brotherliness at last prevail. And that shall be! I will work for it, and I will succeed!"

He seemed so passionate, so lofty, so victorious in his prophetic exaltation, that Jordan, marvelling, turned towards Sœurette to say, "Just look at him, is he not handsome?"

Sœurette herself, quivering, pale with admiration, had not taken her eyes from Luc. It seemed as if a kind of religious fervour possessed her. "Oh! he is handsome," she murmured faintly, "and he is good as well."

"Only, my dear friend," resumed Jordan, smiling, "you are really an Anarchist, however much you may deem yourself to be an evolutionist. But you are right in holding that one begins by Fourier's formula, and ends by the free man in the free commune."

Luc himself had begun to laugh. "At all events," said he, "let's make a start; we shall see whither logic will lead us."

Jordan had become thoughtful, however, and no longer seemed to hear him. He, the cloistered scientist, had been profoundly stirred, and if he still doubted the possibility of hastening mankind's advance, he no longer denied the utility of experiment.

"Individual initiative is no doubt in some respects all-powerful," he said. "To determine facts, one simply needs a man of will and action, some rebel of genius and free mind who brings the new truth with him. In cases of accident, when salvation depends on cutting a cable or splitting a beam, only a man and a hatchet are necessary. Will is everything, the saviour is he who wields the hatchet. Nothing resists, mountains collapse and seas retire before an individuality that acts."

'Twas that indeed; in those words Luc found an expression of the will and conviction glowing within him. He knew not yet what genius he brought with him, but he was pervaded by a strength that seemed to have been long accumulating, a strength compounded of revolt against all the injustice of centuries, and an ardent craving to bring justice into the world at last. His also was the freed mind, he only accepted such facts as were scientifically proved. He was alone too, he wished to act alone, he set all his faith in action. He was the man who dares, and that would be sufficient, his mission would be fulfilled.

Silence reigned for a moment, and then Jordan, with a friendly gesture of surrender, said: "As I have already told you, there are hours of lassitude when I would give Delaveau the whole property, both the smeltery and the mine and the land, so as to rid myself of them and to be able to devote myself in peace to my studies and experiments. So take them, you—I prefer to give them to you, since you think you can turn them to good use. All that I ask of you is to deliver me completely from the burden, to leave me in my corner to work and finish my task, without ever speaking to me of these affairs again."

Luc gazed at him with sparkling eyes, in which all his gratitude, all his affection, glittered. Then, without any hesitation, like one certain of the reply he would receive, he said: "That is not all, my friend. Your great heart must do something more. I can undertake nothing without money, I need five hundred thousand francs[1] to establish the works I dream of, which will be like the foundation of the future city. . . I am convinced that I offer you a good investment, since your capital will enter into the association, and ensure you a large part of the profits."

And as Jordan wished to interpose, he went on: "Yes, I know that you do not desire to become any richer. Nevertheless you must live; and if you give me your money I shall strive to provide for all your material wants in such a manner that your peace as a worker shall never be disturbed."

---

1. 20,000*l*.

Once more did silence, grave, full of emotion, fall in that spacious room, where so much work was already germinating for the harvests of the days to come. The decision that had to be taken was fraught with such great importance for the future that it set something like a religious quiver there during that august interval of suspense.

"Yours is a soul of renunciation and benevolence," said Luc again. "Did you not apprise me of it yesterday when you told me that you would not trade upon the discoveries you pursue, those electrical furnaces which will some day reduce human labour and enrich mankind with new wealth? For my part it is not a gift that I ask of you, it is brotherly help, help to enable me to lessen the injustice of the times and create some happiness in the world."

Then, in very simple fashion, Jordan consented. "I'm willing, my friend," he said. "You shall have the money to realise your dream. Only, as one never ought to tell a falsehood, I will add that, in my eyes, that dream is still only so much generous utopia, for you have not fully convinced me. Excuse the doubts of a scientist. . . But no matter, you are a good fellow; make your attempt—I will be with you!"

Luc, whom enthusiasm seemed to raise from the ground, gave a cry of triumph: "Thanks! I tell you that the work is as good as done, and that we shall know the divine joy of having accomplished it!"

Sœurette hitherto had not intervened—she had not even stirred. But all the kindliness of her heart had made itself manifest in her face, big tears of tender emotion filled her eyes. All at once, under some irresistible impulse, she rose, drew near to Luc, silent, distracted, and kissed him on the face, her tears gushing forth as she did so. Then, in her wondrous emotion, she flung herself into her brother's arms, and long remained sobbing there.

Slightly surprised by the kiss she had given the young man, Jordan anxiously inquired: "What is the matter, little sister? At least you don't disapprove of what is proposed, do you? It is true that we ought to have consulted you. But there is still time—are you with us?"

"Oh, yes! oh, yes!" she stammered, smiling, suddenly radiant amidst her tears; "you are two heroes, and I will serve you—dispose of me."

Late on the evening of that same day, towards eleven o'clock, Luc leant out of the window of the little pavilion, as on the previous night, in order to inhale for a moment the calm fresh air. In front of him, beyond the uncultivated fields strewn with rocks, Beauclair was falling asleep, extinguishing its lights one by one; whilst on the left the Abyss resounded with all the noise of its hammers. Never had the breathing of the pain-racked giant seemed to Luc more hoarse, more oppressed. But again, as on the previous night, a sound arose from across the road, so light a sound that he fancied it was caused by the beating wings of some night-bird. His heart suddenly palpitated, however, when he heard the sound afresh, for he recognised a gentle quiver of approach. And again he saw a vague, delicate, and slender form which seemed to float over the grass. Then, with the spring of a wild goat, a woman crossed the road, and threw him a little bouquet so skilfully that he once more received it on his lips like a caress. As on the previous night, too, it was a little bunch of mountain pansies, gathered just then among the rocks, and of such powerful aroma that he was quite perfumed by it.

"Oh, Josine, Josine!" he exclaimed, penetrated by infinite tenderness.

She it was who had returned, and who, naïve, simple like those very flowers, once again gave him her whole soul, ever with the same gesture of passionate gratitude. And he felt refreshed, revived, amidst all the physical and mental fatigue following upon so decisive a day. Were not those flowers already a reward for his first efforts, for his resolution to proceed to action? And it was in her, Josine, that he loved the suffering toilers, it was she whom he wished to save from monstrous fate. He had found her the most wretched, the most insulted and derided, so near to debasement that she was on the point of falling into the gutter. With her poor hand mutilated by work, she typified the whole race of the victims, the slaves, who gave their flesh for work or for pleasure. When he should have redeemed her, he would have redeemed the entire race. And she, too, was love, love that is needful for harmony, for the happiness of the city of the future.

He gently called her: "Josine! Josine! It is you, Josine!" But without a word she was already fleeing, disappearing into the darkness of the uncultivated moor. Then he again called her: "Josine! Josine! It is you, I know it, Josine; I want to speak to you!"

Thereupon, trembling but happy, she came back with the same light step, and paused on the road below the window. "Yes, it is I, Monsieur Luc," she murmured.

He did not hasten to speak, however—he was trying to see her better, so slim, so vague she was, like some vision which a wave of darkness would soon carry away. At last he spoke: "Will you do me a service? Tell Bonnaire to come to speak with me to-morrow morning. I have some good news for him—I have found him some work."

She showed her pleasure by a laugh, tinged with emotion, and so faint and musical that it recalled the warbling of a bird. "Ah! you are kind! you are kind!" she murmured.

"And," continued he in a lower voice, for he, likewise, was feeling moved, "I shall have work for all who wish to work. Yes, I am going to try to provide a little justice and happiness for everybody."

She must have understood him, for her laugh became yet more gentle, more expressive of passionate gratitude. "Thank you, thank you, Monsieur Luc!" Then the vision began to fade, and Luc again saw the light shadow fleeing through the bushes, accompanied by another and smaller one, Nanet, whom he had not previously seen, but who was now bounding along beside his big sister.

"Josine! Josine! *Au revoir*, Josine!"

"Thank you, Monsieur Luc!"

He could no longer distinguish her, she had disappeared, but he still heard her expressions of gratitude and joy, that bird-like warble which the night breeze wafted to him; and it was instinct with an infinite charm which penetrated and enchanted his heart.

For a long time did he linger at the window, full of rapture and boundless hope. Between the Abyss, where accursed toil was panting, and La Guerdache, whose park formed a great black patch upon the low plain of La Roumagne, he perceived Old Beauclair, the workers' dwelling-place, with its shaky rotting hovels slumbering beneath the crushing weight of misery and suffering. There lay the cloaca which he wished to purify, the antique gaol of the wage-system, which must be razed to the ground with all its hateful iniquity and cruelty, in order that mankind might be cured of the effects of the long efforts to poison it. And on the same spot he was, in imagination, already raising the future city, the abode of truth, justice, and happiness, whose white houses he could already picture smiling freely and fraternally amongst delicate verdure, under a mighty sun of joy.

But, all at once, the whole horizon was illumined, a great pink glow lighted up the roofs of Beauclair, the promontory of the Bleuse Mountains, the entire stretch of country. It was the glow of liquid metal running from the furnace of La Crêcherie, and Luc had, at first, taken it for the dawn. But it was not dawn, it symbolised rather the setting of a planet—old Vulcan, tortured at his anvil, throwing forth his final flames. Work, hereafter, would no longer be aught than health and joy, to-morrow was coming fast.

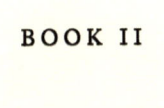

BOOK II

I

There years went by, and Luc established his new factory, which gave birth to a whole town of workers. The land which lay below the ridge of the Bleuse Mountains extended over a space of some twelve hundred square yards, a great moor, which, sloping slightly, stretched from the park of La Crêcherie to the jumbled buildings of the Abyss. And the beginnings were necessarily modest, only a part of the moor was at first utilised, the rest being reserved for the extensions which it was hoped the future would justify.

The works stood against the rocky promontory, just below the blast-furnace, with which they communicated by two lifts. Pending the revolution which Jordan's electrical furnaces would effect, Luc had done little to the smeltery; he had improved it in a few matters of detail, and then left it in Morfain's hands to continue working according to old-time routine. But in the new works, both as regards the buildings and the plant, he had availed himself of all possible improvements in order to increase the output and diminish the labour of the workers. In a like spirit he desired that the houses of the workers, each of which stood in a garden, should be homes of comfort where family life might flourish. Some fifty were already built on the land near La Crêcherie, forming quite a little town advancing towards Beauclair. The building of each new house, indeed, was like a fresh step taken by the future city towards the conquest of the old, guilty and condemned one. Then, in the centre of the land, Luc had erected the common-house, a large building containing schools, a library, a hall for meetings and festivities, baths and so forth. This was all that he had retained of Fourier's phalanstery, leaving everybody free to build as he pleased, and only deeming collective action to be necessary for certain public services. Finally, in the rear of the property some general stores had been established, and grew daily in importance. There was a bakery, a butcher's, a grocery department, not to mention others for clothes, utensils, all sorts of small indispensable articles, the whole being conducted on the principles of a cooperative society of consumers corresponding with the cooperative society of producers which controlled the works. All this, no doubt, was simply a beginning, but there was no dearth of life, and one could already see and judge the work. Luc would not have succeeded in making such rapid progress had not the happy thought occurred to him of interesting workmen of the building trades in the enterprise. One thing, too, which particularly delighted him was that he had managed to capture all the springs scattered among the higher rocks, for they yielded an abundance of fresh and pure water, which cleansed the works and the common-house, gave moisture to the gardens, where thick greenery arose, and brought health and delight to every home.

Now, one morning, Fauchard, the drawer at the Abyss, came strolling up to La Crêcherie to see some of his old mates. He, ever undecided and doleful, had remained under Delaveau, whereas Bonnaire had repaired to the new works, taking with him his brother-in-law Ragu, who in his turn had induced Bourron to follow. Those three then worked with Luc, and Fauchard wished to question them. In the state of hebetude to which fifteen years of labour, ever the same, ever a repetition of similar gestures amidst a similar glare, had reduced him, he felt incapable of arriving at any decision by himself. Such, indeed, had become his indolence of mind, that for long months he had been thinking of this visit without finding sufficient strength of will to make it. From the moment of entering the works of La Crêcherie he felt astonished.

Coming as he did from the grimy, dusty Abyss, into whose heavy, tumbledown halls the light scarcely entered, he marvelled, in the first instance, at the sight of the light airy halls of La Crêcherie, all brick and iron, through whose broad windows the sunshine streamed. All the workshops were paved with slabs of cement, in such wise that there was little dust; and the abundance of water facilitated frequent washings. Moreover, the place remained clean and was easily kept in such a condition, by reason of the new smoke-consuming apparatus with which all the fires were provided. Thus, in lieu of an infernal, cyclopean den there were bright, shiny, spacious workshops in which toil seemed to lose much of its harshness. No doubt the employment of electricity was still very limited; there was still a deafening roar of machinery, and but little relief had been found for human efforts. Only among some of the furnaces had there been trials of mechanical appliances, which, although hitherto defective, encouraged the hope that man would some day be freed from excessive labour. At La Crêcherie they were feeling their way, so to say; and yet how great was the improvement which already resulted from cleanliness, air, and sunlight!

Fauchard had expected to find Bonnaire, the master-puddler, at his furnace, and was surprised to come upon him watching over a large rolling-machine for the making of rails.

"Hallo!" exclaimed the visitor, "have you given up puddling then?"

"No," Bonnaire replied, "but we do a little bit of everything here. That's the rule of the place: two hours on one thing, two hours on another; and really, it's quite true that it rests one."

As a matter of fact Luc did not easily induce the men whom he took on to quit whatever might be their specialty. Later, however, reforms would be realised, for the children were already passing through several apprenticeships, since work could only be made attractive by varying it, and giving but a few hours to any one particular form.

"Ah!" sighed Fauchard, "wouldn't it just amuse me to do something else than draw crucibles out of my furnace! But then I can't, I don't know how!"

The noise made by the rolling-machinery was so violent that he had to raise his voice to its highest pitch. At last he profited by a brief interval to shake hands with Ragu and Bourron, who were busily engaged in receiving the rails. All this again was quite a sight for Fauchard. The rails were not made in the same way as at the Abyss. He looked at them with confused thoughts, which he could not have put into words. That which more particularly made him suffer amidst his downfall, reduced as he was to the status of a mere tool, was the dim consciousness that he might have been a man of intelligence and will. It was indeed so sad to think what a free, healthy, joyful man he might have become if slavery had not cast him into that brutifying gaol, the Abyss! The rails, which ever grew longer before his eyes, seemed to him like an endless railroad over which his thoughts glided away into the future, of which he had neither hope nor clear conception.

Under the hall adjacent to the great foundry the steel was melted in a special furnace, and the fusing metal was received in a large cast-iron pocket lined with refractory clay, which afterwards discharged it into moulds. Electrical rolling bridges, powerful cranes, raised and transported the heavy masses, brought them to the rolling-machines, and conveyed them to the riveting and bolting workshops. There were various sorts of rolling-presses, some of them gigantic, one for large pieces of steel required for bridges, for the frameworks of buildings and so forth; and others for such simple things as girders and rails whose dimensions did not vary. These were made with extraordinary speed and regularity. The steel billet, as dazzling as the sun, but short, and as thick as a man's trunk, was caught in the first cage between two rollers revolving inversely, and when it came forth from the throat it was already more slender. But it entered a second cage and came forth more slender still, and thus from cage to cage it was gradually shaped, till it at last assumed the correct outline and the regulation length of ten mètres. All this, however, was not accomplished without a deafening uproar, a terrible noise of jaws between the cages, something akin to the mastication of a colossus, whom one could imagine munching all that steel. And rails succeeded rails with extraordinary rapidity; you could scarcely follow the billet as it grew thinner and longer, and sprang out at last as a rail, to be added to others and others, as if indeed railways were extending endlessly, penetrating into the depths of the least known lands, and girdling the whole earth.

"Who's all that for?" asked Fauchard in his bewilderment.

"For the Chinese!" answered Ragu by way of a joke.

But Luc was now passing the rolling-mills. He generally spent his mornings in the works, glancing into each hall and chatting like a mate with the men. He had been compelled to retain part of the old hierarchy, master workmen, foremen, engineers, and an office staff for account-keeping and commercial management. Nevertheless, he already effected considerable economy by constant care in reducing the number of managers and clerks. On the other hand, his immediate hopes had been realised. Although high-class lodes like those of former times had not yet been found in the mine, the ore now extracted yielded by chemical treatment cheap iron of fair quality; in such wise that the manufacture of girders and rails, being sufficiently remunerative, ensured the prosperity of the works. They paid their way, the amount of business increased each year, and this was the important point for Luc, whose efforts were directed towards the future of the enterprise, convinced as he was that he should conquer if, at each division of profits, the workmen saw their comfort and happiness increase. None the less his daily life was full of alarms amidst that complicated creation of his; there were considerable advances to make, an entire little army to lead, and worries assailed him both as a reformer, as an engineer, and as a financier. Success seemed certain, yet he fully understood that the enterprise was still in a precarious stage, at the mercy of events.

Amidst the uproar, he only paused for a moment to smile at Bonnaire, Ragu, and Bourron, and he did not even notice Fauchard. He liked that hall where the rolling-machinery was installed, he was cheered by the sight of all the girders and rails made there; it was the good forge of peace, he sometimes exclaimed gaily. And he contrasted it with the evil forge of war—that neighbouring forge, the Abyss, where guns and projectiles were made at such great cost, and with so much care. To think of it! Such perfect appliances, metal worked with so much delicacy and skill, and all that simply to produce monstrous engines of warfare which cost nations millions upon millions, and ruined them whilst they waited for war, when indeed war did not arise to exterminate them. Ah! might the steel girders and frameworks be multiplied, might they build up useful edifices and happy cities, bridges to cross rivers and valleys, might rails for ever gush from the presses and form endless lines to abolish frontiers, bring nations together, and win the whole world over to the brotherly civilisation of to-morrow!

However, just as Luc passed into the large foundry where the great steam-hammer began to pound away, forging the armature of a gigantic bridge, the rolling-machinery was suddenly stopped, and an interval ensued pending the starting of another section. Fauchard then drew nearer to his old mates, and some conversation ensued between them.

"So things are going all right here; you are satisfied, eh?" he inquired.

"Satisfied, no doubt," Bonnaire replied. "The working day is only one of eight hours, and as what one does is diversified, one doesn't get so tired as formerly, and the work seems pleasanter."

He, so tall and strong, with his broad, good-natured, healthy face, was one of the chief mainstays of the new works. He belonged to the council of management, and felt very grateful to Luc for having taken him on at the moment when he had been obliged to quit the Abyss, and could not think of the morrow without apprehension. With his uncompromising Collectivist principles, however, he suffered at seeing La Crêcherie governed by a *régime* of mere association, in which capital retained its great influence. The revolutionary within him, the dreamer of the absolute, protested against such a thing. But at the same time he was sensible, he worked, and urged his mates to work with all devotion, until they should be able to judge the result of the experiment.

"And so," resumed Fauchard, "you earn a lot of money, double what you used to, eh?"

Ragu, with that evil laugh of his, began to jest: "Oh! the double, indeed! Say a hundred francs a day, without counting the champagne and the cigars!"

He had simply followed Bonnaire's example in taking work at La Crêcherie. And though he did not find himself badly off, thanks to the relative comfort he enjoyed there, on the other hand the orderliness and preciseness of everything could scarcely be to his taste, for he was again becoming a railer, turning his happiness into derision.

"A hundred francs!" cried Fauchard in stupefaction. "You earn a hundred francs, you do?"

Bourron, who still remained Ragu's shadow, then tried to improve on what his mate had said: "Oh! a hundred francs just to begin with!" said he. "And one is treated to the roundabouts on Sundays."

But whilst the others sneered, Bonnaire shrugged his shoulders with disdainful gravity. "Can't you see," he exclaimed, "that they are talking folly and making fun of you? Everything considered, after the division of the profits our daily earnings do not amount to much more than they did formerly. Only at each settlement they increase a little, and it's certain that they will some day become superb. Then, too, we have all sorts of advantages, our future is assured, and living costs us much less than formerly, thanks to our co-operative stores and the gay little houses which are let to us almost for nothing. Certainly this isn't yet real justice, but all the same we are on the road to it."

Ragu continued sneering, and a desire came to him to satisfy another hatred, for if he jested about La Crêcherie, he never spoke of the Abyss otherwise than with ferocious rancour.

"And what kind of face does that animal Delaveau pull nowadays?" he inquired. "It amuses me to think that he must be quite wild at having another show erected close to his own, and one too that seems likely to do good business. He's in a rage, isn't he?"

Fauchard waved his arm vaguely and replied: "Of course he must be in a rage, only he doesn't show it over much. And yet I really don't know, because I've enough worries of my own without troubling about those of other people. I've heard say that he doesn't care a fig about your works and the competition. He says, it seems, that cannons and shells will always be wanted, because men are fools and will always go on murdering one another."

Luc, who was just then returning from the foundry, heard those last words. For three years past, since the day when he had prevailed on Jordan to keep the blast-furnace and establish forges and steel-works, he had known that he had an enemy in Delaveau. The blow had been a severe one for the latter, who had hoped to acquire La Crêcherie for a comparatively small sum payable over a term of years, and who in lieu thereof saw it pass into the hands of an audacious young man, full of intelligence and activity, possessed of such creative vigour that at the very outset of his operations he raised the nucleus of a town. Nevertheless after the anger born of his first shock of surprise, Delaveau had felt full of confidence. He would confine himself to the manufacture of ordnance and projectiles, in which line the profits were large ones, and in which he feared no competition. The announcement that the neighbouring works would resume the making of rails and girders had at first filled him with merriment, ignorant as he was that the mine would be worked afresh. Then, on understanding the situation, realising that large profits might be made by treating the defective ore chemically, he did not lose his temper, but declared to everybody that there was room for all enterprises, and that he would willingly leave the making of rails and girders to his fortunate neighbour if the latter left him that of guns and shells. In appearance, then, peace was not disturbed, cold but polite intercourse was kept up. But in the depths of Delaveau's mind lurked covert anxiety, a fear of that centre of just and free work, so near to him, for in time its spirit might gain upon his own workshops and men. And there was yet other uneasiness on his part, an unacknowledged feeling that old scaffoldings were gradually cracking under him, that there were causes of rottenness which he could not control, and that on the day when the power of capital might fail him, his arms, however stubborn and vigorous they might be, would prove powerless to keep up the edifice, which would fall in its entirety to the ground.

In the inevitable and ever fiercer warfare which had begun between La Crêcherie and the Abyss, and which could only end by the downfall of one or the other of the works, Luc felt no pity for the Delaveaus. If he had some esteem for the man on seeing how energetically he worked, and how bravely he defended his opinions, he despised the woman, Fernande, though with his contempt there was mingled a kind of terror on divining in her a terrible force of corruption and destruction. That evil intrigue which he had detected at La Guerdache, the imperious subjugation of Boisgelin, that dull-witted coxcomb whose fortune was melting away in the hands of a devouring creature, filled him with growing anxiety, as if he foresaw in it some future tragedy. All his affection went out towards the good-hearted and gentle Suzanne, for she was the real victim, the only one worthy of his pity. He had been compelled to break off all intercourse with La Guerdache, and his only knowledge of what went on there was derived from chance reports. These indicated, however, that things were going from bad to worse,

Fernande's wild demands increasing, whilst Suzanne only found energy to remain silent, closing her eyes for fear of some scandal. One day when Luc met her, holding her little boy Paul by the hand, in one of the streets of Beauclair, she gave him a long look in which he could read all her distress, and the friendship that she still retained for him in spite of the deadly struggle which now parted their lives.

As soon as Luc recognised Fauchard, he put himself on the defensive, for it was part of his plan to avoid all unnecessary conflicts with the Abyss. He was willing that men should come from the neighbouring works to offer their services, but he did not wish it to be said that he tried to attract them. As a matter of fact, it was the workers of La Crêcherie who decided whether a new hand should be admitted or not. Accordingly, as Bonnaire had on various previous occasions spoken to him of Fauchard, Luc feigned a belief that the latter was trying to gain admittance from his former comrades. "Ah! it's you, my friend," said he; "you've come to see if your old mates will make room for you, eh?"

The other, once more full of doubt, incapable of prompt resolution, began to stammer disjointed words. All novelty frightened him, accustomed as he was to blind routine. Those new works, those large, light, clean halls, filled him with emotion as if they formed part of some awesome place where it would be impossible for him to live. He was already eager to return to his black and pain-fraught *inferno*. Ragu had derided him. What was the good of changing, when nothing was certain? Besides, he dimly realised, perhaps, that it was too late for him to make a change.

"No, no, monsieur, not yet," he stuttered; "I should like to, but I don't know. I'll see a little later—I'll consult my wife."

Luc smiled. "Quite so, quite so—one has to please the women. *Au revoir*, my friend."

Then Fauchard went off in an awkward way, astonished at the turn that his visit had taken, for he had certainly made it with the intention of asking for work, if he found the place to his liking, and one could earn more money there than at the Abyss.

For a moment Luc remained speaking to Bonnaire about some improvements which he wished to introduce into the rolling-machinery. But Ragu had a complaint to make. "Monsieur Luc," said he, "a gust of wind has broken three more panes in the window of our bed-room. And I must warn you that this time we really won't pay. It all comes from our house being the first in the line of the wind that comes from the plain. One freezes in it."

He was always complaining, always finding reasons for discontent. "Besides, it's very simple, Monsieur Luc," he added, "you've only got to call at our house to see how it happens. Josine will show you."

Since Ragu had been working at La Crêcherie Sœurette had prevailed on him to marry Josine; and thus they lived together in one of the little houses of the new town of workers, a house which stood between those of Bonnaire and Bourron, As Ragu had considerably amended his ways, thanks to his new surroundings, there did not as yet seem to be any serious disagreement in his home. Only a few quarrels had broken out, caused chiefly by the presence of Nanet, who also lived in the house. Moreover, whenever Josine was sorrowful and inclined to shed tears, she carefully closed the window in order that her neighbours might not hear her weeping.

But a shadow had passed over Luc's brow. "Very well, Ragu," he simply said, "I will call at your house."

Then the conversation ceased, the machinery had begun to work once more, drowning the voices of one and all with a tremendous noise, which suggested the mastication of a giant. For another moment Luc watched the work, smiling at Bonnaire, encouraging Bourron and Ragu, striving to promote brotherly love among each gang of workers, for he was convinced that nothing can prove substantial and effective if love be lacking. At last he quitted the workshops, and repaired to the common-house, as he did each morning, in order to visit the schools. If it pleased him to linger in the halls of work, dreaming of future peace, he tasted the delight of a yet keener hope among the little world of children, by whom the future was personified.

The common-house, naturally enough, was as yet only a large, clean, gay building, in erecting which Luc had aimed at little beyond making the place as commodious as possible at a small cost. The schools occupied one wing of it, the library, recreation-hall, and baths being installed in the other one, whilst the meeting and festival-hall, together with various offices, occupied the central pile. The schools were divided into three distinct sections, first a kind of infant asylum, where mothers following various avocations could place their little ones, even when these were mere babes in swaddling clothes; secondly a school proper, comprising five divisions, in which a complete system of education was in force; and thirdly a series of workshops for apprentices. The pupils frequented the latter even whilst following their studies, acquiring familiarity with manual callings as their general knowledge developed. And the sexes were not separated, boys and girls grew up side by side, from the cradle to the workshop of apprenticeship, which they quitted in order to marry, passing meantime through the five classes of the school, where they sat side by side on the forms, mingling there as they were bound to mingle in after life. To separate the sexes from infancy, to bring up boys and girls and educate them differently, one in ignorance of the other, does not this render them inimical, and does it not tend to pervert them by heightening the mystery of the laws of natural attraction? Peace will only be complete between the sexes on the common interest which ought to unite them becoming apparent to both, reared as comrades, knowing one another, deriving their knowledge of life from the same source, and setting forth on its road in order to live it logically and healthily even as it ought to be lived.

Sœurette had greatly aided Luc in organising the schools. Whilst Jordan, after giving the money he had promised, had shut himself up in his laboratory, refusing to examine accounts, or to discuss what measures should be adopted, his sister had begun to take a passionate interest in that new town which she saw germinating, rising before her eyes. The feelings of a teacher and a nurse had always been latent within her, and her benevolence, which hitherto had been unable to go beyond a few poor folk pointed out to her by Abbé Marle, Doctor Novarre, or Hermeline the schoolmaster, suddenly expanded in presence of Luc's large family of workers, who needed to be taught and guided and loved. She had at the outset chosen her special task; she did not refuse to help in organising the classes and the workshops for the apprentices, but she more particularly devoted herself to the infant-asylum, where she spent her mornings, satisfying her love for the little ones. One day, when it was suggested that she ought to marry she replied with some slight confusion and a pretty laugh: "But haven't I all the children of others to look after?"

She had ended by finding an assistant in Josine, who, although now married to Ragu, remained childless. Each morning Sœurette employed her among the infants; and drawn together as they were by solicitude for the little ones, they had become good friends, however different in other respects might be the bent of their natures.

That morning, when Luc entered the white cool ward, he found Sœurette alone there. "Josine hasn't been," she explained; "she sent word

ÉMILE ZOLA

that she was not feeling well. Oh! it's merely a trifling indisposition, I believe."

To Luc, however, there came a vague suspicion, and a shadow again darkened his glance. "I have to call at her house—I will see if she needs anything," he simply replied.

Then came the delightful visit to the cradles. They stood all white alongside the white walls. Little pink faces lay smiling or sleeping in them. And there were some willing women with large dazzling aprons, soft eyes, and motherly hands, who, speaking gentle words, watched over all those little ones, those germs of humanity in whom the future was rising. Some of the children, however, were growing fast—there were little men and little women of three and four years of age, and these were at liberty, toddling or running about on their little legs without encountering too many falls. The ward opened on to a flowery verandah, whence a garden extended, and the whole troop disported itself in sunshine and warm air. Toys, such as jumping jacks, hung down from strings to amuse the smallest, whilst the others had dolls, or horses, or carts, which they dragged about noisily like future heroes in whom the need of action was awaking. And it warmed the heart to see those young folk growing thus gaily, and in comfort, for all the tasks of to-morrow.

"Nobody ill?" asked Luc, who lingered with delight amidst all the dawn-like whiteness.

"Oh no! they are all lively this morning," Sœurette replied. "We had two children taken with the measles the day before yesterday. But I did not receive them afterwards—they have been isolated."

She and Luc had now gone out to the verandah, along which they went to visit the adjoining school. The glazed doors of the five class-rooms followed one after the other, allowing a view over the greenery of the garden, and the weather being warm these doors were at that moment wide open, in such wise that Luc and Sœurette were able to glance into each room without entering.

Since the establishment of the school the masters had arranged quite a new programme of education. From the first class, in which they took the child before he could even read, to the fifth, in which they parted from him, after teaching him the elements of general knowledge necessary to life, they particularly strove to place him in presence of things and facts, in order that he might derive his learning from the realities of the world. They also sought to awaken a spirit of orderliness and method in each child; for without method there can be no useful work. It is method which classifies and enables one to go on learning without losing aught of the knowledge one has already acquired. The science of books was not condemned in the school at La Crêcherie, but it was put back to its rightful secondary place, for a child only learns well such things as he sees, touches, or understands by himself. He was no longer bent like a slave over indisputable dogmas; his masters appealed to his initiative to discover, penetrate, and make the truth his own. By this system the individual energy of each pupil was awakened and stimulated. In like manner punishments and rewards had been abolished, no further recourse was had to threats or caresses to force idle lads to work. As a matter of fact there are no idlers, there are only ailing children, children who understand badly what is badly explained to them, children into whose brains obstinate attempts are made to force knowledge for which they are not prepared. This being so, in order to have good pupils at La Crêcherie it was found sufficient to utilise the immense craving for knowledge which glows within each human being, that inextinguishable curiosity of the child for all that surrounds him, a curiosity so great that he never ceases to weary people with questions. Thus learning ceased to be torture; it became a constant pleasure by being rendered attractive, the master contenting himself with arousing the child's intelligence, and then simply guiding it in its discoveries. Each has the right and the duty to develop himself. And self-development is necessary if one wishes a child to become a real man of active energy, with will-power to decide and direct.

Thus the five classes spread out, offering from the very first notions to the acquirement of all the scientific truths, a means for the logical, graduated emancipation of the intelligence. In the garden gymnastic appliances were installed, there were games, exercises of all kinds, in order that the body might be fortified, provided with health and strength whilst the brain developed and enriched itself with learning. In the first classes especially, a great deal of time was allowed for play and recreation. At the outset only short and varied studies, proportionate to the child's powers of endurance, were required. The rule was to confine the children within doors as little as possible: lessons were frequently given in the open air; walks were arranged and the pupils were taught amidst the things on which their lessons turned, now in workshops, now in presence of the phenomena of nature, among animals and plants, or beside watercourses and mountains. Then, too, efforts were made to give the children a notion of what mankind really was, and of the necessity for solidarity. They were growing up side by side, they would always live side by side. Love alone was the bond of union, justice and happiness. In love was found the indispensable and all-sufficient social compact, for it was sufficient for men to love one another to ensure the reign of peace. That universal love which will spread in time from the family to the nation, and from the nation to all mankind, will be the sole law of the happy community of the future. It was developed among the children at La Crêcherie by interesting them in one another, the strong being taught to watch over the weak, and all giving rein to their studies, diversions, and budding passions in common. From all this would arise the awaited harvest—men fortified by bodily exercise, instructed in experience amidst nature, drawn together by brain and heart, and in this wise becoming true brothers.

However, some laughter and some shouts suddenly arose, and Luc felt a little anxious, for at times things did not pass off without disorder. In the middle of one of the class-rooms he perceived Nanet standing up. It was he, no doubt, who had caused the tumult.

"Does Nanet still give you trouble?" he asked Sœurette. "He's a little demon, I fear."

She smiled and made a gesture of indulgent excuse. "Yes, he is not always easily managed," she said. "And we have others too who are very turbulent. They push and fight one another, and show little obedience. But all the same they are dear little fellows. Nanet is very brave and good-natured. Besides, when they keep over-quiet we feel anxious, we imagine that they must be ill."

After the class-rooms, beyond the garden, came the workshops for the apprentices. Instruction was given there in the principal manual callings, which the children practised less in order to acquire them perfectly, than to form an acquaintance with their *ensemble* and determine their own vocations. This teaching went on concurrently with the other studies. Whilst a child was acquiring the first notions of reading and writing, a tool was already placed in his hand; and if during the morning he studied grammar, arithmetic, and history, thereby ripening his intelligence, in the afternoon he worked with his little arms in order to impart vigour and skill to his muscles. This was like useful recreation, rest for the brain, a joyous competition in activity. The principle was adopted that every man ought to know a manual calling, in such wise that each pupil on leaving the school simply had to choose the calling he himself preferred, and perfect himself in it in a real workshop. In like manner beauty flourished; the children passed through courses of music, drawing, painting, and sculpture, and in souls that were well awakened the joys of existence were then born. Even for those who had to confine themselves to the first elements such studies tended to an enlargement of the world, the whole earth taking a voice, and splendour in one or another form embellishing the humblest lives. And in the garden, at the close of fine days, amidst radiant sunsets, the children were gathered together to sing songs of peace and glory, or to be braced by spectacles of truth and immortal beauty.

Luc was finishing his daily visit when he was informed that two peasants of Les Combettes, Lenfant and Yvonnot, were waiting to speak to him in the little office opening into the large meeting-hall.

"Have they come about the stream?" asked Sœurette.

"Yes," he replied, "they asked me to fix an appointment. And for my part I greatly desired to see them, for I was talking again to Feuillat only the other day, and I am convinced that an understanding is necessary between La Crêcherie and Les Combettes if we desire to win the day."

She listened to him smiling, like one who knew all his plans; and after pressing his hand she returned with her discreet, quiet step to her white cradles, whence would arise the future people that he needed for the fulfilment of his dream.

Feuillat, the farmer of La Guerdache, had ended by renewing his lease with Boisgelin under disastrous conditions for both parties. But it was necessary to live, as Feuillat said; and the farming system had become so defective that it could no longer yield any good results. It was leading, indeed, to the very bankruptcy of the soil. And so Feuillat, like the stubborn man he was, haunted by an idea which he imparted to nobody, covertly continued urging on certain experimental work which he desired to see tried near his farm. That is, the reconciliation of the peasants of Les Combettes, whom ancient hatreds parted, the gathering together in a commonalty of all their patches of land, now cut up into little strips, and the creation of one great estate, whence they would derive real wealth by applying the principles of high cultivation on a large scale. And the idea which Feuillat kept back in the depths of his mind most have been that of persuading Boisgelin to let the farm enter the new association, when the first experiments should have succeeded. If Boisgelin should refuse, facts would end by compelling him to consent. In Feuillat moreover, silent man that he was, bending beneath such servitude as appeared inevitable, there was something of the nature of a patient, crafty apostle, who was resolved to gain ground by degrees, undeterred therefrom by any feeling of weariness.

He had just achieved a first success by reconciling Lenfant and Yvonnot, whose families had been quarrelling for centuries. The former having been chosen mayor of the village and the latter "adjoint," or deputy mayor, he had given them to understand that they would be the real masters if they could only agree together. Then he had slowly won them to his idea of a general agreement, by which alone the village could emerge from the wretchedness born of routine in which it vegetated, and once more find in the earth an inexhaustible source of fortune. As the works of La Crêcherie were at that time being established, he cited them as an example, spoke of their growing prosperity, and profiting by some water question which had to be settled between La Crêcherie and Les Combettes, he even ended by putting Lenfant and Yvonnot in communication with Luc. Thus it was that the village mayor and his deputy happened, that morning, to be at the works.

Luc immediately consented to what they came to ask him, and the good nature he evinced in doing so in some degree dispelled their habitual distrust.

"It's understood, messieurs," said he, "La Crêcherie will henceforth canalise all the springs captured among the rocks, and turn those which it does not employ into the Grand-Jean rivulet, which crosses the lands of your village before joining the Mionne. At little cost, if you only establish some reservoirs, you will have abundant means for watering your land and increasing its bearing qualities three times over."

Lenfant, who was short and stout, wagged his big head and reflected: "It will certainly cost too much," said he. Then Yvonnot, who was short and slim, with a dark face and bad-tempered mouth, added: "Besides, monsieur, one thing that troubles us is that this water will lead to a lot more disputes among us when we divide it. You act like a good neighbour in giving it to us, and we are much obliged to you. Only, how are we to manage so that each may have his proper share without thinking that the others are robbing him?"

Luc smiled. The question pleased him, for it would enable him to broach the subject which he had on his mind, and on account of which he had so particularly desired to see the two men. "But water which fertilises," said he, "ought to belong to everybody, just like the sun which shines and warms, and the land, too, which brings forth and nourishes. As for the best way to divide the water, why, the best is not to divide it at all. What Nature gives to all men should be left to all of them."

The two peasants understood his meaning. For a moment they remained silent, with their eyes fixed on the floor. It was Lenfant, the greater thinker of the two, who at last replied. "Yes, yes, we know. The farmer of La Guerdache spoke to us of all that. No doubt it's a good idea for folk to come to an agreement as you have done here, and put their money and land and arms and tools in common, and then share the profits. It seems certain that one would gain more and be happier in that fashion. But, all the same, there would be some risk in it, and I think that one will have to talk of it a good deal longer before all of us at Les Combettes are convinced."

"Ah! yes, that's certain," put in Yvonnot with a sudden wave of his arm. "We two, you see, are now pretty well in agreement, and are not so much opposed to such novelties. But all the others have to be gained over, and that will take a lot of doing, I warn you."

In those words lurked the peasant's distrust of all social changes affecting the conditions under which property is now held. Luc knew it well; he had expected resistance of this kind. However, he continued smiling. How heart-rending to some was the idea of having to give up one's strip of land, which from father to son one had loved for centuries, and to see it merged into the strips of others! Nevertheless all the many bitter disappointments due to that bankruptcy of the over-divided soil, which ended by filling agriculturists with despair and disgust, must help to convince them that the only possible salvation lay in union and joint effort. Luc explained that success would henceforth belong to associations, that it was necessary to operate over large tracts of land with powerful machines for ploughing, sowing, and reaping, with an abundance of manure too, chemically prepared in neighbouring factories, and with continuous waterings by which the crops would be greatly increased. The efforts of the peasant who worked alone, in isolation, were leading to famine, but prodigious plenty would ensue if the peasants of a village would only combine together so as to work upon a large scale and procure the necessary machinery, manure, and water. Extraordinary fertility would be created thereby. Two or three acres would suffice to feed two or three families. The population of France might be trebled, its soil would amply suffice to nourish it if it were cultivated logically, all the creative forces working harmoniously

　　　　　　　　　　　　　　　　　　ÉMILE ZOLA

together. And that would also mean happiness; the peasants' labour would not be one-third as painful as now; he would be liberated from all sorts of ancient servitude, that of the moneylender who preys upon him and that of the large landowner and the State, who likewise do their best to crush him.

"Oh! it's too fine!" declared Lenfant in his thoughtful way.

But Yvonnot took fire more readily. "Ah! dash it!" said he, "if that be true we should be fools not to try it."

"You see how we are situated at La Crêcherie," resumed Luc, who had been keeping a final argument in reserve. "We have hardly been three years in existence, and our business prospers, all our hands who have combined together eat meat and drink wine, and they have no debts left and no fear for the future. Question them, and visit our workshops, our homes, our common house, all that we have managed to create in so short a time. It's all the fruit of union, and you yourselves will accomplish prodigies as soon as you become united."

"Yes, yes, we've seen, we know," the two peasants answered in chorus.

This was true; before asking for Luc they had inquisitively visited La Crêcherie, appraising the wealth already acquired, feeling amazed at the sight of that happy town which was springing up so rapidly, and wondering what gain there might be for themselves if they should combine in the same manner. The force of example was gradually winning them over.

"Well, since you know, it's all simple enough," Luc gaily retorted. "We need bread; our men can't live if you don't grow the corn that's necessary. And you others need tools, spades, ploughs, machines made of the steel which we manufacture. And so the solution of the problem is simple enough—we have only to come to an understanding together—we will give you steel, you will give us corn, and we shall all live very happily. Since we are neighbours, since your land adjoins our works, and we absolutely have need of one another, is it not best to live as brothers, to combine together for the benefit of every one of us, so as to form in future but one sole family?"

Luc's good-natured way of putting the proposal made Lenfant and Yvonnot merry. Never had the desirability of reconciliation and agreement between the peasant and the industrial worker been set forth more plainly. Luc dreamt, indeed, of incorporating in his association all the secondary factories and industries which lived on it or beside it. It was sufficient that there should be a centre producing a raw material—steel—for other manufactories to swarm around. There were the Chodorge works which made nails, the Hausser works which made scythes, the Mirande works which made agricultural machinery; and there was even an old wire-drawer, one Hordoir, whose couple of hammers, worked by water power derived from a torrent, were still active in one of the gorges of the Bleuse Mountains. All of these, if they desired to live, would some day be compelled to join their brothers of La Crêcherie, apart from whom existence would prove impossible. Even the men of the building trades and those of the clothing trades— as for instance Mayor Gourier's boot-works—would be dragged into the combination, and supply houses and garments and shoes even, if in exchange they desired to have tools and bread. The future city would only come about through some such universal agreement, a community of labour.

"Well, Monsieur Luc," at last said Lenfant in his wise way, "all these matters are too big to be decided in an offhand manner. But we promise you that we will think them over and do our best to bring about a cordial agreement at Les Combettes, such as you have here."

"That is just it, Monsieur Luc," said Yvonnot, seconding his companion. "Since we have got so far as to be reconciled, Lenfant and I, we may well do all we can to get the others reconciled in the same way. Feuillat, who's a clever fellow, will help us."

Then, before going off, they once more referred to the water which Luc had promised to turn into the Grand-Jean rivulet. Everything was settled; and the young man accompanied them as far as the garden, where their children Arsène and Olympe, Eugénie and Nicolas, were waiting. They had doubtless brought the little ones in order to show them that famous Crêcherie, which the whole region was talking about. And, as it happened, the pupils of the five classes had just come into the garden to play, so that it was full of turbulent gaiety. The skirts of the girls flew about in the bright sunshine, the boys bounded hither and thither like young goats, there was laughter, and singing, and shouting, a perfect florescence of childish happiness amidst the grass and the foliage.

But Luc caught sight of Sœurette, who stood scolding somebody amidst a cluster of little heads both fair and dark. In the front rank stood Nanet, now nearly ten years old, with a gay, round, bold face under a tumbled shock of hair of the hue of ripe oats, but suggesting the fleece of a young sheep. Behind him were grouped other children from five to ten years of age, the four Bonnaires—Lucien, Antoinette, Zoé, and Séverin—and the two Bourrons—Sébastien and Marthe—all of whom, no doubt, had been detected in fault. It seemed, indeed, as if Nanet had been the leader of the guilty band, for it was he who was answering Sœurette, arguing matters with her like an obstinate urchin who would never admit himself to be in the wrong.

"What is the matter?" Luc inquired.

"Ah! it's Nanet," Sœurette replied, "he has again been to the Abyss, though it is strictly forbidden. I have just learnt that he led these others there yesterday evening; and this time they even climbed over the wall."

At the end of the Crêcherie lands, indeed, there stood a party-wall separating them from those of the Abyss. And at one corner, where Delaveau's garden was situated, there was an old door, which since all intercourse had ceased was kept strongly bolted.

But Nanet raised his voice in protest. "First of all," said he, "it isn't true that we all got over the wall. I got over by myself, and then I opened the door for the others."

Luc, who felt greatly displeased, in his turn lost his temper. "You know very well," he exclaimed, "that you have been told more than a dozen times that you are not to go there. You will end by bringing on us some serious unpleasantness, and I repeat it to all of you that it is very wrong and wicked to disobey in this fashion."

Nanet stood listening and looking with his eyes wide open. A good little fellow at bottom, but unable to appreciate the importance of his transgression, he felt moved at seeing Luc so disturbed. If he had climbed over the wall to let the others in, it was because Nise Delaveau had some playmates with her that afternoon, Paul Boisgelin, Louise Mazelle, and other amusing little *bourgeois*, and because they all wanted to play together. She was very pleasant was Nise Delaveau, according to Nanet.

"Why was it so wrong?" the boy repeated with an air of stupefaction. "We didn't do harm to anybody, we all amused ourselves together."

Then he named the children who had been present, and gave a truthful account of what they had done. They had only played as was allowable; they had not broken any plants, nor had they thrown the stones lying in the paths on to the flower-beds.

"Nise gets on very well with us," he said in conclusion. "She likes me, she told me so, and I like her since we've played together."

Luc forced back a smile. But in his heart a vision was arising—he saw the children of the two rival classes scaling walls to fraternise, and play, and laugh together, in spite of all the hatred and warfare which separated their fathers. Would the peacefulness of the future community flower forth in them?

"It is quite possible," said he, "that Nise may be charming, and that you may agree very well together; only it is understood that she is to remain on her land and you on ours, in order that there may be no complaints."

Then Sœurette, won over by all the charm of that innocent childhood, looked at him with eyes so suggestive of forgiveness that he added more gently: "Well, you must not do it again, little ones, because you might bring some real worry on us."

When Lenfant and Yvonnot had finally taken leave, carrying off their children, who, after mingling in the play of the others, departed very regretfully, Luc, whose daily visit was now finished, thought of going home again. But he suddenly remembered that he had promised to see Josine, and so he resolved to call on her. His morning had hitherto been a good one, and by-and-by he would be able to return home with his heart full of hope.

The house occupied by Ragu and Josine, one of the first that had been built, stood near the park of La Crêcherie, between the houses occupied by the Bonnaires and the Bourrons. Luc was crossing the road when, at some distance, at a corner of the foot pavement, he saw a small group of women, who appeared to be busily chattering. And he soon recognised Madame Bonnaire and Madame Bourron, who were apparently giving some information to Madame Fauchard, she having come that morning, like her husband, to see if the new works were indeed such a Tom Tiddler's ground as some folk asserted. Judging by the sharp voice and harsh gestures of Madame Bonnaire—La Toupe as folks called her—it seemed evident that she was not painting a very seductive picture of the new concern. Cross-grained as she was, she could be happy nowhere, but invariably spent her time in spoiling her own life and that of others. At the very beginning she had seemed pleased to find her husband obtaining work at La Crêcherie, but after dreaming of immediately securing a big share of the profits, she was now enraged at having to wait for it, perhaps for a considerable time to come. Her great grievance, however, was that she could not even succeed in buying herself a watch, an article of which she had coveted the possession for several years already. Quite a contrast to her was Babette Bourron, who was ever in a state of delight, and did not cease extolling the advantages of her new home, her keenest satisfaction arising perhaps from the fact that her husband no longer came home drunk with Ragu. Between the two of them—La Toupe and La Bourron—Madame Fauchard, looking more emaciated, unlucky, and mournful than ever, remained in a state of some perplexity, but she was naturally inclined to favour the pessimism of La Toupe, the more particularly as she was convinced that there was no more joy for her in this life.

The sight of La Toupe and La Fauchard thus distressfully chattering was very disagreeable to Luc. It robbed him of his good humour, the more especially as he knew what a disturbance in the future organisation of work, peace, and justice was threatened by women. He felt that they were all-powerful, and it was by and for them that he would have liked to found his city. Thus his courage often failed him when he met such as were evil, hostile, or simply indifferent—women who, instead of proving a help such as he awaited, might become an obstacle, a destructive force indeed by which his labour might be annihilated. However, he passed the gossips, lifting his hat as he did so, and they suddenly became silent and anxious, as if he had caught them doing wrong.

When he entered Ragu's house he perceived Josine seated beside a window. She had been sewing, but her work had fallen in her lap and, gazing far away, she was now plunged in so deep a reverie that she did not even hear him enter. For a moment he paused and looked at her. She was no longer the wretched girl that he had known scouring the pavements, dying of starvation, badly clad, with a pinched and woeful face under a wild tangle of hair. She was one-and-twenty now, and looked charming in her simple gown of blue linen stuff, her figure supple and slim but by no means thin. And her beautiful hair, light as silk, seemed like a delicate florescence above her rather long face with its laughing blue eyes and its little mouth as fresh as a rosebud. She seemed also to be seated in a fitting frame-work, in that gay and clean little parlour furnished with varnished deal—the room that she most preferred in the little house which she had entered so happily, and in tidying and embellishing which she had taken so much pride and pleasure for three years past.

But of what could Josine now be dreaming, with so sorrowful an expression on her pale face? When Bonnaire had prevailed on Ragu to follow him and join the others at La Crêcherie she had deemed herself saved from all future trials. Thenceforward she would have a nice little home, her daily bread would be assured, and Ragu himself, having no further worries with respect to work, would amend his ways. Luck apparently had not failed her: Ragu had even married her at the express desire of Sœurette; though truth to tell she, Josine, was by no means so pleased with the idea of that marriage as she would have been at the time when she had first met Ragu. Indeed, she had only consented to it after consulting Luc, who for her remained both God and master. And deep in her being there lurked a rapturous feeling born of the momentary hesitation which she had divined in him before he signified his approval. But after all was not that the best, and indeed the only possible, solution? She could not do otherwise than marry Ragu since he was willing. Luc had to appear pleased for her sake, retaining for her the same affection after her marriage as before it, and looking at her with a smile at each of their meetings, as if to ask her whether she were happy. But at those times she often felt her poor heart succumbing to despair, melting with an unsatisfied craving for true affection.

As if some breath had warned her, Josine started and shivered slightly amidst her dolorous reverie. Then turning round she recognised Luc smiling at her in a gentle and anxious way.

"My dear child," said he, "I've come because Ragu asserts that you are very badly lodged in this house, exposed to all the winds from the plain, which, it seems, have broken three panes of your bedroom window."

She listened, looking surprised and confused, at a loss indeed how to contradict her husband and avoid telling a lie.

"Yes, there are some panes broken, Monsieur Luc," said she, "but I'm not sure whether it was the wind that did it. True enough, when it blows from the plain, we get our full share of it."

Her voice trembled as she spoke, and she was unable to restrain two big tears which rolled down her cheeks. As a matter of fact the windows had been broken by Ragu the previous evening when, in a fit of passion, he had wanted to throw everything out of doors.

"What, Josine! Are you crying? What is the matter? Come, tell me all about it. You know that I am your friend," said Luc eagerly.

He had seated himself beside her, full of emotion, sharing her distress. But she had already wiped her tears away. "No, no, it is nothing," said she; "I beg your pardon, but you've come at a bad moment, and found me unreasonable and worrying."

Struggle as she might, however, he at last wrung a full confession from her. Ragu did not become acclimatised to that sphere of order, peacefulness, and slow and continuous effort towards a better life. He seemed to suffer from nostalgia, to regret the misery and the suffering of that wage-system amidst which he had lived, growling against the masters yet habituated to slavery, and consoling himself for it in the wine shops, where he intoxicated himself and poured forth rebellious but powerless words. He regretted the black and dirty workshops, the covert warfare waged with one's superiors, the noisy freaks with comrades, all the abominable days fraught with hatred, which one finished up by beating one's wife and children when one at last returned home. And after beginning with jests he was ending with accusations, calling La Crêcherie a big barracks, a prison where no liberty was left one, not even that of drinking a glass too many if one felt so inclined. Besides, so far, one earned there no more than one had earned at the Abyss; and there were all sorts of worries, anxiety as to whether things were going well, and whether there might be no money for one to take when the time came round for profit-sharing. For instance, during the last two months some very bad rumours had been spreading; it was said that they would all have to tighten their waistbands that year, as a great deal of money had been expended in buying new machinery. Then again the co-operative stores often worked very badly: at times potatoes were sent you when you had asked for paraffin oil; or else you were forgotten and had to return three times to the distribution office before you could get served. For these various reasons Ragu had begun to deride the place, and grow wrathful with it, calling it a dirty hole whence he hoped to "sling his hook," as soon as might be possible.

Painful silence fell between Josine and Luc. The young man had become gloomy, for there was some truth beneath all those recriminations. It was the inevitable grating of new machinery at the first stage of its work. The rumours which were afloat respecting the difficulties of the current year affected Luc particularly, since he did indeed fear that he might be obliged to ask the men to make a few sacrifices in order to prevent the prosperity of the establishment from being compromised.

"And Bourron says 'ditto' to Ragu, does he not?" Luc inquired of Josine. "But you have never heard Bonnaire complain, have you?"

Josine was shaking her head, by way of answering no, when, through the open window, the breeze wafted the voices of the three women who had remained on the foot-pavement. La Toupe was again forgetting herself, carried away by her incessant desire to bark and bite. If Bonnaire remained silent, like a thoughtful man whose sensible mind admitted the necessity of an experiment of considerable duration, that wife of his sufficed to gather together all the backbiters of the rising town. As Luc glanced out of the window he saw her again frightening La Fauchard by predicting the approaching ruin of La Crêcherie.

"And so, Josine," he slowly resumed, "you are not happy?"

She again tried to protest: "Oh! Monsieur Luc, why should I not be happy, when you have done so much for me?"

But her strength failed her, and again two big tears appeared in her eyes and rolled down her cheeks.

"You see very well, Josine, you are not happy," repeated the young man.

"I am not happy, it's true, Monsieur Luc," she at last answered, "only you can do nothing in the matter. It is no fault of yours. You have been a Providence for me, and what can one do if there's nothing that can change Ragu's heart? He is becoming quite malicious again; he can no longer abide Nanet; he nearly broke everything here yesterday evening, and he struck me, because the child, so he said, answered him improperly. But leave me, Monsieur Luc—those are things which only concern me; at all events I promise you that I'll worry as little as I can."

Sobs broke upon her trembling voice, which was scarcely audible. And he, powerless as he was, experienced increasing sadness. A shadow was cast over the whole of his happy morning; he was chilled by doubt and despair—he usually so brave, whose strength lay so much in joyous hope. Although things obeyed him, although material success seemed assured, was he to find himself powerless to change men and develop divine love, the fruitful flower of kindliness and solidarity, in their hearts? If men should remain in a state of hatred and violence his work would never be accomplished. Yet how was he to awaken them to affection, how was he to teach them happiness? That dear Josine, whom he had sought in the very depths, whom he had saved from such awful misery, she to him seemed the very image of his work. That work would not really exist until she was happy. She was woman, wretched woman, the slave, the beast of burden and the toy, that he had dreamt of saving. And if she was still and ever unhappy, nothing substantial could have been founded, everything still remained to be done. Amidst his grief Luc foresaw many dolorous days; a keen perception came to him of the fact that a terrible struggle was about to open between the past and the future, and that he himself would shed in it both tears and blood.

"Do not cry, Josine," said he; "be brave, and I promise you that you shall be happy, for you must be happy in order that everybody may be so."

He spoke so gently that she smiled.

"Oh! I am brave, Monsieur Luc," she answered; "I know very well that you won't forsake me, and that you will end by conquering, since you are so full of kindness and courage. I will wait, I promise you, even if I have to wait all my life."

It was like an engagement, an exchange of promises instinct with hope in coming happiness. Luc rose, and as he stood there clasping both her hands he could feel the pressure of her own. And that was the only token of affection between them, the union of their hands for a few brief seconds. Ah! what a simple life of peacefulness and joy might have been lived in that little parlour, so cheerful and so clean with its furniture of varnished deal!

"*Au revoir*, Josine."

"*Au revoir*, Monsieur Luc."

Then Luc turned his steps homeward. And he was following the terrace, below which ran the road to Les Combettes, when a final encounter made him pause for a moment. He had just caught sight of Monsieur Jérôme, who, in his bath-chair, propelled by a man-servant, was skirting the Crêcherie lands. The sight of the old man recalled to Luc other frequent chance meetings with him, now here, now there, and particularly the first meeting of all, when he had seen him passing the Abyss and gazing with his clear eyes at the smoky and noisy pile where he had formerly founded the fortune of the Quignons. In like fashion he was now passing La Crêcherie and gazing at its new buildings, so gay in the sunlight, with those same clear and seemingly empty eyes of his. Why had he signed to his servant to bring him so far?—was he making a complete round of the place in order to examine everything? What did he think of it then, what comparisons did he wish to establish? Perhaps, after all, this was merely some chance promenade, some mere caprice on the part of a poor old man who had lapsed into second childhood. However, whilst the servant slackened his pace, Monsieur Jérôme, grave and impassive, raised his broad and regular countenance, on either side of which fell his long white hair, and seemingly scrutinised everything, letting neither a wall nor a chimney pass without giving it a glance, as if indeed he wished to thoroughly understand that new town now springing up beside the establishment which he had formerly created.

But a fresh incident occurred, and Luc's emotion increased. Another old man, also infirm, but still able to drag himself about on his swollen legs, was coming slowly along the road in the direction of the bath-chair.

It was Daddy Lunot, corpulent, pale, and flabby, whom the Bonnaires had kept with them, and who in sunny weather took short walks past the works. At first, no doubt, he failed to recognise Monsieur Jérôme, for his sight was weak. Then, however, he started, and drew back close to the wall as if the road were not wide enough for two, and, raising his straw hat, he bent double, bowed profoundly. It was to the Qurignons' ancestor, to the master and founder, that the eldest of the Ragus, wage-earner and father of wage-earners, thus rendered homage. Years—and behind him centuries—of toil, suffering, and poverty, humbled themselves in that trembling salute. The master might be stricken, but the former slave, in whose blood coursed the cowardice of ancient servitude, became disturbed and bowed as he passed. And Monsieur Jérôme did not even see him, but passed on, staring like a stupefied idol, his gaze still and ever fixed on the new workshops of La Crêcherie, which perhaps he likewise failed to see.

Luc shuddered. What a past there was to be destroyed, what evil, deadly tares there were to pluck away! He looked at his town scarce rising from the ground, and understood what trouble, what obstacles it would encounter in growing and prospering. Love alone, and woman, and child could end by achieving victory.

II

During the four years that La Crêcherie had been established covert hatred of Luc had been rising from Beauclair. At first there had only been so much hostile astonishment accompanied by malicious pleasantries, but since folk had been affected in their interests anger had arisen, with a furious desire to resist that public enemy by all possible weapons.

It was more particularly among the petty traders, the retail shopkeepers, that anxiety at first displayed itself. The co-operative stores of La Crêcherie, which had been regarded with derision when first inaugurated, were now proving successful, counting among their customers not only the factory hands, but also all the inhabitants who adhered to them. As may be imagined, the old purveyors were thrown into great emotion by that terrible competition, that new tariff which in many instances meant a reduction of one third on former prices. Ruin would soon ensue if that wretched Luc were to prevail with those disastrous ideas of his, tending to a more just apportionment of wealth, and aiming in the first instance at enabling the humble ones of the world to live more comfortably and cheaply. The butchers, the grocers, the bakers, the wine dealers, would all have to put up their shutters if people were to succeed in doing without them. Thus the tradespeople shouted in chorus that it was abominable. To them society did indeed seem to be cracking and collapsing now that they could no longer levy the profits of parasites, and thereby increase the misery of the poor.

The most affected of all, however, were the Laboques, those ironmongers who, after beginning life as market hawkers, had ended by establishing something like a huge bazaar at the corner of the Rue de Brias and the Place de la Mairie. The prices for the iron of commerce had fallen considerably throughout the district since La Crêcherie had been turning out large quantities; and the worst was that with the co-operative movement now gaining upon the smaller works of the neighbourhood, a time seemed coming when consumers would procure direct at the co-operative stores, without passing through the clutches of the Laboques, such articles as Chodorge's nails, Hausser's scythes and sickles, and Mirande's agricultural appliances and tools. Apart from their output of raw iron and steel the Crêcherie stores were already supplying several of those articles, and thus the amount of business transacted by the

Laboques became smaller every day. Their rage therefore knew no end; they were exasperated by what they termed that "debasement of prices," and regarded themselves as robbed, simply because their useless cogwheels were no longer being allowed to consume energy and wealth with profit for nobody save themselves. Their house had thus naturally become a centre of hostility, opposition, and hatred, in which Luc's name was never mentioned otherwise than with execration. There met Dacheux the butcher, stammering forth his reactionary rage, and Caffiaux the grocer and wine-seller, who, although reeking of rancour, was of a colder temperament and weighed his own interests carefully. Even the beautiful Madame Mitaine, the baker's wife, though inclined to agreement, came at times and lamented with the others the loss of a few of her customers.

"Do you know," Laboque cried, "that this Monsieur Luc, as people call him, has at bottom only one idea, that of destroying trade? Yes, he boasts of it, he shouts the monstrous words aloud: 'Trade is robbery.' For him we are all robbers, and we've got to disappear! It was to sweep us away that he established La Crêcherie."

Dacheux listened with dilated eyes, and all his blood rushing to his face. "Then how will one manage to eat and clothe oneself, and all the rest?" he asked.

"Well, he says that the consumer will apply direct to the producer."

"And the money?" the butcher asked.

"Money? Why, he suppresses that too! There's to be no more money. Isn't it stupid, eh? As if people could live without money!"

At this Dacheux almost choked with fury. "No more trade! no more money! Why, he wants to destroy everything. Isn't there a prison for such a bandit? He'll ruin Beauclair if we don't put a stop to it!"

But Caffiaux was gravely wagging his head. "He says a good many more things. He says first of all that everybody ought to work—he wants to turn the world into a perfect stone-yard, where there'll be guards with staves to see that everybody does his task. He says, too, that there ought to be neither rich nor poor; according to him one will be no richer when one's born than when one dies; one will eat according to what one earns, neither more nor less, too, than one's neighbour; and one won't even have the right to save up money."

"Well, but what about inheritances?" put in Dacheux.

"There will be no more inheritances."

"What! no more inheritances? I shan't be able to leave my daughter

ÉMILE ZOLA

my own money? Thunder! that is coming it too strong!" And thereupon the butcher banged his fist on the table with such violence that it shook.

"He says, too," continued Caffiaux, "that there will be no more authorities of any kind, no government, no gendarmes, no judges, no prisons. Each will live as he pleases, eat and sleep as he fancies. He says also that machinery will end by doing all the work, and that the workmen will simply have to drive it. It is to be the earthly paradise, because there will be no more fighting, no more armies, and no more wars. And he says, moreover, that when men and women love one another they will remain together as long as they please and then bid each other good-bye in a friendly fashion, to take up with others later on if they are so inclined. And as for children, the community will take charge of them, bring them up in a heap as chance may have it, without any need of a mother's or a father's attentions."

Beautiful Madame Mitaine, who hitherto had remained silent, now began to protest: "Oh, the poor little ones!" said she. "I hope that each mother will at least have the right to bring up her own. It's all very well for the children who are forsaken by their parents to be brought up pell-mell by strangers as in orphan asylums. But really it seems to me that what you have been telling us is hardly proper."

"Say at once that it's filthy!" roared Dacheux, who was beside himself. "Why, their famous future society will simply be a house of ill-fame!"

Then Laboque, who did not lose sight of his threatened interests, concluded: "That Monsieur Luc is mad. We cannot let him ruin and dishonour Beauclair in this fashion! We shall have to agree together and take steps to stop it all."

The anger increased, however, and there was a universal explosion when Beauclair learnt that the infectious disease of La Crêcherie was spreading to the neighbouring village of Les Combettes. Stupefaction was manifested, condemnation was passed on all sides—that Monsieur Luc was now debauching, poisoning the peasantry! After reconciling the four hundred inhabitants of the village, Lenfant, the mayor, assisted by his deputy, Yvonnot, had induced them to put their land in common by virtue of a deed of association similar to that which linked capital, talent, and work together at La Crêcherie. Henceforth there would be but one large estate, in such wise that machinery might be used, that manure might be applied on a large scale, and high cultivation practised with a view to increasing the crops tenfold and reaping large profits, which would be shared by one and all. Moreover, the two associations, that of La Crêcherie and that of Les Combettes, would mutually consolidate each other; the peasants would supply the workmen with bread, and the workmen would supply the peasants with tools and manufactured articles necessary for life, in such a way that there would be a conjunction of two inimical classes, tending by degrees to fusion, and forming the embryo of a brotherly people. Assuredly the old world would come to an end if Socialism should win over the peasantry, the innumerable toilers of the country districts, who had hitherto been regarded as the ramparts of egotistical ownership, preferring to die of unremunerative labour on their strips of land rather than part with them. The shock of this change was felt throughout Beauclair, and a shudder passed like a warning of the coming catastrophe.

Again the Laboques were the first to be affected. They lost the custom of Les Combettes. They no longer saw Lenfant nor any of the others come to buy spades, ploughs, tools, and utensils. On the last occasion when Lenfant called he haggled and finally bought nothing, plainly declaring to them that he would gain thirty per cent, by no longer dealing with them, since they were compelled to levy such a profit on articles which they themselves procured at neighbouring works. Henceforth all the folk of Les Combettes addressed themselves direct to La Crêcherie, adhering to the co-operative stores there, which grew and grew in importance. And then terror set in among all the petty retailers of Beauclair.

"One must act, one must act!" Laboque repeated with growing violence each time that Dacheux and Caffiaux came to see him. "If we wait till that madman has infected the whole region with his monstrous doctrines, we shall be too late."

"But what can be done?" Caffiaux prudently inquired.

Dacheux for his part favoured brutal slaughter. "One might wait for him one evening at a street corner and treat him to one of those hidings which give a man food for reflection."

But Laboque, puny and cunning, dreamt of some safer means of killing his man. "No, no, the whole town is rising against him, and we must wait for an opportunity when we shall have the whole town on our side."

Such an opportunity did indeed arise. For centuries past old Beauclair had been traversed by a filthy rivulet, a kind of open drain, which was called the Clouque. It was not known whence it came; it seemed to flow up from under some antique hovels at the opening of the Brias gorges, and according to the common opinion it was one of those mountain torrents whose sources remain unknown. Some very old inhabitants remembered having seen it in full flood at certain periods. But for long years already it had supplied very little water, which various industries contaminated. The housewives dwelling beside it had even ended by using it as a natural sink into which they emptied all sorts of slops, in such wise that it carried with it much of the filth of the poor district, and in summer sent forth an abominable stench. At one moment there had been serious fears of an epidemic, and the municipal council, at the mayor's initiative, had debated whether it should not be covered over. But the expense seemed too great, so the matter was shelved and the Clouque quietly continued perfuming and contaminating the neighbourhood. All at once, however, it quite ceased to flow, dried up apparently, leaving only a hard rocky bed in which there was no longer a single drop of water. As by the touch of some magician's wand Beauclair was rid of that source of infection, to which all the bad fevers of the district had been attributed. And all that remained was a feeling of curiosity as to whither the torrent might have betaken itself.

At first there were only some vague rumours on the subject. Then more precise statements were made, and it became certain that it was Monsieur Luc who had begun to divert the torrent from its usual course by capturing the springs on the slopes of the Bleuse Mountains for the needs of La Crêcherie, whose health and prosperity came largely from its abundant supply of beautiful, clear water. But the climax had come, all the water of the torrent being diverted by Luc, when it had occurred to him to give the overplus of his reservoirs to the peasants of Les Combettes, in that way founding their fortune, and bringing about their happy association; for it was that beneficent water, flowing on for one and all, that had first united them together. Before long proofs became plentiful, the water which had disappeared from the Clouque was streaming along the Grand-Jean, and turned to intelligent use, was becoming wealth instead of filth and death. Then rancour and rage arose and grew against that man Luc, who disposed so lightly of what did not belong to him. Why had he stolen the torrent? Why did he keep it and give it to his creatures? It was not right that people should in that way take the water of a town, a stream which had always flowed there, which people were accustomed to see, and which, whatever might be said to the contrary, had rendered great services. The meagre streamlet, transporting filthy detritus, exhaling pestilence and killing people, was forgotten. Folk talked no more of burying it, each recounted what great benefit he or she had derived from it, for watering, for washing, and for the daily needs of life. Such a theft could not be tolerated; it was absolutely necessary that La Crêcherie should restore the Clouque, that filthy drain which had poisoned the town.

Naturally enough it was Laboque who shouted the loudest. He paid an official visit to Gourier, the mayor, to inquire what decision he intended to propose to the Municipal Council under such grave circumstances. He, Laboque, claimed to be particularly injured, for the Clouque had flowed behind his house, at the end of his little garden; and he alleged that he had derived considerable advantages therefrom. If he had drawn up a protest and sought to collect signatures he would undoubtedly have obtained those of all the inhabitants of his district. But, in his opinion, the town itself ought to take the affair in hand, and commence an action against La Crêcherie, claiming the restitution of the torrent, and damages for the temporary loss of it. Gourier listened, and in spite of his own hatred against Luc, contented himself with nodding approval. Finally he declared that he must have a few days to reflect, look into the matter, and consult those around him. He fully understood that Laboque was urging the town to take up the matter, in order that he might not have to do so himself. And no doubt Sub-Prefect Châtelard, whom all complications terrified and with whom Gourier shut himself up for a couple of hours, was able to convince him that it was always wise to let others embark in law-suits; for when the mayor sent for the ironmonger again, it was only to explain to him at great length that an action started by the town would drag on and lead to nothing serious, whereas one brought by a private individual would prove far more disastrous for La Crêcherie, particularly if after a first condemnation other private individuals followed suit, prolonging matters indefinitely.

A few days later Laboque issued a writ and claimed five and twenty thousand francs damages. Taking as a pretext a kind of treat offered by his son and daughter, Auguste and Eulalie, to their young friends, Honorine Caffiaux, Évariste Mitaine, and Julienne Dacheux, Laboque held quite a meeting at his house. The young folk were now fast growing up—Auguste was sixteen and Eulalie nine; Évariste, now in his fourteenth year, was already becoming serious, and Honorine, nineteen, and thus of an age to marry, showed herself quite motherly towards little Julienne, who was but eight years old, and therefore the youngest of the party. The young people, it should be said, at once installed themselves in the strip of garden, where they played and laughed merrily, for their consciences were clear and gay, and they knew nothing of hatred and anger such as consumed their parents.

"We hold him at last!" said Laboque to his friends. "Monsieur Gourier told me that if we carried things to a finish we should ruin the works! Let us admit that the court only awards me ten thousand francs. Well, there are a hundred of you who can all bring similar actions, so he would have to dip in his pockets for a million! And that is not all—he will have to give us back the torrent and demolish the works he raised. That will deprive him of that fine fresh water which he is so proud of. Ah! my friends, what a good business!"

They all grew excited and triumphant at the idea of ruining the works of La Crêcherie and lowering that fellow Luc, that madman who wished to destroy trade, inheritances, money—in a word all the most venerable foundations of human society. Caffiaux alone reflected.

"I should have preferred to see an action brought by the town," said he. "Whenever it's a question of fighting the gentlefolk always want others to do so. Where are the hundred people who will issue writs against La Crêcherie?"

At this Dacheux exploded: "Ah! I would willingly join in, if my house were not on the other side of the street. And even as things stand I shall see if I cannot do something, for the Clouque passes at the end of my mother-in-law's yard. Yes, thunder! I must make one of you."

"But to begin," resumed Laboque, "there is Madame Mitaine, who is circumstanced exactly as I am, and whose house suffers like mine since the stream has ceased to flow. You will issue a writ, won't you, Madame Mitaine?"

He had craftily invited her that day with the express intention of compelling her to enter into a formal agreement. He knew her to be desirous of living in peace herself and of respecting the peace of others. Nevertheless he hoped to win her over.

She at first began to laugh. "Oh! as for any harm done to my house by the disappearance of the Clouque, no, no, neighbour; the truth is that I had given orders that not a drop of that bad water was ever to be used, for I feared I might render my customers ill. It was so dirty and it smelt so bad that whenever it is given back to us we shall have to spend the necessary money to get rid of it by making it pass underground as there was formerly a question of doing."

Laboque pretended that he did not hear this. "At all events, Madame Mitaine," said he, "you are with us, your interests are the same as ours, and if I win my suit you will act with all the other river-side people, relying on the *chose jugée*, won't you?"

"We'll see, we'll see," replied the baker's beautiful wife, becoming grave. "I'm willing enough to be on the side of justice, if it is just."

Laboque had to rest content with that conditional promise. Besides, his state of excitement and rancour deprived him of all sense; he thought that victory was already won, and that he was about to crush all those socialist follies which in four years had diminished his sales by one half. It was society that he avenged by banging his fist on the table in company with Dacheux, whilst the prudent Caffiaux, before definitely committing himself, waited to see which side would triumph.

Beauclair was quite upset when it heard of Laboque's writ, and his demand for an indemnity of twenty-five thousand francs. This was indeed an ultimatum, a declaration of war. From that moment there was a rallying-point around which all the scattered hatreds grouped themselves into an army which pronounced itself vigorously against Luc and his work, that diabolical factory, where the ruin of ancient and respectable society was being forged. All Beauclair ended by belonging to this army, the injured tradesmen drew their customers together, and all the gentlefolk joined, since the new ideas quite terrified them. Indeed, there was not a petty *rentier* who did not feel himself threatened by some frightful cataclysm, in which his own narrow egotistical life would collapse. The women, too, were indignant and disgusted now that La Crêcherie was depicted to them as a huge disorderly house, the triumph of which, with its doctrine of free love, would place them at any man's mercy. Even the workmen, even the starving poor, became anxious, and began to curse the man who dreamt of saving them, but whom they accused of aggravating their misery by increasing the pitilessness of their employers and the wealthy. What distracted Beauclair more than all else, however, was a violent campaign which the local newspaper, the little sheet published by Lebleu the printer, started against Luc. This journal now appeared twice a week, and Captain Jollivet was suspected of being the author of the articles whose virulence was creating such a sensation. The attack, it should be said, reduced itself to a cannonade of lies and errors, all the muddy trash which is cast at Socialism by way of caricaturing its intentions and besmirching its ideal. It was, however, certain that such tactics would prove successful with poor ignorant brains, and it was curious to see how greatly the indignation spread, uniting against the disturber of the public peace all the old inimical classes, which were furious at being disturbed in their ancient cesspool by a pretended desire to reconcile them and lead them to the just, happy, and healthy city of the future.

Two days before Laboque's action was heard in the civil court of Beauclair, the Delaveaus gave a grand lunch, with the secret object of enabling their friends to meet and arrive at an agreement prior to the battle. The Boisgelins naturally were invited, and so were Mayor Gourier, Sub-Prefect Châtelard, Judge Gaume, with his son-in-law Captain Jollivet, and finally Abbé Marle. The ladies of the various families also attended, in order that the meeting might retain all the semblance of a private pleasure party.

Châtelard that day, according to his wont, called on the mayor at half-past eleven to fetch him and his wife, the ever-beautiful Léonore. Ever since the success of La Crêcherie Gourier had been living in anxiety. He had divined that a quiver was passing through the hundreds of hands that he employed at his large boot-works in the Rue de Brias. The men were evidently influenced by the new ideas, and inclined to combine together. And he asked himself if it would not be better to yield, to help on such combination himself, for he would be ruined by it if he did not contrive to belong to it. This, however, was a worry which he kept secret, for there was another which filled him with great rancour, and made him Luc's personal enemy. His son, indeed, that tall young fellow Achille, so independent in his ways, had broken off all connection with his parents and sought employment at La Crêcherie, where he found himself near Ma-Bleue, his sweetheart of the starry nights. Gourier had forbidden any mention of that ungrateful son, who had deserted the *bourgeoisie* to join the enemies of social security. But although the mayor was unwilling to say it, his son's departure had aggravated his secret uncertainty, and brought him a covert fear that he might some day be forced to imitate the youth's example.

"Well," said he to Châtelard, as soon as he saw the latter enter, "that lawsuit is at hand now. Laboque has been to see me again, as he wanted some certificates. He is still of opinion that the town ought to intervene, and it is really difficult to refuse him a helping hand after egging him on as we did."

The sub-prefect contented himself with smiling. "No, no, my friend," he answered, "believe me, don't involve the town in it. You were sensible enough to yield to my reasoning, you refused to take proceedings, and you allowed that terrible Laboque, who thirsts for vengeance and massacre, to act by himself. That was fitting, and, I beg you, persevere in that course, remain simply a spectator; there will always be time to profit by Laboque's victory if he should be victorious. Ah! my friend, if you only knew what advantages one derives by meddling in nothing!"

Then by a gesture he expressed all that he had in his mind, the peace that he enjoyed in that sub-prefecture of his since he allowed himself to be forgotten there. Things were going from bad to worse in Paris, the central authorities were collapsing a little more each day, and the time was near when *bourgeoise* society would either crumble to pieces or be swept away by a revolution. He, like a sceptical philosopher, only asked that he might endure till then, and finish his life happily in the warm little nest which he had chosen. His whole policy therefore consisted in letting things go, in meddling with them as little as possible; and he was convinced that the Government, amidst the difficulties of its last days, was extremely grateful to him for abandoning the beast to its death without creating any further worries. A sub-prefect whom one never heard of, who by his intelligence had effaced Beauclair from the number of governmental cares, was indeed a precious functionary. Thus Châtelard got on extremely well; his superiors only remembered him to cover him with praises, whilst he quietly finished burying the old social system, spending the autumn of his own days at the feet of the beautiful Léonore.

"You hear, my friend," he continued, "don't compromise yourself, for in such times as ours one never knows what may happen on the morrow. One must be prepared for everything, and the best course therefore is to include oneself with nothing. Let the others run on ahead and take all the risk of getting their bones broken. You will see very well afterwards what you ought to do."

However, Léonore now came into the room, gowned in light silk. Since she had passed her fortieth year she had been looking younger than ever, with her blonde majestic beauty and her candid eyes. Châtelard, as gallant now as on the very first day, took her hand and kissed it, whilst the husband with an air of relief glanced at the pair affectionately.

"Ah! you are ready," said he. "We will start then—eh, Châtelard? And be easy, I am prudent, and have no desire to thrust myself into any turmoil, which would destroy our peace and quietness. But by-and-by, at Delaveau's, you know, it will be necessary to say like the others."

At that same hour Judge Gaume was waiting at home for his daughter Lucile and his son-in-law Jollivet, who were to fetch him in order that they might all repair to the lunch together. During the last four years the judge had greatly aged. He seemed to have become yet more severe, and sadder; and he carried strict attention to the letter of the law to the point of mania, drawing up the preambles of his judgments with increasing minuteness of detail. It was said that he had been heard sobbing on certain evenings, as if he felt everything connected with his life giving way, even that human justice to which he clung so despairingly as to a last piece of wreckage which might save him from sinking. Amidst his dolorous remembrance of the tragedy which weighed upon his life—his wife's betrayal and violent death—he must above all else have suffered at seeing that drama begin afresh with his daughter Lucile, of whom he was so fond, and who was so virginal of countenance, and so strikingly like her mother. She in her turn was now deceiving her husband. Indeed, she had not been married six months to Captain Jollivet before she had taken a lover, a solicitor's petty clerk, a tall fair youth with blue girlish eyes, younger than herself. The judge having surprised the intrigue, suffered from it as if it were a renewal of that betrayal which had left an ever-bleeding wound in his heart. He recoiled from a painful explanation, which would have brought him perchance a repetition of the awful day when his wife had killed herself before his eyes after confessing her fault. But how abominable was that world in which all that he had loved had betrayed and failed him! And how could one believe in any human justice when it was the most beautiful and the best who made one suffer so cruelly!

Thoughtful and morose, Judge Gaume was seated in his private room, where he had just finished reading the "Journal de Beauclair," when the Captain and Lucile made their appearance. The violent article against La Crêcherie which he had just read seemed to him foolish, clumsy, and vulgar. And he quietly expressed his opinion to that effect.

"It is not you, I hope, my good Jollivet, who write such articles, as is rumoured. No good purpose is served by insulting one's adversaries," he said.

The Captain made a gesture of embarrassment: "Oh, write!" he retorted, "you know very well that I don't write, it is not to my taste. But it's true that I give Lebleu some ideas, some notes, you know, on scraps of paper, and he gets somebody or other to write articles based on them." Then, as the judge still pursed his lips disappprovingly, the captain went on: "What else can one do? One fights with such weapons as one has. If those cursed Madagascar fevers had not compelled me to send in my papers, I should have fallen sabre and not pen in hand on those idealogues who are demolishing everything with their criminal utopian schemes. Ah! yes indeed, it would relieve me to be able to bleed a dozen of them!"

Lucile, short and *mignonne*, had hitherto remained silent, with her usual keen enigmatical smile upon her lips. But now she turned so plainly ironical a glance upon her husband, that great man with the victorious moustaches, that the judge easily detected in it all the merry disdain she felt for a swashbuckler whom her little hands toyed with as a cat may toy with a mouse.

"Oh, Charles!" said she, "don't be wicked, don't say things that frighten me!"

But just then she met her father's glance, and feared lest her true feelings should be divined; so putting on her candid, virginal air again, she added: "Isn't it wrong of Charles to get so heated, father dear? We ought to live quietly in our little corner."

But Gaume detected that she was still jeering. "It is all very sad and very cruel," said he by way of conclusion, virtually speaking to himself. "What can one decide, what can one do when all deceive and devour one another?"

He rose painfully, and took his hat and gloves in order to go to Delaveau's. Then in spite of everything, when once he was in the street, and Lucile—of whom he was so fond, whatever the sufferings she caused him—took hold of his arm, he enjoyed a moment of delightful forgetfulness as after a lovers' quarrel.

Meantime, when noon struck at the Abyss, Delaveau joined Fernande in the little *salon* opening into the dining-room of the pavilion built by the Qurignons, which was now the home of the manager of the works. It was a rather small dwelling; for, apart from the dining and drawing rooms and the domestic offices, the ground floor only contained one other apartment, which Delaveau had made his private room, and which communicated by a wooden gallery with the general offices of the works. Then on the first and second floors were some bed-rooms. Since a young woman passionately fond of luxury had been living in the house, carpets and hangings had imparted to the old floors and dark walls some little of the splendour that she dreamt of.

Boisgelin was the first guest to arrive, and came unaccompanied.

"What!" exclaimed Fernande, as if greatly distressed, "is not Suzanne with you?"

"She begs you to excuse her," Boisgelin replied in very correct fashion. "She woke up this morning with a sick headache, and has been unable to leave her room."

Each time that there was any question of going to the Abyss matters took this course—Suzanne found some pretext for avoiding such an aggravation of her grief, and only Delaveau, in his blindness, failed to understand the truth.

Moreover, Boisgelin immediately changed the conversation. "Ah! so here we are on the eve of the famous law-suit," said he. "It is as good as settled, eh? La Crêcherie will be condemned!"

Delaveau shrugged his broad shoulders. "What does it matter to us whether it be condemned or not?" he replied. "It does us harm, no doubt, by lowering the price of metal, but we don't compete in manufactured articles, and there is nothing very serious as yet."

Fernande, who looked wondrously beautiful that day, stood quivering, gazing at her husband with flaming eyes. "Oh! you don't know how to hate!" she cried. "What! that man set himself to thwart all your plans, founded at your very door a rival enterprise, the success of which would be the ruin of the one you manage—a man, too, who never ceases to be an obstacle and a threat—and you don't even desire to see him crushed! Ah! if he's flung naked into a ditch I shall be only too pleased!"

From the very first day she had felt that Luc would be the enemy, and she could not speak calmly of that man who threatened her enjoyment of life. Therein for her lay his one great unique crime. With her ever-increasing appetite for pleasure and luxury, she required ever larger profits, an abundance of prosperity for the works, hundreds and hundreds of workmen, kneading, fashioning steel at the flaming doors of their furnaces. She was the devourer of men and money, the one whose cravings the Abyss with its steam hammers and its huge machinery no longer sufficed to satisfy. And what would become of her hopes of future pomp and vanity, of millions amassed and devoured, if the Abyss should fall into difficulties, and succumb to competition? With that thought in her mind, she left neither her husband nor Boisgelin any rest, but ever urged them on, worried them incessantly, seizing every opportunity to give expression to her anger and her fears.

Boisgelin, who feigned a superior kind of way—never meddling with business matters, but spending the profits of the works without counting them, setting his only glory in being a handsome ladykiller, an elegant horseman, and a great sportsman—was none the less accustomed to shiver when he heard Fernande speak of possible ruin. Thus, on the present occasion, turning towards Delaveau, in whom he retained absolute confidence, he inquired, "You have no anxiety, eh, cousin? All is going on well here?"

The engineer again shrugged his shoulders. "I repeat that the works are in no wise affected as yet. Moreover, the whole town is rising against that man—he is mad. We shall all see now how unpopular he is; and if at bottom I am well pleased with that law-suit, it is because it will finish him off in the opinion of Beauclair. Before three months have elapsed all the workmen that he has taken from us will be coming with hands clasped to beg me to take them back. You will see, you will see! Authority is the only sound principle, the enfranchisement of labour is arrant stupidity, for the workman no longer does anything properly when once he becomes his own master."

Silence fell, then he added more slowly, with a faint shade of anxiety in his eyes, "All the same, we ought to be prudent. La Crêcherie is not a competitor that one can neglect, and what would alarm me would be any lack of the necessary funds for a struggle in some sudden emergency. We live too much from day to day, and it is becoming indispensable that we should establish a substantial reserve fund, by setting apart, for instance, one third of the annual profits."

Fernande restrained a gesture of involuntary protest. That was indeed her fear: that her lover might have to reduce his expenditure, and that she, in her pride and pleasures, might suffer therefrom. She had to content herself for the moment with looking at Boisgelin. But he, of his own accord, plainly answered: "No, no, cousin, not at the present moment. I can't set anything aside, my expenses are too heavy. At the same time I must thank you once more, for you make my money yield even more than you promised. We will see about the rest later on—we will talk it over."

Nevertheless Fernande remained in a nervous state, and her covert anger fell upon Nise, who had just lunched alone, under the supervision of a maid, who now brought her into the *salon* before taking her to spend the afternoon with a little friend. Nise, who was now nearly seven years old, was growing quite pretty, pink and fair, and ever merry, with wild hair which made her resemble a little curly sheep.

"There, my dear Boisgelin," said Fernande, "there's a disobedient child who will end by making me quite ill. Just ask her what she did the other day at that treat which she offered to your son Paul and little Louise Mazelle!"

Without evincing the slightest alarm, Nise, with her limpid blue eyes, continued gaily smiling at those about her.

"Oh!" continued her mother, "she won't admit any wrong-doing. But do you know, although I had forbidden it a dozen times, she again opened the old door in our garden wall to admit all the dirty urchins of La Crêcherie into our grounds. There was that little Nanet, a frightful little rascal for whom she has conceived an affection. And your boy Paul was mixed up in it, and so was Louise Mazelle, all of them fraternising with the children of that man Bonnaire, who left us in such an insolent fashion. Yes, Paul with Antoinette, and Louise with Lucien, and Mademoiselle Nise and her Nanet, leading them to the assault of our flower-beds. Yet she has not even a blush of shame on her cheeks, you see!"

"It isn't just," Nise simply answered in her clear voice; "we did not break anything, we played together very nicely. He is funny, is Nanet."

This answer made Fernande quite angry: "Ah! you think him funny, do you? Just listen to me. If ever I catch you with him, you shall have no dessert for a week. I don't want you to get me into any unpleasantness with those people near us. They would go about everywhere saying that we attract their children here in order to render them ill. You hear me? This time it is serious; you will have to deal with me if you see Nanet again."

"Yes, mamma," said Nise in her quiet, smiling way. And when she had gone off with the maid, after kissing everybody, the mother concluded: "It is very simple—I shall have the door walled up. In that way I shall be certain that the children won't communicate. There is nothing worse than that—it corrupts them."

Neither Delaveau nor Boisgelin had intervened; for on the one hand they saw in this affair only so much childishness, and on the other they approved of severe measures when good order was in question. But the future was germinating. Stubborn Mademoiselle Nise had carried away in her little heart the thought of Nanet, who was funny and played so nicely.

At last the guests arrived, the Gouriers with Châtelard, then Judge Gaume with the Jollivets. Abbé Marle was the last to appear, late according to his wont. Though the Mazelles had expressly promised to come and take coffee, some obstacle prevented them from sharing the repast. Thus there were only ten at table; but then they had desired to be few in number in order that they might be able to chat at their ease. Besides, the dining-room, of which Fernande felt ashamed, was such a small one that the old mahogany sideboard interfered with the service whenever there were more than a dozen round the table.

From the serving of the fish, some delicious trout of the Mionne, the conversation naturally fell on La Crêcherie and Luc. And what was said by those educated *bourgeois*, in a position to know the truth about what they called "socialist utopia," proved scarcely one whit more sensible or intelligent than the extraordinary views expressed by such people as Dacheux and Laboque. The only man who might have understood the real position was Châtelard. But then he preferred to jest.

"You know," said he, "that the boys and girls there grow up all together in the same class-rooms and workshops, so that we may expect the little town to become a populous one, very rapidly. With their loose theories, they will all be papas and mammas, and there will be quite a tribe of children running about?"

"How horrible!" exclaimed Fernande, with an air of profound disgust, for she affected extreme prudishness.

Then, for a few moments, the free love theories attributed to the denizens of La Crêcherie formed the topic of conversation. But a matter of that kind did not worry Delaveau. In his estimation the serious point was the undermining of authority, the criminal dream of living without a master.

"Such a conception as that is beyond me," he exclaimed. "How will their future city be governed? To speak only of the works, they say that by association they will suppress the wage system, and that there will be a just division of wealth when only workers are left, each giving his share of toil to the community. But I can conceive of no more dangerous dream than that, for it is irrealisable, is it not, Monsieur Gourier?"

The mayor, who was eating with his face bent over his plate, spent some time in wiping his mouth before he answered, for he noticed that the sub-prefect was looking at him.

"Irrealisable, no doubt," he said at last. "Only one must not lightly condemn the principle of association. There is great strength in association, and we ourselves may be called upon to make use of it."

This prudent reply incensed the captain, who retorted angrily, "What! wouldn't you condemn once and for all the execrable deeds which that man—I speak of that Monsieur Luc—is planning against all that we love, that old France of ours, such as the swords of our fathers made it and bequeathed it to us?"

Some mutton cutlets served with asparagus heads were now being handed round, and a general outcry against Luc arose. The mention of his hated name sufficed to draw them all together, unite them closely, in alarm for their threatened interests, and with an imperious craving for resistance and revenge. Somebody, however, was cruel enough to ask Gourier for news of his son, Achille the renegade, and the mayor had to curse the lad once again. Châtelard alone tried to tack about and keep the discussion on a jocular footing. But in this he failed, for the captain continued prophesying the worst disasters if the factious-minded were not immediately kicked into obedience and order. And his words disseminated such a panic that Boisgelin, becoming anxious again, appealed to Delaveau, from whom there happily came a reassuring declaration.

"Our man is already hit," declared the manager of the Abyss. "The prosperity of La Crêcherie is only on the surface, and an accident would suffice to bring everything to the ground. Thus, for instance, my wife was lately giving me some particulars—"

"Yes," broke in Fernande, happy to have an opportunity of relieving her feelings, "the information came to me from my laundress. She knows one of our former hands, a man named Ragu, who left us in order to go to the new works. Well, it seems that Ragu is declaring everywhere that he has had quite enough of that dirty den, that the men are bored to death there, that he isn't the only one to complain, and that one of these fine days they will all be coming back here. Ah! who will begin, who will deal the blow necessary to make that man Luc totter and fall to pieces?"

"But there's the Laboque lawsuit," said Boisgelin, coming to the young woman's help. "I hope that will suffice for everything."

Fresh silence ensued whilst some roast ducks made their appearance. Although the Laboque lawsuit was the real motive of that friendly gathering, nobody as yet had dared to speak of it in presence of the silence which Judge Gaume preserved. He ate but little, his secret sorrows having brought him a complaint of the digestive organs, and he contented himself with listening to the others and gazing at them with his cold grey eyes, whence he knew how to withdraw all expression. Never had he been seen in a less communicative mood, and this ended by embarrassing the others, who would have liked to know on what footing to treat him, and at least have some certainty as to the judgment which he would deliver. Although no thought of possible acquittal at his hands entered anybody's mind, they all hoped that he would have the good taste to pledge himself in a sufficiently clear fashion.

Again it was the captain who advanced to the assault. "The law is formal, is it not, Monsieur le Président?" he inquired. "All damage done to anybody must be repaired?"

"No doubt," answered Gaume.

More was expected from him, but he relapsed into silence. And thereupon, by way of compelling him to pledge himself more thoroughly, the Clouque affair was noisily discussed. That filthy stream became one of the former adornments of Beauclair; it was not right that people should steal a town's water in such a fashion as that man Luc had done, particularly to give it to peasants whose brains had been turned to such a point that they had converted their village into a hotbed of furious anarchy which threatened the whole region. All the terror of the *bourgeoisie* now became apparent, for assuredly the ancient and holy principle of property was in sore distress if the sons of the hard-fisted peasants of former times had reached such a point as to place their strips of land in common. It was high time that justice should interfere and put a stop to such a scandal.

"Oh! we may be quite easy," Boisgelin ended by saying in a flattering tone. "The cause of society will be in good hands. There is nothing above a just judgment, rendered in all liberty by an honest conscience."

"Without doubt," Gaume simply repeated.

And this time it was necessary to rest content with that vague remark, in which they all strove to detect the certainty of Luc's conviction. The meal was now virtually over, for after a Russian salad there were only some strawberry ices and the dessert. But the guests' stomachs were comforted, and they laughed a good deal, for they were convinced of victory. When they had gone into the *salon* to take coffee and the Mazelles arrived, the latter were, as usual, greeted with somewhat jocose friendliness. Those worthy folk, living on their income, and personifying the delights of idleness, moved one's heart! Madame Mazelle's complaint was no better, but she was delighted at having obtained from Doctor Novarre some new wafers which enabled her to eat anything with impunity. It was only such matters as the abominable stories of La Crêcherie, the threat that Rentes would be done away with, and that the right of inheritance would be abolished, that now gave her a turn. But what was the use of talking about disagreeable things? Mazelle, who watched over his wife with profound satisfaction, winked at the others and begged them to raise those horrid subjects no more, since they had such a bad effect on Madame Mazelle's failing health. And then the gathering became delightful, they all hastened to revert to the happiness of life, a life of wealth and enjoyment, of which they plucked all the flowers.

At last, amidst growing anger and hatred, the day of the famous lawsuit dawned. Never had Beauclair been so upset by furious passion. Luc in the first instance had felt astonished at Laboque's writ, and had simply laughed at it, particularly as it seemed to him impossible that the claim for twenty-five thousand francs by way of damages could be sustained. If the Clouque had dried up it would in the first place be difficult for anybody to prove that this had been caused by the capturing of hillside springs at La Crêcherie; and moreover those springs belonged to the estate, to the Jordans, and were free from all servitude, in such wise that the owner had a full right to dispose of them as he pleased. On the other hand Laboque must assuredly base his claim for damages on facts proving that he had really sustained injury and loss, but he simply made such a feeble and clumsy attempt to do so that no court of justice in the world could possibly decide in his favour. As Luc jocularly put it, it was he who ought to have claimed a public grant as a reward for having delivered the waterside landowners from a source of infection, of which they had long complained. The town now simply had to fill up the bed of the stream and sell the land for building purposes, thereby putting a few hundred thousand francs into its coffers. Thus Luc laughed, not imagining that such a lawsuit as Laboque's could be at all serious. It was only afterwards, on finding rancour and hostility rising against him on every side, that he began to realise the gravity of the situation, and the peril in which his work would be placed.

This was a first painful shock for him. He was not ignorant of the maliciousness of man. In giving battle to the old world, he had fully expected that the latter would not yield him place without anger and resistance. He was prepared for the Calvary he foresaw, the stones and mud with which the ungrateful multitude usually pelt precursors. Yet his heart wavered as he realised the approach of folly, cruelty, and betrayal. He understood that behind the Laboques and the other petty traders there was the whole *bourgeoisie*, all who possess and are unwilling to part with aught of their possessions. His attempts at association and co-operation placed capitalist society, based on the wage-earning system, in such peril that he became for it a public enemy, of which it must rid itself at any cost. And it was the Abyss and La Guerdache and the whole town and authority in every form that were now bestirring themselves, joining in the struggle and striving to crush him. If he fell that pack of wolves would rush upon him and devour him. He knew the names of those enemies, functionaries, traders, mere *rentiers* with placid faces who would have eaten him alive had they seen him fall at a street corner. And therefore, mastering his distress of heart, he prepared for battle, full of the conviction that one can found nothing without battling, and that all great human work is sealed with human blood.

It was on a Tuesday, a market day, that Laboque's action was heard by the civil court, over which Judge Gaume presided. Beauclair was in a state of uproar, all the folk who had come in from the neighbouring villages helped to increase the general feverishness on the Place de la Mairie and in the Rue de Brias. Sœurette, who felt anxious, had therefore begged Luc to ask a few strong friends to accompany him. But he stubbornly refused to do so, he resolved to go to the court alone, just as he had resolved to defend himself in person, having engaged an advocate simply as a matter of form. When he entered the court-room, which was small and already crowded with noisy people, silence suddenly fell, and the eager curiosity which greets an isolated, unarmed victim ready for sacrifice became manifest. Luc's quiet courage increased the rage of his enemies, who pronounced his demeanour to be insolent. He remained standing in front of the bench allotted to defendants, and whilst quietly gazing at the closely packed people around him, he recognised Laboque, Dacheux, Caffiaux, and other shopkeepers among all the many furious enemies with ardent faces, whom he saw for the first time. However, he felt a little relieved on finding that the intimates of La Guerdache and the Abyss had at least had the good taste to refrain from coming to see him delivered to the beasts.

Long and exciting proceedings were anticipated, but there was nothing of the kind. Laboque has chosen one of those provincial advocates with a reputation for maliciousness who are the terror of a region. And, indeed, the best time which Luc's enemies spent was when this man spoke. Knowing how flimsy were the legal grounds on which the demand for damages was based, he contented himself with ridiculing the reforms attempted at La Crêcherie. He made his hearers laugh a good deal with the comical and distorted picture which he drew of the proposed future society. And he raised general indignation when he pictured the children of both sexes being corrupted, the holy institution of marriage being abolished, and free love and all such horrors taking its place. Nevertheless, the general opinion was that he had not found the supreme insult or argument, the bludgeon blow by which a suit is gained and a man for ever crushed. And so great, therefore, became the anxiety that when Luc in his turn spoke, his slightest words were greeted with murmurs. He spoke very simply, refrained from replying to the attacks made upon his enterprise, and contented himself with showing with decisive force that Laboque's demands were ill-founded. Would he not rather have rendered a service to Beauclair if he had, indeed, dried up that pestilential Clouque, and presented the town with good building land? It was not even proved, however, that the works carried out at La Crêcherie had caused the disappearance of the torrent, and he was waiting for the other side to give proof of it. When he concluded, some of his bitterness of heart appeared, for he declared that if he desired nobody's thanks for whatever useful work he might have done, he would be happy if people would but allow him to pursue his enterprises in peace, without seeking groundless quarrels with him. On several occasions Judge Gaume had to enjoin silence on the audience; nevertheless when the public prosecutor also had spoken, in a designedly confused manner, in turn praising and condemning both parties, Laboque's advocate replied in so violent a fashion, calling Luc an Anarchist bent on destroying the town, that loud acclamations burst forth, and the judge had to threaten that he would order the court to be cleared if such demonstrations were renewed. Then he postponed judgment for a fortnight.

When that fortnight was past, the popular passions had become yet more heated, and folk almost came to blows on the market-place in discussing the probable terms of the judgment. Nearly everybody, however, was convinced that it would be a severe one, fixing the damages at ten or fifteen thousand francs, and ordering the defendant to restore the Clouque to its former condition. At the same time some people wagged their heads and felt sure of nothing, for they had not been satisfied with Judge Gaume's demeanour in court. Anxiety was caused, too, by the manner in which the judge had shut himself up at home on the morrow of the hearing, under the pretence of suffering from some indisposition. It was said that he was really in perfect health, and had simply desired to place himself beyond any pressure, refusing to see people lest they might try to influence his judicial conscience. What did he do in that silent house of his, whose doors and windows were kept strictly closed, and which his daughter even was not allowed to enter? To what moral struggle, what internal drama had he fallen a prey amidst his wrecked life, the collapse of all that he had loved and all that he had believed in? Those were questions which occupied many people, but which none could answer.

Judgment was to be delivered at noon at the outset of the court's sitting. And the room was yet more crowded and excited than on the former occasion. Laughter rang out, and words of hope and violence were exchanged from one to the other end. All Luc's enemies had come to see him annihilated. And he had again refused to let anybody accompany him, preferring to present himself alone, the better to express the peacefulness of his mission. He stood up smiling and looking around him without even appearing to suspect that all that growling anger was directed against himself. At last, punctual to the minute, Judge Gaume came in, followed by his two assessors and the public prosecutor. There was no need for the usher to command silence, the chatter suddenly ceased, and the faces of one and all were stretched forward, aglow with anxious curiosity. The judge had in the first instance seated himself, then he rose holding the paper on which his judgment was written; and for a moment he remained thus, motionless and silent, with his eyes gazing far away beyond the crowd. At last, slowly and without the faintest emphasis, he began to read his judgment. It was a long business, for "whereas" followed "whereas" with monotonous regularity, presenting the various questions submitted to the court in full detail and under every possible aspect. The people present listened without understanding much of what was read, and without managing to foresee the conclusion, so incessantly and closely did arguments on either side follow one another. It seemed, however, at each forward step that Luc's contentions were adopted by the court, that no real damage had been done to another, and that every landowner had a right to execute what work he pleased on his own land when no servitude existed to restrain him. And the decision at last burst forth—Luc was acquitted, the action was dismissed.

At first a moment of stupefaction ensued in the court-room. Then, everybody having understood the position, there came hooting and

ÉMILE ZOLA

violent threatening shouts. What! the excited crowd, maddened by lies for months past, was robbed of its promised victim! It demanded that victim, it claimed him that it might tear him to pieces, since an attempt to rob it of him was made at the last moment by a judge who had evidently sold himself. Was not Luc the public enemy, the stranger who had come nobody knew whence to corrupt Beauclair, ruin its trade, and foment civil war in its midst by banding the workmen together against their masters? And had he not with diabolical wickedness stolen the town's water, dried up a stream whose disappearance was a disaster for all who had property near its banks? The "Journal de Beauclair" had repeated those accusations every week, all the authorities, all the gentlefolk had spread them abroad, and now the humbler ones, blinded and enraged, convinced that a pestilence would come from La Crêcherie, "saw red" and demanded death. Fists were thrust forward, and the cries increased:

"To death with the thief! To death with the poisoner, to death with him!"

Very pale, with his features rigid, Judge Gaume remained standing amidst the uproar. He wished to speak and give orders for the court to be cleared, but he had to renounce all hope of making himself heard. And for dignity's sake he had to rest content with suspending the sitting by withdrawing from the court followed by his two assessors and the public prosecutor.

Luc had remained calm and smiling beside his bench. He had been as much surprised as his adversaries by the tenor of the judgment, for he knew in what a vitiated atmosphere the judge lived. It was comforting to meet a just man amid so much human baseness. When, however, the cries of death burst forth, Luc's smile became a sad one, and his heart filled with bitterness as he turned towards that howling throng. What had he done to those petty *bourgeois*, those tradesmen, those workmen? Had he not desired to benefit all, was he not working in order that all might become happy, loving, and brotherly? But the fists still threatened him, and the shouts lashed him more violently than ever: "To death! to death with the thief! To death with the poisoner!"

To see those poor folk so wild, maddened by falsehoods, caused Luc profound grief, for he loved them in spite of everything. He restrained his tears, for he wished to remain erect, proud, and courageous beneath those insults. The public thinking itself braved, would have ended, however, by breaking down the oaken partitions in order to get at him, if some guards had not at last succeeded in thrusting him out of the court-room and securing the doors. Then, on behalf of Judge Gaume, the clerk of the court came to beg Luc to refrain from leaving immediately, for fear of some accident; and eventually the clerk prevailed on him to wait a few minutes in the room of the doorkeeper of the Palace of Justice, whilst the crowd was dispersing.[1]

But if Luc consented to do this he none the less experienced a feeling of shame and revolt at being obliged to hide himself. He spent in that doorkeeper's room the most painful fifteen minutes of his life, for he thought it cowardly not to face the crowd, and was indignant that the position of an apparent culprit should thus be forced upon him. Directly the approaches of the Palace of Justice had been cleared, he insisted on going home, on foot, and unaccompanied by anybody. He had merely a light walking-stick with him, and was even sorry that he had brought it, for fear lest anybody should imagine that he had done so for purposes of defence. He had all Beauclair to cross, and he set out slowly and quietly along the streets. Until he reached the Place de la Mairie nobody seemed to notice him. The people who had quitted the court had waited for him for a few minutes; then feeling certain that he would not venture out for some hours, they had gone off to spread the news of the acquittal through the town. But on the Place de la Mairie, where the market was being held, Luc was recognised. He was pointed out and a few persons even began to follow him, not as yet with evil intentions, but solely to see what might happen. There were only some peasants and their customers present, mere sightseers who were not mixed up in the quarrel. Thus matters only took a serious turn when the young man turned into the Rue de Brias, at the corner of which, in front of his shop, Laboque, infuriated by his defeat, was venting his anger amidst a small crowd of people.

All the tradespeople of the neighbourhood had hastened to Laboque's establishment directly they had heard the disastrous tidings. What! was it true then? La Crêcherie would be free to finish ruining them with its co-operative stores, since the judges took its part? Caffiaux, who looked overwhelmed, preserved silence, full of thoughts which he would not express. But Dacheux the butcher, with all his blood rushing to his

---

1. All who remember M. Zola's trial in Paris in connection with the Dreyfus case will recognise that the above passages and others in this chapter are in part founded on his personal experiences at the time referred to.—*Trans.*

ÉMILE ZOLA

face, showed himself one of the most violent, eager to defend his meat, sacred meat, meat the privileged food of the wealthy! And he even talked of killing people rather than reduce his prices by a single centime. Madame Mitaine, for her part, had not come. She had never been in favour of the lawsuit, and she simply declared that she should go on selling bread as long as she found buyers, and that, for the rest, she would see afterwards. Laboque, however, boiling over with fury, was for the tenth time recounting the abominable treachery of Judge Gaume when all at once he perceived Luc quietly walking past his shop—that ironmongery shop whose ruin he was consummating. Such audacity brought Laboque's rage to a climax; and he almost threw himself on the young man as, half stifled by his rising bile, he growled, "To death with the thief! To death with the poisoner!"

Luc, without pausing, contented himself with turning his calm brave eyes on the tumultuous throng whence came Laboque's husky invectives. This was taken by all as an act of provocation, and a general clamour arose, gathered force, and became like a tempest blast. "To death with the thief! To death with the poisoner! To death with him!"

Luc meantime, as if he himself were not in question, quietly went his way, glancing to right and left, like one who is interested in the sights of the streets. But almost the whole band had begun to follow him with louder and louder hoots, and threats, and the outrageous words, "To death with the thief! To death with the poisoner! To death with him!"

And those shouts never ceased, but grew and spread as he went at a leisurely pace up the Rue de Brias. Out of each shop came fresh tradespeople to join the demonstration. Women showed themselves in the doorways and hooted the young man as he passed. Some in their exasperation even rushed up and shouted with the men: "To death with the thief and poisoner!" Luc saw one of them, a fair young woman, a fruiterer's wife, charmingly beautiful, showing her fine white teeth as she shouted insults after him, and threatening him with her hands, whose rosy finger-nails seemed eager to tear him to pieces. Children also had begun to run after him, and there was one, some five or six years old, no bigger than a jack-boot, who almost threw himself between the young man's legs in order that he might be the better heard: "To death with the thief! To death with the poisoner!" Poor little urchin! Who could have already taught him to raise that shout of hatred? But matters became worse when Luc passed the factories situated in the upper part of the street. The workgirls of Gourier's boot manufactory appeared at their windows, clapped their hands and howled. Then there were even the workmen of the Chodorge and Mirande factories, who stood smoking on the foot-pavement waiting for the bells to ring the close of the dinner-hour, and who, brutified by servitude, likewise joined in the demonstration. One thin little fellow, with carroty hair and big blurred eyes, seemed stricken with insanity, so furiously did he rush about, shouting louder than all the others: "To death with the thief! To death with the poisoner! To death with him!"

Ah! that ascent of the Rue de Brias, with that growing band of enemies at his heels, amidst that ignoble torrent of threats and insults! Luc remembered the evening of his arrival at Beauclair four years previously, when the black tramp, tramp of the disinherited starvelings along that same street had filled him with such active compassion that he had vowed to devote his life to the salvation of the wretched. What had he done for four years past, that so much hatred should have sprung up against him? He had made himself the apostle of the morrow, the apostle of a community all solidarity and brotherliness, organised by the ennoblement of work—work, the regulator of human wealth. He had given an example of what he desired to establish, at that La Crêcherie where the future city was germinating, and where such additional justice and happiness as was for the time possible already reigned. And that had sufficed—the whole town regarded him as a malefactor; for he could feel that the whole of it was behind the band now barking at his heels. How bitter was the suffering that accompanied that Calvary-ascent, which all just men must make amidst the blows of the very beings whose redemption they seek to hasten! Yet as for those *bourgeois* whose quiet digestions he troubled, Luc excused them for hating him; for were they not terrified by the thought of having to share their now egotistical enjoyment with others? He also excused those shopkeepers who ascribed their ruin to his malice, when he simply dreamt of a better employment of social forces, and of preventing all useless waste of the public fortune. And he even excused those workmen whom he had come to save from misery, and for whom he was so laboriously raising a city of justice, yet who hooted and insulted him, to such a degree, indeed, had their brains been fogged and their hearts chilled. Only if he excused them all, in his sorrowful brotherliness, he bled, indeed, at finding, amongst the most insulting, those very toilers of factory and workshop whom he desired to make the nobles, the free and happy men of to-morrow.

Luc was still ascending that endless Rue de Brias, and the pack of wolves was still increasing in numbers, their shouts knowing no cessation: "To death with the thief! To death with the poisoner! To death with him!"

For a moment he paused, turned, and looked at all those people in order that they might not imagine that he was fleeing. And as there happened to be some piles of stones thereabouts, one man stooped down, took up a stone and flung it at him. Immediately afterwards others stooped, and the stones began to rain upon him amidst ever-growing threats.

"To death with the thief! To death with the poisoner! To death with him!"

So now he was being stoned. However, he made not a gesture even, but resumed his walk, persevering in the ascent of his Calvary. His hands were empty, he had with him no weapon save his light walking-stick, and this he had slipped under his arm. But he remained very calm, full of the idea that if he were destined to fulfil his mission it would render him invulnerable. His grief-stricken heart alone suffered, cruelly rent as it was by the sight of so much error and madness. Tears rose to his eyes, and he had to make a great effort to prevent them from flowing down his cheeks.

"To death with the thief! To death with the poisoner! To death with him!" Still and ever did those cries resound.

A stone at last struck one of Luc's heels, then another grazed his hip. It had become a game now—the very children took part in it. But they were unskilful, and most of the stones rebounded over the ground. Twice, however, did pebbles pass so near Luc's head, that one might have thought him struck. He no longer turned round, but still and ever ascended the Rue de Brias at the same leisurely pace as before, like one who, after going for a stroll, is returning home. But at last a stone did hit him, tearing his right ear; and then another, striking his left hand, cut the palm of it open. At this his blood gushed out, and fell in big red drops upon the ground.

"To death with the thief and poisoner! To death with him!" some of the crowd still cried. But an eddy of panic momentarily stayed the advance. Several people ran off, seized with cowardice, now that the moment to kill the man seemed to have arrived. Some of the women, too, shrieked, and carried the children away in their arms. Only the most furious fanatics then kept up the pursuit. Luc, still continuing his painful journey, just glanced at his hand; then, after wiping his ear with his handkerchief, he wrapped the latter over his bleeding palm. But he had slackened his pace, and could hear his pursuers drawing quite near to him. When on the nape of his neck he detected the ardent panting of the throng, he turned round for the last time. Rushing on frantically, in the front rank, was the short and scraggy workman with carroty hair and big dull eyes. He was a smith belonging to the Abyss, it was said. With a final bound he reached the man whom he had been following from the bottom of the street, and though there seemed to be no motive for his frenzied hatred, he spat with the greatest violence in his face.

"To death with the thief! To death with the poisoner! To death with him!"

Luc had at last ascended his Calvary—he was at the top of the Rue de Brias now. But he staggered beneath that final abominable outrage. His face became frightfully pale, and an involuntary impulse of his whole being prompted him to raise his uninjured hand and clench it vengefully. He looked like some superb giant beside a wretched dwarf, for with one blow he could have felled the little workman to the ground. But his consciousness of strength enabled him to restrain himself. He did not bring down his fist. From his eyes, however, flowed two big tears, tears of infinite grief which hitherto he had been able to keep back, but which he could now no longer hide, such had become the bitterness of his feelings. He wept to think that there should be so much ignorance, so terrible a misunderstanding, that all those poor, unhappy, well-loved toilers should refuse to be saved! And they, after sneering at him, allowed him to return home, bleeding, and all alone.

In the evening Luc shut himself up in the little pavilion which he still occupied at the end of the park, alongside the road to Les Combettes. His acquittal did not leave him any illusions. The violence displayed towards him that afternoon, the savage pursuit of the crowd, told him what warfare would be waged against him now that the whole town was rising. These were the supreme convulsions of an expiring social system which was unwilling to die. It resisted and struggled furiously, with the hope of staying the march of mankind. Some, the partisans of authority, set salvation in pitiless repression; others, the sentimentalists, appealed to the past and its poetry, to all indeed that man weeps for when he is forced to quit it for ever; and others, again, seized with exasperation, joined the revolutionaries as if eager to finish matters at once. And thus Luc felt that he had virtually been pursued by all Beauclair, which was like a miniature world amidst the great one. And if he remained brave and still resolved for battle, he was none the less bitterly distressed, and anxious to hide it. During the hours, few and far between, when he felt weakness coming over him, he preferred to shut himself up and drain his cup of sorrow to the dregs in privacy, only showing himself once more when he was hale and brave again. That evening therefore he barred both the doors and windows of the pavilion, and gave orders that nobody was to be admitted to see him.

About eleven o'clock, however, he fancied that he could hear some light footsteps on the road. Then came a low call, scarce audible, which made him shiver. He went to open the window, and on looking between the laths of the shutters he perceived a slender form. Then a very gentle voice ascended, saying: "It is I, Monsieur Luc, I must speak to you at once."

It was the voice of Josine. Luc did not even pause to reflect, but at once went to open the little door communicating with the road. And then he led her into his closed room, where a lamp was burning peacefully. But on looking at her he was seized with terrible anxiety, for her garments were in disorder and her face was bruised.

"Good heavens! what is the matter, Josine? What has happened?" he cried.

Tears were falling from her eyes, her hair drooped about her delicate white neck, and the collar of her gown was torn away.

"Ah, Monsieur Luc, I wanted to see you," she began. "It isn't because he beat me again when he came home, but on account of the threats he made. It's necessary you should know of them this very evening."

Then she related that Ragu, on learning what had happened in the Rue de Brias, the ignominious manner in which "the governor," as he called Luc, had been escorted out of the town, had gone off to Caffiaux's wine-shop, leading Bourron and others astray with him. And he had but lately returned home, drunk, of course, and shouting that he had had quite enough of La Crêcherie, and would not stop a day longer in a dirty den where one was bored to death, and had not even the right to drink a drop too much if one wanted to. At last, after jeering and laughing and indulging in all sorts of foul language, he had wished to compel her, Josine, to pack up their clothes at once in order that they might go off in the morning to the Abyss, where all the hands leaving La Crêcherie were readily taken on. And as she had desired him to pause before coming to such a decision, he had ended by beating her and turning her out of the house.

"Oh! I don't count, Monsieur Luc," she continued. "It's you who are insulted and whom they want to injure. Ragu will certainly go off in the morning—nothing can restrain him—and he will certainly carry off Bourron as well as five or six others whom he didn't name to me. For my part, I can't help it, but I shall have to follow him, and it all grieves me so much that I felt I must tell it you at once, for fear lest I might never see you again."

Luc was still looking at her, and a wave of bitterness submerged his heart. Was the disaster even greater then than he had supposed? His workmen now were leaving him, returning to the hard toil and filthy wretchedness of former times, seized with nostalgia for the hell whence he had so laboriously striven to extricate them. In four years he had won naught of their minds or their affection. And the worst was that Josine was no happier; she now came back to him as on the first day, insulted, beaten, cast into the street! Thus nothing was done, and everything remained to be done; for did not Josine personify the suffering people? It was only on that evening, when he had met her grief-stricken and abandoned, a victim of accursed toil, imposed on human kind like slavery, that he had yielded to his desires to act. She was the most humble, the lowest, the nearest to the gutter, and she was also the most beautiful, the gentlest, the saintliest. Ah! as long as woman should suffer, the world would not be saved.

"Oh! Josine, Josine, how grieved I am for you—how I pity you!" he murmured with infinite tenderness, whilst he also began to weep.

When she saw his tears thus falling, she suffered yet more grievously than before. What! he was weeping thus bitterly, he, her god, he whom she adored, like some superior power, in gratitude for all the help he had brought her, the joy with which he had henceforth filled her life! The thought, too, of the outrages that he had undergone, that awful ascent of the Rue de Brias, increased her adoration, drew her near to him as with a desire to dress his wounds. What could she do to comfort him, how could she efface from his face the insult spat upon him, enable him to feel himself respected, admired, and worshipped?

"Oh, Monsieur Luc," said she, "you do not know how grieved I am at seeing you so unhappy, and how I should like to relieve your sorrows a little."

They were so near together that the warmth of their breath passed over their faces. And their mutual compassion filled them with increasing tenderness. How she suffered! how he suffered! And he only

ÉMILE ZOLA

thought of her, even as she only thought of him, with immensity of pity and a craving for love and felicity.

"I am not to be pitied," said Luc at last; "there is only you, Josine, whose suffering is a crime, and whom I must save."

"No, no, Monsieur Luc, I do not count; it is you who ought not to suffer, for you are the providence of us all."

Then, as she let herself sink into his arms, he clasped her passionately to his breast. It was a crisis not to be resisted—the mingling of two flames in order that they might henceforth become but one sole flame of affection and strength. Thus was their destiny accomplished. All had led them to it; a sudden vision appeared to them of their love born one stormy evening, then slowly growing in intensity, in the depths of their hearts. Nothing henceforth could part them. They were two beings meeting in a long-awaited kiss, attaining to florescence. No remorse was possible; they loved even as they existed, in order that they might be healthy and strong and fruitful. And as Luc sat in that quiet chamber with Josine he became conscious that a great help had suddenly come to him. Love alone could create harmony in the city he dreamed of. Josine was his; and his union with the disinherited was thereby sealed. Apostle that he was of a new creed, he felt that he had need of a woman to help him to redeem mankind. The poor little beaten workgirl whom he had met one evening dying of starvation had now for him become a very queen. She had known the uttermost depths, and she would help him to create a new world of splendour and joy. She was the only one whose help he needed to complete his task.

"Give me your hand, your poor injured hand, Josine," he gently said to her.

She gave it him; it was the hand which had been caught in some boot-stitching machinery, and the forefinger of which had been cut off. "It is very ugly," she murmured.

"Ugly, Josine? Oh no! it is so dear to me that I kiss it with devotion."

He pressed his lips to the scar left by the injury, he covered the poor, slender, maimed hand with caresses.

"Oh, Luc!" she cried, "how you love me, and how I love you!"

As that cry of happiness and hope rang out they once more flung their arms around each other's necks. Outside, over the heavy sleep of Beauclair sped the thuds of hammer-strokes, the clang of steel coming from La Crêcherie and the Abyss, both working, competing one with the other through the night. And doubtless the war was not yet over, the terrible battle between Yesterday and To-morrow was destined to become fiercer still. But in the midst of all the torture there had come a halt of happiness, and whatever sufferings might lie ahead, love at least was sown for the harvest of the future.

III

From that time forward, at each fresh disaster which fell upon La Crêcherie, when men refused to follow Luc or impeded him in his endeavours to establish a community of work, justice, and peace, he invariably exclaimed: "But they don't love! If they only loved, all would prove fruitful, all would grow and triumph in the sunlight."

His work had reached the torturing all-deciding hour of regression, that hour when, in every forward march, there comes a struggle, a forced halt. One ceases to advance, one even recedes, the ground that has been gained seems to crumble away, and it appears even as if one would never reach one's goal. And this, too, is the hour when with firmness of mind and unconquerable faith in final victory heroes make themselves manifest.

Luc strove to restrain Ragu when he found him desirous of withdrawing from the association and returning to the Abyss. But he was confronted by an evilly disposed ranter, one who felt happy in doing wrong, since defection on the part of the men might ruin the new works. Besides there was something deeper in Ragu's case, a form of nostalgia, a craving to return to slavish labour and black misery, all that horrid past which he carried with him in his blood. In the warm sunlight, amidst the gay cleanliness of his little home, girt round with verdure, he had ever regretted the narrow evil-smelling streets of Old Beauclair, the soiled hovels through which swept a pestilential atmosphere. Whenever he spent an hour in the large clear hall of the common-house, where alcohol was not allowed, he was haunted by the acrid smells of Caffiaux's tavern. Even the orderly manner in which the co-operative stores were now managed angered him, and prompted him to spend his money after his own fashion with the dealers of the Rue de Brias, whom he himself called thieves, but with whom he at least had the pleasure of quarrelling. And the more Luc insisted, pointing out how senseless was his departure, the more stubborn did Ragu become, full of the idea that if such efforts were made to retain him, it must be because his departure would deal the works a severe blow.

"No, no, Monsieur Luc," said he, "there's no arrangement possible. Perhaps I am acting stupidly, though I don't think so. You promised us all sorts of marvels—we were all to become rich men; but the truth is that we don't earn more than elsewhere, and that we have additional worries that are not at all to my taste."

It was indeed a fact that the shares in the profits made at La Crêcherie had, so far, amounted to little more than the salaries earned at the Abyss. But Luc made haste to answer. "We live, and is it not everything to live when the future is certain? If I have asked sacrifices of you, it has been in the conviction that everybody's happiness lies at the end. But patience and courage are certainly necessary, together with faith in the task and a great deal of work also."

Such language was not of a nature to influence Ragu. One expression alone had struck him. "Oh! everybody's happiness," he said jeeringly, "that's very pretty. Only I prefer to begin by my own."

Luc then told him that he was free, that his account would be settled, and that he might leave when he pleased. After all, he had no interest in retaining a malicious man, whose evil disposition might prove fatally contagious. But the thought of Josine's departure wrung Luc's heart, and he felt slightly ashamed when he realised that he had only shown so much warmth in seeking to retain Ragu at La Crêcherie because he wished to retain her there. The thought that she would go back to live amidst the filth of Old Beauclair, with that man who, relapsing into his passion for drink, would assuredly treat her with violence, was unbearable to Luc. He pictured her once more in the Rue des Trois Lunes, in a filthy room, a prey to sordid, deadly misery; and he would no longer be near to watch over her. Yet she was his now, and he would have liked to have had her always with him in order to render her life a happy one. On the following night she came back to see him, and there was then a heart-rending scene between them: tears, vows, wild suggestions and plans. But reason prevailed; it was needful that they should accept facts as they were, if they did not wish to compromise the success of the work which was now common to both of them. Josine would follow Ragu, since she could not refuse to do so without raising a dangerous scandal; whilst Luc at La Crêcherie would continue battling for everybody's happiness in the conviction that victory would some day unite them. They were strong, since love, the invincible, was with them. She promised that she would come back to see him; nevertheless how painful was the rending when she bade him good-bye, and when, on the morrow, he saw her quit La Crêcherie, walking behind Ragu, who with Bourron was pushing a little hand-cart containing their few chattels!

Three days later Bourron followed Ragu, whom he had met each evening at Caffiaux's wine-shop. His mate had joked to such a degree about the "syrups" of the common-house, that he fancied he was acting as became a free man when in his turn he again went to live in the Rue des Trois Lunes. His wife, Babette, after at first attempting to prevent such foolish conduct, ended by resigning herself to it with all her usual gaiety. *Bah!* things would go on right enough, for her husband was a good fellow at bottom, and sooner or later would see things clearly. Thereupon she laughed, and moved her goods, simply saying *au revoir* to her neighbours; for she could not believe that she would never return to those pretty gardens which she had found so pleasant. She particularly hoped to bring back her daughter, Marthe, and her son, Sébastien, who were making so much progress at the schools. And, Sœurette having spoken of keeping them there, she consented to it.

However, the situation at La Crêcherie became yet worse, for other workmen yielded to the contagion of bad example by taking themselves off in the same fashion as Bourron and Ragu had done. They lacked faith quite as much as love, and Luc found himself battling with human bad will, cowardice, defection in various forms, such as one always encounters when one works for the happiness of others. He felt that even Bonnaire, always so reasonable and loyal, was secretly shaken. His home was troubled by the daily quarrels picked by his wife, La Toupe, whose vanity remained unsatisfied, for she had not yet been able to buy either the silk gown or the watch which she had been coveting ever since her youth. Besides, she was one of those women who regret that they have not been born princesses; and thus ideas of equality and of a community of interests angered her. She kept a hurricane perpetually blowing in the house, rationed out Daddy Lunot's tobacco more gingerly than ever, and was for ever hustling her children, Lucien and Antoinette. Two more had been born to her, Zoé and Séverin, and this again she regarded as a disaster, for ever complaining of it to her husband. Bonnaire, however, remained very calm; he was accustomed to those storms, and they simply saddened him. He did not even answer when she shouted to him that he was a poor beast, a mere dupe, who would end by leaving his bones at La Crêcherie.

All the same Luc fully perceived that Bonnaire was scarcely with him. The man never allowed himself to speak a word of censure, he remained an active, punctual, conscientious worker, setting a good example to all his mates. But, in spite of this, there was disapproval, almost lassitude and discouragement, in his demeanour. Luc suffered greatly from it; he felt something like despair on finding such a man, whose heroism he knew and for whom he had so much esteem, drifting away so soon. If he, Bonnaire, was losing faith, could it be that the work was bad?

They had an explanation on the subject one evening, whilst seated on a bench at the door of the workshops. They had met just as the sun was setting in a quiet sky, and, sitting down, they talked together.

"It is quite true, monsieur," said Bonnaire frankly, in reply to a question from Luc, "I have great doubts about your success. Besides, you will remember that I never quite shared your ideas, and that your attempt seemed to me regrettable on account of the concessions you made. If I joined in it, it was, so to say, by way of experiment. But the further things go the more I see that I wasn't wrong. The experiment is made now, and something else, revolutionary action, will have to be attempted."

"What! the experiment made!" exclaimed Luc. "Why, we are only beginning it! It will require years—several lifetimes possibly; it may be a century-long effort of will and courage. And it is you, my friend, you a man of energy and bravery, who begin to doubt at this stage?"

As he spoke Luc gazed at Bonnaire, with his giant build, and broad, peaceful face on which one read so much honest strength. But the man gently shook his head. "No, no," said he, "goodwill and courage will do nothing. It's your method which is too gentle, which places too much reliance on men's wisdom. Your association of capital, talent, and work will go on always at a jog-trot, without establishing anything substantial and final. The fact is the evil has reached such a degree of abomination that one can only heal it by applying a red-hot iron."

"Then what ought one to do, my friend?"

"It is necessary that the people should at once seize all the implements of labour; it is necessary that it should dispossess the *bourgeoise* class and dispose of all the capital itself in order to organise compulsory universal work."

Once more did Bonnaire explain his ideas. He had remained entirely on the side of Collectivism, and Luc, who listened sorrowfully, felt astonished that he had in no wise won over that thoughtful but rather obtuse mind. Even as he had heard him speaking in the Rue des Trois Lunes on the night when he had quitted the Abyss, so did he find him speaking now, still holding to the same revolutionary conceptions, his faith in no degree modified by the five years which he had spent at La Crêcherie. He held evolution to be too slow, saying that progress merely by association would demand far too many years for realisation;

and he was weary of such an attempt, and only believed in immediate and violent revolution.

"We shall never be given what we don't take," said he by way of conclusion. "To have everything we must take everything."

Silence fell. The sun had set, and the night shifts had started work in the resounding galleries. Luc, whilst listening to those renewed efforts of labour, could feel an indescribable sadness stealing over him as he foresaw that his work would be compromised by the eager haste of even the best to bring about their social ideal. Indeed, was it not often the furious battling of ideas which hindered and retarded the realisation of facts?

"I won't argue with you again, my friend," he at last replied. "I don't think that any decisive revolution is possible or likely to give good results in the circumstances in which we find ourselves. And I am convinced that association and co-operation offer the preferable road, one along which progress may be slow, but which will all the same end by leading us to the promised city. We have often talked of those matters without altogether agreeing. So what use would it be to begin afresh and thereby sadden ourselves? One thing that I do hope of you is, that in the difficulties through which we are passing you will remain faithful to the enterprise we founded together."

Bonnaire made a sudden gesture of annoyance. "Oh, Monsieur Luc!" he exclaimed, "have you doubted me? You know very well that I am not a traitor, and that since you one day saved me from starving, I'm ready to eat my dry bread with you as long as may be necessary. Don't be anxious; I never say to others what I've just said to you; those are matters between you and me. Naturally, I'm not going to discourage our men here by announcing that we shall soon be ruined. We are associated, and we will remain associated until the walls fall down on our heads."

Greatly moved, Luc pressed both his hands. And during the ensuing week he witnessed a scene in the hall where the rolling-machinery was installed, which touched him even more. He had been warned that two or three wrong-headed fellows wished to follow Ragu's example and carry off with them as many of their mates as possible. Just as he was arriving to restore order, however, he saw Bonnaire intervening vehemently in the midst of the mutineers. He thereupon stopped short and listened. Bonnaire was saying precisely what it was requisite one should say in such a difficulty, recalling the benefits that had come from the works, and calming the anxiety of his mates by promises of a better future, provided that they all worked bravely. He looked so superb, so handsome, and spoke so well that the others speedily became quiet. Influenced by the fact that one of themselves had used such sensible arguments, none spoke any further of quitting the association; and thus defection was stopped. Luc could never forget that spectacle of Bonnaire pacifying his revolted comrades with the broad gestures of a good giant, the courage of a hero of work, full of respect for freely accepted toil. Since they were fighting for the happiness of all, he would indeed have thought himself a coward had he deserted his post, even though he was of opinion that they ought to have fought the battle in another manner.

When Luc, however, expressed his thanks he was again distressed by this quiet reply. "It was simple enough," said Bonnaire; "I merely did what it was my duty to do. All the same, Monsieur Luc, I shall have to bring you round to my ideas, for otherwise we shall all end by dying of starvation here."

A few days later Luc's gloom was increased by another conversation. He was coming down from the smeltery—with Bonnaire as it happened—when the pair of them passed before the kilns of Lange the potter, who obstinately clung to the narrow strip of land which had been left him beside the rocky ridge of the Bleuse Mountains, and which he had enclosed with a little wall of stones. In vain had Luc proposed to take him on at La Crêcherie, offering him the management of a crucible-making department which he had found it necessary to establish. Lange's reply was that he wished to remain free "without either God or master." So he continued dwelling in his wild den and making common pottery, pans, stock-pots, and pitchers, which he afterwards carted to the markets and fairs of the neighbouring villages, he himself drawing the cart whilst Barefeet pushed it from behind. That evening, as it happened, they were returning together from one of their rounds when Luc and Bonnaire passed before their little enclosure.

"Well, Lange, is business prospering?" the young man cordially inquired.

"Oh! always well enough to give us bread, Monsieur Luc. As you're aware, that is all that I ask for," answered Lange.

Indeed, he only carted his wares about when bread was lacking in his home. Throughout his spare time he lingered over pottery which was not intended for sale, remaining for hours in contemplation of the things he thus made, his eyes having the dreamy expression of those of some rustic poet full of a passion to impart life to things. Even the coarse goods which he fashioned, his very pans and stock-pots, displayed a *naïveté* and purity of lines, a proud and simple gracefulness which bespoke poetic fancy. A son of the people, as he was, he had instinctively lighted upon the old primitive popular beauty, that beauty of the humble domestic utensil which arises from perfection of proportions and absolute adaptability to the uses to which the utensil is intended to be put.

Luc was struck by that beauty on examining a few unsold pieces in the little hand-cart. And the sight of Barefeet, that tall, dark, comely girl, with the strong, slender limbs of a wrestler and the firm bosom of an Amazon, likewise filled him with mingled admiration and astonishment.

"It is hard to push that along all day, isn't it?" he said to her.

But she was a silent creature, and contented herself with smiling with her big, wild eyes, whilst the potter answered in her stead: "Oh! we rest in the shade by the wayside when we come upon a spring," said he. "Things are all right, aren't they, Barefeet, and we are happy."

The young woman had turned her eyes on him, and they glowed with boundless adoration, as for some beloved, powerful, benign master, a saviour, a god. Then without a word she pushed the little hand-cart into the enclosure and set it in place under a shed.

Lange, on his side, had watched her with a glance of deep affection. At times he feigned some roughness, as if he still regarded her as a mere gipsy picked up by the wayside, But truth to tell she was now the mistress. He loved her with a passion which he did not confess, which he hid beneath the demeanour of an uncouth peasant. In point of fact that thick-set little man with square-shaped head, bushy with a tangle of hair and beard, was of a very gentle and amorous nature.

All at once, again turning towards Luc, whom he affected to treat as a "comrade," he said to him in his rough, frank way: "Well, isn't everybody's happiness getting on, then? Aren't those idiots who consent to shut themselves up in your barracks willing to be happy in the fashion you want?"

Each time that he met Luc he thus jeered at the attempt at Fourierist Communism which was being made at La Crêcherie. And as the young man contented himself with smiling, he added: "I'm hoping that before another six months have gone by you'll be with us, the Anarchists. I tell you once again that everything is rotten, and that the only thing is to blow old society to pieces with bombs!"

At this Bonnaire, hitherto silent, abruptly intervened. "Oh! with bombs—that's idiotic!"

He, a pure Collectivist, was not in favour of crime, so called "propaganda by deeds," although he believed in the necessity of a general and violent revolution.

"What, idiotic?" cried Lange, who felt hurt. "Do you imagine that if the *bourgeois* are not properly prepared for it your famous socialisation of the instruments of labour will ever take place? It's your disguised Capitalism which is idiotic. Just begin by destroying everything so as to have the ground clear for building up things properly."

They went on arguing, the Anarchism of one contending with the Collectivism of the other, and Luc remained listening to them. The distance between Lange and Bonnaire, he noticed, was as great as the distance between Bonnaire and himself. By the extreme bitterness of their dispute one might have taken them to be men of different races, hereditary enemies, ready to devour one another, and beyond all possibility of agreement. Yet they desired the very same happiness for one and all, they met at the very same point: justice, peace, and a reorganisation of work giving bread and joy to all. But what fury, what aggressive, deadly hatred became manifest on either side as soon as there was a question of agreeing on the means to be employed to attain that end! All along the rough road of progress at each halt the brothers on the march, one and all inflamed by the same desire for enfranchisement, waged bloody battles together on the simple question whether they would do best to turn to the right or to the left.

"After all each of us is his own master," Lange ended by declaring. "Go to sleep in your *bourgeoise* niche, if it amuses you, mate. I know what I myself have got to do. They are getting on, they are getting on, those little presents of mine, those little pots which we shall deposit some fine morning at the sub-prefect's, the mayor's, the judge's, and the parson's. Isn't that so, Barefeet? We shall have a fine round that morning! Ah! shan't we push our cart on gaily?"

The tall and beautiful girl had now returned to the threshold, and stood out sculpturally, in sovereign fashion amongst the ruddy clay of the little enclosure. Her eyes again blazed, and she smiled like one who is all submission, ready to follow her master to the point of crime.

"She belongs to it, mate," added Lange in all simplicity. "She helps me."

When Luc and Bonnaire had quitted him, without any show of animosity on either side, though they agreed together so little, they walked on for a few moments in silence. Then Bonnaire felt a desire to renew his argument and demonstrate yet once again that no salvation was possible outside of the Collectivist faith. He anathematised the Anarchists, even as he anathematised the Fourierists—the latter because they did not immediately possess themselves of the capital, now in the hands of the *bourgeois*, the former because they suppressed it by violence; and it again appeared to Luc that reconciliation would only be possible when the future community should be founded, for then, in presence of the realisation of the common dream, all sects would necessarily be contented. But what a long road yet remained to be travelled, and how grievously he feared lest his brothers should devour one another on the way!

He returned home saddened by all that constant clashing which impeded the progress of his work. No sooner, apparently, had two men resolved to act than they began to disagree. Then, on finding himself alone, the cry which ever inflated Luc's heart burst forth from him: "But they do not love! If they loved, all would prove fruitful and grow and triumph in the sunlight!"

Morfain was also now causing the young man a deal of worry. In vain had he tried to civilise the smelter by offering him one of the gay little houses of La Crêcherie if he would only quit his cave in the rocks. The other stubbornly refused, on the pretext that up yonder he was near his work and able to watch over it unceasingly. Luc had now confided to him the whole management of the smeltery, which worked on in the ancient fashion, pending the invention of those electrical furnaces which Jordan, never wearying, was still striving to devise.

However, the real cause of Morfain's obstinacy in refusing to come down and dwell among the men peopling the new town was the disdain, the hatred almost, with which he regarded them. He who personified the Vulcan of the primitive days, a tamer of fire, later on crushed down by prolonged slavery, toiling with heroic resignation, and ending by loving the sombre grandeur of the inferno in which fate kept him, felt irritated with those new works where toilers were to become gentlemen, using their arms but sparingly, since they would be replaced by machinery, which mere children would soon know how to drive. That desire to toil as little as possible, to cease battling personally with fire and iron, seemed to Morfain abject and wretched. He could not even understand it, but simply shrugged his shoulders whenever he thought of it during his long days of silence. And, alone and proud, he remained on his mountain-ridge reigning over the smeltery and looking down upon the new works, which the dazzling flow of liquid metal crowned as with flames four times every four-and-twenty hours.

But there was yet another reason which angered Morfain with those new times which he wished to ignore; and this was a reason which must have made the heart of the taciturn smelter bleed frightfully. Ma-Bleue, his daughter, whose blue eyes were to him like the blue of heaven, that tall and beautiful creature, who since her mother's death had worked as the well-loved housewife of the wild home, had become *enceinte*. Morfain flew into a rage when he discovered it, and then forgave her, saying to himself that she would assuredly some day have got married. But forgiveness was suddenly recalled, and became impossible when his daughter gave him her lover's name—that of Achille Gourier, the son of the mayor of Beauclair. The intrigue had been going on for years now, amidst the evening breezes, under the starry sky, along the paths of the Bleuse Mountains, and over their rocks and patches of thyme and lavender. Achille, breaking off all intercourse with his family, like a young *bourgeois* whom the *bourgeoisie* bored and disgusted, had at last begged Luc to take him on at La Crêcherie, where he had become a designer. He thus severed every tie connecting him with his former life; he lived as he listed, resolved to toil for her whom he had chosen, like a scion of the old condemned social system whom evolution led towards the new age. What angered Morfain to such a point that he drove his daughter from home was precisely the fact that she had suffered herself to be led astray by a *monsieur*, in such wise that to him there seemed naught but rebellion and devilry in her conduct. The whole antique edifice must be tumbling to pieces since so good and beautiful a girl had shaken it by listening to, and perhaps even angling for, the son of the mayor.

As Ma-Bleue, on being turned out of doors, naturally sought a refuge with Achille, Luc was compelled to intervene. The young people did not even speak of marriage. What was the use of any such ceremony since they were quite sure that they loved one another, and would never part? Besides, in order to get married Achille would have had to address "judicial summonses" to his father; and this seemed to him useless and vexatious trouble. In vain did Sœurette insist on the matter, in the idea that morality and the good repute of La Crêcherie still required that there should be a legal marriage. Luc ended by prevailing on her to close her eyes, for he felt that with the new generations one would be gradually compelled to accept the principle of free union.

Morfain, however, did not consent to the position so readily, and Luc had to go up one evening to reason with him. Since he had driven his daughter away the master-smelter lived alone with his son, Petit-Da, and between them they cooked their meals, and attended to the various household duties in their rocky cave. That evening, after partaking of some soup, they had remained seated on their stools at the roughly-hewn table which they had made themselves, while the little lamp which lighted them threw the shadows of their burly figures upon the smoky stone walls.

"Yet the world advances, father," Petit-Da was saying. "One can't remain motionless."

Morfain banged his fist on the table and made it shake. "I lived as my father lived," said he, "and your duty is to live as I do."

As a rule the two men scarcely exchanged four words a day. But for some time past a feeling of uneasiness had been growing up between them, and although they did all they could to avert it, disputes sometimes arose. The son, who could read and write, was being more and more affected by the evolution of the times, which penetrated even to the depths of the mountain gorges. And the father, in his proud and stubborn determination to remain merely a strong toiler, able to subjugate fire and conquer iron, indulged in sorrowful outbursts, as if his race were degenerating through all the science and useless ideas of the new era.

"If your sister hadn't read books and hadn't busied herself about what went on down below, she'd still be with us," said he. "Ah! it was that new town, that cursed town, that took her from us!"

This time he did not strike the table, but thrust his fist through the open doorway, into the dark night, towards La Crêcherie, whose lights twinkled like stars below the rocky ridge.

Petit-Da did not answer, in part from a sense of respect, in part because he felt embarrassed, for he knew that his father had been displeased with him ever since meeting him one day with Honorine, the daughter of Caffiaux, the tavern-keeper. Honorine, short, slender, and dark, with a gay wide-awake face, had fallen passionately in love with that gentle young giant; and he for his part thought her charming. In the discussion which had broken out that evening between the father and the son, the question at bottom was really one of Honorine. And thus the direct attack which Petit-Da had all along anticipated ended by coming.

"And you," suddenly said his father, "when are you going to leave me?"

This idea of a separation seemed to upset Petit-Da. "Why, do you want me to leave you, father?" he asked.

"Oh, when a girl's in question there can only be quarrels and ruin. And besides, what girl have you chosen? Will her people even let you have her? Is there any sense in such marriages, which mix one class with another, and turn the world topsy-turvy? It's the end of everything. I've lived too long."

Gently and tenderly his son strove to pacify him. The young man did not deny his love for Honorine. Only he spoke like a sensible lad, who was resolved to remain patient as long as might be necessary. They would see about the matter later on. Nevertheless, when he and the girl chanced to meet what harm could there be in wishing one another a friendly good day? Although folks might not be of the same position, that did not always prevent them from caring for one another. And even if different classes were to mingle a little, would that not have its good side, since they would thus learn to know each other and esteem each other more?

Morfain, however, full of wrath and bitterness, did not listen to those arguments. He suddenly rose up, and with a great tragic wave of his arm under the rocky ceiling which his head almost touched, he replied: "Be off! be off as soon as you like! Do as your sister has done! Spit on everything that's respectable, leap into shamelessness and madness. You are no longer my children, I no longer recognise you; somebody has changed you! So leave me here alone in this wild den, where I hope the rocks will soon fall down on me and crush me to death!"

Luc, at that moment just arriving, paused on the threshold and heard those last words. He was greatly affected by them, for he held Morfain in much esteem. For a long time he reasoned with him. But the smelter, on the arrival of the young man whom he regarded as a master, had forced back his grief to become once more a mere workman, a submissive subordinate with no thoughts beyond his duties. He did not even allow himself to judge Luc, although the latter was the primary cause of the abominations which were upsetting the region and causing him so much pain. The masters after all had a right to act as they pleased, and it was for the workmen to remain honest and do their work as their elders had done it before them.

"Do not be alarmed, Monsieur Luc," he said, "if I happen to have some ideas of my own, and get angry when I find them thwarted. It seldom happens, for you know that I'm no talker. And you may be quite sure that the work does not suffer from it; for I always keep one eye open, and no metal is ever run out otherwise than in my presence. After all, when one's heart is full one works all the harder. Isn't that so?"

Then, however, as Luc again strove to make peace in that unhappy family, ravaged by the evolution of which he had made himself the apostle, the master-smelter all but flew into a passion once more.

"No, no, that's enough, let me be! If you came up, Monsieur Luc, to speak to me about Ma-Bleue you did wrong, because that's the very way to make things worse. Let her stop where she is, while I stop where I am!"

Then, desirous of changing the conversation, he brusquely gave Luc some bad news, which indeed had largely brought about his fit of ill-temper.

"I should probably have gone down to you by-and-by," he said, "for I wanted to tell you that I went to the mine again this morning, and that we've again been disappointed in our hope of finding the rich vein. Yet I could have sworn that it would certainly be met at the end of the gallery I indicated. What would you have? An evil spell seems to have been cast over all we have undertaken for some time past. Nothing succeeds!"

Those words resounded in Luc's ears like the knell of his great hopes. He lingered for a moment talking with the father and the son, and then went down the hillside again, overcome by bitter sadness, and wondering upon what ever-increasing mass of ruins he would have to found his city.

Even at La Crêcherie he encountered reasons for discouragement. Sœurette still received Abbé Marle, Schoolmaster Hermeline, and Doctor Novarre, and it apparently gave her so much pleasure to have her friend Luc to lunch on those occasions that he dared not decline her invitations, in spite of the secret discomfort into which he was thrown by the everlasting disputes of the schoolmaster and the priest. Sœurette, whose mind was at peace, did not suffer from them, and even thought that they interested Luc; whilst Jordan, wrapped in his rugs and dreaming of some experiment which he had begun, seemed to listen with a vague smile.

One Tuesday, after they had risen from table, the dispute in the little drawing-room became exceptionally violent. Hermeline had tackled Luc with respect to the education which was being given to the children at La Crêcherie; he spoke of the boys and girls mingling in the five classes, of the long intervals of play that were allowed, and of the numerous hours spent in the workshops. This new school, where methods diametrically opposed to his own were pursued, had robbed him of several of his own pupils, a thing which he could not forgive. And his angular face, with its long brow and thin lips, turned pale with suppressed rage at the idea that anybody could believe otherwise than himself.

"I might consent to see those boys and girls brought up together," said he, "though it seems to me scarcely proper, for they already evince an abundance of evil instincts when the sexes are separated, and the extraordinary idea of uniting them can only pervert them the more. But what I hold to be inadmissible is that the master's authority is destroyed and discipline reduced to nothingness. Did you not tell me that each pupil followed his own bent, applied himself to those studies which pleased him, and was free to argue about his lessons? You call that raising energy, it seems. But what can those studies be when the pupils are always at play, when books are held in contempt, when the master's word ceases to be infallible, and when the time not spent in the garden is spent in workshops, planing wood or filing iron? A manual calling is a good thing to learn, no doubt; but there is a time for everything, and the first thing is to force as much grammar and arithmetic as possible into the brains of all those idlers!"

Luc had ceased arguing, weary as he was of coming into collision with the stubborn uncompromising views of that sectarian, who having decreed a dogma of progress according to his own lights refused to stir from it. Thus the young man quietly contented himself with replying: "Yes, we think it necessary to render the pupils' work attractive, to change classical studies into constant lessons of things, and our object above all else is to create will, to create men!"

Hermeline thereupon exploded: "Well, do you know what you will create?" he cried. "You will create so many *déclassés*, so many rebels! There is only one way to give citizens to the State, and that is to make them expressly for it, such as it needs them in order to be strong and glorious. Thence comes the necessity for discipline and a system of education preparing, according to the programmes which are recognised as the best, the workmen, the professional men, and the functionaries which the country needs. Outside the pale of authority there is no certainty. For my part I am an old republican, a free-thinker, an atheist. Nobody, I hope, will ever picture me as a man with a retrograde mind; and yet your system of education sets me beside myself, because in half a century, with such a system of work, there would be no more citizens, no more soldiers, no more patriots. Yes, indeed, I defy you to make soldiers of your so-called free men; and in that case how could the country defend itself in the event of war?"

"No doubt, in the event of war, it would be necessary to defend it," answered Luc, unmoved. "But of what use will soldiers be some day, if men no longer fight? You talk like Captain Jollivet writes in the 'Journal de Beauclair,' when he accuses us of being traitors—men without a country."

This touch of sarcasm, although slight, brought Hermeline's anger to a climax. "Captain Jollivet is an idiot for whom I feel nothing but contempt," said he. "But it is none the less true that you are preparing a disorderly generation, in rebellion against the State, and one which would assuredly lead the Republic to the worst catastrophes."

"All liberty, all truth, all justice are catastrophes," said Luc, again smiling.

But Hermeline went on drawing a frightful picture of to-morrow's social system, if indeed the schools should cease to turn out citizens on a given pattern for the needs of his authoritarian republic. There would be no more political discipline, no more government possible, no more sovereignty of the State, but in lieu thereof would come disorderly license, leading to the worst forms of corruption and debauchery. And all at once Abbé Marle, who had been listening and nodding his head approvingly, could not resist an impulse to exclaim, "Ah! yes, you are quite right, and all that is put very well indeed!"

His broad, full face, with its regular features and aquiline nose, was radiant with delight at that furious attack upon the new society, in which he felt his Deity would be condemned, regarded simply as the historical idol of a dead religion. He himself, each Sunday in the pulpit, brought forward the same accusations, prophesied the same disasters as Hermeline. But he was scarcely listened to, his church became emptier every day, and he felt deep, unacknowledged grief thereat, confining himself more and more, as his sole consolation, within his narrow doctrines. Never had he shown himself more attached to the letter of dogma, never had he inflicted severer penance on his penitents, as if indeed he were desirous that the *bourgeois* world, over whose rottenness he threw the cloak of religion, might at least show a brave demeanour when it was submerged. On the day when his church would fall, he at any rate would be at his altar, and would finish his last mass beneath the ruins.

"It is quite true," said he to Hermeline, "that the reign of Satan is near at hand, what with all those lads and girls brought up together, every evil passion let loose, authority destroyed, the kingdom of God set, not in Heaven, but on earth as in the time of the pagans. The picture that you have drawn of it all is so correct that I myself could add nothing stronger."

Embarrassed at being thus praised by the priest, with whom he never agreed on anything, the schoolmaster suddenly became silent, and gazed at the lawns of the park as if he did not hear.

"But," resumed Abbé Marle, addressing himself this time to Luc, "apart from the demoralising education given in your schools, there is one thing that I cannot pardon, which is that you have turned the Divinity out of doors, and have voluntarily neglected to build a church in the centre of your new town, among so many handsome and useful edifices. Do you pretend then that you can live without God? No State hitherto has been able to do so. A religion has always been necessary for the government of men."

"I pretend nothing," Luc replied. "Each man is free with respect to his belief, and if no church has been built it is because none of us has yet felt the need of one. But one can be built should there be faithful to attend it. It will always be allowable for a group of citizens to meet together for such satisfactions as may please them. And with regard to the necessity of a religion, that is indeed a real necessity when one desires to govern men. But we do not desire to govern them at all; on the contrary, we wish them to live free in the free city. Let me tell you, Monsieur l'Abbé, it is not we who are destroying Catholicism, it is destroying itself, it is dying slowly of old age, like all religions, after accomplishing their historical task, necessarily die at the hour indicated by human evolution. Science destroys all dogmas one by one; the religion of humanity is born and will conquer the world. What is the use of a Catholic church at La Crêcherie, since yours at Beauclair is already too large, growing more and more deserted, and destined one of these days to topple over?"

The priest was very pale, but he would not understand. With the stubbornness of a believer who places his strength in affirmation without reason or proof, he contented himself with repeating: "If God is not with you, your defeat is certain. Believe me, build a church."

Hermeline was unable to restrain himself any longer. The priest's words of praise were still suffocating him, particularly as they had been followed by that declaration of the necessity of a religion. "Ah, no! ah, no, Abbé!" he shouted, "no church, please! I make no concealment of the fact that matters are hardly organised in the new town in accordance with my tastes. But if there is one thing that I approve, it is certainly the relinquishment of any State religion. Govern men? Why yes, only instead of the priests in their churches, it is we, the citizens in our municipal buildings, who will govern them. As for the churches, they will be turned into public granaries, barns for the crops!"

Then as Abbé Marle, losing his temper, declared that he would not allow sacrilegious language to be used in his presence, the dispute became so bitter that Doctor Novarre, as usual, was forced to intervene. He had hitherto listened to the others with his shrewd air, like a gentle and somewhat sceptical man who was not put out by any words, however violent, that might be exchanged. However, he fancied he could detect that the dispute was beginning to pain Sœurette.

"Come, come!" said he, "you almost agree, since both of you put the churches to use. The Abbé will always be able to say mass provided he leaves a little space in his church for the fruits of the earth, in years of great abundance." Then the doctor went on to speak of a new rose that he had just raised, a superb flower, its outer petals very white and pure, and its heart warmed by a pronounced flush of carmine. He had brought a bunch of the flowers, which had been placed in a vase on the table, and Sœurette looking at it smiled once more at the sight of that florescence all charm and perfume, though she still felt saddened and tired by the violence which nowadays marked the quarrels attending her Tuesday lunches. If things went on in that fashion, it would soon be impossible for them to see one another.

And it was only now that Jordan emerged from his reverie. He had not ceased to appear attentive, as if indeed he were listening to the others. But he made a remark which showed how far away his mind had been. "Do you know," exclaimed he, "that a learned electrician in America has succeeded in storing enough solar heat to produce electricity?"

When the priest, the schoolmaster, and the doctor had departed and Luc found himself alone with the Jordans profound silence fell. The thought of all the poor men who tore one another and crushed one another in their blind struggle for happiness rent the young man's heart. As time went by, seeing with what difficulty one worked for the common weal, having to contend against the revolts even of those whom one worked to save, Luc was sometimes seized with discouragement which he would not as yet confess, but which left both his limbs and his mind strengthless as after some great useless exertion. For a moment his will would capsize and seem on the point of sinking. And again that day he raised his cry of distress: "But they don't love! If they loved all would prove fruitful, all would grow and triumph in the sunlight!"

A few days later, one autumn morning, at a very early hour, Sœurette experienced a terrible heart-blow which threw her into the greatest anguish. She invariably rose betimes, and that morning she was going to give some orders at a dairy which she had established for the infants of her *créche*, when, as she went along the terrace which ended at the pavilion occupied by Luc, it occurred to her to glance down at the road which the terrace overlooked. And precisely at that moment the door of the pavilion opening into the road was set ajar, and she saw a woman steal out, a woman of slender form, who immediately afterwards disappeared amidst the pinkish morning mist. Nevertheless Sœurette had time to recognise her: it was Josine, leaving Luc at break of day.

Since Ragu's departure from La Crêcherie Josine, indeed, had returned to see Luc every now and then. On this occasion she had come to tell him that she should not again return, for she feared lest she might be surprised when leaving her home or returning thither by some of her inquisitive neighbours. Moreover, the idea of lying and hiding herself in order to join the man whom she regarded as a god had become so painful to her that she preferred to await the day when she might proclaim her love aloud. Luc, understanding her, had resigned himself to this separation; but how full of passion and despair was their hour of farewell! They lingered there, exchanging vows, and the daylight had already come when Josine was at last able to tear herself away. Only the morning mist in some degree veiled her flitting, though not sufficiently to prevent Jordan's sister from recognising her.

Sœurette, in the shock of her discovery, had stopped short, rooted to the spot, as if she saw the earth opening before her. Such was her agitation, such a buzzing filled her ears, that at first she could not reason. She forgot that she was going to the dairy to give an order, and all at once she fled, retracing her steps at a run, returning to the house and climbing wildly to her room, the door of which she locked behind her. And then she flung herself upon her bed, striving to cover both her eyes and her ears with her hands, so that she might see and hear nothing more. She did not weep, she had not recovered full consciousness as yet, but a feeling of awful desolation, blended with boundless fright, filled her being.

Why did she suffer thus, why did she feel such a rending within her? She had hitherto thought herself to be simply Luc's affectionate friend, his disciple and helper, one who was passionately devoted to the work which he was striving to accomplish. Yet now she was all aglow, shaken by burning fever, and this because her eyes could ever picture that other woman quitting him at daybreak. Did she love Luc then? And had she only become conscious of it on the day when it was too late for her to win his love? That, indeed, was the disaster: to learn in such a brutal fashion that she loved, and that another already possessed the heart over which she might perchance have reigned like some all-powerful, beloved queen. All the rest vanished: she recalled neither how her love had sprung up, nor how it had grown, nor how it was that she had remained ignorant of it, artless still in her thirtieth year, happy simply in the enjoyment of affectionate intimacy, untouched till now by passion's dart. Her tears gushed forth at last, and she sobbed over her discovery, over the sudden obstacle which had risen to part her from the man to whom unknowingly she had given both heart and soul. And now naught but the knowledge of her love existed for her; and she asked herself, What should she do—how should she succeed in making herself loved? For it seemed impossible that she should not be loved in return, since she herself loved and would never cease to love. Now that her love was known to her, it began to consume her heart, and she felt that she would no longer be able to live unless it were shared. At the same time all remained confusion within her, she struggled amidst vague and contradictory thoughts, obscure plans, like a woman who, despite her years, has remained childish and suddenly finds herself confronted by the torturing realities of life.

Long must she have remained striving to annihilate herself, with her face close pressed to her pillow. The sun climbed the heavens, the morning sped on; and yet in her increasing distress she could devise no practical solution for the problem that tortured her. Ever and ever did the haunting questions come back: how would she manage to say that she loved, and how would she manage to secure love in return? All at once, however, she bethought herself of her brother. It was in him that she must confide, since he alone really knew her—knew that her heart had never lied. He was a man, he would surely understand her, and he would teach her what it is meet for one to do when a craving for happiness possesses one. Accordingly, without reasoning any further, she sprang off her bed and went downstairs to the laboratory, like a child who has at last discovered a solution for its grief.

That morning Jordan himself had experienced a disastrous check. Of recent months he had believed that he had devised a safe and cheap system for the transport of electric force. He burnt coal beside the pit it came from, and he carried electricity over long distances without the slightest loss of power, in such wise as to lessen cost price considerably. He had given four years of study to that problem amidst all the recurring ailments to which his puny frame was subject. He made the best use possible of his weak health, sleeping a great deal, wrapped round with rugs, and then methodically employing the few hours which he was able to wrest from his unkind mother Nature. For fear of disturbing his studies, the crisis through which La Crêcherie was passing had been hidden from him. He thought that things were going on satisfactorily at the works, and, besides, it was out of the question for him to take any interest in such matters, cloistered as he was in his laboratory, absorbed in his work, apart from which nothing seemed to exist in the whole world. That very morning at an early hour he had resumed his studies, feeling his mind to be quite clear, and wishing to profit by it, in order to make a last experiment. And that experiment had absolutely failed; he found himself confronted by an unforeseen obstacle, some error in his calculations, some detail which he had neglected, and which suddenly became important and all-destructive, indefinitely postponing the solution that he had long sought with respect to his electrical furnaces.

It was the downfall of his hopes: so much hard work had yielded nothing, so much more of it would be necessary! Yet he remained calm, and had just wrapped himself in his rugs again, and ensconced himself in the arm-chair in which he spent so many hours, when his sister came into the laboratory. She looked so pale, so greatly distressed, that he immediately felt anxious on her account, he who had witnessed the failure of his experiment with unruffled brow, like a man whom nothing can discourage.

"What is the matter, my dear?" he asked her; "are you not well?"

Her confession in no wise embarrassed her. Without any hesitation, like a poor creature whose heart opens with a sob, she said: "The matter, brother dear, is that I love Luc, and that he does not love me. Ah! I am very unhappy!"

Then, simple and artless, she told her brother the whole story—how she had seen Josine leaving the pavilion, and how she had then felt such a heart-pang that she had come in search of consolation and cure: she loved Luc, and Luc did not love her!

Jordan listened in a state of stupefaction, as if she had apprised him of some unexpected, extraordinary cataclysm.

"You love Luc! you love Luc!" he repeated. "Love, why love?" The thought that love possessed that fondly treasured sister whom he had always seen beside him like his second self, filled him with amazement. He had never thought that she might some day love, and from that cause become unhappy. Love was a craving of which he himself knew nothing, a sphere into which he had never entered. And thus, artless and ignorant as he himself was, his embarrassment became extreme.

"Oh! tell me, brother, why does Luc love that Josine, why does he not love me?" Sœurette repeated. She was sobbing now. She had wound her arms around her brother's neck, resting her head upon his shoulder, so weighed down by distress that he was utterly distracted. And yet what could he say to console her?

"I don't know, little sister; I don't know," he answered. "No doubt he loves her because it is his nature to love. There can be no other reason. He would love you if he had loved you the first."

There was truth in this. Luc loved Josine because she was an *amorosa*, a woman of charm and passion, whom he had found suffering, and who had kindled into flame all the love of his heart. And besides, beauty was hers, with the passion which peoples the world.

"But, brother," said Sœurette, "he knew me before he knew her, so why did he not love me first?"

More and more embarrassed by these questions, Jordan anxiously sought for delicate and kindly words: "Perhaps," he answered, "it was because he lived here like a friend, a brother. He has become a brother for you and me."

Whilst speaking thus, Jordan looked at his sister, and this time he did not tell her all that he thought. He observed her resemblance to himself. She was so slender, so frail, so insignificant. She did not represent love; she was too pale and puny. Charming no doubt, very gentle and very kind; but then, ever clad in black, sombre-looking and sad, as are all the silent and devoted ones. For Luc she had never been aught but an intelligent and a benevolent creature.

"You will understand, little sister," Jordan presently resumed, "that if he has become as it were your brother and mine, he cannot love you in the same way as he loves Josine. Such a thing would not have entered his mind. But none the less I am sure that he loves you a great deal; he loves you indeed all the more, as much in fact as I myself love you."

But Sœœurette would not admit it. Her whole being protested dolorously, and amidst a fresh explosion of sobs she cried her distress aloud: "No, no; he does not love me the more; he does not love me at all! To love a woman as a brother! what is that when I suffer as I am suffering now that I see him lost to me? If I knew naught of all those things a little while ago, at least I divine them now, and I feel as if I should die—yes, die!"

Like herself, Jordan was becoming more and more distressed, and only with difficulty was he able to restrain his tears. "Little sister, little sister," said he, "you grieve me deeply. It is scarcely reasonable of you to make yourself ill like this. I no longer recognise you. You are usually so calm and sensible, and you are well aware what firmness of spirit one ought to evince in order to resist the worries of life."

Then he wished to reason with her. "Come," he said, "you have no reproach to address to Luc?"

"Oh! none. I know that he has a great deal of affection for me. We are very good friends," she answered plaintively.

"Then you must not complain. He loves you as he is able to love, and you do wrong in getting angry with him."

"But I am not angry! I have no hate for anybody; I only suffer."

Again did her sobs burst forth; again did distress master her, and wring from her lips the cry: "Why does he not love me? Why does he not love me?"

"If he does not love you as you desire to be loved, little sister," said Jordan, "it is because he does not know you well enough. No, he does not know you as I do; he does not know that you are the best, the gentlest, the most devoted and affectionate of women. You would have been a fit companion and helper; the one that makes life's pathway softer and easier. But the other came with her beauty, and that assuredly was a powerful force, since he followed her without perceiving you, and this although you already loved him. Come, my dear, you must resign yourself."

He had taken her in his arms, and he kissed her hair. But she still went on struggling.

"No! no! I cannot."

"Yes, you will resign yourself; you are too good, too intelligent to do otherwise. Some day you will forget."

"No! Never!"

"I did wrong to say that; I will not ask you to forget. Keep the memory of it in your heart. But I do ask you to be resigned, because I well know that you are capable of resignation, even to the point of sacrifice. Think of all the disasters which would follow if you were to rebel—to speak out! Our life would be broken up, our enterprises shattered, and you would suffer a thousand times more than you do now."

She interrupted him, quivering: "Well, let our life be broken up! let our enterprises be shattered! At least I shall have satisfied myself. It is cruel of you, brother, to speak to me like that. You are an egotist!"

"An egotist!" replied Jordan. "When I am only thinking of you, my dear little sister. At this moment grief is turning your wonted kindliness to exasperation. But how bitter would be your remorse if I were to allow you to destroy everything! You would no longer be able to live in presence of the ruins that you would have piled up. Poor, dear girl! you will resign yourself, and find happiness in abnegation and pure affection."

Tears were choking him, and their sobs mingled. That battle between brother and sister, both so artless and so loving, was fraught with the most exquisite fraternal affection. In a tone of intense compassion, blended with boundless kindliness, Jordan repeated: "You will resign yourself; you will resign yourself."

She still protested, but like one who is surrendering. Her moan now was that of a poor, stricken creature whose hurt one strives to soothe: "Oh, no! I cannot, I do not resign myself."

As it happened, Luc that very day was to take *déjeuner* with the Jordans, and when at half-past eleven he joined the brother and sister in the laboratory, he found them still agitated, with red, blurred eyes. But he himself was so distressed, so downcast, that he noticed nothing. Josine's farewell, the necessity of that separation, filled him with despair. The severance of the love which he deemed essential for his mission seemed to deprive him of his last strength. If he did not save Josine he would never save the unhappy multitude to whom he had given his heart. And that day, from the moment of rising, all the obstacles which hindered his advance had risen up before him like insurmountable impediments. A black vision of La Crêcherie had appeared to him. La Crêcherie on the path to ruin, wrecked already, to such a point indeed that it was madness to hope to save it. Men devoured one another there; it had been impossible to establish brotherly accord between them; every human fatality weighed upon the enterprise. And thus, bowed down by the most frightful discouragement he had ever known, Luc lost his faith. The heroism within him wavered; he was almost on the point of renouncing his task, fearing as he did that defeat was near at hand.

Sœurette noticed his perturbation directly she saw him, and, with divine solicitude, she expressed her anxiety: "Are you not well, my friend?" she asked him.

"No, I do not feel well," he answered. "I spent an awful morning. I have heard of nothing but misfortunes since I rose."

She did not insist, but gazed at him with increasing anxiety, wondering what his sufferings could be, since he loved and was loved in return. To hide in some slight degree her own intense emotion, she had seated herself at her little table, and pretended to be writing out some notes for her brother; whilst the latter, who now seemed overwhelmed, again lay back in his arm-chair.

"In that case, my good Luc," said he, "none of us is any better off than the others; for if I felt well enough when I got up this morning, I have since had no end of worry."

For a moment Luc walked about the room, silent, with a frown upon his face. He came and went, pausing at times before one of the large windows to glance over La Crêcherie, the budding town, whose roofs spread out before him. At last, unable to restrain his despair any longer, he exploded: "I must speak out, my friend. I owe you the truth. We did not wish to worry you in the midst of your researches, and we have hitherto hidden from you the fact that things are going on very badly at La Crêcherie. Our men are leaving us; disunion and revolt have sprung up among them, the fruit of egotism and hatred. All Beauclair is rising against us, the traders, and even the workmen themselves, whose long-acquired habits we interfere with; and thus our position is day by day becoming more and more disquieting. I don't know if I see things in too gloomy a light this morning, but they appear to me to be beyond cure. Everything seems to be lost, and I cannot hide from you any longer that we are going towards a catastrophe."

Jordan listened with an expression of astonishment, though he remained very calm. He even smiled slightly: "Are you not exaggerating things a little, my friend?" said he.

"Suppose that I am exaggerating; suppose that ruin will not actually fall on us to-morrow, none the less I should be acting wrongly if I failed to tell you that I fear ruin is approaching. When I asked you for your land and your money, to undertake that work of social salvation which I dreamt of, did I not promise you not only the accomplishment of something great and beautiful, worthy of a man like you, but also a good investment? And now it appears that I did not speak the truth, for your money is likely to be swallowed up in the disaster. Is it not natural therefore that I should be haunted by remorse?"

Jordan tried to interrupt him by waving his hand, as if to say that the pecuniary question was of no importance. But Luc continued: "It is not merely a question of the large sums which have already been swallowed up; more money is, each day, becoming necessary to continue the struggle. And I no longer dare to ask it of you; for if I can sacrifice myself entirely, I have no right to pull you and your sister down with me."

He sank upon a chair like one overcome, whilst Sœurette, still very pale, and seated at her little table, looked both at him and at her brother, awaiting developments in a state of deep emotion.

"Ah, really! so things are so very bad," Jordan quietly resumed. "Yet your idea was a very good one; you ended by convincing me of that. I did not hide from you that I took no personal interest in such political and social enterprises, being convinced that science is the only revolutionary, and will alone bring about the evolution of to-morrow, leading man towards truth and justice in their entirety. But your theory of solidarity was so beautiful. Sitting at this window after my day's work, I often looked at your town, and it was with interest that I saw it growing. It amused me; and I said to myself that I was working for it, since electricity would one day prove its chief helpmate. Must everything be abandoned, then?"

A cry of supreme renunciation came from Luc: "My energy is exhausted," he exclaimed, "I have no courage left, all my faith has departed. It is all over, and I came to tell you that I am prepared to abandon everything rather than impose a fresh sacrifice upon you. How could you give me the money which we should need? How could I even have audacity enough to ask you for it?"

Never had man raised a more despairing cry. This was the evil hour, the black hour, well known to all heroes, all apostles, the hour when grace departs, when the mission becomes obscured, and the task appears impossible. Forsooth a passing defeat, a momentary spell of cowardice, accompanied, however, by the most frightful suffering.

But Jordan again smiled quietly. He did not immediately answer the remark which Luc with a shudder had addressed to him respecting the large amount of money which would be needed if the work were to be carried on. In a chilly way he pulled his rugs over his spare limbs, then gently said: "Do you know, my good friend, I'm not very well pleased either. Yes, a perfect disaster befell me this morning. You know how I thought that I had planned a perfect scheme for transmitting electric force cheaply and without any loss over long distances. Well, I was mistaken; I have discovered nothing of what I thought I had. An experiment which I made this morning by way of checking everything failed completely, and I have convinced myself that it is necessary to begin all over again. That means a fresh labour of years, and you will understand how worrying it is to encounter defeat when one imagines victory to be certain."

Sœurette had turned towards her brother, quite upset at hearing of that defeat of which she had hitherto been ignorant. In like manner Luc, prompted to compassion by his own despair, stretched out his hand in order to grasp his friend's with brotherly sympathy. And Jordan alone remained calm, apart from the slight feverish tremulousness which always came over him when he had exerted himself unduly.

"In that case what do you intend to do?" Luc inquired.

"What do I intend to do, my good friend? Why, I shall set to work again. I shall make a fresh start to-morrow; I shall begin my work anew from the very beginning. There is evidently nothing else to be done. It is simple enough. You hear me! One ought never to throw up a task. If it needs twenty years, thirty years, a whole lifetime, one still ought to persevere with it. If one makes a mistake, one must retrace one's steps and go over the whole ground afresh as many times as may be necessary. Obstacles and hindrances are inevitable on the road, and must be anticipated. A task, an *œuvre*, however, is like a sacred child, and it would be criminal not to persevere during the period of gestation. There is some of our blood in it, we have no right to refuse to perfect it, we owe it all our strength, soul, flesh, and mind. Even as a mother dies at times through the dear little one whom she hopes to bring into the world, so should we be ready to die if our task exhaust us. And if it does not cost us life, we have but one thing to do when it is accomplished, and that is to begin another, never pausing, but taking up one task after another as long as we are erect, full of intelligence and virility."

As Jordan spoke he seemed to become tall and strong—shielded against all discouragement by his belief in human effort, convinced of conquering provided that he devoted to the fight the last drop of blood in his veins. And to Luc, who was listening, it seemed as if a gust of energy came to him from that weak and puny being.

"Work! work!" continued Jordan; "there is no other force in the world. When one has set one's faith in work one is invincible. Why should we doubt of to-morrow since it is we ourselves who create to-morrow by our work to-day? All that is now being sown by our work will prove to-morrow's harvest. Ah! holy work, creative, all-saving work, thou art my life, the one sole reason why I live!"

His eyes wandered afar as communing with himself he repeated those last words—that hymn to work which ever returned to his lips in moments of great emotion. And once again he related how work had ever consoled and sustained him. If he were still alive it was because he had taken into his life a task for which he had regulated all the functions of his being. He was convinced that he would not die so long as his work should remain unfinished. Bad as was his health, he had never entered his laboratory without feeling relief. How many times had he not sat down to his task with pain-racked limbs and tearful heart; yet on each occasion work had healed him. His uncertainties, his infrequent moments of discouragement had only come from his hours of idleness.

All at once he turned towards Luc with his kindly smile, and said by way of conclusion: "You see, my friend, if you let La Crêcherie die, you yourself will die of it. That task is your very life, and you must live it to the end."

Luc had risen, upbuoyed once more, for his friend's faith in work, his passionate love for his chosen task, filled him again with a spirit of heroism and restored both his faith and his strength. In his hours of lassitude and doubt there was nothing like the bath of energy which he found beside Jordan, that weak and sickly friend of his from whom peace and certainty seemed to radiate.

"Ah! you are right," he cried; "I am a coward, I feel ashamed that I despaired. Human happiness only exists in the glorification and reorganisation of all-saving work. It will found our city. But then, my friend, that money—all that money which must again be risked!"

Jordan, exhausted by his own passionate outburst, was now drawing his rugs more closely around his puny shoulders, and in a faint voice he simply said, "I will give you the money. We will economise; we shall always be able to get on. Here we need very little, you know—milk, eggs, and fruit. Provided that I am still able to pay the expenses of my experiments, the rest will be all right."

Luc had caught hold of his hands, and was pressing them with deep emotion.

"But my friend, my friend," said he; "there is your sister. Are we to ruin her also?"

"True," replied Jordan, "we have forgotten Sœurette."

They turned towards her. She was silently weeping at her little table, on which she had leant her elbows, whilst her chin rested between her hands. Big tears were streaming down her cheeks. Her poor, tortured, bleeding heart was venting all its woe. She, as well as Luc, had been stirred to the depths of her being by all that she had heard. Everything which her brother had said to his friend had resounded with equal energy within her own heart. The necessity of work, of abnegation in the presence of one's task, did that not also mean acceptance of life, whatever it might be, and resolution to live it loyally in order that all possible harmony might accrue therefrom? Like Luc, she now would have thought herself evil-minded and cowardly had she sought to hinder the great work, had she not devoted herself to it even to renunciation of all else besides. The great courage of her simple, kindly, sublime nature had returned to her once more.

She rose and pressed a long kiss upon her brother's brow; and whilst she remained beside him, with her head resting on his shoulder, she whispered to him gently, "Thank you, brother. You have healed me; I will sacrifice myself."

Luc, however, once again eager for action, was now bestirring himself. He had gone back towards the window, and was gazing at the glow which fell upon the roofs of La Crêcherie from the broad blue heavens. And as he came back towards the others he once more repeated his favourite cry: "Ah! they do not love! On the day they love all will prove fruitful; all will spread, and grow, and triumph in the sunlight!"

Then, with a last quiver of her subjugated flesh, Sœurette, who had affectionately drawn near to him, replied: "And one must love even without wishing to be loved in return, for it is only by loving others that the great work can ever be."

Those words, from one who gave herself unreservedly, for the sole joy of doing so and without hope of reward, were followed by a deep, quivering silence. They no longer spoke, but all three, united by close brotherliness, gazed towards the greenery amidst which the rising city of justice and happiness would gradually but ever spread its roofs, now that so much love was sown.

From that time forward Luc the builder, the founder of cities, recovered his self-possession, spoke his will and acted; and men and stones arose at his bidding. He became very gay, and carried on the struggle of La Crêcherie against the Abyss with triumphant joyousness, little by little winning over both folk and things, thanks to the craving for love and happiness which he inspired all around him. He himself felt that the secure establishment of his city would bring him back Josine. With her all the woeful ones of the whole world would be saved. In this he set his faith, and he worked by and for love, in the conviction that he would ultimately conquer.

One bright day, when the sky was radiantly blue, he came upon a scene which again heightened his spirits and filled his heart with tenderness and hope. As he was going round the dependencies of the works, desirous of giving an eye to everything, he was surprised to hear some light, fresh voices and bursts of laughter rising from a corner of the property at the foot of the mountain ridge, a spot where a wall separated the land of La Crêcherie from that of the Abyss. Approaching prudently, for he wished to see without being seen himself, Luc perceived to his delight a party of children playing freely in the sunshine, restored to all the fraternal innocence of nature.

On Luc's side of the wall, Nanet, who daily returned to La Crêcherie in search of playmates, stood beside Lucien and Antoinette Bonnaire, whom he had doubtless persuaded to accompany him on some terrible lizard hunt. All three of them stood there with upturned faces, laughing and calling, whilst on the other side of the wall, other children who could not be seen were laughing and calling also. It was easy to understand that Nise Delaveau had had some young friends to lunch, and that the party on being dismissed to the garden had heard the calls of those outside it, one and all becoming eager to see each other, join hands, and amuse themselves together. Unfortunately, the former doorway had been walled up, for their elders had grown tired of scolding them. At Delaveau's the children were even forbidden to go to the bottom of the garden, and were punished if they were found doing so; whilst at La Crêcherie there were many efforts to make them understand that their disobedience might bring about some unpleasant affair, complaints, and even a lawsuit. But, like artless young creatures yielding to the unknown forces of the future, they continued meeting and mingling, fraternising together in total forgetfulness of all class rancour and hostility.

Shrill, pure, and crystalline voices continued rising, almost suggesting the notes of skylarks.

"Is that you, Nise? Good day, Nise!"

"Good day, Nanet! Are you by yourself, Nanet?"

"Oh, no! I'm with Lucien and Antoinette! And you, Nise, are you alone?"

"Oh! no, no, I'm with Louise and Paul! Good day, good day, Nanet!"

"Good day, good day, Nise!"

At each "good day," again and again repeated, came peals of laughter, so amused did they feel at talking together without seeing one another.

"I say, Nise, are you still there?"

"Why, yes, Nanet, I'm still here."

"Nise, Nise, listen! Are you coming?"

"Oh, Nanet, how can I, since the door's walled up?"

"Jump, jump, Nise, jump, my little Nise!"

"Nanet, my little Nanet, jump, jump!"

Then came perfect delirium, all six of them repeated "jump, jump!" whilst dancing before the wall, as if indeed they imagined that by bounding higher and higher they would at last find themselves together. They turned and waltzed, and bowed to the pitiless wall, and with that childish power of imagination which suppresses all obstacles played as if they could really see one another.

At last a flute-like voice again arose. "Listen, Nise! do you know what?"

"No, Nanet, I don't know."

"Well, I'm going to get on the wall, and I'll pull you up by the shoulders and get you over here."

"Oh! that's it, Nanet, that's it! Climb up!"

In a trice Nanet, clinging to the stone wall with hands and feet, as agile as a cat, found himself on the top of the wall. And as he sat there, bestriding it, he looked quite comical, with his big round head, his large blue eyes, and his tumbled fair hair. He was already fourteen, but he remained little, though very strong and resolute.

"Lucien, Antoinette!" he cried, "just you keep watch."

Then bending over Delaveau's garden, quite proud of overlooking everything on both sides of the wall, he added: "Come on, Nise, let me catch hold of you."

"Oh, no! not me first, Nanet! I'll keep watch over here."

"Then who's coming, Nise?"

"Wait a minute, Nanet, be careful. Paul's climbing up. There's a trellis. He'll try it to see if it breaks."

Silence followed. One only heard the cracking of some old woodwork, mingled with stifled laughter. And Luc began to ask himself if he ought not to restore order by scattering both bands of urchins even as one scatters sparrows on surprising them in a barn. How many times already had not he himself scolded those children, from fear lest their playfulness should prove the cause of some annoying trouble. Yet there was something very charming about the bravery and joyousness which they displayed in seeking to join one another in spite of every prohibition and every obstacle!

At last a cry of triumph arose. Paul's head appeared just above the wall, and Nanet was seen hoisting him up, and then passing him over in order that he might fall into the arms of Lucien and Antoinette. Although Paul himself was more than fourteen, he was not a heavy weight. He had remained slim and delicate, a handsome, fair-complexioned lad, very good-natured and gentle, with quick and intelligent eyes. Directly he had fallen into Antoinette's embrace he kissed her, for he knew her well, and was fond of being near her, for she was tall and pretty, and very graceful, although but twelve years old.

"That's done, Nise!" cried Nanet. "I've, passed one over. Whose turn next?"

But Nise was heard replying in a loud anxious whisper: "Hush, hush, Nanet! There's something moving near the fowls' run. Lie down on the wall. Quick, quick!" Then the danger being past, she added: "Look out, Nanet! It's Louise's turn now; I'll push her up!"

This time, indeed, it was Louise's head which appeared above the wall: a comical, goatish head with black and somewhat obliquely-set eyes, a slender nose and pointed chin. With her vivacity and gaiety she was very amusing. At eleven years of age she had already become a self-willed little woman, quite upsetting her parents, the worthy Mazelles, who were stupefied to find that such a riotous, enthusiastic wilding had sprung from their placid egotism. She did not even wait for Nanet to pass her over, but jumped of her own accord into the arms of Lucien, her favourite playmate, who was the oldest of all of them. A tall, sturdy lad of fifteen, endowed with great ingenuity and inventive talent, he made her some extraordinary playthings.

But Nanet was again calling. "That makes two, Nise," said he. "There's only you now. Come up, quick! There's something moving again over yonder near the well."

A sound of cracking wood was once more heard; a large piece of the trellis-work must have fallen to the ground, for Nise burst out: "Oh! dear me, dear me, Nanet, I can't! Louise broke it with her feet, and now it's all down."

"Never mind—it doesn't matter! Give me your hands, Nise, and I'll pull you up."

"No, no, I can't! I'm too little; can't you see, Nanet?"

"But I tell you I'll pull you. Stretch out your arms—there! Now I'll stoop and you must stand on tip-toes. There we are! You see very well that I can pull you up."

Evincing great dexterity, he had raised Nise with his strong young arms and seated her on the wall in front of him. She looked even more tumbled than usual, with her fair curly pate, her pink and ever-smiling mouth, and her pretty blue eyes. She and her friend Nanet formed a pair, both of them with locks of the same soft golden hue, curling and waving hither and thither.

For a moment they remained astride the wall, face to face and delighted at finding themselves so high up.

"Ah! all the same you're strong, Nanet, to have pulled me up as you did," said the girl.

"But then you've grown quite tall, Nise. I'm fourteen now; how old are you?"

"I'm eleven, Nanet. But, I say, isn't this like being on a horse, a very tall horse, made of stone?"

"Yes, but I say, Nise, shall I stand upright?"

"Yes, upright, Nanet! I'll do the same!"

But again a stir was heard down the garden, this time in the direction of the kitchen, and the two children, full of anxiety, caught hold of each other, and fell to the ground together, locked in a close embrace. They might have killed themselves, but they laughed gaily, unhurt and delighted with their tumble. Paul and Antoinette, Lucien and Louise on their side, were already running wildly among the bushes and fallen rocks which helped to form many a delightful nook at the feet of the Bleuse Mountains.

Thinking it too late to intervene, Luc went off very softly. As the children had not seen him, they would not know that he had closed his eyes to their escapade. After all, was it not best that they should yield to the glow of youth within them, and meet and play in spite of all the prohibitions? They were like the very florescence of life, which well knew for what future harvests it thus flowered in them. And they brought with them, perchance, the reconciliation of classes, the morrow full of justice and peace which was awaited. That which their fathers could not accomplish would be accomplished by them, and yet more completely by their children, thanks to the evolution which was ever spreading. And thus Luc, as he quietly walked away, refraining from alarming them, laughed to himself as he heard them laughing, heedless of the difficulties that they would encounter when they might wish to climb over the wall again. That glimpse of the kindly future had inspired the young man with a hope, a courage to continue fighting, and a determination to achieve victory such as he had never known before.

For long months the desperate, pitiless struggle went on between La Crêcherie and the Abyss. Luc, who had momentarily thought his enterprise in jeopardy, toppling towards ruin, exerted every effort to keep it on its legs. He did not expect to gain any more ground for a long time to come, but he wished to lose none; and it was already an achievement to remain stationary, to continue living amidst the blows which were aimed at La Crêcherie from all sides. And how mighty was the toil, and with what joyous bravery was it accomplished! Luc was always here, there, and everywhere, encouraging the men in the workshops, promoting brotherliness between one and all at the common-house, and watching over the management of the co-operative stores. He was constantly seen too in the sunlit avenues of the little town, amidst the women and the children, with whom he liked to laugh and play, as if he were the father of the young nation now springing up around him. Thanks to his genius and creative fruitfulness, things arose and grew methodically, as if in obedience to a wave of his hand. But his greatest achievement was the conquest of his workmen, amidst whom discord and rebellion had for a moment swept. Although his views were not always shared by Bonnaire, he had won that brave and kindly man's affection in such wise as to secure in him the most faithful, the most devoted of lieutenants, one without whose help it would have been impossible to carry on the enterprise. And indeed the affection which radiated from Luc had influenced all the workers of La Crêcherie, who, finding him so loving and brotherly, intent on securing happiness for others, in the conviction that he would therein find happiness himself, had gradually grouped themselves around him. Thus the staff was becoming a large family linked more and more closely together, each ending by understanding that he worked for his own delight when he worked for that of all. Over a period of six months not a single hand quitted the works, and if those who had previously left did not as yet return, the others who remained devoted themselves entirely to the enterprise, even leaving a part of their profits untouched in order that a substantial reserve fund might be formed.

At that critical period it was assuredly the solidarity evinced by all the associated workers that saved La Crêcherie from falling beneath the blows with which egotistical and jealous hatred inspired Beauclair. The reserve fund, prudently increased and managed, proved a decisive help. It enabled the folk of La Crêcherie to face difficult moments, and to avoid borrowing at heavy interest. Thanks to this fund, moreover, they were twice able to purchase new machinery, which had been rendered requisite by changes in various processes, and which largely diminished the cost of manufacture. Then, too, there came a few strokes of luck. About that time there were some important enterprises: the laying down of railways, the building of bridges and other things in which metal work was largely used, and thus considerable quantities of rails, girders, and structural material were required. The long peace in which Europe lived vastly developed metallurgical industry in its pacific and civilising branches. Never before had iron entered so largely into the dwellings of men. Thus the output of La Crêcherie increased, though the profits did not become very large, for Luc particularly wished to sell cheaply, in the belief that cheapness would control the future. At the same time he strengthened the works by wise management and constant economy, and by gathering together that reserve fund of ready money in order that it might be brought into use at the first sign of danger; whilst the workers' devotion to the common cause, their abnegation in foregoing a portion of their due, did the rest, enabling one to wait for the arrival of triumph without excessive hardship.

The Abyss, meantime, apparently remained in a flourishing situation; there had been no falling-off in its turnover, and great success seemed to attend its costly output of guns and projectiles. Still this prosperity was only on the surface, and Delaveau, though he did not confess it, experienced at times serious anxiety. He certainly had on his side the whole of Beauclair—the whole of that *bourgeoise*, capitalist society whose existence was threatened. And he remained convinced that he represented truth, authority, and power, and that ultimate victory was certain. Nevertheless, after a time secret doubts began to assail him: he was disturbed at finding so much vitality in La Crêcherie, whose prompt collapse he prophesied every three months or so. He could no longer contend against the neighbouring works with respect to commercial iron and steel—those rails, girders, and structural materials which La Crêcherie turned out so well and so cheaply. There only remained to him the manufacture of superfine steel, of carefully made articles valued at three and four francs per kilogramme, and as it happened these were also made at two very important establishments in a neighbouring department. The competition of those establishments was terrible, and Delaveau felt that of the three—the Abyss and the two others—there was one too many. The question was which two of them would devour the third. Weakened as it was by the rivalry of La Crêcherie, would not the Abyss prove to be the establishment fated to disappear? This question preyed upon the manager, although he showed more activity than ever, and professed serene confidence in the good cause, that religion of the wage system of which he had constituted himself the defender. But another matter worried him even more than the competition of rivals and the chances of industrial warfare. This was the absence of any reserve fund, such as might enable him to face some emergency, some unforeseen catastrophe. If a crisis were to arise—some strike, or simply some falling-off in trade—the result would be disastrous, for the works would not possess the wherewithal to await a revival of business. The necessity of purchasing some new plant had already compelled him to borrow three hundred thousand francs, and the heavy interest on the loan now weighed upon his annual budget. But what if he were compelled to borrow again and again, until at last he should find himself swallowed up by an abyss of indebtedness?

About this time Delaveau tried to make Boisgelin listen to reason. When he had induced the latter to confide to him the remnants of his fortune, he had certainly promised that if the Abyss were purchased he would hand him heavy interest on his capital, and enable him to continue leading a luxurious life. Now, however, that difficulties were likely to arise, he wished Boisgelin to be reasonable enough to cut down his style of living for a time. He assured him that fortune would soon smile once more, and that he would then be able to live again on his former footing, and indeed in finer style than ever. Delaveau's desire was to induce Boisgelin to content himself for a while with one half of the profits, the other half being employed to constitute a reserve fund which would enable the Abyss to emerge victoriously from such bad times as might present themselves. But Boisgelin would not listen; he demanded every penny, refusing to forego any one of the pleasures of the costly life which he was leading. Quarrels even broke out between the two cousins. Now that it seemed as if the invested capital might no longer yield the expected interest, that the toil of more than a thousand human beings might no longer suffice to keep an idler in luxury, the capitalist accused his manager of failing to keep his promises. Delaveau, though irritated by the other's idiotic thirst for perpetual enjoyment, still entertained no suspicion that behind that coxcomb, his cousin, there stood his own wife Fernande, the all-corrupting, devouring creature, for whom all the money was squandered in caprices and folly. Life at La Guerdache was nought but a round of festivities, amidst which Fernande enjoyed such pleasing triumphs that any pause in her delights would have seemed to her to be absolute downfall. She egged on Boisgelin, she told him that her husband's powers were declining, that he did not extract from the works nearly so large a revenue as he might have done; and, according to her, the only way to spur him on was to overwhelm him with demands for money. The demeanour preserved by Delaveau—who was one of those authoritative men who never take women into their confidence, making no exception even of his wife, although he was passionately attached to her—had ended by convincing Fernande that her view was the right one, and that if she wished to realise her dream of returning to Paris with millions of francs to squander, she must harass him without cessation.

One night, however, Delaveau forgot himself in Fernande's presence. A hunt had taken place at La Guerdache that day, and in the course of it Fernande, whose delight it was to gallop about on horseback, had for a time disappeared in the company of Boisgelin. A great dinner had followed in the evening, and it was past midnight when a carriage brought the Delaveaus back to the Abyss. The young woman, who seemed overcome with fatigue, satiated as it were with the consuming enjoyment of which her life was compounded, hastened to get to bed, whilst her husband, after taking off his coat, went hither and thither about the room, looking both angry and worried.

"I say," he ended by inquiring, "did not Boisgelin tell you anything when you went off with him?"

At this Fernande, who was closing her eyes, opened them again in surprise. "No," she answered, "nothing interesting at all events. What would you have him tell me?"

"Oh! the fact is that we had previously had a discussion together," Delaveau resumed. "He asked me to let him have another ten thousand francs for the end of the month. But this time I positively refused. It's impossible, it's madness!"

Fernande raised her head, and her eyes glittered. "Madness—how's that?" said she, "why don't you give him those ten thousand francs?"

As it happened it was she herself who had suggested the application for this money in order that Boisgelin might purchase an electrical motor car in which she ardently desired to travel about the country at express speed.

"Why?" cried Delaveau forgetting himself. "Because that idiot with his extravagance will end by ruining the works. We shall have a smash up if he doesn't cut down his style of living. There can be nothing more idiotic than that life of festivity which he leads, that stupid vanity of his which prompts him to let everybody despoil him."

Startled by these words, Fernande sat up in bed looking rather pale, whilst Delaveau, with the *naïveté* of a husband blind to his wife's misconduct, went on: "There's only one sensible person left at La Guerdache, the only one, too, who enjoys nothing there. I mean poor Suzanne. It grieves me to see her always looking so sad. However, when I begged her to-day to intervene with her husband she answered, forcing back her tears, that she was resolved to meddle in nothing."

The idea that her husband had appealed to her lover's wife, the poor sacrificed creature, who showed such lofty dignity in her life of renunciation, brought Fernande's exasperation to a climax. But she was still more moved by the thought that the works—the very source of her enjoyment—might be in peril.

"We shall have a smash up—why do you say that?" she asked, "I thought that the business was going on very well?"

She put this question in so anxious a tone that Delaveau, fearing that if she knew everything she might amplify the fears which he strove to hide from himself, became distrustful, and forced back the truth which anger well nigh wrung from him.

"The business is going on all right, no doubt," said he, "only it would go on a great deal better if Boisgelin did not perpetually empty the safe in order to continue leading an idiotic life. The man's a fool, I tell you; he has only the poor paltry brain of a coxcomb."

Reassured by this reply, Fernande stretched herself out in bed once more. Her husband was simply an individual with a gross mind, a miser, whose desire was to part as little as possible with the large sums which were received at the works. As for his denunciation of Boisgelin, this was an indirect attack upon herself.

"My dear," said she by way of conclusion, "all people are not made to brutify themselves with work from morning till night; and those who have money do right to enjoy themselves and taste the pleasures of a higher life."

Delaveau was about to reply violently, but by an effort he managed to calm himself. Why should he try to convert his wife to his views? He treated her as a spoilt child, and let her act as she listed, never complaining of any lapses on her part, such as he condemned when others were in question. He did not even notice the folly of her life, for she was his own folly, the prized jewel which he had longed to grasp with his big, hard-working hands. She remained through all the object of his admiration and adoration, the idol for whom one sets aside both dignity and reason, and whom it is impossible to suspect.

A little later, when Delaveau in his turn had got into bed, his anxiety with respect to the position of the works came back to him. His wife lay fast asleep beside him, but he himself was unable to close his eyes, and amidst his painful insomnia the difficulties by which he was menaced seemed to become greater. Never yet, indeed, had he surveyed the future with so much insight and seen it under darker colours. He became fully conscious that the cause of the impending ruin was that mad craving for enjoyment, that sickly impatience which Boisgelin displayed to spend his money the moment it was earned. There was an abyss somewhere into which all that money sank, some abominable sore also by which exuded all the strength and gain which work should have brought with it. Accustomed as he was to be very frank with himself, Delaveau passed his life in review, and could find nothing to reproach himself with. He rose early, and was the last to leave the workshops at night, remaining on the watch throughout the day, directing the labour of his large staff as he might have directed the movements of a regiment. He incessantly brought all his remarkable faculties into play, showing a great deal of rectitude amidst his roughness, together with rare powers of logic and method and the loyalty of a fighter who has vowed to conquer and is determined to do so or to perish. Thus he suffered frightfully at feeling that in spite of all his heroism he was gliding to disaster through the collapse of everything that he set on foot, a kind of daily destruction which came he knew not whence and which his energy was powerless to stay. What he called Boisgelin's imbecile life, that gluttonous craving for pleasure, was doubtless the evil that preyed upon the works. But who, then, was it that made the wretched man so stupid? whence came that insanity of his, which he, Delaveau, could not understand, sensible and sober worker that he was himself, hating idleness and excessive enjoyment since he knew that they destroyed all creative health?

And still he had no suspicion that the demolisher of Boisgelin's fortune, the poisoner of his mind, was his own well-loved Fernande, she who now lay beside him, looking so charming in her slumber. Whilst he, amidst the black smoke of the Abyss and the burning glow of its furnaces, exhausted himself in efforts to wring money from the toil of pain-racked workmen, she on her side strolled in gay apparel under the shady foliage of La Guerdache, flung money to the four winds of fancy, and with her white teeth crunched the hundreds of thousands of francs which more than a thousand wage-earners coined for her amidst the resounding thuds of the great hammers. That night, too, whilst her husband, with his eyes wide open in the darkness, remained tortured by the thought of future payments, wondering by what fresh efforts he might make the works produce the amounts promised to one and another, she lying by his side slept off her intoxication of the day, so weary with enjoyment that only the faintest breath came from her glutted breast. At last Delaveau himself ended by falling asleep, and dreamt that some weird, perverse, diabolical powers were at work beneath the Abyss, eating away the soil in such wise that the whole establishment would suddenly be engulfed on some fulgural, tempestuous night.

During the days which followed Fernande recalled the fears which her husband had expressed to her that evening. Whilst making every allowance for what she regarded as his passion for heaping up money, and his hatred of the pleasures of luxury, she could not help shuddering at the thought of a possibility of ruin. Boisgelin ruined indeed! In such a case what would become of her? That ruin would not simply mean an end to the delightful life which she had always desired as compensation for the wretched poverty of her earlier years, but it would imply their return to Paris like vanquished beings, with a flat of a thousand francs annual rental in the depths of some suburban district, and some petty employment for Delaveau in which he would vegetate whilst she herself would relapse into all the loathsome coarseness of a home of penurious toil. No! no! she would not consent to that; she would not allow her golden prey to escape her; every muscle of her covetous being hungered for triumph. Within her slender form, instinct with such delicate charm, such light gracefulness, there was the keen appetite of a she-wolf, the most furious predatory instincts. She was resolved that she would in no wise check that appetite, that she would take her pleasure to the very end, allowing none to rob her of it. No doubt she was full of contempt for those grimy, muddy works where day and night she heard the monstrous-looking hammers forging pleasure for her; and as for the men, those toilers who roasted amidst hellish flames in order that she might lead a life of happy idleness, she regarded them as domestic animals that gave her food and spared her all fatigue. She never risked her little feet on the uneven soil of the workshops; she never evinced the faintest interest in the human flock which passed to and fro before her door, bowed down by accursed labour. Nevertheless those works and that flock were hers, and the idea that fortune might be wrested from her by the ruin of the business roused her to revolt, prompted her to defend herself as energetically as if her life itself were threatened. Whosoever harmed the works became her personal enemy, a dangerous evil-doer, of whom she was resolved to rid herself by all imaginable means. Thus her hatred of Luc had gone on increasing ever since the Sunday when they had first met at lunch at La Guerdache, where, with a woman's keen acumen, she had guessed that he was the man who would strive to bar her path. Since that time, moreover, she had frequently come into collision with him, and now it was he who threatened to destroy the Abyss and to cast her back into all the loathsomeness of mediocrity. If she should allow him a free hand her happiness would be over; he would rob her of everything that she cared for in life. And thus, beneath her seeming graciousness, she was consumed by murderous fury. One thought alone possessed her—that of suppressing that man, and she dreamt of devising some catastrophe in which he might perish.

Eight months had now gone by since Josine had bidden farewell to Luc, and since that time she had become *enceinte*. Ragu had discovered the truth one day, when in a fit of drunkenness he had wished to beat her. He himself had reverted to his old life of debauchery, leading astray all the factory girls who were foolish enough to listen to him, and utterly neglecting his own wife. Thus his discovery both amazed and exasperated him, and terrible scenes followed it. At first he had recourse to brutality, and it was a wonder that Josine escaped alive. Then he kept her shut up for days together, or else watched her every movement. He had long spoken of casting her into the streets, he had long neglected her for the most shameless of creatures, but at present he quivered with jealous fury whenever he saw her speaking with any man out of doors. He tried by every means he could devise to wring from her her lover's name, but this she steadfastly refused to tell him, whatever might be his threats, his violence, or his promises; for after striking her he would sometimes exclaim: "Tell me his name, tell me his name! And I promise you that I'll leave you alone!"

No suspicion of Luc entered Ragu's mind, for nobody, apart from Sœurette, was aware of Josine's visit to the pavilion. Thus Ragu sought the culprit among his own mates; but however much he might watch, however much he might question, he learnt nothing, and the efforts he made in this respect only increased his fury.

Josine meantime hid herself as much as possible; she dreaded the result for Luc should the truth be discovered. So far as she was personally concerned, she was overjoyed by what had happened, and would have gladly hastened to her lover to tell him of it. But fears for his safety came upon her, and she thought that it was best to wait; in such wise that a chance meeting alone apprised Luc of the truth. And even then Josine was only able to acquaint him with her secret by a gesture; for others were present, and it was impossible for the lovers to exchange a word.

Filled with emotion by the tidings thus imparted to him, Luc sought for further information, and soon heard of Ragu's wrath and violence, and of the close watch which he kept upon Josine. Had he, Luc, retained any doubts on the matter, the other's ferocious jealousy and exasperation would have sufficed to destroy them. From that moment he regarded Josine as his own wife. She was his, and his alone, since she was soon to become a mother—and the father of the child, and not the other, was the real and sole husband. Ragu had vowed that he would never be burdened with children, and thus there was no bond whatever between him and Josine. There can, indeed, be but one bond between man and woman, one firm and eternal bond—the bond which comes from the birth of a child. Apart from that, whatever human laws may say, there is no real union, no real marriage. Thus Josine now for ever belonged to Luc alone, and assuredly she would come back to him, and the child would be the living florescence of their love.

All the same, Luc suffered terribly when he learnt that Josine was constantly being reviled and ill-treated, ever in danger of receiving some dastardly blow. It was unbearable to the young man that he should have to leave that fondly loved woman in the clutches of Ragu, when he longed to set her in a paradise of affection. But what could he do since she so stubbornly cloistered herself in order to spare him all embarrassment and worry? She even refused to see him, for fear of some surprise that would have revealed the secret which she so tenderly buried in the depths of her dolorous heart. Thus Luc had to watch for her, in order to be able to say a few words. At last, one very dark evening, while hiding in a dim corner of the wretched Rue des Trois Lunes, he was able to stop her for a moment as she was passing.

"Oh, Luc! is it you? How imprudent!" she gasped. "Kiss me and run off, I beg you."

But he, quivering, had clasped her round the waist, and was whispering passionately, "No, no, Josine, I want to tell you. . . You are suffering too much, and it is criminal of me to leave you, who are so dear, so precious, in such suffering. . . Listen, Josine, I have come to fetch you, and you must come with me, so that I may place you in my home, your home, like a well-loved happy woman."

She was already yielding to his gentle and consoling embrace. But all at once she freed herself. "Oh! what are you saying, Luc? Have you no more reason than that?" she asked. "Follow you, good heavens! when that would be confession, and would draw the greatest dangers down upon you! It is I who would then be acting wrongly, criminally, creating embarrassment for you in the work that you are accomplishing. Be off, quick! He may try to kill me, but I will never, never give him your name."

At this Luc tried to convince her of the uselessness of such a sacrifice to the hypocrisy of the world. "You are my wife, since I am the father of your child," said he, "and me it is that you ought to follow. By-and-by, when our city of justice is built, there will be no other law save that of love, and our union will be respected by one and all. Why should we trouble about the people whom we may scandalise to-day?"

Then as she seemed stubbornly bent on sacrifice, saying that she took only the present into account, for she wished him to be spared all obstacles, in order that he might become powerful and triumphant, he raised a cry of grief: "What, will you never return to me then? Will that child never be mine, in the presence of one and all?"

Again she clasped him with her delicate, endearing arms, and with her lips near his she softly murmured: "I will come back on the day when you need me, when I shall be not a source of embarrassment but a help, and then I will bring with me that dear child whose presence will endow us both with increase of strength."

Black Beauclair, the old, pestilential den of accursed toil, lay around them, agonising in the darkness beneath the crushing weight of its centuries of iniquity, whilst those words, instinct with hope in a future of peace and happiness, were spoken.

"You are my husband," resumed Josine; "you alone will have formed part of my life; and ah! if you only knew with what delight I refrain from speaking your name, no matter how much I may be threatened. I keep it secret like a hidden flower, like hidden armour, too. Oh! do not pity me; I am strong and I am very happy."

And Luc made answer: "You are my wife; I loved you on the very first evening when I met you, so wretched yet so divine. And if you keep my name secret so will I keep yours; it shall be my worship and my strength till you yourself deem it time to cry our love aloud."

"Oh, Luc! how good, how reasonable you are, and how happy we shall be!"

"It is you, Josine, who have made me good and reasonable, and it is because I succoured you one evening that we shall be so very happy later on, amidst the happiness of all."

Without again speaking they remained yet another moment linked in a close embrace. Then Josine freed herself and returned, glorious and invincible, to martyrdom, whilst Luc disappeared amidst the gloom, strengthened by that interview and ready to resume the battle which would lead to victory.

A few weeks later, however, chance placed Josine's secret in Fernande's hands. Fernande knew Ragu, whose sudden return to the Abyss had created quite a sensation there, in such wise that Delaveau had made a pretence of esteeming him, and had even appointed him master-puddler, and favoured him in other ways, although his conduct was execrable. That Fernande should have heard of the drama which had upset Ragu's home was not surprising. He made no attempt whatever to conceal the facts, but openly denounced his wife as a shameless creature, with the result that the affair became a common subject of conversation in the workshops. It was even spoken about at the manager's house, and one day in Fernande's presence Delaveau expressed his great annoyance at it all; for Ragu, now that he was wild with jealousy, worked like a madman, at times never touching a tool for three days in succession, and at others rushing upon his task and stirring the fusing metal with all the fury of a man who is seized with a longing to strike and kill.

At last one winter morning, when Delaveau was absent in Paris, whither he had gone the previous day, Fernande questioned her maid, who had just brought her the tea and toast which composed her first breakfast. Nise was seated there drinking her own milk and casting covetous eyes at her mother's tea, for tea was a thing which she was not usually allowed to drink, though she was very fond of it.

"Is it true, Félicie," Fernande inquired, "that the Ragus have been quarrelling again? The laundress told me that Ragu had half killed his wife."

"I don't know if that's so, madame," replied the maid, "but I think she must have exaggerated, for I saw Josine pass the house a little while ago, and she looked no worse than she usually does."

A pause followed, and then the maid, as she went off, added, "All the same, it's pretty certain that he will end by killing her one of these days. He tells everybody that he means to do so."

Silence fell again, and Fernande slowly ate her toast, absorbed the while in a gloomy reverie. But all at once, amidst the heavy stillness, Nise, letting her thoughts escape her unawares, began to hum in an undertone: "Ragu isn't Josine's real husband; her husband is Monsieur Luc, Monsieur Luc, Monsieur Luc!"

At this her mother raised her eyes in stupefaction, and gazed at the child fixedly. "What is that you are saying, Nise?" she exclaimed. "Why are you saying it?"

Thunderstruck at having unwittingly hummed those words aloud, Nise lowered her face over her cup, and strove to assume an innocent air. "Oh, for nothing! I don't know."

"You don't know, you little falsehood-teller! You certainly did not make up those words yourself. If you repeat them somebody must have told them you."

Nise, although she was becoming more and more disturbed, feeling that she had landed herself in a nasty scrape which might have far-reaching consequences, nevertheless held out against all evidence. "I assure you, mamma," said she, in the most artless manner that she could assume, "one sings things without knowing, just as they come into one's head."

Then Fernande, seeing her repeat her fib with all the demeanour of a genuine *gamine*, suddenly felt enlightened: "It was Nanet who told you what you sang; it can only have been Nanet."

Nise blinked; it was indeed Nanet who had told her. But she was afraid of being again scolded and punished, as on the day when her mother had caught her returning from La Crêcherie with Paul Boisgelin and Louise Mazelle by climbing over the wall, so she persisted in her falsehood: "Oh! Nanet, Nanet—but I haven't seen him at all since you forbade it."

Feverishly desirous of ascertaining the truth, her mother suddenly assumed great gentleness of manner. Such was her emotion that she forgot all question of scolding—Nise's escapades with Nanet being of little moment compared with the important matter on which she desired full enlightenment. "Listen, little girl," she said, "it is very wrong to tell falsehoods. That day when I said that you should have no dessert it was because you wanted to make me believe that you and the others had climbed over the wall simply to fetch a ball. Well, to-day, if you tell me the truth, I promise that you shall not be punished. Come, be frank—it was Nanet?"

Nise, who at bottom was a good little girl, immediately replied: "Yes, mamma, it *was* Nanet."

"And he told you that Josine's real husband was Monsieur Luc?"

"Yes, mamma."

"And, pray, what does he know about it? Why does he say that Monsieur Luc is Josine's real husband?"

Thereupon Nise became perplexed, and innocently lowered her face over her cup again. "Oh! he knows—he knows—well, he says he knows it."

Greatly as Fernande desired to obtain precise information on the subject, she felt that she could not put any further questions to her child. And by way of precaution she sought to destroy the effect of the eager curiosity which she had hitherto displayed: "Nanet knows nothing," she said; "he talks foolishly, and you are a little stupid to repeat what he says. Don't go singing such silly things again, or else you shall never have any dessert at all."

Then the meal was finished in silence, the mother absorbed in what she had learnt, and the child well pleased at having escaped so lightly.

Fernande spent the day in her room, reflecting. She began by asking herself if what Nanet had said could really be the truth. But how was she to doubt it? The lad had certainly heard something—discovered something—and he was too much attached to his sister to tell any falsehood about her. Moreover, a number of little incidents which Fernande now recalled rendered the story quite probable—in fact, certain. But then how could she make use of the weapon which chance had placed in her hand? In a confused way she dreamt of steeping that weapon in poison, so as to render it deadly. Never had she hated Luc so much as she hated him now. If Delaveau was at present in Paris, it was solely for the purpose of trying to negotiate a fresh loan, for the Abyss was sinking a little more each day. How great, then, would be her victory if she could succeed in suppressing the hated master of La Crêcherie, the man who threatened her life of luxury and pleasure! The enemy killed, the competition would be killed as well. With such a man as Ragu, a drunkard, full of jealousy and wrath, a prompt finish might be expected. It would doubtless suffice to inflame him, to prompt him to draw his knife. But then, again, how was she to bring this about— how was she to act? The proper course was evidently to warn Ragu, to acquaint him with the name of the man whom he had been trying to discover for three months past. Then, however, came a difficulty: how was she to warn him, where, and by whom? At first she thought of sending him an anonymous letter, and decided that she would cut the words she needed out of some old newspaper, paste them on a sheet of paper, and post the letter in the evening. She had, indeed, already begun to cut out such words as she desired, when it suddenly occurred to her that her plan might not prove efficacious, for Ragu might pay little heed to a letter, whereas it was necessary to exasperate him. If he were not excited, fired to the point of madness, perhaps he would never strike. The truth must be cast at him like a blow—a whip stroke in the face, and under such circumstances as might madden him. But whom could she send? Whom could she choose to poison the man's mind? When night came and she went to bed, she had grown convinced that there was nobody whom she could employ, and that she herself must speak the fatal words. Chance favoured her in this design. Her husband was absent, and, on awaking at an early hour, she was able to go down and waylay Ragu as he quitted the night shift. She had an excuse quite ready; she would tell him that she wanted a woman to do some needlework, and had thought of employing his wife, if he were willing to let her come. That proposal would enable her to raise the subject which she had at heart. And, indeed, at the first words that Fernande addressed to him with respect to his wife, Ragu burst into invectives; and when she, in a seemingly innocent way, declared that she imagined he had become reconciled to the position, for she had heard that the child was to be provided for by its father, Monsieur Luc, the man's fury became uncontrollable. The die was cast, and it was certain that he would wreak summary vengeance, for there was murder in his glance as he wildly rushed away.

It was nearly nine o'clock, and the pale morning light of winter was rising, when Luc was stabbed by Ragu. The former was about to pay his usual morning visit to the school—his greatest daily pleasure—when Ragu, who had been watching for him, secreted the while behind a clump of spindle trees, suddenly sprang forward and thrust his knife into his back, between his shoulders. Luc, standing at that moment on the very threshold of the school, laughing with some of the little girls who had come forward to meet him, gave a loud cry and fell to the ground, whilst his assailant fled up the Bleuse Mountains, where he disappeared amidst the rocks and the bushes. As it happened Sœurette had not yet arrived; she was busy at the dairy on the other side of the park. The children present fled in their terror, calling for help, and shrieking that Ragu had just killed Monsieur Luc. Some minutes elapsed, however, before some of the men of the works heard these calls and were able to pick up the stricken man, who had swooned away. The blood that had gushed from him already formed quite a pool, and the steps of the right wing of the common-house, which the school occupied, seemed to have been baptized with gore. For the time being nobody thought of pursuing Ragu, who must have been far away already. The attention of one and all was given to Luc, who, just as the men were about to carry him into a hall adjoining the class-rooms, emerged from his swoon and gasped in a faint, entreating voice; "No, no! to my home, my friends."

They had to obey him, and carry him to the pavilion on a stretcher; but it was only with difficulty that they were able to lay him on his bed, and then such was the agony he experienced that he again lost consciousness.

At that moment Sœurette arrived. One of the little girls, retaining her presence of mind, had gone to warn her at the dairy, whilst, on the other hand, one of the workmen ran down to Beauclair in order to fetch Doctor Novarre. When Sœurette entered the pavilion and saw Luc lying there, with his face quite white and his body covered with blood, she believed him to be dead. Thus she at once fell upon her knees beside the bedstead, a prey to such keen grief that the secret of her love escaped her. She took hold of one of Luc's inert hands and kissed it, and sobbed, and stammered forth all the passion against which she had battled, and which she had buried deep within her. In losing him she felt that she was losing her own heart; she would love no more, she would be unable to live another day. And amidst her despair she did not perceive that Luc, upon whom her tears were falling, had at last recovered consciousness, and was listening to her with infinite affection, infinite tenderness. At last he faintly breathed the words, "You love me. Ah! poor, poor Sœurette!"

Full of blissful surprise at finding him yet alive, Sœurette regretted nought of her confession; rather was she delighted at no longer having to lie to him, for she felt that her love was so great and so lofty it would never bring suffering on him.

"Yes, I love you, Luc!" she gasped, "but do I count, I? You live, and that is sufficient. I am not jealous of your happiness. Oh, Luc, you must live! you must live! and I will be your servant."

At that tragic moment, when death seemed so near at hand, the discovery of Sœurette's mute and absolute love, which had long surrounded and accompanied him like that of some guardian angel, filled Luc with immense but dolorous rapture.

"Poor, poor Sœurette! Oh, my divine, sad friend!" he murmured in his failing voice.

But the door opened and Doctor Novarre entered in a state of keen emotion. He immediately wished to examine the wound, with the assistance of Sœurette, with whose skill as a nurse he was well acquainted. Deep silence fell. There came a moment of inexpressible anguish; then followed unhoped-for relief, a glow of hope. The knife had struck the shoulder-blade and had swerved, reaching no vital organ, but simply gashing the flesh. At the same time the wound was a frightful one, and it seemed as if the bone might be broken, in which event complications might arise. Even if there were no immediate danger convalescence would at all events be a long time coming. Yet how joyful was the thought that death had been averted!

Luc was holding Sœurette's hand and smiling feebly at the sight of her happiness. "And my good Jordan, does he know of it?" he asked.

"No, he knows nothing as yet; for three days past he has shut himself up in his laboratory. But I will bring him to you. Ah! my friend, how happy the doctor's assurance makes me!"

In her rapture Sœurette still let her hand rest in Luc's, when once again the door of the room opened. And this time it was Josine who entered. At the first news of the crime she had hastened to the spot, distracted, wild with grief. That which she had feared had happened! Some scoundrel had surprised and revealed her secret, and Ragu had killed Luc, her husband, the father of her child. Her life was over, there was nothing more for her to hide, she would die there, in her real home.

Luc raised a light cry at the sight of her. And quickly dropping Sœurette's hand, he held out both his arms.

"Ah! Josine," he gasped, "it is you—you have come back to me!"

Then, as she, staggering forward, sank down beside him, he understood her anguish, and sought to reassure her. "Do not grieve," he said, "you have come back to me with the dear little one, and I shall live—the doctor tells me so—live for both of you."

She listened and drew a long breath, as though recovering life. Had she then reached the realisation of her hopes, that which she had awaited from life, which seems so harsh whilst it accomplishes its needful work? He would live! And it was that abominable knife-thrust which brought them together once more—they who were already for ever linked one to the other.

"Yes, yes, I have come back to you, Luc," she said, "and it is all over; we shall never part again since now we have nothing more to hide. Remember that I promised to return to you whenever you might have need of me, whenever I should no longer be a source of embarrassment to you. All other ties are severed: I am your wife before one and all, and my place is here, at your bedside."

Luc was so moved, so thrilled with rapture, that tears gathered in his eyes. "Ah! dear, dear Josine, love and happiness have come with you."

But all at once he remembered Sœurette, and then he raised his eyes and saw her standing erect once more, on the other side of the bed; and although she looked very pale she was smiling. With an affectionate gesture he took hold of her hand again.

"My good Sœurette," he said, "this was a secret which I was compelled to hide from you."

She shivered slightly, then simply answered: "Oh! I knew it, I had seen Josine leave the pavilion one morning."

"What! you knew it!"

Then he divined everything, and the compassion, the admiration, the affection he felt for her became infinite. Her renunciation of hope, the love which she still retained for him, and which she manifested in boundless affection, in a gift of her whole life, touched him like an act of the loftiest heroism. Drawing quite close to him she whispered: "Have no fear, Luc, I knew it; and I shall never be aught but the most devoted and most sisterly of friends."

"Ah, Sœurette!" he repeated, in so faint a breath that he could scarcely be heard, "ah! my divine, sad friend!"

Noticing his exhaustion, Doctor Novarre intervened, and forbade any further talking. The doctor smiled discreetly at all that he had learnt at that bedside. It was very nice that the injured man should have a sister, a wife to nurse him. But it was necessary to be reasonable and to refrain from encouraging fever by excess of emotion. Luc promised, however, that he would be very good; he spoke no more, but only turned soft glances upon Josine and Sœurette, his two good angels, who stood one on the right, the other on the left of his bed.

A long pause followed. The blood of the reformer had flowed, and this was the Calvary, the passion whence triumph would arise. As the two women moved gently around him the injured man opened his eyes to smile at them again. Then he fell asleep, murmuring: "Love has come at last, and now we shall be the conquerors."

V

Before long complications arose, and Luc barely escaped the clutches of death. For a couple of days it was thought that he was dying. Josine and Sœurette never quitted him, and Jordan came to seat himself beside the bed of anguish, thus forsaking his laboratory, a thing which he had not done since his mother's last illness. And how great was the despair of those loving hearts which from hour to hour expected to see their dear one drawing his last breath!

The knife-thrust which Ragu had dealt Luc had quite upset La Crêcherie. Work went on in the mourning workshops, but at every moment the men desired tidings. There was great solidarity among them, and all felt an anxious affection for the victim of that crime, which did more to tighten the bonds of fraternity between them than many years of experimental humanitarianism. Even in Beauclair sympathy became apparent; a great many people there felt for that young, handsome, and active man, whose one crime, apart from his work of justice, consisted in having loved a very charming woman, who had been incessantly reviled and beaten by her husband. Briefly, nobody seemed to be scandalised at seeing Josine instal herself at Luc's bedside. It was indeed thought quite natural, for was he not the father of the child? And had they not purchased at the cost of many tears the right to live together? On the other hand, the gendarmes despatched after Ragu had found no trace of him; for a fortnight all the researches proved fruitless, but at last, in the depths of a ravine of the Bleuse Mountains, the remains of a man, half devoured by wolves, were discovered; and in these remains the searchers asserted that they could recognise the body of Ragu. It was impossible to draw up a death certificate on such evidence, but a legend arose to the effect that Ragu had perished either accidentally or by suicide amidst the furious madness born of his crime. In this case, if Josine were a widow, why should she not live with Luc? And why should not the Jordans accept the situation? The union of the young couple seemed so natural, so firm, so indissoluble, that later on the idea that they were not legally married occurred to nobody.

At last, one bright February morning, Doctor Novarre declared that he thought he might answer for Luc; and, indeed, a few days later the latter was quite convalescent. Then Josine, who had not spared herself throughout his illness, in her turn required to be nursed, for she gave birth to a vigorous boy, named by his parents Hilaire. During the weeks which followed, Luc often spent an hour, seated in an arm-chair, near Josine's bed. The early springtide filled the room with sunshine; on the table there was always a fresh bunch of lovely roses which the doctor brought from his garden, like a prescription of youth, health, and beauty, as he was wont to say. Between the parents was the cradle occupied by little Hilaire, whom Josine herself nursed. Yet greater strength and hope than they had previously known now flowered from their lives in the person of that child. As Luc constantly repeated, amidst the many plans for the future in which he indulged pending the time when he might set to work once more, he was now at ease, convinced that he would found the city of justice and peace, since in Josine and Hilaire he had love—fruitful love—upon his side. Nothing is founded without a child. A child is living work, the broadening and the propagation of life, the assurance that to-morrow will duly follow to-day. The mated couple alone brings life, alone works for human happiness, and will alone save poor men from iniquity and wretchedness.

On the first day when Josine, erect once more, was able to begin her new life by the side of Luc, he caught her in his arms, exclaiming: "Ah! you are mine alone! your child is mine also! And now we are perfected, and fear nothing more from fate!"

As soon as Luc was able to resume the management of the works, the sympathy which had gone out to him on all sides helped him to accomplish prodigies. Moreover, it was not only the baptism of blood which brought about the success of La Crêcherie, a success which now ever increased, continuously and invincibly. There was also a lucky discovery: the mine once more became a source of great wealth, for they fell at last upon considerable lodes of excellent ore, thus proving that Morfain had been right. From that time forward iron and steel were turned out of such excellent quality, and at such a low cost, that the Abyss was even threatened in its manufacture of superfine articles. All competition became impossible. And then there was also the effect of the great democratic movement which now tended on all sides to an increase in the means of communication, to an endless extension of railway lines, and to the erection of bridges, buildings, whole cities indeed, in which iron and steel were employed to a prodigious and ever larger and larger extent. Since the days of the first Vulcans who had smelted ore in a pit for the purpose of forging weapons to defend themselves and conquer dominion over beings and things, the employment of iron had been steadily spreading, and when its conquest by science should be perfect, when it would be possible to work it for next to nothing and adapt it to all usages, iron itself would become a source of justice and peace. That, however, which more particularly brought about the prosperity and triumph of La Crêcherie was its improved management, into which there entered increase of truth, equity, and solidarity. Its success had been certain from the day when it had been founded on the provisional system of an association between capital, labour, and intelligence; and the difficult days through which it had passed, the obstacles of all kinds, the various crises which had been deemed deadly, were simply so many inevitable jolts upon the road during the first trying days of the advance, when it is necessary that one should brace oneself for resistance if one desires to attain one's goal. All this was now clearly manifest; the enterprise had ever been full of life, laden with sap whence the harvests of the future would spring.

The works were now like a practical lesson, a decisive experiment which would gradually convince everybody. How was it possible to deny the strength of that association of capital, labour, and intelligence when the profits became larger from year to year, and the workmen of La Crêcherie earned twice as much as those of other establishments? How could one do otherwise than admit that eight hours', six hours', three hours' work—work rendered attractive by variety, and accomplished in bright, gay workshops with the help of machinery which children might have directed—was the fundamental principle necessary for future society, when one saw the wretched wage-earners of yesterday born anew, becoming healthy, intelligent, cheerful, and gentle men again as things progressed towards complete liberty and justice? How also could one do otherwise than conclude in favour of the necessity of co-operation which would suppress all intermediary parasitic growths, mere trading in which so much wealth and strength is swallowed up, when the general stores of La Crêcherie worked so smoothly, ever increasing the comfort of those who yesterday had been famished, and loading them with enjoyments hitherto reserved for the rich alone? How again could one do otherwise than believe in the prodigies accomplished by solidarity, which renders life so pleasant and makes it a continual festival for one and all, when one attended the happy meetings at the common-house, destined to become the people's royal palace, with its libraries, its museums, its concert-halls, its gardens, and its many diversions? And how could one do otherwise than renew the whole system of educating and rearing children in such wise that this system should no longer be based on a theory of the innate idleness of man, but on his inextinguishable craving for knowledge? And how refuse to render study agreeable and leave each pupil in possession of his individual energy, and allow the two sexes to mingle from infancy—since they are destined to share life side by side—when one beheld the prosperity of the schools of La Crêcherie, whence all excessive book-learning was banished, where lessons were mingled with play and rudimentary notions of professional apprenticeship, so as to help each fresh generation to draw nearer to that ideal community towards which mankind has been marching for so many centuries?

Thus the extraordinary example which La Crêcherie day by day displayed in the broad sunlight became contagious. There was no longer any question of theories, but one of facts evident to the eyes of all. And naturally the association gained more and more support; crowds of fresh workmen presented themselves for admission, attracted by the larger earnings, the increase of comfort; and new buildings arose on all sides, continually adding themselves to those which had been first erected. In three years the population was doubled, and the pace of the progress was increased till it became one of incredible rapidity. This was the dreamt-of city, the city of reorganised work, restored to its status of nobility, the city of happiness at last conquered, springing naturally from the soil around the works, which likewise grew and spread, becoming, as it were, a metropolis, a central heart, the source of life, dispensing and regulating social existence. The workshops, the great halls became larger and larger until they covered acres of ground, whilst the little bright, gay dwelling-houses, standing amidst the greenery of their gardens, multiplied incessantly even as the number of workers increased. And this overflowing wave of new buildings advanced towards the Abyss, which it threatened to destroy and submerge. At first, between the two establishments there had been a great bare space made up of all the uncultivated land which Jordan owned below the ridge of the Bleuse Mountains. Now, beyond the few houses first built near La Crêcherie, there had come others and ever others, lines of houses invading everything like a rising tide, which only some two or three hundred yards separated from the Abyss. And whenever the waves might advance against it, would it not be covered, carried away, to be replaced by a triumphant florescence of health and joy? Even Old Beauclair was threatened, for one part of the new city was marching thither, and would sweep off that black and evil-smelling den of the old-time workers, that nest of pain and pestilence, where the wage-system lay at its last gasp under the crumbling ceilings of the hovels.

One evening, when Luc stood gazing at his new city, which he could already picture covering the whole estuary of the Brias gorges, Bonnaire brought Babette, Bourron's wife, to him. Said she, with her everlasting expression of good humour, "It's like this, Monsieur Luc. My man would very much like to come back to work at La Crêcherie. Only he wasn't bold enough to come and speak to you himself, for he remembers that he took himself off in a very wrong fashion. So I've come for him."

Then Bonnaire added: "One ought to forgive Bourron. That wretched Ragu led him astray. There's no malice in Bourron; he's only weak, and perhaps we can still save him."

"Oh, let him come back!" Luc gaily exclaimed. "I do not desire the death of a sinner—rather the reverse! How many there are who only take to bad courses because they are led to them by their mates, idlers and revellers whom they cannot resist! Bourron will be a good recruit; we'll make an example of him for the benefit of the others."

Never had Luc felt so happy. Bourron's return seemed to him a decisive symptom, albeit the man had become a mediocre worker. But, then, as Bonnaire said, would not his redemption be a victory over the wage-system? And besides, this would mean another household in the new town, another little wave added to all the others which helped to swell the tide by which the old world would be swept away.

Some days later Bonnaire again came to ask Luc to admit one of the men of the Abyss. On this occasion, however, the recruit was such a pitiable one that the former master-puddler was not disposed to insist on the matter.

"It's that poor Fauchard," said Bonnaire; "he's made up his mind at last. He prowled about La Crêcherie on several occasions, as you may remember; but he could come to no resolution, he was afraid to choose, to such a degree had he been brutified, exhausted by excessive labour, ever the same. He's no longer a man, you know; he's simply an old warped bit of mechanism. I fear that we shall never get anything good out of him."

Luc was reflecting, recalling the first days that he had spent at Beauclair. "Ah! yes," he said, "I know; he has a wife called Natalie, isn't that so? A woman of complaining mind, full of care, who is always in search of credit. And he has a brother-in-law, Fortuné, who when I first met him was only sixteen years old, and looked so pale, so bewildered, so shattered already by mechanical toil! Ah! the poor creatures! Well, let all of them come; why shouldn't they? This will be another example, even if we cannot make Fauchard a free and cheerful man again."

Then in a jocular, joyful manner he added: "This will mean another family, another house added to the others. La Crêcherie is becoming populous, eh? Do you know, Bonnaire, we are now on the high road to that beautiful great city of which I used to speak to you at the very beginning, when you were so incredulous! Do you remember? You were anxious as to the result of the experiment; and if you remained on my side it was chiefly out of gratitude. But are you convinced now?"

Bonnaire, who seemed somewhat embarrassed, did not immediately reply. At length, in his usual frank way, he said: "Is one ever convinced? It's necessary that one should be able to touch the result with one's finger. The works are prosperous, no doubt; our association is growing, the men live in more comfort; there is a little more justice and happiness. But you know my ideas, Monsieur Luc; it is still the accursed wage-system, and I don't yet see any realisation of Collectivism."

It was only as a theorist that Bonnaire now defended himself. If he did not give up his ideas, as he expressed it, he at least showed admirable activity and courage in helping on the work which was going forward. He was the hero-worker, the real leader, whose brotherly example of solidarity had decided the battle in favour of La Crêcherie. When he appeared in the workshops, looking so tall, so strong, and so good-natured, all hands were stretched towards him. And he was more won over to the cause than he was willing to admit, for it delighted him to see that his comrades suffered less, tasted all sorts of delights, and dwelt in healthy homes with flowers around them. After all it seemed as if he would not go off without seeing the fulfilment of his life dream, that dream of a world in which there would be less wretchedness and more equity.

"Yes, yes, Collectivist society," said Luc, laughing, for he knew Bonnaire well, "we shall bring it about, even in a better way perhaps than many of its partisans imagine; and if we don't, our children will. Be confident, Bonnaire, and remember that the future henceforth belongs to us, since our town is growing, always growing."

Then, with a broad gesture Luc pointed to the houses which stood among the young trees, and whose roofs of coloured faïence showed so gaily in the light of the setting sun. Ever and ever did he return to those living houses which seemed to rise from the ground at his command, and which he really pictured on the march like some pacific army which had set forth to sow the future on the ruins of Old Beauclair and the Abyss.

If, however, the industrial workers of La Crêcherie alone had triumphed, the result would simply have been a happy one, with consequences still open to discussion. But it was rendered decisive by the fact that the peasant workers of Les Combettes triumphed on their side also in the association which had been formed between the village and the factory. Here again there was only a beginning, but how great was the promise of prodigious fortune! Since the day when, realising that agreement was necessary if they were to struggle on and live, Mayor Lenfant and his assessor Yvonnot had become reconciled, and had prevailed on all the petty landowners of the village to combine together in order to constitute one large estate of several hundreds of acres, the land had developed extraordinary fertility. Previously it had seemed as if it were becoming bankrupt, even like the great plain of La Roumagne which had once been so fruitful, and which now presented such a sorry spectacle with its poor, stunted, meagre crops. In point of fact this was simply the effect of man's stubborn laziness and ignorance, his adherence to old-fashioned methods, and the lack of proper manure, machinery, and agreement. Thus what a lesson was given to others when the peasants of Les Combettes began to cultivate their land in common. They purchased manure cheaply and procured tools and machinery at La Crêcherie in exchange for the bread, wine, and vegetables with which they supplied it. Strength came to them now that they were no longer isolated, but had formed a solid and henceforth indestructible bond between the village and the factory. And this was the long-dreamt-of reconciliation between peasant and mechanic, which for so many years had seemed impossible: the peasant supplying the corn that nourishes, and the other supplying iron and steel in order that the land might be sown with corn. If La Crêcherie needed Les Combettes, Les Combettes on the other hand could not have thriven without La Crêcherie. At all events union was at last effected, there was a fruitful alliance whence the happy community of to-morrow would spring. And what a miraculous spectacle was presented by that plain, now reviving to life. A short time previously it had been almost abandoned, and now it overflowed with crops! Amidst the other stretches of land stricken by disunion and incompetence, Les Combettes formed as it were a little sea of rich verdure which the whole region contemplated at first with stupefaction and then with envy. Such dryness, such sterility yesterday, and so much vigour and abundance to-day! Why not follow, then, the example of the folk of Les Combettes? Neighbouring villages were already making inquiries, and showing a desire to join the movement. It was said that the mayors of Fleuranges, Lignerolles, and Bonneheux were drawing up articles of association and collecting signatures. Thus the little green sea would soon grow, join other seas, and spread its waves of greenery afar until the whole expanse of La Roumagne would form but one sole domain, one sole pacific ocean of corn, vast enough to nourish the whole of a happy people.

For pleasure's sake, Luc often took long walks through those fertile fields, and he occasionally met Feuillat, Boisgelin's farmer, who likewise strolled about, with his hands in his pockets, whilst contemplating in his silent enigmatical way the growth of the fine crops which sprang from that well-tilled land. Luc knew what a large part Feuillat had had in prompting Lenfant and Yvonnot to take the initiative, and he was aware that the farmer still advised them nowadays. Thus the young man remained full of surprise at seeing in what a lamentable condition the other left the land which he himself farmed—the land belonging to La Guerdache, whose sorry fields looked like an uncultivated desert beside the rich domain of Les Combettes.

One morning, as Luc and Feuillat were chatting whilst they sauntered along the road which separated the two estates, the former could not help remarking: "I say, Feuillat, don't you feel ashamed at keeping your land in such poor condition, when over the way your neighbours' land is so admirably cultivated? Surely your own interest ought to urge you to active and intelligent work, such as I know you to be quite capable of."

At first the farmer simply smiled; then he fearlessly spoke out: "Oh, Monsieur Luc! shame is far too fine a sentiment for such poor devils as we are. As for my interest, it is just to get a living, and no more, out of this land which does not belong to me. That's what I do; I cultivate it just sufficiently to procure bread. I should simply be a dupe if I were to work it properly, manure it and improve it; for all that would only enrich Monsieur Boisgelin, who each time my lease expires is free to turn me out of doors. No, no! To make a field a good field it ought to belong to oneself, better still to everybody."

Then he began to jeer at the folk who shouted to the peasants: "Love the land! Love the land!" No doubt he was willing to love it: but all the same he wished to be loved in return, or rather he did not desire to love it for the sake of others. As he repeated, his father, his grandfather, and his great-grandfather had loved it in all good faith, bending beneath the rod of those who exploited them, and never drawing from it aught save wretchedness and tears. For his own part he would have none of the system by which landlords ferociously imposed upon their tenants that farming system which meant that the farmer was to love and caress and fructify the soil in order to increase the owner's wealth.

A pause followed. Then in a lower voice, with an expression of concentrated ardour, Feuillat added: "Yes, yes, the land to everybody, so that one may love it again and cultivate it properly. For my part, I'm waiting."

Greatly struck by these words, Luc again glanced at the farmer. Close as he might keep, he was evidently a man of keen intelligence. Behind the peasant, who simply seemed unobtrusive and somewhat shy, Luc now divined a skilful diplomatist, a keen-eyed precursor, one who gazed into the future and helped on the experiment at Les Combettes with a distant object, known to him alone, in view. Luc suspected the truth, and, wishing to make certain on the point, he said: "So, if you leave your land in that condition, it is in part to make people compare it with the neighbouring land and understand the reasons of the difference. But is it not all a dream? Surely Les Combettes will never invade and swallow up La Guerdache."

Again did Feuillat break into a silent laugh. Then he contented himself with saying: "Something big would have to happen between now and then. But, after all, who knows? I'm waiting."

They took a few steps, and then, with a sweeping gesture which embraced the whole scene, the farmer resumed: "All the same, things are moving. Do you remember what a horrid view one had from here with all those little patches of ground which yielded such poor crops? And now just look! With everything united in one estate, and cultivation in common with the help of machinery and science, the crops overflow on all sides. Ah, it is indeed a splendid sight!"

The ardent love which he had secretly retained for the soil was manifest at that moment in the fire of his glance and the enthusiasm of his voice. And Luc himself was impressed by the great gust of fruitfulness which passed, quivering, over that sea of corn. If he felt so strong and competent at La Crêcherie, it was because he now had his granary and was assured of bread, through having added a community of peasants to his community of industrial workers. And the delight he experienced when he saw his city marching on, its waves of houses ever advancing to the conquest of the Abyss and Old Beauclair, was no greater than that which he felt when he came to view the fertile fields of Les Combettes, which on their side were likewise marching on, stretching into the neighbouring fields, and gradually spreading out into an ocean of crops which would cover La Roumagne from one to the other end. Here as there the effort was identical; the same civilisation was coming—mankind was marching towards truth, justice, peace, and happiness.

The first effect of La Crêcherie's success was to make the petty factories of the region understand the advantage they would reap by following its example and combining with it. The Chodorge works—nail works which purchased all their raw material from their powerful neighbours—were the first to come to a decision, allowing themselves to be absorbed by La Crêcherie in the interest of both sides. Then the Hauser works, which after manufacturing sabres had made scythes and sickles their specialty, likewise joined the association, forming as it were a natural adjunct of the great forge. Some difficulties arose with another establishment, that of Mirande & Co., who built agricultural machinery, for one of the two partners was a reactionist, and fought against all novelties. But the position of the firm became so critical that, fearing a catastrophe, he withdrew from it, and the other partner hastened to save his works by merging them into those of La Crêcherie. All the establishments thus drawn into the movement of association and solidarity accepted the same statutes—a division of profits based upon an alliance between capital, work, and intelligence. They ended by constituting one sole family made up of various groups, ever ready to welcome fresh adherents, and in this wise capable of spreading indefinitely. And in this there was a re-casting of society, which reconstituted itself on the basis of a new organisation of work, tending to the freedom and happiness of mankind.

Beauclair was astonished and disconcerted, and its anxiety soon reached a climax. What! would La Crêcherie grow without cessation, absorb every little factory it might meet, this one, that one, and then that other? And would the town itself and the immense plain beside it be swallowed up and become the dependencies, the domain, the very flesh of La Crêcherie? Men's hearts were disturbed, and their brains began to wonder in what direction might lie the true interest of one and all, and the possibility of fortune. The perplexity of the petty traders, particularly the usual household purveyors, increased and increased as day by day their takings diminished. It became a question whether they would not be soon obliged to put up their shutters. The sensation was general when people learnt that Caffiaux, the grocer and taverner, had come to an arrangement with La Crêcherie by which his establishment would be turned into a simple *dépôt*, a kind of branch of the factory's general stores. Caffiaux had long been regarded as the hireling of the Abyss, more or less a spy, one who poisoned the worker with alcohol and then sold his secrets to his masters, for taverns are the strongest pillars of the wage-system. At all events the man was a suspicious character, one who ever watched to see which side would prove victorious, and who was always prepared to commit some act of treachery, readily turning his coat with the ease of one who is by no means partial to defeat.

Thus the circumstance that he had so jauntily set himself on the side of La Crêcherie greatly increased the anxiety of his neighbours, who, for their own parts, wished to take up the most profitable position as soon as possible. A pronounced movement of adherence to the association then set in, and was destined to proceed more and more rapidly. Beautiful Madame Mitaine, the bakeress, had not waited for Caffiaux's conversion to express approval of the developments at La Crêcherie, and she was quite disposed to enter the association, though her establishment remained prosperous, thanks to the reputation for beauty and kindliness which she had imparted to it. Butcher Dacheux alone persevered in obstinate resistance, full of fury at the downfall of all his cherished notions. He declared that rather than yield to the current he would prefer to die amongst his last quarters of beef on the day when he should no longer find a *bourgeois* disposed to buy them at their proper price. And it seemed indeed as if this would come to pass, for his customers were gradually deserting him, and such were his fits of wrath that assuredly he was threatened with some sudden stroke of apoplexy.

One day Dacheux betook himself to Laboque's establishment, whither he had begged Madame Mitaine also to repair. It was a question, said he, of seeing to the moral and commercial interests of the whole district. A rumour was current that the Laboques, in order to avoid bankruptcy, were on the point of making peace with Luc and joining La Crêcherie, in such a way as to become mere depositaries of its goods. Since the works had been directly exchanging their iron and steel, their tools and machinery for the bread of Les Combettes and the other syndicated villages, the Laboques had lost their best customers, the peasants of the environs, without counting the housewives and even the *bourgeoises* of Beauclair, who effected great savings by making their purchases at the stores of La Crêcherie, which Luc by a happy inspiration had ended by throwing open to everybody. This meant the death of trade, such as it had hitherto been understood, such as it was personified by the middleman who intervened between producer and consumer, increasing the cost of life, and living like a parasite on the needs of others. And thus amidst their deserted bazaar the Laboques poured forth their lamentations.

When Dacheux arrived, the woman, dark and scraggy, sat behind her counter doing nothing, for she lacked even the courage to knit herself some stockings; whilst the man, with the eyes and the snout of a ferret, came and went like a soul in distress, before the pigeon-holes full of unsold, dust-covered goods.

"What's that I hear?" cried the butcher, flushing purple. "You've turned traitor, Laboque, so people say, you are on the point of surrendering! To think of it! You who lost that disastrous lawsuit, you who swore that you'd kill the bandit even if it should cost you your skin! Would you now set yourself against us, then, and add to the disaster?"

But Laboque, whose hopes were all shattered, burst into a rage. "I've quite enough worry; just leave me in peace," he answered. "As for that idiotic lawsuit, you all urged me to it. And now you don't spend enough money with me to enable me to make my monthly payments. So you need not come taunting me about saving my skin." And pointing to his dusty goods he went on: "My skin's there, and if I don't come to an arrangement the bailiffs will be here next Wednesday. Yes, it's quite true, since you want me to say it; yes, I'm negotiating with La Crêcherie, I've come to an understanding with them, and I shall sign the papers to-night. I was still hesitating, but I'm being worried beyond endurance."

He sank upon a chair, whilst Dacheux, quite thunderstruck, and almost choking, was only able to stammer oaths. Then in her turn Madame Laboque, huddled up behind her counter, poured forth her plaint in a low and monotonous voice: "To have worked so hard, *mon Dieu*, to have taken so much trouble when we first started in business and went selling ironmongery from village to village! And then too, all the efforts that we had to make here in order to open this shop, and enlarge it from year to year! We were rewarded, no doubt; the business prospered, and we dreamt of buying a house right in the country and of retiring to it and living on our income. But now everything is crumbling away, Beauclair has gone mad, though I can't yet understand why, *mon Dieu!*"

"Why, why?" growled Dacheux; "why, because the Revolution has come, and the *bourgeois* are cowards and don't even dare to defend themselves. For my part, if I'm hustled too much I'll take my knives one morning, and then you'll see something."

Laboque shrugged his shoulders. "A lot of use that would be!" he exclaimed. "It's all very well when folk are with one, but when a man feels that to-morrow he will be left quite alone, the best is to go where the others are going, however much it may enrage one to do so. Caffiaux understood it well enough."

"Ah! that filthy Caffiaux!" shouted the butcher, full of fury once more. "There's a traitor for you—a man who sells himself! You know that Monsieur Luc, that bandit, gave him a hundred thousand francs to desert us."

"A hundred thousand francs," repeated the ironmonger, whose eyes glowed, although he feigned ironical scepticism. "I only wish he'd offer them to me, I'd take them at once. But no, it's stupid to be obstinate, and the sensible course is always to side with the stronger."

"How awful! how awful!" resumed Madame Laboque in her whining voice. "The world is certainly being turned upside down; it is coming to an end."

Beautiful Madame Mitaine, who was just then entering the shop, heard those last words. "What! the end of the world," said she gaily, "why there were two babies, two fine big boys, born yesterday. And your children, Auguste and Eulalie, how are they? Aren't they here?"

No, they were not there, they were never there. Auguste, now nearly two-and-twenty, had acquired a passion for mechanical arts, holding trade in horror; whilst Eulalie, who was a very sensible girl, already a little housewife at fifteen, lived for the most part with one of her uncles, a farmer of Lignerolles, near Les Combettes.

"Oh! the children," said Madame Laboque, again in a complaining voice, "one can't rely on the children."

"They are all so ungrateful," declared Dacheux, who was indignant at finding no trace of his own nature in his daughter Julienne, a plump, good-looking girl of a compassionate disposition, who, although she had passed her fourteenth birthday, still played with all the little ragamuffins that infested the Rue de Brias. "When one relies on one's children one may be sure of dying of misery and grief."

"Well, I certainly rely on my Évariste, I do," resumed the baker's wife. "He's close on twenty now, but we shan't quarrel because he has refused to learn his father's calling. These young people naturally grow up with ideas different from ours, for they are born for times when we shall no longer be here. All I ask of my Évariste is to love me well, and that he does."

She then plainly stated her position to Dacheux. If she had come to Laboque's shop at his request it was in order that it might be fully understood between them that each tradesman of Beauclair ought to retain full freedom of action. She did not as yet belong to the association of La Crêcherie, but she relied upon joining it when she might be so pleased, that is to say, when she might feel convinced that she would be acting in the general interest as well as in her own.

"It's evident that we ought to be free," put in Laboque by way of conclusion. "As I can't do otherwise, I shall sign to-night."

Then Madame Laboque's moan began once more: "I told you so, the world is topsy-turvy, this is the end of it."

"No, no!" the beautiful Madame Mitaine again exclaimed. "How can the world be coming to an end when our children are just getting to an age when they may marry and have children of their own, who in their turn will marry and have children too? The young people are pushing the others aside, the world is being renewed, that's what it is—the end of *a* world, if you like."

Those last words fell from her so sharply and decisively that Dacheux, banging the door behind him, went off exasperated, with bloodshot eyes and a quiver of the apoplexy by which he was threatened. As Madame Mitaine had said, it was indeed the end of *a* world, the end of iniquitous and rotting trade, that trade which only creates the wealth of a few at the expense of the greater number.

But Beauclair was to be upset by another and greater blow. Hitherto the success of La Crêcherie had reacted only on establishments of a similar nature, and on the petty traders, those who lived from day to day on passing customers. Thus the emotion became great indeed when one fine morning it was learnt that Mayor Gourier himself had been won over to the new ideas. He—firmly established, needing nobody, as he declared in a spirit of vanity—did not intend to join the association of La Crêcherie. But he founded another one of a similar character, dividing his large boot-works of the Rue de Brias into shares, on the basis of a partnership between capital, work, and intelligence, amongst which the profits were to be apportioned in three parts. This was simply the establishment of a new group, what may be called the clothing group, by the side of that which dealt in iron and steel. And the resemblance between the two became the more pronounced when Gourier succeeded in syndicating all the branches of the clothing industry: the tailors, hatters, hosiers, linendrapers, and mercers. Then, too, yet another group was spoken of, one which a big building contractor proposed to establish by associating all the workers of the building trade, masons, stonecutters, carpenters, locksmiths, plumbers, tilers, and painters. And this group would assuredly absorb the architects and artists, as well as the workers of the furniture trade, the cabinetmakers, upholsterers, and bronze-workers, and in time even the clockmakers and the jewellers. All this was simply logical; the example of La Crêcherie had sown that fruitful idea of so many associations forming natural groups, which grew up by themselves, in an imitative spirit, through a craving to reach the greatest possible sum of life and happiness. The law of human creation was working, and it would certainly work with increasing energy if such were necessary for the happy existence of the species. It already became apparent that a general bond was in process of formation above these groups, a common link which would some day join them all together in a vast system of social reorganisation, which would prove the one code of the future community.

However, the idea of escaping from La Crêcherie by imitating it seemed too good a one to have emanated from a man of Gourier's intellect. Thus the general opinion was that it must have been suggested to the mayor by Sub-Prefect Prefect Châtelard, who kept himself more and more in the background and displayed more and more quiet indifference as Beauclair gradually transformed itself. The guess was a correct one, for the matter had been settled at a little *déjeuner*, when the mayor and the sub-prefect had sat face to face with only the ever-beautiful Léonore beside them.

"My dear fellow," had said the sub-prefect, with his amiable smile, "I believe that we are at the end of our tether. Everything is going from worse to worse in Paris, and the Revolution is approaching to sweep away whatever remains of the old, rotting, ruinous social edifice. Here, our chief man, Boisgelin, is a poor, vain creature, who will be drained of his last copper by little Madame Delaveau. Nobody excepting her husband is ignorant of what becomes of the money that he still makes at the Abyss in his heroic struggle against bankruptcy. And you'll see what a disaster there will be presently. So it would really be foolish if one did not think of oneself if one does not wish to be dragged down with the others."

At this Léonore showed some anxiety. "Are you, yourself, threatened, my friend?" she asked.

"I? Oh, no! Who thinks of me? No Government will trouble about my paltry self, for I am clever enough to do as little as possible in the way of administrative duties, and I am always of precisely the same opinion as my superiors, whoever they may be. I shall die here, forgotten and happy, when the last Ministry collapses. But it is of you that I am thinking, my good friends."

Thereupon he explained his ideas and enumerated all the advantages that would accrue from anticipating the Revolution by making a second Crêcherie of the Gourier boot-works. The profits would not be diminished—on the contrary. Besides, he was convinced—he was too intelligent, said he, to fail to understand the truth—the future lay in that direction, reorganised labour would end by sweeping the old iniquitous *bourgeoise* society away. As Châtelard proceeded it became manifest that in that peaceful, sceptical functionary who deliberately preserved an attitude of absolute inactivity, there had sprung up a genuine Anarchist, though in public he carefully kept this concealed beneath a demeanour of diplomatic reserve.

"You know, my dear Gourier," he concluded with a laugh, "all this won't prevent me from declaring myself openly against you when you have gone over to the new community. I shall say that you are a traitor or that you have lost your reason. But I shall embrace you whenever I come here, for you will have played them all a fine trick, which will bring you in a deal of money. You'll see what faces they'll pull!"

All the same, Gourier was quite scared by the other's suggestions. He did not consent, but argued the matter at great length. The whole of his past life rose up in protest. He rebelled at the idea of becoming nothing more than the partner of hundreds of workers, of whom hitherto he had been absolute master. Beneath his heavy exterior, however, there was a very shrewd business mind; he fully understood that he would risk nothing by the change, but, on the contrary, would assure his establishment against all the dangers of the future should he adopt the advice of Châtelard. Besides, he himself had been touched by the passing gale, that exaltation, that passion for reform, whose contagious fever at times of Revolution transports the very classes which are about to be despoiled. Gourier, indeed, ended by believing that the other's idea was his own, even as Léonore, by the advice of her friend Châtelard, repeated to him every morning, and thus he at last set to work.

The whole *bourgeoisie* of Beauclair was scandalised. Deputations called upon Judge Gaume to beg him to intervene with the mayor, since the sub-prefect, anxious to avoid compromising the Government, had formally declined to meddle in this sorry affair, which he proclaimed to be scandalous. Judge Gaume now led a very retired life, seeing virtually nobody since his daughter Lucile, compromised it seemed beyond remedy by an intrigue with a notary's clerk, had been obliged to seek a refuge with him. On being approached he followed the same course as Châtelard, and showed great unwillingness to go to the mayor with representations which the latter would doubtless take in very bad part. It was then resolved to bring pressure to bear upon the judge. Captain Jollivet, his son-in-law, after Lucile's flight from her home, had, with growing wrath, thrown himself into reactionary courses. He contributed such violent articles to the "Journal de Beauclair" that Lebleu, the printer and proprietor, becoming anxious at the turn which things were taking, feeling that it was necessary to be on the side of the stronger, and thus pass from the Abyss to the Crêcherie party, one day closed his door to him. The captain, thus disarmed and reduced to idleness, spent his time in airing his futile rancour abroad, when the idea suddenly occurred to his fellow-townsmen that he alone might compel the judge to range himself on their side. As a matter of fact the captain had not broken off all intercourse with his father-in-law; they exchanged salutes whenever they met. Accordingly, on being entrusted with the delicate mission, Jollivet presented himself at the judge's house in the most ceremonious fashion, and two long hours elapsed before he came out of it again. It was then learnt that he had only been able to extract some evasive replies from his father-in-law, but that he had become reconciled with his wife. On the following day she returned to the conjugal roof, the captain having forgiven her on her solemn promise that she would never transgress again. All Beauclair was stupefied by this *dénouement* to a very scandalous business, and the affair ended in a great outburst of laughter.

It was the Mazelles who ultimately succeeded in drawing from Gaume an expression of his views, and this purely by chance, without having been entrusted with any mission whatever. As a rule the judge went out every morning and made his way to the Boulevard de Magnolles, a long, deserted avenue, where he walked up and down in a gloomy reverie, with his head bent and his hands clasped behind him. He stooped as if beneath some final collapse, as if weighed down by the failure of his whole life, the harm he had done, or the good which he had found he could not do. And whenever he raised his eyes for a moment and gazed far away, he seemed to be looking and waiting for something which did not come, which perchance he would never see. Now one morning, on the Boulevard de Magnolles, the Mazelles, who had risen early to go to mass, mustered sufficient courage to approach the judge in order to ask him his opinion on public affairs, so greatly did they fear that these would lead to some disaster for themselves.

"Well, Monsieur le Président, and what do you think of all that is happening?" asked Monsieur Mazelle.

The judge raised his head, and for a moment gazed into the distance. Then, reverting to his torturing reverie, thinking aloud as though nobody were listening to him, he said: "I say that the hurricane is a long time coming—yes, the hurricane of truth and justice which will end by sweeping this abominable world away."

"What! what!" stammered the Mazelles, thunderstruck, and imagining that they had misunderstood him. "You want to frighten us, eh, because you think that we are not over-brave? That's in a measure true, and people tease us about it."

But Gaume had recovered his self-possession, and as soon as he recognised the Mazelles, who stood before him scared, with pale faces, perspiring with anxiety for their money and their idle lives, his lips became curved into an expression of disdainful irony. "What do you fear?" he resumed; "the world will well last another twenty years, and if you are still alive then you will console yourselves for the *ennuis* of the Revolution by witnessing some very interesting things. It is your daughter who ought to think of the future."

At this Madame Mazelle sorrowfully exclaimed: "Ah! that's the very thing that Louise does not think about—ah! not at all. She is scarcely thirteen as yet, and when she hears us talking of what goes on, as we naturally do from morning till evening, she finds it very funny. While we despair she simply laughs. Whenever I say to her, 'You wretched girl, why, you won't have a penny,' she jumps about like a goat, and answers: 'Oh! I don't mind that—no, not a bit; I shall be all the merrier!' But, all the same, she's a very dear girl, although she does so little of what we desire."

"Yes," said Gaume; "she dreams of mapping out her life for herself. There *are* girls like that."

Mazelle remained perplexed, for he feared that the judge was again poking fun at him. The idea that he had made a fortune in ten years, that he had since been leading the delightful life of sloth of which he had dreamt already in his youth, and that his felicity might now come to an end, that he might, perhaps, be compelled to work again if work should become the general rule, filled him with ceaseless, intolerable anguish, which was like a first punishment for his sins.

"But the Rentes, Monsieur le Président, what would become of them, in your opinion, if all those Anarchists should succeed in turning the world topsy-turvy? As you may remember, that Monsieur Luc, who is behaving so badly, used to make fun of us, saying that the Rentes would be suppressed. In that case they may as well cut our throats."

"Sleep in peace, I tell you," Gaume repeated with quiet irony, "the new social fabric will feed you if you won't work."

Then the Mazelles went off to church, where they now burnt tapers to the Virgin in the hope of inducing her to cure Madame Mazelle; for Doctor Novarre had one day been brute enough to tell the old lady that she was not ill at all. Not ill, indeed! when she had been nursing her illness so lovingly for so many years—that illness which was her very life—to such a point had she made it her occupation, her joy, her *raison d'être*! If the doctor forsook her it must be that he deemed her incurable; at which thought, full of terror, she had addressed herself to religion, in which she now found great relief.

There was another promenader on the Boulevard de Magnolles, that desert whose quietude was so seldom disturbed by any passer-by. This was Abbé Marle, who came thither to read his breviary. But he often let the hand which held the book fall beside him, whilst still slowly walking on, absorbed, like the judge, in a gloomy reverie. Since the last events, those incidents of the evolution which was bearing the town towards a new destiny, his church had become still emptier. By way of congregation, there only remained some very old women of the people, dull-witted, obstinate creatures, and a few *bourgeoises* who supported religion because they deemed it to be the last rampart of fine society which was now crumbling to pieces. When the last of the faithful should desert the Catholic churches, leaving them to brambles and nettles like the ruins of a dead social system, another civilisation would begin. And with this threat above his head, the presence of the few *bourgeoises* and old women of the people in no wise consoled Abbé Marle, who felt that the void around him was ever increasing. Léonore, the mayor's wife, looked very decorative, no doubt, at high mass on Sundays, and opened her purse widely to contribute to the expenses of public worship; but he knew her indignity, her life of sin, which the whole town accepted, and over which he himself had been compelled to cast the cloak of his holy office, though he regarded that life as one leading to eternal perdition, for which he himself would be accounted responsible. And still less did the support of the Mazelles content him. They were so childish and so basely egotistical. If they came to him, it was solely in the hope of extracting some personal felicity from heaven. Even as they had invested their money, so did they invest their prayers—that is, with the object of deriving Rentes from them on high. And one and all were the same in that dying society, all lacked the true faith which in the first centuries had given Christianity its force, all lacked the spirit of renunciation and absolute obedience—a spirit which was more than ever necessary nowadays if the power of the Church was to be maintained. Thus the priest no longer hid it from himself—the days were numbered, and if God in His mercy did not soon call him hence, he would, perhaps, behold the awful catastrophe—the steeple of his church falling, bursting through the roof of the nave, and crushing the altar of the Divinity.

It was in such sombre reveries that he indulged for hours whilst he walked about the Boulevard de Magnolles. He kept them well within him, and affected to remain brave and haughty, full of disdain for passing events, under the pretext that the Church was the mistress of eternity. But whenever he met Hermeline the schoolmaster, who was in a continuous rage over the successes of La Crêcherie, and ready to go over to the reactionists in order to save the Republic, he no longer discussed things with his former bitterness, but declared that he placed his trust in the Divinity, who must certainly be allowing these Anarchist saturnalia with the object of ultimately striking down the enemies of religion, and thus making it triumphant. Doctor Novarre jestingly said that the Abbé abandoned Sodom on the eve of the rain of fire. By Sodom he meant Beauclair, that plague-spot, *bourgeois* Beauclair, devoured by egotism, the town condemned to be destroyed and of which the earth must be purified, if on its site one desired to see the city of health and delight, justice and peace arise. Every symptom pointed to the approach of the final rending: the wage-system was at its last gasp, the distracted *bourgeoisie* was passing over to the revolutionists, the despairing desire to save something of one's interests was bringing all the living strength of the country over to the conquerors; and as for what remained, the scattered, worn-out, unusable remnants of the old system, they would be swept away by the wind. The radiant Beauclair of to-morrow was already emerging from the ruins; and when Abbé Marle, as he strolled under the trees of the Boulevard de Magnolles, let his breviary fall, and slackening his pace, half-closed his eyes, it was assuredly a vision of that coming city that arose before him and filled him with such intense bitterness.

At times, Judge Gaume and Abbé Marle met in the course of those silent solitary walks. At first they did not see one another, but walked on with lowered heads, so absorbed in the contemplation of what they pictured that nothing of their surroundings remained visible to them. Each on his own side chewed the cud of his own despair—the one his regret for the world which was disappearing, the other his appeal to the world which was now rising from the ground. Exhausted religion was unwilling to die; justice, awaiting birth, was in despair that its advent should be so long delayed. However, the two men at last raised their heads, and recognised one another. Then it became necessary for them to exchange a few words.

"This is very gloomy weather, Monsieur le Président. We shall have some rain," the priest would say.

"I fear so, Monsieur l'Abbé," replied the judge. "It is quite cold for the month of June."

"Ah! how can it be otherwise? The seasons are all out of order now. There is no equilibrium left."

"True; yet life goes on. The good sun will perhaps set everything right again."

Then each resumed his solitary perambulations, sank into his reflections, carrying hither and thither the eternal battle between the past and the future.

It was, however, especially at the Abyss that one felt the effects of the evolution of Beauclair which the reorganisation of labour was gradually transforming. At each fresh success achieved by La Crêcherie Delaveau had to display more activity, intelligence, and courage; and naturally everything which contributed to the prosperity of the rival works to him brought disaster. Thus the discovery of excellent lodes of ore in the once-abandoned mine dealt him a terrible blow, since it so greatly reduced the price of raw material. He could no longer continue struggling so far as commercial iron and steel were concerned. And the manufacture of guns and projectiles likewise suffered. There had been a marked falling off in orders since the money of France had been more particularly spent on manufactures that symbolised peace and social solidarity—such as railways, bridges, structures of all kinds in which iron and steel triumphed. The worst was that the orders for ordnance, which went to only a few establishments, no longer sufficed to enable all of them to pay their way, and, if the market was to be cleared, one of them at least must be killed. The least firmly established of all being at that moment the Abyss, it was the latter which the other competing foundries savagely resolved to destroy.

The difficulties of the Abyss were becoming the greater since its workmen no longer remained faithful to it. Ragu's attempt to kill Luc had thrown the comrades that he left behind him into confusion. And when Bourron, converted, brought round to reason, had returned to La Crêcherie followed by Fauchard, a general movement set in, most of the other men asking themselves why they should not follow Bourron's example, since so many advantages awaited them yonder. The success of Luc's experiment was now evident; the men employed at La Crêcherie earned twice as much as at the Abyss, and yet they only worked eight hours. And, besides, there were other attractions—the pleasant little houses, the schools where the children learned things so well and so merrily, the common-house which was ever *en fête*, and the general stores, whose prices were fully a third lower than those of other places, the whole tending to increase of health and increase of comfort.

Nothing is of any avail against figures. The men of the Abyss, wishing to earn as much as those of La Crêcherie demanded a rise in wages. As it was impossible to grant this demand, many of them naturally went off. And, finally, Delaveau was paralysed by the lack of a reserve fund. He did not yet confess himself conquered; he would have held out for a long time, and would, in his own opinion, have ended by triumphing if he had possessed a few hundred thousand francs to help him to pass through this crisis, which he obstinately believed to be a temporary one. Only how was he to continue fighting? how was he to face pay-days when money failed him? Moreover, the money which he had already borrowed was proving a crushing charge on the business. Yet he struggled on heroically, ever erect, devoting all his intelligence, his very life, to his work, in the hope that he might still save the crumbling past which he supported, and that he might wring from the capital entrusted to him the revenue that he had promised.

Delaveau's worst sufferings, indeed, arose from the fact that he could no longer hand Boisgelin the profits which he had covenanted to extract from the business, and his defeat became materialised in the most cruel fashion on the days when he was compelled to refuse his cousin money. Although on the last occasion when accounts had been balanced the position had proved to be disastrous, Boisgelin would in no respect curtail his expenditure at La Guerdache. In this matter he was inflamed by Fernande, who treated her husband like an ox at the plough, one that needed to be goaded till it bled in order to discharge its work properly. Never had the young woman shown herself more ardent, more insatiable than now. She was consumed by a passion for excesses. There was something wild in her glance, something that suggested a desire for the impossible. Her acquaintances felt anxious about her, and Sub-Prefect Châtelard confidentially told Mayor Gourier that the little woman would assuredly end by perpetrating some great piece of folly, from which all of them would suffer. Hitherto she had contented herself with changing her home into a hell by urging Boisgelin upon her husband, pressing him with continual demands for money, whereby Delaveau was thrown into such a state of exasperation that he even continued growling at night when resting his head on the conjugal pillow. Fernande, by her remarks, maliciously kept his wound open. Nevertheless, he still adored her, set her upon one side like an innocent, immaculate being whom it was impossible to suspect.

November came with intense early cold. The payments which fell due that month were so large that Delaveau fancied he could feel the very ground he walked upon trembling beneath him. He had not the necessary amount of money in the safe. On the evening before the day on which the payments had to be made he shut himself up in his private room to reflect and write some letters, whilst Fernande went to dine at La Guerdache, whither she had been invited. Though she was unaware of it, he himself had gone thither in the morning, and had had a decisive conversation with Boisgelin, in which, after plainly stating the terrible position, he had at last prevailed on him to reduce his expenditure. He meant to limit him to a proper allowance for several years, and had even advised him to sell La Guerdache. And now, alone in his private room, Delaveau walked about slowly, every now and then mechanically stirring the large coke fire which was burning in a kind of stove before the chimney-piece. The only possible means of salvation was to secure time: he must write to the creditors, who could not possibly desire to see the works closed. However, he did not hurry about it; he would write his letters after dinner. Meantime, he continued thinking whilst going from one window to the other, ever returning to the one whence he could see the far-spreading lands of La Crêcherie, even to the distant park and the pavilion where Luc resided. The cold, frosty atmosphere was very clear, and the sun was setting in a sky as pure as crystal, a pale golden glow bringing the growing town into delicate relief against a purple background. Never had Delaveau seen it so plainly. It seemed to palpitate with life; he could have counted the light slender branches of the trees, and he was able to distinguish the smallest details of the houses, down to the decorations of faïence which rendered them so gay. There came a moment when, under the oblique rays of the sun, all the windows began to flame and sparkle like hundreds of bonfires. It was like a triumph, a glory. And Delaveau remained there, drawing the cretonne curtains aside, and gazing at that triumph with his face close to the window-pane.

Even as Luc over yonder, at the other end of the lands of La Crêcherie, occasionally watched his town marching on, spreading out and threatening the Abyss with invasion, so Delaveau on his side often came to gaze at it, and found it ever growing, threatening him with conquest. How many times of recent years had he not lingered at that window, and on each occasion he had seen the rising tide of houses growing larger and drawing nearer to the Abyss. It had started from a remote point of a great stretch of uncultivated, deserted land; one house had appeared there like a little wave, then another, and another. And those waves had covered the whole space before them, and now they were only a few hundred yards away, and were rolling in a sea of incalculable power, ready to carry off everything which might oppose them. To-morrow would witness an irresistible invasion; all the past would be swept away, the Abyss and Beauclair, too, would be replaced by the young and triumphant city. At one moment, when a very severe crisis had fallen on La Crêcherie, Delaveau had hoped that the advance would stop, but before long the new town had resumed its march so impulsively that the old walls of the Abyss were now already shaking. Yet he would not despair; he tried to stiffen himself against the evidence of facts, and flattered himself that he would find the necessary dyke and rampart in his own energy.

That particular evening, however, he was enervated by anxiety, and began to feel some covert regrets. Had he not formerly made a mistake in letting Bonnaire take himself off? He remembered certain prophetic words spoken by that strong, yet simple, man at the time of the great strike. And it was on the morrow of that strike that Bonnaire, like a good worker, had helped to found La Crêcherie. Since then the Abyss had scarcely ever ceased to decline: Ragu had besmirched it with attempted murder; Bourron, Fauchard, and others were quitting it as they might have quitted an accursed ruin-breeding spot. And afar off the new town was still flaming in the sunlight. At the sight of it sudden anger seized upon Delaveau—anger whose violence restored him to himself, to the beliefs of his whole life. No, no! he had been right, the truth was in the past; nothing could be extracted from men unless one bent them beneath the authority of dogma; the wage-system remained the true law of labour, and beyond its pale there could be naught save madness and catastrophe. Then Delaveau, intent on seeing nothing more, drew the large cretonne curtains together, lighted his little electric lamp, and again began to reflect as he strolled about his well-closed room, which the glowing stove rendered extremely warm.

At last, after dinner, Delaveau sat down at his writing table to attend to his letters, in accordance with the plans which he had been maturing for hours, plans whereby he hoped to save the business. Midnight struck and he still sat there, completing that worrying and difficult correspondence. And doubts had now come to him, he was again possessed by fear. Did salvation really lie in the direction he was taking? What would he be able to do, even if the delays he asked for should be granted? Exhausted by the superhuman effort he was making to save the Abyss, he at last bowed his head and let it rest upon his hands. And thus he remained, deep in anguish. But at that same moment the rattle of a carriage was heard, and words rang out. Fernande had just returned from the dinner at La Guerdache, and was sending the servants to bed.

When she entered her husband's private room it was with hasty gestures and excited speech, like a woman who is beside herself, one who has been restraining and nursing her anger for hours.

"Good heavens, how hot it is here! How can one live with such a fire?"

Then sinking back in an armchair she unclasped and threw off the magnificent furs which covered her shoulders, and appeared in all her marvellous beauty, gowned in silk and white lace, with arms and bosom bare. Her husband expressed no surprise at her luxurious ways—he did not even notice them—he loved her solely for herself, her beauty; and passion always rendered him obedient to her whims, deprived him of both foresight and strength. Never, too, had a more intoxicating charm emanated from her person than at this period.

That evening, however, when Delaveau, with his head still buzzing, looked up at her, he became anxious: "What is the matter with you, my dear?" he asked.

It was evident that she was greatly upset. Her large dark blue eyes, which as a rule had such a caressing expression, now glowed with a sombre fire. Her little mouth, which usually smiled in such a tenderly deceitful way, opened, showing her strong teeth, whose lustre nothing could tarnish, and which seemed ready to bite. And the whole of her face, which displayed such a charming oval under her black hair, was swollen as by a craving for violence.

"What is the matter with me?" she ended by saying, whilst she still quivered, "Nothing."

Silence fell again, and amidst the lifeless quietude of that winter night one heard the growling of the busy Abyss, the blows of whose hammers continuously shook the house. As a rule the Delaveaus remained unconscious of it, but that night, in spite of the falling off in business, the huge steam-hammer had been set to work to forge the tube of a great gun in all haste; and the ground quaked, the vibrations of each blow seemed to resound in that very room, coming thither along the light wooden gallery which connected it with the works.

"Come, there is something the matter with you," Delaveau resumed. "Why won't you tell me what it is?"

A gesture of wrathful impatience escaped Fernande, who replied: "Let us go to bed, that will be better."

Nevertheless she did not stir; with feverish hands she continued twisting her fan, whilst her breath came short and quick, and her bosom heaved. At last she blurted out what was stifling her.

"So you went to La Guerdache this morning?"

"Yes, I went there," answered Delaveau.

"And what Boisgelin has just told me is true, then? The works are in danger of bankruptcy, we are on the eve of ruin—such ruin, indeed, that I shall have to content myself with woollen gowns and dry bread!"

"I had to tell him the truth."

Fernande was trembling, and had to restrain herself from bursting forth into reproaches and insults at once. It was all over, her life of enjoyment was threatened—nay, ended. No more festivities, neither dinners, nor balls, nor hunts, would be given at La Guerdache. Its doors would be closed to her, for had not Boisgelin confessed that he would perhaps be compelled to sell the property? And her dream of returning to Paris with millions to squander was ended also. All that she had imagined she held within her grasp, fortune, luxury, and pleasure, had crumbled to pieces. Nought but ruin encompassed her, and that wretched Boisgelin had increased her exasperation by his supineness, his cowardice in bending his head beneath the disaster.

"You never tell me anything about our affairs," she continued bitterly. "I'm treated as if I were a fool. That news fell on me as if the very ceilings were coming down. But if things are like that what are we going to do, just tell me?"

"We shall work," Delaveau simply answered; "there is no other means of salvation possible."

But she did not hear his last words, she had ceased to listen. "Did you for a moment imagine," said she, "that I should consent to remain with nothing to wear, to trudge about in worn-out boots and begin afresh that wretched life which I remember like a nightmare? Ah, no! I'm not like you others, I won't have it, I won't. You will have to arrange something, you and Boisgelin between you, for I won't be poor again."

Then she went on pouring forth all that was distracting her mind. There was her wretched youth, when living with her mother, the music teacher, she had failed to capture the prize which her great beauty had seemed to promise her—for after seduction she had been abandoned. And following upon that odious adventure, the memory of which she hid deep within her, had come her marriage, all calculation and diplomacy, the acceptance of that ugly insignificant Delaveau whom she had taken because she felt the need of some support, a husband whom she might put to use. And then had come a lucky stroke, the acquisition of the Abyss, the success of her plans, her husband procuring victory for her, Boisgelin conquered, La Guerdache and every luxury and enjoyment at her disposal. Twelve years had followed, replete with all the pleasures that she had tasted there, like the enjoyer, the perverter she was, satisfying her endless appetites and the dark rancour amassed within her since childhood, happy in lying, betraying, bringing ruin and disorder with her, and, in particular, exulting over the tears which she drew from Suzanne's eyes. But now, to think that this was not to last, that she was destined to relapse, vanquished, into the poverty of her former days!

"You must arrange something—arrange something," she repeated. "I won't go bare; I won't dispense with anything to which I have been accustomed!"

Delaveau, growing impatient, shrugged his sturdy shoulders. He was still resting his massive bulldog head, with projecting jaws, upon his two fists, whilst looking at her with his big dark eyes, his face reddened the while by the great heat of the fire.

"You were right, my dear," said he, "don't let us talk of these matters, for you seem to me to be scarcely reasonable to-night. I am very fond of you, as you know, and am ready to make any sacrifice to spare you suffering. But I hope that you will resign yourself to doing as I myself intend to do. I mean to fight as long as there is breath in my body. If necessary I shall get up at five in the morning, live on a crust of bread, give my whole day to work, and no doubt I shall go to bed at night feeling quite content. Besides, what if you do have to wear more simple gowns, and have to go out on foot! Only the other evening you yourself were telling me how all these pleasures, ever the same, wearied and disgusted you!"

This was true. Fernande's blue, caressing eyes darkened till they almost became black as she thought of it. For some time past she had failed to satisfy her passion for enjoyment. Though she was unwilling to give up her present life, it palled upon her. She was full of rancour against both her husband and her lover, who no longer amused her, and she often wondered wrathfully whether she would ever feel amused again. Thus, it was with insulting contempt that she had greeted the lamentations of Boisgelin when the latter had told her of his despair at being compelled to cut down his expenses. And this also was why she had returned home in such a passion, eager to bite and to destroy.

"Yes, yes," she stammered, "those pleasures which are always the same! Ah! it isn't you who'll ever give me any new ones!"

In the works the heavy blows of the steam hammer still resounded, making the ground tremble. Long had that hammer forged delight for her, by wringing from steel the wealth she coveted, whilst the grimy flock of toilers gave their lives in order that her own might be one of full and free enjoyment. For a moment she listened to the dolorous commotion of labour sounding amidst the heavy silence. Then, with her savage hatred increasing, she turned upon her husband. "It is all your fault if this has happened!" she cried, "I told Boisgelin so. If you had begun by strangling that wretched Luc Froment, we should not now be on the eve of ruin. But you have never known how to conduct business."

At this Delaveau abruptly rose from his chair, and, resisting the anger which was gaining on him, retorted, "Let's go to bed. If we went on discussing, you would end by making me say things which I should regret afterwards."

But she did not stir; she continued speaking so bitterly, so aggressively, accusing her husband of having wrecked her life, that he, on his side, waxing brutal, at last exclaimed: "Why, when I married you, my dear, you hadn't a halfpenny; it was I who had to buy you some clothes. You were on the point of falling to the streets, and where would you have been now?"

At this, thrusting her face and bosom forward, she answered, with a murderous glance, "What! do you imagine that, beautiful as I was, a prince's daughter, I should have accepted such a man as you, ugly, common, and without position, if I had only had bread? Just look at yourself, my friend! I took you because you promised to win a fortune, a royal position for me. And if I tell you this it is because you have kept none of your engagements."

Delaveau was now standing before her, letting her talk on, whilst clenching his fists and striving to retain his *sangfroid*.

"You hear!" she repeated, with furious obstinacy, "none of your engagements—none! No more with Boisgelin than with me, for it's certainly you who have ruined the poor fellow. You prevailed on him to trust his money to you; you promised him a fabulous income, and now he won't oven have enough money left him to buy a pair of shoes. When a man isn't capable of managing a large business, my friend, he remains a petty clerk, and lives in a hovel with a wife ugly enough and stupid enough to wash a pack of children, and mend their socks. Yes, bankruptcy has come, and it is your fault; you hear me, your fault—yours! yours alone!"

Delaveau was unable to restrain himself any longer. Those savage words tortured him as if a knife had been turned round and round in his heart and conscience. To think that he had loved that woman so well, and to hear her speak of their marriage as a base bargain, in which on her side there had only been so much necessity and calculation! For nearly fifteen years he had been striving so loyally and so heroically to keep the promise he had made his cousin, and yet she accused him of incapacity and lack of business knowledge! He caught hold of her bare arms with both hands, and shook her, saying in a low tone, as if he feared that the sound of his own voice might unhinge him, "Be quiet, you unhappy woman; do not madden me!"

But she in her turn arose and freed herself, stammering with anger and pain at the sight of the red circles which his rough grasp had left round her delicate white arms. "You beat me now, you blackguard, you brute!" she cried. "Ah! you beat me, you beat me!"

And again she thrust forward her beautiful face, now convulsed by wrath, and spat out all her contempt full in that man's countenance which she longed to lacerate with her nails. Never had she hated him so much; never had the sight of his massive bulldog figure irritated her to such a degree as now. All the rancour amassed within her arose once more, urged her on to some irreparable insult which should end everything. With instinctive cruelty she sought a means of inflicting some poisonous wound, something that should make him howl and suffer.

"You are only a brute!" she cried. "You are not capable of directing a gang of ten men!"

At this singular insult, which seemed to him stupid and childish, Delaveau burst into convulsive laughter. And this laughter exasperated Fernande to such a point that she became half delirious. What could she say to him that would prove a mortal blow and bring his laughter to an end?

"Yes, it was I who made you what you are!" she exclaimed. "If it had not been for me you would not have remained director of the Abyss a single year!"

At this he laughed all the louder: "You are mad, my dear; you say such stupid things that they don't affect me!"

"I say foolish things, do I? So it was not thanks to me that you kept your place?"

Confession had suddenly risen to her throat. Ah! to shout it full in his dog's face, to shout that she had never loved him, and that she was another's mistress. That was the knife-thrust which would make his laughter cease. And how it would relieve her! what terrible and ferocious and voluptuous enjoyment she would taste in that collapse of her life which was already crumbling to pieces! She flung herself into the pit with a cry of horrible delight: "The things I say are not stupid, for I've been Boisgelin's mistress for twelve years past."

Delaveau did not immediately understand her. Those horrible words, striking him full in the face, had almost stunned him.

"What is that you say?"

"I say that I've been Boisgelin's mistress for twelve years past, and since there's nothing left, since all is falling to pieces, well, there, that's the end of it!"

In his turn half delirious, stammering, with his teeth clenched, Delaveau rushed upon her, caught hold of her arms, shook her, and threw her into the arm-chair. He would have liked to pound and annihilate all that provoking nudity which she displayed, her bare shoulders and bare bosom, to prevent her from ever insulting and torturing him again. The veil was at last torn away, and he saw and divined things clearly. She had never loved him; her life beside him had never been aught but hypocrisy, ruse, falsehood, and betrayal. From that beautiful, polished, charming woman whom he had adored there suddenly emerged a she-wolf, all sombre fury and brutal instinct. Many things of the cause of which he had been ignorant had sprung from her; she was the perverter, the poisoner, who had slowly corrupted all around her; hers was the flesh of cruelty and treachery, whose enjoyment had been made up of the tears and blood of others.

But whilst he was still struggling with his stupefaction she insulted him again: "With your fists, eh, you brute! Oh! go on, hit, hit, like your workmen do when they are drunk!"

Then, amidst the frightful silence which fell between them, Delaveau heard the rhythmic blows of the steam-hammer, the commotion of labour which, without a pause, accompanied both his days and his nights. The sound came to him like a well-known voice, whose clear language acquainted him with the whole of the horrible adventure. Was it not Fernande, with her little teeth of unchangeable lustre, who had devoured all the wealth which yonder hammer had forged? That burning thought possessed his brain: she was the devourer, the one cause of the disaster, of the squandering of millions, of the inevitable, approaching bankruptcy. Whilst he had been heroically striving to keep

ÉMILE ZOLA

his promises, working eighteen hours a day, endeavouring to save the old and crumbling world, it was she who had gnawed at the edifice and rotted it. She had lived there beside him, looking so quiet, with her soft smiling face, and yet she herself was the poison, the destructive agent who had paralysed his efforts and annihilated his work. Yes, ruin had ever been present beside him, at his table, in his bed, and he had not seen it. She had shaken everything with her little agile hands, and pulverised everything with her little white teeth. He remembered nights when she had returned from La Guerdache, intoxicated by the caresses of her lover, by the wine she had drunk, by the waltzes she had danced, by the money which she had flung around her, and, when she had slept off that intoxication, lying by his side, whilst he, with his eyes wide open, peering into the darkness, tortured his brain in striving to devise some means for saving the Abyss, and did not even stir for fear of disturbing her slumber. And this, which seemed to him the supreme horror of all, inspired him with mad fury and made him shout: "You shall die!"

She sat up in the chair, her elbows resting on its arms, her bare bosom and her charming face again thrust forward under her black casque of splendid hair: "Oh! as for that I'm agreeable. I've had enough of you and the others, and myself, and life as well! I'd rather die than live in wretchedness."

"You shall die! you shall die!" he howled, growing wilder and wilder.

But he had no weapon, and vainly sought one whilst he turned around the room. He had not even a knife, nothing save his two hands, with which he might strangle her. But what use would that be? What could he do afterwards—could he go on living? A knife would have sufficed for both.

She noticed his embarrassment, his momentary hesitation, and triumphed over it, believing that he would not again find the strength to kill her. And in her turn she began to laugh, with an insulting, taunting laugh. "What! are you not going to kill me, then? Kill me, kill me then, if you dare!"

All at once, in the midst of his wild search for a weapon, Delaveau perceived the sheet-iron stove in which such a brasier of coke was glowing that the room seemed to be on fire already. And utter dementia suddenly fell upon him, making him forget everything, even his daughter, his fondly-loved Nise, who was sleeping quietly in her little room on the second floor. Oh! to make an end of himself, annihilate himself amidst the fury which transported him! Oh! to carry that hateful woman to death, so that she might never more belong to another, and to go with her, and cease to live, since life was now utterly soiled and wrecked!

She was still urging him on with her lashing, contemptuous laugh. "Kill me! kill me then! You are far too big a coward to kill me!"

Yes, yes, thought Delaveau, to burn everything, to destroy everything by a huge conflagration in which the house and the works alike would disappear, a conflagration which would complete the work of ruin carried on by that woman and her idiotic lover! Ay, a gigantic pyre on which he himself would crumble into ashes with that malignant, devouring, lying creature, amidst the smoking ruins of that old social system which he had so foolishly striven to defend.

With a terrible kick, he overturned the stove, and projected it into the middle of the room, ever repeating his shout: "You shall die! you shall die!"

The red-hot coke spread in a red sheet over the carpet. Some pieces rolled as far as one of the windows. Then the cretonne curtains were the first to flare, whilst the carpet began to burn. The furniture and the walls flamed in their turn with overwhelming rapidity. The house, which was but lightly built, caught fire and sparkled and smoked like a mere wisp of hay.

The rest was frightful. Fernande had sprung up in her terror, gathering the silk and lace of her skirts together, and seeking a passage where the flames would not reach them. She darted towards the door opening into the hall, feeling certain that she would have time to escape, that she would reach the garden at a bound. But in front of the door she found Delaveau, whose arms barred her passage. He looked so terrible that she then sprang towards the other door, the one which opened into the wooden gallery, connecting the room with the works. But it was too late to flee in that direction—the gallery was burning, acting like a chimney, in which the draught urged on the flames with such rapidity that the adjacent business offices were already threatened. So she came back to the centre of the room, stumbling, blinded, suffocating, full of rage and terror at feeling that her dress was flaring, that her uncoiled hair also was catching fire, covering her bare shoulders with burns. And in a frightful voice she gasped:

"I will not die! I will not die! let me pass, murderer! murderer!"

Then again she threw herself towards the door opening into the hall,

ÉMILE ZOLA

and strove to force a passage, rushing upon her husband, who still stood there, erect and motionless, full of fierce determination. Without any violence he simply repeated: "I tell you that you are going to die."

To force him to give way, she dug her nails into his flesh, and then only did he catch hold of her again and bring her back into the centre of the room, which had now become a perfect brasier. And here there was a horrible battle. She struggled with all her strength, which was increased tenfold by the dread of death; she sought the doors, the windows with the instinctive eagerness of a wounded animal; whilst he still kept her amidst the flames in which he wished to die, and in which he wished her to perish with him, in order that the whole of their abominable existence might be annihilated. And to accomplish this he needed all the strength of his strong arms, for the walls were cracking, and ten times in succession did he have to drag her from the outlets by which she might have escaped. At last he imprisoned her in a final savage embrace, and they fell together amidst the embers of the flooring, whilst the last hangings burnt away like torches, and ardent brands rained from the woodwork overhead. And although she bit him, he did not release her, but held her fast, carrying her away into nothingness, both of them burning together with the same avenging fire. Soon all was over, the ceiling fell upon them with a great crumbling of flaming beams.

THAT NIGHT AT LA CRÊCHERIE, as Nanet left the machinery gallery, where he was now serving his apprenticeship as an electrician, he perceived a red glow in the direction of the Abyss. At first he imagined that it came from the cementing furnaces. But its brightness increased, and all at once he understood the truth—the manager's house was on fire. He experienced a sudden shock, for he thought of Nise, and then ran off wildly and came into collision with the party-wall, over which, in former times, they had both climbed so nimbly in order to be together. And once again, with the help of hands and feet, he somehow got over the wall and found himself in the garden, alone as yet, for no alarm had been given. It was, indeed, the house that was burning, and the frightful feature of the conflagration was that like a fire lighted at the base of some huge pyre, it spread from ground-floor to roof, without anybody within showing sign of life. The windows remained closed, and the door was already burning, in such wise that one could neither go in nor out. It merely seemed to Nanet that he could hear some loud cries and a commotion like that of some horrible death struggle. But at last the shutters of one of the second-floor windows were flung back violently, and then, amidst the smoke, appeared Nise, all in white, wearing only her chemise and a petticoat. She called for help and leant out, terrified.

"Don't be frightened, don't be frightened," cried Nanet in distraction, "I'm going up."

He had perceived a long ladder lying alongside a shed. But on going to take it he found that it was chained. A moment of terrible anguish ensued. The lad took up a large stone and struck the padlock with all his strength in order to break it. Meantime the flames were roaring, and the whole of the first floor took fire amidst such an outpouring of smoke and sparks, that at certain moments Nise, up above, quite disappeared from sight. Nanet still heard her cries, however, which grew wilder and wilder, and he struck and struck the padlock, whilst calling in response: "Wait! wait! I'm coming!"

At last the padlock was crushed and he was able to take the ladder. He never remembered afterwards how he had managed to set it erect. It was a prodigious feat; but he was able to rear it under the window. Then, however, he perceived that it was too short, and such was his despair at the discovery that his courage wavered. Boy hero that he was, only sixteen years of age, he was resolved to save that young girl of thirteen, his friend and playmate; but he was losing his head, and no longer knew how to act.

Nevertheless, he called again: "Wait! wait! It doesn't matter, I'll come somehow!"

At that moment one of the two servant girls, whose garret bedroom had a window opening on to the roof, managed to get out, clutching hold of the guttering. But, maddened by terror, imagining that the flames were already reaching her, she suddenly leapt into space and fell, dead, with her skull broken, beside the flight of steps.

Nanet, unhinged by Nise's cries, which had become more and more frightful, fancied that she also was about to jump out. He pictured her lying at his feet, covered with blood, and he raised a last terrible call: "Don't jump; I'm coming, I'm coming!"

Then, in spite of everything, the young fellow ascended the ladder, and when he reached the burning first floor he entered the house by one of the windows whose panes had been burst by the violence of the heat. Help was now arriving; there were a number of people already on the road and in the garden. And the throng spent some minutes of frightful

ÉMILE ZOLA

anxiety in watching one child save the other with such wild bravery. The conflagration was still and ever spreading; the walls cracked, and the very ladder seemed to ignite as it stood against the house front, whilst neither the boy nor the girl reappeared. But at last Nanet came back, carrying Nise on his shoulders as a shepherd may carry a lamb. He had managed to climb through the furnace from one story to the other, take her up, and come down again; but his hair was singed and his clothes were burning, and when he had slipped, rather than stepped, down the ladder with his well-loved burden, both he and she were covered with burns and fell fainting in one another's arms, clasped in so close an embrace that they had to be carried thus to La Crêcherie, whither Sœurette, who had now been warned, repaired to nurse them.

Half an hour later the house fell; not a stone of it remained standing. And the worst was that the fire, after reaching the general offices by way of the wooden gallery, had now gained the neighbouring buildings, and was devouring the great hall where the puddling-furnaces and the rolling-machinery were installed. The entire works were in danger; the fire blazed amidst those old buildings, almost all of which were of dry woodwork. It was said that the Delaveaus' other servant, having managed to escape by way of the kitchen, had been the first to give the alarm to the night-shifts, who had hurried up from the works. But they had no fire-engine, and nothing could be done till their comrades of La Crêcherie, headed by Luc himself, came in brotherly fashion to the help of the rival establishment with both engine and firemen. The Beauclair fire brigade, whose organisation was very defective, only turned up afterwards. And it was too late to save the Abyss; it was now blazing from one to the other end of its sordid workshops over an expanse of several acres, forming a huge brasier whence emerged only the lofty chimneys and the tower in which great cannon were tempered.

When the dawn rose after that night of disaster numerous groups of people still stood before the smouldering wreckage under the livid, chilly November sky. The Beauclair authorities, Sub-Prefect Châtelard and Mayor Gourier, had not quitted the scene of the catastrophe, and Judge Gaume was with them, as well as his son-in-law, Captain Jollivet. Abbé Marle, warned late, only arrived when it was light, and was soon followed by a stream of inquisitive folk, *bourgeois* and shopkeepers, the Mazelles, the Laboques, the Caffiaux, and even Dacheux. A gust of terror was sweeping by; one and all spoke with bated breath, their great anxiety being to know how such a catastrophe could possibly have taken place. Only one witness remained, the servant-girl who had managed to escape. She related that Madame had returned from La Guerdache about midnight, and that immediately afterwards there had been some loud shouting, after which the flames had suddenly appeared. People listened to her, and repeated her story in low tones; and those who had been intimate with the Delaveaus divined the frightful tragedy which had taken place. It was evident, as the servant said, that Monsieur and Madame had perished in the fire. The horror, which was spreading, increased still further on the arrival of Boisgelin, who had to be helped out of his carriage, such was his faintness and pallor. He ended by swooning, and Doctor Novarre had to attend to him there, before that field of ruin where the remnants of his fortune were smoking, and where the bones of Delaveau and Fernande were at last crumbling into dust.

However, Luc continued directing the last efforts made by his men to save the still burning gallery where the steam-hammer was installed. Jordan, wrapped in a rug, obstinately remained in spite of the intense cold. Bonnaire, who had arrived one of the first, had distinguished himself by his courage in saving such machinery and appliances as was possible. Bourron, Fauchard, and all the other former hands of the Abyss who had gone to La Crêcherie, helped him, exerted themselves devotedly on that ground which they knew so well, where they had toiled for so many dolorous years. But destiny in its fury seemed to have transformed itself into a hurricane. In spite of all the efforts, everything was carried, swept away, and annihilated. Fire the avenger, fire the purifier had fallen upon the walls like lightning, razed everything, cleared the expanse of the ruins with which the downfall of the old world had littered it. And now the work was done, the ground stretched away clear and open, and the rising city of justice and peace might carry its conquering waves of houses even to the end of the great plains.

All at once Lange, the potter, the Anarchist, who stood in one of the groups of people, was heard saying in his rough but jovial voice: "No, no, I haven't to pride myself on it, for I didn't light it. But, no matter, it's fine work, and it's rather funny that the masters should help us by roasting themselves."

He was referring to the conflagration. And such was the shudder that passed through all his listeners that none attempted to silence him. The feelings of the throng impelled it towards the victorious forces; the authorities of Beauclair congratulated Luc on his devotion; the tradespeople and petty *bourgeois* surrounded the workers of La

Crêcherie, at last openly ranging themselves upon their side. Lange was right; there are tragic hours when decaying societies, stricken with madness, fling themselves upon the pyre. And now, of all those grimy works of the Abyss, where the wage-system had gasped in the last hours of dishonouring, accursed toil, there only remained against the grey sky a few crumbling walls supporting the frameworks of roofs, above which the high chimneys and the tempering tower alone rose up, useless and woebegone.

That morning, about eleven o'clock, when the sun at last made up its mind to show itself, Monsieur Jérôme passed by in his bath-chair propelled by a servant. He was making his usual promenade. He had just followed the Combettes road, skirting the works and the growing town of La Crêcherie, which looked so bright and gay in the dry, sunshiny weather. And now he beheld the field of defeat, the Abyss sacked and destroyed by the justice-dealing violence of the flames. For a long time his clear and empty eyes, as transparent as spring water, gazed upon the scene. He spoke no word, he made no gesture; he simply looked, and then was wheeled away, nothing about him telling whether he had really seen and understood.

BOOK III

I

The blow was a terrible one at La Guerdache. Ruin suddenly fell upon that residence of luxury and pleasure, which had continually resounded with festivities. A hunt had to be countermanded, and it was necessary to stop the grand Tuesday dinners. The numerous domestics would have to be discharged *en masse*, and there was already some talk of the sale of the carriages, horses, and kennels. All the noisy life of the gardens and park, the endless affluence of visitors, had ceased. In the huge house itself the drawing-rooms, dining-room, billiard-room, and smoking-room became so many deserts, quivering with the blast of disaster. It was a stricken dwelling agonising in the sudden solitude born of misfortune.

To and fro through that infinite sadness went Boisgelin like a woeful shadow. Utterly overcome, with his mind almost unhinged, he spent the most frightful days, at a loss what to do with himself, wandering about like a soul in distress amidst the downfall of his life of enjoyment. He was at bottom a sorry being, a horseman and clubman, an amiable mediocrity whose fine presence and correct, proud mien—the mien of the fool who wears a single eyeglass—collapsed entirely at the first tragic gust of truth and justice. He had hitherto taken his pleasures like one convinced that they were due to him; he had never done the slightest work in his life; he imagined himself to be different from others—a privileged being, one of the elect, born to be fed and amused by the labour of others—and so how could he have understood the catastrophe which had so logically fallen upon him? His egotistical creed had received too severe a shock, and he remained in dismay before the future, respecting which he had not previously felt any disquietude. In the depths of his bewilderment there was particularly the terror of the idler, the kept-man, one who was utterly upset by the thought that he was incapable of earning his living. As Delaveau was gone, from whom could he now demand the profits which had been promised him on the day when he had invested his capital in the Abyss? The works were burnt, the capital had vanished in the ruins, and where would he now find the money to live? He roamed like a madman through the deserted gardens and the lugubrious house without finding an answer to that question.

At first, on the evening following the tragedy, Boisgelin was haunted by thoughts of the frightful death of Delaveau and Fernande.

He could have no doubt on the matter, for he remembered in what a mood the young woman had left him—full of wrath and pouring forth threats against her husband. It was certainly Delaveau who, after some terrible scene, had set fire to the house in order to destroy both the guilty woman and himself. In that vengeance, for a mere enjoyer of life like Boisgelin, there was a sombre ferocity, a monstrous violence, which inspired him with unending fright. But the greatest blow was to understand that he was deficient in strength of intellect, and that he lacked the necessary energy to set his affairs in order. From morning till evening he ruminated over various plans without knowing which to adopt. Would it be best to try to resuscitate the works, seek money and an engineer, endeavour to establish a company to carry on the business? He feared that he might not succeed in such attempts, for the losses were very great, and must in the first instance be made good. Ought he not rather to wait for a purchaser who would take the land, and such plant and materials as had been saved, at his risk and peril? But Boisgelin greatly doubted whether such a purchaser would ever turn up, and in particular he doubted whether he would obtain from him a sufficiently large sum to liquidate the situation. Moreover, the question of his future life still remained to be settled; for the estate of La Guerdache was an expensive one to keep up, and perhaps at the end of the month he would no longer have enough money to buy even bread.

In this emergency one sole creature took pity on the wretched, trembling, forsaken man, who roamed about his empty house like a lost child, and this was Suzanne, his wife, that woman full of heroic gentleness whom he had so cruelly outraged. At the outset, when he had imposed his *liaison* with Fernande upon her, she had again and again resolved upon asserting herself and driving the intruder, the strange woman, from her house; but in the end she had invariably refrained from taking that course, for she felt certain that if she were to drive Fernande away, her infatuated husband would follow her. Then, their relative positions being settled, Suzanne had taken a room for herself and had become a wife in name only, keeping up appearances in the presence of visitors, but devoting herself entirely to the education of Paul, whom she wished to save from disaster. Had it not been for that dear child, fair and gentle like herself, she would never have become, resigned to the position. It was he who had brought about her renunciation, her sacrifice. She had removed him as much as possible from the influence of his unworthy father, anxious that his mind and heart, in which by way of consolation she hoped to cultivate sense and kindliness, should belong to herself alone. In this wise years went by, amidst the delight of seeing him grow up reasonable and affectionate; and it was only from a distance, so to say, that Suzanne had beheld the slow ruin of the Abyss and the growing prosperity of La Crêcherie. Like her husband, she had no doubt whatever that Delaveau, informed of the truth, had personally fired that huge pyre in order to destroy himself with that corrupting, devouring creature, his guilty wife. Suzanne shuddered as she thought of it, and asked herself if she had not in some small degree contributed to the catastrophe by her own resignation, her weakness, in tolerating betrayal and shame in her own home during so many years. If she had only rebelled at the outset, perhaps the crime would never have reached that climax. And her qualms of conscience quite upset her, and moved her to compassion for the wretched man whom, since the days of the catastrophe, she had seen roaming about like one demented, through the deserted garden and the empty house.

One morning, as she herself was crossing the grand drawing-room where Boisgelin had given so many *fêtes*, she perceived him there huddled up on an arm-chair, and sobbing and weeping like a child. She was quite stirred, filled with pity at the sight. And she, who for many years had never spoken to him unless it were necessary to do so in the presence of guests, drew near and said, "It is not in despairing that you will find the strength you need."

Amazed at seeing her there, at hearing her speak to him, he looked at her through the tears which blurred his eyes.

"Yes," she continued, "it is of no use roaming about from morning till night—you must find courage in yourself, you will not find it elsewhere."

He made a gesture expressive of desolation, and answered in a faint voice: "I am so much alone."

He was not by nature an evilly disposed man; he was simply a fool and a weakling, one of those cowards whom egotistical pleasure turns into brutes. And it was with such utter dejection that he complained of the solitude in which she left him amidst his misfortune, that she again felt very touched.

"You mean," she said, "that you wished to be alone. Since those frightful occurrences why have you not come to me?"

"Good God!" he stammered, "can you forgive me?"

Then he caught hold of her hands, which she left in his grasp, and, overwhelmed and wildly repentant, confessed his fault. He acknowledged nothing but what she knew already, his long betrayal, the mistress whom he had brought into his home, that woman who had maddened him and urged him on to ruin; but in accusing himself he displayed such passionate frankness that Suzanne was touched as by some spontaneous confession which he might have spared himself.

"It is true," he ended by saying, "I have wronged you so long, I have behaved abominably. Ah! why did you abandon me, why did you try nothing to win me back?"

His words awoke in her those qualms of conscience, the covert remorse which she felt at the thought that she had perhaps not done all her duty, that she had erred in not trying to stop him on his downward course. And the reconciliation which pity had initiated was completed by a feeling of indulgence. Are not the most pure, the most heroic partially responsible at times, when the weak and the erring succumb around them?

"Yes," she said, "I ought to have battled more, but I was too intent on sparing my pride and procuring quietude. We both have need of forgetfulness, we must regard all the past as dead."

Then, as their son Paul happened to pass through the garden under the windows, she called him indoors. He was now a big fellow of eighteen, intelligent and refined, a son after her own image, very affectionate and very sensible, free from all caste prejudices, and ready to live on the fruit of his own exertions whenever circumstances might require it. He had begun to take a passionate interest in the land, and spent whole days at the farm, busy with questions of culture, the germination of seed and harvesting of crops. As it happened, when his mother asked him to come in for a moment, he was about to repair to Feuillat's to see a new type of plough.

"Come in, my boy, your father is in great grief, and I wish you to kiss him," said Suzanne.

There had been a rupture between father and son as between husband and wife. Won over entirely to his mother's side, Paul, in growing up, had felt nothing but cold respect for his father, whose conduct, he divined, must be the cause of his mother's frequent sorrow. Thus he now came into the drawing-room, feeling both surprised and moved, and for a few seconds remained gazing at his parents, whom he found so pale, so upset by emotion. Then, understanding the position, he kissed his father very affectionately, and flung his arms around his mother's neck, anxious to embrace her also with all his heart. The family bond was formed once more, and there came a happy moment, when one might have believed that agreement would henceforth be complete between them.

When Suzanne in her turn had kissed her son, Boisgelin had to restrain a fresh flow of tears. "Good, good! now we all agree. Ah! that gives me some courage again. We are in such a terrible position! We shall have to come to some arrangement, take some decision."

They went on talking for a little while, all three of them seated there together; for Boisgelin felt a desire to unburden himself and confide in that woman and that lad after roaming about alone so distressfully. He reminded Suzanne how they had bought the Abyss for a million, and La Guerdache for five hundred thousand francs, out of the two millions which had remained to them, the one which had formed her dowry, and the other which had been saved in the wreck of his own fortune. The five hundred thousand francs left out of the two millions had been handed to Delaveau, and had served as working capital for the Abyss. All their money was thus invested in that enterprise, but unfortunately during recent financial embarrassments it had been necessary to borrow six hundred thousand francs, a debt which had weighed heavily upon the business. It really seemed as if the works were quite dead since they were burnt, and besides, before erecting them afresh it would be necessary to pay the debt of six hundred thousand francs.

"Then what do you intend to do?" Suzanne inquired.

Boisgelin thereupon explained the two solutions between which he hesitated, unable to adopt either, so great were the difficulties which attended both. On the one hand they might rid themselves of everything, sell what remained of the Abyss for what it would fetch— that is, no doubt, barely enough to pay the outstanding debt of six hundred thousand francs; or, on the other hand, they might try to find fresh funds, and establish a company, to which he would belong by contributing the land and the plant that had been saved. But here again there seemed little hope of effecting such a combination. Meantime, a solution was every day becoming more necessary, for their ruin was growing more and more complete.

"We also have La Guerdache—we can sell it," remarked Suzanne.

"Oh! sell La Guerdache!" he answered in a despairing way. "Part with this property to which we are so accustomed, so attached! And all to go and hide ourselves in some wretched hovel! What a downfall it would be, what a lot more grief it would bring!"

Suzanne became grave again, for she well perceived that he was not resigned to the idea of leading a reasonable modest life. "We shall inevitably have to come to it, my friend," said she. "We cannot continue living upon such a footing."

"No doubt, no doubt, we shall sell La Guerdache, but later on, when an opportunity presents itself. If we were to put it up for sale now we should not obtain half its value, for in doing so we should confess our ruin, and the whole district would league itself against us to rejoice and speculate on our misfortunes." Then he added more direct arguments: "Besides, my dear, La Guerdache belongs to you. As is stated in the deeds, the five hundred thousand francs of the purchase money were taken from your dowry, the remaining five hundred thousand francs of which formed half of the million which the Abyss cost us. Whilst we are co-proprietors of the works, La Guerdache is entirely your own property, and I simply desire to keep it for you as long as possible."

Suzanne did not wish to insist on the subject, but she made a gesture as if to say that she had long since resigned herself to every sacrifice. Her husband was looking at her, and all at once he seemed to remember something.

"Oh, by the way," he exclaimed, "I've a question to ask you. Have you ever seen your old friend, Monsieur Luc Froment, again?"

She remained for a moment stupefied. Following upon the foundation of La Crêcherie and the acute rivalry which had ensued between that enterprise and the Abyss, had come a rupture with Luc, a rupture which had not been the slightest of her sorrows amongst her many bitter experiences. She felt that she had lost in Luc a cordial, consoling, brotherly friend who would have helped and sustained her. But once again she had resigned herself, and whenever she had chanced to meet him at long intervals, on one of the few occasions when she went out, she had never spoken to him. He imitated her discretion and renunciation, and it seemed as if their old intimacy were quite dead. Still this did not prevent Suzanne from taking quite a passionate interest in Luc's enterprise, an interest of which she spoke to nobody. In secret she remained upon his side in the generous efforts which he was making to set a little more justice and love upon the earth. Thus she had suffered with him and triumphed with him, and when at one moment she had imagined him to be dead, killed by Ragu's knife-thrust, she had for forty-eight hours shut herself up alone, far away from everybody.

In the depths of her grief she had then discovered an intolerable anguish; that *liaison* with Josine which Ragu's crime had revealed to her left a torturing wound in her heart. Had she then been in love with Luc without knowing it? Perhaps so, for had she not dreamt of the joy, the pride that she would have felt at having such a husband as he, one who would have turned fortune to such good and magnificent use? Had she not thought, too, that she would have helped him, and that between them they would have accomplished prodigies in the cause of peace and kindness? But he grew well again, and was now the husband of Josine; and Suzanne felt everything crumbling once more, leaving her nought but the abnegation of a sacrificed wife, of a mother who only continued living for her son's sake. From that moment Luc ceased to exist for her, and the question which her husband had now put revived what seemed to be such a distant past that she was unable to hide her surprise.

"How can I have seen Monsieur Froment again?" she at last answered. "You know that for more than ten years all intercourse between us has been broken off."

But Boisgelin quietly shrugged his shoulders. "Oh! that doesn't prevent it; you might have met him and have spoken to him. You agreed so well together formerly. So you have kept up no relations with him at all?"

"No," she answered, somewhat sharply. "If I had, you would know it."

Her astonishment was increasing; she felt hurt by her husband's insistence; ashamed, too, at being questioned in that manner. What could be his object? why did he wish that she had kept up relations with Luc? In her turn she felt inquisitive, and inquired: "Why do you ask me that?"

"Oh! for nothing—only an idea which occurred to me just now."

Finally, he reverted to the subject, and revealed what he had on his mind. "This is it. I was telling you a little while ago that we could adopt one of two courses; either sell the Abyss, rid ourselves of everything, or start a company to which I should belong. Well, there's also a third course, a combination, as it were, of both the others, and that would be to sell the Abyss to La Crêcherie, but in such a way as to reserve to ourselves the larger part of the profits. Do you understand?"

"No, not exactly."

"But it is very simple. That fellow Luc must have a great desire to acquire our land. Well, he has done us enough harm; is that not so? And it is quite legitimate that we should get a large sum out of him. And our salvation certainly lies in that direction, particularly if we acquire an interest in the business which would enable us to keep La Guerdache without need of retrenchment in our manner of life."

Suzanne listened with sorrow and dismay. What! he was still the same man as formerly; that frightful lesson had not corrected him! He only dreamt of speculating on others, of deriving profit from the situation in which they found themselves. And in particular he still had one sole object, that of doing nothing, of remaining an idler, a kept-man, otherwise a capitalist. In the wild despair amidst which he had been struggling since the catastrophe there had been but terror, hatred of work, and one haunting thought: how could he so arrange matters that he might continue to live, doing nothing? His tears were already dry, and now, all at once, he reappeared such as he really was—a man intent on enjoyment.

However, Suzanne wished to know everything.

"But what have I to do with this matter?" she inquired; "why did you ask me if I had kept up any relations with Monsieur Froment?"

"Oh, *mon Dieu!*" he quietly replied; "because that would have facilitated the overtures which I think of making to him. As you can understand, after years of rupture, it is not easy to approach a man to discuss questions of interest, whereas things would be much easier if he had remained your friend. In that case you yourself, perhaps, might have seen him, spoken to him—"

With a sudden wave of her hand Suzanne stopped her husband: "I would never have spoken to Monsieur Froment under such circumstances. You forget that I had a sisterly affection for him."

Ah, the wretched being! So now he had sunk to so low a degree of baseness that he was ready to speculate on such affection as Luc might have retained for her, and it was she whom he thought of employing to touch his adversary, in such wise that the latter might then be more easily conquered.

Boisgelin must have understood that he had hurt Suzanne's feelings, for he could see that she had become much paler and colder, as if she had again withdrawn from him. He wished to efface that bad impression. "You are right," said he, "business is not a thing for women to attend to. As you say, also, you could not have undertaken such a commission. But all the same I am well pleased with my idea, for the more I think it over, the more convinced I feel that our salvation lies in it. I shall prepare my plan of attack, and find a means of opening up intercourse with the director of La Crêcherie—unless, indeed, I allow him to take the first steps, which would be a more skilful course."

He was quite enlivened by the hope of duping another and deriving sustenance and pleasure from him as he had hitherto done. There would still be something good in life if one could live it with white and idle hands, ignorant of work. He rose, gave a sigh of relief, and looked on the great park. It seemed more extensive still on that clear winter day, and he hoped to give fêtes in it again as soon as the spring should come. Finally he exclaimed: "It would really be too stupid for us to distress ourselves. Can folk like ourselves ever become paupers?"

Suzanne, who had remained seated, felt her painful sadness increase. For a moment she had entertained the naïve hope of reforming that man, and now she perceived that every tempest and revolution might pass over him without bringing amendment, or even understanding of the new times. The ancient system of the exploitation of man by man was in his blood, he could only live on others. He would always remain a big bad child who would fall to her charge later on should justice ever do its work. And thus she could only regard him with great and bitter pity.

Throughout that long conversation Paul had remained motionless, listening to his parents with his usual gentle, intelligent, and loving expression. All the feelings which in turn agitated his mother were reflected in his large pensive eyes. He was in constant communion with her, and suffered like herself at seeing how unworthy his father was. She at last perceived his painful embarrassment, and asked him: "Where were you going just now, my child?"

"I was going to the farm, mother; Feuillat must have received the new plough for the winter ploughing."

Boisgelin laughed: "And that interests you?" he asked.

"Why yes, father. At Les Combettes they have steam ploughs which turn up furrows several thousand yards long now that all the fields have been joined together; and it is superb to see the land turned up like that and fertilised."

He was overflowing with youthful enthusiasm. His mother, who felt touched by it, smiled at him. "Go, go, my boy," she said, "go and see the new plough, and work—your health will be all the better for it."

During the ensuing days Suzanne noticed that her husband evinced no haste in putting his project into execution. It seemed as if he deemed it sufficient to have discovered a solution which in his opinion would save them all. That done he relapsed into indolence, incapable of any effort. However, there was another big child at La Guerdache, whose manner suddenly caused Suzanne considerable disquietude. Monsieur

Jérôme, her grandfather, who had just reached the advanced age of eighty-eight, in spite of the species of living death to which paralysis had reduced him, still led a silent and retired existence, having no intercourse with the outer world apart from his frequent promenades in the bath-chair which a servant propelled. Suzanne alone entered his room and ministered to his wants, evincing the same loving attention as she had already shown when a mere girl, thirty years previously, in that same large ground-floor room looking towards the park. She was so accustomed to the old man's clear, fathomless eyes, which seemed, as it were, full of spring water, that she was able to detect the slightest shadow that passed over them. Now, since the recent tragical events, those eyes had darkened somewhat after the fashion of water when rising sand renders it turbid. For many monotonous years Suzanne had seen nothing in them, and finding them so limpid and so empty had imagined that power of thought had for ever departed from her grandfather. But was it now returning? Did not those shadows in Monsieur Jérôme's eyes, and his feverishness of manner, indicate a possible awakening? Perhaps, indeed, he had always retained his consciousness and intelligence; perhaps, too, by some kind of miracle, now when he was drawing nigh to death, the hard physical bond of paralysis was relaxing in some slight measure, releasing him from the silence and immobility in which he had so long lived imprisoned. It was with growing astonishment and anguish that Suzanne watched that slow work of deliverance.

One night the servant who propelled Monsieur Jérôme's bath-chair ventured to stop her just as she was coming from the old man's room, quite stirred by the living glance with which he had watched her depart. "Madame," said the servant, "I made up my mind to tell you. It seems to me that there is a change in Monsieur. To-day he spoke."

"What! he spoke?" she answered, thunderstruck.

"Yes, even yesterday I fancied that I could hear him stammering words in an undertone when we halted for a little while on the Brias road in front of the Abyss. But to-day, when we passed before La Crêcherie, he certainly spoke, I'm sure of it."

"And what did he say?"

"Ah, madame, I did not understand, his words were disconnected, one couldn't make sense of them."

From that moment Suzanne, full of anxious solicitude, had a close watch kept upon her grandfather. The servant received orders to report to her every evening what had happened during the day. In this wise she was able to follow the growing fever which seemed to have come upon Monsieur Jérôme. He was possessed by a desire to see and hear, he made it plain by signs that he wished to have his outings prolonged, as if he were eager for the sights which he found upon the roads. But he particularly insisted on being taken each day to the same spots, either the Abyss or La Crêcherie, and he never wearied of contemplating the former's sombre ruins and the latter's gay prosperity. He compelled his servant to slacken his pace, made him go past the same spot several times, and all the while he more and more distinctly stammered those disjointed words, whose sense was not yet apparent. Suzanne, quite upset by this awakening, at last sent for Doctor Novarre, whose opinion she was anxious to ascertain.

"Doctor," said she, after explaining the case to him, "you cannot conceive how it frightens me. It is as if I were witnessing a resurrection. My heart contracts, it all appears to me like some prodigious sign announcing extraordinary events."

Novarre smiled at her nervousness, and wished to see things himself. But it was not easy to deal with Monsieur Jérôme; he had closed his door to doctors as well as to others; and besides, as his ailment admitted of no treatment, Novarre had for years abstained from making any attempt to enter his room. In the present instance the doctor had to wait for the old man in the park, where he bowed to him as he passed in his bath-chair. Next he followed him along the road, and on drawing near saw that his eyes began to gleam whilst his lips parted, and a vague stammering came from them. In his turn Novarre felt astonished and stirred.

"You were quite right, Madame," he came to tell Suzanne, "the case is a very singular one. We are evidently in presence of some crisis affecting the whole organism, and arising from some great internal shock."

"But what do you expect will happen, doctor?" Suzanne anxiously inquired, "and what can we do?"

"Oh, we can do nothing, that is unfortunately certain, and as for foreseeing what such a condition may lead to, I won't attempt it. Yet I ought to tell you that if such cases are very rare they do occasionally occur. Thus I remember examining at the asylum of Saint-Cron an old man who had been shut up there for nearly forty years, and whom the keepers, to the best of their remembrance, had never once heard speak. Quite suddenly, however, he appeared to awake, at first speaking in a confused manner, and then very plainly, whereupon an interminable flow of speech set in—whole hours of ceaseless chatter. But the extraordinary part of it was that this old man, who was regarded as an idiot, had seen, heard, and understood everything during his forty years of apparent slumber. And when he recovered the power of speech it was an endless narrative of his sensations and recollections stored within him since his entry into the asylum that poured from his lips."

Although Suzanne strove to hide the frightful emotion into which this example threw her, she could not help shuddering. "And what became of that unhappy man?" she asked.

Novarre hesitated for a second, then replied: "He died three days afterwards. I must own it, madame, a crisis of that sort is almost always a symptom of approaching dissolution. One finds in it the eternal symbol of the lamp which throws up a last flame before going out."

Deep silence reigned. Suzanne had become very pale. The icy breath of death swept by. But it was not so much the thought that her unhappy grandfather would soon die that pained her—she had another poignant fear. Had he seen, heard, and understood everything throughout his long paralysis, even after the fashion of the old man of Saint-Cron?

At last she summoned sufficient bravery to ask another question: "Do you think, doctor," she inquired, "that intelligence has quite departed from our dear patient? In your opinion does he understand, does he think?"

Novarre made a vague gesture, the gesture of the scientist who does not consider it right to venture on any pronouncement respecting matters outside the pale of scientific certainty.

"Oh! you ask me too much, madame," said he. "Everything is possible in that mystery, the human brain, into which we still penetrate with so much difficulty. Intelligence can certainly remain intact after the loss of speech; because one cannot speak it does not follow that one is unable to think. However, I may say that I should formerly have believed in a permanent weakening of all Monsieur Jérôme's mental faculties, I should have thought him sunk in senile infancy for ever."

"Still, it is possible that he may have retained his faculties intact."

"Quite possible; I even begin to suspect that such is the case, as is indicated by that awakening of his whole being, and that return of speech which seems to be coming back to him gradually."

This conversation left Suzanne in a state of dolorous horror. She could no longer linger in her grandfather's room and witness his slow resurrection without a secret feeling of alarm. If amidst the mute rigidity in which he had been chained by paralysis he had indeed seen, heard, and understood everything, what a terrible drama must have filled his long silence! For more than thirty years he had remained an impassive witness, as it were, of the decline of his race, those clear eyes of his had beheld the rout of his descendants, a downfall accelerated from father to son by the vertigo born of wealth. In the devouring blaze of enjoyment two generations had sufficed to consume the fortune which his father and he had built up, and which he had deemed so firm. He had seen his son Michel ruin himself for worthless women directly he became a widower, and blow his brains out with a pistol-shot; whilst his daughter Laure, losing her head in mysticism, entered a convent; and his second son, Philippe, married to a hussy, perished in a duel after an imbecile career. He had also seen his grandson Gustave impel his father Michel to suicide by robbing him of his mistress and of the hundred thousand francs that he had collected for his business payments; whilst at the same time his other grandson André, Philippe's child, was relegated to a lunatic asylum. He had further seen Boisgelin, the husband of his granddaughter Suzanne, purchase the imperilled Abyss, and confide its management to a poor cousin, Delaveau, who, after restoring it to prosperity for a brief period, had reduced it to ashes on the night when he had discovered the betrayal of his wife Fernande and that coxcomb Boisgelin—the pair of them maddened by such a craving for luxury and pleasure that they had destroyed all around them. And he had seen the Abyss, his well-loved work, so small and modest when he had inherited it from his father, so greatly enlarged by himself, he had seen that Abyss, which he had hoped his race would make a city, the empire as it were of iron and steel, decline so rapidly that with the second generation of his descendants not a stone of it remained standing. Finally, he had seen his race, in which creative power had accumulated so slowly through a long line of wretched toilers, till it had burst forth at last in his father and himself; he had seen his race spoilt, debased, and destroyed by the abuse of wealth, as if nothing of the Quirignons' heroic passion for work glowed among his grandchildren. And thus how frightful must be the story amassed in the brain of that octogenarian, what a procession of terrible occurrences, synthetising a whole century of effort, and casting light on the past, the present, and the future of a family! And what a terrifying thing, too, it was that the brain in which that story had seemed to slumber should at last slowly awaken to life, and that everything should threaten to come forth from it, in a great flood of truth, if indeed the tongue that already stammered should end by speaking plainly!

It was for that terrible awakening that Suzanne now waited with growing anxiety. She and her son were the last of the race; Paul was the sole heir of the Quignons. Aunt Laure had lately died in the Carmelite convent where she had lived for nearly forty years; and Cousin André, cut off from the world since infancy, had been dead for many years already. Thus nowadays, whenever Paul went with his mother into Monsieur Jérôme's room, the old man's eyes, once more gleaming with intelligence, rested on him for a long while. That lad was the sole frail wattle of the oak from whose powerful trunk he had once hoped to see a number of vigorous branches, a whole swarming family, fork and grow. Was not that family tree full of new sap, health, and vigour, derived from sturdy, toiling forerunners? Would not his line blossom forth and spread around to conquer all the wealth and all the joy of the world? But, behold the sap was already exhausted with the coming of his grandchildren; in less than half a century a misspent life of wealth had consumed the whole strength amassed through a long ancestry! How bitter it was when that unhappy grandfather, the supreme witness surviving amidst so much ruin, found himself confronted by one sole heir, that gentle, delicate, refined Paul, who was like the last gift vouchsafed by life, which perhaps had left him to the Quignons in order that they might grow afresh and flower in new soil! But what dolorous irony there was in the fact that only that quiet, thoughtful lad remained in that huge, royal residence of La Guerdache which Monsieur Jérôme had originally purchased at such great cost, in the hope of seeing it some day peopled by his numerous descendants. He had pictured its spacious rooms occupied by ten households; he had imagined that he could hear the laughter of an ever-increasing troop of boys and girls; in his imagination the place became the happy, luxurious family estate where the ever-fruitful dynasty of the Quignons would reign. But, on the contrary, the rooms had grown emptier day by day; drunkenness, madness, and death had swept by, accomplishing their destructive work; and then a final corrupting creature had come to complete the ruin of the house; and since the last catastrophe two-thirds of the rooms were kept closed, the whole of the second floor was abandoned to the dust, and even the ground-floor reception-rooms were only opened on Saturdays in order to admit a little sunshine. The race would end if Paul did not raise it up afresh; the empire in which it should have prospered was already naught but a large empty dwelling which would crumble away in abandonment unless new life were imparted to it.

Another week went by. The servant who attended Monsieur Jérôme could now distinguish certain words amidst his stammering. At last a distinct phrase was detected, and the man came to repeat it to Suzanne.

"Oh! he did not manage it without difficulty, madame, but I assure you that this morning Monsieur repeated: 'One must give back, one must give back.'"

Suzanne was incredulous. The words seemed to have no meaning. What was to be given back?

"You must listen more attentively," she said to the servant; "try to distinguish the words better."

On the morrow, however, the man was still more positive. "I assure madame," said he, "that Monsieur really says: 'One must give back, one must give back.' He says it twenty and thirty times in succession in a low but persistent voice, as if putting all his strength into it."

That same evening Suzanne determined to watch her grandfather herself, in order that she might understand things better. On the following day the old man was unable to get up. Whilst his brain seemed to be freeing itself from its bonds, his legs and soon his trunk were attacked by paralysis, and became quite lifeless. Suzanne was greatly alarmed by this, and again sent for Novarre, who was unable to do anything, and warned her that the end was approaching. From that moment she did not quit the room.

It was a very large room, with very thick carpets and heavy hangings. A deep ruddy hue and a substantial and rather sombre luxury prevailed there. The furniture was of carved rosewood, the bed was a large four-poster, and there was a tall mirror in which the park was reflected. When the windows were open the view, beyond the lawns, between the old trees, stretched over an immense panorama in which one saw first the jumbled roofs of Beauclair, and then the Bleuse Mountains with La Crêcherie and its smeltery, and the Abyss, whose gigantic chimneys still rose erect.

One morning Suzanne sat down near the bed, after drawing back the window curtains, in order to admit the winter sunshine; and all at once she felt greatly moved on hearing Monsieur Jérôme speak. For a few moments his face had been turned towards one of the windows through which he had been looking at the distant horizon. And at first he only uttered two words:

"Monsieur Luc."

Suzanne, who had distinctly heard them, was quite overcome with surprise. Why Monsieur Luc? Her grandfather had never had any intercourse with Luc, he ought to have been ignorant of his existence, unless indeed he was aware of what had lately occurred, had seen everything, and understood everything, even as hitherto she had only suspected and feared. Indeed, those words "Monsieur Luc," falling from his lips which had been sealed so long, were like a first proof that he had retained a lively intelligence amidst his silence, and could see and understand. Suzanne felt her anguish increasing.

"Is it really Monsieur Luc that you say, grandfather?" she asked.

"Yes, yes, Monsieur Luc."

He pronounced the name with increasing distinctness and energy, keeping his ardent glance fixed upon her.

"But why do you speak to me of Monsieur Luc?" she said. "Do you know him then? Have you something to say to me about him?"

Monsieur Jérôme hesitated, doubtless because he could not find the words he wished; then with childish impatience he repeated:

"Monsieur Luc!"

"He used to be my best friend," resumed Suzanne, "but for long years now he has ceased coming here."

Monsieur Jérôme quickly nodded his head, and then, as if his tongue were gradually acquiring the power of speech, he said: "I know, I know—I wish him to come."

"You wish Monsieur Luc to come to see you—you wish to speak to him, grandfather?"

"Yes, yes, it is that. Let him come at once—I will speak to him."

The surprise and the vague fright that possessed Suzanne were now increasing. What could Monsieur Jérôme wish to say to Luc? There were such painful possibilities, that for a moment she tried to avoid granting the old man's request, as if indeed she imagined him to be delirious. But he was in full possession of his senses, and entreated her with increasing fervour, all the strength indeed remaining in his poor infirm frame. And at this Suzanne felt profoundly disturbed, asking herself if it would not be wrong of her to refuse the dying man's request for that interview, although she shuddered at the thought of the dimly threatening things which might result from it.

ÉMILE ZOLA

"Cannot you say what you wish to me, grandfather?" she ultimately asked.

"No, no—to Monsieur Luc. I will speak to him at once—oh, at once!"

"Very well, then, grandfather, I will write to him, and I hope that he will come."

When Suzanne sat down to write, however, her hand trembled. She penned only two lines: "My friend, I have need of you, come at once." Nevertheless she was twice compelled to pause, for she lacked strength to trace even those few words, so painful were the memories that they aroused within her—memories of her lost life and of the happiness beside which she had passed, and which she would never know. At last, however, the note was written, and it was scarcely ten in the morning when one of the servants, a lad, set out to take it to La Crêcherie.

Luc, as it happened, was standing outside the common-house, finishing his morning inspection, when the note was handed to him; and without delay he followed the young messenger. But how great was the emotion which he felt on reading those simple yet touching words: "My friend, I have need of you, come at once." Events had parted him from Suzanne for twelve long years, yet she wrote to him as if they had met only the previous day—like one, too, who was certain that he would respond to her appeal. She had not doubted his friendship for a moment, and he was touched to tears at finding her ever the same, still full of sisterly affection as in former times. The most frightful tragedies had burst forth around them, every passion had run riot, sweeping away men and things, yet after those years of separation they found themselves hand in hand once more. Whilst walking on quickly, and drawing near to La Guerdache, Luc began to wonder, however, why she had sent for him. He was not ignorant of Boisgelin's desire to speculate on the situation and sell the Abyss for as much money as possible; but he had resolved that he would never buy it. The only acceptable solution of the matter in his opinion was the entry of the Abyss into the association of La Crêcherie, after the fashion of the other smaller factories. For a moment it occurred to him that Boisgelin might have asked his wife to make overtures to him, but he knew her, and felt that she was incapable of playing such a part. It seemed to him that she must be exhausted by some great anxiety, that she must need his help in some tragic circumstance. And so he puzzled his mind no more—she herself would soon tell him what service she required of his affection.

Suzanne was waiting for him in one of the little drawing-rooms, and when Luc entered it she thought she was about to faint, so great became her perturbation. He himself felt upset, and at first neither of them could utter a word. They looked at one another in silence.

"Oh, my friend, my friend!" Suzanne murmured when she was at last able to speak.

Those simple words were fraught with all the emotion she felt at the thought of those last twelve years—their separation, broken only by a few silent chance meetings, the cruel life which she herself had led in her defiled home, and the work which he meantime had accomplished, and which she had watched from afar, enthusiastically. He had become a hero for her, she had worshipped him, and had longed to throw herself at his knees, nurse his wounds, and become his consoling helpmate. But another had stepped between them—Josine, who had caused her so much suffering that now all passionate love seemed dead. Nevertheless, at the sight of Luc standing once more before her all those hidden things rose from the depths of her being, and the intensity of her emotion moistened her eyes and made her hands quiver.

"Oh, my friend, my friend!" she repeated, "so it was sufficient that I should send for you!"

Luc quivered with a similar sympathy, and he also recalled the past. He knew how unhappily she had lived beneath the horrible insult offered to her, the presence of her husband's mistress in her home. He knew, too, what dignity and heroism she had shown in remaining in that home with head erect, for her son's sake and her own. Thus in spite of separation she had never been absent from his mind and heart—he had pitied her more and more at each fresh trial that fell upon her. He had often wondered how he might help her. It would have greatly delighted him to be able to prove that he had forgotten nothing, that he was still the same good friend as formerly. And this was why he had now hastened to respond to her first summons, full of an anxious affection which made his heart swell and prevented him from speaking.

At last, however, he was able to reply: "Yes, your friend, one who has never ceased to be so, and who only awaited your summons to hasten here."

They were at that moment so keenly conscious of the bond that for ever united them like brother and sister, that they embraced and kissed each other on the cheeks, even as friends who fear nought of human folly or suffering, but are certain that they will only impart peacefulness and courage to one another. All the strength and tenderness with which the friendship of man and woman may be instinct bloomed in their smiles.

"If you only knew, my friend," said Luc, "how great my fears were when I realised that my competition would end by destroying the Abyss! Was it not you whom I was ruining? And what faith in my work I needed to prevent those thoughts from staying my hand! Great sorrow often came upon me—I believed that you must curse me, that you would never forgive me for being the cause of the worries in which you must be struggling."

"Curse you, my friend! But I was with you, I prayed for you—your victories were my only joy. And living in a sphere that hated you, it was very sweet for me to have a secret affection, to be able to understand and love you, unknown to everybody."

"None the less I have ruined you, my friend," Luc retorted. "What will become of you now, accustomed as you have been since childhood to a life of luxury?"

"Oh, ruined! That would have come about without you! It was the others who ruined me. And you will see how brave I can be, no matter how delicate you may think me."

"But Paul, your son?"

"Paul! Why, nothing happier could have befallen him. He will work. You know what wealth has done to my people."

Then Suzanne at last told Luc why she had sent him such a pressing summons. Monsieur Jérôme, the wondrous awakening of whose intelligence she revealed, wished to speak to him. It was the desire of a dying man, for Doctor Novarre believed in his imminent dissolution. Astonished by these tidings even as she had been, seized too, like herself, with vague alarm at the thought of this resurrection in which he was so strangely desired to intervene, Luc none the less answered that he was entirely at her disposal, and ready to do whatever she might request.

"Have you warned your husband of Monsieur Jérôme's desire and my visit?" he inquired.

Suzanne looked at him and shrugged her shoulders. "No, I did not think of it—besides, it is useless," said she; "for a long time past it has seemed as if my grandfather no longer knew that my husband existed. He does not speak to him, he does not even seem to see him. Moreover, my husband went out shooting early this morning, and he has not yet come home." Then she added, "If you will follow me, I will take you to my grandfather at once."

When they entered Monsieur Jérôme's room, the old man, who was sitting up in the large rosewood bed supported by several pillows, still had his eyes turned towards the window whose curtains had been drawn back. In all probability he had never ceased gazing over the park and the spreading horizon, with the Abyss and La Crêcherie showing yonder, beside the Bleuse Mountains, above the jumbled roofs of Beauclair. It was a scene which seemed to attract him irresistibly, like some symbolism of the past, the present, and the future, which he had had before him during all his long silent years.

"Grandfather," said Suzanne, "I have had Monsieur Luc Froment fetched for you. Here he is, he was kind enough to come at once."

The old man slowly turned his head, and looked at Luc with his large eyes, which had grown it seemed yet larger than formerly, and which were now full of deep light. He said nothing, no word of greeting or thanks came from his lips, and the heavy silence lasted several minutes, whilst he kept his gaze fixed upon that stranger, the founder of La Crêcherie, as if he were anxious to know him thoroughly, to dive indeed into his very soul.

At last Suzanne, who felt slightly embarrassed, resumed, "You do not know Monsieur Froment, grandfather; but perhaps you may have noticed him when you were out."

Monsieur Jérôme did not appear to hear his granddaughter, for he still returned no answer. After a moment, however, he once more turned his head and looked round the room. And failing to find what he sought he ended by speaking one word—a name—"Boisgelin."

This caused Suzanne fresh astonishment as well as anxiety and embarrassment. "You are asking for my husband, grandfather—do you wish him to come here?" she inquired.

"Yes, yes, Boisgelin."

"But I am afraid that he has not come home yet. Meantime you ought to tell Monsieur Froment why you wished to see him."

"No, no, Boisgelin, Boisgelin."

It was evident that he wished to speak in Boisgelin's presence. Suzanne therefore apologised to Luc and left the room to seek her husband. Meanwhile Luc remained face to face with Monsieur Jérôme, conscious that the latter's bright glance was still and ever fixed upon him. In his turn he then began to scrutinise the old man, and found him looking wondrously handsome in his extreme old age, with his white face and regular features, to which the approach of death seemed to impart an expression of sovereign majesty. The wait was a long one, and not a word was exchanged by those two men, whose eyes dived into one another's. All around them the room with its heavy hangings and massive furniture seemed to be slumbering. Not a sound arose—there was naught but the quiver which came through the walls from the large empty closed rooms, the stories and stories which had been abandoned to dust. And nothing could have been more tragical or solemn than that spell of silent waiting. At last Suzanne returned, bringing with her Boisgelin, who had just come home. He still wore his shooting-jacket, gloves, and gaiters, for she had not allowed him time to change his clothes. And he came in with an anxious, bewildered air, astonished at such an adventure. All that his wife had just rapidly told him of the summoning of Luc, his presence in Monsieur Jérôme's room, the old man's recovery of his intelligence, and the statement that he was awaiting him—Boisgelin—before speaking, all those unforeseen occurrences quite upset Suzanne's husband, who had not been allowed even a few minutes of reflection.

"Well, grandfather," said Suzanne, "here is my husband. Speak if you have something to tell us. We are listening."

But again the old man looked round the room, and once more he asked, "Paul, where is Paul?"

"Do you want Paul to be here too?"

"Yes, yes, I want him."

"But the fact is that he must be at the farm. Fully a quarter of an hour will be necessary to fetch him."

"He must come—I want him, I want him!"

Suzanne yielded, and hastily despatched a servant for her son. And then the waiting began afresh, and proved even more solemn and tragic than before. Luc and Boisgelin had simply bowed to one another, finding nothing to say on meeting after so many years in that room which an august breath already seemed to fill. Nobody spoke, and amidst the quiver of the air one only heard the somewhat heavy respiration of Monsieur Jérôme. Once again his large eyes, full of light, were turned towards the window, towards that horizon symbolical of the labour of manhood, where the past had undergone accomplishment, and where the future would be born. And the minutes went by, slowly, regularly, in that anxious wait for what was to come, the act of sovereign grandeur whose approach could be divined.

Some light footsteps were heard at last, and Paul came in, his face glowing healthily from contact with the open air.

"My boy," said Suzanne, "it is your grandfather who has brought us all together here. He wishes you to be present while he speaks."

On the hitherto rigid lips of Monsieur Jérôme a smile of infinite tenderness had at last appeared. He signed to Paul to approach, and made him sit down as near as possible, on the edge of the bed. It was particularly for him, the last heir of the Qurignons, through whom the race might flower anew and yet yield excellent fruit, that he desired to speak. And on seeing how moved the youth looked, full of grief at the thought of a last farewell, he continued for a moment trying to reassure him with his affectionate glances, like one to whom death was sweet since he was about to bequeath as inheritance to his great-grandson an act of goodness, justice, and pacification.

At last he began to speak, amidst the religious silence of one and all. He had turned his face towards Boisgelin, and at first he merely repeated the words which his servant had for two days past heard him stammering in an undertone, amidst other confused utterances:

"One must give back, one must give back!"

Then, seeing that the others did not appear to understand what he meant, he turned to Paul and repeated with growing energy:

"One must give back, my child, give back!"

Suzanne shuddered, and exchanged a glance with Luc, who also was quivering; whilst Boisgelin, seized with uneasiness and alarm, pretended to detect in all this some rambling on the old man's part. But Suzanne inquired: "What do you desire to tell us, grandfather—what is it that we must give back?"

Monsieur Jérôme's speech was fast becoming easier and more distinct. "Everything, my child—the Abyss yonder must be given back; La Guerdache must be given back. One must give back the land of the farm. Everything must be given, because nothing ought to belong to us, because everything ought to belong to all."

"But explain to us, grandfather—to whom are we to give these things?"

"I tell you, my girl, they must be given back to all. Nothing of what we thought to be our property belongs to us. If that property has poisoned and destroyed us, it is because it belonged to others. For our happiness, and the happiness of all, it must be given back, given back!"

Then came a scene of sovereign beauty, incomparable grandeur. The old man did not always find the words he desired, but his gestures indicated his meaning. Amidst the silence of those who surrounded him, he went on slowly, and in spite of all difficulties succeeded in making himself understood. He had seen everything, heard everything, understood everything, and even as Suzanne had divined with quivering anguish, it was all the past which now came back, all the truth of the terrible past, pouring forth in a flood from that hitherto silent, impassive witness, so long imprisoned within his own body. It seemed as if he had only survived the many disasters, a whole family of happy, then stricken, beings, in order to draw from everything the great lesson. On the day of awakening, before going to his death, he spread out all the torture he had suffered as one who, after believing in the triumphant reign of his race over an empire established by himself, had lived long enough to see both race and empire swept away by the blast of the future. And he told why all this had happened, he judged it, and offered reparation.

At the outset came the first Qurignon, the drawer who with a few mates had founded the Abyss, he being as poor as they were, but probably more skilful and economical. Then came himself, the second Qurignon, the one who had gained a fortune, and piled up millions in the course of a stubborn struggle, in which he had displayed heroic determination, ceaseless and ever-intelligent energy. But if he had accomplished prodigies of activity and creative genius, if he had gained money, thanks to his skill in adapting the conditions of production to those of sale, he knew very well that he was simply the outcome of long generations of toilers from whom he had derived all his strength and triumph. How many peasants perspiring as they tilled the glebe, how many workmen exhausted by the handling of tools had been required for the advent of those two first Qurignons who had conquered fortune! Among those forerunners there had been a keen passion to fight for life, to make money, to rise from one class to another, to pursue all the slow enfranchisement of the poor wretch who bends in servitude over his appointed task. And at last one Qurignon had been strong enough to conquer, to escape from the gaol of poverty, to acquire the long-desired wealth, and become in his turn a rich man, a master! But immediately afterwards, that is in two generations, his descendants collapsed, fell once more into the dolorous struggle for existence, exhausted already as they were by enjoyment, consumed by it as by a flame.

"One must give back, one must give back, one must give back!" repeated Monsieur Jérôme.

There was his son Michel, who after years of excesses had killed himself on the eve of a pay-day; there was his other son Philippe, who, having married a hussy, had been ruined by her, and had lost his life in a foolish duel. There was his daughter Laure, who had died in a convent, her mind weakened by mystical visions. There were his two grandsons, André, a rachitic semi-maniac, who had passed away in an asylum, and Gustave, who had met a tragic death in Italy after impelling his father to suicide by robbing him of his mistress and the money he needed for his business payments. Finally, there was his granddaughter Suzanne, the tender-hearted, sensible, well-loved creature, whose husband after repurchasing the Abyss and La Guerdache had completed the work of destruction. The Abyss was now in ashes, and La Guerdache, where he had hoped to see his race swarming, had become a desert. And whilst his race had been collapsing, carrying off both his father's work and his own, he had seen another work arise, La Crêcherie, which was now full of prosperity, throbbing with the future that it brought with it. He knew all those things because his clear eyes had witnessed them in the course of his daily outings, those hours of silent contemplation, when he had found himself outside the Abyss at the moment when one or another shift was leaving, or outside La Crêcherie where the men who had deserted his own foundation took off their caps to him. And again he had passed before the Abyss on the morning when of that well-loved creation he had found nought but smoking ruins left.

"One must give back, one must give back, one must give back!"

That cry, which he constantly repeated amidst his slowly flowing words, which he emphasised each time with more and more energy, ascended from his heart like the natural consequence of all the disastrous events which had caused him so much suffering. If everything around him had crumbled away so soon, was it not because the fortune which he had acquired by the labour of others was both poisoned and poisonous? The enjoyment that such fortune brings is the most certain of destructive ferments—it bastardises a race, disorganises a family, leads to abominable tragedies. In less than half a century it had consumed the strength, the intelligence, the genius which the Qurignons had amassed during several centuries of rough toil. The mistake of those robust workers had been their belief that to secure personal happiness they ought to appropriate and enjoy the wealth created by the exertions of their companions. And the wealth they had dreamt of, the wealth they had acquired, had proved their chastisement. Nothing can be

ÉMILE ZOLA

worse from the moral point of view than to cite as an example the workman who grows rich, who becomes an employer, the sovereign master of thousands of his fellow-men who bend perspiring over their toil, producing the wealth by which he triumphs! When a writer says: "You see very well that with order and intelligence a mere blacksmith may attain to everything," he simply contributes to the work of iniquity, and aggravates social disequilibrium. The happiness of the elect is really compounded of the unhappiness of others, for it is their happiness which he cuts down and purloins. The comrade who makes his way, as the saying goes, bars the road to thousands of other comrades, lives upon their misery and their suffering. And it often happens that the happy one is punished by success, by fortune itself, which coming too quickly and disproportionately, proves murderous. This is why the only right course is to revert to salutary work, work on the part of all—all earning their livings and owing their happiness solely to the exertion of their minds and their muscles.

"One must give back, one must give back, one must give back!" repeated Monsieur Jérôme.

One must give back, indeed; one must restitute because one is liable to die of that which one steals from another. One must give back, because the sole cure, the only certainty of happiness lies in doing so. One must give back in a spirit of justice, and even more in one's own personal interest, since the happiness of each can only reside in the happiness of all. One must give back in order that one may enjoy better health and live a happy life in the midst of universal peace. One must give back because if all the unjust victors of life, all the egotistical holders of the public fortune, were to restore the wealth that they squander for their personal pleasures—the great estates, the great industrial enterprises, the roads, the towns—peace would be restored to-morrow, love would flower once more among men, and there would be such an abundance of possessions that not one single being would be left in penury. One must give back because one must set the example if one desires that other wealthy folk may understand, may realise whence have come all the evils from which they suffer, and may be inspired to endow their descendants with renewed vigour by plunging them once more into active life, daily work. One must give back, too, whilst there is yet time to do so, whilst there is still some nobility in returning to one's comrades, in showing them that one was mistaken, and that one returns to one's place in the ranks to participate in the common effort, with the hope that the hour of justice and peace will soon strike. And one must give back in order to die with a clear conscience, a heart joyful at having accomplished one's duty, at leaving a repairing and liberating lesson to the last of one's race, so that he may restore it, save it from error, and perpetuate it in strength, delight, and beauty.

"One must give back, one must give back!"

Tears had appeared in Suzanne's eyes as she perceived the exaltation with which her son Paul was filled by her grandfather's words; whilst Boisgelin expressed his irritation by impatient movements.

"But, grandfather," said she, "to whom and how are we to give back?"

The old man turned his bright eyes upon Luc. "If I desired the founder of La Crêcherie to be present," said he, "it was in order that he might hear me and help you, my children. He has already done much for the work of reparation, he alone can intervene and restore what remains of our fortune to the sons and grandsons of those who were my own and my father's comrades."

Luc was filled with emotion by the wondrous nobility of the scene, yet he hesitated, for he could divine Boisgelin's keen hostility. "I can only do one thing," said he—"that is, if the owners of the Abyss are willing I will procure them admission into our association at La Crêcherie. In the same way as other factories have already done, the Abyss will increase our family—double, in fact, the importance of our growing town. If by 'giving back' you mean a return to increase of justice, a step towards the absolute justice of the future, I will help you, I will consent to what you say with all my heart."

"I know you will," Monsieur Jérôme slowly answered; "I ask nothing more."

But Boisgelin, unable to restrain himself any longer, began to protest. "Ah! that is not what I desire. However much it may distress me to do so, I am willing to sell the Abyss to La Crêcherie. A price will have to be agreed upon, and in addition to the amount which may be fixed I desire to retain an interest in the enterprise, which also will have to be arranged. I need money and I wish to sell."

This was the plan which he had been maturing for some days past, in the idea that Luc was eager to secure possession of the Abyss land, and that he would be able to obtain a considerable sum from him at once, as well as a future income. But this plan entirely collapsed when Luc declared in a voice expressive of irrevocable determination: "It is impossible for us to buy. It is contrary to the spirit which guides us. We are simply an association, a family open to all those brothers who may wish to join us."

Then Monsieur Jérôme, whose bright eyes had been fixed on Boisgelin, resumed with sovereign tranquillity of manner: "It is I who wish it and who order it. My granddaughter, Suzanne, here present, is co-proprietress of the Abyss, and she will refuse her consent to any other arrangement than that which I desire. And, like myself, I am sure that she will have but one regret, that of being unable to restore everything, of having to accept interest on her capital, which she will dispose of as her heart may dictate."

And as Boisgelin remained silent, submitting to the others with the weakness that had come with his ruin, the old man continued: "But that is not all, there remain La Guerdache and the farm—they must be given back, given back."

Then, though he was again experiencing a difficulty in speaking and was well-nigh exhausted, he made his last desires known. As the Abyss would be blended with La Crêcherie, he wished the farm to join the association of Les Combettes, so as to enlarge the fields which had been united by Lenfant, Yvonnot, and all the other peasants, who had been living together like brothers since a proper understanding of their interests had reconciled them. There would be but one stretch of earth, one common mother, loved by all, tilled by all, and feeding all. The whole plain of La Roumagne would end by yielding one vast harvest to fill the granaries of regenerated Beauclair. And as for La Guerdache, which entirely belonged to Suzanne, he charged her to restore it to the poor and suffering, so that she might keep nothing of the property which had poisoned the Quirignons. Then, reverting to Paul, who still sat on the edge of the bed, and taking his hand in his own, and looking at him earnestly with his eyes which were now growing dim, Monsieur Jérôme said in a lower and lower voice: "One must give back, one must give back, my child. You will keep nothing, you will give yonder park to the old comrades, so that they may rejoice there on high days, and so that their wives and children may walk there and enjoy hours of gaiety and good health under the fine trees. And you will also give back this house, this huge residence which we did not know how to fill in spite of all our money, for I wish it to belong to the wives and the children of poor workmen. They will be welcomed here and nursed when they are ailing or when they are weary. Keep nothing, give all, all back, my child, if you wish to save yourself from poison. And work and live solely on the fruits of your work, and seek out the daughter of some old comrade who still works and marry her, so that she may bring you handsome children, who also will work, who will be just and happy beings, and in their turn have handsome children for the eternal work of futurity. Keep nothing, my child, give everything back, for therein alone lies salvation, peace, and joy."

They were all weeping now—never had a more beautiful, a loftier, a more heroic breath passed over human souls. The great room had become august. And the eyes of the old man, which had filled it with light, faded slowly, whilst his voice likewise became fainter, returning to eternal silence. He had at last accomplished his sublime work of reparation, truth, and justice, to help on the advent of the happiness which is the primordial right of every man. And his duty done, that same evening he died.

Before then, however, when Suzanne and Luc left Monsieur Jérôme's room together, they found themselves alone for a moment in the little *salon*. They were so overcome by emotion that their hearts rose to their lips.

"Rely on me," said Luc. "I swear to you that I will watch over the fulfilment of the supreme desires which have been committed to you. I will attend to matters from this moment."

She had taken hold of his hands. "Oh! my friend," she answered, "I place my faith in you. I know what miracles you have already performed, and I do not doubt the prodigy which you will accomplish by reconciling us all. Ah! there is nothing but love. Ah! if I had only been loved as I myself loved!"

She was trembling. The secret of which she herself had been ignorant so long, escaped her at that solemn moment. "My friend, my friend," she repeated, "what strength I should have had for doing good, what help might I not have given had I felt beside me the arm of a just man, a hero, one whom I should have made my god! But if it be too late for that, will you at least accept what help I may be able to give as a friend, a sister—"

He understood her. It was a repetition of Sœurette's sweet, sad case. She had loved him without revealing it, without even owning it to herself, like an honest woman eager for tenderness, who amidst the torments of her household dreamt of happy love. And now that Josine was chosen, now that all else was dead without possibility of resurrection, she gave herself, even as Sœurette had done, as a sisterly companion, a devoted friend, who longed to participate in his mission.

"If I will accept your help!" cried Luc, who was touched to tears. "Ah! yes indeed, there is never enough affection, enough help and active tenderness. The work is vast, and you will have ample opportunities for giving without stint your heart. Come with us, my friend, and stay with us, and you will be part of my thoughts and my love."

She was transported by his words, she threw herself into his arms, and they kissed. An indissoluble bond was being formed between them, a marriage of sentiment, of exquisite purity, in which there was nought but a common passion for the poor and the suffering, an inextinguishable desire to obliterate the misery of the world.

Months went by, and the liquidation of the affairs of the Abyss, which were extremely involved, proved a most laborious matter. Before everything else it was necessary to get rid of the debt of six hundred thousand francs. Arrangements were at last entered into with the creditors, who agreed to accept payment in annuities levied upon the share of profits to which the Abyss would be entitled when it entered the Crêcherie association. Then it was necessary to value the plant and materials saved from the fire. These, with all the land stretching along the Mionne as far as Old Beauclair, formed the share of capital which the Boisgelins brought into the association; and a modest income, levied on the profits before they were divided among the creditors, was ensured them. Old Qurignon's desires were but half fulfilled during that period of transition, when capital still held a position similar to that of work and intelligence, pending the time when, with the victory of sovereign work, it would altogether disappear.

At least, however, La Guerdache and the farm returned completely to the commonalty, the heirs of the toilers, who had formerly paid for them with the sweat of their brows, for as soon as the farm lands—entering the Combettes association in accordance with the long-planned schemes of Feuillat—began to prosper and yield gain, the whole of the money was employed to transform La Guerdache into a convalescent home for weak children and women who had recently become mothers. Free beds were installed there, with gratuitous board, and the park now belonged to the humble ones of the world, forming a huge garden, a paradise as of dreamland, where children played, where mothers recovered their health, where the multitude enjoyed recreation as in some palace of nature which had become the palace of one and all.

Years went by. Luc had ceded one of the little houses of La Crêcherie, near the pavilion which he still occupied, to the Boisgelins. And at first that modest life proved very hard for Boisgelin, who did not become resigned to it without violent fits of revolt. At one moment he even wished to go to Paris to live there chancewise, as he listed. But his innate sloth and the impossibility of earning his own living rendered him as weak as a child, and placed him in the hands of whoever cared to take him. Since his downfall Suzanne, so sensible, so gentle, and yet so firm, had acquired absolute authority over him, and he always ended by doing what she wished, like a poor rudderless creature carried away by the stream of life. Soon, too, among that active world of workers he felt idleness weighing upon him to such a degree that he began to desire some occupation. He felt weary of dragging himself about all day long, he suffered from a secret feeling of shame, a need of action, for he could no longer tire himself with the management and squandering of a large fortune. Shooting remained a resource for him during the winter months, but as soon as the fine weather came there was nothing for him to do except to ride out occasionally, and dismal *ennui* then crushed him down. And so when Suzanne prevailed on Luc to confide an inspectorship to him, a kind of control over a department of the general stores, which meant employment for three hours of his time every day, he ended by accepting the offer. His health, which had suffered, then improved; still he always displayed anxiety, wearing a lost, unhappy air, such as one might find in a man who had fallen from one planet to another.

And years again went by. Suzanne had become the friend and sister of Josine and Sœurette, in whose work she participated. All three surrounded Luc, sustaining him and completing him, like personifications of kindness, love, and gentleness. He called them with a smile his three virtues. They busied themselves with the *crèches*, the schools, the infirmaries, and the convalescent homes, they went wherever there might be weakness to protect, pain to assuage, joy to initiate. Sœurette and Suzanne, in particular, took on themselves the most ungrateful tasks, those which require personal abnegation, entire renunciation; whilst Josine, having to attend to her children, her ever-growing home, naturally bestowed less of her time upon others. She, moreover, was the *amorosa*, the flower of beauty and desire, whilst Sœurette and Suzanne were the friends, the consolers, and the counsellors. At times some very bitter trials still fell on Luc, and often, on quitting his wife's embrace, it was to his two friends that he listened, charging them to dress the wounds they spoke of and devote themselves to the common work of salvation. It was by and for women that the future city had to be founded.

Eight years had already elapsed when Paul Boisgelin, who was seven-and-twenty, married Bonnaire's eldest daughter, then twenty-four years old. As soon as the lands of La Guerdache had entered the Combettes association, Paul, with Feuillat, the former farmer, had begun to take a passionate interest in promoting the fertility of the vast expanse which those fields had enlarged. He had become an agriculturist, and directed one of the sections of the domain, which it had been necessary to divide into several groups. And it was at his parents' little house at La Crêcherie, whither he returned to sleep every night, that he had renewed his acquaintance with Antoinette, who lived with her parents in a neighbouring house. Close intercourse had sprung up between that simple family of workers and the former heiress of the Qurignons, who now lived so modestly and welcomed every one so kindly. And although Madame Bonnaire, the terrible La Toupe, had remained a rather difficult customer to deal with, the simple nobility of character displayed by Bonnaire, that hero of work, one of the founders of the new city, had sufficed to render the intercourse intimate. It was charming to see the children loving one another, and drawing yet closer the links which had thus been formed between the representatives of two classes which had formerly fought one against the other. Antoinette, who resembled her father, being a good-looking, sturdy brunette, possessed of no little natural gracefulness, had passed through Sœurette's schools, and now helped her at the big dairy which was installed at the end of the park beside the ridge of the Bleuse Mountains. As she said with a laugh, she was simply a dairymaid, expert with milk, and cheese, and butter. When the young people married, he, Paul, a *bourgeois* by birth, who had gone back to the soil, and she, Antoinette, a daughter of the people working with her hands, a great *fête* was given, for there was a desire to celebrate as gloriously as possible those symbolical nuptials, which proclaimed the reconciliation, the union of repentant capitalism and triumphant work.

During the ensuing year, one warm June day, shortly after the birth of Antoinette's first child, the Boisgelins, accompanied by Luc, once more found themselves together at La Guerdache. Nearly ten years had now elapsed since the death of Monsieur Jérôme and the restitution of the estate to the people in accordance with his desire. Antoinette had for some time been a *pensionnaire* in the convalescent home which had been installed in the château where the Quirignons had reigned; and, leaning on the arm of her husband, she was now able to stroll under the beautiful foliage of the park, whilst Suzanne, like a good grandmother, carried the baby. A few paces in the rear walked Luc and Boisgelin. And what memories arose at the sight of that princely house, those copses, those lawns, those avenues where the uproar of costly *fêtes*, the galloping of horses and the baying of hounds no longer resounded, but where the humble of the world at last enjoyed the health-giving open air, and the restful delight that came from the great trees! All the luxury of that magnificent domain was now theirs, the convalescent home opened its bright bed-rooms, its pleasant *salons*, its well-stocked larders to them, the park reserved for them its shady paths, its crystalline springs, its lawns where for their delight gardeners cultivated beds of perfume-shedding flowers. They found there their long-withheld share of beauty and grace. And it was delightful to see infancy, youth, and motherhood—which for centuries had been condemned to suffering, shut up in sunless hovels, dying of filthy wretchedness—suddenly summoned to partake of the joy of life, the share of happiness belonging by right to every human creature, that luxury of happiness at which innumerable generations of starvelings had gazed from afar without ever being able to touch it!

As the young married couple, followed by the others, at last reached a pool of water glistening with mirror-like limpidity under the blue sky, beyond a row of willows, Luc began to laugh softly.

"Ah, my friends!" said he, "what a gay and pretty scene this recalls to me! You know nothing about it, eh? Nevertheless it was at the edge of this calm water that Paul and Antoinette were betrothed a score or so of years ago."

Then he spoke of the delightful scene which he had witnessed beside that pond on the occasion of his first visit to La Guerdache—the invasion of the park by three youngsters of the streets, Nanet bringing his companions, Lucien and Antoinette Bonnaire, through a gap in the hedge in order that they might play beside the pond; then Lucien's ingenious invention, the little boat which travelled all alone over the water; and the arrival of the three little *bourgeois*, Paul Boisgelin, Nise Delaveau, and Louise Mazelle, who all marvelled at the boat, and immediately made friends with the intruders. And couples had been formed quite naturally, there had been betrothals at once, Paul with Antoinette, Nise with Nanet, Louise with Lucien, amidst the smiling complicity of kind-hearted Nature, the eternal mother.

"Don't you remember it?" asked Luc gaily.

The young couple, who joined in his laughter, declared that he went back too far. "If I was only four years old," said Antoinette, who felt highly amused, "my memory could not have been a very strong one."

But Paul, gazing fixedly into the past, was making an effort to recall the scene. "I was seven," said he. "Wait a moment! It seems to me that I vaguely remember—the little boat had to be brought back with a pole whenever its wheels ceased turning; and then one of the little girls narrowly missed falling into the pond; and afterwards the intruders, the little bandits, ran away on seeing some people approach."

"That was it!" cried Luc. "Ah! so you remember! Well, for my part, I remember that day experiencing a quiver of hope in the future, for that scene in some measure suggested the reconciliation which was to come. Childhood in its naïve fraternity was at work here, taking a first step towards justice and peace. And whatever fresh happiness you may bring about, you know, will be yet increased by that little gentleman yonder."

He pointed to the baby, little Ludovic, now lying in the arms of Suzanne, who felt so happy at being a grandmother. She, on her side, jestingly retorted: "For the time being he is very good, because he is asleep. Later on, my dear Luc, we will marry him to one of your granddaughters, and in that manner the reconciliation will be complete, all the combatants of yesterday will be united and pacified in the persons of their descendants. Are you willing? Shall we have the betrothal to-day?"

"Am I willing? Certainly I am! Our great-grandchildren will push on our work hand in hand."

Paul and Antoinette felt moved, and kissed one another, whilst Boisgelin, who was not listening, looked round the park, his former estate, in a mournful manner, though without any bitterness, to such a degree indeed had the new world upset and stupefied him. And then they all resumed their walk along the shady paths, Luc and Suzanne silently exchanging smiles which told their joy.

When they all came back to the house they paused for a moment before it, to the left of the steps, under the windows of the very room where Monsieur Jérôme had died. From that point one perceived—between the crests of the great trees—the distant roofs of Beauclair, and then La Crêcherie and the Abyss. They gazed upon that spreading panorama in silence. They could plainly distinguish the Abyss, now built afresh on the same plan as La Crêcherie, and forming with it one sole city of work—work, reorganised and ennobled, transformed into man's pride, health, and gaiety. More justice and more love were born there every morning. And the waves of little smiling houses, set in greenery, those waves which the anxious Delaveau had seen always advancing, had flowed over the once black land without a halt, ever enlarging the future city. They now occupied the whole expanse from the ridge of the Bleuse Mountains to the Mionne, and they would soon cross the narrow torrent, to sweep away Old Beauclair, that sordid agglomeration of the hovels of servitude and agony. And as they advanced they built up stone by stone—under the fraternal sun, even to the verge of the fertile fields of La Roumagne—the city where all at last would be freedom, justice, and happiness.

II

Whilst evolution was carrying Beauclair towards its new destiny, love, young, gay, and victorious, asserted itself, and on all sides there came frequent marriages, drawing various classes together and hastening the advent of harmony and final peace. Love the victorious overthrew all obstacles, triumphed over the greatest resistance with a passion full of happy vitality, an explosion of joy which proclaimed in the broad sunlight what happiness there was in being, in loving, in creating yet more and more.

Luc and Josine had set the example. During the last ten years a family of three boys and two girls had sprung up around them. Hilaire, the eldest, born before the collapse of the Abyss, was already eleven. Then, at intervals of two years, had come the others: Charles, who was now nine years old; Thérèse, who was seven; Pauline, who was five; and Jules, who was three. To the old pavilion another structure had been added, and there these children romped, filling the place with gaiety and hope, and growing up for future unions. As Luc, in delight, often said to the smiling Josine, the constancy of their affection sprang largely from that triumphant fruitfulness. In Josine, the *amorosa* had now largely given way to the mother; yet she and Luc were still lovers, for love does not age, it remains the eternal flame, the immortal brazier whence the life of the world derives its being. Never had a home resounded with brighter gaiety than theirs, full as it was of children and flowers. And they loved one another so well there, that misfortune passed them by. Whenever any recollection of the dolorous past returned, when Josine recalled her sufferings and the downfall in which she would have perished had it not been for Luc's helping hand, she flung her arms around his neck in a transport of inexhaustible gratitude, whilst he, full of emotion, felt that the iniquitous opprobrium from which he had saved her rendered her all the dearer to him.

Nanet, little Nanet, who was now becoming a man, lodged with Luc, beside his "big sister," as he still called Josine. Gifted with keen intelligence and an enterprising bravery which was ever on the alert, the young fellow captivated Luc, whose dearest pupil he became, a youthful disciple full of the master's lessons. And meantime, at the Jordans', whose house was so near to Luc's, Nise, little Nise, was likewise growing up in the affectionate charge of Sœurette, who had given her a home on the morrow of the destruction of the Abyss, happy in being able to adopt the young girl, in whom she found a charming companion and assistant. And it followed that Nanet and Nise, seeing one another every day, ended by living solely one for the other. As a matter of fact, did not their betrothal date from infancy, from the distant days when child-love, divine ingenuousness, had filled them with a craving to be together, impelling them to brave all punishments and even to scale walls in order to meet? They had been fair and curly like little lambs in those days, and how silvery had seemed their laughter when at each meeting they embraced, knowing nothing of what parted them socially, she the *bourgeoise* by birth, the master's daughter, and he the urchin of the streets, the penniless son of a wretched manual worker. Then had come the frightful tempest of flames, Nise saved by Nanet, to whose neck she had clung, both of them covered with burns, and at one moment in danger of death. And to-day also they were both fair and curly, they gave vent to the same light laughter as in childhood, and displayed a similarity of demeanour as if one matched the other. But Nise had now become a big girl, Nanet a big youth, and they adored one another.

The idyll lasted for nearly seven years longer, whilst Luc was making a man of Nanet, and Sœurette was helping Nise to grow up in kindliness and beauty. Nise had been thirteen years of age at the time of the terrible death of her father and mother, whose remains had been reduced to ashes, in such wise that nothing of them was found under the remnants of the burnt house. For long years the girl shuddered at the recollection of that night. There was no reason to hurry her marriage; so far as that was concerned, indeed, her friends wished to wait until she should be twenty in order that she herself might come to a free and sensible decision. Besides, Nanet himself was very young, her elder by scarcely three years, and still an apprentice. With their gay playful natures, moreover, simply intent as they were on making merry together, they themselves were in no hurry. They met every evening, and found a simple enjoyment in telling one another what they had done during the day. They would often sit hand in hand, and when they parted for the night they exchanged an affectionate kiss. But amidst their cordial agreement there were at times some little quarrels. Nanet occasionally found Nise too proud and wilful; she put on her princess's airs, as he was wont to remark. Again, he sometimes thought her too coquettish, too fond of fine attire and of the *fêtes* at which she displayed it. Of course it was not forbidden to appear beautiful—on the contrary; but it was not right to spoil one's beauty by assuming an air of contempt for others. At first Nise, in whom reappeared some little of her mother's passion for enjoyment and her father's despotic disposition, grew angry when she was reproved, and endeavoured to demonstrate that she was perfection itself. But as she worshipped Nanet she ended by confiding in him, listening to him, and striving to please him by becoming the best and gentlest of little women. And when, as sometimes happened, she did not succeed in this, she remarked with a laugh that if she should ever have a daughter the latter would no doubt be much better than herself, because it was necessary that the blood of the princes of this world should have time to become democratised among a more brotherly line of descendants.

The wedding at last took place, when Nise was twenty and Nanet twenty-three years old. It had long been wished for, foreseen, and awaited. For seven years not a day had elapsed without a step towards this *dénouement* of the long and happy idyll. And as this marriage of Delaveau's daughter with the brother of Josine, who was now to all intents and purposes Luc's wife, extinguished all hatred, and sealed a pact of alliance, there was a desire that it should be made a festival celebrating forgiveness of the past and the new community's radiant entry into the future. With this object it was decided that there should be singing and dancing on the very site of the Abyss, in one of the halls now erected there as an adjunct to La Crêcherie, which at present spread over acres and acres of ground, and ever and ever grew.

Luc and Sœurette were the organisers and masters of the ceremonies of this marriage festival, as well as the witnesses of the bridal pair, Luc being witness for Nanet, and Sœurette for Nise. They wished to impart to the festival all the splendour of a triumph, to endow it with the gaiety of hope's fulfilment, to make it like the very victory of the city of work and peace, now founded and prosperous. It is good that communities should indulge in great rejoicings; public life needs frequent days of beauty, joy, and exultation. Thus Luc and Sœurette chose the great foundry hall, where so many of the monster-like hammers, the gigantic rolling bridges, the movable cranes of prodigious strength were gathered together. The new buildings, all bricks and steelwork, were clean and healthy, and full of joyous brightness with their large windows through which streamed both air and sunlight. And the plant was left in position, especially as, for a festival of triumphant work, one could not have devised any better decorations than were provided by those gigantic appliances, whose powerful forms were instinct with a sovereign beauty compounded of logic, strength, and certainty. However, they were decorated with foliage and crowned with flowers, even as were altars in ancient times. The brick walls, too, were ornamented with garlands of verdure, and the very pavement was strewn with roses and broom flowers. The whole seemed like the blossoming of man's effort to attain happiness, an effort which had ended by flowering there, scattering perfume around the toil of the worker, a toil once unjust and hard, but now attractive and leading solely to happiness.

Two processions set forth, one from the home of the bridegroom, the other from that of the bride. On his side Luc, followed by his wife Josine and their children, brought the hero Nanet; on hers, Sœurette, with her brother Jordan, brought their adopted daughter, the heroine Nise. The whole population of the new city, where all work was stopped in token of rejoicing, lined the road to acclaim the bridal pair. The beautiful sun shone out, the gay houses were decked with bright colours, the greenery was full of flowers and birds. And in the rear of either *cortège* followed the crowd of workers, a vast concourse of joyous people who gradually invaded the great halls of the works, which were as lofty and as broad as the naves of the old-time cathedrals. The foundry hall, whither the bridal couple repaired, was soon crowded to excess in spite of its immensity. In addition to Luc, his family, and the Jordans, there were the Boisgelins with Paul, who at that time had not yet married Antoinette, for their wedding was only to take place four years later. Then came the Bonnaires, the Bourrons, even the Fauchards, indeed, all those whose arms had contributed to the victory of work. Those men of good will and faith, those workers of the first days, had increased and multiplied. Was not the throng of comrades around them an enlargement of their families, an assemblage of brothers whose numbers still increased daily? There were five thousand of them, and soon there would be ten. They would increase to a hundred thousand, to a million, and would at last absorb all mankind.

The ceremony, in the midst of the powerful machinery decked with flowers and garlands of verdure, was one of sovereign and touching simplicity.

With smiling mien Luc and Sœurette placed Nanet's and Nise's hands one in the other.

"Love one another with all your hearts," they said to them, "and have handsome children who will love one another as you yourselves will be loved."

The crowd raised acclamations, and shouted the word "Love!" For it was King Love who alone could render work fruitful, by making the race ever more and more numerous, and inflaming it with desire, the eternal source of life.

But in all this there was already too much solemnity for Nanet and Nise, who had loved one another so playfully ever since childhood. Although those two little curly lambs had grown up, they remained like toys in their festival raiment, both clad in white, charming and delightful. And they were not content with a ceremonious hand-shake. They fell upon each other's neck.

"Ah! my little Nise, how happy I am to have you for my wife at last, after waiting for you for years and years!"

"Ah! my little Nanet, how happy I am to belong to you, for it is quite true, you have earned it!"

"And little Nise, do you remember when I pulled you up by the arms to help you over the walls, and when I carried you pick-a-back, and played at being a rearing horse?"

"And little Nanet, do you remember when we played at hide-and-seek, and you ended by finding me among the rosebushes, so well hidden there that it was enough to make me die of laughing?"

"Little Nise, little Nise, we'll love each other as we played, very heartily, with all, all the strength of health and gaiety."

"Little Nanet, little Nanet, we played so much, and we will love one another so much, that we shall love yet again in our children, and play again even with our children's children."

And they embraced, and laughed, and played together, raised to the highest felicity. The throng, filled with enthusiasm by the sight, traversed by a wave of sonorous gaiety, clapped hands and acclaimed love, almighty love, which without cessation creates more and more life and happiness. Then the singing began, chorus singing, in which the aged sang their well-earned rest, the men the triumph of their toil, the women the helpful sweetness of their love, the children the confident cheerfulness of their hopes. Afterwards came the dances, with a great final round and chain, which brought all that brotherly little people hand in hand, stretching out and revolving for hours to the strains of gay music, through the halls of the huge works. They had formerly toiled so much and suffered so much in the dirty, grimy, unhealthy inferno which had stood there, and which the flames had swept away. The sunshine, the air, and life, now entered freely. And the marriage *ronde* still came and went around the huge appliances, the colossal presses, the formidable steam hammers, the gigantic planing-machines, which wore a smiling aspect beneath their adornments of flowers and foliage, whilst the young married couple led the dance, as if in them rested the soul of all those things, that morrow of increase in equity and fraternity, which the victory of their long affection had ensured.

Luc was preparing a surprise for Jordan, for he also wished to celebrate the labour of the scientist whose endeavours would contribute more than a hundred years of politics could have done to the happiness of the city. When the night had fallen and it was quite dark, the whole works suddenly glowed, thousands of lamps casting the gay light of day-time over the place. Jordan's researches, it should be said, had at last yielded fruit. After many defeats he had devised a system for the transport of electrical force without loss, employing new appliances, ingenious means of transmission. Henceforth the cost of conveying coal was saved, it was burnt at the pit's mouth, and the machinery which transformed calorical into electrical energy sent it to La Crêcherie by special cables, which allowed of no loss on the way, in such wise that the cost price was now only half of what it had formerly been. This then was a first great victory, La Crêcherie profusely illumined, power distributed abundantly among both the large and the small appliances, comfort increased, work facilitated, and fortune augmented. And at the same time it was virtually a fresh step towards happiness.

When Jordan, on beholding the festive illumination, understood Luc's affectionate intention, he began to laugh like a child.

"Ah! my friend, so you give me a bouquet too! As a matter of fact, I rather deserve it, for as you must remember I had been striving to solve the problem for ten long years! What obstacles, what defeats did I not encounter when I imagined success to be a certainty! But, no matter, I set to work afresh on the morrow, on the ruins of all the experiments that had failed. A man always ends by succeeding when he works."

Luc was laughing with his friend, whose courage and faith he shared.

"I know that very well," said he in reply; "you are the living proof of it. I know no greater, loftier master of energy than you, and I have tried to follow your example. Well, so night is now vanquished, you have put darkness to flight, and as electricity at present costs so little, we shall be able to light up a planet above La Crêcherie, to replace the sun as soon as evening comes. And you have also wrought economy in human toil, for, thanks to the abundance of mechanical power yielded by your system, one man now suffices for work in which two had to be employed. Thus we acclaim you as the master of light and warmth and power."

Jordan, wrapped in a rug which Sœurette, fearing the coolness of the evening, had thrown over his shoulders, was still looking at the huge pile around him, now sparkling like a palace of fairyland. Short and puny, with a pale face and the feeble air of one who is on the point of dying, he strolled about those glowing halls, examining them curiously, for during the last ten years he had scarcely stirred from his laboratory. Thus he marvelled at the results already obtained, the success of a work of which he had been both the least known and the most active artisan.

"Yes, yes," he muttered, "the result is very good already, no little ground has been gained. We are advancing, the future we dreamt of is nearer to us. And I owe you my apologies, my dear Luc, for I did not hide from you at the outset that I scarcely believed in the success of your mission. But you still have a great deal to accomplish, and for my part, alas! I have done next to nothing by the side of all that I should like to do."

He became grave and thoughtful. "Though we have reduced the cost of electricity by one half, it still remains too high," he said; "and, besides, all the intricate and expensive installations at the mouths of the pits, the steam engines and the boilers, without mentioning the miles of cables which have to be kept in repair, are barbarous, and consume time and money. Something else is needed, something more practical, simple, and direct. I know very well in what direction I ought to look, but such a search seems madness, and I don't dare to tell people what work I have undertaken, for I myself can't describe it clearly. Yet yes, one ought to suppress the engine and the boiler, which are cumbersome intermediaries between the coal extracted and the electricity which is produced. In a word, one ought to be able to transform the calorical energy contained in the coal into electrical energy, without having to bring mechanical energy into play. I don't yet know how that is to be done, but I have set to work, and I hope to succeed. And if I do, you'll then see that electricity will cost scarcely anything. We shall be able to give it to everybody, spread it broadcast, and make it the victorious agent of universal comfort."

He grew more and more enthusiastic, drawing himself up with passionate gestures as he spoke, he who as a rule remained so silent and thoughtful.

"The day must come," he resumed, "when electricity will belong to everybody, like the water of the rivers and the breezes of the heavens. It will be necessary to give it abundantly to one and all, and to allow men to dispose of it as they choose. It must circulate in our towns like the very blood of social life. In each house one must merely have to turn on a switch or a tap to obtain a profusion of power, heat, and light. At night-time, in the black sky, electricity will set another sun, which will extinguish the stars. And it will suppress winter, it will bring eternal summer into being, warming the old earth, and ascending to melt the snow even among the clouds. This is why I am not particularly proud of what I have done as yet, for it is very little by the side of all that has to be accomplished."

And with an air of quiet disdain he concluded: "I can't even get a practical result from my electrical furnaces. They are still mere experimental furnaces. Electricity is still too costly—one must wait till its employment proves remunerative, and for that to be it should not cost us more than the waters of the rivers and the atmosphere of the heavens. When I am able to give it in a flood without counting, my furnaces will revolutionise metallurgy. Oh! I well know the only path to follow, and I have already set to work!"

The night festival was a marvellous one. The dancing and singing had begun afresh in the dazzling halls, where the throng continued celebrating the marriage until the time came to escort Nanet and Nise to their nuptial home, amidst acclamations in honour of the love which had united them.

About this time love likewise revolutionised the *bourgeoisie* of Beauclair, and it was in the home of the Mazelles, those idlers living on their income, that the tempest first burst forth. Their daughter Louise had always surprised and upset them, so different was her nature from their own. An extremely active and enterprising girl, she was ever at work in the house, declaring that idleness would kill her. Her parents, who placed their great delight in doing nothing, could not understand how it was that she spoilt her days by useless agitation. She was an only child, said they, and would have a very fine fortune invested in State Rentes, and so was she not unreasonable in refusing to shut herself up in her cosy nook, well sheltered from the worries of life? They, her parents, were content with their egotistical happiness, and why therefore did she trouble about the passing beggar, the ideas which were changing the world, the incidents which disturbed the streets? But whatever might be said, she remained all of a quiver, full of life, taking a passionate interest in everything; and thus, amidst her parents' deep love for her, there was a great deal of stupefaction at having a daughter so utterly unlike themselves. At last she utterly upset them by a *coup de passion*, at which they had at first simply shrugged their shoulders, thinking it some mere fancy or whim. But things soon came to such a climax that they almost believed the end of the world to be at hand.

Louise Mazelle had remained a great friend of Nise Delaveau, whom she had frequently met at the home of the Boisgelins, since the latter had been installed at La Crêcherie. There also she had again met Lucien Bonnaire, her former playmate, now a tall and handsome fellow of twenty-three, whilst she herself was twenty. Lucien no longer made little boats which travelled by themselves over the water, but under Luc's guidance he had become a very intelligent and inventive mechanician, destined to render great services to La Crêcherie, where he already fitted up the machinery. He was not a "monsieur," he took a sort of courageous pride in remaining a simple workman, like his father, whom he revered. And no doubt, in the ardent love with which Louise was inspired for him, there was some little of the natural rebellion which urged her on to flout *bourgeois* notions, and to behave differently from the folk of her sphere. At all events her old friendship for Lucien became a passionate love that chafed at obstacles. He, touched by the keen attachment of that pretty, active, smiling girl, ended by loving her quite as deeply; but he was certainly the more reasonable of the two, and desired to hurt nobody's feelings. He suffered at the idea that she was too refined and too rich for him, and simply spoke of remaining a bachelor if he could not have her; whereas she, at the mere thought of opposition to their marriage, became wildly rebellious, and talked of throwing up position and fortune to go and live with him.

During nearly six months the battle went on. Lucien's parents looked on the proposed marriage with covert distrust. Bonnaire, with his common sense, would much have preferred to see his son marry some mate's daughter. Time had already done its work, and there was no reason to be proud of seeing one's son rise to another class, on the arm of a daughter of the expiring *bourgeoisie*. All the profit of such an alliance would soon be on the side of the *bourgeoisie* itself, which would intermarry with the people in order to regain blood and health and strength. Quarrels on the subject of the match at last broke out in Bonnaire's household. His wife, the proud and terrible Toupe, would doubtless have consented to it, on condition that she also became a lady, with fine gowns and jewels to wear. Nought of the evolution now in progress around her had lessened her craving for domination and display. She retained her hateful disposition even in her present easy circumstances, often reproaching her husband for not having made a big fortune like Monsieur Mazelle, an artful fellow, who had done no work for years past. However, when she heard Lucien declare that even if he should marry Louise, not a copper of the Mazelles' money should ever enter his home, she quite lost her head, and in her turn opposed the match, since it would not bring her any profit.

One evening there was a stormy explanation between La Toupe, Bonnaire, and Lucien, in the presence of Daddy Lunot, who was still alive, and more than seventy years old. They had just finished dining in the bright, clean dining-room, whose window opened on to the garden greenery. There were even flowers on the table, where nowadays food was always plentiful. Daddy Lunot, who at present had as much tobacco as he cared for, had just lighted his pipe, when La Toupe, for the mere pleasure of getting into a temper, according to her old habit, turned to Lucien and said to him sourly: "So it's decided, eh—you still mean to marry that *demoiselle*? I saw you with her again this morning at Boisgelin's door. It seems to me that if you cared anything for us you might have ceased meeting her, since you know that both your father and myself are by no means over-pleased with the idea of that marriage."

Lucien, like a good son, avoided argument, particularly as he knew it to be useless. Turning towards Bonnaire, he simply said: "But I think that my father is ready to consent."

To La Toupe this was like a whip-stroke, which urged her upon her husband: "What!" she exclaimed. "You give your consent without warning me of it? You told me less than a fortnight ago that such a marriage wasn't reasonable to your thinking, and that you would have fears for our lad's happiness if he were so foolish as to make it! So you turn about like a weather-cock, eh?"

Bonnaire quietly began to explain things: "I should have preferred to see the lad make another choice, but he's nearly four-and-twenty, and I'm not going to force my will on him in a matter which concerns his own heart. He knows what I think, and he'll do what he thinks best."

"Ah!" shouted back La Toupe, "you're easily got over; you fancy yourself a free man, but you always end by saying the same as the others. During the twenty years that you've been here with Monsieur Luc you've repeated that his ideas and yours are not the same, and that he ought to have begun by seizing the instruments of work without accepting money from the *bourgeois*. But all the same, you give way to Monsieur Luc's wishes, and to-day, perhaps, you begin to like what you've done together."

She rattled on, striving to hurt her husband's feelings and pride. She had often exasperated him by trying to prove that his actions were in contradiction with his principles. This time, however, he simply shrugged his shoulders. "There's no doubt that what we've done together is very good," said he. "I may still regret that Monsieur Luc did not follow my ideas; only you ought to be the last to complain of what exists here, for we know nothing more of want, we are happy, happier than any one of those *bourgeois* whom you dream about."

This reply irritated her the more. "As for what exists here, it would be kind of you to explain it to me, for I've never understood anything of it, you know," she said. "If you are happy, so much the better for you; but I'm not happy, no, I'm not. Happiness is when one has plenty of money and can retire and do nothing afterwards. All your rigmarole, your division of profits, your stores where one gets things cheaply, your coupons and your cash-desks, will never put a hundred thousand francs into my pocket so that I may spend them as I please, on things which I like—I am an unhappy woman, a very unhappy woman!"

She was exaggerating things with the desire to make herself disagreeable, yet there was truth in what she said. She had never grown accustomed to La Crêcherie, she suffered there like a coquettish, extravagant woman, whose instincts were wounded by Communistic solidarity. A clean and active housewife, but of a quarrelsome, stubborn, dull-witted nature, she continued making her home a hell, when it should have been full of comfort.

Bonnaire at last lost his patience so far as to say to her: "You are mad; it is you who make yourself unhappy and us too!"

Thereupon she began to sob. Lucien, who felt very embarrassed whenever such disputes arose between his parents, had to emerge from his silence and kiss her and tell her that he loved and respected her. Nevertheless she clung to her views, and shouted to her husband, "Ah! just ask my father what he thinks of your factory in which everybody has a share, and that wonderful justice and happiness of yours, which are to regenerate the world. He's an old workman, he is! You won't accuse him of saying foolish things like a woman. And he's seventy years old, so you can believe in his experience and sense!"

Turning to Daddy Lunot, who was sucking the stem of his pipe, with the blissful expression of a child, she went on: "Isn't that so, father? Aren't they idiots with all their inventions to do without masters, and won't they end by making their own fingers smart?"

The old man looked at her in his bewildered way before answering in a husky voice: "Of course—the Ragus and the Qurignons, ah! they were comrades once upon a time. There was Monsieur Michel, who was five years my senior. As for me, it was under Monsieur Jérôme that I entered the works. But before the others there was Monsieur Blaise, with whom my father, Jean Ragu, and my grandfather, Pierre Ragu worked. Pierre Ragu and Blaise Qurignon were mates together, two wire-drawers, who used the same anvil. And now you see the Qurignons are masters and great millionaires, and the Ragus have remained poor devils as they were before. Things can't change, and so one must believe that they are well as they are."

He rambled slightly in the somnolence that had come over him, as over some very old, maimed, and forgotten beast of burden, who by a miracle had escaped the universal slaughterhouse. There were often days when he failed to remember what had happened on the previous one.

"But Daddy Lunot," said Bonnaire, "it so happens that things have changed a good deal for some time past. Monsieur Jérôme, whom you speak of, has long since been dead, and he gave back all that remained of his fortune."

"Gave back—how's that?"

"Yes, he gave back to his old comrades the wealth which he owed to their toil and suffering. Don't you remember? it occurred a long time ago already."

The old man searched in his dim memory. "Ah! Yes, yes, I recollect—a funny business it was! Well, if he gave his money back he was a fool."

The words were spoken sharply and contemptuously, for Daddy Lunot had never dreamt of anything but making a big fortune like the Qurignons, in order to enjoy life like a master, an idle gentleman, who amused himself from morning till night. That had remained his ideal, even as it was that of the whole generation of broken-down, exploited slaves, whoso sole regret was that they had not been born among the exploiters.

La Toupe burst into an insulting laugh. "You see!" she cried, "Father isn't such a fool as you others are; he's not the man to start on a wild-goose chase! Money's money; and when a man's rich he's the master!"

Bonnaire shrugged his broad shoulders, whilst Lucien gazed in silence through the window at the roses in the garden. What was the use of arguing? She represented the stubborn past, she would pass away in the Communist paradise, in the midst of fraternal happiness, denying its very existence and regretting the days of wretchedness when she had been obliged to save up ten sous one by one in order to buy herself a strip of ribbon.

Just then, however, Babette Bourron came in. Unlike La Toupe, she was ever gay, ever delighted with her new position. By her smiling and comforting optimism she had helped to save her simpleton of a husband from the pit into which Ragu had fallen. She had invariably shown confidence in the future, feeling certain that things would eventually turn out all right. And she often jestingly remarked that La Crêcherie, where work had become light, cleanly, and pleasant, where one and all lived amidst comforts formerly reserved to the *bourgeois* alone, was like a fulfilment of her dreams of Paradise. Her doll-like face remained fresh-looking under her carelessly twisted hair, and radiant with the delight she felt at finding her husband cured of his passion for drink, and at living in a gay house of her own with two handsome children whom she would soon be marrying off.

"Well, so it's decided, eh?" she exclaimed. "Lucien is going to marry Louise Mazelle, that charming little *bourgeoise* who isn't ashamed of us?"

"Who told you that?" roughly asked La Toupe.

"Why, Madame Luc, Josine, whom I met this morning."

La Toupe turned white with restrained wrath. Amidst her ceaseless irritation with La Crêcherie there was a great deal of hatred against Josine, whom she had never forgiven for having become the wife and helpmate of Luc, that hero whom all admired, and for having, moreover, a number of handsome children, who were now growing up for lives of happiness. Could she not remember the days when that wretched creature had been turned starving into the streets by her brother? Yet now she met her wearing a bonnet like a lady. That was a crushing blow. She would never be able to stomach the idea of that creature being happy.

"Josine," she roughly exclaimed, "would do better to make people forget what she calls her own marriage before meddling with marriages which don't concern her. And as for me, you do nothing but aggravate me, so just let me be!"

Then she rushed out of the room, banging the door behind her, and leaving the others in silent embarrassment. Babette was the first to laugh, accustomed as she was to the manners of her friend, whom she indulgently pronounced to be a good woman, though a wrong-headed one. Tears, however, had risen to the eyes of Lucien, for it was his future life that was at stake amidst all that quarrelling. His father pressed his hand in a friendly way, as if to promise that he would arrange matters. None the less Bonnaire himself remained very sad, quite upset at finding happiness at the mercy of family jars. Would a spiteful temper always suffice then to spoil the fruits of brotherliness? he wondered. Daddy Lunot alone retained his blissful unconsciousness, sitting there half asleep, with his pipe in his mouth.

If Lucien entertained no doubt of the eventual consent of his parents, Louise felt the resistance of hers increasing, and thus the battle became fiercer every day. The Mazelles adored their daughter, and it was in the name of this adoration that they refused to give way to her. There were no violent explanations between them, but they persevered in a kind of good-natured inertia, by which they fancied that the girl's patience would be tired out. In vain did she fill the house with the incessant rustling of her skirts, play feverishly on the piano, fling flowers out of the window, though they were by no means faded, and give many other signs of perturbation. They still peacefully smiled at her, made a pretence of understanding nothing, and strove to glut her with dainties and presents. She was enraged at being thus overwhelmed with douceurs when she was denied the one thing which would have pleased her; and at last she made up her mind to fall ill. She took to her bed, turned her face to the wall, and refused to answer her parents when they questioned her. Novarre, on being summoned, declared that such ailments did not come within the scope of his profession. The only way to cure girls who fell love-sick was to allow them to love as they desired. Thereupon the Mazelles, quite distracted, realising that the matter was becoming a serious one, held counsel together as to whether they ought to give way. They spent a whole night talking it over, and it seemed such a serious business, the consequences of which might be so great, that they lacked the courage to come to a decision between themselves. They

ÉMILE ZOLA

resolved to bring their friends together in order to submit the matter to them. In the revolutionary state of affairs with which Beauclair was struggling, would it not be desertion on their part to give their daughter to a workman? They felt that such a union would be decisive, a final abdication on the part of the *bourgeoisie*, the mercantile and propertied folk. And it was therefore natural that the authorities, the leaders of the wealthy governing classes, should be consulted. Thus, one fine afternoon, they invited Sub-Prefect Châtelard, Mayor Gourier, Judge Gaume, and Abbé Marle to take tea with them in their flowery garden, where they had spent so many idle days, stretched face to face in large rocking chairs, and gazing at their roses, without even tiring themselves by talking.

"You see," said Mazelle to his wife, "we will do what those gentlemen advise. They know more about such matters than we do, and nobody will be able to blame us for following their counsel. For my part I am quite losing my head, for all this business tortures my brain from morning till night."

"It's like me," said Madame Mazelle. "It isn't living to be obliged to keep on thinking and thinking. Nothing could be worse for my complaint, I'm sure of it."

The tea was served in an arbour of greenery in the garden one beautiful, sunshiny afternoon. Sub-Prefect Châtelard and Mayor Gourier were the first to arrive. They had remained inseparable, linked it seemed even more closely together since the death of Madame Gourier, the beautiful Léonore, who, during her last five years had remained an invalid in an arm-chair, afflicted with paralysis of the legs, but most devotedly nursed, her lover taking her husband's place to watch over her and read to her whenever the other was obliged to absent himself. It was, indeed, in Châtelard's arms that Léonore had suddenly expired one evening while he was helping her to drink a cupful of lime-water, whilst Gourier was outside smoking a cigar. When he came in again, the two men wept together for the dear departed. And nowadays they were inseparable, their duties leaving them plenty of leisure, for it was only in a theoretical kind of way that they now governed the town, the sub-prefect having prevailed on the mayor to follow his example, and let things take their own course, rather than spoil his life by trying to oppose the evolution, the progress of which nobody in the world could have prevented. Nevertheless, Gourier, who often felt afraid of the future, had some difficulty in taking this philosophical course.

He had become reconciled to his son Achille, whom Ma-Bleue had presented with a very charming daughter, Léonie, who had the eyes of her beautiful mother, big blue eyes suggesting some large blue lake, some vast stretch of blue sky. Nearly twenty years of age at present, fit to be married, Léonie had captivated her grandfather. And he had resigned himself to opening his door to her parents, that son who had formerly rebelled against his authority, and that Ma-Bleue, of whom he still occasionally spoke as a savage. As he himself expressed it, it was hard for him, a mayor, the celebrant of lawful marriage, to receive at his fireside a couple of revolutionaries, who had simply espoused one another under the stars one warm summer's night. But the times were so strange, such extraordinary things happened, that a charming granddaughter become a very acceptable present, even although she were the offspring of impenitent free love. Châtelard had gaily insisted on reconciliation; and Gourier, since his son had been bringing Léonie to see him, had been more and more won over to the cause of La Crêcherie, though, to his thinking, it had hitherto remained a source of catastrophes.

Judge Gaume and Abbé Marle were late in arriving that day at the Mazelles', but the latter could not refrain from explaining their position to the sub-prefect and the mayor. Ought they to resign themselves to their daughter's unreasonable whim?

"As you will certainly understand, Monsieur le Sous-Préfet," said Mazelle in an anxious but pompous manner, "apart from the grief which such a marriage would cause us, we have to consider the deplorable effect which it would have socially, and our heavy responsibility towards distinguished persons of our class. We really seem to be going towards some abyss."

They were seated in the warm shade, perfumed by the climbing roses, at a table with gay-coloured napery, on which stood several dishes of little cakes; and Châtelard, still a well-groomed, fine-looking man in spite of his years, smiled in a discreetly ironical manner. "We are already in the abyss, dear Monsieur Mazelle," he replied. "It would be very wrong of you to put yourself out about the Government, the authorities, or even fine society, for only a semblance of these things now exists. I am still sub-prefect and my friend Gourier is still mayor, no doubt. Only we are scarcely more than shadows, and there is no longer any real, substantial State behind us. And it is the same with the powerful and the wealthy, a little of whose power and wealth is carried off each succeeding day by the new organisation of work. So don't take the trouble to defend them, particularly as they themselves, yielding to vertigo, are now becoming active artisans of the revolution. Don't resist then, yield to the current!"

He was fond of that style of jesting, which terrified the last *bourgeois* of Beauclair. Moreover, it was an amiable and jocular way of telling the truth, for he indeed felt convinced that the old world was done for, and that a new one was springing from the ruins. Most serious events were taking place in Paris, the ancient edifice was falling stone by stone, giving place to a provisional structure, in which one could already plainly detect the outlines of the future city of justice and peace.

But the Mazelles had turned pale. Whilst the wife sank back in her armchair with her eyes fixed on the little cakes, the husband exclaimed: "Really! do you think us threatened to such a point as that? I know very well that people think of reducing the interest on Rentes."

"Rentes," said Châtelard quietly, "they will be suppressed before another twenty years have gone by; or, rather, some plan will be found for dispossessing the *rentiers* by degrees. A scheme to that effect is already being studied."

Madame Mazelle heaved such a desperate sigh that one might have imagined she was giving up the ghost. "Oh, I hope we shall be dead by then!" said she; "I hope that we shan't have the grief of witnessing such infamy! But our poor daughter will suffer by it, and that is an additional reason for compelling her to make a good marriage."

But Châtelard pitilessly went on: "Why, good marriages are no longer possible, since the right of inheritance is about to disappear. That is virtually resolved upon. In future each married couple will have to work out its own happiness. And whether your daughter Louise marries a *bourgeois'* son or a workman's son, the capital of the newly-wedded pair will soon be identical—so much love, if they are lucky enough to love one another, and so much activity if they are intelligent enough not to be idlers."

Deep silence fell, and one could hear the faint whirr of a warbler's wings, as it flew about among the roses.

"And so," Mazelle, who was overwhelmed, ended by asking, "that is the advice you give us, Monsieur le Sous-Préfet? According to you, we can accept that Lucien Bonnaire as our son-in-law, eh?"

"Oh, *mon Dieu*, yes! The world will none the less continue peacefully revolving. And as the two children are so fond of one another, it is at least certain that you will make them happy."

Gourier had hitherto said nothing. He felt ill at ease at being called upon to decide such a question—he, whose son had gone off to live with Ma-Bleue, that wild girl of the rocks, whom he now received in his highly respectable middle-class home. At last an avowal of his embarrassment escaped him: "That's true; the best thing after all is to marry them. When their parents don't marry them the young people take themselves off and get married as they fancy. Ah! in what times are we living!"

He raised his arms towards heaven, and Châtelard had to exercise all his influence to prevent him from falling into black melancholy. Gourier's old age—following on a somewhat dissolute life—was full of stupor; he constantly fell asleep, at table, in the midst of conversation, even whilst walking out of doors. With the resigned air of a once terrible employer of labour, whom facts had vanquished, he ended by saying: "Well, what else can be expected? After us the deluge, as many of our class now say. We are done for."

It was at this moment that Judge Gaume arrived, much behind his time. Nowadays his legs swelled, and it was only with difficulty that he could walk, helping himself along with a stick. He was nearly seventy, and was awaiting his pension, full of secret disgust for that human justice which he had administered during so many years, contenting himself the while with strictly applying the written law, like a priest who no longer believes, but is sustained solely by dogma. In his home, however, the drama of love and betrayal which had wrecked his life had pursued its course, stubbornly and pitilessly. The disaster, which had begun with the suicide of his wife, had been completed by his daughter Lucile, who had caused her husband, Captain Jollivet, to be killed in a murderous duel by one of her lovers, with whom she had afterwards eloped. The police were seeking her, and Gaume now lived alone with her one child, André, a delicate, affectionate youth of sixteen, over whom he watched with anxious affection. Sufficient misfortune had fallen, he felt; avenging destiny, punishing some old unknown crime, must go no further. Yet he still wondered to what good power, what future of true justice and faithful love he might guide that youth in order that his race might be renewed and at last win happiness.

On being questioned by Mazelle respecting the advisability of a marriage between Louise and Lucien Bonnaire, Judge Gaume immediately exclaimed: "Marry them, marry them—particularly if they feel for one another such great love as to enter into contest with their parents and to pass over all obstacles. Love alone decides happiness."

Then he regretted, like an avowal, that cry which the bitterness of his whole life had wrung from him, for he was intent on preserving during his last days his wonted mendacious rigidity of demeanour, his austerity and coldness of countenance. "Do not wait for Abbé Marle," he resumed. "I met him just now, and he begged me to apologise to you. He was hastening to the church for the holy vessels, in order to take extreme unction to old Madame Jollivet, an aunt of my son-in-law's, who is in the last pangs. Poor Abbé, in her he is losing one of his last penitents; he had his eyes full of tears."

"Oh! the fact that the clergy is being swept away is the one good feature of what is happening!" exclaimed Gourier, who had remained a devourer of priests. "The republic would still be ours if the clergy had not tried to take it from us. It was they who urged the people on to upset everything and become the masters."

But Châtelard remarked compassionately: "Poor Abbé Marle! it grieves me to see him in his empty church. You do quite right, Madame Mazelle, in still sending him some bouquets for the Virgin."

Silence fell again, and the tragic shadow of the priest seemed to flit by in the bright sunlight amidst the perfume of the roses. In Léonore he had lost his dearest and most faithful parishioner. Madame Mazelle doubtless remained to him, but she was not really a believer; all that she sought in religion was something ornamental—a kind of certificate that she was a right-minded *bourgeois*. And the Abbé was not ignorant of his destiny—he would some day be found dead at his altar under the remnants of his church, which threatened ruin, but which, for lack of money, he could not repair. Neither at the sub-prefecture nor at the town-hall was there any fund left for such work. He had appealed to the faithful, and in response had with difficulty obtained a ridiculously small sum of money. And now he was resigned to his fate; he awaited the fall, still celebrating the offices as if he were unaware of the threat of annihilation hanging above his head. His church was becoming emptier and emptier, dying a little more each day, and he would die also when the old structure cracked around him and fell crushing him beneath the weight of the great crucifix, which still hung from the wall. And they would have one and the same grave: the earth whither all returns.

As it happened Madame Mazelle was far too much upset by her personal worries to take any interest at that moment in the dolorous fate of Abbé Marle. If there should not be a prompt solution with respect to the marriage, she feared that she might fall seriously ill—she who had derived so many hours of nursing and petting from the malady without a name with which she had embellished her existence. All her guests having now arrived, she quitted her armchair to serve the tea, which steamed in the cups of bright porcelain, whilst a sunray gilded the little cakes lying in the crystal dishes. And she went on shaking her big, placid head, for she was not yet convinced: "You may say what you like, my friends, but that marriage would really be the last blow, and I cannot make up my mind to it."

"We will wait," declared Mazelle; "we will exhaust Louise's patience."

But all at once both husband and wife were thunderstruck, for Louise herself stood before them among the sunlit roses at the entrance of the arbour. They had fancied her in her room, on her couch, suffering from that love-sickness which, according to Doctor Novarre, contentment alone could cure. No doubt she had guessed that the others were deciding her fate, and with her beautiful black hair just caught up in a knot, wearing a dressing-gown with a pattern of little red flowers, she had come down in all haste. Quivering with the passion that animated her, she looked charming with her somewhat obliquely-set eyes gleaming in her slender face. Not even grief could entirely extinguish their gay sparkle. She had heard the last words spoken by her parents. "Ah, mamma! ah, papa! what was that you were saying?" she cried. "Do you imagine that some merely childish caprice is in question? I've told you already, and I tell you again, I wish Lucien to be my husband, and so he shall!"

Although half-conquered by the sudden apparition of his daughter, Mazelle still tried to struggle against the inevitable. "But just think of it, you unhappy child! Our fortune, which you were to have inherited, is already in jeopardy, so it is quite possible that one of these days you will find yourself without a penny," he said.

"Just understand the situation," remarked Madame Mazelle in her turn. "With our money, even though it is in danger, you might still make a sensible marriage."

Then Louise exploded with superb, joyous vehemence, "Your money! I do not care a pin for it I You can keep it! If you were to give it me Lucien would no longer take me as his wife. Money, indeed! what should I do with it? Money! of what use is it? It does not help one to love and be happy. Lucien will earn my bread for me, and I'll earn it too if necessary. It will be delightful."

She cried these things aloud with such strength of youth and hope that the Mazelles, fearing for her reason, were anxious to quiet her by at last yielding to her desires. Besides, they were not people to continue battling; they wished to end their days in peace. As for Sub-Prefect Châtelard, Mayor Gourier, and Judge Gaume, whilst drinking their tea they smiled with some embarrassment, for they felt the girl's free love sweeping them away like bits of straw. One must needs consent to what one cannot prevent.

It was Châtelard who summed up everything in his amiable, bantering way, the irony of which was scarcely perceptible. "Our friend Gourier is right—we are done for, since it is our children who make the laws now."

The marriage of Lucien Bonnaire and Louise Mazelle took place a month later. Châtelard for his personal amusement prevailed on his friend Gourier to give a grand ball at the town-hall on the wedding night, as if by way of honouring their friends the Mazelles. At heart he thought it a good joke to make the *bourgeoisie* of Beauclair dance at this wedding, which became a symbol of the multitude's accession to power. They would dance on the ruins of authority in that town-hall which was gradually becoming the real common-house, where the mayor was no longer anything but a link between the various social groups. The hall was most luxuriously decorated, and there was music and singing as at the wedding of Nanet and Nise. And acclamations once more arose at the sight of the bridal pair, Lucien, so strong and sturdy, followed by all his mates of La Crêcherie, and Louise, so slim and passionate, followed by all the fine society of the town, whose presence had been desired by her parents as a kind of supreme protest. Only it came to pass that the fine folk were swamped by the multitude, won over to the rush of delight, carried away and conquered to such a point that a great many more marriages between the lads and girls of the different classes ensued. Once more, then, love triumphed, all-powerful love which inflames the living universe, and bears it onward to its happy destiny.

Youth flowered on all sides, other alliances were concluded, couples which everything seemed to separate set out together for the future city of happiness. The old trading class of Beauclair, now on the point of disappearing, gave its daughters and sons to the artisans of La Crêcherie and the peasants of Les Combettes. The Laboques set the example by allowing their son Auguste to marry Marthe Bourron, and their daughter Eulalie to marry Arsène Lenfant. They had ceased struggling for some years already, for they realised that the trade of old times, the useless cogwheel which had consumed so much energy and wealth, was vanquished and dying. At the outset they had been obliged to allow their shop of the Rue de Brias to be turned into a mere *dépôt* of the articles manufactured at La Crêcherie and the other syndicated factories. Then, taking a further step, they had consented to close the shop, which had been merged into the general stores, where Luc's indulgence had procured them an inspectorship by way of occupation. And now old age had come, and they lived in retirement, full of bitterness, and scared by the sight of that new world which evinced none of their own passion for lucre. The new generations had grown up for other forms of activity and delight than moneymaking. And thus their children, Auguste and Eulalie, yielding to love, the great artisan of harmony and peace, married as they pleased, encountering no obstacle on their parents' side save the covert disapproval of old folk who regret the past. It was arranged that the two weddings should be celebrated on the same day at Les Combettes, now a large township, a very suburb of Beauclair, with large bright buildings redolent of the inexhaustible wealth of the earth. And the weddings took place at harvest-time—indeed, on the very last day of the harvesting, when huge ricks already arose upon every side over the great golden plain.

Feuillat, the former farmer of La Guerdache, had already married his son Léon to Eugénie, daughter of Yvonnot, the assessor, whom he had formerly reconciled with Feuillat, the mayor—that reconciliation whence had sprung the good agreement of all the inhabitants of the place, and that impulse to combine together which had made the wretched village, consumed by hatred, a fraternal and flourishing town. Nowadays Feuillat, who was very aged, had become like the patriarch of that agricultural society, for it was he who had dreamt of it, secretly sought to establish it, in former days, when combating the deadly tenant-farming system, and foreseeing what incalculable wealth the tillers of the soil might draw from it when they should agree together to love it like men of science and method. A true love for that soil which for centuries had been exhausting his ancestors, seemed to have sufficed to enlighten that simple farmer, who originally had been a hard-headed and rapacious man like all of his class. He had perceived in what direction lay salvation, peace among all the peasants, a combination of efforts, the earth becoming once more the sole mother, ploughed, sown, and cropped by one family. And he had beheld the fulfilment of his dream, he had seen his neighbours' fields joined together, the farm of La Guerdache merged into the parish of Les Combettes, other smaller villages joined thereto, a vast estate created, and set on the march for the conquest, by successive annexation, of the whole of the vast plain of La Roumagne. Feuillat, who had remained the soul of the association, formed with Lenfant and Yvonnot, its founders, a kind of "Conseil des Anciens," who were consulted on all things, and whose advice was always found profitable.

Thus, when the wedding of Lenfant's son Arsène with Eulalie Laboque was decided upon, and the latter's brother Auguste determined to celebrate his marriage with Marthe Bourron at the same time, it occurred to Feuillat, whose idea was accepted and acclaimed by all, to organise a great *fête* which should be like the festival of the pacification and triumph of Les Combettes. They would drink to fraternity between the peasant and the industrial worker, formerly so bitterly opposed to one another, but whose alliance alone could establish social wealth and peace. They would drink also to the end of all antagonism, to the disappearance of that barbarous thing called trade which had perpetuated a hateful struggle between the dealer who sold a tool, the peasant who made corn grow, and the baker who sold bread, at a price increased by the thefts of a number of intermediaries. And what better day could be chosen to celebrate the reconciliation than that when the enemies of former days, the castes which had seemed bent on devouring and destroying one another, ended by exchanging their lads and girls, consenting to marriages which would hasten the advent of the future! Thus it was decided that the *fête* should take place in a large field near the town, a field where lofty ricks, golden under the bright sun, arose like the symmetrically disposed columns of some gigantic temple. The colonnade stretched indeed to the very horizon; other ricks and other ricks arose, proclaiming the inexhaustible fruitfulness of the soil. And it was there that they sang, that they danced, amidst the pleasant odour of the ripe corn, amidst the great fertile plain, whence the work of man, now at last reconciled, drew bread enough for the happiness of all.

The Laboques brought in their train all the former tradesmen of Beauclair, whilst the Bourrons brought the whole of La Crêcherie. The Lenfants were there, at home, and never yet had folk fraternised so fully, the groups fast mingling and uniting in one sole family. The Laboques, no doubt, remained grave and somewhat embarrassed, but the Lenfants made merry with all their hearts, whilst the great sight of all was

Babette Bourron, whose everlasting good humour, her certainty, even amidst the greatest worries, that things would turn out well at last, now proved triumphant. She personified hope, marching radiant behind the two bridal couples; and when these arrived—Marthe Bourron on the arm of Auguste Laboque, Eulalie Laboque on the arm of Arsène Lenfant—they brought with them such a blaze of youth and strength and delight, that endless acclamations rolled from one to the other end of the stubbles. The onlookers called to them affectionately, they were loved, they were praised because they indeed personified sovereign and victorious love, that love which had already drawn all those folk together, by giving them those overflowing harvests amidst which they would henceforth swarm like a free and united people, ignorant alike of hatred and of want.

That same day other marriages were decided upon, as had already happened at the wedding of Lucien Bonnaire and Louise Mazelle. Madame Mitaine, the former bakeress, who had remained for everybody the "beautiful Madame Mitaine," in spite of her sixty-five years, kissed Olympe Lenfant, sister to one of the bridegrooms, and told her that she would be happy to call her "daughter," for her son Évariste had confessed that he adored her. The beautiful bakeress's husband had been dead for ten years, and her establishment had been merged into the general stores of La Crêcherie, as was the case with most of the retail businesses of the town. She lived like a retired worker with her son Évariste, both very proud of the fact that Luc had given them the charge of the electrical kneading appliances, which yielded an abundance of white light bread. Whilst Évariste in his turn was bestowing a betrothal kiss on Olympe, who had turned pink with pleasure, Madame Mitaine suddenly recognised in a thin, dark little woman seated beside a rick, her old neighbour, Madame Dacheux, the butcher's wife. She thereupon went and sat down beside her. "Must it not all finish in weddings," she asked gaily, "since all these young folk were ever playing together?"

Madame Dacheux, however, remained silent and gloomy. She also had lost her husband, who had died from the effects of a badly aimed blow with his chopper, which had struck off his right hand. According to some folk, clumsiness had nothing to do with it, the butcher having voluntarily cut off his hand in a fit of furious anger, rather than sign a transfer of his shop to La Crêcherie. Decent occurrences, and the idea that holy meat, the meat of the wealthy, was now being placed within the reach of all and appearing at the tables of the poorest, must have maddened that violent, reactionary, and tyrannical man. He had died from the effects of gangrene improperly treated, leaving his wife in a state of terror from the oaths which he had heaped upon her during his final agony.

"And your Julienne, how is she?" Madame Mitaine inquired in her amiable way. "I met her the other day. She looked superb."

The butcher's widow was at last obliged to answer. Pointing to a couple figuring in one of the quadrille sets, she said: "She's dancing yonder. I'm watching her."

Julienne indeed was dancing on the arm of a tall, good-looking fellow, Louis Fauchard, the son of the former drawer. Sturdy of build, white of skin, her whole face beaming with health, Julienne evidently enjoyed the embrace of that vigorous yet gentle-looking youth, who was one of the best smiths of La Crêcherie.

"Oh! does that mean another marriage, then?" asked Madame Mitaine, laughing.

But Madame Dacheux shuddered and protested: "Oh! no, no! How can you say such a thing? You know what my husband's ideas were. He would rise from his tomb if I let our daughter marry that workman, the son of that wretched Mélanie, who was always trying to get a bit of soup-beef on credit, and whom he drove out of our shop so often because she never paid!"

In a low and tremulous voice the butcher's widow went on to relate what a torturing life she led. Her husband appeared to her at night-time. Although he was dead he still made her bow beneath his despotic authority, tormenting her, upbraiding her, frightening her with devilish threats in her dreams. The poor, scared, insignificant woman was so unlucky that even widowhood had not brought her peace.

"If I were to let Julienne marry contrary to his wishes," she concluded, "he would certainly come back every night to beat me!"

She was shedding tears now, and Madame Mitaine strove to comfort her, assuring her that she would soon get rid of her nightmares if she would only set a little happiness around her. Just then, as it happened, Mélanie, the ever-complaining Madame Fauchard, whom for years one had seen perpetually running about to procure the four quarts of wine which her husband required for his shift, drew near with a hesitating step. She no longer suffered from want. She occupied one of the bright little houses of La Crêcherie with Fauchard, who, infirm and stupefied, had now ceased all work. Lodging with her, moreover, was her brother Fortuné, now forty-five years of age, and already an old man, half-blind, and deaf, owing to the brutish, mechanical, uniform toil to which he had been condemned at the Abyss from his fifteenth year onward. Thus, in spite of the comforts which La Fauchard owed to the new pension and mutual relief system, she had remained a complaining creature, a wretched waif of the past, with two old children on her hands. Therein lay a lesson, an example of the shame and grief which the wage-system had brought with it.

"Have you seen my men?" she asked Madame Mitaine, referring to her husband and brother. "I lost them in the crowd. Oh! there they are!"

With halting gait, arm-in-arm, by way of propping up each other, the brothers-in-law passed by—Fauchard, wrecked and done for, suggesting some ghost of the painful toil of the past; and Fortuné, looking less aged but quite as downcast, stricken seemingly with imbecility. Through all the sturdy crowd, overflowing with new life and hope amidst the sweet-smelling ricks, in which was piled the corn of a whole community, the two unfortunate men strolled hither and thither, freely displaying their decrepitude, understanding nothing of what went on around them, and not even acknowledging the salutations of acquaintances.

"Leave them in the sunshine—it does them good," resumed Madame Mitaine, addressing La Fauchard. "Your son is sturdy and gay enough!"

"That's true; Louis has the best of health," the other replied. "The sons are not much like the fathers, now that the times have changed. Just see how he dances! He will never know cold and hunger."

Thereupon Madame Mitaine, in her good-natured way, resolved to promote the happiness of the young couple who were smiling at each other so lovingly whilst they danced before her. She brought the two mothers, Madame Fauchard and Madame Dacheux, together, and made them sit down side by side, and then she moved the butcher's widow and convinced her that she ought to consent to her daughter's marriage. It was solitude that made the poor old creature suffer; she needed grandchildren to climb up on her knees and put all troublesome phantoms to flight.

"Ah, *mon Dieu!*" she ended by exclaiming, "I'm agreeable all the same, on condition that I'm not left alone. I myself never said no to anybody. It was *he* who wouldn't have it. But if you all wish it, and promise to defend me, then do, do as you like."

ÉMILE ZOLA

When Louis and Julienne learnt that their mothers consented to their wedding, they hastened to them and fell in their arms with tears and laughter. And thus amidst the general joy fresh joy was born.

"How could you think of parting these young people?" Madame Mitaine repeated; "they seem to have grown up one for the other. I've given my Évariste to Olympe Lenfant, whom I remember as quite a little girl, when she used to come to my shop and my boy gave her cakes. It's the same with Louis Fauchard. How many times have I not seen him prowling near your shop, Madame Dacheux, and playing with your Julienne! The Laboques, the Bourrons, the Lenfants and the Yvonnots, whose marriages are now being celebrated, why, they all grew up together, at the very time when their parents were attacking one another, and now you see their harvest time has come."

She laughed yet more loudly as she recalled the past, while an expression of infinite kindness spread over her face. And joy was rising around her. People came to say that other betrothals had just taken place—that of Sébastien Bourron with Agathe Fauchard, and that of Nicolas Yvonnot with Zoé Bonnaire. Love, sovereign love, was incessantly perfecting the reconciliation, blending all classes together. And the *fête* lasted until night-time, until the stars came out, whilst love thus triumphed, bringing heart nearer to heart and merging one into another, amidst the dances and songs of those joyous people marching towards future unity and harmony.

Amidst the growing fraternity, however, there was one man, one of the old ones, Master-smelter Morfain, who remained apart from all the rest, mute and wild, unable and unwilling to understand. He still dwelt, like one of the prehistoric Vulcans, in the rocky cavity near the smeltery under his charge, and now he was quite alone there, like a *solitaire* who had broken off all intercourse with the rising generations. When his daughter Ma-Bleue had gone off to realise her dream of love with Achille Gourier, the Prince Charming of her blue nights, Morfain had already felt that the new times were robbing him of the best part of himself. Then another love affair had carried away his son Petit-Da, that tall young fellow who had become so passionately enamoured of Honorine, a quick, alert little brunette, daughter of Caffiaux, the grocer and taverner. Morfain had at first peremptorily refused to consent to their marriage, full of contempt as he was for that shady family of poisoners, the Caffiaux, who on their side returned his disdain with interest, and in their vanity were by no means inclined to allow their daughter to marry a worker. Nevertheless, Caffiaux was the first to give way, for he was of a supple and crafty nature. After closing his tavern he had secured a very comfortable post as chief guardian at the general stores of La Crêcherie, and the nasty stories once told of him were being forgotten; whilst for his part he feigned too much devotion to the principles of solidarity to cling obstinately to a decision which might have harmed him. Thus Petit-Da, carried away by his passion, took no further notice of his father's opposition, and the result was that a terrible quarrel, a frightful rupture, between the two men ensued. From that time forward the master-smelter no longer spoke, save to direct the furnace work, but shut himself up in his cavern like some fierce and motionless spectre of the dead ages.

Though years and years went by Morfain did not appear to age. He was always the same old-time conqueror of fire, a colossus with a huge head, a nose like an eagle's beak, and flaming eyes set between cheeks which a flow of lava seemed to have ravaged. His twisted lips, now seldom parted, retained their tawny redness suggestive of burns. And it seemed as if no human considerations would again weigh with him in the depths of the implacable solitude in which he had shut himself on perceiving that his daughter and his son had joined the party of to-morrow. Ma-Bleue had presented Achille with a sweet little girl, Léonie, who was growing up all grace and tenderness. And Petit-Da's wife, Honorine, had given birth to a strong and charming boy, Raymond, now an intelligent young man who would soon be old enough to marry. But the children's grandfather did not soften—he repulsed them, shrank even from seeing them.

On the other hand, however, amidst the collapse of his affection for his kin, the species of paternal passion which he had always evinced for his furnace seemed to increase. That growling monster ever afire, whose flaming digestion he controlled both day and night, was seemingly regarded by him as some child. The slightest disturbance in its work threw him into anguish; he spent sleepless nights in watching over the working of the twyers, displaying all the devotion of a young lover amidst the embers whose heat his skin no longer feared. Luc, rendered anxious by Morfain's great age, had spoken of pensioning him off, but renounced the idea at the sight of the quivering rebellion, the inconsolable grief which was displayed by that hero of toil, who was so proud of having exhausted, consumed his muscles in pursuing the conquest of fire. However, the hour for retirement would come forcibly from the inevitable march of progress, and Luc indulgently decided to wait awhile.

Morfain had already felt that he was threatened. He was aware of the researches which Jordan was making with the view of replacing the old, slow, barbarous smeltery by batteries of electrical furnaces. The idea that one might extinguish and demolish the giant pile which flamed during seven and eight years at a stretch, quite distracted the master-smelter, and he became seriously alarmed when Jordan effected a first improvement by burning coal at the mouth of the pit from which it was extracted, and bringing electricity without loss to La Crêcherie by cable. However, as the cost price still remained too high for electricity to be employed for smelting ore, Morfain was able to rejoice over the futility of Jordan's victory. During the ensuing ten years each fresh defeat which fell on Jordan delighted him. He indulged in covert irony, feeling convinced that fire would never suffer itself to be conquered by that strange new power, that mysterious thunder, whose flashes were not even visible. He longed for his master's defeat, the annihilation of the new appliances which were ever being constructed and improved. But all at once the position became very threatening, a rumour spread that Jordan had at last completed his great work, having discovered a means of transforming calorical energy direct into electrical energy, without the help of mechanical energy being required. That is, the steam engine, that cumbersome and costly intermediary, was suppressed. And in thiswise the problem was solved, the cost of electricity would be lowered by one-half, and it would be possible to employ it for the smelting of ore. A first battery of electrical furnaces was indeed already being fitted up, and Morfain, full of despair, prowled fiercely around his blast-furnace, as if anxious to defend it.

Luc did not immediately give orders for its demolition. He wished first of all to make some conclusive experiments with the battery. Thus, during a period of six months, the work went on in both forms, and the old smelter spent some abominable days, for he now realised that the well-loved monster in his charge was condemned. He saw it forsaken now, nobody came up the hill to see it, whereas the inquisitive thronged around those electrical furnaces below, which occupied such little space, and did their work, it was said, so well and so speedily. Morfain, for his part, full of rancour, never went down to see them, but spoke of them disdainfully as of toys for children. Was it possible that the ancient method of smelting which had given man the empire of the world could be dethroned? No, no, one would have to revert to those giant furnaces which had burnt for centuries without ever being extinguished! And, alone with the few men under his orders, who remained silent like himself, Morfain looked down contemptuously on the shed in which the electrical furnaces were working, and still felt happy at night-time, when he was able to set the horizon all aglow with a "run" of dazzling metal.

But the day at last came when Luc passed sentence on the blast-furnace, whose work was now shown to be both slower and more costly than the other. Thus it was decided that following upon a final run it should be allowed to go out, after which it might be demolished. Morfain, on being warned of this, did not answer, but remained impassive, his bronze countenance revealing nothing of the tempest in his soul. His calmness frightened people; Ma-Bleue came up to see him, accompanied by her daughter Léonie, and Petit-Da, moved by the same affectionate impulse, brought his son Raymond. For a moment the family found itself assembled, as in former days, in the rocky hillside cavern, and the old man allowed himself to be kissed and caressed, without repulsing his grandchildren as he had usually done. Still he did not return their caresses, but seemed far away, like one who belonged to a past period, one in whom no human feeling was left. It was a cold and gloomy autumn day, and the crapelike veil of the early twilight was falling from a livid sky over the dark earth. At last Morfain arose and broke the silence, saying, "Well, they are waiting for me, there is yet another run."

It was the last. They all followed him to the blast-furnace. The men under his orders were present, already shadowy in the increasing gloom, and once again, for the last time, the usual work was accomplished. A bar was thrust into the plug of refractory clay, the hole was enlarged, and finally the tumultuous flood of fusing metal poured forth, a stream of flames rolling along the channels in the sand and filling the moulds with blazing pools. And once again, too, from those tracks and fields of fire arose a harvest of sparks, blue sparks of delicate ethereality, and golden fusees delightfully refined, a florescence of cornflowers, as it were, amidst golden ears of wheat. And a blinding glow burst on the mournful twilight, illumining the furnace, the neighbouring buildings, the distant roofs of Beauclair, and the whole of the great horizon. Then everything disappeared, deep night reigned all around; the end had come, the furnace's life was over.

Morfain, who without a word had stood looking at it all, remained there in the gloom motionless like one of the neighbouring rocks which the shades of night again enveloped.

"Father," said Ma-Bleue gently, "now that there is no more work to be done here, you must come down to us. Your room has long been ready for you."

And Petit-Da in his turn exclaimed: "Father, you've certainly got to rest now. There is a room for you in my place too. You must let each of us have you in turn, you must live sometimes with one and sometimes with the other."

But the old master-smelter did not immediately answer. A great sigh made his breast heave dolorously. At last he said: "That's it, I'll go down, I'll have a look. But you can go away now."

For another fifteen days it was impossible to induce Morfain to quit the furnace. He watched it cooling, as one watches beside a death-bed. Every evening he felt it in order to make sure that it was not quite dead. And as long as he found a little warmth remaining, he lingered obstinately beside it as if it were a friend whose remains it would be wrong to abandon. But at last the demolishers arrived, and then one morning the grand old vanquished man was seen to descend from his cavern to La Crêcherie, where he repaired with a still firm step to the large glazed shed in which the battery of electrical furnaces was working.

As it happened, both Jordan and Luc were there with Petit-Da, whom they had appointed to direct the smelting in conjunction with his son Raymond, the latter already being a good electrician. The work was being brought to greater precision day by day; and Jordan scarcely quitted the shed, eager as he was to perfect the new method which had cost him so many years of study and experiment.

"Ah! Morfain, my old friend!" he exclaimed joyously. "So you've become sensible!"

The other's face, the colour of old iron, remained impassive, and he contented himself with replying: "Yes, Monsieur Jordan, I wanted to see your machine."

Luc, however, scrutinised him rather anxiously. He had given orders to have him watched, for he had learnt that he had been found leaning over the mouth of the blast furnace, when the latter was still full of glowing embers, like a man preparing to fling himself into that frightful hell. One of the smelters under his orders, however, had saved him from that death which he had contemplated, perchance as a last gift of his scorched frame to the monster, as though indeed he set his pride in dying by fire, after loving and serving it so faithfully for more than half a century.

"It is pleasant to find you still inquisitive at your age, my good Morfain," said Luc, without taking his eyes from him. "Now, just examine these toys."

The battery stretched out before them, showing ten furnaces, ten cubes of red brick-work over six feet high and nearly five feet long. And above them one only saw the powerful electrodes, thick cylinders of carbon, to which the electric cables were attached. The operations were very simple. An endless screw, worked by a switch, served the ten furnaces, bringing the ore and discharging it into them. A second switch set up the current, the arc whose extraordinary temperature of two thousand degrees sufficed to melt almost four hundredweight of metal in five minutes. And it was only necessary to turn a third switch for the platinum door of each oven to rise up and for a kind of rolling way, lined with fine sand, to start off on the march and receive the ten pigs, each of four hundredweight, and carry them into the cool air outside.

"Well, my good Morfain," asked Jordan with the gaiety of a happy child, "what do you think of it?"

Then he told him of the output. Those toys, each yielding four hundredweight of metal every five minutes, could turn out altogether a total of two hundred and forty tons daily, if they were allowed to work ten hours at a stretch. This was a prodigious output when one considered that the old blast-furnace, burning day and night alike, could not supply one-third of the quantity. As a matter of fact the electrical furnaces were seldom kept working more than three or four hours, and the advantage was that they could be lighted and extinguished as one pleased, in accordance with one's needs, whatever quantity of raw material that was required being immediately obtained. And how easily they worked, and what cleanliness and simplicity there was! As the electrodes themselves supplied the carbon necessary for the carburisation of the ore, there was little dust. The gases alone escaped, and the quantity of slag was so small that a daily cleaning sufficed to get rid of it. There was no longer any need of a barbarous colossus whose digestion caused disquietude, nor of any of the numerous and cumbersome appendages, the purifiers, the heaters, the blast machinery, and the constant current of water, with which it had been necessary to surround it. There was no longer any fear of stoppages or cooling down, nor any talk of demolishing or emptying the monster whilst still ablaze, because a twyer simply went wrong. Loaders watching at the mouth, and smelters piercing the plug and broiling in the flames of the "runs" were no longer required to be on the alert, following one another incessantly with day and night shifts. The battery of the ten electrical furnaces, extending over a surface under fifty feet in length and some sixteen feet in width, was at its ease in the large, bright, glazed shed which sheltered it. And three children would have sufficed to set everything going, one at the switch of the endless screw, a second at the switch of the electrodes, and a third at that of the rolling way.

"What do you think of it? What do you think of it, my good Morfain?" repeated Jordan triumphantly.

The old master-smelter still looked at the furnaces without moving or speaking. Night was already at hand, shadows were filling the shed, and the working of the battery, with its gentle mechanical regularity, was quite impressive. Cold and dim, the ten furnaces seemed to slumber, whilst the little cars of ore, moved by the endless screw, were emptied one by one. Then every five minutes the platinum doors opened, the ten white jets of the ten "runs" blazed upon the gloom, and the ten pigs, flowery with cornflowers amidst ears of wheat, slowly and continuously journeyed off on the rolling way.

However, Petit-Da, who hitherto had remained silent, wished to give some explanations, and pointing to the thick cable which, descending from the rafters, brought the current to the furnaces, he said, "You see, father, the electricity comes along that cable, and such is its force that if the wires were severed everything would be blown up!"

Luc, whom Morfain's calmness had reassured, began to laugh. "Don't say that," he exclaimed, "you would frighten our young people. Nothing would be blown up. Only the imprudent man who touched the wires would be in danger. Besides, the cable is a strong one."

"Yes, that's true," Petit-Da resumed; "a strong wrist would be needed to break it."

Morfain, still impassive, drew near. To reach the cable he simply had to raise his hands. However, for a moment longer he remained there motionless, nothing on his scorched face revealing what his thoughts might be. But all at once such a flame shot from his eyes that Luc again felt anxious, as if with a vague presentiment of a catastrophe.

"A strong wrist, you say?" Morfain at last exclaimed, making up his mind to speak. "Just let us see, my lad."

And before the others had time to intervene he caught hold of the cable with his hands, hardened by fire and as strong as iron pincers. And he bent the cable and broke it, even as an irritated giant might break the string of some child's toy. And lightning came, the wires met, and a mighty dazzling flash burst forth. Then the whole shed was plunged into darkness, amidst which one heard nought but the fall of that tall, lightning-stricken old man, who dropped, all of a piece, like an oak felled in the forest.

Lanterns had to be fetched. Jordan and Luc, utterly distracted, could only pronounce Morfain to be dead, whilst Petit-Da shrieked aloud and wept. Stretched upon his back, the old smelter did not appear to have suffered. He lay there like some colossal figure of old iron. However, his garments were smouldering, and the fire had to be put out. Doubtless he had been unwilling to survive the well-loved monster, that blast-furnace of which he had been the last fervent worshipper. With him had finished the first battle: man, the subduer of fire, the conqueror of metals, bending beneath the slavery of dolorous toil, and so proud of that long and overwhelming labour—the labour of humanity marching towards future happiness—as to make it a title of nobility. He had even shrunk from knowing that new times were born, bringing to each by the victory of a just apportionment of work, a little rest, a little gaiety, a little happy enjoyment, such as hitherto only a few privileged beings had tasted, deriving it from the iniquitous suffering of the greater number. And he had fallen like some fierce, obstinate hero of the ancient and terrible *corvée*, like a Vulcan chained to his forge, a blind enemy of all that would have freed him, setting his glory in his servitude, and regarding the possible diminution of suffering and effort as mere downfall. And the force of the new age, the lightning which he had come to deny and insult, had annihilated him. And now he slept.

Three years later three more marriages took place, still further blending the classes together and tightening the bonds of that fraternal and peaceful people which was ever and ever spreading. Hilaire Froment, the eldest son of Luc and Josine, a strong young man already twenty-six, espoused Colette, the daughter of Nanet and Nise, a delightful little blonde in all the flowery springtide of her eighteen summers. And the blood of the Delaveaus became calmer on mingling with that of the Froments and Josine, the erstwhile wretched wanderer, who had been picked up, half dead of starvation, almost on the threshold of the Abyss. Then yet another Froment, Thérèse, the third-born, a tall, gay, good-looking girl, became when seventeen the wife of Raymond, son of Petit-Da and Honorine Caffiaux, her senior by two years. And this time the blood of the Froments was allied with that of those epic toilers the Morfains and that of the Caffiaux, the representatives of the old trade system, which the advent of La Crêcherie had swept away. Finally Léonie, the amiable daughter of Achille Gourier and Ma-Bleue, married one of Bonnaire's sons, who was twenty, like herself. This was Séverin, Lucien's younger brother; and in this marriage the expiring *bourgeoisie* became united to the people, the resigned and mighty toilers of the dead ages, and the revolutionary workers who were attaining to freedom.

Great *fêtes* were given, for the happy descendants of Luc and Josine were about to increase and multiply, helping to people the new city which Luc had founded in order that Josine and all others might be saved from iniquitous want. The torrent of Love was flowing forth, life was incessantly spreading, doubling the harvests, ever creating more and more men for increase of truth and increase of justice. Love the victorious, young and gay, bore couples, and families, and the whole town towards final harmony and happiness. Each marriage led to the building of another little house among the greenery; and the march of those houses never ceased. Old Beauclair had long since been invaded and swept away. The ancient leprous district, the filthy hovels where labour had agonised for centuries, had been razed to the ground, over which now stretched broad roads planted with trees and edged with smiling dwellings. Even the *bourgeois* quarter of Beauclair was threatened; the piercing of new streets enabled one to enlarge and turn to other uses the old public edifices such as the sub-prefecture, the law courts, and the prison. The ancient church alone remained, cracking and crumbling in the centre of a small deserted square, which suggested a field of nettles and brambles. On all sides the old-time houses where people had lived cooped up in flats, had given place to healthier dwellings scattered through the huge garden, which Beauclair was becoming, each of them gay with light and with streaming water. And the city was founded, a very great and very glorious city, whose sunlit avenues ever stretched away, overflowing already into the neighbouring fields of the fertile Roumagne.

III

Ten more years went by, and love which had united so many couples, victorious and fruitful love, brought each household a florescence of children, a new growth going towards the future. At each fresh generation a little more truth, justice, and peace would spread and reign throughout the world.

Luc, who was already sixty-five years old, evinced, with increasing age, a livelier, a keener affection for children. Now that he saw his long-dreamt-of city in being, his mind went out to the rising generations. To them he gave all his time with the thought that the future rested with them. Ripe men, who have long lived amidst certain beliefs and habits, and who perchance are chained to the past by atavism, cannot be altered; whereas children may be influenced, freed from false ideas, helped to grow and progress, in accordance with the natural inclination towards evolution which is within them.

Thus, during the visits which on two mornings every week Luc continued to pay to his work, he devoted most of his attention and time to the schools and the *crèches* where the very little ones were kept. He began by inspecting them before proceeding to the workshops and the stores, and as he changed his visiting days every week, he generally took all the turbulent young people by surprise.

One Tuesday, a delightful morning in spring, he set out for the schools at about eight o'clock. The sunrays were scattering golden rain amidst the young greenery, and as Luc walked slowly down one of the avenues past the house where the Boisgelins resided, he heard a well-loved voice calling him. It was that of Suzanne, who, having seen him passing, had come to the garden-gate. "Oh! pray come in for a moment, my friend," said she. "The poor man has another attack, and I feel very anxious."

She was speaking of Boisgelin, her husband. As his idleness made him feel ill at ease in that busy hive, he had at one time tried to work, and Luc, at Suzanne's request, had given him a kind of inspectorship at the general stores. But the man who has never done anything, who has been an idler from birth, lacks will-power, and can no longer bend to rule or method. Thus Boisgelin soon found that he was incapable of following any continuous occupation. His mind fled, his limbs ceased to obey him, he became sleepy, overwhelmed. He suffered from his impotence and gradually relapsed into the emptiness of his former life, a succession of idle days, all spent in the most futile fashion. As there was no longer any round of pleasure and luxury to daze him he sank into increasing boredom, from which he could not be roused. He was spending his last years in a state of stupor, like a man who had fallen from another planet, amazed at the unexpected, extraordinary things which took place around him.

"Does he have any violent fits?" Luc inquired of Suzanne.

"Oh, no!" she replied. "He simply remains very sombre and suspicious; but my anxiety comes from his insane fancies having taken hold of him again."

It seemed indeed that Boisgelin's mind had been weakened by the idle life he led in that city of activity and work. From dawn till dusk he was to be seen wandering, like a pale, scared phantom, about the bustling streets, the buzzing schools, and the resounding workshops. He alone did nothing, whereas all the others busied themselves, overflowing with the delight and health which come from action. And, by degrees, as he found that he himself was the only one who did not work amidst that nation of workers, the insane idea seized upon him that he was the king, the master, and that this nation was a nation of slaves, working solely for his benefit, amassing incalculable wealth, which he would dispose of as he pleased for his sole enjoyment. Although olden society was crumbling to pieces, the capitalist idea had survived in him, and he remained the mad capitalist, the god-capitalist, who, possessing all the capital of the earth, had made all other men his slaves, the wretched artisans of his own egotistical happiness.

Luc found Boisgelin on the threshold of the house, dressed with all the care that he still evinced as regards his personal appearance. Even at seventy years of age he remained a vain-looking coxcomb, always well groomed, freshly shaved, and wearing that distinctive mark of conceit, a single eyeglass. His wavering glance and weak mouth alone revealed the collapse of his mind. At that moment he was about to go out, and a light cane was in his hand, and a shiny hat was tilted over his ear.

"What, already up! Already out and about!" exclaimed Luc, affecting a good-natured manner.

"Oh, it's necessary, my dear fellow," replied Boisgelin, after giving him a suspicious glance. "Everybody deceives me. How can I sleep in peace with all those millions which my money brings me in, and which this nation of workmen earns for me every day? I am obliged to see to things, for otherwise there would be a leakage of hundreds of thousands of francs every hour."

Suzanne made a sign of despair, then addressing Luc she said: "I was advising him not to go out to-day. What is the use of worrying like that."

But her husband silenced her: "It isn't merely to-day's money that worries me, there are all the sums piled up already—those milliards which fresh millions increase every evening. I quite lose myself among them; I no longer know how to live in the midst of such a colossal fortune. It is necessary that I should invest it, manage it, watch over it, in order to save myself from being robbed—is that not so? And, oh! it's hard work, terribly hard work, and makes me absolutely wretched—more wretched even than the poor who have neither fire nor bread."

His voice had begun to tremble dolorously, and big tears rolled down his cheeks. He looked a pitiable object, and, although he generally annoyed Luc, who regarded him as an anomaly in that industrious city, the other was now stirred to the depths of his heart. "Oh!" said he, "you can at least take a day's rest. I'm of your wife's opinion. If I were you I shouldn't go out to-day, I should stop in my garden and watch my flowers bloom."

But Boisgelin again scrutinised him and, as if yielding to a desire to confide in him, as in a safe friend, resumed: "No, no, it is indispensable that I should go out. What bothers me even more than exercising supervision over my men and my fortune, is that I don't even know where to put my money. Just think of it! there are milliards and milliards! They end by becoming an encumbrance—no rooms are built big enough to hold them. And so it has occurred to me to have a look round and try to find some pit which might be deep enough. Only, don't say a word of it; nobody ought even to suspect it."

Then as Luc, shuddering and terrified, turned towards Suzanne, who was very pale, and scarce able to restrain her tears, Boisgelin profited by the opportunity to slip out of the garden and go off. He could still walk rapidly, and, turning down the sunlit avenue, he speedily disappeared. Luc's first impulse was to run after him and bring him back by force.

"I assure you, my friend," he said to Suzanne, "that you act wrongly in letting him wander about; I can never meet him prowling around the schools or through the workshops and stores without fearing some disaster."

However, Suzanne strove to reassure him. "He is inoffensive, I am sure of it," she said. "True, I sometimes tremble for him, for he becomes so gloomy beneath the burden of all that imaginary money of his that a sudden impulse to have done with it all is to be feared. But how can I shut him up? He is only happy out of doors, and to place him in confinement would be useless cruelty, especially as he never even speaks to anybody, but remains as wild and as timid as a truant schoolboy."

Then the tears, which she had been restraining, flowed forth. "Ah! the unhappy man, he has caused me much suffering; but never before did I feel so grieved."

On learning that Luc was going to the schools Suzanne resolved to accompany him. She also had aged; she was sixty-eight already. But she had remained healthy and active, ever desirous of showing her interest in others, and helping on good work. And since she had been living at La Crêcherie, and had had nothing more to do for her son Paul, who was now married and the father of several children, she had created a larger family for herself by becoming a teacher of *solfeggio* and singing for some of the youngest pupils in the schools. This helped her to live happily. It delighted her to arouse the musical instinct in those little children. She herself was a good musician, but after all her ambition was not so much to impart exceptional science to them, as to render their singing natural, like that of the warblers of the woods. And she had obtained marvellous results—there was all the sonorous gaiety of an aviary in her class, and the young ones who left her hands afterwards filled the other classes, the workshops, and indeed the whole town, with perpetual mirthful melody.

"But you don't give your lesson to-day, do you?" Luc inquired.

"No, I only want to profit by the play-hour to make my little cherubs rehearse a chorus. But there are also some matters for me to consider with Sœurette and Josine."

The three women had become great, and indeed inseparable, friends. Sœurette had retained the management of the central *crèche*, where she watched over the very little ones—the children still in their cradles and those who could scarcely walk. As for Josine, she directed the needlework and household lessons, turning all the girls who passed through the schools into good wives and mothers, well able to manage their homes. In addition, the three friends formed together a kind of council which looked into all important questions concerning women in the new city.

Luc and Suzanne, following the avenue, at last reached the large square where the common-house arose, surrounded by green lawns decked with shrubs and flower-beds. The building was not the modest pile of earlier years; in its stead there had been erected a perfect palace, with a long polychromatic façade, in which decorated stoneware and painted faïence were blended with ironwork. In the large halls erected for meetings, theatrical performances, spectacular displays, and games, the people found themselves at their ease, at home as it were. They frequently fraternised at the festivities which were interspersed among the days of work. If the little houses, where each lived as he listed, were modest ones, the common-house, on the contrary, displayed dazzling luxury and beauty, such as was appropriate for the sovereign abode of the people-king. The common-house even tended to become a town in the town, so frequently was it enlarged in accordance with increasing needs. Other buildings, too, arose behind it—libraries, laboratories, and lecture-halls, which facilitated free study, research, experiment, and the diffusion of the acquired truths. There were also courts and covered buildings for athletic exercises, without mentioning some admirable free baths, flooded with the fresh and pure water captured on the slopes of the Bleuse Mountains, that water to whose inexhaustible abundance the city owed its cleanliness, health, and gaiety. But the schools especially had become a little world by themselves, occupying a number of buildings near the common-house, for several thousand children now studied in them. To avoid all unhealthy crowding numerous divisions had been arranged, each occupying its own pavilions, whose large bay windows overlooked spacious gardens. Thus the whole formed, as it were, a city of childhood and youth, in which one found children of all ages, from infants still in their cradles to big lads and lassies who were completing their apprenticeships after passing through the five classes in which education proper was imparted to them.

"Oh!" said Luc, with his kindly smile, "I always begin at the beginning; I always go first to see those little friends of mine who are still being suckled."

"Well, of course," replied Suzanne, smiling also. "I will go in with you."

In the first pavilion on the right-hand, amidst a garden planted with roses, Sœurette reigned over a hundred cradles and as many rolling-chairs. She also watched over some of the adjacent pavilions, but she invariably returned to this one, which sheltered three of Luc's granddaughters and one of his grandsons, of whom she was very fond. Luc and Josine, knowing how the city benefited by the rearing of the children together, had set an example in this respect, desiring that their own grandchildren should be brought up with those of others.

As it happened, Josine was in the pavilion with Sœurette that morning. The former was now fifty-eight, and the latter sixty-five years of age. But Josine retained her supple gracefulness and fair delicacy beneath her beautiful hair, whose golden hue had simply paled; whilst Sœurette, as often happens with plain, thin, dark women, did not appear to age, but seemed to acquire with advancing years a particular charm, derived from her active kindliness and persistent youth. Suzanne, now sixty-eight, was the elder of both of them; and all three surrounded Luc like a trio of faithful hearts, one the loving wife and the others devoted friends.

When Luc went in with Suzanne, Josine was holding on her knees a little boy scarcely two years old, whose right hand Sœurette was examining.

"Why, what is the matter with my little Olivier?" asked Luc, already feeling anxious. "Has he hurt himself?"

The little fellow was his last-born grandson, Olivier Froment, the child of his eldest son Hilaire, and of Colette, the daughter of Nanet and Nise.

"Oh!" replied Sœurette, "it is merely a splinter which must have come from the table of his chair. There, it's out now!"

The boy had raised a slight cry of pain and then had begun to laugh again; while a little girl, a four-year-old, who ran about in all freedom, hastened up with open arms as if to take hold of him and carry him off.

"Will you let him be, Mariette?" exclaimed Josine, full of alarm. "One must not turn one's little brother into a doll."

Mariette protested, declaring that she would be very good. And Josine, like a kind grandmother, already calmed, glanced at Luc, and the pair of them smiled, well pleased to see all those young folk who had sprung from their love around them. However, Suzanne was bringing them two other fair-headed little granddaughters, Hélène and Berthe, who were twins, in their fourth year. Their mother was Pauline, Luc's second daughter, now the wife of André Jollivet, who had been brought up by his grandfather Judge Gaume, after the captain's tragical death and Lucile's disappearance. Of their five children, Luc and Josine had already married three, Hilaire, Thérèse, and Pauline, whilst the two others, Charles and Jules, were as yet merely "engaged."

"And these darlings—you were forgetting them," said Suzanne gaily.

Hélène and Berthe, the twins, threw their arms around the neck of their grandfather, of whom they were extremely fond; Mariette also tried to climb upon his knees, whilst little Olivier thrust out his hands, which no longer hurt him, and frantically implored grandpapa to take him on his shoulders. Luc, half stifled by caresses, began to jest:

"That's it, my friend, you have now only to fetch Maurice, your nightingale as you call him. Then there would be five of them to devour me. Good heavens! what shall I do when there are dozens?"

Then, setting the twins and Mariette on the floor, he took hold of Olivier and threw him up into the air, at which the child raised cries of rapturous delight.

"Come, be reasonable, all of you," Luc resumed when he had set the boy on his chair again, "one can't be always playing, you know; I must attend to the others."

Guided by Sœurette and followed by Josine and Suzanne, he next went round the rooms. Those nurseries of the little folk were very charming with their white walls, their white cradles, their babes in white, a universal whiteness which seemed so gay in the sunshine which streamed through the lofty windows. Here also there was an abundance of water—one could feel its crystalline freshness, hear its murmur, as if indeed clear streams were flowing through the place, ensuring all the extreme cleanliness which was apparent on every side. Cries occasionally came from the cradles, but for the most part one only heard the pretty prattle, the silvery laughter of those who could already walk. Amongst them there was yet another little community, a silent community of toys, dolls, jumping-jacks, horses, and carts, all leading a naïve and comical existence. And these were the property of one and all, of both the boys and the girls who mingled like members of one sole family, growing up together from their cradles, and destined hereafter to live side by side, now as brothers and sisters, now as husbands and wives.

This practice of bringing up the children of both sexes together had already yielded good results. Among the young married couples Suzanne noticed a happy peacefulness, a closer blending of intelligence and sentiment, something resembling fraternity in love. And in the schools she observed that the presence of the sexes side by side aroused a new spirit of emulation, imparting gentleness to the boys, decision to the girls, and preparing both for a more perfect intermingling of natures, in such wise that they would become one joint spirit at the family hearth. Nothing of that which some had feared had taken place; on the contrary the moral level was higher than formerly, and it was wonderful to see those lads and girls seek the studies which might prove most useful to them, in accordance with the liberty which was granted to each pupil to work out his or her future in conformity with individual taste.

"They are virtually betrothed in their cradles," said Suzanne jestingly, "and divorce is done away with, for they know one another too well to select either wife or husband lightly. But come, my dear Luc, playtime has begun and I want you to hear my pupils sing."

Sœurette remained with her little folk, for it was also the time when some of them took their baths, and Josine for her part had to go into her needlework ward, where several of the little girls preferred to spend their play-hour in learning to make dresses for their dolls. Thus Luc alone followed Suzanne down the covered gallery into which opened the five class-rooms.

It had long since been necessary to subdivide the classes, provide more spacious buildings, and even enlarge the dependencies, the gymnasiums, the apprenticeship workshops, and the gardens into which the children were turned in all liberty every two hours. After a few trials a definite system of education had been arrived at, and this system, which rendered study attractive by leaving the pupil all his personality, and only requiring of him attention to such lessons as he preferred, as he freely chose, yielded admirable results, providing the city each year with a new generation that tended more and more towards truth and justice. This was, indeed, the only good way to hasten the future, to create such men as might be entrusted with the realisation of to-morrow, free from all lying dogmas, reared amidst the necessary realities of life, and won over to proven scientific facts. And now that the new system worked so well nothing seemed more logical or more profitable than to abstain from bending a whole class beneath the rod of some master who would have tried to impose his personal views upon some fifty pupils of varying disposition and sensibility. It seemed indeed quite natural that one should simply awaken a desire to learn among those pupils, then direct them on their journey of discovery, and favour the individual faculties which each might display. The five classes had thus become experimental grounds, where the children gradually explored the field of human knowledge, not to devour that knowledge gluttonously without digesting any of it, but to awaken individual intellect, assimilate knowledge in accordance with personal comprehension, and in particular make sure of one's specialities.

Luc and Suzanne had to wait another moment for the school work to cease. From the covered gallery they were able to glance into the large class-rooms, where each pupil had his or her little table and chair. Long tables and forms had been discarded, and the new system made the pupil feel as if he were virtually his own master. But how gay was the sight of all these lads and girls mingled together promiscuously! And with what deep attention they listened to the professor who went from one to another, teaching in a conversational manner, and at times even provoking contradiction. As there were no longer any punishments or prizes the children set their budding desire for glory in competing together as to who could best show that he or she had understood some knotty point. It often happened that the professor ceased speaking to listen to those whom he guessed to be full of the subject, and the lesson then acquired all the interest of a discussion. Indeed one of the chief objects that the masters had in view was to put life into the studies, to draw the pupils from inanimate books, to make them cognisant of living things, and impart to them the passion of ideas. And pleasure was born of it all, the pleasure of learning and knowing; and through the five classes was spread the *ensemble* of human knowledge, the real stirring drama of the world, which each of us ought to know, if he wishes to take part in it and find happiness in its midst.

But a joyous clamour arose, playtime had come round. Every two hours the gardens were invaded by a rush of boys and girls, fraternising together. A sturdy, good-looking lad, some nine years old, ran up and flung himself in Luc's arms, exclaiming: "Good morning, grandfather."

This was Maurice, the son of Thérèse Froment, who had married Raymond Morfain.

"Ah!" said Suzanne gaily, "here's my nightingale! Come, children, shall we repeat our pretty chorus on that lawn between those big chestnut trees?"

Quite a band already surrounded her. Among a score of others there were two boys and a girl whom Luc kissed. Of the former one was Ludovic Boisgelin, a lad eleven years old, the son of Paul Boisgelin and Antoinette Bonnaire, whose marriage had first announced the fusion of the classes. Then there was Félicien Bonnaire, now fourteen, the son of Séverin Bonnaire and Léonie Gourier, the daughter of Achille and Ma-Bleue, whose love had flowered among the wild perfumed rocks of the Bleuse Mountains. And the girl was Germaine Yvonnot, a granddaughter of Auguste Laboque and Marthe Bourron. A handsome, dark-haired laughing girl she was, and in her one found blended the blood of workman, peasant, and petty trader, who had so long warred one against the other. It amused Luc to unravel the intricate skeins of those alliances, those frequent crossings of the race; and he was skilful in identifying the young faces, whose endless increase enraptured him.

But Suzanne spoke: "You shall hear them," she said; "it is a hymn to the rising sun, a salute on the part of childhood to the planet which will ripen the crops."

Some fifty children assembled together on the lawn amidst the chestnut trees. And the chant arose, very fresh, pure, and gay. There was no great musical science in it. It was merely a series of couplets, sung by a girl and a boy alternately, and emphasised by choral repetition. But it was so lively, so expressive of naïve faith in the planet of light and kindliness, that it possessed a stirring charm as sung by those young and somewhat shrill voices. For his part Maurice Morfain, the little boy who replied to Germaine Yvonnot, the girl, possessed, even as Suzanne had said, an angel voice of crystalline lightness, rising to the most delightful, high-toned, flute-like notes. And the chorus-singing suggested the warbling and chirruping of birds in freedom on the branches. Nothing could have been more amusing.

Luc laughed, like a well-pleased grandpapa, and Maurice, full of pride, again rushed into his arms.

"Why, it's true, my lad," said Luc, "you sing like a little nightingale! And do you know that is very nice, because in life, you see, you will be able to sing in your hours of worry, and your songs will bring back your courage. One ought never to weep, one ought always to sing."

"That is what I tell them!" exclaimed Suzanne. "Everybody ought to sing, and I teach them in order that they may sing here, and in studying, and in their workshops, and afterwards throughout their lives. The nation that sings is a nation of health and gaiety."

She displayed no severity nor vanity in the lessons which she gave in this fashion amidst the garden greenery. Her only ambition was to open those young souls to the mirth of fraternal song and the clear beauty of harmony. As she expressed it, whenever the day of universal justice and peace should dawn, the whole happy city would sing beneath the sun.

"Come, my little friends," she exclaimed, "once again, and carefully, in time. There is no occasion to hurry."

Once again the chant arose, but towards the finish of it the young vocalists were disturbed. A man appeared amidst some shrubbery behind the chestnut trees—a man who furtively turned round as if to hide himself. Luc, however, perceived that it was Boisgelin, and was greatly surprised by the maniac's strange behaviour; for he stooped and explored the grass as if seeking some hiding-place, some secret cavity. At last Luc understood the meaning of it. The poor fellow was looking for some nook where he might store away his incalculable wealth in order that it might not be stolen from him. He was often met behaving in this wild way, trembling with fear, at a loss where he might bury all that surplus fortune, the weight of which bowed him down. Luc shuddered with pity at the sight, and became yet more concerned when he perceived that the children were alarmed by the apparition, even like a party of gay chaffinches put to flight by the wild fluttering of some night-bird.

However, Suzanne, who had turned somewhat pale, repeated in a louder voice: "Keep time, keep time, my dears! Bring out the last bar with all your fervour!"

Haggard and suspicious, Boisgelin had disappeared, like a black shadow vanishing from amidst the flowering shrubs. And as soon as the children, recovering their composure, had saluted the sovereign sun with a last joyful cry, Luc and Suzanne complimented them on their efforts and dismissed them to their play. Then they walked together towards the apprenticeship workshops on the other side of the garden.

"Did you see him?" Suzanne asked in a low voice, after a moment's silence. "Ah! the unhappy man, how anxious he makes me!" But as Luc thereupon expressed his regret that he had been unable to follow Boisgelin and take him home again, she once more protested: "Oh! he would not have followed you; you would have had to struggle with him, and there would have been quite a scandal. My only fear, I repeat it to you, is that he may be found some day in a pit with his head broken."

They relapsed into silence, for they were now reaching the workshops. A good many pupils spent a part of their playtime there, planing wood, filing iron, sewing or embroidering, whilst others who reigned over a neighbouring strip of ground busied themselves with digging, sowing, and weeding. And now Luc and Suzanne again met Josine, standing in a large room where sewing, knitting, and weaving machines, placed side by side, were worked sometimes by girls and sometimes by boys.

Here again several of the children were singing, and a joyous spirit of emulation seemed to animate the workshop.

"Do you hear them?" exclaimed Suzanne, whose gaiety had returned. "They will always sing, those warblers of mine."

Josine was explaining to a big girl of sixteen, named Clémentine Bourron, the manner in which she ought to manage a sewing-machine in order to do certain embroidery, whilst another pupil, a girl of nine, Aline Boisgelin by name, was waiting to be shown how she ought to turn down a seam. Clémentine was the daughter of Sébastien Bourron and Agathe Fauchard, her grandfather on her mother's side being Fauchard, the old drawer of the Abyss, and on her father's Bourron the puddler. Aline, who was a younger sister of Ludovic, the son of Paul Boisgelin and Antoinette Bonnaire, laughed affectionately when she perceived her grandmother, Suzanne, who was very fond of her.

"Oh, grandmamma!" said she, "I can't turn my seams down very well as yet, but I sew them very straight—don't I, friend Josine?"

Suzanne kissed her, then watched Josine, who turned down a seam to serve as a pattern for the child. Luc himself took an interest in these little matters, aware as he was that everything has its importance, that happy life depends upon the happy employment of one's hours. Then, as Sœurette came up, at the moment when he was about to quit Josine and Suzanne in order to repair to the works, he found himself for a moment in the flower garden with the three women, those three loving and devoted hearts that helped him so powerfully to bring about the fulfilment of his dream of goodness and happiness. They surrounded him like symbols of the affectionate solidarity, the universal love which he wished to disseminate among mankind. Taking each other by the hand they stood there smiling at him, old no doubt, with their white hair, but still beautiful, with the wondrous beauty of kindliness. And when, after discussing some details of organisation with them, Luc departed, going towards the works, their loving eyes long followed his footsteps.

The factory halls and workshops, which were now much more extensive than formerly, were full of the healthy gaiety which comes from an abundance of sunshine and air. On all sides fresh water washed the cement pavement, carrying off the slightest particles of dust in such wise that the abode of work, once so grimy, muddy, and pestilential, now shone with cleanliness. Most of the work, too, was now performed by machines which stood around in serried array, like an army of docile, indefatigable artisans, ever ready for the effort required of them. If their metal arms wore out they simply had to be replaced. They themselves did not know what pain was, and they had in part suppressed human pain. They, too, were friendly machines, not the machines of the earlier days, the competitors which aggravated the workman's want by producing a fall in wages, but liberating machines, universal tools toiling for man whilst man rested. Around those sturdy workers, propelled by electricity, there were only so many drivers and watchers, whose sole duties consisted in moving levers or switches, and in making sure that the mechanism acted properly. The working day did not exceed four hours, and a workman never spent more than two upon one task, being relieved at the expiration of his two hours by a mate, whilst he himself passed to some other form of work, industrial art, agriculture, or public function. Again, the general employment of electric power had virtually done away with the uproar with which the workshops had once resounded, and now they were enlivened by the songs of the workmen, the vocal mirth which the latter had brought from their schools like a florescence of harmony embellishing their whole lives. And the singing of those men around that silent machinery, at once so powerful and so easy to manage, proclaimed the delight of just, glorious, and all-saving work.

As Luc passed through the hall containing the puddling furnaces, he paused for a moment to exchange a few friendly words with a strong young man of twenty or thereabouts, who managed one of those furnaces without any need of assistance.

"Well, Adolphe, are things going on satisfactorily, are you satisfied?" Luc inquired.

"Oh! certainly they are! I've just completed my two hours, and the 'bloom' is just fit for removal."

Adolphe was a son of Auguste Laboque and Marthe Bourron. Unlike his maternal grandfather, Bourron the puddler, who had now retired, he did not have to perform the terrible task of stirring the ball of fusing metal with a long bar amidst all the flaring of the fire. The stirring was now performed by mechanical means, and, indeed, an ingenious contrivance brought the dazzling ball out of the furnace and placed it on the chariot which carried it to the helve hammer without the workman having to intervene.

"You shall see," Adolphe gaily resumed, "it's of first-rate quality, and the work's so easy."

He lowered a lever, a door opened, and the ball, like some planet, setting the horizon aglow with its luminous trail, slid down to the chariot, whilst the young man continued smiling, without a drop of perspiration appearing on his brow, his limbs remaining nimble and supple, undeformed by excessive toil. The chariot had already started off to deposit its burden under the hammer, one of a new pattern, worked by electricity, and doing everything that had to be done by itself, without need of any smith to turn the lump over, now upon this side and now upon that. And the hammer also worked so easily and the sound it gave out was so clear and light that it became like a musical accompaniment to the mirth of the workmen.

"I must make haste," said Adolphe again, after washing his hands. "I have to finish a table in which I'm greatly interested, and I shall do a couple of hours in the carpenters' workshop."

He was indeed a carpenter as well as a puddler, having learnt various callings, like all the young folk of his age, in order that he might not be brutified by clinging to some particular specialty. Varied in this manner, work became both delight and recreation.

"Well, amuse yourself!" cried Luc, sharing his delight.

"Yes, yes, thanks, Monsieur Luc. That's the right thing to say—good work, good amusement."

One spot where Luc spent a few enjoyable minutes on the mornings when he visited the works was the hall where the crucible furnaces were installed. He there felt himself to be far indeed from the old hall at the Abyss, that hall with its glowing pits growling like volcanoes, whence the wretched workers, amidst a blaze of fire, had to lift at arm's length their hundred pounds' weight of fusing metal. Instead of the old-time grimy, filthy place, there was now a spacious gallery, having broad windows through which the sunshine streamed, and a pavement of large slabs between which opened batteries of symmetrically disposed furnaces. As electricity was employed to work them they remained cold, silent, clean, and bright. And here again mechanical appliances performed all the work, lowered the crucibles, lifted them all aglow, and emptied them into moulds under the eyes of the men directing them. Women were even employed in this department, attending to the distribution of the electric power, for it had been noticed that they displayed more care and precision than men in working the delicate appliances.

Luc walked up to a tall and good-looking girl of twenty, Laure Fauchard, daughter of Louis Fauchard and Julienne Dacheux, who, standing near one apparatus, was carefully directing the current towards one of the furnaces in accordance with the indications of a young workman, who on his side watched the progress of the fusion.

"Well, Laure, you are not tired, are you?" Luc asked her.

"Oh! no, Monsieur Luc, it amuses me. How can I get tired from merely turning this little switch?"

The young workman, Hippolyte Mitaine, who was now nearly three-and-twenty, had drawn near. He was the son of Évariste Mitaine and Olympe Lenfant, and was reported to be betrothed to Laure Fauchard.

"Monsieur Luc," said he, "if you would like to see some billets cast we are ready."

The machinery on being started quietly and easily removed the incandescent crucibles, and then emptied them into the moulds, which another mechanism brought forward in turn. In five minutes, whilst the young man and the girl looked on, the work was properly performed and the furnace was ready to receive yet another charge.

"There!" exclaimed Laure, laughing. "When I think of all the terrible stories which my poor grandfather Fauchard used to tell me when I was a child I can hardly believe them. He hadn't got much of his wits left, and he related things about his old calling as a drawer that were fit to make one shudder. It was as if he had spent his life in the midst of a fire, with the flames licking his limbs. All the old folk think us very happy nowadays."

Luc had become grave, and emotion moistened his eyes. "Yes, yes," said he, "the grandfathers suffered a great deal. And that is why the grandchildren enjoy a better life. Work well, and love one another well, the lives of your sons and daughters will be better still."

Then Luc resumed his round, and wherever he repaired throughout those spacious works he found the same healthy cleanliness, the same tuneful gaiety, the same easy and attractive work, thanks to the variety of the duties entrusted to the staff and the sovereign help of the machinery. The worker was no longer an overpowered beast of burden, held in contempt; with freedom he had recovered conscience and intelligence.

As Luc concluded his inspection in the hall where the rolling-machinery had its place, near the puddling furnaces, he again paused to say a few friendly words to a young man, about twenty-six years of age, who was just arriving.

"Yes, Monsieur Luc," was the reply, "I've come from Les Combettes, where I've been helping my father. There was some sowing to finish, so I did two hours at it over yonder. And now I mean to do another two hours here, for there is an urgent order for some rails."

The young man was named Alexandre, and was a son of Léon Feuillat and Eugénie Yvonnot. Gifted with a lively fancy, he amused himself after completing his regular four-hours' work by preparing ornamental designs for Lange the potter.

However, he had already set himself to his task, which was the superintendence of a train of rollers for the making of rails. Luc, who felt very happy, looked on in a kindly way. Since electrical force had been employed the terrible uproar of the machinery had ceased; one only heard the silvery ring of each rail as it spurted forth, following those which were cooling. 'Twas all the good and constant production of an epoch of peace, rails and yet more rails, in order that every frontier might be crossed, and that the nations, drawn closer and closer together, might become but one sole nation, spread over the surface of the earth, which was becoming a perfect network of roads. And in addition to the rails there were the great steel ships—not the hateful vessels of war, carrying devastation and death across the ocean, but vessels of solidarity and brotherliness, enabling continents to exchange their products, and helping on the increase of mankind's fortune to such a degree that prodigious abundance reigned everywhere. And there were also the bridges facilitating communication, and the girders and all the structural materials for the erection of the innumerable edifices which the reconciled communities needed for their public life, the common-houses, the libraries, the museums, the asylums for infancy and old age, the huge general stores and the granaries, all vast enough for the life and keep of the federated nations. And finally, there were the innumerable machines and appliances which upon all sides and in all forms of labour replaced the arms of men: those which tilled the soil, those which toiled in the workshops, those which travelled along the roads, athwart the waves and through the sky. And Luc rejoiced that all that iron and steel should have become pacific, that the metal of conquest which mankind had so long employed solely to make the swords and spears that it needed for its bloodthirsty struggles, which it had afterwards turned into the guns and shells of its latter days of carnage, should be used, now that peace was won, solely for the erection of its city of fraternity, justice, and happiness.

Before returning home that day Luc desired to give a last glance at the battery of electrical furnaces which had replaced Morfain's smeltery. The battery, as it happened, was then at work, amidst a blaze of sunshine which filled the glazed shed where it was placed. Every five minutes the mechanism charged the furnaces afresh, after the rolling way had carried off the ten pigs whose glow was dimmed by the bright light of the planet. And here again, watching over the electrical appliances, there were two girls each about twenty, one of them a charming blonde, Claudine, the daughter of Lucien Bonnaire and Louise Mazelle, and the other a superb brunette, Céline, the daughter of Arsène Lenfant and Eulalie Laboque. As it was needful that they should give all their attention to switching the current on and off, they were at first only able to smile at Luc. But a short rest ensued, and on perceiving a group of children who stood inquisitively on the threshold of the shed, they came forward.

"Good-day, my little Maurice! Good-day, my little Ludovic! Good-day, my little Aline! Are lessons over, since you have come to see us?"

It should be mentioned that the children by way of recreation, and in the idea that they would acquire some first notions of various forms of work, were allowed to run about the place in comparative freedom. Luc, well pleased at seeing his grandson Maurice again, made the whole party enter the shed. And he answered their numerous questions, and explained the mechanism of the furnaces, and even made the appliances work again by way of showing the children how it sufficed for Claudine or Céline to turn a little lever, in order to fuse the metal and enable it to flow forth in a dazzling stream.

But Maurice, with all the importance of a little man who, though only nine years old had already learnt a great many things, exclaimed "Oh! I know, I've already seen it. Grandfather Morfain showed me everything one day. But tell me, grandfather Froment, is it true that there used to be furnaces as high as mountains, and that one had to burn one's face day and night in order to get anything out of them?"

The others all began to laugh at this, and it was Claudine who answered: "Of course there were! Grandfather Bonnaire has often told me of it, and you, Maurice, ought to know the story, for your great-grandfather—the great Morfain as he is still called—was the last to wrestle with fire like a hero. He lived up yonder in a cavern in the rocks, and never came down to the town, but from one end of the year to the other watched over his gigantic furnace, the monster whose ruins one can still see on the mountain-side, like those of some storm-rent castle-keep of the ancient days."

Maurice's eyes dilated with astonishment, and he listened with all the passionate interest of a child to whom some prodigious fairy-tale is being told. "Oh! I know, I know! Grandfather Morfain told me all about his father and the furnace as high as a mountain. But, all the same, I thought he was inventing it just to amuse us, for he does invent stories when he wants to make us laugh. And so it's true?"

"Why yes, it's true!" Claudine continued. "Up above there were workmen who loaded the furnace, by emptying into it truck-loads of ore and coal, and down below there were other workmen ever on the watch, ever nursing the monster so that it might not have an attack of indigestion which would have prevented the work from being properly performed."

"And that lasted seven and eight years at a stretch," said Céline, the other young woman; "the monster remained alight all that time, always flaming like a crater, without it being possible for one to let it cool, for if it did cool, there was a great loss, it had to be broken open, and cleaned, and almost entirely rebuilt."

Then Claudine resumed: "So you see, my little Maurice, your great-grandfather Morfain had a vast deal of work to do, since he could hardly quit that fire for a moment during seven or eight years; besides which, every five hours, he had to clear the tap-hole with an iron bar, in order to release the smelted ore, which ran out like a perfect river of flames, hot enough to roast one, as if one were a duck on the spit."

At this the hitherto stupefied children burst into loud laughter. Oh! the idea of it, a duck on the spit, Old Morfain roasting like a duck!

"Ah well!" said Ludovic Boisgelin, "it can't have been very amusing to work in those days. It must have given one too much trouble."

"Of course," his sister Aline exclaimed, "I'm glad that I was born after all that, for it's very amusing to work nowadays."

Maurice, however, had become serious and thoughtful, turning over in his mind all the incredible things which had been told him. And by way of summing up everything, he ended by saying: "All the same, grandfather's father must have been awfully strong, and if things go better nowadays it is perhaps because he had such a lot of trouble formerly."

Luc, who hitherto had contented himself with smiling, was delighted by this remark. He caught up Maurice and kissed him on both cheeks.

"You are right, my boy," said he. "And in the same way, if you work with all your heart nowadays, your great-grandchildren will be yet happier than you are—even now, you see, one no longer roasts like a duck."

By his orders the battery of electrical furnaces was started once more, Claudine and Céline turning the current on or off by a simple gesture. The children wished to direct the mechanism themselves, and how delightful did that easy work seem after the legend-like narrative of Morfain's hard toil—the toil, it seemed, of some pain-racked giant living in a world that had disappeared!

All at once, however, there came an apparition, and the children, perturbed by it, ran off. Then Luc again perceived Boisgelin, who this time stood at one of the doorways of the shed, watching the work in an angry, mistrustful way, like some master who is for ever afraid that his men may rob him. He was often to be seen in this fashion in one or another part of the works, distracted by the idea that the place was too vast to be properly inspected by him, and maddened more and more by the thought of all the millions that he must every day be losing through his inability to check the work of all those people who were earning milliards for him. They were too numerous, he was never able to see them all. He looked so haggard, so exhausted by his fruitless roaming through the workshops, that Luc, stirred by pity, this time wished to join him, calm him, and lead him gently home. But Boisgelin was on his guard, and springing back, ran off towards the large workshops.

His morning ramble over, Luc now returned home, and just as the daylight was waning in the afternoon, after glancing round the general stores, he went to spend an hour with the Jordans. In the little drawing-room overlooking the park he found Sœurette chatting with schoolmaster Hermeline and Abbé Marle; whilst Jordan, stretched on a sofa and wrapped in a rug, remained thinking, according to his wont, with his eyes fixed upon the setting sun. Amiable Doctor Novarre had lately been carried off after an illness of a few hours, his only regret being that he would not behold the realisation of so many beautiful things in the possibility of which he had at the outset scarcely believed. Thus Sœurette nowadays received but the schoolmaster and the priest, and these only called at long intervals, when yielding to their old habit of meeting at her house. Hermeline, now seventy years of age and retired, was ending his days in a state of growing bitterness and anger against all that passed before him. He had reached such a point in this respect that he reproached the old priest with lack of warmth. As a matter of fact Abbé Marle, who was five years older than the other, sought refuge in dolorous dignity, silence which became more and more haughty as he beheld his church becoming empty and his religion expiring.

As Luc entered and took a chair beside Sœurette, who sat there silent, gentle, and patient, it so happened that the schoolmaster was again badgering the priest, like the sectarian and dictatorial republican that he still was. "Come, come, abbé," he said, "since I fall in with your views you ought to help me. This is surely the end of the world. Children's passions, evil growths which we the educators were formerly appointed to crush, are nowadays cultivated, it seems. How is it possible for the State to have any disciplined citizens reared for its service when a free rein is given to anarchical individuality? If we, the men of method and sense, don't manage to save the Republic, it is surely lost!"

Since the day when he had thus begun to speak of saving the Republic from those whom he called the Socialists and the Anarchists, he had gone over to the side of reaction, joining the priest in his hatred of all who dared to free themselves otherwise than by his own narrow Jacobin formula.

And he went on yet more violently: "I tell you, abbé, that your church will be swept away if you do not defend it! Your religion, no doubt, was never mine. But I have always admitted the necessity of a religion for the people; and Catholicism was certainly an admirable governing machine. So stir yourself! We are with you, and we will have an explanation afterwards, when we have re-conquered the lost ground together."

At first Abbé Marle simply shook his head. As a rule nowadays he did not take the trouble to answer or get angry. At last he slowly said: "I do the whole of my duty—I am at my altar every morning, even when my church is empty, and I implore God to perform a miracle. He will surely do so, if He deems it necessary."

This brought the old schoolmaster's exasperation to a climax. "Pooh! one must help oneself! It is cowardly to do nothing."

Sœurette, smiling and full of tolerance for those vanquished men, thereupon thought it necessary to intervene: "If the good doctor was still here," said she, "he would beg you not to agree so well together, since your seeming agreement only makes your quarrel worse. You grieve me, my friends; I should have been so happy—not to convert you to our ideas, but to see you admit, by virtue of experience, a little of all the good which our ideas have effected in this region."

They had both retained great deference for Sœurette, and indeed their presence in that little drawing-room, beside the very hearth, so to say, of the new city, showed what ascendancy she still exercised over them. For her sake they even put up with the presence of Luc, their victorious adversary, though he, it should be admitted, discreetly avoided all appearance of triumphing over them. Thus, on this occasion, he refrained from intervening, however furiously Hermeline might deny all that he had created. After all, thought Luc, this was simply the last revolt of the principle of authority against the liberation of man both naturally and socially. On seeing the nations so near the point of escaping from civil as well as religious servitude, the once all-powerful State and the once all-powerful Church, which had voraciously contended for possession of them, now tried to come to an agreement, and league themselves together in order to reconquer the nations.

"Ah!" cried Hermeline again, "if you own yourself beaten, abbé, it must be all over. In that case I can only keep silent as you do, and withdraw into my corner to die."

The priest once more shook his head, preserving silence. But eventually, for the last time, he said: "God cannot be beaten; it is for God Himself to act."

The night was now slowly falling over the park, lengthening shadows were filling the little *salon*, and nobody spoke any further. Only a great quiver, coming from the melancholy past, swept through the room. Finally the schoolmaster rose and took his leave. Then, as the priest was about to do the same, Sœurette wished to slip into his hand the sum which at each recurring visit she had been accustomed to give him for his poor. This time, however, he refused the alms which he had been accepting so regularly for more than forty years; and in a low voice he slowly said: "No, thank you, mademoiselle; keep that money. I should not know what to do with it; there are no more poor!"

Ah! what words those were for Luc: "No more poor!" His heart had leapt as he heard them. No more poor, no more starvelings in that town of Beauclair, which he had known so black, so wretched, peopled by such an accursed race of famished toilers! Would all the frightful sores which had come from the wage-system be healed then? would shame and crime soon disappear, even as want did? The reorganisation of work in accordance with justice had sufficed already to bring about a better apportionment of wealth. And thus, when work should on all sides

ÉMILE ZOLA

become honour and health and joy, an entirely peaceful and a brotherly race would assuredly people the happy city.

Jordan, who still lay upon the sofa, wrapped in his rug, had hitherto remained motionless, his eyes fixed upon space, through which no doubt his mind was roaming. At last, Abbé Marle and Hermeline having departed, he woke up, and without taking his eyes off the sunset which he seemed to be watching with passionate interest, he said in a dreamy manner: "Each time that I see the sun set I become dreadfully sad and anxious. Suppose it were not to come back, suppose it were never to rise again over the black and frost-bound earth, what a terrible death would then overtake all life! The sun is the father, the fructifier, without whom all germs would wither or rot. And it is in the sun that we must place our hope of relief and future happiness, for if it were not to help us life would some day dry up."

Luc had begun to smile. He knew that Jordan, in spite of his great age—he was now nearly seventy-five—had for some years been studying the problem of how he might capture solar heat and store it in vast reservoirs in order to distribute it afterwards as the one, great, eternal, living force. A time would come when the coal in the mines would be exhausted, and where would one then find the necessary energy for the torrent of electricity which had become so needful for life? Thanks to his first discoveries, Jordan had succeeded in supplying an abundance of electrical force for next to nothing. But what a victory it would be if he should succeed in making the sun the universal motor—if he should be able to take from it direct the caloric power which was now found slumbering in coal—if he should manage to employ it as the one sole fructifier, the very father of immortal life! He had but a last discovery to effect, and then his work would be accomplished and he would be ready to die.

"Don't alarm yourself!" said Luc gaily, "the sun will rise to-morrow and you will succeed at last in snatching the sacred fire from it."

However, Sœurette, whom the evening breeze now coming in cool gusts through the open window rendered somewhat anxious, stepped forward to ask her brother: "Don't you feel cold? Wouldn't you like me to shut the window?"

He declined the offer with a motion of his hand, and all that he would allow was that she should wrap him round with the rug to his very chin. He now seemed to live solely by a miracle, solely because he wished to live, having adjourned death until the evening of his last day of work, the triumphant evening when, his task accomplished, he might at last sink into the good sleep of a loyal and contented worker. His sister surrounded him with greater precautions than ever; her extreme care prolonged his strength, and still gave him two hours of physical and intellectual energy each day—two hours which by force of method he put to wonderful use. And thus that poor, old, puny being, whom the slightest draught threatened with annihilation, was completing the conquest of the world simply because he was still a stubborn worker, one who did not throw his task aside.

"You will live to be a hundred years old!" said Luc, with an affectionate laugh.

At this Jordan likewise made merry. "No doubt," said he, "if a hundred years prove necessary."

Again deep silence fell in the little *salon*, full of such affectionate intimacy. It was delightful to see the warm twilight stealing slowly over the park, whose deep paths were gradually steeped in the gloom. Vague gleams still hovered just above the lawns, whilst the great trees faded away and became like light and quivering apparitions in the blue distance. And it was now the sweethearts' hour—the sweethearts to whom the park of La Crêcherie remained open, and who therefore came thither in the twilight after their daily work. Nobody troubled about the roaming, shadowy couples, who, holding one another by the hand, gradually melted away and disappeared amidst the greenery. They were confided to the keeping of the friendly old oaks. Reliance was placed on the freedom to love that was granted them, for this would render them gentle and chaste, like future spouses whose embrace becomes an indissoluble tie if mutually desired. To love always one need only know why and how one loves. Those who choose one another, knowing and consenting, never part. And already, along the dim avenues, over the lawns where the shadows stretched, there came sauntering couples, who peopled, as with apparitions, the mysterious gloom amidst the quiver of delight which the fresh odours of spring brought from the earth.

As other couples arrived Luc recognised among them several of the lads and girls whom he had seen in the workshops that morning. Were not yonder shadowy forms, so close one to the other that they seemed carried by one and the same flight over the tips of the grass, those of Adolphe Laboque and Germaine Yvonnot? And those others, whose hair mingled, their heads resting one against the other, were they not Hippolyte Mitaine and Laure Fauchard? And those others too, whose arms were tightly clasped around each other's waist, were they not Alexandre Feuillat and Clémence Bourron? Yet softer emotion came to Luc's heart when he fancied that he recognised his son Charles with his arm around the dark-haired Céline Lenfant, and his son Jules leading away in his embrace the fair Claudine Bonnaire. Ah! the young folk, the messengers of the new springtide, the last to awaken to love, to feel kindling within them the glow of life which the generations transmit one to the other! As yet they knew but the chaste quiver which comes at the first whispered words, and the innocent caress, the clasp in which ignorant hearts seek one another, and the furtive kiss whose sweetness suffices to open the portals of heaven. But before long the sovereign flame would unite and blend them in order that yet other artisans of love might spring from them, other couples, who in years to come would repair to this same park to exchange the vows of budding affection. For there would ever be more and more happiness and more and more free passion tending to increase of harmony. Even now other couples, and others still, were arriving, the park was gradually becoming populous with all the sweethearts of the happy city. This was the exquisite evening after the good day of work, the gloaming spent amidst lawn and cover, shadowy like dreamland, steeped in mystery and perfume, with nought breaking upon the silence save light sounds of laughter and kisses.

All at once, however, a shadowy form stopped outside the *salon*. It was Suzanne, who had anxiously been seeking Luc. And on finding him there she told him how greatly she was worried by Boisgelin's prolonged absence, for he had not yet returned home. Never before had he lingered like this out of doors after nightfall.

"You were right," she repeated; "I did wrong in leaving him to his mad fancies. Ah! the unhappy man, the poor old child!"

Luc, who shared her fears, bade her go home again. "He may return at any moment," he said; "it is best that you should be there. For my part I will have a look round and bring you tidings."

He at once took two men with him and crossed the park, with the intention of beginning the search among the workshops. But he had scarcely taken three hundred steps, and was near the little lake, fringed with willows, quite a nook of paradise, when he halted on hearing a light cry of terror which came from an adjacent clump of greenery. From amidst that foliage there ran a pair of frightened lovers, who he fancied were his son Jules and the fair Claudine Bonnaire. "What is the matter? What has alarmed you?" he called.

But they did not answer, they fled as beneath a blast of terror, like love birds whose caresses have been disturbed by some frightful encounter. And when Luc himself decided to enter the copse, he also gave vent to an exclamation of horror. For he had almost knocked against a body which hung from a branch there, blocking the narrow pathway. In the last gleam of light falling from the sky where the stars were now appearing Luc recognised the body as that of Boisgelin.

"Ah! the unhappy man, the poor old child!" he murmured, repeating Suzanne's words, and feeling quite upset by that horrible tragedy which would cause her such deep grief.

With the help of his companions he cut down the body and laid it on the ground. But it was already quite cold. The unhappy man must have hanged himself there early in the afternoon, after his desperate ramble through the busy works. Luc fancied that he could divine everything when at the foot of the tree he noticed a large hole which Boisgelin had apparently dug with his hands, a hole in which he had no doubt meant to bury the prodigious fortune which his people of workers earned for him, that fortune which he knew not how to manage or how to store away. And despairing, perchance, of his power to make a pit of sufficient size for so much wealth, he had ended by resolving to die there and thus rid himself of the horrible embarrassment in which he was placed by his ever-growing and crushing fortune. His day of wild roaming, his madness, his inability to live, idler that he was, in the new city of just work, had culminated in that tragic death, and he had hung there whilst the park, in the clasp of warm and nuptial night, was filled with the rustling of caresses and the whispering of loving vows.

In order to avoid frightening the shadowy couples gliding between the trees around him, Luc at once sent the two men to fetch a stretcher at La Crêcherie, at the same time begging them to tell nobody of the lugubrious discovery. And when they had returned and laid the lifeless body between the little curtains of grey canvas, the mournful *cortège* set off along the blackest of the paths in order to escape observation. In this wise death, frightful death, passed along silently, steeped in shadows, through the delightful awakening of spring, now all a-quiver with new life. Lovers seemed to arise on all sides, springing up at the bends of each avenue, in the recesses of each clump of bushes. A perfume of flowers made the air quite balmy, hands sought hands, and lips met. Love was budding, a fresh wave was coming to increase humanity's broad stream, death was incessantly vanquished, to-morrow and to-morrow were ever

ÉMILE ZOLA

sprouting in order that there might be yet more truth, more justice, more happiness in the world.

Suzanne stood waiting in a state of anguish, at the door of the house, her eyes gazing into the night. When she perceived the stretcher she understood, and gave vent to a low moan. And when Luc in a few words had acquainted her with the wretched end of the useless being now slumbering there, she was only able to repeat, as she thought of that empty, poisoned, and poisonous life which had brought her so much suffering: "Ah, the unhappy man, the poor old child!"

Other catastrophes took place amidst the crumbling of the rotten society of the old days now fated to disappear. But the greatest stir of all was caused by one that occurred during the ensuing month—the collapse of the old church of Saint Vincent one bright sunshiny morning when Abbé Marle was at the altar celebrating mass solely for the sparrows which flew through the deserted nave.

The priest had long been aware that his church would some day fall upon him. It dated from the sixteenth century, and was in a very damaged condition, cracking upon all sides. The steeple had certainly been repaired some forty years previously, but from lack of funds it had been necessary to postpone all work on the roofing, whose beams, half eaten away, were already yielding. And since that time every application for a grant had been made in vain. The State, overburdened with debts, abandoned that church of a remote region. The town of Beauclair refused to contribute anything, Mayor Gourier having never been on the side of the priests. Thus Abbé Marle, reduced to his own resources, had been obliged to seek among the faithful the large sum which became more and more urgently required if the edifice was not to fall upon his shoulders. But in vain did he knock at the doors of wealthy parishioners, the faithful were dwindling away, their zeal was fast cooling. During the lifetime of the beautiful Léonore, the mayor's wife, whose extreme piety proved some compensation for her husband's atheism, the priest had found precious help in her. Subsequently, however, only Madame Mazelle had remained to him, and not only did her fervour decline, but she was in no wise of a generous disposition. In course of time worries respecting her fortune consumed her, and she came less and less frequently to Saint Vincent, in such wise that nobody was left to the priest save a few poor creatures who in their wretchedness clung obstinately to the hope of a better life. And finally when no poor remained, the church became quite empty, and the abbé lived there in solitude, amidst the abandonment in which mankind now at last left his religion of error and wretchedness.

The abbé then felt that a world was indeed expiring around him. His complaisance had been powerless to save the life of the lying, poisonous *bourgeoisie* which was devoured by its own iniquities. In vain had he cast the cloak of religion over its last agony; it had died amidst a final scandal. And in vain, too, had he sought a refuge in the strict letter of dogma, in order that he might concede nothing to the truths of science, which, he could realise, were mounting to the supreme and victorious assault by which the ancient edifice of Catholicism would be destroyed. Science, indeed, had at last effected its breach, dogma was finally swept away, and the Kingdom of God was about to be set, not in some fabulous paradise, but upon this very earth, in the name of triumphant justice. A new religion, the religion of man, at last truly conscious, free, and master of his destiny, was sweeping away the ancient mythologies, the forms of symbolism amidst which he had lost himself during the anguish of his long struggle against nature. After the temples of ancient idolatry, the Catholic churches in their turn had to disappear, now that a fraternal people set its certain happiness in the sole force of its living solidarity without need of any political system of punishments and rewards. Thus the priest, since confessional and holy table alike had been deserted, since the faithful had departed from his church, beheld each day when he celebrated mass there the cracks in the walls spreading, and the beams of the roofs yielding more and more. It was a constant crumbling, a gradual process of destruction and ruin, the slightest premonitory sounds of which he could detect. But since he had been unable to summon the builders even for the most urgent repairs, he must necessarily allow the work of death to follow its course and culminate in the natural end of things. Thus he simply waited and continued to say his mass, like a hero of faith, alone with his forsaken creed, whilst the roof cracked more and more above the altar.

A morning came when Abbé Marle perceived that another large stretch of the vaulting of the nave had split during the previous night. And although he now felt certain of the downfall which he had been anticipating for months past, he nevertheless came to celebrate his last mass, clad in his richest vestments. Very tall and broad-shouldered, with a nose like an eagle's beak, he still held himself firm and upright in spite of his advanced age. He dispensed with servers now, he came and went, spoke the sacramental words, and made the usual gestures, as if a great throng were pressing together before him, docile to his voice. But in the state of abandonment in which the church was left, only some broken chairs lay upon the flag-stones, suggesting the wretched-looking mouldy garden seats that are left forgetfully out of doors exposed to the rains of winter. Weeds grew round the columns, over which moss was spreading. All the winds of heaven streamed in through the broken windows, and the great doorway being half unhinged, remained partially open, allowing the animals of the neighbourhood to flock in. On that fine bright day, however, it was particularly the sunshine that poured into the edifice, like a conqueror, setting as it were a triumphal invasion of life amidst that tragic ruin where birds flew hither and thither, and where wild oats germinated even among the stone mantles of the old saints. Above the altar, however, there still reigned a great crucifix of painted and gilded wood, displaying a long, livid, pain-racked effigy, splashed with some blackish blood that dripped like tears.

Whilst Abbé Marle was reading the Gospel he heard a louder cracking, and some dust and some fragments of plaster fell upon the altar. Then, at the moment of the Offertory, the sinister rending began again, and it seemed as if the edifice were shaking before it fell. But the priest, collecting all the remaining strength of his faith together for the Elevation, prayed with his whole soul for the miracle for whose glorious, all-saving splendour he had so long been waiting. If it should so please God, the church would regain its vigorous youth, and be endowed with sturdy pillars upholding an indestructible nave. Masons were not necessary, the Almighty power would suffice, and a magnificent sanctuary would arise there, with chapels of gold, windows of purple, wood-work marvellously carved, and dazzling marble, whilst a multitude of the faithful on their knees would sing the hymn of Resurrection amidst the blaze of thousands of candles and the loud pealing of bells. But at the very moment when the priest, finishing his prayer, raised the chalice, it was not the miracle he asked for that came, it was annihilation. He stood there erect, with both arms raised in a superb gesture of heroic belief, and the vaulted roof was rent asunder as if by a bolt from heaven, and crashed downward in a whirlwind of fragments with a roar like that of thunder. The shaken steeple tottered and then in its turn fell, ripping the remainder of the roof open, and dragging down the rest of the sundered walls. And nought remained beneath the bright sun save a huge litter of stones and tiles, amidst which a fruitless search was made for Abbé Marle. He had disappeared as if the remnants of the shattered altar had consumed his flesh, drunk his blood. And in like way nothing was ever found of the great crucifix of painted and gilded wood. That also had been shattered to atoms, reduced to dust. Thus yet another religion was dead, the last priest saying his last mass had perished with the last of the churches.

For a few days old Hermeline, the retired schoolmaster, was seen prowling about the ruins, and talking aloud as old folk are wont to do when haunted by some fixed idea. His words could not be plainly distinguished, but he seemed to be still arguing and reproaching the abbé for having failed to obtain the needed miracle. Then, one morning, he was found dead in his bed. And later on, when the ruins of the church had been cleared away, a garden was planted there, with fine trees and shady walks, skirting sweet-smelling lawns. Lovers went thither on pleasant evenings, even as they went to the park of La Crêcherie. The happy city was ever spreading, children were growing and becoming lovers in their turn, lovers whose kisses in the shade again sowed future harvests. After the gay day of work came love amidst the roses blooming upon every side. And in that delightful garden where slept the dust of a religion of wretchedness and death, one now beheld the growth of human joy, the overflowing florescence of life.

IV

During yet another ten years the city continued growing, and organising new society in accordance with the principles of justice and peace. And at last, one 20th of June, on the eve of one of the great Festivals of Work, which took place four times a year, coinciding with the seasons, Bonnaire met with a strange experience.

He, Bonnaire, now nearly eighty-five years of age, had become the patriarch, the hero of work. Still straight and tall, with an energetic head under a crown of thick white hair, he remained active and gay, in the enjoyment of good health. Old revolutionary that he was, a theoretical Collectivist pacified by the sight of his comrades' happiness, he now tasted all the reward of his long efforts—the conquest of that harmonious solidarity amidst which he saw his grandchildren and great-grandchildren growing in all felicity.

That evening then, just as the daylight was waning, Bonnaire happened to be strolling near the entrance of the Brias gorges. He often walked abroad in this fashion, with the sole assistance of a stick, for the pleasure of viewing the countryside once more and recalling old-time memories. On this occasion he had just reached the spot where in former days had stood the gates of the Abyss, which had long since disappeared. Near that spot also a wooden bridge had once spanned the Mionne, but no trace of it remained, for the torrent had been covered over for a distance of about a hundred yards, to admit of the passage of a broad boulevard.

What changes there were! thought Bonnaire. Who would ever have recognised the former black and muddy threshold of the accursed factory in that broad, open space, over which there now passed a quiet, bright-looking avenue, lined with smiling houses? As he lingered there for a moment, erect and handsome, like the happy old man he was, he experienced great surprise on perceiving another old man, a stranger, huddled up on a wayside bench near him. And this other seemed to have been wrecked by misery, for his clothes were in tatters, his face ravaged and bushy with hair, his frame emaciated and trembling as if with some evil fever.

"A poor man!" muttered Bonnaire, speaking aloud in his astonishment.

It was certainly a poor man, and years had now gone by since Bonnaire had seen one. It was evident, however, that he who sat on the bench did not belong to the region. His shoes and clothes were white with dust, and he must have sunk upon that bench near the entry of the town from sheer fatigue, after tramping the roads for days and days. His staff and his empty wallet had fallen from his weary hands and lay at his feet. With an air of exhaustion he let his gaze wander around him, like one who is lost, who knows not where he may be.

Full of pity Bonnaire drew near to him. "Can I help you, my poor fellow?" he asked; "your strength is exhausted, and you seem to be in great distress."

Then, as the other did not answer, but still let his eyes roam in a scared way from one point of the horizon to the other, Bonnaire continued: "Are you hungry? do you need a good bed? Let me guide you—you will here find all the help you need."

Thereupon the old and wretched-looking beggar began to stammer in a low voice, as if speaking to himself: "Beauclair, Beauclair—is this really Beauclair?"

"Of course it is; you are at Beauclair, that's certain," declared the former master-puddler with a smile. But on seeing the other give signs of increasing surprise and anxiety, he ended by understanding the truth: "You knew Beauclair formerly, no doubt," said he. "It is perhaps a long time since you were last here?"

"Yes, it was more than fifty years ago," the stranger answered in a husky voice.

Then Bonnaire burst into good-natured laughter. "In that case I am not astonished if you find a difficulty in recognising the place," he retorted. "There have been some changes. For instance, here the Abyss works have disappeared, whilst yonder the sordid hovels of old Beauclair have been razed to the ground. And you can see that a new city has been built; the park of La Crêcherie has spread over everything, invading the former town with its greenery and turning it into a vast garden, where the little white houses peep brightly from among the trees. And thus one naturally has to reflect before one can recognise the place."

The stranger had followed the explanations, turning his glance upon the various points which Bonnaire with gentle gaiety indicated. But again he wagged his head as if he could not believe what was told him. "No, no," said he, "I don't recognise it; this can't be Beauclair. Yonder are the two promontories of the Bleuse Mountains, between which the Brias gorge opens; and yonder, too, far away, is the plain of La

ÉMILE ZOLA

Roumagne. That's certain, but all the rest—those fine gardens and those houses belong to some other spot, some wealthy and smiling land which I never saw before. Ah! well, I shall have to walk further; I must have made a mistake in the road."

After picking up his staff and his wallet, he was making an effort to rise from the bench when his eyes at last rested on the old man who had shown himself so obliging and friendly. And at the first glance which he gave Bonnaire he shuddered, and became anxious to depart. Had he recognised Bonnaire then, although he could not recognise the town? Bonnaire, for his part, was so stirred by the sudden flame which shot from the other's hairy countenance that he examined him more attentively. Where had he previously seen those bright eyes, which blazed in moments of savage violence? All at once his memory awoke, and in his turn he shuddered, whilst all the past lived anew in the cry which burst from his lips:

"Ragu!"

For fifty years people had believed him to be dead! But the crushed and mutilated body found in a gorge of the Bleuse Mountains, on the morrow of his flight, after his crime, had not been his. He lived, he lived, good heavens! He had come back, and to Bonnaire that extraordinary resurrection after so many events and so many years brought anguish— anguish respecting all that had happened in the past, and all that might happen to-morrow.

"Ragu, Ragu, it is you!" Bonnaire repeated.

The other already had his staff in his hand, his wallet on his shoulder. But as he was recognised why should he go off? It was certain now that he had not mistaken his road.

"It's me, sure enough, my old Bonnaire," he replied; "and since you are still alive, though you are ten years older than I, I have certainly a right to be alive also—though it's true that I'm very battered."

Then, in the jeering tone of former times, he resumed: "So you give me your word for it, that splendid big garden yonder, with those pretty houses, is really Beauclair? Well, since I've got here, I've only to look for an inn where they'll let me sleep in a corner of the stables."

Why had he come back? What plans were rife under that bald skull, behind that wrinkled face, ravaged by so many years of evil and vagabond life? Bonnaire, who grew more and more anxious, could already picture Ragu disturbing the festival on the morrow by some scandal or other. He dared not question him at once, but he felt that it would be best to have him in his charge. Moreover, he was full of pity; his heart was quite stirred at finding the unhappy man in such a state of destitution.

"There are no more inns," he answered; "you will have to come to my place. You'll be able to eat as much as you like there, and you will sleep in a comfortable bed. Then we can have a chat. You'll tell me what you want, and I'll help you to content yourself if possible."

But Ragu jeered again: "Oh! what I want," he retorted—"why, the wishes of an old beggar like me, more or less infirm, are of no account at all. What I want, indeed! Why, I wanted to see you all again, to give a glance in passing at the place where I was born. The idea worried me, and I shouldn't have died easy in mind if I hadn't come for a stroll in this direction. That's a thing anybody may do, isn't it? The roads are still free."

"No doubt."

"Well, so I started—oh! years ago. When a man's got bad legs and never a copper, he doesn't make much progress. All the same, one reaches one's destination at last, since here I am. And, it's understood, let's go to your place, since you offer me hospitality like a good comrade."

The night was falling, and the two old men were able to cross new Beauclair without being remarked. On the way Ragu's astonishment increased; he glanced to right and to left, but could not recognise a single spot. At last, when Bonnaire stopped before one of the most charming of the dwellings, a house standing amidst a clump of fine trees, an exclamation escaped Ragu, showing that he still retained his ideas of former times: "What! you've made your fortune; you've become a *bourgeois* now!"

The former master-puddler began to laugh. "No, no; I've never been anything but a workman, and I'm only one to-day. But in a sense it's true that we've all made our fortunes and all become *bourgeois*."

As if his envious fears were quieted by that answer, Ragu began to sneer once more: "A workman can't be a *bourgeois*," said he, "and if a man still works it's because he hasn't made his fortune."

"All right, my good fellow, we'll have a chat about it, and I'll explain things to you. Meantime go in, go in."

Bonnaire for the time being was dwelling alone in this house, which was that of his granddaughter, Claudine, now the wife of Charles Froment. Daddy Lunot had long since been dead, and his daughter, Ragu's sister, the terrible Toupe, had followed him to his grave during the previous year, after a frightful quarrel, which, as she expressed it, had turned her blood. When Ragu heard of the loss of his sister and father, he simply made a little gesture, as if to say that by reason of their age he had anticipated it. After an absence of half a century one is not surprised to find nobody one knew left among the living.

"So here we are in the house of my granddaughter, Claudine," continued Bonnaire; "she's the daughter of my eldest son, Lucien, who married Louise Mazelle, the daughter of the Rentiers, whom you must remember. Claudine herself has married Charles Froment, a son of the master of La Crêcherie. But she and Charles have taken their daughter Aline, a little girl of eight, to see an aunt at Formeries, and they won't be back till to-morrow evening." Then he concluded gaily: "For some months now the children have taken me to live with them, by way of petting me. Come, the house is ours; you must eat and drink your fill, and then I'll show you to your bed. To-morrow, when it's daylight, we'll see to all the rest."

Ragu's head swam as he listened. All those names, those marriages, those three generations flitting by at a gallop quite scared him. How was he ever to understand things when so many unknown events and so many marriages and births had taken place? He did not speak again, but, seated at a well-spread table, ate some cold meat and fruit ravenously in the gay room, which was brilliantly illumined by an electric lamp. The comfort and ease which he felt around him must have weighed heavily upon the old vagabond's shoulders, for he seemed yet more aged, more utterly "done for," as with his face lowered over his plate he devoured the food, glancing askance the while at all the encompassing happiness in which he had no share. His very silence, his downcast mien at the sight of so much comfort, was expressive of all his long stored-up rancour, his powerless thirst for vengeance, his now irrealisable dream of triumphing and seeing disaster fall on others. And Bonnaire, again uneasy at the sight of his gloominess, wondered through what adventures he had rolled during the last half-century, and felt more and more astonished at finding him still alive and in such destitution.

"Where have you come from?" he ended by inquiring.

"Oh, from everywhere more or less!" Ragu answered with a sweeping gesture.

"Ah! so you've seen a good many countries and people and things?"

"Oh, yes; in France, Germany, England and America, and elsewhere. I've dragged my carcase, indeed, from one end of the world to the other."

Then, lighting his pipe, he gave Bonnaire, before retiring to bed, some idea of his life as a wanderer, in rebellion against work, idle by nature and coveting enjoyment. He typified the spoilt fruit of the wage-system—the wage-earner who dreams of suppressing the masters in order to take their place, and in his turn crush down his fellows. In his estimation there could be no other happiness than that of making a big fortune and enjoying it, with the satisfaction that one had known how to exploit the misery of the poor. And, violent in language, but all the same cowardly in the master's presence, dishonest, addicted to drink, and incapable of steady work, he had rolled from workshop to workshop, from country to country, at times dismissed, at others impelled by some silly whim to take himself off. He had never been able to put a copper by, wherever he had found himself want had become his companion, each succeeding year bringing about a fresh decline in his fortunes. When old age arrived it was a wonder that he did not die, famished and forsaken, in some gutter. Until he was nearly sixty, however, he had still found some petty jobs to do. Then he had stranded in a hospital, but had been obliged to leave it, though only to fall into another one. For the last fifteen years he had thus been clinging to life—how, he could hardly tell; and now he begged and tramped the roads for the crust of bread and truss of straw that he needed. And nothing of his old nature had departed from him, neither his covert rage and jealousy, nor his eager desire to be a master and enjoy himself.

Restraining a flood of questions which rose to his lips, Bonnaire at last exclaimed, "But all the countries you passed through must now be in a state of revolution! I know very well that we have progressed quickly here, and are in advance of the others. But the whole world is now stirring, is it not?"

"Yes, yes," Ragu answered in his jeering way, "they are fighting and building up a new society on all sides, but all that did not prevent me from starving."

He had passed through strikes and terrible risings in Germany, in England, and especially in the United States. In all the countries through which his rancour and idleness had carried him, he had witnessed tragic events. The last empires were crumbling, republics were springing up in their place, while frontiers were being suppressed by the confederation of neighbouring nations. It was like a smash up of the ice at the advent of springtide, when the ice melts and disappears, uncovering the fertilised soil, where germs sprout and flower forth in a

ÉMILE ZOLA

few days, under the glow of the great brotherly sun. All mankind was certainly in evolution, busying itself at last with the foundation of the happy city. But he, Ragu, bad workman, discontented reveller that he was, had simply suffered from all the catastrophes he had witnessed, merely encountering blows therein without ever finding an opportunity even to pillage a rich man's cellar, and, for once in his life, drink his fill. Nowadays, having become a confirmed old vagabond and beggar, he cared not a curse for the so-called city of justice and peace. It would not bring him back his twentieth birthday, it would not give him a palace full of slaves, where he might have ended his days amidst a round of pleasures, like the kings that books speak of. And he jeered bitterly at the idiocy of the human race which took so much trouble to prepare a somewhat cleaner social edifice for the great-grandchildren of the next century—an edifice which the men of nowadays would only know in dreams!

"But that dream has long sufficed for happiness," quietly said Bonnaire. "However, what you say is not true, the edifice is almost rebuilt even now, and is very beautiful and healthy and gay. I will show it to you to-morrow, and you will see if one does not taste pleasure in dwelling in it."

Then he explained that on the following day he would take Ragu to witness one of the four Festivals of Work, which filled Beauclair with delight on the first day of each season. Each of these festivals was marked by some particular rejoicings appropriate to the seasons. The one on the morrow, the summer festival, would be bright with all the flowers and fruits of the earth, overflowing in prodigious abundance, amidst the sovereign splendour of horizon and sky, in which the powerful sun of June would blaze.

Ragu, however, relapsed into gloomy anxiety, a covert fear, indeed, lest he should really find the ancient dream of social happiness fulfilled at Beauclair. Was it a fact then that after traversing so many countries where the society of to-morrow was coming forth amidst such frightful struggles—was it a fact that he would behold it virtually installed in that town, his own, whence he had fled on a day of murderous madness? Had that happiness, for which he had sought so frantically on all sides, come into being on his native spot, during his absence? Had he returned merely to behold the felicity of others, now that he himself could no longer expect any joy in life? The idea that he had spoilt his existence to the very end seemed to him like a supreme crushing blow amidst his misery and weariness whilst he sat there silently finishing the bottle of wine which had been placed before him. And when Bonnaire rose to show him to his room—a sweet-smelling white room with a large white bed in it—he followed with a heavy step, suffering from the open-handed brotherly hospitality offered to him with such happy ease.

"Sleep well, my good fellow," said Bonnaire, "till to-morrow morning!"

"Yes, till to-morrow—unless this cursed world should fall to pieces during the night."

Bonnaire, who also went to bed, found some difficulty in getting to sleep, for he still felt worried with respect to Ragu's intentions. He had a dozen times resisted his desire to put plain questions to him on the subject, from fear of provoking some dangerous explanation; for he thought it might be preferable to keep the matter in reserve and act hereafter according to circumstances. He feared some frightful scene; for perhaps that wretched vagabond, maddened by want and disaster, might have come back in order to provoke a scandal, insult Luc, insult Josine, and even attempt murder again. Bonnaire therefore resolved that he would not leave him alone for a moment on the following day. Moreover, in his desire to show him everything at Beauclair, there was the hope of morally paralysing him by an exhibition of such an abundance of wealth and power as would make him realise how futile would be the rage and rebellion of any one individual. When he should have seen and learnt everything he would no longer dare to stir, his defeat would be definitive. And thus Bonnaire at last fell asleep, resolved on waging that final battle for the sake of general harmony, peace, and love.

Already at six o'clock on the following morning a joyous flourish of trumpets sped over the roofs of Beauclair, announcing the Festival of Work. The sun was already high in the beautiful blue heavens. Windows opened, greetings flew through the greenery from one house to another, and one could feel that joy was already stirring the soul of the city, whilst the trumpet calls continued, arousing from garden to garden the cries of children and the laughter of loving couples.

Bonnaire, having quickly dressed himself, found Ragu up, washed and clad in some clean garments, which had been laid for him the previous evening on a chair. Now that he had well rested, the vagabond had become quite the jeerer of former days, resolved upon deriding everything and refusing to acknowledge the existence of the slightest progress. On seeing his host enter he indulged once more in his old evil insulting laugh.

"I say, old man!" he exclaimed, "what a row they make with those trumpets! That must be precious disagreeable for those who don't like to be startled out of their sleep. Are you wakened every morning in your barracks by that music?"

The old master-puddler preferred to find his guest in this mood. He smiled quietly, and answered: "No, no, that's only the *réveil* of our high days and holidays. On other mornings one can oversleep oneself if one chooses, for the quiet is delightful. But when life's so pleasant one always gets up early, and only the infirm regret having to lie in bed."

Then, with his attentive kindness, he added: "Have you slept well? Did you find everything you wanted?"

Ragu tried to make himself disagreeable again. "Oh! I can sleep anywhere," said he. "For years past I've been sleeping among hayricks, and they are worth the best beds in the world. It's just the same as regards all those inventions you have here—baths, and cold and hot water taps, and electrical heating appliances, which you only have to switch on. They may be useful, no doubt, when one's in a hurry, but it's still preferable to wash in the river and warm oneself before a good old stove." And, as his host did not reply, he concluded by saying: "You have too much water in your houses, they must be damp!"

What blasphemy! The idea of it, those streaming beneficent waters, so pure and so fresh, which were now the very health and joy and strength of Beauclair, whose streets and gardens they bathed as with eternal youth!

"Our water is our friend, the good fairy of our happy destiny," Bonnaire replied. "You will see it gushing forth on every side and fertilising our city. But come and have some breakfast; we will go out directly afterwards."

That first breakfast in the bright dining-room, illumined by the rising sun, was delightful. On the white cloth there were eggs, milk, and fruit, with bread which was so golden and smelt so sweet that one could divine it had been kneaded by carefully worked machinery for a happy people. And the old host lavished on his wretched guest the most delicate attentions, a simple and affectionate hospitality, which set an atmosphere of gentleness and kindness all around.

Whilst they ate they again began to chat. As on the previous evening, Bonnaire prudently refrained from asking Ragu any direct questions. Yet he felt persuaded that the other, after the fashion of all criminals, had returned to the scene of his crime, consumed by an invincible craving to behold it again and know what had taken place during his absence. Was Josine still alive, and if so what was she doing? Had Luc been saved from death, and had he taken her to live with him? At all events, what had become of them both? Surely it was an ardent curiosity with respect to all those matters which glittered in the vagabond's bright eyes. As he did not mention them, however—preferring apparently to keep his secret locked within him—Bonnaire had to content himself with putting into execution the plan which he had thought of the previous night. Without mentioning Luc's name he began to explain the greatness of his work.

"For you to understand things properly, my good fellow," said he, "it's necessary that I should tell you something about our position before we take a stroll through Beauclair. We have now got to the triumph, the full florescence of the movement, which was scarcely beginning when you went away."

Then he reverted to the origin of the evolution, the establishment of the works of La Crêcherie, based on an association between capital, labour, and brains, and its struggle with the Abyss, where the barbarous wage-system had been enforced. At last the latter had been vanquished and replaced, and La Crêcherie, with its pleasant white houses, had gradually spread over the site of Old Beauclair, the wretched home of want. Then Bonnaire showed how, both in a spirit of imitation and by reason of the necessities of the position, all the neighbouring works had ended by joining the original association; and how in due course other groups had been formed, every calling of a similar kind gradually being syndicated together, every family, as it were, meeting and uniting. Then the co-operation of producers on the one hand and of consumers on the other had completed the victory, work being reorganised on a basis of human solidarity, and bringing in its train a new form of society. There was now only four hours' work a day, and it was work freely chosen and constantly varied, in order that it might remain attractive; whilst machinery, the enemy of former days, had at present become a docile slave, upon whom all great efforts were cast. Then, moreover, the co-operation of consumers had swept away old-time trade, which had simply absorbed so much energy and gain. Huge general stores centralised products of all kinds, and distributed them according to consumers' needs, and in this manner millions of money were saved, agiotage and theft abstracting nothing on the way. Indeed, life was becoming greatly simplified: there was a tendency towards the complete suppression of specie and the closing of law courts and prisons; for disputes on matters of private interest ceased, and no longer urged man against man in some mad fit of fraud, pillage, or murder. Why should there be any crime left since there were no more poor, no more disinherited ones, since brotherly peace was being established more and more firmly every day, all being at last convinced that individual happiness came from the happiness of all? A long peace reigned, the blood tax—the conscription—had disappeared like all other taxes; there were no longer any rates of any kind or any prohibitive laws, but in lieu thereof full liberty for production and exchange. And in particular, since the parasites—the innumerable *employés*, functionaries, magistrates, barrack-men, and churchmen—had been suppressed, the greatest wealth had set in, such a prodigious heap of riches accumulating that from year to year the granaries became too small and threatened to burst beneath the ever-growing abundance of the public fortune.

"That's all right," interrupted Ragu when Bonnaire had reached this point. "But all the same, the real pleasure is to do nothing; and if you still work you are not a gentleman. To my idea there's no getting away from that. Besides, in one manner or another you are still paid, so that you still have a wage-system. But you are converted, eh?—you, who always demanded the absolute destruction of capital?"

Bonnaire laughed with joyous frankness. "It's true, they've ended by converting me," he said. "I believed in the necessity of a sudden revolution, some stroke which would have placed power in our hands, together with possession of the soil and all the instruments of work. But how can one resist the force of experience? For so many years past I've been witnessing here the assured victory of social justice and brotherly happiness, which I dreamt of so long! And thus patience has come to me; I'm weak enough—if you like to put it that way—to rest content with to-day's conquests, certain as I am of to-morrow's final victory. Of course, I'm ready to grant that a great deal remains to be done—our liberty and justice are not complete, capital and the wage-system must entirely disappear, the social pact must be rid of all forms of authority, we must have the free individual in the free community. And we try to act in such wise that our grandchildren's children may bring about the reign of justice and liberty in their entirety."

Then he explained the new educational methods which were in force, the working of the *crèches*, schools, and apprenticeship workshops, the adoption and cultivation of all the forms of energy springing from the passions, and the up-bringing of boys and girls together with the view of drawing yet closer the ties of love on which the city's strength would depend. The cause of greater freedom in the future rested with the couples of to-morrow; it might be taken that each generation growing up amidst an increase of equity and kindliness would contribute its stone to the final edifice. Meantime, the city's wealth would continue accumulating now that the suppression of the right of inheritance—almost entirely accomplished—prevented the building up of huge, scandalous, and poisonous individual fortunes; in such wise that the prodigious output of the work of all was becoming the property of all. Such things as the State Funds were also falling to pieces, the Rentiers, the idlers who lived on the work of others or on egotistical savings of their own, were disappearing. All citizens were equally rich, since the city—overflowing with work, freed from obstacles and hindrances, preserved from waste and theft—was piling up such immense wealth, that production would assuredly some day have to be moderated. Enjoyments once reserved for a few privileged beings were to-day already within the reach of all, and if family life remained simple the public edifices had become wonderfully sumptuous, large enough to hold huge multitudes, and so charming and so commodious as to be indeed true palaces of the people, centres of enjoyment where it loved to live. There were museums, and libraries, theatres, bathing establishments, places for diversions of one and another kind, together with simple "porches," opening out of meeting and lecture halls which the whole town frequented in its hours of rest. There was also a great number of hospitals, special isolated hospitals, for each kind of disease, and asylums which the infirm and the aged could enter freely; others, too, particularly for mothers and children, for pregnant women, who were carefully nursed from an early stage until their babes were born, and they themselves had fully recovered their strength. In this wise the new city affirmed its faith in motherhood and childhood—the mother who is the source of eternal life, the child who is the victorious messenger of the future.

"And now," Bonnaire gaily concluded, "since you have finished breakfast, let us go to see all those fine things, our Beauclair in its festive gaiety. I shan't spare you a single interesting nook of it."

At this Ragu, who had resolved upon no surrender, simply shrugged his shoulders, repeating what he deemed to be his decisive argument: "As you like; but all the same you are not gentlemen, you are still poor devils if you still work. Work's your master, and, when all's said, you've remained a people of slaves."

At the door of the house a little electric car with accommodation for two persons was waiting. Similar cars were at the disposal of all. The old master-puddler, who, despite his advanced years, had retained a clear eyesight and a firm hand, made his companion get in, and then took his own seat as driver.

"You don't mean to cripple me for good with this mechanism, eh?" asked Ragu.

"No, no, don't be alarmed. We get on very well together, electricity and I," Bonnaire replied, adding: "You will find it everywhere; it is the one force which drives our machinery, and it is in general use in our homes, just like a domestic servant. Oh! it has been necessary to produce it in incalculable quantities, and yet it seems that there's not enough, and that the former master of La Crêcherie is trying to provide us with a still larger supply, in order that we may have something like a planet blazing over Beauclair at night-time, and live amidst the glow of eternal day."

He laughed at this idea of putting all darkness to flight, whilst the car glided rapidly along the broad avenues. Before exploring Beauclair he proposed to go as far as Les Combettes, in order to show his companion the magnificent estate which was changing La Roumagne into a paradise of fertility. The festive morning was bright with sunshine, the roads resounded with gaiety, laughter and songs arising from all the other electric cars which were continually met on the way. A great many foot passengers were also arriving from neighbouring villages, mostly in bands, lads and girls brave in their ribbons, who joyously saluted Bonnaire the patriarch. And on cither side of the road stretched a perfect sea of grain. Instead of the old-time narrow patches of ground, badly manured and badly tilled, one found but one sole, huge field, richly cultivated by thousands of associates. Whenever the soil showed sign of impoverishment, the properties it lacked were imparted to it by a chemical dressing; it was warmed, too, and screened, and high cultivation brought forth two crops of vegetables and fruit each season. Thanks to machinery, man was spared many efforts: the harvests sprang up as if by enchantment over leagues and leagues of ploughed land. It was even said that one would become master of the clouds, directing them upon one or another point at one's will by means of electric currents, in such wise as to obtain days of rain or days of sunshine, according to the needs of cultivation.

"You see, my good fellow," resumed Bonnaire with a sweeping gesture, "we have the wherewithal for bread—bread for all, the bread to which each acquires a right as soon as he is born."

"So you feed even those who don't work?" asked Ragu.

"Certainly we do; but with very few exceptions only the sick and the infirm refrain from working. When one's in good health it bores one too much to remain doing nothing."

The car was now traversing some orchards, and the endless rows of cherry trees covered with red fruit presented a delightful spectacle. The apricots, farther on, were not yet ripe, and green was the fruit which weighed down the apple and pear trees. Nevertheless there was extraordinary abundance, enough dessert indeed for a whole nation until the ensuing spring. But they were at last reaching Les Combettes. The sordid village of former days had disappeared, and white houses had been built among the greenery alongside the Grand-Jean, the once filthy stream, which was now canalised, its pure water contributing to all the surrounding fertility. One no longer beheld the country side of the old times, all abandonment, dirt, and wretchedness, in which the peasantry had wallowed for centuries with the obstinacy born of routine and hatred of each other. The spirit of truth and liberty had visited that spot, and an evolution had set in towards science and harmony, enlightening minds, reconciling hearts, and bringing health, wealth, and joy in its train. Since all had consented to co-operate the happiness of each had come into being.

"You remember old Combettes," said Bonnaire, "the hovels standing in mud and dung, and the fierce-looking peasants, who complained of dying of starvation? See what association has done for all that!"

In his savage jealousy, however, Ragu would not let himself be convinced. With that hatred of work which had remained in his blood, the hereditary hatred of a wage-earner chained to toil, he replied: "If they work they are not happy. Their happiness is mendacious; the sovereign enjoyment is to do nothing." And though in former times he had often reviled the priests, he now added: "Doesn't the catechism say that work is man's punishment and mark of degradation? When once one gets to heaven one has nothing to do there."

On the way back to Beauclair the car passed La Guerdache, which was now enlarged, and whose grounds were full of young mothers, their babes, and playful children. But even the sight of that palace of the people and its beautiful park did not influence Ragu. "After all, what's the value of luxury and enjoyment which everybody can share?" said he. "A thing that one can't have entirely to oneself isn't worth much."

However, the little car was still speeding along, and they soon found themselves in Beauclair once more. The town, as Ragu had remarked on first perceiving it, did indeed present the aspect of a large garden. The houses, instead of being pressed close one to the other, as in the days of tyranny and terror, seemed to have dispersed in order that their inmates might enjoy more freedom, quietude, and health. Land cost nothing since all had been put in common from one to the other promontory of the Bleuse Mountains. Why, therefore, should folk have heaped themselves together when the whole great plain spread before them? Are a few thousand square yards of land too much for a family when so many immense tracts of the earth are absolutely uninhabited? Thus, each family had chosen its lot, and had built according to its fancy. Broad avenues ran past the gardens, supplying abundant means of communication, but people were not required to build their houses in line; they simply set them amongst the trees in the manner they pleased. Still, the dwellings had a family aspect, for all were clean and gay, and decorated with stoneware and faïence of bright colours, enamelled tiles, and so forth, which formed gables, borders, panels, friezes, and cornices, the convolvulus-blue, the dandelion-yellow, and the poppy-red of all this ornamentation imparting to the houses much the appearance of huge nosegays amidst the verdure of the trees. Then, on the squares, at the points where the avenues met, rose the many public buildings, huge piles in which triumphed steel and iron. Their magnificence was compounded of simplicity, of logical fitness for the purpose for which they were intended, and of intelligence in the choice of materials and style of decoration. In these buildings it was intended that the people should be at home; the museums, libraries, theatres, baths, laboratories, meeting and amusement halls were but so many common-houses, open to the entire community. Moreover, some portions of the avenues were already being covered with glass, and it was proposed to warm them in winter, so as to enable people to stroll there in comfort during cold and rainy weather.

Ragu gave so many signs of surprise, and seemed so lost, that Bonnaire began to laugh. "Ah! it isn't easy to identify the place," said he, "but we are now on the old Place de la Mairie, whence started the four great thoroughfares—the Rue de Brias, the Rue de Formeries, the Rue de Saint-Cron, and the Rue de Magnolles. Only, as the old town-hall was falling to pieces from sheer rottenness, it was demolished, together with the old schools, where the boys learned to spell under the master's rod. And now, you see, there is a series of large pavilions, chemical and physical laboratories, where all are free to study and experiment when they think they have made some discovery which may prove useful to the community. Then, too, the four streets have been transformed, their hovels have been swept away, and little of them remains save the gardens and houses of the gentlefolk, in which sundry marriages have ended by placing the children of the poor devils of former times."

Then Bonnaire went on to explain other transformations brought about by the victory of the new social system. For instance, although the sub-prefecture had been preserved and two wings had even been added to it, it had been converted into a public library. In the same way the law-courts had become a museum, whilst it had been possible at no very great cost to turn the prison with its cells into a bath-house where water abounded. Then there was the garden, which had been planted on the site of the fallen church—a garden where some fine shady verdure already arose around a little lake which now filled the ancient underground crypt. In this wise, as the various forms of authority disappeared, the buildings once allotted to them had reverted to the people, who had disposed of them in such a manner as to increase their own comfort and enjoyment.

However, whilst the car was ascending another fine long avenue Ragu again felt lost, and inquired of his guide: "Where are we now?"

"In the old Rue de Brias," Bonnaire answered. "Ah! its aspect has greatly changed. Petty trade having completely disappeared, the shops shut up one after the other, and at last the old houses were demolished to make room for those new ones which smile so pleasantly among the hawthorns and lilac bushes. The Clouque, that poisonous sewer, has been covered up, and the side walk of this avenue, on the right, passes over it."

He went on recalling the narrow, dark Rue de Brias of former times, with its ever-muddy pavement, over which weary workers had trudged day by day. Hunger and prostitution had prowled there at night, whilst poor housewives went from shop to shop to beg a petty credit. There had reigned the Laboques, levying tribute on all purchasers, whilst Caffiaux poisoned the workers with doctored alcohol, and Dacheux kept jealous watch over his meat, holy meat—the chosen food of the wealthy. Only the beautiful Madame Mitaine had been willing to close her eyes when a loaf or two happened to disappear from her shop-front on the days when the street urchins were unable to restrain their hunger. But now all the misery and suffering had been swept away, and the avenue ascended, broad, clean, and flooded with sunlight, with only the houses of happy workers upon either hand, whilst the multitude strolled about laughing and singing on that bright festive morning.

"But if La Clouque flow's under that grassy bank," exclaimed Ragu suddenly, "Old Beauclair must have been over yonder, on the site of that new park, where the white house-fronts are peeping out of the greenery?"

And this time he remained aghast. The spot he mentioned had indeed been Old Beauclair, the sordid mass of hovels spread out like an evil-smelling stagnant pond, with its streets lacking both light and air, and infected by their open drains. He particularly remembered the Rue des Trois Lunes, the darkest, narrowest, and filthiest of them all. But the blast of avenging justice had purified the spot, carried away the abominable cloaca, and in place thereof had set that greenery, amidst which had sprung dwellings of health and joy.

Bonnaire, amused by Ragu's astonishment, now drove him more slowly along the new thoroughfares of the happy City of Work. In honour of that day of rejoicing all the houses were gay with bunting; bright oriflammes flapped in the light morning breeze, and vivid drapery hung about doors and windows. The thresholds of the houses, too, were covered with roses, the streets even were bestrewn with them; such an abundance of roses being grown in the vast plantations of the neighbourhood that the whole town was able to adorn itself with them, like a woman on her bridal morn. Music resounded on all sides, the chorus singing of maids and youths flew past in sonorous waves, whilst the pure voices of the children soared aloft to the very sun itself. It seemed as if the limpid and rejoicing orb were also participating in the festival, as it cast great sheets of gold under the sky's sumptuous tent, so aerial and silken, and so delightfully blue. All the people were now flocking into the streets, arrayed in light-coloured garments adorned with beautiful stuffs, which had once been so dear and which were now at the disposal of all. New fashions, very simple in their magnificence, made the women look adorable. Gold—since money had gradually disappeared—was now simply used for purposes of adornment. Each little girl that was born found in her cradle her necklets, her bracelets, and her rings, even as the little ones of former days had found their toys. But jewellery now had no value, gold had simply become so much beauty. And, moreover, the electrical furnaces were about to produce incalculable quantities of diamonds and precious stones, sacks of rubies, emeralds, and sapphires—gems enough, indeed, to cover all the women of the world. The maids who passed hanging on their lovers' arms already had their hair adorned with constellations of flashing stars. And there was an endless procession of couples, those whom love in its freedom had just betrothed; the young folk of twenty, too, who had recently mated and were never more to part; and those also who had grown old amidst mutual affection, and whose hand-clasp had tightened with each succeeding year.

"Where are they all going like that?" Ragu at last inquired.

"Oh! they are calling on one another," Bonnaire answered, "inviting one another to the grand dinner which is to be given this evening, and which you will attend. And many are just strolling about in the sunshine for the love of the thing, because they feel gay and at home in our beautiful brotherly streets. Besides, there are entertainments and games on all sides, with admission gratis, of course, for one may freely enter all our public establishments. Those parties of children are being taken to one or another circus, and others of the crowd are going to meetings, theatrical performances, and concerts. Our theatres, you know, enter into our system of social education."

Then, all at once, on reaching a house whose occupiers, it seemed, were about to go out, Bonnaire stopped the car. "Would you like to visit one of our new houses?" he asked. "This is where my grandson Félicien lives, and as we have just caught him at home, he will receive us."

Félicien was the son of Séverin Bonnaire, who had married Léonie, the daughter of Ma-Bleue and Achille Gourier. He, Félicien, only a fortnight previously had for his part espoused Hélène Jollivet, daughter of André Jollivet and Pauline Froment. But when Bonnaire wished to explain those relationships to Ragu, the latter made the gesture of a man who feels quite lost amidst such a tangle of alliances. The young people were charming—the wife very young and adorably fair; the husband also fair, and tall and strong. Love perfumed all the bright, gay, simple, yet elegantly furnished rooms of their home, which, like the streets, was that day full of roses; for it seemed as if roses had rained upon Beauclair—there were some everywhere, even on the roofs. The whole house was visited, and then they returned to a room which served as a workshop—a large, square apartment, where an electrical motor was installed. Besides following three or four other callings, Félicien was by taste a metal-turner, and preferred to work at this avocation in his own home. Several of his comrades, young men of his own age, were similarly inclined, and a new movement was thus arising among the generation just reaching manhood. One found the worker on a small scale following some calling at home in all freedom, irrespective of work in the great general workshops. For these individual artisans the supply of electric power, which they found in their homes even as they found water there, was of wonderful assistance. Home-work under such conditions proved easy, and clean, and light, and some houses were gradually becoming family workshops and tending to the realisation of the formula: The free workman in the free city.

"Till this evening, my children," said Bonnaire, taking leave. "Shall you dine at our table?"

"Oh! it's impossible this time, grandfather," was the reply; "we have our places at grandmother Morfain's table. But we shall see one another at dessert."

Ragu took his seat in the car again without speaking a word. He had remained silent throughout the visit, though for a moment he had paused before the little motor. At last, he once again managed to throw off the emotion which he had felt in the midst of so much comfort and happiness.

"Come," he exclaimed, "can one call those the houses of well-to-do *bourgeois*, when there's machinery in the largest room? I grant that your men are better lodged, and have more enjoyment, since want has disappeared. But they are still workmen, mercenaries condemned to labour! In the old days there were at least a few happy, privileged folk who did nothing. All your progress consists in reducing the entire community to common slavery!"

At this despairing cry from that devotee of sloth, whose religion was fast crumbling, Bonnaire gently shrugged his shoulders. "One must understand, my good fellow," said he, "what it is that you call slavery. If it be slavery to breathe and eat and sleep—in a word, to live—why, then work is slavery. But if you live you must necessarily work; one cannot live an hour without doing work of some kind. However, we'll talk of all that by-and-by. For the present let us go home to lunch, and we'll spend the afternoon in visiting the workshops and the stores."

After their meal, indeed, they went out again, but this time on foot, walking along leisurely. They crossed the entire works, all the sunlit halls, where the steel and copper of the new machinery shone like jewels in the bright radiance. That morning, moreover, some of the workers—parties of youths and girls—had come to decorate the machinery with garlands of verdure and roses; for was it not right that it should participate in the festival of work, powerful, gentle, and docile artisan that it was, bringing relief both to man and to beast? And nothing could have been gayer or more touching. The roses that adorned the presses, the huge hammers, the giant planing, rolling, and turning machines, proclaimed how attractive work had become, bringing comfort to the body and delight to the mind. Songs rang out, too, chains were formed, and amidst general laughter quite a *farandole* began, spreading gradually from one hall to another, and transforming the entire works into an immense palace of rejoicing.

Ragu, who still remained impassive, walked about, raising his eyes to the lofty windows, which were bright with sunshine, or glancing now at the slabs under foot, and now at the walls of speckless brightness, or else examining the machines, many of which were unknown to him. They were huge creatures, provided with all sorts of intricate works, in order that they might perform most of the tasks once allotted to man, the most trying as well as the most delicate. Some had legs, arms, feet, and hands, so that they might move, embrace, clutch, and manipulate metal with fingers at once supple, nimble, and strong. The new puddling furnaces, in which the "bloom" was kneaded mechanically, particularly struck Ragu. Was it possible that the "bloom" came out like that, quite ready to pass under the hammer! And then there was the electricity that propelled the bridges, that set the huge hammers in motion, that worked the rolling-machinery, which could have covered the whole world with rails. On each and every side one found that sovereign electric force. It had become like the very blood of the factory, circulating from one to the other end of the workshops, giving life to all things, acting as the one source of movement, heat, and light.

"It's good, no doubt," Ragu grunted. "The place is very clean and very large, and ever so much better than our dirty dens of former times, where we found ourselves like pigs in their styes. There has certainly been a good deal of progress; but the worry is that one hasn't yet found a way to give each man an income of a hundred thousand francs."

"Oh! but we have our income of a hundred thousand francs," retorted Bonnaire jestingly. "Just come and see."

Then he took the other to the general stores—great barns, huge granaries, vast magazines—where all the produce and wealth of the city was accumulated. They had been enlarged, perforce, year by year; for one no longer knew where to store the crops, and indeed it had even been necessary to check the production of manufactured goods, to avoid encumbrance. Nowhere else could one better realise what an incalculable fortune a nation might amass when all intermediaries were done away with—the drones and the thieves, all those who had lived upon the work of others without producing anything themselves.

"There are our Rentes!" Bonnaire repeated; "each of us can help himself here without counting. And don't you think that it all represents a hundred thousand francs' worth of happy life for each of us? We are all equally rich, it's true, and, as you have said, that would spoil your pleasure, fortune being nothing to you unless it be seasoned with the misery of others. Yet it has an advantage; for one no longer incurs the risk of being robbed or murdered some evening at a street corner, just for the sake of gain."

Then he mentioned a movement that was setting in, quite apart from the working of the general stores—that is, a movement of direct exchange between producers, a movement which had originated among the petty family workshops. Perhaps then the great workshops and the huge general stores would end by disappearing in the course of the advance towards increase of liberty: the sovereign freedom of the individual amidst the freedom of all mankind.

Ragu listened, more and more upset by that conquest of happiness which he still wished to deny. And at a loss as to how he might hide the fact that he was sorely shaken, he exclaimed: "So you're an Anarchist now!"

This time Bonnaire burst into noisy merriment. "Oh! my good fellow, I used to be a Collectivist, and you reproached me for having ceased to be one. Now you make an Anarchist of me. But the truth is that we are no longer anything at all since the common dream of happiness, truth, and justice has been realised. But, now that I think of it, come a little way with me and see something else by way of finishing up our visit."

He led him to the rear of the general stores, to the base of the mountain ridge, to the very spot, indeed, where Lange the potter had formerly installed his rudimentary kilns in an enclosure barricaded with dry stones. To-day a large building stood there, a manufactory of stoneware and faïence, whence came the enamelled bricks and tiles, the thousand bright-hued decorations which adorned the whole city. Yielding indeed to the friendly entreaties of Luc, and seeing a little equity arise to relieve the misery of the people, Lange had decided to take some pupils. Since the masses were reviving to joy he would be able to realise an old dream of his by making and scattering broadcast all the bright earthenware, glowing like golden wheatears, cornflowers and poppies, with which he had so long desired to enliven the house-fronts peeping out of the garden greenery. And beauty had blossomed forth under the touch of his big, genial hands—beauty in an admirable form of art, coming from the people and returning to it, instinct with all the popular primitive strength and grace. He had not renounced the making of humble utensils, kitchen and table pottery, pans, pots, pitchers, and plates—all exquisite in form and colour, setting the glorious charm of art in the most commonplace daily life; but he had each year increased his production, adorning the public buildings with superb friezes, peopling the promenades with graceful statues, setting up in the squares lofty fountains which looked like nosegays, and whence the water of the springs flowed with all the freshness of eternal youth. And the band of artists whom he had created in his own image now set the beauty of art in the very pots which the housewives used as receptacles for their preserves and jam.

As it happened, Lange was at the top of the little flight of steps on the threshold of the factory. Although he had nearly completed his seventy-fifth year, his short squat figure had remained robust. He still had the same rustic-looking square head, bushy with hair and beard, now white like snow. But at present all the kindliness, long hidden beneath his rough bark, gleamed from his eyes in clear smiles. A party of playful children stood before him, boys and girls, who pushed one another and stretched out their hands whilst he went on with a distribution of little presents, as was indeed his habit every *fête* day. He thus apportioned among them some little clay figures modelled with a few thumbstrokes, coloured and baked by the gross, yet very graceful, and in some instances charmingly comical. They represented the most simple subjects, everyday occupations, the petty incidents and fugitive delights of the passing hour. There were children laughing or crying, young girls attending to their household duties, men at work—in fact, all life in its everlasting, marvellous florescence.

"Come, come, my children," said Lange, "don't be in a hurry, there are enough for all of you. Here, my pet, take this little girl who's putting on her stockings; and for you, my lad, here's this boy coming back from school. Ah! you little darky, yonder, take this smith with his hammer."

He shouted and laughed, vastly amusing himself in the midst of all those children, who struggled for the possession of his exquisite little figures.

"Ah! be careful!" he cried, "you must not break them. Put them in your rooms, so that you may have some pretty colours and pleasant lines before your eyes. And in that wise when you grow up you will love what's beautiful and good, and be handsome and good yourselves."

It was his theory that the people needed beauty in order to become healthy and brotherly. Everything that surrounded them, particularly all objects of current use—utensils, furniture, and dwellings—ought to suggest beauty. And belief in the superiority of aristocratic art was imbecile. The greatest, most touching and most human art was that into which most life entered. Moreover, the work that proved immortal and defied the centuries was one that sprang from the multitude and summed up for it an epoch or a civilisation. And it was ever from the people that art flowered forth in order that it might embellish the people themselves and impart to them the perfume and the radiance which were as necessary to their life as was daily bread.

"Ah! here's a peasant reaping, and a woman washing linen. Take that one, my big lassie; and you, my little man, there's one for you. Well, it's over now. Mind you are very good; kiss your mammas and papas for me. Ah! my little lambs, my little chicks, life is beautiful, life is good!"

Ragu had listened motionless and silent, but he was evidently more and more surprised. At last, with a ferocious sneer he exploded: "Ah! Master Anarchist!" said he, "so you no longer talk of blowing up the whole show, eh?"

Lange turned sharply and looked at Ragu without recognising him. However, he displayed no anger, but simply began to laugh again: "Ah! so you know me," he said, "though what your name is I can't remember. Well, yes, it's true, I did wish to blow up the whole show. I cried it everywhere, to all the winds of the sky, and I heaped malediction after malediction upon the accursed city, announcing its approaching destruction by iron and fire. I had even resolved to do justice myself and raze Beauclair as by lightning. But things turned out otherwise. Enough justice came to disarm me. The town was purified, and rebuilt, and I can't destroy it now that all I wanted, all I dreamt of, is being realised—isn't that so, Bonnaire; we've made peace, eh?"

Thereupon Lange, the former Anarchist, held out his hand to the ex-Collectivist with whom he had once had such bitter quarrels: "We were ready to eat one another, were we not, Bonnaire?" he resumed. "We agreed as to the city of liberty, equity, and cordial understanding which we wished to reach; only we differed as to the best road to follow, and those who thought that they ought to turn to the right were ready to massacre those who showed a desire to turn to the left. But now that we've all reached our destination, it would be too stupid of us to continue quarrelling. Is that not so, Bonnaire? As I said before, peace is made."

Bonnaire, who had retained the potter's hand in his grasp, pressed and shook it affectionately.

"Yes, yes, Lange," he replied; "we did wrong in not coming to an understanding, it was perhaps that which prevented us from making progress. Or perhaps we were all right, since now here we are, hand in hand, willing to admit that at bottom we all wanted the same thing."

"And if things are not yet altogether such as absolute justice would require," Lange resumed, "we can rely on those lads and lassies to continue the work and some day finish it. You hear, my little chicks, my little lambs, love each other well."

The shouting and laughing was beginning afresh, when Ragu in his brutal fashion intervened once more: "But I say, you spoilt Anarchist, what about your Barefeet, have you made her your wife, eh?"

Tears started to Lange's eyes. Nearly twenty years previously the tall and beautiful creature whom he had compassionately picked up on the roads, and who had worshipped him like a slave, had died in his arms, the victim of a frightful and mysterious accident. He had spoken of an explosion in one of his kilns, saying that its iron door had been carried away, and had struck Barefeet full in the bosom. But the truth was assuredly different. She had assisted him in his experiments with explosives, and must have been struck down during some attempts to charge those famous little "stock-pots," of which he had spoken so complacently, intending to deposit them at the town-hall, the sub-prefecture, the law-courts—in all the places, indeed, where there was any form of authority to be destroyed. For months and for years that tragic death had made Lange's heart bleed, and even nowadays, after the attainment of so much happiness, he still wept for the loss of that

ÉMILE ZOLA

gentle yet impassioned woman who, in return for the alms of a piece of bread, had for ever bestowed on him the royal gift of her beauty.

He strode roughly towards Ragu: "You are a bad man," he cried, "why do you stab me in the heart like that? Who are you? Where have you sprung from? Don't you know that my dear wife is dead, and that every evening I still ask her forgiveness, accusing myself of having caused her death? If I haven't become a bad man, I owe it to her dear memory, for she is always with me, she is my good counsellor. But you, you are a bad man, I don't want to recognise you, I don't want to know your name. Go away, go away from our city!"

He was superb in his dolorous violence. The poetic spirit that dwelt within his rugged form, and which had formerly manifested itself in vengeful flights of fancy of a sombre grandeur, had now softened, tempering his heart with infinite quivering kindliness.

"Have you recognised him then?" asked Bonnaire anxiously. "Who is he? Tell me."

"I do not wish to recognise him," Lange repeated yet more rigorously. "I shall not say anything—let him go his way, let him go his way at once! He isn't fit to be one of us."

Thereupon Bonnaire, feeling convinced that the potter had recognised Ragu, gently led the latter away in order to avoid any painful explanations. For his part Ragu evinced no desire to linger and quarrel, but retired in silence. All that he had seen and heard had dealt him blow after blow in the heart, filling him with bitter regret and boundless envy. He had begun to stagger beneath the shock of that happiness, in which he had not, and would never have, the slightest part.

But it was particularly the aspect of Beauclair in the evening that upset him. It had become a custom for each family to set its table in the street and dine there on that first day of summer. The repast was like a fraternal communion of the whole city, the bread was broken, and the wine was drunk in public, and the tables were at last brought together in such wise that they formed but one table, the whole town changing into a vast banqueting-hall, where the people became one sole family.

At seven o'clock, whilst the sun was still shining, the tables were set out, decorated with roses, that rain of roses which had perfumed Beauclair ever since the morning. The white cloths, the decorated crockery, the glass and the silver reflected the purple glow of the sunset. As silver money, like gold money, was fast disappearing, each now had his or her silver goblet, even as in olden time one had goblets or mugs of pewter. And Bonnaire insisted on Ragu taking his seat at his table, or rather at that of his granddaughter Claudine, who had married Luc's son, Charles Froment.

"I have brought you a guest," he simply said to the others, without naming Ragu. "He is a stranger, a friend."

And all made answer: "He is welcome."

Bonnaire kept Ragu near him. But the table was a long one, for four generations elbowed one another. When Bonnaire the patriarch looked round he could see his son Lucien and his daughter-in-law Louise Mazelle, both of whom were now over fifty. He could also see his granddaughter Claudine and his grandson-in-law, Charles Froment, both in their prime; and he could likewise see his great-granddaughter Alice, a charming little maid, eight years of age. And all manner of kith and kin followed. Bonnaire explained to Ragu that a gigantic table would have been needed if his three other children, Antoinette, Zoé, and Séverin, had not arranged to dine at other tables with their own offspring. At dessert, however, they would bring the tables together in a neighbourly fashion, in suchwise that they would end by being all together.

Ragu more particularly turned his eyes upon Louise Mazelle, who still looked very charming and active. He was no doubt surprised by the sight of that daughter of the *bourgeoisie*, who invariably displayed so much affection for her husband Lucien, the scion of a working-class stock. Leaning towards Bonnaire, the old vagabond at last asked him in an undertone: "Are the Mazelles dead then?"

"Yes; the dread of losing their money killed them. The conversions which upset everything and foreshadowed the approaching suppression of Rentes altogether, fell upon them like so many thunderbolts. The husband was the first to die, killed by the idea that his idle days were over and that he would perhaps have to work again. Then the wife dragged on for a while, cloistering herself at home and no longer daring to go out, convinced as she was that as violent hands had been laid on Rentes people must nowadays be murdered at every street-corner. It was in vain that her daughter proposed to take her with her; she stifled at the thought of being fed by others, and at last one day she was found dead—stricken by apoplexy, her face quite black, and resting among a package of her Rente certificates, which had virtually lost all value. Poor people! They died in a state of stupefaction, absolutely overcome, and declaring that the world had been turned topsy-turvy."

ÉMILE ZOLA

Ragu wagged his head. He was not inclined to weep for those *bourgeois*, but at the same time he was of opinion that a world whence idleness was banished was not worth living in. Then he again looked round him, and became yet gloomier as he noticed the rising spirits of one and all, and the abundance and luxury which prevailed at the table, though to the others those things were now only natural, and gave no cause for vanity. The women were all arrayed in similar festive garb, similar light, charming silks; and precious stones—rubies and sapphires and emeralds—glittered in the hair of all. But the roses, the superb roses, were preferred to the gems by far, for they lived, and were therefore the more precious.

Already in the middle of the meal, which was made up of delicate and simple viands, vegetables, and fruit especially, everything being served on silver dishes, joyous songs began to arise, saluting the setting sun and bidding it *au revoir*, in the certainty that in a few hours' time it would happily arise again. And all at once, amidst the singing, a delightful incident occurred. All the birds of the neighbourhood—the robins, the blackcaps, the finches, even the sparrows, flew down on the tables before retiring to rest among the darkening greenery. They alighted boldly on one's shoulders, hopped down to peck the crumbs on the cloth, and accepted dainties from the hands of the children and the women. Since Beauclair had become a town of concord and peace they had been aware of the change there; they no longer feared aught from its kindly inhabitants—neither snares nor gunshots. And they had grown familiar in their way; they formed part of the various families; each garden had its denizens, who at meal-time flew down to take their share of the common food.

"Ah! here are our little friends!" cried Bonnaire. "How they chatter! They know very well that to-day is a festival. Crumble some bread for them, Alice!"

Ragu, with his face darkening and a dolorous expression in his eyes, watched the birds as they flew down from every side, like a very whirlwind of small light feathers to which the last sunbeams imparted a golden glow. Those birds made the dessert quite lively, so many were the little feet hopping jauntily among the cherries and the roses. And of all the felicity and splendour that Ragu had witnessed since the morning, nothing had so clearly and so charmingly told him how peaceful and how happy was that young community. For him it was like a supreme blow; he suddenly arose and said to Bonnaire: "I'm stifling, I must walk about. And besides, I want to see everything, all the tables, all the people."

Bonnaire understood him well. Was it not Luc and Josine whom he wished to see? Was not all the ardent curiosity that he had displayed since his return culminating in a desire to behold them? Still avoiding a decisive explanation, Bonnaire answered: "Very well, I will show you; we will make the round of the tables."

The first they reached—the one set out before the next house—was that of the Morfains. Petit-Da presided over it beside his wife, Honorine Caffiaux, both of them with snowy hair; and with them were their son Raymond, their daughter-in-law Thérèse Froment, and their eldest grandson, Maurice Morfain, a tall youth, nineteen years of age already. Then, on the other side, came Achille Gourier's line, with his widow, Ma-Bleue, whose large sky-blue eyes retained all their intensity, though she was now nearly seventy years old. She would soon be a great-grandmother, through her daughter Léonie, married to Séverin Bonnaire, and her grandson, Félicien, born of that marriage, and lately wedded to Hélène, the daughter of Pauline Froment and André Jollivet. All were present, even both of the last named, who had come with their daughter. And some of them were making merry with Hélène, suggesting that if her firstborn should be a son he ought to be called Grégoire. Meantime her sister Berthe, though she was scarcely fifteen, already laughed at the soft things said to her by her cousin Raymond, thus offering promise of another love-match in the future.

The arrival of Bonnaire was hailed with joyous acclamations. Ragu, who was losing himself more and more amidst the tangle of matrimonial alliances, particularly desired that the two Froments seated at this table should be pointed out to him. They were two of Luc's daughters, Thérèse and Pauline, both well on the road to their fortieth year, but still displaying a bright and healthy beauty. Then, as the sight of Ma-Bleue reminded Ragu of old Mayor Gourier and Sub-Prefect Châtelard, he wished to know how they had ended. Bonnaire told him that they had passed away, one a few days later than the other, after spending their last years in close intimacy, linked together by the loss of the beautiful Léonore. Gourier, the first to depart, had with difficulty accustomed himself to the new state of things. He had often raised his arms to heaven in astonishment at being an employer of labour no longer; and he had been wont to talk of the past with all the melancholy of an aged man, who, although he would willingly have devoured the priests in former days, had actually begun to regret the ceremonies of the Catholic Church, the First Communions and processions, the incense and the pealing bells. Châtelard, on the other hand, had gallantly fallen asleep in the skin of an Anarchist, for such he had gradually become in the midst of his diplomatic reserve, accomplishing his destiny such as he had wished it to be—living happy and forgotten in the midst of that Beauclair which was now rebuilt and triumphant—and at last disappearing in silence with the *régime* whose funeral procession he had so complacently followed, he himself swallowed up, as it were, in the collapse of the last ministry.

But there was a finer, a more noble, death to be mentioned, the death of Judge Gaume, which was recalled by the presence at that table of his grandson André and his great-granddaughters Hélène and Berthe. Alone with his grandson, Gaume had lived to the age of ninety-two in all the desolation of his spoilt and dolorous life. On the day, however, when the law courts and the prison were closed, he had felt himself in a measure delivered from the haunting torture of his career as a judge. A man judging men, consenting to play the part of infallible truth, absolute justice, in spite of all the possible infirmities of his mind and his heart, the thought of it made Gaume shudder, filled him with excessive scruples, dreadful remorse, terror lest he should indeed have been a bad judge. However, the justice which he had long awaited, which he had feared he might never see, had dawned at last—not the justice of an iniquitous social system, reigning with the sword, with which it defends a small minority of despoilers, and with which it strikes the great multitude of wretched slaves, but justice as between free man and free man—justice allotting to each his share of legitimate happiness, and bringing in its train truth and brotherliness and peace.

On the morning of the day he died Gauine sent for an old poacher whom he had formerly condemned to a heavy punishment for killing a gendarme who had dealt him a sabre stroke, and he publicly expressed his contrition, and cried aloud all the doubts which had poisoned his career. He proclaimed all the crimes of the Code, all the errors and falsehoods of the Statutes, those weapons of social oppression and hatred, those corrupt foundations of the social system whence spring perfect epidemics of theft and murder.

"And so," Ragu resumed, "those young folk seated at that table, that Félicien and his wife Hélène, at whose house we called this morning, are at once the grandchildren of the Froments, the Morfains, the Jollivets, and the Gaumes? But doesn't the blood of such enemies poison those in whose veins it now flows?"

"No, indeed," Bonnaire quietly replied, "that commingling of blood has brought reconciliation, and the race has acquired more beauty and strength from it."

Fresh bitterness awaited Ragu at the next table—that of Bourron, his old chum, the boon companion of his days of sloth and drunkenness, whom he had ruled and led astray so easily. The idea of it! Bourron happy, Bourron saved, when he himself remained in his hell! In spite of his many years Bourron did indeed look quite triumphant as he sat there beside his wife Babette, she who had ever remained cheerful, whose unchangeable hopes and optimism had found fulfilment without even moving her to astonishment. Was it not natural? One was happy because one always ends by being happy.

And around the Bourrons there had been no limit to the swarming of offspring. There was first their eldest daughter, Marthe, who had married Auguste Laboque and had given birth to Adolphe, who in his turn had married Germaine, the daughter of Zoé Bonnaire and Nicholas Yvonnot. There was next their son Sébastien, who had married Agathe Fauchard, and had begotten Clémentine, who on her side had married Alexandre Feuillat, the son of Léon Feuillat and of Eugénie Yvonnot. The fourth generation proceeding from those two branches of Bourron's family was already represented by two little girls, Simonne Laboque and Amélie Feuillat, each of them in their fifth year. And by virtue of the kinship established by marriage the party further included Louis Fauchard, married to Julienne Dacheux, who had given him a daughter, Laure; and Évariste Mitaine, married to Olympe Lenfant, by whom he had had a son Hippolyte. Then there was the aforesaid Hippolyte himself, now the husband of Laure Fauchard, and the father of a lad in his eighth year, named François, in such wise that the fourth generation was sprouting vigorously on this side also. Throughout festive Beauclair one could not have found a larger table than that where intermingled the descendants of the Bourrons, the Laboques, the Bonnaires, the Yvonnots, the Fauchards, the Feuillats, the Dacheux, the Lenfants, and the Mitaines.

Bonnaire, who here again found one of his own children, Zoé, gave Ragu some particulars respecting those whom death had carried off. Old Fauchard and his wife Natalie—he always in a state of stupor and she always complaining—had gone off without understanding the great changes which were taking place. Feuillat, on his side, had beheld the triumph of his work, that vast estate of Les Combettes, ere he departed. Lenfant and Yvonnot had lately followed him to their graves, in that earth which was now loved with intelligence and fertilised with virile power. And after the Dacheux, the Caffiaux and the Laboques, those relics of the vanished trading system, the beautiful bakeress, the good Madame Mitaine, had passed away full of years, kindliness, and beauty.

But Ragu was no longer listening—he could not take his eyes from Bourron. "He looks quite young," he muttered, "and his Babette still has her pretty laugh."

He recalled the sprees of other days, Bourron and he lingering late in Caffiaux's den, railing against the masters, and at last staggering home, dead drunk. And he recalled his own long life of wretchedness, the fifty years that he had squandered in rolling from workshop to workshop through the world. To-day the experiment had been made and made successfully. Work, reorganised and regenerated, had saved his old chum when he was already half lost, whereas he, Ragu, had come back annihilated by the old labour system, full of misery and suffering, that iniquitous wage-system, which poisoned and destroyed.

All at once there came a charming incident which brought Ragu's anguish to a climax. Simonne Laboque, the daughter of Adolphe and Germaine, a fair-haired little maid about five years old, took some rose petals, scattered over the table, in her chubby little hands, and smilingly poured them over her great-grandfather's white head.

"There! grandpa Bourron, there you are, and there's some more! They're to make you a crown. Oh! you've some in your hair, and in your ears, and on your nose too. You've some everywhere! And *bonne fête, bonne fête*, grandpa Bourron!"

The whole table laughed, applauded, and acclaimed the old man. But Ragu fled, dragging Bonnaire with him. He was trembling, he could scarcely remain erect. When they had got a little distance away, however, he suddenly said to Bonnaire in a husky voice: "Listen, what's the use of keeping it back any longer? I only came to see *them*. Where are they? Show them me!"

He was speaking of Luc and Josine; and, as Bonnaire, who had fully understood it, delayed replying, he continued: "You have been taking me about ever since this morning and I have seemed to be interested in everything, yet I can only think of them. It was the thought of them indeed that brought me back here amidst so much fatigue and suffering.

I heard while I was far away that I hadn't killed him. They are both still alive, are they not? They have had several children—they are happy, triumphant, is that not so?"

Bonnaire was reflecting. For fear of a scandal he had hitherto delayed the inevitable meeting. But had not his tactics succeeded? Had not a kind of holy awe come over Ragu in presence of the grandeur of the accomplished work? Bonnaire could tell that his companion was quivering, distracted, too nerveless to think of committing another crime. And so, with his air of serene good nature, he finished by replying, "You want to see them, my good fellow; well, I will show them to you. And it's quite true, you will see happy folk."

Luc's table came immediately after that of Bourron. He sat on one side of it, in the centre, with Josine on his right, whilst on his left hand were Sœurette and Jordan. Suzanne also was present, seated in front of Luc; and near her Nanet and Nise had taken their places. They in their turn would soon be great-grandparents, but their eyes still laughed under their fair hair, which had now become somewhat paler in hue, as in the distant days when they had looked like two little toys—two little curly lambs. All around the table sat the younger members of Luc's family. There was Hilaire, his eldest son, who had married Colette, the daughter of Nanette and Nise, and had become the father of Mariette, now nearly fifteen years of age. In like manner from Paul Boisgelin and Antoinette Bonnaire had sprung Ludovic, who would soon be twenty; and there was a promise of marriage between Ludovic and Mariette, who dined side by side, spending much of their time in whispering together, having little secrets of their own to communicate. Then came Jules, the last of the Froments, who had married Céline, the daughter of Arsène Lenfant and Eulalie Laboque; this pair having a boy of six named Richard, a child of angelic beauty, the particular favourite of his grandfather Luc. And afterwards followed all the kinsfolk; this being the table where the blood of old-time enemies was most closely blended, that of the Froments, the Boisgelins, and the Delaveaus mingling with that of the Bonnaires, the Laboques, and the Lenfants, the artisans, traders, and tillers of the soil; in such wise that the whole social communion whence the new city, the Beauclair of justice and peace, had sprung, was represented here.

At the moment when Ragu drew near to the table, a last ray of the setting sun enveloped it as with a glory, and the clumps of roses, the silver plate, the light silk gowns and the diamond-spangled hair of the women coruscated amidst the splendour. But the most charming incident that attended the orb's farewell was another flight of the birds of the vicinity, who yet once again flew around the diners before retiring to rest among the branches. There came such coveys and such a flapping of little wings that the table was covered as with a snow of warm living down. Friendly hands took hold of the birds, caressed them, and then let them go. And the confidence thus displayed by the robins and the finches was fraught with adorable sweetness. In that calm evening atmosphere it seemed like a sign that an alliance was henceforth formed between all creatures, that universal peace reigned at last between men and animals and things.

"Oh, Grandpa Luc!" cried little Richard, "just look, there is a blackcap drinking water out of Grandma Josine's glass!"

It was true; and Luc, the founder of the city, felt both amused and touched by it. The water came from those fresh and pure springs which he had captured among the rocks of the Bleuse Mountains, and which had given birth to the whole town of gardens and avenues and plashing fountains. When the bird had flown away Luc took up the glass, and raised it amidst the purple glow of the sunset, saying: "Josine! we must drink—we must drink to the health of our happy city!"

And when Josine, who all her life had remained an *amorosa*, a creature of tender heart beneath her white hair, had laughingly moistened her lips with the water, Luc in his turn drank of it and resumed, "To the health of our city, whose *fête* it is to-day! May it ever increase and spread, may it grow in liberty, prosperity, and beauty, and may it win the whole world over to the work of universal harmony!"

In the last sunray, which set an aureola round his head, he looked superb—still young even, overflowing with triumphant faith and joy. Without pride or emphasis he simply expressed the delight he felt at seeing his work so full of life and strength. He was the founder, the creator, the father; and all those joyous people, all who sat at those tables celebrating work and the fruitfulness of summer, were his people, his friends, his kinsfolk, his ever-spreading, brotherly, and prosperous family. An acclamation greeted the ardently loving wishes which he offered up for his city, ascending into the evening air, and rolling from table to table even to the most distant avenues. One and all had risen to their feet, in their turn holding their glasses aloft and drinking the health of Luc and Josine, the heroes, the patriarchs of work; she, the redeemed one, glorified as spouse and as mother, and he the saviour, who, to save her, had saved the whole wretched world of the wage-earners from iniquity and suffering. And it was a moment full of exaltation and magnificence, testifying to the passionate gratitude of the vast throng for all the active faith which had been shown, and proclaiming the community's final entry into the reign of glory and love.

Ragu turned ghastly pale and trembled in all his limbs as that gust of triumph swept by. He could not endure the sight of Luc and Josine, so radiant with beauty and kindliness. He recoiled and staggered, and was on the point of fleeing when Luc, who had noticed him, turned towards Bonnaire.

"Ah! my friend, you were lacking to make my joy complete," said he. "You have ever been like my other self, the bravest, sturdiest, most sensible artisan of our work, and people must not praise me without praising you also. But who is that old man that I see with you?"

"He is a stranger."

"A stranger! Let him approach then. Let him break with us the bread of our harvests, and drink the water of our springs. Our city is a city of welcome and peace for all men. Make room, Josine! And you, friend, whom we do not know, come, seat yourself between my wife and me, for we should like to honour in you all our unknown brothers of the other cities of the world."

But Ragu, as if seized with holy horror, retreated yet farther away.

"No, no, I cannot."

"Why not?" Luc gently asked. "If you come from afar, if you are weary, you will here find helping and comforting hands. We ask you neither your name nor your past. Here all is forgiven; brotherliness reigns alone, in order that the happiness of all may produce the happiness of each. And you, dear wife, repeat all that to him—the words will come gently and convincingly from your lips, for it seems as if I only frighten him."

Thereupon Josine herself spoke: "Here! my friend," said she, "here is our glass, why should you not drink our health and your own? You come from afar, and you are a brother, in you we shall have the pleasure of still enlarging our family. It is a custom at Beauclair now, on days of festival, to exchange a kiss of peace which effaces everything. Take this glass and drink, for the love of all!"

But Ragu again recoiled, paler and trembling more violently than before, stricken with terror indeed as at some idea of sacrilege: "No, no, I cannot!"

Did Luc and Josine at that moment suspect the truth, did they recognise the wretched man who had returned merely to experience fresh suffering after so long dragging about with him his destiny of sloth and corruption? As they looked at him an expression of deep sadness came into their eyes which had beamed so kindly. And by way of conclusion Luc simply said: "Go then, since you desire it, since you cannot belong to our family, at the hour when it is drawing yet more closely together, pressing around on all sides, hand in hand. Look! it is mingling, tables are joining tables, and soon there will be but one board for the whole of our city of brothers!"

This was true; the people were gathering together in neighbourly fashion—each table seemed to set out on the march towards the next one, in such wise that they all met and joined, as invariably happened at the close of that repast in honour of the festival of Summer. And it was all quite natural, the children at first served as messengers, going from table to table, for there was a tendency among the scattered members of particular families to gather together and seat themselves side by side. How could Séverin Bonnaire, who sat at the table of the Morfains, Zoé Bonnaire, who sat at that of the Bourrons, and Antoinette Bonnaire, who sat at that of Luc, help feeling drawn towards the paternal table, where their elder brother Lucien had his place? And was it not natural that the Froments, scattered like the seed corn which one casts into different furrows—Charles being among the Bonnaires, Thérèse and Pauline among the Morfains—should desire to join their father, the founder and creator of the city? Thus one beheld the tables marching and uniting together in such wise that not a break soon remained along the avenues, before the doors of the gay houses. The paschal feast of that brotherly people was about to continue under the stars, in a vast communion, all being seated elbow to elbow, at the same board, among the same scattered rose petals. The whole city thus became a gigantic banqueting-hall, the families were blended into one, the same spirit animated every breast, and the same love made every heart beat. Meantime from the far-spreading pure heavens fell a delightful, sovereign peace, the harmony of spheres and men.

Bonnaire had not intervened, but he had kept his eyes on Ragu, watching for the change that he expected after that day of surprises which, one by one, had shaken the wanderer until at last he was terrified and transported by that final blaze of glory. At last realising that he was sorely stricken, and tottering, Bonnaire gave him his hand. "Come, let us walk a little," he said, "the evening air is so mild. And tell me, do you now believe in our happiness? Surely you must now see that one may work and at the same time be happy. Indeed, joy and health and perfect life are to be found in work. To work is to live. And only a religion of suffering and death could have made work a curse, and eternal sloth the happiness of heaven! Work is not our master, it is the breath of our lungs, the blood of our veins, the one sole reason why we love and create and form immortal humanity!"

But Ragu, as if exhausted by fatigue, weary unto death amidst his defeat, ceased arguing: "Oh, leave me, leave me," said he. "I am only a coward, a child would have had more courage, and I hold myself in contempt." Then in a whisper he went on: "I came to kill them both. Ah! that never-ending journey, the roads that followed the roads, the years of roaming through unknown lands with one rageful thought in my heart—that of returning to Beauclair, of finding that man and that woman once more, and of planting in their flesh the knife I had used so clumsily! But you met me, amused me, and just now I trembled before them, and retreated like a coward, when I saw them looking so beautiful, so great, so radiant!"

Bonnaire shuddered on hearing that confession. Already on the previous night he had apprehended a crime. But now, at the sight of the woeful wretch's collapse, he felt stirred by pity. "Come, come, you unhappy being," he exclaimed, "come and sleep again to-night at my house. To-morrow we'll see—"

"Sleep again at your house! Oh! no, no! I'm going, I'm going at once!"

"But you cannot start off at this hour—you are too tired, too weak. Why won't you stay with us? You will become calmer, you will know our happiness."

"No, no! I must start at once, at once. The potter said the truth, I'm not of the sort to make one of you." And like some damned and tortured wretch full of suppressed wrath Ragu added: "Your happiness—why, I can't bear the sight of it! It would make me suffer too much!"

Bonnaire then ceased to insist; secret horror and uneasiness had come over him also. In silence he led Ragu to his house again, and the other, unwilling even to wait till the end of the meal, took up his wallet and his staff. Not a word was exchanged between them, not even a gesture of farewell. Bonnaire watched the miserable old man go off with tottering steps, and vanish at last, far away in the night, which was gradually falling.

It was impossible, however, for Ragu to lose sight of festive Beauclair in a moment. He slowly went up the Brias gorge, and at each step climbed higher and higher among the rocks of the Bleuse Mountains. Before long he was above the town, the whole of which on turning round he once more beheld. The sky, of a dark yet pure blue, was glittering with stars. And, beneath the sweetness of the lovely June night, the town spread out like another stretch of sky, swarming, as it were, with innumerable little planets—the thousands and thousands of electric lamps which had just been lighted on the banquet tables and amidst the greenery. Once more then Ragu beheld those tables, outlined, so to say, with fire, and thus emerging victoriously from the darkness. They spread along without end till they filled the whole space below him. And he could hear laughter and singing arising, and still and ever behold that giant festival of a whole people, gathered together at table in one sole brotherly family.

Then he once more sought to flee the sight, and ascended still higher; but when he next turned round, he again saw the city glowing yet more brightly than before. He went higher still, he ever and ever climbed upward, but at each further ascent, each time that he turned round the city seemed to have grown, till at last it spread over the entire plain, becoming like the very heavens with its infinite expanse of sombre blue and glittering stars. The sounds of laughter and of song reached him more and more distinctly; it was as if the whole great human family were celebrating the joy of work, upon the fruitful earth. Then, for the last time, he again set out, and walked for hours and for hours until he became lost in the darkness.

V

Yet other years rolled by, and death, necessary death, the good helpmate of eternal life, performed his work, carrying off one by one those who had accomplished their tasks. Bourron was the first to go, followed by his wife Babette, who retained her good humour to the last. Then came the turn of Petit-Da and that of Ma-Bleue, whose blue eyes partook of the infinite of the blue heavens. Lange died too, whilst putting the finishing touch to a last little figure, a delightful barefooted girl, the very image of the Barefeet he had loved. Then Nanet and Nise went off, exchanging a last kiss, whilst still young; and finally Bonnaire succumbed like a hero amidst the stir of work one day when he had repaired to the factory to see a new giant hammer, whose every stroke forged a great piece of metal-work.

Of all their generation, of all the founders and creators of triumphant Beauclair, Luc and Jordan alone remained, loved and surrounded with the affectionate attentions of Josine, Sœurette, and Suzanne. It seemed as if the three women, whose health and courage in their old age were marvellous, lived on simply to be the helpmates and nurses of the men. Since Luc had scarcely been able to walk, his legs gradually failing him till he was almost fastened to his arm-chair, Suzanne had come to reside in his house, lovingly sharing with Josine the glory of waiting upon him. He was more than eighty now, of unchangeable gaiety and in full possession of his intelligence—quite young indeed, as he said with a laugh, had it not been for those wretched legs of his which were becoming like lead. And in the same way Sœurette did not quit her brother Jordan, who now never left his laboratory, but worked there in the day-time and slept there at night. He was Luc's elder by ten years, and had retained at ninety the slow and methodical activity to which he was indebted for the accomplishment of such a vast amount of work—ever seemingly on the point of expiring, but introducing such logic and such well-reasoned determination into his labour, that he was still working when the sturdiest toilers of his generation had long been sleeping in the grave.

He had often said in his weak little voice: "People die because they're willing; one doesn't die when one still has something to do. My health is very bad, but all the same I shall live to a good old age, I shall only die on the day when my work is finished. You'll see, you'll see! I shall know

ÉMILE ZOLA

when the time has come, and I will warn you, my good friends, saying: 'Good-night, my day's over, I'm going to sleep now.'"

Thus Jordan still worked because in his estimation his work was not yet finished. He lived on, wrapped in rugs; his drinks were warmed in order that he might not catch cold, and he took long rests on a couch between the brief hours which he was able to devote to his researches. Two or three such hours sufficed him, however, for the accomplishment of a considerable amount of work, in such a methodical manner did he exert himself. Sœurette, all attention and abnegation, was like his second self, at once a nurse, a secretary, and a preparator, allowing nobody to approach and disturb him. On the days, moreover, when his hands were too weak for any exertion, it was she who carried out his thoughts for him, becoming as it were a prolongation of his own life.

To Jordan's thinking his work would only be completed when the new city's supply of beneficent electricity should be as unlimited as the inexhaustible water of the rivers, or the air which one can breathe in all freedom. During the past sixty years he had accomplished a great deal of work tending to that solution. He had diminished the cost of electricity by burning coals when they quitted the pit, and then despatching the electric force he obtained by cable to numerous factories. And after long researches he had devised a new appliance by which he even transformed the calorical energy contained in coal into electrical energy, without mechanical energy having to be employed. He had in this manner done away with boilers, which meant a saving of more than fifty per cent, in the cost price. The dynamos being charged direct, by the simple combustion of the coal, he had been able to work his electrical furnaces cheaply and well, revolutionise metallurgy, and provide the town with an abundance of electricity for all social and domestic purposes. Nevertheless, in his opinion it still remained too costly; he wished to have it for nothing, like the passing breeze which is at the disposal of all. Besides, a fear had come to him, born of the possibility—in fact, the certainty—that the coal mines would in time become exhausted. Before another century perhaps coal would fail one; and would not that mean the death of the world, the cessation of all industry, the suppression of the chief means of locomotion—mankind reduced to immobility, a prey to the cold, like some big body whose blood has ceased to circulate? It was with growing anxiety that Jordan saw each ton of coals burnt; that made a ton the less, he often said. And although he was so puny, feverish, racked by coughing, already with one foot in the grave, he incessantly tortured his mind in thinking of the catastrophe which threatened the future generations. He vowed that he would not die until he should have presented those generations with a flood of power, a flood of endless life, which would prove the source of their civilisation and their happiness. Thus he had set to work again, and for more than ten years already he had been working on the problem.

In the first instance Jordan had naturally thought of the waterfalls. They constituted a primitive mechanical force which had been employed successfully in mountain regions in spite of the capriciousness of the torrents, and the interruptions which dry seasons brought about. Unfortunately, the few watercourses still to be found in the Bleuse Mountains—apart from the springs utilised for the town's water-supply—did not possess the necessary energy. And, besides, no mountain spring would ever yield such a constant, regular, and abundant motive power as was necessary for his great design. Jordan therefore thought of the tides, the continual flux and reflux of the ocean, whose power, ever on the march, beats against the coasts of the continents. Scientists had already given attention to the tides, and he turned to their researches and even devised some experimental appliances. The distance of Beauclair from the sea was not an obstacle, for electrical force could already be transmitted without loss over considerable distances. But another idea haunted him, and gradually took complete possession of him, throwing him into a prodigious dream, full of the thought that if he could bring it to fulfilment he would give happiness to the whole world.

Puny and chilly as he was, Jordan had always evinced a passion for the sun. He often watched it pursuing its course. With a quivering fear of the spreading darkness he saw it set at evening, and at times he rose early in the morning in order that he might have the joy of seeing it appear again. If it should be drowned in the sea; if it should some day never reappear, what endless, icy, deadly night would fall upon mankind! Thus Jordan almost worshipped the sun, regarding it as something divine, the father of our world, the creator and regulator, which after drawing beings from the clay, had warmed them, helped them to develop and spread, and nourished them with the fruits of the earth, throughout an incalculable number of centuries. The sun was the eternal source of life since it was the source of light, heat, and motion. It reigned in its glory like a very powerful, very good, and very just king, a necessary god, without whom there would be nothing, and whose

ÉMILE ZOLA

disappearance would bring about the death of all things. This being so, Jordan asked himself why should not the sun continue and complete his work? During thousands of years it had stored its beneficent heat away in the trees of which coal was made. During thousands of years the earth had preserved in its bosom that immense reserve stock of heat, which had come to us like a priceless gift at the hour when our civilisation needed new splendour. And it was to the all-helping sun that one must again apply, it was the sun which would continue giving to that which it had created, the world and man, increase of life, and truth, and justice, all the happiness indeed of which one had dreamt so long. Since the sun vanished each evening, since it disappeared at winter-time, one must ask it to leave us a plentiful share of its blaze, in order that one might without suffering await its return at dawn, and take patience during the cold seasons. The problem was at once a simple and a formidable one; it was necessary to address oneself direct to the sun, capture some of the solar heat, and by special appliances transform it into electricity, of which immense quantities must be stored in air-tight reservoirs. In this fashion one would always have an unlimited source of power, of which one might dispose as one pleased. The rays would be harvested during the scorching days of summer, and stored away in endless granaries. And when the nights grew long, when winter arrived with its darkness and its ice, there would be light and warmth and motion for all mankind. That electrical power, ravished from the all-creating sun and domesticated by man, would then at last prove his docile and ever-ready servant, relieving him of much exertion, and helping him to make of work not only gaiety and health, and just apportionment of wealth, but the very law and cult of life.

The dream which possessed Jordan had already occupied other minds. Scientists had succeeded in devising little appliances which captured solar heat and transformed it into electricity, but in infinitesimal quantities, the instruments being suited merely for laboratory experiments. It was necessary to be able to operate on a large scale, and in a thoroughly practical manner, in order to fill the huge reservoirs which would be needed for the requirements of a whole nation. For years, then, Jordan was seen superintending the building—in the old park of La Crêcherie—of some strange appliances, species of towers, whose purpose could not be divined. For a long while he would not speak out, but kept the secret of his researches from everybody. In fine weather, during the hours when he felt strong enough, he repaired with the short, slow step of a weak old man to the new works which he had set up, and shut himself up inside them with some chosen men. And in spite of repeated failures he clung to his task, wrestled with it, and ended by overcoming the sovereign planet—he, the little hardworking ant, whom too hot a sunray would have killed. Never was there greater heroism, never did the pursuit of an idea afford the spectacle of a loftier victory over the natural forces—forces which yesterday had been deadly thunderbolts for man, and which to-day were conquered, subjected to his service. He succeeded in solving the problem, the great and glorious sun parted with some little of that inexhaustible glow with which, never cooling, it has warmed the earth through so many centuries. After some final trials new works were definitively planned and erected, and supplied Beauclair throughout a whole year with as much electricity as its inhabitants required, even as the springs of the mountains supplied them with water. Nevertheless, an annoying defect was observed: the loss from the reservoirs remained very large, and some last improvements had to be devised, a means of storing without fear of diminution the necessary winter reserve of power, in such wise that another sun, as it were, might be lighted above the town throughout the long cold nights of December.

Again did Jordan set to work. He sought, he struggled still, resolved upon keeping alive until his task should be completed. His strength declined, he was at last unable to go out, and had to rest content with sending his orders to the works respecting the final, long-debated ameliorations. In this fashion several months went by. Shut up in his laboratory he there perfected his work, resolved to die there on the day when this work should be ended. And that day arrived: he found a means of preventing all loss, of rendering his reservoirs absolutely impermeable, capable of holding their store of electric force for a long period. And then he had but one desire—to bid farewell to his work, embrace his friends, and return again into universal life.

The month of October had come, and the sun was still gilding the last leaves with warm, clear gold. Jordan requested Sœurette to have him carried in an arm-chair, for the last time, to the works where the new reservoirs had been installed. He wished to gaze upon his creation, to make sure that enough sunshine was stored away to enable Beauclair to wait for the return of spring. And so one delightful afternoon he was taken to the works, and spent two hours in them, inspecting everything and regulating the action of the appliances. The works were built at the very foot of the Bleuse Mountains, in a part of the old park which looked towards the south, and which had formerly been an overflowing paradise of fruit and flowers. There were towers rising above large buildings with long roofs of steel and glass, but nothing connected with the work could be seen from the outside, for all the conducting cables passed underground.

At last, by way of finishing his visit, Jordan bade his bearers halt for a moment in the central courtyard, where he gave a long supreme glance around him at that nucleus of a new world, endowed with the source of eternal life, his creation, the passion of his whole life. And finally he turned towards Sœurette, who, never quitting him, had followed his arm-chair step by step. "Well," said he with a smile, "it's finished, and it seems quite satisfactory; so now I can go off. Let us return to the house, sister."

He was very gay, radiant like a toiler who thinks that he will at last be able to rest since his work is done. However, his sister, hoping that he might benefit by the sunshine, told the men carrying the arm-chair not to hurry, but to go back to the house by a somewhat roundabout way. And thus it happened that on emerging from one of the paths Jordan suddenly found himself in front of the pavilion where Luc still dwelt, reduced like his friend to immobility, since he had lost the use of his legs. For some months now the two friends had not seen one another. They could only correspond, obtain news of each other through their dear nurses, their guardian angels, who were ever coming and going between them. And a final desire, the last desire of his heart, suddenly upbuoyed the sinking Jordan.

"Oh! sister, I beg you," said he, "let them stop and place my chair yonder, under that tree, at the edge of the tall grass. And go up to Luc at once and tell him that I am here, at his door, waiting for him."

Sœurette hesitated for a moment, feeling somewhat anxious at the thought of all the emotion which such an interview would bring with it. "But Luc is like yourself, my friend," she said, "he cannot stir. How would you have him come downstairs?"

The gay smile which revived the brilliancy of Jordan's eyes, again appeared upon his face.

"My bearers will carry him down, sister," he replied. "Since I have come so far in my arm-chair he can surely come here in his." And he added tenderly: "It is so pleasant here, we can have a last chat together, and bid one another goodbye. How can we part for ever without embracing?"

It was impossible for Sœurette to refuse his request any longer, so she went into the pavilion for Luc. Jordan waited quietly amidst the caress of the declining sun; and his sister soon returned, announcing that his friend was coming. Deep was the emotion when Luc appeared, likewise carried by the men in his arm-chair. He was brought towards the greenery, followed by Josine and Suzanne, who did not leave him. At last the bearers deposited him near Jordan, the chairs touching one another, and the two friends were then able to press each other's hands.

"Ah! my good Jordan, how much I thank you," said Luc; "how kind of you to have thought of bringing us together in order that we might see one another again and bid one another a last good-bye!"

"You would have done the same, my dear Luc," Jordan answered. "As I was passing and you were there it was natural that we should meet for the last time on this grass, under one of our dear trees, whose shade we have loved so well."

The tree under which they sat was a big silvery lime-tree, a superb giant that had already shed its leaves. But the sunshine still gilded it delightfully, and the golden dust of the planet fell in a warm rain athwart its branches. The evening too was exquisite, an evening of intense peacefulness, fraught with the sweetest charm. A broad sun ray enveloped the two old men as with a loving splendour, whilst the three women, standing in the rear, watched over them with solicitude.

"Just think of it, my friend!" Jordan resumed. "For so many years past whilst we have been pursuing parallel tasks, our lives have been mingled. I should have gone off full of remorse if I had not again excused myself for having placed such little faith in your work when you first came to me and asked my help to build the future city of Justice. I was at that time convinced that you would encounter defeat."

Luc began to laugh: "Yes, yes, as you said, my friend, political, economical, and social struggles were not your business. No doubt there has been much futile agitation among men. But was one to abstain on that account from taking part in what went on, was one to allow evolution to take place as it listed, and refrain from hastening the hour of deliverance? All the compromises—often necessary ones—all the base devices to which the leaders of men have stooped, have had their excuse in the double march which they have at times helped mankind to effect."

Jordan hastily interrupted him: "You were right, my friend," said he, "and you have proved it magnificently. Your battle here has created, hastened the advent of a new world. Perhaps you have snatched a hundred years from human wretchedness. At all events this new town of Beauclair, where more justice and happiness now flower, proclaims the excellence of your mission, the beneficent glory of your achievement. I am with you entirely, you see, in mind and in heart, and I do not wish to quit you without telling you once more how thoroughly you won me over to your work, and with what growing affection I watched you whilst you were realising so many great things. You were often an example for me."

But Luc protested: "Oh! do not let us speak of any example of mine, my friend. It was you who ever gave me one, the loftiest, the most magnificent! Remember my lassitude, my occasional attacks of weakness, whereas I always found you erect, endowed with more courage, more and more faith in your work, even on the days when everything seemed to be crumbling around you. That which made you invincible was that you believed solely in work, in which, alone, you set health and the one reason for living and doing. And your own work became your very heart and brain, the blood pulsing in your veins, the thought ever on the alert in the depths of your mind. Your work alone existed for you, building itself up with all the life that you bestowed on it, hour by hour. And what an imperishable monument, what a gift of splendour and happiness you will leave to mankind! I might never have been able to carry out my own work, as a builder of towns, and leader of men, and at all events it would as yet be as nothing, had it not been for yours."

Silence fell, and some birds flew by, whilst through the bare branches of the lime-tree the autumn sunshine streamed more gently as evening advanced. Sœurette, in her motherly fashion, became anxious, and drew Jordan's rug over his knees, whilst Josine and Suzanne bent over Luc, fearing lest he should tire himself.

But the latter replied to Jordan: "Science remains the great revolutionary. You told me so at the outset, and every forward step in our long lives has shown me how right you were. Would our town of Beauclair, now all comfort and solidarity, have been possible as yet if you had not placed at its disposal that electrical power which has become the necessary agent of all work, all social life? Science, truth, will alone emancipate man, make him master of his destiny, and give him sovereignty over the world by reducing the natural forces to the status of obedient servants. Whilst I was building, my friend, you gave me what was needed to infuse life into my stones and mortar."

"It is true, no doubt, that science will free man," Jordan quietly replied in his weak little voice, "for at bottom truth is the one powerful artisan of fraternity and justice. And I'm going off, feeling well pleased with myself, for I've just paid my last visit to our factory, and it is working now as I desired it to work, for the relief and felicity of all."

He went on giving explanations and instructions respecting the working of the new appliances, the employment of those reservoirs of force, as if indeed he were dictating his last will and testament to his friend. Electricity already cost nothing, and was so abundant that it might be given to the inhabitants of Beauclair in whatever measure they desired, like the streams whose flood was inexhaustible; like the air which came freely from the four corners of the heavens. And given in this wise electricity was life.

In every public edifice and private house, even the most modest, light, heat, and motive power were distributed without counting. It was only necessary to turn on a few switches and the house was illumined and warmed, food was cooked, and various trade and household appliances were set working. All sorts of ingenious little mechanisms were being invented for household requirements, relieving women of the work which they had formerly done, substituting mechanical action for manual toil. In a word, from the housewife to the factory-worker, the ancient human beast of burden had been altogether relieved of physical exertion and useless suffering; a subjugated and domesticated natural force now replacing the old-time toilers and performing all the work allotted to it, in silence and cleanliness, with merely an attendant to check its action. And this also meant relief and freedom for the mind, a moral and intellectual rise for every brain, hitherto weighed down by excessive work, badly apportioned and fraught with savage iniquity for the greater number of the disinherited, whom it had plunged in ignorance, baseness and crime. And it was not slothful idleness that now reigned in the place of excessive toil, but work into which more freedom and conscience entered; man really becoming the king of work, devoting himself to the occupations he preferred, and creating more truth and beauty according to his tastes, after the few hours of general work which he gave to the community. And meantime also the unhappy domestic animals, the sad-looking horses, all the beasts used for draught, burden, and servitude were freed from the carts they had been compelled to drag, the millstones they had turned, the loads they had carried, and were restored to happy life in the fields and the woods.

But the purposes for which the electric force could be used were innumerable, and each day brought with it some fresh benefit. Jordan had invented some lamps of such great power that two or three sufficed to illumine an avenue. Thus the dream of lighting another sun above Beauclair at night-time would assuredly be fulfilled. Some huge and splendid glass houses had also been erected, in which by means of an improved system of heating, flowers, vegetables, and fruits could be easily grown at all seasons. The town was full of them, they were distributed broadcast, and winter, like night, ceased to exist. Moreover, transport and locomotion were facilitated more and more, thanks to the free motive power which was applied to an infinity of vehicles, bicycles, carriages, carts, and trains of several coaches.

"Yes, I am going off feeling well pleased," Jordan repeated with serene gaiety. "I've done my own work, and the general task is sufficiently well advanced to allow me to fall asleep in all peacefulness. To-morrow the secret of aerial navigation will be discovered, and man will conquer the atmosphere even as he conquered the oceans. To-morrow he will be able to correspond from one to the other end of the earth without wire or cable. Human speech, human gesture will dart round the world with the rapidity of lightning. And that indeed, my friend, is the deliverance of the nations by science, the great invincible revolutionary, who will ever bring them increase of peace and truth. You yourself long ago obliterated the frontiers, so to say, by your rails, your railway lines which have extended further and further, crossing rivers, transpiercing mountains, gathering the nations together in a closer and closer network of intercourse. And what will it be when one capital can chat in friendly fashion with another, however far away, when the same thought at the same minute occupies the attention of distant continents, and when the balloon cars travel freely through the infinite, man's common patrimony, without knowing aught of customs' tariffs? The air which we all breathe, that space which is the property of all, will prove a field of harmony, in which the men of to-morrow will assuredly become reconciled. And this is why you have always seen me so composed, my friend, so convinced of final deliverance. Men might do all they could to devour one another, religions might pile error upon error in order to retain their domination, but science was taking a step forward every day, creating more light, more brotherliness, more happiness. And by the irresistible force of truth it will at last sweep away all the dark and hateful past, liberate the minds of men, and draw their hearts closer and closer together under the great and beneficent sun, the father of us all."

Jordan was growing tired, and his voice became very faint. Nevertheless he laughed again as he concluded: "You see, my friend, I was as much of a revolutionist as you."

"I know it," Luc replied with affectionate gentleness. "You have been my master in all things. I shall never be able to thank you sufficiently for the admirable lesson of energy you gave me by your superb faith in work."

The sun was now fast declining, and a light quiver had passed between the branches of the great lime-tree, whence fell the planet's golden dust, now of a paler hue. Night approached, and a delightful stillness spread slowly over the tall herbage. The three women, still standing there, silent and attentive, full of respect for that supreme interview, nevertheless became anxious, and gently intervened. However, as Josine and Sœurette covered Luc, in his turn, with a rug, he said to them: "I don't feel cold, the evening is so beautiful."

But Sœurette turned to glance at the sun, which was about to disappear from the horizon, and Jordan following her glance, exclaimed: "Yes, night is falling. But the sun may go to bed now—it has left some of its beneficence and power in our granaries. If it now sets the meaning is that my day is over. I am going to sleep. Good-bye, my friend."

"Good-bye, my friend," Luc rejoined; "I shall soon go to sleep also."

This was their farewell, full of poignant affection, simple yet wondrous grandeur. They knew that they would never more see one another, and they exchanged a last glance and spoke a few last words.

"Good-bye, my friend," Jordan repeated. "Do not be sad, death is good and necessary. One lives again in others, one remains immortal. We have already given ourselves to others, we have worked for them only, and we shall be born again in them, and thus enjoy our share of our work. Goodbye, my friend."

Then Luc once again repeated: "Good-bye, my friend, all that will remain of us will tell how much we loved and hoped. Each is born for his task, that is the sole reason of life; nature brings a fresh being into the world each time that she needs another workman. And when his day's work is over, the workman can lie down, the earth will take him again for other uses. Good-bye, my friend."

He leant forward, for he wished to embrace Jordan; but he was unable to do so until the three affectionate women came to the help of both of them, sustaining them whilst they exchanged that last embrace. They laughed at it like children, they were full of gaiety and serenity at that moment of separation, feeling neither regret nor remorse, since they had done all their duty, all their work as men. And they had no fears, no terror of the morrow of death, certain as they were of the deep quietude in which good workmen slumber. They exchanged a long and very tender embrace, putting all the strength that remained to them into that last kiss.

"Good-bye, my dear Jordan."

"Good-bye, my dear Luc."

Then they spoke no more. The silence became intense and holy. The sun disappeared from the great heavens, vanishing behind the vague and distant horizon. A bird perched on the lime-tree ceased singing, and delicate shadows stole over the branches, whilst the lofty herbage, and all the park with its clumps of trees, its paths and its lawns, sank into the delightful quietude of twilight.

Then, at a sign from Sœurette, the bearers took up Jordan's chair, and slowly, gently carried him away. Luc had asked that he might be allowed to remain under the tree a little longer, and as he still sat there he watched his friend going off along a broad, straight pathway. At one moment Jordan looked round, and a last glance and a half-stifled laugh were exchanged. Then all was over, Luc saw the arm-chair disappear, whilst the park was invaded by the gathering gloom. And Jordan, on returning to his laboratory, went to bed there; and even as he had said to Luc—his work being done, his day being ended—he let death take him, dying on the morrow very peacefully, with a smile upon his lips, in Sœurette's loving arms.

Luc was destined to live five years longer in that arm-chair of his which he seldom quitted, and which was placed near a window of his room whence he could see his city spreading and growing day by day. A week after Jordan's death Sœurette came to join Josine and Suzanne, and from that day forward all three women encompassed Luc with their loving attentions. During the long hours which he spent gazing upon his happy city he often lived through the past again. He once more saw his point of departure, the distant night of insomnia when he had taken up a little book in which the doctrines of Fourier were set forth. And Fourier's ideas of genius: the honouring, the utilisation, the acceptance of the human passions as the very forces of life; the extrication of work from its prison, its ennoblement, its transformation into something attractive, into a new social code, liberty and justice being gradually won by pacific means, thanks to a confederation of capital, work, and brain power—all those ideas of genius had suddenly illumined Luc's mind and prompted him to action on the very morrow. It was to Fourier that he was indebted if he had dared to make that experiment at La Crêcherie. The first common-house with its school, the first bright clean workshops, the first dwelling-houses with their white walls smiling amidst the greenery, had all sprung from Fourierist ideas, ideas which had been left slumbering like good grain in winter fields, ever ready to germinate and flower. Even like Catholicism, the Religion of Humanity might need centuries to be firmly established. But what an evolution afterwards, what a continuous broadening of principles as love grew and the city spread! By proposing combination between capital, work, and brain power as an immediate experiment, Fourier, the evolutionist, a man of method and practicability, virtually led one first to the social organisation of the Collectivists, and afterwards even to the Libertarian dream of the Anarchists. In that association capital gradually became annihilated, and work and intelligence became the only regulators and basis of the new social compact. At the end lay the disappearance of ordinary trade, and the suppression of money, the first a cumbersome cogwheel levying toll and consuming energy, the second a fictitious value, which became useless in a community in which all contributed to produce prodigious wealth, that circulated in continual exchanges. And thus, starting with Fourier's experiment, the new city was fated to transform itself at each fresh advance, marching on to more and more liberty and equity, and conquering on its way all the socialists of the various hostile sects, the Collectivists and even the Anarchists, and finally grouping them in a brotherly people, reconciled amidst the fulfilment of their common ideal, the kingdom of heaven set at last upon the earth.

And that was the admirable spectacle which Luc ever had before his eyes, a spectacle summed up in that city of happiness whose bright roofs spread out among the trees before his window. The march which the first generation, imbued with all the ancient errors, spoilt by iniquitous surroundings, had begun so painfully, amidst so many obstacles and so much hatred, was pursued with a joyous easy step by the ensuing generations which the new schools and workshops had created. They were attaining to heights which had once been declared inaccessible. Thanks to continuous change, the children and the children's children seemed to have hearts and brains different from those of their forerunners, and brotherliness became easy to them in a community in which the happiness of each was virtually compounded of the happiness of all.

With trade, theft had disappeared. With money, all criminal cupidity had vanished. Inheritance no longer existed, and so no more privileged idlers were born, and men no longer butchered each other to benefit by somebody's will. What was the use of hating one another, of being envious of one another, of seeking to acquire somebody's property by ruse or force, when the public fortune belonged to one and all, each being born, living and dying, in as good circumstances as his neighbour? Crime became senseless, idiotic, and the whole savage apparatus of repression and chastisement, instituted to protect the thefts of a few rich beings from the rebellion of the wretched multitude, had fallen to pieces like something useless, gendarmes and law courts and prisons alike being swept away. Living among that people who knew not the horrors of war, who obeyed the one law of work, with a solidarity simply based upon reason and individual interest, properly understood, a people, too, saved from the monstrous falsehoods of religion, well informed, knowing the truth and bent on justice, one realised how possible became the alleged "utopia" of universal happiness. Since the passions, instead of being combated and stifled, had been cultivated like the very forces of life, they had lost all criminal bitterness, and had become social virtues, a continuous flowering of individual energies. Legitimate happiness lay in the development and education of the five senses and the sense of love. The long efforts of mankind ended in the free expansion of the individual, and in a social system satisfying every need, man being man in his entirety, and living life in its entirety also. And the happy city had thus secured realisation in the practice of the religion of life, the religion of humanity freed from dogmas, finding in itself its *raison d'être*, its end, its joy, and its glory.

But Luc particularly beheld the triumph of Work, the saviour, creator, regulator of the world. He had at the very outset desired to destroy the iniquitous wage-system, and had dreamt of a new compact which would allow of a just apportionment of wealth. But what a deal of ground it had been necessary to traverse! In this respect again the evolution had started from Fourier, for to him could be traced the association of workers, the varied, attractive, limited labour of the workshops, the groups of workers forming successive series, parting to meet again and mingling with all the constant play of free organs—the play of life itself. The germs of the Libertarian Commune may be found in Fourier, for if he repudiated brutal revolution, and began by making use of the existing mechanism of society, his doctrines tended in their result to that society's destruction. No doubt the wage-system had long lingered at the works of La Crêcherie, passing through various stages of association, division of profits, a percentage of interest in the common toil. At last it had been transformed in such a manner as to satisfy the Collectivists, realising their formula, a regulated circulation of "vouchers for work." Nevertheless it still remained the wage-system, attenuated, disguised, but refusing to die. And the doctrine of the Libertarian Commune alone had swept it away in the course of a last advance, that of deliverance by liberty and justice in their entirety, that chimera of other days, that unity and harmony which now really lived. At present no authority remained, the new social compact was based solely on the bond of necessary work, accepted by all, and constituting both law and cult. An infinity of groups practised it, starting with the old groups of the building, clothing, and metal trades, the industrial workers and the tillers of the soil, but multiplying and varying incessantly, in such wise as to be adapted to all individual desires as well as to all the needs of the community. Nothing hindered individual expansion, each citizen formed part of as many groups as he desired, passed from the cultivation of the soil to factory work, gave his time as best suited his faculties and his desires. And there was no longer any contention between classes, since only one class existed, a whole nation of workers, equally rich, equally happy, educated to the same level, with no difference either in attire, or in dwelling-place, or in manners and customs. Work was king, the only guide, only master, and only deity, instinct with sovereign nobility, since it had redeemed mankind when it was dying of falsehood and injustice, and had restored it to vigour and to the joy of life, and to love, and to beauty.

Luc laughed gaily when the morning breeze wafted towards him all the sonorous gaiety of his city. How good, easy, and delightful was the work performed there! It lasted only a few hours each day, and so much of it, the most delicate as well as the mightiest task, was performed by the new machinery which completed man's conquest of nature and loaded him with wealth and abundance. Freed from long hours of rough toil, man was the better able to exert his mind; art and science soared; the level of current mentality was ever rising; great intelligence ceased to be an exception, and men of genius sprang up in crowds.

The science of alimentation had already been revolutionised by chemistry, the earth might have yielded no more wheat, no more olives, no more grapes, and yet enough bread, oil, and wine for the whole city would have come from its laboratories. In physics, in electricity especially, fresh inventions were ever and ever enlarging the domain of the possible, and endowing men with the power of gods, knowing all, seeing all, and capable of all. Then came the flight of art, the growth and diffusion of beauty in every respect, an extraordinary florescence of all the arts, now that the soul of the multitude throbbed in every soul, and that life was lived with all its passions freed, love given and received in its entirety. Inspired by the universal loving kindness, music became the very voice of the happy people, through and for whom musicians found the most sublime chants, in whose continual harmony theatres, workshops, dwellings, and streets were ever steeped. And for the people architects built vast and superb palaces, made in its own image, of a size and a majesty at once varied and yet all one, like the multitude itself, all the charming variations of thousands of individualities finding expression in them. Then sculptors peopled the gardens and museums with living bronze and marble; and painters decorated the public edifices, the railway stations, the markets, the libraries, the theatres, and the halls for study and diversion with scenes borrowed from daily life. Writers moreover gave to that innumerable people, who all read them, vast, strong, and powerful works, born of them, created for them. Genius expanded, acquiring fresh strength from increase of knowledge and freedom among the community; never before had it displayed such splendour. The narrow, cramped, aristocratic, hot-house literature of the past had been swept away by the literature of humanity, poems overflowing with life, which all had helped to create with their blood, and which returned to the hearts of all.

Full of serenity, without fear for the future, Luc watched his town growing like a beautiful being, endowed with eternal youth. It had descended from the Brias gorges, between the two promontories of the Bleuse Mountains, and was now spread over the meadow-land of La Roumagne. In fine weather its white house-fronts smiled amidst the verdure without a single puff of smoke besmirching the pure atmosphere, for there were no chimneys left, electricity having everywhere replaced coal and wood for heating purposes. The light silk canopy of the broad blue sky spread over all, immaculate, without a speck of soot. Thus in aspect the town remained a new one, bright and gay under the refreshing breezes, whilst on all sides one heard the carolling of water, the crystalline streaming of springs, whose purity brought health and perpetual delight. The population steadily increased, fresh houses were built, fresh gardens were planted. A happy people, free and brotherly, becomes a centre of attraction, and thus the little towns of the neighbourhood, Saint-Cron, Formerie, and Magnolles, had found it necessary to follow the example of Beauclair, and had ended by becoming so many prolongations of the original city. It had been sufficient to make an experiment on a small scale, and by degrees the *arrondissement*, the department, the whole region was won over. Irresistible happiness was on the march, and nothing will be able to withstand the force of happiness when men possess a clear and decisive perception of it. Mankind has known but one struggle through the ages, the struggle for happiness, which is to be found beneath every form of religion, every form of government. Egotism is merely an individual effort to acquire the greatest possible sum of happiness for self; and why should not each set his egotism in treating his fellows as brothers when he becomes convinced that the happiness of each rests in the happiness of all? If there was contention between different interests in the past, it was because the old social pact opposed them one to the other, making warfare the very soul of society. But let it be demonstrated that work reorganised will apportion wealth justly, and that the passions, playing freely, will lead to harmony and unity, and then peace will at once ensue, and happiness will be established in a brotherly contract of solidarity. Why should one fight one against the other, when interests cease to clash? If all the desperate, pain-fraught exertions of generations, the prodigious sum of efforts, blood, and tears that mankind has given to mutual slaughter throughout so many centuries, had only been devoted to the conquest of the world, the subjugation of the natural forces, man would long since have been the absolute, happy sovereign of creatures and things. When humanity at last became conscious of its imbecile dementia, when man ceased to be wolfishly inclined towards his brother, and resolved to devote some of the genius and wealth hitherto squandered in mutual annihilation, to the common work of happiness, the mastery of the elements, on that day the nations first started on their march towards the happy city. And no! it is not true that a nation having its every need satisfied, having to battle no longer for existence, would thereby gradually lose the strength it requires to live, and sink into torpor and catalepsy. The human dream will always be without a limit, there will always remain much of the Unknown to be conquered. Each time a new craving is contented, desire will give birth to another, the satisfaction of which will exalt men and make them heroes of science and beauty. Desire is infinite, and if men long battled together in order to steal happiness one from the other, they will battle side by side to increase it, to make it an immense banquet, resplendent with joy and glory, vast enough to satiate the passions of thousands of millions of human creatures. And there will be only heroes left, and each fresh child born into the world will receive as his birthgift the whole earth, the unbounded expanse of heaven, and the paternal sun, the source of immortal life.

As Luc gaily contemplated his triumphant town he often repeated that love alone had created all the prodigies he beheld. He had sown the seed, and now he reaped inexhaustible harvests of kindliness and brotherliness. At the very outset he had felt that it was necessary to found his city by and for woman if it was to prove fruitful and for ever desirable and beautiful. Woman saved—Josine set in her due place of beauty, dignity, and tenderness—was not that the symbol of the future alliance, the union of the sexes, ensuring social peace, and free and just life in common? Then, too, the new system of education, the sexes being reared together and acquiring the same knowledge, had brought them to a complete understanding, and made them sincerely desirous of attaining to the one object of life, that object which was reached by loving a great deal in order that one might be loved a great deal in return. True wisdom lay in creating happiness, it was thus that one logically became happy oneself. And now love chose freely; no law, mutual consent alone, regulated marriage. A young man, a young girl had known one another since their schooldays, had passed through the same workshops together, and when they bestowed themselves one on the other, that bestowal was simply like the florescence of their long intimacy. They gave themselves to one another for life, long and faithful unions predominating; they grew old together, even as they had grown up together, in a bestowal of their whole beings, their rights being equal, their love equal also. Yet their liberty remained entire, separation was always possible for those who ceased to agree, and their offspring remained with one or the other, as they decided, or when difficulties supervened in the charge of the community. The bitter duel of man and woman, all the questions which had so long set the sexes one against the other, like savage, irreconcilable enemies, came to an end in that solution: woman free in all respects, woman the free companion of man, resuming her position as an equal, as an indispensable factor in the union of love. She had a right to abstain from marrying, to live as a man, to play a man's part as far as she desired, if she chose; but why should she deny desire, and set herself apart from life? Only one thing is sensible and beautiful, and that is life in its entirety. And so the natural order of things had come about, peace was signed between the reconciled sexes, each finding happiness in the happiness of a common home tasting at last all the delights of the bond of love, which was freed from the baseness of pecuniary and social considerations. One could no longer sell himself for the other's dowry, families could no longer barter their sons and daughters like mere merchandise.

Thus the fulness of love reigned in the community. The sense of love, developed and purified, became the perfume, the flame, the focus of existence. It was widespread, general, universal love, springing from the mated couple, and passing to the mother, the father, the children, the relations, the neighbours, the citizens, the men and women of the whole world in ever-broadening waves, a sea of love which ended by bathing the entire earth. Loving kindness was like the pure air on which every breast fed; there remained but one breath of brotherly affection, and that alone had at last brought about the long-dreamt-of unity, the divine harmony. Humanity—equilibrated like the planets, by force of attraction, by the law of justice, solidarity and love—would henceforth journey happily through the eternal infinite. And such was the ever-recurring harvest, the immense harvest of tenderness and kindliness, which Luc each morning saw arising from all sides; from all the furrows which he had sown so abundantly; from his entire city, where for so many years he had cast the good seed by the handful into the schools, into the workshops, into every home, and even into every heart.

"Look! look!" he said with a laugh some morning when Josine, Sœurette, and Suzanne remained near his arm-chair before the open window. "Look, there are trees which have flowered since last night, and it seems as if kisses were winging their flight, like song-birds, from some of the roofs. There, yonder, both on the right and on the left, love flaps his wings, as it were, in the rising sunlight."

The three women joined in his laughter, and jested in a tender way to please him. "Certainly," Josine would say, "on that side, above that house with the blue tiles spangled with white stars, there is a great quiver of the sunlight, telling of internal rapture. That must be the house of some newly-wedded pair."

"And straight before us," said Sœurette, "see how the window-panes are flashing with the splendour of a rising planet, in that house-front where the faïence ornaments are decorated with roses! Assuredly a child has been born there."

"And on all sides, over all the dwellings, over the whole town the rays are pouring," said Suzanne in her turn. "They form sheaves of wheat, a field of prodigious fertility. Is it not the peace springing from the love of all that grows and is harvested there each day?"

Luc listened to them with rapture. What a delightful reward was that which he himself had won from love, which had surrounded him with the sublime affection of those three women, whose presence filled his last days with perfume and brilliancy! They were full of solicitude, infinitely good, infinitely loving, with serene eyes which ever brought him joy in life, and gentle hands which sustained him to the very threshold of the grave. And they were very old and quite white, light and aerial like souls, like gay, active, pure flames, glowing with youthful, eternal passion. He lived on; and they lived on also, and were like his force, his activity and intelligence, healthy and strong as they were in spite of everything, coming and going for him when he himself could no longer move, like guardians, housewives, and companions, who prolonged and broadened his life far beyond the usual limits.

At seventy-eight years of age Josine remained the *amorosa*, the Eve, who had long ago been saved from error and suffering. Extremely slim, suggesting a dry, pallid flower that had retained its perfume, she had preserved her supple gracefulness, her delicate charm. In the bright sunlight her white hair seemed to recover some of its golden hue, the sovereign gold of youth. And Luc adored her still, as on the distant day when he had succoured her, setting in his love for her his love for the whole suffering people, for all tortured women; choosing her, indeed, as the most wretched, the most dolorous, in order that with her—should he save her—he might likewise save all the disinherited of the world whom shame and hunger were clutching at the throat. Even nowadays it was religiously that he kissed her mutilated hand, the wound dealt by iniquitous labour, in the prison of the wage-system, from which his compassion and love for her had helped him to extricate the workers. He had not remained unfruitful in his mission of redemption and deliverance; he had felt the need of woman, the necessity of being strong and complete in order to redeem his brothers. It was the mated couple, the fruitful spouse, that had given birth to the new people. When she had borne him children his work itself had begun to create, had become lasting. And on her side she likewise adored him, with the adoration of their first meeting, a flame of tender gratitude, a gift of her whole person, a passion and a desire for the infinite of love, whose inextinguishable flame age had not weakened.

Sœurette, born the same year as Luc, her eighty-fifth birthday being near at hand, was the most active of the three women, on her feet, busy the whole day long. It had long seemed as if she had ceased to grow older. Small of frame, shrunken even, she had nevertheless been beautified by gentle age. So dark, so thin, so graceless in former times, she had become a delightful little old woman, a little white mouse, whose eyes were full of light. Long ago, in the distressing crisis of her love for Luc, amidst her grief at loving and remaining unloved, her good brother Jordan had told her that she would become resigned, and would sacrifice her passion to the love of others. And each day she had indeed become more and more resigned, her renunciation proving at last a source of pure joy, a force of divine delight. She still loved Luc, she loved him in each of his children and grandchildren, with whom she had long assisted Josine. And she loved him with a deeper and deeper love, freed from all egotism, a chaste flame, that glowed with sisterly affection and motherliness. The delicate attentions, the discreet comforts which she had lavished on her brother, were now bestowed on her friend. She was always on the watch, in order to make his every hour delight. And all her happiness lay in that: to feel how greatly he himself was attached to her, to end almost a century of life in that passionate friendship, which was as sweet as love itself.

Suzanne, now eight-and-eighty years of age, was the eldest, the most serious, the most venerable of the women. Slender of figure, she remained upright, showing a tender countenance, whose only charm, as in days before, rested in its expression of kindliness, indulgence, and sterling good sense. But nowadays she could scarcely walk, and her compassionate eyes alone expressed her craving to interest herself in others and expend her strength in good work. As a rule she remained seated near Luc, keeping him company, whilst Josine and Sœurette quietly and attentively trotted around them. She, on her side, had loved Luc so tenderly in her sad younger days, loved him with a consoling love, of which she had long remained ignorant. She had given herself without knowing it amidst her dream of a hero whom she would have liked to encourage, assist with her affection. And on the day when her heart had spoken, the hero was already in another's arms, and only room for a friend remained at his hearth. She had been that friend for numerous years now, and had found perfect peace in the communion of heart and mind in which she had lived with the man who had become her brother. Doubtless, too, as in the case of Sœurette, if that friendship proved so delightful, it was because it had sprung from a brasier of love, and retained its eternal fire.

Thus Luc, very aged, glorious, and handsome, lived his last days encompassed by the love of those three women, who also were very old, glorious, and beautiful. His eighty-five years had failed to bend his lofty figure, he remained healthy and strong, save for that stiffening of his legs which kept him at his window like a happy spectator of the city he had founded. His hair had not fallen from above his lofty, towering brow, it had simply whitened, surrounding his head with a great white mane, like that of some old, resting lion. And his last days were brightened and perfumed by the adoration with which Josine, Sœurette, and Suzanne surrounded him. He had loved all three of them, and still loved them with that vast love of his, whence flowed so much desire, so much brotherliness and kindness. But signs appeared. As with Jordan, no doubt, the work being done, Luc was soon to die. Somnolence came over him, like a foretaste of the well-earned repose whose advent he awaited with joyous serenity. It was with good spirits that he saw death approaching, for he knew it to be necessary and gentle, and he had no need of any mendacious promise of a heaven in order to accept it with a brave heart. Heaven henceforth was set upon the earth, where the greatest possible sum of truth and justice realised the ideal, the entirety of human happiness. Each being remained immortal in the generations born of him, the torrent of love was increased by each fresh love that came into being, and rolled and rolled along, assuring eternity to all who had lived, loved, and created. And Luc knew that, although he might die, he would continually be born anew in the innumerable men whose lives he had desired to see improved, more fortunate. That was the only certainty of survival, and it brought him delightful peace. He had loved others so much, and had expended his strength so much for the relief of their wretchedness, that he found reward and beatitude in falling asleep in them, in profiting himself by his work in the bosom of generations which would ever become happier and happier.

Anxious though they felt at seeing him thus gently sinking, Josine, Sœurette, and Suzanne did not wish to be sad. They opened the windows every morning in order that the sun might enter freely, they decorated and perfumed the room with flowers, huge nosegays possessing all the brightness and aroma of youth. And knowing how attached Luc was to children, they surrounded him with a joyous party of little lads and lassies, whose fair and dark heads were like other nosegays—the flowery to-morrow, the strength and beauty of the years to come. And when all those little folk were present, laughing and playing around his arm-chair, Luc smiled at them tenderly and watched their play with an air of amusement, enraptured at heart at departing amidst such pure delight, such living hope.

Now, on the day when death, very just and very good, was to come upon Luc with the twilight, the three women, who divined its approach by the expression in the clear eyes of the grand old man, sent for his great-grandchildren, the very little ones, those who would set the most childhood, the most future promise around him in his last moments. And these children brought others, playmates and so forth, some of them their elders, and all of them descendants of the workers by whose solidarity and exertion La Crêcherie had formerly been founded. It was a charming spectacle, that sunlit room full of children and roses, and the hero, the old lion with the white mane, still cheerfully and lovingly taking an interest in the little ones. He recognised them all, named them, and questioned them.

A tall lad of eighteen, François, the son of Hippolyte Mitaine and Laure Fauchard, strove to restrain his tears as he looked at him.

"Come and shake hands with me, my handsome François," said Luc. "You must not be sad, you see how cheerful we all are. And be a good man. You have grown taller lately, you will make a superb sweetheart for some charming girl."

Then came the turn of two girls of fifteen, Amélie, the daughter of Alexandre Feuillat and Clémentine Bourron, and Simonne, the daughter of Adolphe Laboque and Germaine Yvonnot. "Ah! you at least are gay, my pretty ones," said Luc, "and it is right that you should be so. Come and let me kiss you on your fresh cheeks, and be always gay and beautiful, for therein lies happiness."

Then he only recognised his own descendants, whose number was destined to multiply without cessation. Two of his grandchildren were present, a granddaughter aged eighteen, Alice, who had sprung from

Charles Froment and Claudine Bonnaire, and a grandson of sixteen, Richard, who had sprung from Jules Froment and Céline Lenfant. Only the unmarried grandchildren had been invited, for the room could not have held the married ones with their wives and families. And Luc laughed yet more tenderly as he called Alice and Richard to him. "Sly fair Alice," said he, "you are of an age to marry now. Choose a lad who is joyous and healthy like yourself. Ah! is it done already? Then love one another well, and may your children be as healthy and joyous as you are.—And you Richard, my big fellow, you are about to begin your apprenticeship as a bootmaker, I hear, and you also have a perfect passion for music. Well, work and sing, and be a genius!"

But at this moment he was surrounded by a stream of little ones. Three boys and a girl, all of them his grandchildren, tried to climb upon his knees. He began by taking the eldest, a boy of seven, Georges, the son of a pair of cousins, Maurice Morfain and Berthe Jollivet, Maurice being the son of Raymond Morfain and Thérèse Froment, whilst Berthe was one of the daughters of André Jollivet and Pauline Froment.

"Ah! my dear little Georges, the dear little grandson of my two daughters—Thérèse the brunette, and Pauline the blonde. Your eyes used to be like my Pauline's, but now they are becoming like those of my Thérèse. And your fresh and laughing mouth, whose is that? Is it Thérèse's or Pauline's? Give me a good kiss, a good kiss, my dear little Georges, so that you may remember me for a long, long time."

Then came the turn of Grégoire Bonnaire, who was barely five years old. He was the son of Félicien Bonnaire and Hélène Jollivet; Félicien having sprung from Séverin Bonnaire and Léonie Gourier, and Hélène being the daughter of André Jollivet and Pauline Froment.

"Another of my Pauline's little men!" said Luc. "Eh, my little Grégoire, isn't grandmamma Pauline very kind, hasn't she always plenty of nice things in her hands? And you love me, too, your great-grandpapa, don't you, Grégoire? And you will always wish to be good and handsome when you remember me, eh? Kiss me, give me a good kiss."

By way of conclusion he took up the two others, Clément and Luce, brother and sister, one on his right and the other on his left knee. Clément was five and Luce two years old. They were the children of Ludovic Boisgelin and Mariette Froment. But at the thought of Ludovic and Mariette a host of memories arose, for he was the son of Paul Boisgelin and Antoinette Bonnaire, and she, the daughter of Hilaire Froment and Colette, the eldest child of Nanet and Nise. The

Delaveaus, the Boisgelins, the Bonnaires mingling with the Froments, were born anew in those pure brows, that light and curly hair.

"Come, little Clément, come little Luce, my pets," said Luc. "If you only knew all that I recognise, all that I read in the depths of your bright eyes. You are already very good and strong, little Clément, I know it well, for grandfather Hilaire has told me, and is well pleased to hear you always laughing! And you, little Luce, my little mite who can scarcely talk, one knows that you are a brave little girl, for you never cry, but gaily stretch your chubby little hands towards the good sun. You also must kiss me, my beautiful well-loved children, the best of myself, all my strength and all my hope!"

The others had drawn near, and he would have liked to have had arms long enough to embrace and press every one of them to his heart. It was to them that he confided the future, that he bequeathed his work as to new forces which would ever enlarge it. He had always relied on the children, the future generations, to complete the work of happiness. And those dear children who had sprung from him and by whom he was so lovingly surrounded in the serene peacefulness of his last hour, what a testament of justice, truth, and kindness he left them, and with what intense passion he appointed them the executors of his will, his dream of humanity freed more and more, and dwelling together in happiness!

"Go, go, my dear children! Be good, very good, and very just with one another! Remember that you all kissed me to-day; and always love me well, and love each other well also! You will know everything some day, you will do as we have done, and it will be for your children to do as you do. Let there be plenty of work, plenty of life, and plenty of love! Meantime, my dear children, go and play, and keep full of health and gaiety!"

Josine, Sœurette, and Suzanne then wished to send the joyous band home, for fear of a noise, as they could see that Luc was growing weaker and weaker. But he would not consent to this—he desired that the children might remain near him, in order that he might gently depart amidst the joyous sounds of their laughter. It was then arranged that they should play in the garden under his window. He could thus hear and see them, and felt well pleased.

The sun—a great summer sun which made the whole town resplendent—was already sinking on the horizon. It gilded the room as with a glory, and Luc, seated in his arm-chair amidst that splendour,

ÉMILE ZOLA

long remained silent, gazing the while far away. Josine and Sœurette, silent like himself, came and leant one on his right, the other on his left, whilst Suzanne, seated close by, appeared to be sharing his dream. At last, in a voice which seemed to become more and more distant, he slowly said: "Yes, our town is yonder. Regenerated Beauclair scintillates in the pure atmosphere, and I know that the neighbouring towns—Brias, Magnolles, Formerie, and Saint-Cron—have followed us, won over by our example to the cause of all-powerful happiness. But what is becoming of the world beyond the horizon, on the other side of the Bleuse Mountains, and beyond the great dim plain of La Roumagne—what point have the provinces and nations reached in the long struggle, the difficult and bloody march towards the happy city?"

Again he became silent, full of thought. He was aware that the evolution was in progress everywhere, spreading each hour with increasing speed. From the towns the movement had gained the provinces, then the whole nation, and then the neighbouring nations; and there were no more frontiers, no more insurmountable mountains and oceans—deliverance flew from continent to continent, sweeping away governments and religions and uniting races. However, things did not on all sides take the same course. Whilst the evolution, in the form of a slow advance towards the conquest of every liberty, had progressed at Beauclair without too much battling, thanks to the experiment of association made there, on other sides it was revolution which had broken out, and blood had flowed amidst massacre and conflagration. No two neighbouring states indeed had taken the same road; it was after following the most varied and contrary paths that the nations were to meet at last in one and the same fraternal city, the metropolis of the human federation.

And Luc, as in a dream, repeated in his failing voice: "Ah! I should like to know—yes, before quitting my work I should like to know how far the great task has now advanced. I should sleep better; I should carry yet more certainty and hope away with me."

Silence fell again. Josine, Sœurette, and Suzanne, very old, very beautiful, and very good, were, like himself, still dreaming, with their glances wandering afar.

It was at last Josine who began: "I have heard of things—a traveller told them me," she said. "In one great Republic the Collectivists became the masters of power. For years they had waged the most desperate of political battles in order to gain possession of the legislature and the government. And as they were unable to do so in legal fashion, they had recourse to a *coup d'état* when they felt strong enough for one, and certain of substantial support among the nation. On the morrow, by laws and decrees, they put their entire programme into force. Expropriation *en masse* began, all private wealth became the wealth of the nation, all the instruments of work reverted to the workers. No landowners, nor capitalists, nor employers were left; the State reigned alone, master of everything, both landowner and capitalist and employer, regulator and distributor of social life. But, of course, that tremendous shock, those sudden radical changes, could not take place without terrible troubles arising. The classes would not allow themselves to be dispossessed even of property they had stolen, and there were frightful outbreaks on all sides. Landowners preferred to get killed on the threshold of their estates. Other people destroyed their property, flooded mines, broke up railroads, annihilated factories and goods, whilst capitalists burnt their scrip and flung their gold into the sea. Certain houses had to be besieged, whole towns had to be taken by assault. That frightful civil war lasted for years, and the pavements of the towns became red with blood, whilst the rivers still and ever carried corpses to the ocean. Then the sovereign State experienced all sorts of difficulties in getting the new order of things to work smoothly. An hour's work became the standard of value, exchanges being facilitated by a system of vouchers. At first a statistical commission was established to watch over production and distribute products in accordance with each person's amount of work. Then other controlling offices were found necessary, and little by little an intricate organisation grew up, impeding the working of the new social system. People fell into a kind of regimentation and barrack life; never had men been penned up in smaller compartments. And yet evolution was taking place, even this was a step towards justice; for work rose to honour once more, and wealth was each day divided with more equity. At the end, assuredly, there lay the disappearance of the wage-system and of capital—the suppression of trade and money. And I have been told that this Collectivist State, ravaged by so many catastrophes, deluged with so much blood, is to-day entering the sphere of peace, coming at last to the fraternal solidarity of the free, working nations."

Josine ceased speaking, and again relapsed into a mute contemplation of the great horizon. But Luc gently replied: "Yes, that was one of the bloody paths, one of those which I would not follow. But now, what matters it, since it has led them to the same unity, the same harmony as our own?"

Then Sœurette, still gazing far away, as if exploring the world behind the gigantic promontories of the Bleuse Mountains, in her turn took up the tale: "I also heard a story—some eye-witnesses told me these frightful things. They happened in a vast neighbouring empire where the Anarchists by means of bombs and shrapnel succeeded in blowing up the old social framework. The people had suffered so dreadfully that they ended by leaguing themselves with the Anarchists in order to complete the liberating work of destruction, and sweep away the last crumbs of the rotten world. For a long time the cities flared like torches in the night, amidst the howling of the old butchers of the people, who in their turn were now being slaughtered, and who did not wish to die. And this was the prophesied deluge of blood, the fruitful necessity of which had long been foretold by the prophets of Anarchy. Afterwards the new times began. The cry was no longer: 'To each according to his work,' but: 'To each according to his needs.' Man had a right to life, lodging, clothing, and daily bread. So all the wealth was heaped together and divided, people only being rationed when there was a lack of abundance. But with all mankind at work, and nature exploited scientifically and methodically, there must come incalculable produce, an immense fortune, sufficient to satisfy the appetites of all. When the thieving and parasitic society of olden time had disappeared, together with money, the source of all crimes, and the savage laws of restriction and repression which had been the sources of every iniquity, peace would reign in the Libertarian community, in which the happiness of each would be derived from the happiness of all. And there was to be no more authority of any kind, no more laws, no more government. If the Anarchists had accepted iron and fire as their instruments, believing in the sanguinary necessity of extermination as a first step, it was because they were convinced that they could not utterly destroy monarchical and religious atavism, and for ever crush the last surviving germs of authority, unless the ancient sore should be thus brutally cauterised. In order that one might not be caught in the toils again it was necessary to sever every living link with a past of error and despotism. All politics were evil and poisonous, because they were fatally compounded of compromises and bargains, in which the disinherited were duped. And the lofty, pure dream of Anarchy had sought realisation when the old world had been ruined and swept away. That dream was the broadest and the most ideal conception of a just and peaceful human race, man free in a free state of society, and each man delivered from every hindrance and shackle, living in the full enjoyment of all his senses and faculties, fully exercising his right to live and to be happy through his share in the possession of all the wealth of the earth. But then, Anarchy had gradually become merged into the Communist evolution, for in reality it was only a form of political negation, and simply differed from other kinds of socialism by its determination to throw everything down before building up afresh. It accepted association, the constitution of free groups living by exchanges, constantly circulating, expending their strength and reconstituting themselves, like the very blood of the human body; and thus the great empire where it triumphed amidst massacre and conflagration, has now joined the other freed nations in the universal federation."

Sœurette ceased speaking and remained motionless and dreamy, with her elbow resting on the back of Luc's arm-chair. He, whose voice was thickening, slowly said: "Yes, the Anarchists, after the Collectivists, were bound to follow the disciples of Fourier on the last day on reaching the threshold of the promised land. If the roads were different, the goal remained identical." And after thinking a while he resumed: "Yet, how many tears, how much blood, how many abominable wars there have been in order to win that fraternal peace which all equally desired! How many centuries of fratricidal slaughter have followed one after the other when the question was simply whether one ought to turn to right or left in order to reach happiness more quickly!"

Then Suzanne, who hitherto had remained silent, and whose eyes also had been wandering beyond the horizon, at last spoke in a voice which quivered with compassion: "Ah! the last war, the last battle! It was so frightful that when it was over men for ever destroyed their swords and their guns. It took place during the earlier stage of the great social crises which have renewed the world, and I was told of it by men who had well nigh lost their senses amidst that supreme shock of the nations. In that crisis which distracted them, whilst they were pregnant with the future, one-half of Europe rushed upon the other half, and other continents followed them, and fleets of ships battled on all the oceans for dominion over water and earth. Not a single nation was able to remain apart, in a state of neutrality, they all dragged one another forward; and two immense armies entered into line, glowing with hereditary fury, and resolved upon exterminating one another, as if out of every two men there was one too many in the empty, barren fields. And the two huge armies of hostile brothers met in the centre of Europe, on some vast plains where millions of beings had space to murder one another. Over leagues and leagues did the troops deploy, followed by reinforcements; such a torrent of men, indeed, that the battle lasted for a month. Each day that dawned there still remained human flesh for bullets and shells. The combatants did not even take time to remove their dead; the piles of corpses formed walls, behind which new regiments ever advanced in order to get killed. And night did not stay the battle, men murdered one another in the darkness. Each time that the sun arose it illumined yet larger pools of blood, a field of carnage where death in his horrible harvesting piled the corpses of the soldiers in loftier and loftier ricks. And on all sides there was lightning, entire army corps disappeared amidst a clap of thunder. It was not necessary that the combatants should draw near or even see each other, their guns carried long miles, and threw shells which in exploding swept acres of ground bare, and asphyxiated and poisoned all around. Balloons also threw bombs from the very heavens, setting towns ablaze as they passed. Science had invented explosives and murderous engines which carried death over prodigious distances, and annihilated a whole community as suddenly as an earthquake might have done. And what a monstrous massacre showed forth on the last evening of that gigantic battle! Never before had such a huge human sacrifice smoked beneath the heavens! More than a million men lay there in the great ravaged fields, alongside the watercourses, across the meadows. One could walk for hours and hours, and one ever met a yet larger harvest of slaughtered soldiers, who lay there with their eyes wide open, and their black mouths agape, as if to cry aloud that mankind was mad! And that was the last battle, to such a degree did horror freeze every heart when men awakened from that frightful intoxication, born of greed for dominion, lust for power; whilst the conviction came to all that war was no longer possible, since science in its almightiness was destined to be the sovereign creator of life, and not the artisan of destruction."

Then Suzanne in her turn relapsed into silence, quivering the while, but with bright eyes, radiant indeed with the peace of the future. And Luc, whose voice was becoming a mere breath, concluded: "Yes, war is dead, the supreme *étape* has been reached, the brotherly kiss comes after the long, rough, dolorous journey. And my day is over, I can now go to sleep."

He spoke no more. That last minute was august and sweet. Josine, Sœurette, and Suzanne did not stir, but waited, exempt from sadness, full indeed of tender fervour in that calm room, gay with flowers and sunshine. Under the window the joyous children were still playing— one could hear the shrill cries of the very little ones, and the laughter of their elders, all the mirth of the future on the march to broader and broader joys. And then there was the friendly sun resplendent on the horizon, the sun, the fertiliser, the father, whose creative force had been captured and domesticated. And under the flaring of its rays of glory appeared the glittering roofs of triumphant Beauclair, the busy hive where by a just apportionment of this world's riches regenerated work now only created happy folk. And yet again beyond La Roumagne, and on the other side of the Bleuse Mountains, there was the coming federation of the peoples, the one sole brotherly nation, mankind at last fulfilling its destiny of truth and justice and peace.

Then, for the last time, Luc gazed around him, his glance embracing the town, the horizon, the whole earth, where the evolution which he had started was progressing, and drawing nigh to completion. The work was done, the city was founded. And Luc expired, entered into the torrent of universal love and of everlasting life.

THE END

A Note About the Author

Émile Zola (1840–1902) was a French novelist, journalist, and playwright. Born in Paris to a French mother and Italian father, Zola was raised in Aix-en-Provence. At 18, Zola moved back to Paris, where he befriended Paul Cézanne and began his writing career. During this early period, Zola worked as a clerk for a publisher while writing literary and art reviews as well as political journalism for local newspapers. Following the success of his novel *Thérèse Raquin* (1867), Zola began a series of twenty novels known as *Les Rougon-Macquart*, a sprawling collection following the fates of a single family living under the Second Empire of Napoleon III. Zola's work earned him a reputation as a leading figure in literary naturalism, a style noted for its rejection of Romanticism in favor of detachment, rationalism, and social commentary. Following the infamous Dreyfus affair of 1894, in which a French-Jewish artillery officer was falsely convicted of spying for the German Embassy, Zola wrote a scathing open letter to French President Félix Faure accusing the government and military of antisemitism and obstruction of justice. Having sacrificed his reputation as a writer and intellectual, Zola helped reverse public opinion on the affair, placing pressure on the government that led to Dreyfus' full exoneration in 1906. Nominated for the Nobel Prize in Literature in 1901 and 1902, Zola is considered one of the most influential and talented writers in French history.

A Note from the Publisher

Spanning many genres, from non-fiction essays to literature classics to children's books and lyric poetry, Mint Edition books showcase the master works of our time in a modern new package. The text is freshly typeset, is clean and easy to read, and features a new note about the author in each volume. Many books also include exclusive new introductory material. Every book boasts a striking new cover, which makes it as appropriate for collecting as it is for gift giving. Mint Edition books are only printed when a reader orders them, so natural resources are not wasted. We're proud that our books are never manufactured in exce
quantity they need to be read and enjoyed.

bookfinity™

Discover more of your favorite classics with Bookfinity™.

- Track your reading with custom book lists.
- Get great book recommendations for your personalized Reader Type.
- Add reviews for your favorite books.
- AND MUCH MORE!

Visit **bookfinity.com** and take the fun Reader Type quiz to get started.

Enjoy our classic and modern companion pairings!

Classic & Modern